From OLIVER NORTH, bestselling author, combat-decorated military hero, and devoted patriot, comes a blisteringly authentic novel of duty, treason, corrupted truth, and stolen honor—a breathtaking adventure ripped from today's headlines.

Major Peter Newman, U.S.M.C., has always answered his country's call—but now he's being asked to prove his loyalty as never before. Named as head of the White House Special Projects Office, Newman is given an assignment that is essential to his nation's future: to hunt down and eliminate the world's most dangerous terrorists before they can unleash terrifying weapons of mass destruction on the U.S. Only a handful of the Washington elite know of his covert mission, and undertaking it will place Peter Newman in the center of a raging maelstrom of intrigue, revenge, lies, and ultimate betrayal, pitting one man against devastating forces that could destroy everything he holds dear.

MISSION COMPROMISED

"**N**icely plotted . . . An inspiring, exciting, tell-it-like-it-is story of military honor and political betrayal."

Washington Post Book World

"**A** well-written, fast-moving military espionage thriller . . . The pages fly by as fast as those of a John Grisham novel."

Nashville Tennessean

"**A** Tom Clancy-esque tale . . . [North] mixes a few uncomfortable facts in with his fiction."

New York Times

Also by Oliver North

ONE MORE MISSION
UNDER FIRE

OLIVER NORTH

with JOE MUSSER

MISSION COMPROMISED

HarperTorch
An Imprint of HarperCollins*Publishers*

❦

HARPERTORCH
An Imprint of HarperCollins*Publishers*
10 East 53rd Street
New York, New York 10022-5299

Copyright © 2002 by Oliver L. North
Author photo by Griff Jenkins
ISBN: 0-06-055584-X

Unless otherwise noted, Scripture quotations are from the New King James Version, © 1979, 1980, 1982, Thomas Nelson, Inc., Publishers

Published previously in hardcover by Broadman & Holman Publishers.

First HarperTorch paperback printing: September 2003

HarperCollins®, HarperTorch™, and ❦ ™ are trademarks of HarperCollins Publishers Inc.

Printed in the United States of America

Visit HarperTorch on the World Wide Web at www.harpercollins.com

10 9 8 7 6 5 4 3

For Betsy
and all the other wives and mothers
who know what it means to receive
a "Next of Kin Notice"

Contents

Acknowledgments

USS Bataan, LHD-5
Arabian Sea
14 December 2001

The Marines and sailors I'm with aboard this 884-foot warship are preparing to go ashore tonight. Within hours they will embark in helicopters and air cushion landing craft and race for a beach thirty miles over the horizon. They will then move quickly inland to a small airfield where they will be picked up by C-130s and C-17s and flown more than four hundred miles to a lonely outpost near Kandahar, Afghanistan. Their mission: to help hunt down the terrorist Osama bin Laden.

Unlike all other amphibious operations I've been on, this time I'm not in command of anyone. Tonight I'm just going along for the ride—as a war correspondent for FOX News Channel. These brave young men, and the thousands of others with whom I served for more than twenty years, are the inspiration for this book.

I'm grateful to Roger Ailes, my boss at FOX News, for sending me out here. And to Vice Admiral Willy Moore, my Naval Academy classmate and Commander of the Fifth Fleet; Jim Roberts, President of Radio America Network; Griff Jenkins, my radio producer; and Pamela Browne, my FOX News producer—all of whom helped to make this trip to the "war zone" possible.

When I started this book, America was at peace. By the time I finished, we were at war. With the war came new demands on my time and energy. This work would never have been finished but for the inspiration, discipline, devotion, and talents of my friend Joe Musser and the willingness of his wife Nancy. If the pen is mightier than the sword, Joe's laptop is mightier than the calendar, and his gift for words has made my military phraseology comprehensible to civilians.

Two years ago, Pastor Ken Whitten put me in touch with David Shepherd, now my publisher, and Ken Stephens, the president of Broadman & Holman. Had they not believed in this project, this story would still be in my laptop.

Gary Terashita, the "editor of editors," knew when to exhort and when to admonish. For those times (and there were more than a few) when a "kinder, gentler" hand was needed, I could always count on the two Kims: Kim Terashita for proofing, promoting, and prayers, and Kim Overcash for always finding a way for Gary and me to communicate—even when Marsha Fishbaugh, my long-suffering assistant, had to find a way to connect us half a world apart. Thankfully for all of us, project editor Lisa Parnell helped to keep the book on track through the editorial process.

Mary Beth Shaw in Author Relations deserves a medal for keeping me informed, as do Dr. Robert Stacey and Jed Haven of Patrick Henry College who devoted their time and considerable talents to ensuring that I had my facts straight. And Marketing Director John Thompson, Sales Director Susanne Anhalt, Publicity Director Heather Hulse, Senior Publicist Robin Patterson, Duane Ward of the Premiere Group, and Cathy Saypol Public Relations all deserve a Meritorious Unit Citation for making sure that everyone in America got to see Greg Pope's great cover design—and a chance to buy this book.

As in every other part of my life for more than three decades, my greatest inspiration and encouragement came from my wife and our children. Many years ago, Betsy taught Tait, Stuart, Sarah, and Dornin to pray for me—and I am grateful for that and their affection. They are the ones who made it possible for a warrior to live a love story and to see God's love manifest in their lives.

Semper Fidelis,
Oliver L. North

Glossary

AmCits. American Citizens

AMEMB. American Embassy

Amn Al-Khass. Iraq's Special Security Services; also SSS

AOB. Advanced Operations Base

AWS. Amphibious Warfare School

Ba'ath Party. Iraqi political party of Saddam Hussein

BUD/S. Basic Underwater Demolition School

Canked. Military slang for canceled

CONUS. Continental United States

COS. Chief of Station, a country's top-ranking CIA official

C & C. Command and Control

CRAF. Civil Reserve Air Fleet

CTG. Counter Terrorism Group

CTOC. Counter Terrorism Operations Center

CT OPS. Counter Terrorism Operations

DCI. Director of Central Intelligence; the head of the CIA

Delta. Elite special-operations unit of the U.S. Army; its existence has never been officially confirmed

DIS. Distribution

DOD. Department of Defense

Drone. Remotely piloted aircraft; also RPV or UAV

DSC. Distinguished Service Cross, the second highest decoration for valor in the Army and Air Force, equivalent to the Navy Cross for sailors and Marines

DZ. Drop Zone, the spot on the ground designated for a parachute drop of personnel, equipment, or supplies.

E and E. Escape and Evade

EmCon. Emission Control

E/T. Emergency Termination

E-PRB. An emergency radio beacon that begins to transmit when an aircraft or vessel has suffered a catastrophic event; e.g., a crash or sinking

EWO. Electronic Warfare Officer

FAC. Forward Air Controller

FLOTUS. First Lady of the United States

GCHQ. British Signals and Intelligence Agency, similar to U.S. National Security Agency

GPS. Global Positioning System

GRU. Soviet Military Intelligence Service

GSA. General Security Administration of U.S. government

Gulags. Soviet-era labor prisons

Gunner. Slang for Marine Warrant Officer

Gunny. Slang for Marine Gunnery Sergeant

Gutra. Arab headdress

HA-HO. High Altitude-High Opening parachute deployment.

HARM. High-speed Anti-Radiation Missile

HQMC. Headquarters, Marine Corps

HM. Hospitalman or medical corpsman, the Navy and Marine equivalent of a medic in the Army and Air Force

IAEA. International Atomic Energy Agency, a United Nations organization

Igal. The black, braided cord that holds the Arab *gutra* or headdress

ISEG. International Sanctions Enforcement Group; a thirty-eight-man, joint U.S.-UK unit

ISET. International Sanctions Enforcement Team; each

joint U.S.-UK team has seven men

IT. Information Technology

JCS. Joint Chiefs of Staff

JSOC. The Joint Special Operations Command

KIA. Killed in Action

Klicks. Military slang for kilometers

LIMDIS. Limited Distribution

LTD. Laser Target Designator

MEU. Marine Expeditionary Unit; a reinforced Infantry Battalion of approximately eighteen hundred men

Mishlah. Arab clothing, a long cloak worn over the *thobe*

MOS. Military Occupational Specialty, the codified list of military job classifications

Mossad. Israeli Foreign Intelligence Service

MoveRep. Movement Report

NCO. Non-commissioned officer

NIC. Nicaragua or Nicaraguan

NMCC. National Military Command Center; located at the Pentagon

NODIS. No Distribution

NOK. Next of Kin

NSA. National Security Agency

NSC. National Security Council

OEOB. Old Executive Office Building

OPSEC. Operational Security

OSD. Office of Secretary of Defense

OTH Imaging. Over the Horizon imaging technology

PAO. Public Affairs Office(r)

PCS. Permanent Change of Station

PFC. Private First Class

PFLP. Popular Front for the Liberation of Palestine

PM. Prime Minister

POTUS. President of the United States

PRI-1. Priority One, the highest priority assigned for the assignment of personnel or the acquisition of military equipment or material

PT. Physical Training

QRF. Quick Reaction Force

R/F. Radio Frequency

RP. Rendezvous Point

RPG. Rocket Propelled Grenade

RPT. Repeat

RPV. Remotely Piloted Vehicle, UAV, or drone

S. Secret

S and R. Search and Recovery

SAM. Surface to Air Missile

SAR. Search and Rescue

SAS. Special Air Service, elite unit of the British Royal Army and Air Force

SEALs. Naval special operations unit: "Sea, Air, Land"

SEAL Team 6. U.S. Navy's crack counterterrorist unit

SecDef. Secretary of Defense

SG. Secretary General (of the United Nations)

SitRep. Situation Report

SOCOM. Special Operations Command

Solidarity. Polish labor and political movement that was opposed to the Communist regime during the 1970s and '80s

SOP. Standard Operating Procedure

SOT. Special Operations Training

SSS. see Amn Al-Khass

STARS. Surface-to-Air Recovery System

SWO. Senior Watch Officer

S-1. Administrative and Personnel function on a military staff or command

S-2. Intelligence and Counterintelligence function on a military staff or command

S-3. Operations and Training function on a military staff or command

S-4. Logistics and Supply function on a military staff or command

S-5. Communications function on a military staff or command

Tagia. Small skull cap that keeps the *gutra* (headdress) from slipping from the head

"The Tank." Secure conference room adjacent to the National Military Command Center at the Pentagon, where the Joint Chiefs of Staff and their deputies meet

Thobe. Arab traditional dress, a long, sometimes hooded, sleeved over-garment

TOW. BGM-71 TOW, a short-range, wire-guided, air-to-surface missile.

TS. Top Secret

UAVs. Unmanned Aerial Vehicles, also Drone or RPV

UN OPS CTR. United Nations Operations Center

UNHCR. United Nations High Commission for Refugees, a refugee relief agency

UNSCOM. United Nations Special Commission for weapons inspections in Iraq

USO Club. United Services Organization, an arm of the Salvation Army devoted to serving the U.S. military

USG United States Government

Vetted. Cleared, as in security clearance

VPOTUS. Vice President of the United States

"Wally World." Slang for Delta Force HQ at Fort Bragg, N.C.

WHCA. (pronounced "wha-cah") White House Communications Agency

WHDB. White House Data Base, euphemism used to describe the White House computer systems in the 1990s

MISSION
COMPROMISED

PROLOGUE

The Assassins

Paris, France
Friday, 14 November 1986
2130 Hours, Local

When the tiny dart hit Pierre Sirois behind his right ear, his right hand reached up as though to swat an insect. His arm never made it past his shoulder. A terrible gagging sound came from the young Frenchman's throat as the cyanide-toxin mix shut down his central nervous system with lightning speed. His fiancée's smile turned to horror as she watched her husband-never-to-be slump to the sidewalk. Maria Therndola screamed at the top of her lungs.

It did no good. Pierre Sirois, age twenty-nine, a successful multinational investment banker and engaged to one of the most beautiful women in France—and former unilateral asset of the CIA—was already dead. By the time Maria's pitiful cries summoned the apartment building's aging concierge, the nimble, shadowy figure hidden in the boxwood trees twenty feet from the apartment door had already slipped silently into the darkness of the alley behind the building. In another twelve seconds the black-clad perpetrator was in the backseat of a dark gray Citröen, pulling off his ski mask and coveralls. Two other men sat in the front seat with the engine idling.

Well before the discordant warble of the ambulance siren could be heard plying its way on a fruitless mission, the Citröen sped east out of the alley, turning on its lights only when it reached the side street. The auto raced south, down Boulevard de Sebastopol and onto the St. Michel Bridge. At the span's midpoint over the Seine, the car squealed to a stop in the dark space between the pools of light from two street-lamps. The man in the backseat got out, walked calmly to the rail, and dropped a bundle—the coveralls and ski mask, along with a compressed air pistol and the remaining six poison darts—into the water, seventy feet below.

Two young lovers heard the muffled splash and paused in their embrace just long enough to see the faint ripple from the object thrown into the river, but they thought nothing of it. The lovers never knew how close they had come to dying that night. But it didn't matter— the Paris police would never question the couple.

After disposing of the evidence, the shooter quickly rejoined his two comrades in the Citröen, and the car again sped off to the south, past the Montparnasse Cemetery where Pierre Sirois would be buried, and headed onto the *autoroute* for Troyes.

Shortly before noon the following morning, the three arrived in Marseilles, and by early afternoon were on the afternoon ferry to Algiers. Just after 4:30 P.M., the Marseilles Prefecture Police discovered the still-smoking, burned-out hulk of a 1986 Citröen, reported stolen from a pharmacist in Reims. They dutifully wrote out their report that the vehicle was a total loss and that the Citröen had been "presumably stolen by drug dealers."

At the hospital where they took Pierre Sirois in a futile effort to revive him, the medical examiner found in the young man's wallet a business card for "William P. Goode, National Security Company" with an American post office box address and a telephone number in the state of Maryland.

The tiny dart that killed Pierre had fallen out of his neck while his body was being loaded into the ambulance and was never found. Nor was the microscopic puncture wound on his neck. There was no redness or swelling around the entry site, so the medical examiner concluded that based on the apparent symptoms, the death was from natural causes.

When Maria came to claim his body, the medical examiner gave her the contents of Pierre's pockets. In the plastic bag were his wallet, some franc notes and coins, a ring that his father had given him, and a tiny metal fish, less than an inch long. He always had the fish with him, and he'd had an identical one made out of gold that Maria wore on a gold chain as a necklace. She had asked him about the significance of the little metal fish, but all he would ever say was, "Someday I'll tell you all about it." Now he never would.

Lisbon, Portugal
Friday, 14 November 1986
2200 Hours, Local

As he did every night at this time, five days a week, Sr. Alvaro Cabral got up from his desk, closed his office door, bid his receptionist *boa noite,* and walked out the

front door of the Cabral Shipping Company building
that his family had owned on Rua Miradouro for nearly
three centuries. Alvaro Cabral, age sixty-two, was a
man of precision. His family had made its fortune by
delivering the goods of a once-proud empire—where
they were wanted and when. And he carried on that
legacy from his office overlooking the port of Lisbon.
From his windows he could see his company's piers and
warehouses on the Rio Douro.

Those who thought they knew Alvaro Cabral described him as a careful man, a person of character with
no known vices who kept to himself. Few people even
knew his political leanings. He steered clear, they would
say, of the political firestorms that had swept his country,
from autocratic rule to socialism, in the 1970s. Sr. Cabral
had no enemies, only competitors. And even his competitors admired how Cabral had somehow saved the family
holdings in Angola when the former Portuguese colony
was torn apart by civil war in the early 1980s.

As a result of his precise routine, everyone agreed that
Sr. Cabral was a man of habit. He arrived at work every
morning at precisely 9:00 A.M. At exactly 2:30 every
afternoon, following a modest meal, he would take a
glass of good wine and lie down for a siesta, rising again
at 3:30 to work straight through until 10:00 P.M. And,
as was his practice, each and every Friday he would dis-
miss Paolo, his longtime loyal chauffeur, and drive himself to the palatial home set back from the Avenida da
Boavista where he and his wife Marabella had raised
seven children. Tonight, as every night, he looked forward to a comfortable and quiet, late dinner with
Marabella.

At four minutes past ten, two quick explosions ripped
Alvaro Cabral's Mercedes apart, and its only occupant

was shredded into fragments along with the expensive automobile. One of the bombs had been placed inside the driver's headrest, the other beneath the fuel tank. It took firefighters nearly twenty-five minutes to arrive and even longer to put out the blaze. By then a positive identification of the victim might have been impossible were it not for the tiny metal fish that survived intact in what was left of the victim's pocket. Everyone who knew Alvaro recalled that he'd had the little metal fish for years. Some speculated that it had been a symbol of Cabral Shipping in colonial times. An hour after the fire was out, the hastily summoned chief inspector of Lisbon's constabulary appeared on the doorstep of the house on Avenida da Boavista to inform Dona Marabella that she was now a widow.

Though the chief inspector's message was the worst news a loving wife could receive, she betrayed little of her horror and dismay as he delivered the awful pronouncement. She was, after all, a lady. And the chief inspector was a mere public servant.

After the police left, but before she called her children to tell them the terrible news about their father, Marabella picked up the phone and calmly dialed a phone number in Maryland, U.S.A. There was no answer at the only number she had for the American named Goode, so she then called her dead husband's friend at the U.S. Embassy in Lisbon. The widow Cabral never told the police or any of the many government ministers who attended her husband's funeral that Alvaro Cabral had, up until a year before his death, provided "delivery services" for the CIA.

The murder of one of Portugal's most successful shipping magnates was never solved. The Lisbon police and investigators from the Ministry of the Interior later told the black-clad Marabella that they suspected her late husband had been assassinated by a bomb intended for someone else, no doubt planted by one of the factions vying for power in Angola. But just in case, they jailed, without trial, Paolo, the faithful family chauffeur.

Warsaw, Poland
Saturday, 15 November 1986
0100 Hours, Local

Father Wenceslas Korzinski shivered. It was a normal condition for anyone north of Warsaw this time of year, even inside. But out here, on the banks of the frozen River Vistula in the middle of the night, it felt like the wind had arrived directly from the Siberian steppes. It cut through a man like a knife.

Tonight's clandestine meeting with the Solidarity organizers had not gone well. There were those in the group who didn't trust him simply because he was a priest. They wouldn't give a cold kielbasa for the fact that he had been a Vatican code clerk, or that he knew the Polish Pope, John Paul II, personally. Some of the men saw religion as a weakness, a view that came as a by-product of living all their lives under Communism— the very system they intended to overthrow. They feared that, if captured, the priest would not have the strength to withhold information about their activities; he might betray them out of this weakness.

Their prejudice troubled Father "Ski." They really didn't trust him—just because he wore a cassock instead of coveralls. *Somehow,* thought the thirty-eight-year-old full-time parish priest and part-time spy, *I've got to find a way to let them know they can trust me.*

Not everyone in the small Solidarity cell distrusted Father Ski. Two among them, Nikolas and Winold, the Krukshank brothers, had helped him divert boxcars from a Soviet munitions train in February. The three of them had braved cold worse than this to disconnect seven cars loaded with AK-47s, mortars, machine guns, and ammunition from the Russian freight train while it was on a siding near Plonsk.

But as Father Ski trudged along with his vaporized breath swirling around his head in the moonlight, he had to admit to himself that stealing the stuff wasn't nearly as hard as shipping it all the way east across Poland, through East Germany, and on to the West. That was the really hard part. And he knew that there were many others who were involved. He prayed frequently and fervently that all involved would be forgiven for breaking the Eighth Commandment. He prayed even more fervently that they would never be caught.

There were times, too, that he wondered why they were shipping Russian weapons to the West. Weren't NATO weapons supposed to be far superior to anything made by the Russians and their satellites? But he didn't let these incongruities or the fear of discovery stop him. If stealing Russian munitions would help bring down godless Communism, so be it.

Some Solidarity members had been picked up by the Ministry of Interior and questioned, but none were from the group that had hijacked the munitions train. Despite the harshness of the regime, cracks were beginning to show like fissures in the ice on the frozen Vistula. Word of an imminent Communist collapse was getting around—it even seeped through the walls of Lud Prison. Sometimes it came all the way back from those who had been dispatched to the *gulags,* the labor camps in Siberia. He used to report all this information, carefully encoded, to his CIA "handler," until contact was abruptly severed last December; his CIA interlocutor had been replaced. A new man, named Goode—a man who spoke very poor Polish and cared little about information—had taken his place. All Goode wanted was action—and Russian rifles and grenades.

Goode had told him that he wasn't a part of the CIA. Father Ski didn't know whether to believe that, but there was one thing for certain: Goode's cash was fine. With it, earlier that year, Father Ski had financed the brazen train robbery. He bought train manifests, freight schedules, and even troop deployment orders. Goode's cash had paid for the entire operation and covered the cost of dispatching seven boxcars of Russian weapons on a long journey across Poland, into Germany, south to Austria, into northern Italy, through France, across Spain, and all the way to Lisbon. As much as he understood it, this oblique route was taken primarily to elude the more careful border checks between Western Germany and Belgium, where NATO had its headquarters.

Once the weapons arrived in Portugal, Goode had sent Father Ski and the Krukshank brothers a generous bonus. The priest used the additional funds to buy warm clothing, blankets, and some decent food for the frailest of his parishioners.

Father Ski was almost back to his tiny rectory and still musing about good deeds and forgiveness when they grabbed him. At first he thought it was the police and that he would simply be arrested for breaking curfew. He was about to tell them that he was on his way to visit a sick member of his parish—a story that Mrs. Schotler would verify—just as Goode had instructed.

But before he could utter the lie, his head was shoved into a bucket of ice-cold water. They held him as he struggled, but he was not a physically powerful man. He held his breath as long as he could, but finally his instinctive processes overwhelmed the logical ones. He no longer had control over his natural motor functions. His head still submerged in the bucket of water, Father Korzinski sucked in the deep breath that he had to have to stay alive. Instead, water filled his lungs. He struggled some more but not for long. Once he no longer had a pulse, the men poured a little schnapps in the dead priest's mouth and splashed some on his shirt. One of them placed the half-empty bottle in the pocket of Father Ski's overcoat, and then they dumped his body off the riverbank into the icy Vistula.

When a policeman walking his beat found the body at the river's edge just after dawn, he first thought it was just another drunk who had frozen to death, not at all uncommon in Polish winters. When the policeman saw the youthful face and the Roman collar, however, he immediately called his superiors.

Two hours later the priest's body was laid out on a porcelain table in the city morgue. When the aging coroner pried open the Reverend Father Wenceslas Korzinski's frozen fingers, he found a tiny metal fish. Though the body and clothes reeked of alcohol, the coroner found none in the young clergyman's stomach—information he didn't share with anyone. Why offer answers to questions that no one was asking?

The old medical examiner never did believe the story the authorities put in the next day's newspaper about the drunken priest drowning on his way back from visiting a prostitute. But the coroner didn't share that either.

Counter-Terrorism Operations Center
CIA Headquarters
Langley, VA
Saturday, 15 November 1986
1730 Hours, Local

"Uh-oh . . . go get the boss, Al. We've got a *flash-eyes only* cable for the director coming in from the London Chief of Station," Communications Watch Officer Joe Kent said as he waited by a machine that looked for all the world like an ordinary computer printer, quietly chattering as it decrypted and stored the high priority message. But before it could be printed on duplication-proof paper, an authorization code would have to be entered on the keyboard next to the decrypter.

Alvin Dewar had the weekend duty in the Counter-Terrorism Operations Center on the seventh floor of the CIA headquarters building. He groaned, "It's going to be another lousy weekend in the CTOC—I can see it coming." Then the balding watch officer pushed himself back from his computer console and shuffled down the quiet hallway to a door labeled *DEPUTY DIRECTOR FOR COUNTER-TERRORISM*. Dewar knocked twice, opened the door without waiting, and said, "Mr. Charles, we have a *flash-eyes only* coming in from COS London. Do you want me to enter your access code and bring it down?"

Alan Charles, the number-four man in the CIA chain of command, looked up with bloodshot eyes, gratefully distracted from the pile of paper on his desk, and glanced at his wristwatch. He replied, "No, I'll come down and acknowledge receipt. Thank you, Alvin."

Alvin Dewar shrugged and walked back down the silent hallway to the door marked *CT OPS—RESTRICTED AREA*. He pressed his palm against the stainless-steel print-reader on the wall, simultaneously pressing his forehead against the optical scanner; he heard the electronic lock snap open.

Meanwhile, Alan Charles pushed himself back from his government-issue mahogany desk, hauled his fifty-eight-year-old, six-foot-two-inch frame out of his government-issue leather chair, and took his government-issue headache down the hall to where Alvin Dewar and the communications duty officer were standing. They were looking at the decryption machine as though staring at it would make it function faster or allow them to see the contents of the message for which they weren't authorized clearance.

The CIA's communications system, perhaps the most sophisticated in the world, was designed so that only those with a legitimate "need to know" could gain access to certain messages and information. This message, from the CIA's senior officer in London, was addressed to the director of Central Intelligence and could only be read and printed at the top of the hierarchy—by Director Casey himself or by the Deputy DCI, Paul Mahan; the Director of Operations, Martin Mason; or by the Deputy Director for Counter-Terrorism, Alan Charles.

As Charles bent over the keyboard to enter his access code, Dewar and the duty officer looked away—the way honest people do when the person in front of them at the ATM machine enters their PIN.

In response to the typed-in code sequence, the machine printed out the message it had stored in its memory:

TOP SECRET /WINTEL/NOFORN
FLASH
EYES ONLY FOR THE DIRECTOR

DTG: 152330ZNOV86
FROM: COS LONDON
TO: DCI
SUBJ: EXTREME MEASURES

1. COS PARIS, COS LISBON, AND BASE CHIEF FRANKFURT REPORT-
ING DEATHS OF FORMER REPEAT, FORMER AGENCY ASSETS IN PARIS,
LISBON, AND WARSAW WITHIN PAST 12 HRS.

2. COS PARIS REPORTS FORMER ASSET DK LIMA DOA AT PARIS
HOSPITAL W/O VISIBLE TRAUMA AT 2200 HRS LAST NIGHT. PRELIMINARY
CAUSE OF DEATH: HEART ATTACK OR STROKE. FAMILY HAS REQUESTED
AUTOPSY. WILL MONITOR AND APPRISE.

3. COS LISBON REPORTS FORMER ASSET GH WILLING KILLED BY
CAR BOMB LIKELY DETONATED BY REMOTE CONTROL. LIAISON W/ NA-
TIONAL POLICE INDICATES INVESTIGATORS SUSPECT ANGOLAN TER-
RORISTS AND A CASE OF MISTAKEN IDENTITY. WILL APPRISE ON NATURE
OF EXPLOSIVES USED WHEN AVAIL.

4. BASE CHIEF FRANKFURT ADVISES THAT FORMER ASSET BT ROVER
FOUND DROWNED IN VISTULA RIVER N OF WARSAW. LOCAL AUTHORI-
TIES CLAIM BT ROVER WAS QUOTE A PHILANDERING CLERGYMAN WITH-
OUT SCRUPLES WHO DRANK TOO MUCH AND WHO FELL THROUGH ICE
ON HIS WAY BACK FROM ILLICIT LIAISON WITH A PROSTITUTE. UN-
QUOTE.

5. REQUEST ADVISE DCI ASAP. ALL THREE ASSETS WERE TERMI-
NATED BY PARIS AND LISBON STATIONS AND WARSAW BASE LAST YEAR
AT DCI DIRECTION AND TURNED OVER TO GOODE AT NSC.

6. PER GUIDANCE FROM DCI, THERE HAS BEEN NO REPEAT NO
AGENCY CONTACT WITH ANY OF THE DECEASED ASSETS FOR MORE
THAN A YEAR. AS DIRECTED BY DCI, GCHQ AND THIS OFFICE HAVE

MONITORED GOODE'S CONTACT WITH THESE ASSETS SINCE AND RE-
PORTED SAME VIA BACK-CHANNEL COMMUNICATIONS TO AVOID
COMPROMISE.

7. AS DIRECTED, THESE DEATHS NOT REPEAT NOT REPORTED
THROUGH NORMAL OPS CHANNELS. BREAK. END TEXT.

Without showing the cable to his two colleagues,
Charles thanked them and returned to his office
where he sat at his desk. When he had read the message through twice, Alan Charles picked up the secure telephone on his desk and waited for the
Director of Central Intelligence to answer. It only
rang twice. After Charles read the text of the message
from London to the aging spy master, he paused for
a few seconds, said "yes sir," and set the phone back
in its cradle.

The CIA's top counterterrorist officer then got up
from his desk, went to his door, locked it, and, using a
key from his pocket, opened a drawer in his desk and
removed a device that looked remarkably similar to a
TV remote control. On the plastic shell in small raised
letters was the word *EncryptionLok-1A*.

Charles disconnected the line to his phone and
plugged it into the end of the little device labeled *OUT-
PUT*. From a jack on the wall beside his desk, he then
disconnected the wire running from his computer
modem and plugged it into the opposite end of the
EncryptionLok-1A labeled *INPUT*. Only then did he sit
down at his computer keyboard.

Typing quickly and flawlessly, the CIA's director of
counterterrorism drafted a message that would go only
to four men: one each at the State Department, the Pentagon, the FBI, and the White House:

DTG: 151900RNOV86
FROM: DIR CT OPS CIA
TO: CTG
SUBJ: URGENT TERMINATION NOTICE

1. THREE FOREIGN NATIONALS WORKING IN EUROPE WITH GOODE ON NIC RESISTANCE INITIATIVE HAVE BEEN KILLED WITHIN PAST 12 HOURS. ALL DECEASED WERE ENGAGED IN DIVERSION OF SOVIET-BLOC WEAPONS FROM POLAND TO NIC RESISTANCE LAST FEB.

2. DCI BELIEVES GOODE TO BE IN JEOPARDY AND THAT ENTIRE OPERATION HAS BEEN COMPROMISED. DCI HAS ORDERED URGENT SHUTDOWN OF ALL CTG OPERATIONS IN SUPPORT OF GOODE. GOODE TO BE REASSIGNED TO USMC ON RETURN TO CONUS.

3. GOODE PHONE DROP IN MARYLAND IS TERMINATED EFFECTIVE IMMEDIATELY.

4. ALL CTG CONTACT WITH GOODE TO BE SEVERED EFFECTIVE 0800 HOURS LOCAL 16 NOVEMBER EXCEPT AS INDICATED BELOW.

FOLLOWING GUIDANCE APPLIES AS INDICATED:

STATE: CONTACT AMEMB BEIRUT ASAP AND ADVISE GOODE TO RETURN CONUS DIRECTLY. REQ ADVISE GOODE OF PERSONAL JEOPARDY.

DOD/JCS: REQUEST U.S. MIL ASSIST TO MOVE GOODE FROM BEIRUT TO LARNACA, CYPRUS, FOR TRANSPORT TO CONUS ASAP.

FBI: POST COUNTERSURVEILLANCE LOOKOUT ON GOODE FAMILY IN VA TO ENSURE SAFETY. ACTIVATE PROTECTIVE MEASURES WITH DOD IF THREAT SITUATION WARRANTS.

ALL: DCI ADVISES ALL MATERIAL PERTAINING TO GOODE AND ANY REFERENCES TO SOVIET ARMS DIVERSION AND NICARAGUAN RESISTANCE ACTIVITIES BE PURGED FROM FILES ASAP. ALL FURTHER COMMS RE GOODE AND HIS ACTIVITIES VIA THIS CHANNEL ONLY. NO REPEAT NO COMMS RE GOODE THROUGH NORMAL CLASSIFIED COMMS.

DO NOT PRINT/RETAIN THIS MSG IN FILES.

BT

✪

Ten days later, on Tuesday, November 25, at five minutes past noon, President Ronald Reagan and Attorney General Edwin Meese marched into a crowded White House briefing room to tell the press and the world about what came to be called the "Iran-Contra affair."

Exactly a month later, the director of the CIA was stricken during a routine medical examination at his office at Langley. He was rushed to Georgetown University Hospital where he was operated on for a brain tumor but never regained consciousness.

The Iran-Contra affair continued with congressional hearings, trials, and investigations well into the 1990s. There was more to the story.

CHAPTER ONE

Duty Station
1600 Pennsylvania Ave.

Office of the National Security Advisor
The White House
Washington, D.C.
Tuesday, 29 November 1994
1000 Hours, Local

Major Peter J. Newman, U.S. Marines, reporting as ordered, sir."

"You don't have to call me, 'sir,' Major. I'm a civilian," replied the President's National Security Advisor seemingly absorbed by the papers on his desk. For more than a minute he never looked up.

Major Peter Newman was a startling contrast to the bloated and disheveled man in the two-thousand-dollar Armani suit seated before him. The Marine stood just over six feet and was trim and muscular. He was thirty-eight but looked much younger. His only "blemishes" were a broken nose that he'd earned during the second round of a Naval Academy boxing match and a two-inch scar above his left eyebrow made from a piece of hot shrapnel during the Gulf War. Major Newman stood at rigid attention in front of the desk.

Dr. Simon Harrod looked up at the ramrod-straight Marine standing in front of him, eyes fixed at the wall in the space above Harrod's head. Harrod was annoyed. Apparently letting this military martinet cool his well-polished heels for two hours in the West Wing reception lobby hadn't done much to instill timidity. He decided to put this Marine in his place right away.

"Look at *me* when I'm talking to you, not the wall! In this administration, we don't go for all that military mumbo jumbo!" Harrod barked.

"Whatever you say, sir."

It wasn't that Simon Harrod, Ph.D., disliked military men. Like the President, he *loathed* them. He'd had his fill of these close-cropped, cleanly shaven boneheads when he had been a professor of international studies at Harvard's Kennedy School. Now the grossly over-weight, rumpled, former antiwar activist had a dozen high-ranking Army, Navy, and Air Force officers toiling for him on the National Security Council staff. And he knew that behind his back, they contemptuously re-ferred to him as "Jabba the Hutt." He didn't care. He was content that now they had to dance to the beat of *his* drum or their careers were finished.

"Sit down." The Marine did as ordered, and Harrod went back to perusing the *Officer's Qualification Record and Confidential Personnel Summary* before him in the disarray of his desk. Newman's "short" bio ran seven pages, and the National Security Advisor took his time with it even though he already knew everything he needed to know about the officer now sitting as stiffly as he'd been standing. Without looking up, Har-rod ticked off the high points: "You're a regular military machine aren't you, Newman? Father is a retired Army brigadier . . . mother was an Army nurse . . . born at the post hospital at Fort Drum, New York . . . graduate of the Naval Academy . . . served in Grenada, Beirut, Panama, Desert Storm." Newman said nothing as Harrod continued reading.

"It says here that you didn't want this assignment, Major Newman. Why?"

"I'd rather be commanding Marines, sir."

"I told you not to call me 'sir.' I thought Marines were capable of following a simple order."

"What do you want me to call you—Mr. Harrod?"

"*Dr.* Harrod will do," said Jabba the Hutt.

Newman nodded but said nothing, so Harrod went back to the file and the *Personnel Summary* and started asking questions to which he already had the answers.

"You're married. What does your wife do?" asked Harrod in a more conciliatory tone.

"She's a flight attendant."

"Children?"

"No."

"You talk to your wife about your work?"

"Not if I'm not supposed to," replied the Marine.

"Well, here you're not supposed to. You got it?"

Newman nodded, knowing as he did so that he and his wife were barely speaking about anything of significance anyway, so this directive hardly mattered.

"What year did you graduate from Annapolis, Newman?"

"Class of '78."

"What was your class standing?"

"Number 143, top 15 percent."

"It says here you were 'deep selected for captain and major.' What's 'deep selected' mean?"

"I was promoted early, as they say, 'ahead of my peers.' "

"Is that because you have the Navy Cross and a Purple Heart from Desert Storm?" Harrod asked with a thinly disguised sneer.

"I don't know."

"Well, I'm not impressed. If you guys had done the job right, we wouldn't have this mess on our hands with Saddam Hussein."

Once more Newman didn't reply, so Harrod again buried himself in the officer's paperwork for a full five minutes. The Marine looked around the well-appointed office. Thick carpet. Nice furniture. Three phones. Large mahogany desk covered with piles of paper, many bearing classified cover sheets labeled *TOP SECRET.* Several bore the additional admonition *EYES ONLY FOR THE PRESIDENT.* On the walls, an eclectic collection of what appeared to Newman's unschooled eye to be original artwork: he recognized some of them—a Wyeth nude, a Remington landscape, and several modern pieces that he didn't recognize. Behind the cluttered desk was a watercolor of uncertain origin, depicting what could only be the grisly violence of General George Armstrong Custer's final moments at the Little Big Horn.

The National Security Advisor looked up to see Newman staring at the painting. "It's by a Native American artist. I got the idea from Hafez al Assad. In his presidential palace in Damascus, he has a painting of Saladin and the Saracens butchering crusaders. It reminds his visitors whom they are dealing with. I put this one here to remind all you green- and blue-suit types how stupid and costly military operations can be."

Harrod glanced down at the file and then back at Newman. "Now, it says here that up until yesterday you were assigned to the Operations and Plans Division at the Marine headquarters here in Washington. Is that right?"

"At the Navy Annex, yes."

"What did they tell you when they ordered you to report to the Secretary of the Navy and SecDef? Did any of them tell you what your assignment here on the NSC staff was to be?"

"No, I was only told that I should report to you for a two-year assignment."

"You may not last two years if you don't lighten up. You probably know this already, but I want to reiterate— you're the only Marine on the White House staff besides the captain who's assigned as one of the President's military aides."

"That's what I understand."

"Do you also understand that as long as you are assigned here you are to have *nothing* to do with the White House military office or your Marine Corps, and that after today you are not to wear a uniform here, ever, and that as the head of the NSC's Special Projects Office, you report only to me?"

"I do now."

"Good. I want you to go now and take care of the necessary paperwork to keep the paper shufflers happy. After you've done that, go home and get out of that monkey suit with all those ribbons, bells, and whistles. Medals and ribbons don't impress me or anyone else around here. Put on some civilian attire. You do have real clothes, don't you?"

"Yes," Newman said to the bloated figure behind the desk.

"Good. After you take care of filling out all the forms and get changed, come back here at 3:00 P.M. sharp. Tell my secretary to take care of getting you a White House

ID badge. And tell her I said to get you a staff-parking pass to hang on your rearview mirror so you can park inside 'the fence.' That's a big perk around here. And as fast as you can, grow some hair on your head. That GI haircut looks ridiculous. Go."

Major Newman stood, did an about-face, and left. It felt good to get a final military dig at his new boss.

●

Notwithstanding rumors Newman had heard to the contrary about this White House administration, the National Security Council's administrative and security office in the Old Executive Office Building was a hub of efficiency. The people who worked in the third-floor office of this gray stone building next door to the White House were older. He surmised that these were professionals, not political appointees. Unlike others he had seen that morning in the West Wing, the men were wearing coats and ties instead of jeans, and the women had on dresses and skirts. He noted, as any U.S. Marine would, that the men in this office had what he considered to be decent haircuts, and here, at least, it was the *women* who wore ponytails and earrings.

A woman who introduced herself as Carol Dayton, and identified herself as the NSC's administrative and security officer, handed Newman a checklist of offices to visit, forms to fill out, and documents to sign. In less than two hours, the Marine major had taken care of all the obligatory paperwork, been photographed for the treasured blue White House pass, had his retinas scanned, had his fingers printed, had signed reams of nondisclosure agreements for classified security "compartments" he had never known existed, been issued access codes for the White House Situation Room cipher locks, and been taken on a quick, cursory tour of the old structure so he wouldn't get lost on his way to work. He still didn't have an office, a desk, or a phone, and each time he asked one of the otherwise helpful and amiable administrative clerks where the Special Projects Office was, they shrugged or replied, "I dunno. Guess that's up to Dr. Harrod."

It was, all in all, relatively painless—even the stop at the small medical clinic on the second floor, where a Navy corpsman drew three vials of his blood. He asked why, given that the Marine Corps already maintained his medical records, but the young man only shrugged and said, "Got me, Major Newman. Guess they just want to have your blood type on hand in case you get a paper cut."

The corpsman thought this line was hilariously funny. But Newman made a mental note to keep one of his military dog tags, with his blood type stamped into it, on a chain around his neck, even if he wasn't allowed to wear his uniform.

By the time he had finished crossing all the t's, dotting all the i's, and all but signing his life away, it was shortly after noon. Newman decided he had just enough time to race out to his house in Falls Church—where he and his wife sometimes lived together—for a change of clothes.

As he strode out of the towering gray granite structure, a cold autumn rain was being wind-whipped up West Executive Avenue between the West Wing of the White House and the Old Executive Office Building. He turned right, toward the South West Gate, the wind and rain lashing his gray, military-issue raincoat, the drops darkening it as he walked. By the time he reached the Ellipse, where he had left his six-year-old Chevy Tahoe, Newman was soaked.

He found his car and a ticket citing him for parking without a White House sticker. Newman got in, backed out, and wheeled around the circle, south of the white mansion he had already come to dislike, and headed west on Constitution Avenue, across the Roosevelt Bridge, and onto Route 50 into Virginia and toward his home, five miles away, in Falls Church.

✪

Newman and his wife Rachel had bought the three-bedroom, brick split-level on Creswell Drive nine years earlier—when they were still in love with each other instead of their separate careers. Newman had met Rachel on a blind date arranged by his sister Nancy. She and Rachel had been roommates at the University of Virginia, and they had driven up from Charlottesville on a lark to "meet some Marines" while Peter was attending the Officer's Basic Course at Quantico in September '78, after he'd graduated from the Naval Academy.

Despite their differences, Newman was smitten by his sister's friend. Like Newman's sister, Rachel was a nursing student, but Rachel didn't want to work in a hospital—she wanted to fly. "Didn't you know that the first flight attendants all had to be nurses?" she asked him one day. Besides, she said with her ravishing smile, "Flying is more romantic."

Rachel really was a romantic. She had grown up on a comfortable farm in Culpepper, Virginia, riding horses and searching for wildflowers in the meadows. Often she'd ride horseback into the countryside with a picnic lunch and spread a blanket to read sonnets or write poetry. He, on the other hand, was both a military man and a sports nut. Many of their early dates consisted of football games at UVA and Annapolis, parades at Quantico and Washington, and visits to the many Revolutionary and Civil War battlefields that dot the Virginia countryside.

After graduating from the Officer's Basic Course, Newman had been ordered to take command of a rifle platoon in the Second Marine Division at Camp Lejeune, North Carolina. And until he deployed to the Mediterranean with the Third Battalion, Eighth Marine Regiment later that year, he spent every weekend when he wasn't on duty somewhere between Camp Lejeune and Charlottesville, trying to be near Rachel while she finished up her last year at "Mr. Jefferson's University."

When Rachel graduated in June of '79, she did what she said she was going to do: she got hired by TWA and went off to their flight attendant training school. By the time she finished the TWA training course in Saint Louis, Missouri, Newman was deployed with his infantry company in the Mediterranean aboard the USS *Fairfax County*. He wrote to her every day and proposed to her over the phone from Athens, Greece, while the ship was in port for repairs.

They married in the chapel at Camp Lejeune soon after Newman returned from his first deployment, which coincided with his promotion to first lieutenant. By then TWA had decided that Rachel should be based at Dulles Airport in Virginia—meaning that her flights would originate and terminate there, even though she was trying to make a home for herself with her new husband on the coast of North Carolina.

Rachel had a difficult time adjusting to military life. In fact, she never quite did, though to be fair, she did her best. She watched how many other new service wives reacted to their husbands' line of work, but she never felt like she fit in. No matter how hard she tried, Rachel couldn't tell a corporal from a colonel and wasn't about to surrender her life to simply become an extension of her husband's career. And with deployment following deployment, she figured out why her husband's friends would joke, "If the Marine Corps had wanted you to have a wife, they would have issued you one." Stuck miles from her family and exhausted from racing up and down Interstate 95 for her flight assignments, Rachel was heartsick and terribly lonely. When he was home, her husband seemed totally unaware of the problem.

Newman wasn't quite as oblivious as he seemed. He just didn't know what to do about his wife's growing unhappiness. He had confided to one or two of his comrades that his wife "wasn't really happy." One of them had suggested that he might want to try marriage counseling. But to a self-made man like Peter Newman, that implied weakness, and besides, he thought, real men don't need outsiders to solve their marital problems.

By 1985, Newman was a captain—already decorated for service in Grenada, Beirut, and Central America—and on the fast track to future promotions. He was assigned as a tactics instructor back at the "Basic School" in Quantico, where he and Rachel had met seven years earlier. He decided that if they bought a house, she'd feel like she had more ties to him and it might give them a place of their own from which to build a relationship.

They found a place in Falls Church, Virginia. Newman knew it would be a long daily commute for him, but Rachel had loved the place at first sight—it was convenient to Dulles and she'd simply had enough of living in the cramped, run-down quarters on sprawling bases like Lejeune and Quantico.

When they first saw the house on Creswell Drive, surrounded by towering oaks and maples, complete with a fenced backyard and quiet neighborhood, Rachel had excitedly said, "It's perfect for raising a family! We can put a sandbox over there, and you can hang a swing from that branch right there and give our kids lots of rides!" Rachel, the romantic, dreamed about how she could turn a house into a home.

Now, almost a decade later, there was no swing, no sandbox, and no kids. And every time Newman looked at that inviting branch on the maple tree in the backyard, he would think of Rachel's two miscarriages and hate the tree for mocking his virility and his wife's infertility.

After completing his three-year stint teaching tactics to new officers at the Basic School, Newman had been rewarded with a year as a student at Quantico's Amphibious Warfare School. While there, he was deep-selected for major, and after graduation, he was assigned to command the Second Force Reconnaissance Company at Camp Lejeune, North Carolina. He and Rachel rented what they called "the house on Creswell" to a Navy commander assigned to the Pentagon. When Newman and his wife moved back into the house in 1992, he'd insisted on repainting the entire interior. The Navy commander and his family had decorated one of the upstairs bedrooms as a nursery. Newman now used it as his home office.

●

As Newman made the turn off Sleepy Hollow Drive, he noticed for the first time a dark-blue, late-model Chrysler sedan making the turn behind him. It hung back about a block, but he saw it as it followed him onto Creswell. And as he turned into his driveway, the Chrysler cruised past, two men in suits sitting in the front seat. Newman memorized the license plate number, make, and model, for later, in case it was something to warrant his suspicion. His first thought was that this was Harrod's way of keeping tabs on him, and he resented it.

He let himself in from the attached garage, shut off the security alarm, ran upstairs to the bedroom that he occasionally shared with his wife, and began changing clothes. He figured that Dr. Harrod wouldn't be hard to please—he'd be happy with anything that wasn't a uniform. He chose a dark blue pinstripe suit and a white shirt. As he was putting a half-Windsor knot in his best blue-and-gold regimental-striped tie, he saw the note on his dresser.

> *Dear P. J.—I drew this afternoon's flight to Chicago. Tomorrow I fly to San Diego and then back here. I'll stay at the airport and nap. My next assignment is to fly to London from Dulles and the turnaround back here. I should be back Friday night. I left a salad for your dinner. Love, R.*

"Great. More rabbit food," Newman mumbled to himself. For whatever reason, the Rachel who had once loved a good steak had suddenly become a vegetarian. On those rare evenings when they actually sat down to eat together, she would serve him up a big plate of green stuff with the admonition, "If you eat this you'll live longer."

And he would invariably reply, "If this is all I get to eat, who wants to live any longer?" The humor she initially found in this line was very short-lived.

Knowing that weather or mechanical problems could cancel her flight, Newman flipped over his wife's note and wrote,

> *R— Couldn't get out of the White House assignment. Don't have an office phone number yet. Will leave a message on your pager when I know what it is. Will probably be late. Don't wait up. Love, P. J.*

He left the note on her dresser, wondering as he did so why he even bothered.

After checking his outfit in the mirror, Newman set the security alarm, locked up the house, and eased his car down the driveway onto the street. It was still raining hard, and as he was wondering half aloud if it was going to change to snow, he noticed the blue car easing away from the curb nearly a block away. It followed him onto Route 50 as he headed back into Washington, but stayed a respectable ten to twenty car lengths back all the way into the city. Newman took the E-Street Expressway off the Roosevelt Bridge and soon pulled up to the South West Gate on West Executive Avenue.

A uniformed Secret Service officer came out from the guard booth as he pulled his Tahoe up to the gate. Newman rolled down the window and showed the officer his new White House ID and the "West Exec" parking pass. The guard checked the ID, the parking pass, the car's license, and said, "You're Space 73, Mr. Newman. It's about halfway up on the left, just past the OEOB entrance."

"OEOB?"

"Old Executive Office Building."

Newman nodded, wondering what else he needed to know just to work here every day. One thing he had just learned was that the White House Access System computers somewhere in the OEOB had already been updated to reflect his new status. He had been "Major Newman" the first time he'd entered the eighteen-acre White House complex that morning. Now he was "Mr. Newman."

As he pulled into the numbered space, he noticed that the dark-blue Chrysler hadn't pulled into the gate behind him. Newman couldn't see it turn north on 17th and pull into the garage beneath the modern, red brick façade of the New Executive Office Building, just across Pennsylvania Avenue from the White House.

As he entered the green-canopied West Wing entrance, the civilian-clad Marine removed his raincoat and walked up to the Secret Service agent who was seated at a desk just inside the door. Before he could even take out his White House ID, the agent said, "Dr. Harrod will see you in the Situation Room, Mr. Newman."

Instead of going up the stairs to the National Security Advisor's office where he had been earlier in the day, Newman turned right, down a corridor past the White House Mess—"the most exclusive restaurant in Washington"—and walked up to a massive wooden door at the end of the hallway. Before he could slide his White House pass through the card reader and put his forehead up against the optical scanner, he heard the metallic click of the electronic lock being opened. Somewhere above him there was a camera he couldn't see. And at someplace he didn't know, a person he'd probably never meet already knew who *he* was—and that he was expected. It made Newman vaguely uneasy.

A cheerful young man greeted him enthusiastically as he entered. "Good afternoon, Mr. Newman. I'm Specialist Jonathan Yardley; welcome to the Situation Room. Dr. Harrod's in the conference room on the phone with the President. He'll signal us when it's time for you to go in." Yardley gestured to two lights—one green, the other red—above a door in front of them. The red light was illuminated.

"While we're waiting, why don't I show you around?" And without waiting for an answer, the younger man started walking Newman around and introducing him to the five men and two women on duty. The facility was smaller than Newman had thought it would be, but it looked for all intents and purposes like any other headquarters operations center—except that everyone was in civilian-clothes.

"This is the second watch. We have five watch sections, seven duty officers, and a senior watch officer for each. I'm the SWO for this watch. Unless there's a major crisis, we rotate the watch every eight hours. Most of us are warrant officers in the military, but some are detailed here from the CIA, NSA, State Department, FBI, Treasury, and Department of Energy. Everyone here has clearances for every security compartment. And nearly all of us have been here for ten years or more."

There was a quiet hum of activity. Newman noticed that the phones chirped instead of ringing, and that everyone had a computer console in a small carrel. He also saw that the phones didn't have standard dial pads; rather, the dial pad was on the computer screen. Each screen had rows of colored boxes with labels: *POTUS, FLOTUS, VPOTUS, STATE, OSD, DCI, NMCC, FBI OPS, JUSTICE, TREASURY,* and *COAST GUARD.* Newman was surprised to note that one of the boxes was labeled: *UN OPS CTR.*

Yardley continued, "Every department and agency has its own watch center. We can connect with any one of them or contact them all simultaneously in the event of a crisis. Over here," Yardley gestured to a carrel in the corner, "we're having WHCA"—he pronounced it *wha-cah*—"install a monitoring system for the watch officer who will be keeping track of you."

"What's WHCA?" Newman asked.

"Sorry," responded Yardley. "We get so used to the

local lingo, we sometimes forget that not everybody knows it. WHCA stands for the White House Communications Agency. You never hear about it, even though more than five hundred people are assigned to it— mostly from the Air Force and Army—though there are a few Marines, I think. WHCA is responsible for all presidential communications, both secure and unclassified. They handle all of the encryption systems, make sure that the President can launch or stop a nuclear war, and generally install and maintain everything from computers to telephones to secure video links so that the President can be in touch with anyone, anywhere, anytime."

Before Newman could ask what "keeping track" of him meant, there was an electronic *ping* and Yardley looked toward the lights over the conference room door. The green light had come on. "It looks like the National Security Advisor is ready for you now. We don't want to keep the doctor waiting, do we?"

"No, I suppose not," Newman muttered, wanting to ask a litany of questions but knowing that they'd have to wait.

"Well, welcome aboard and good luck," said the loquacious watch officer, holding out his hand. And then as Newman shook it, "I sure hope you'll fare better than your predecessor."

Taken aback, Newman started to ask what had happened to his predecessor when the conference room door swung open and Jabba the Hutt bellowed, "I can't wait all day, Newman. What's going on here?"

It occurred to Newman that it was an entirely appropriate question.

CHAPTER TWO
Massacre in Mogadishu

Situation Room
The White House
Washington, D.C.
Tuesday, 29 November 1994
1510 Hours, Local

Nice of you to make it, Newman," Dr. Harrod said sarcastically. His reprimand was loud enough for the whole staff to hear it. "It might occur to you that I don't have time for you to socialize with these people—they have work to do, and so do I." Newman's face flushed with embarrassment, and as he entered the conference room, he was aware that Yardley and all of his situation room personnel had their eyes riveted on him.

The National Security Advisor was in his shirtsleeves, his suit coat draped over one of the twenty or so chairs in the room where presidents had been meeting with their most trusted advisors since Dwight David Eisenhower. It was, Newman observed, a very small room for so many big decisions.

As they moved into the wood-paneled conference room, Harrod closed the door behind them and said,

"Those are better clothes. Now all you need is hair."
Harrod laughed at his own little joke. Newman did not.

"Sit down." Newman sat, taking a seat across the
smooth, polished mahogany table from Harrod—unaware
that the Director of Central Intelligence usually occupied the chair that he had chosen during meetings of the
National Security Council. On the table was a file folder
with a green-bordered cover sheet. Although it was upside down from where he sat, Newman could read the
bold print:

TOP SECRET
CODEWORD ACCESS REQUIRED
EYES ONLY FOR THE PRESIDENT

Harrod, still standing, looked totally unkempt. His
tie had been loosened to keep from choking his fat neck,
but it still ended abruptly a good four inches above his
belt. The National Security Advisor's considerable
paunch made the gap between the buttons on his shirt
front swell into little ovals, and it seemed to Newman
that they were about to pop. And despite the November
weather and cool temperature in the room, Harrod's
shirt was sweat-soaked beneath his arms. Lighting a
cigar, he sat down, shoved several loose pages of paper
into the file folder, and looked up at the Marine. "I just
got off the phone with the President. He's authorized me
to proceed. You are now officially the director of the
Special Projects office. I'll give you a list of who can
know about this assignment; it'll be short. As far as anyone else is concerned, you're a military assistant to the
National Security Advisor. Understood?"

"No, Dr. Harrod, it's not understood. Nor do I understand why I was followed home and then back here

by a dark-blue, late-model Chrysler with smoked-glass windows, more antennas than a cell-phone tower, and a D.C. license, ISL-355."

"Very good, Newman. I'm glad you noticed. *I* had you followed. The men in that car will very shortly be working for you. I had you tailed for three reasons. First, to make sure that you didn't go running back to the Marines to whine about this assignment; second, it's good training for *them;* and third, to see how observant you are. You passed. They failed."

"Exactly what is this job, Dr. Harrod?" Newman asked. There was still anger in his voice.

"Relax, Mr. Newman. This is going to take a few minutes. After I'm finished you can ask all the questions you want. Then I'll take you over to the OEOB, show you your office, and introduce you to your new colleagues.

"You may not want to be here, Newman, but you're here for a reason. Even though you only got your orders last Friday to report to the NSC, you were very carefully selected. You're here because of what happened in Mogadishu, Somalia, in October of last year." At that, Harrod paused, for Newman reacted just the way he expected—as if he had been struck—though the Marine said nothing.

Quieter, in a whisper that he substituted for sympathy and sincerity, Harrod continued. "I know that your brother was one of those Army Rangers who were killed. I'm sorry. It never should have happened." Harrod paused again.

Harrod had brought up images and feelings that Newman had tried to repress for more than a year. He moistened his lips but said nothing. His new boss continued. "You're here because we want to make sure that what happened to your brother James never happens again. The President is adamant that those who did it be appropriately punished. We think that you're the right person to make sure that Mohammed Farrah Aidid never commits another atrocity and that he becomes an example to the entire world of what happens to those who kill Americans and UN peacekeepers." Harrod waited to let his words sink in.

The Marine stared hard at the polished tabletop, struggling for control and adamant that this civilian not see his emotion. It seemed awkward to hear his brother called James. Newman knew his younger brother as Jimmy, and then Jim. His brother—not quite four years his junior—had been buried in Arlington Cemetery for a little more than a year.

Peter Newman recalled those events and felt, ironically, that the man responsible for sending his only brother to his death was only one floor above, in the Oval Office. And now Newman would be working for him.

Harrod flicked the ash off his cigar and watched to see if he had wrung any emotion out of the Marine. Only a brief glistening in his eyes betrayed any feelings he'd had over the events of last year. And Newman blinked a few times more than usual. But other than that, Harrod couldn't tell whether he was getting through to the Marine or not—or even how much the Marine cared about his brother.

Harrod was going to change the subject, but the interview was interrupted by a beeping from his pager. "Excuse me, Newman. I've gotta take this call." He went to the other end of the room and punched one of the numbers listed in the phone's speed-dial list. He droned on for several minutes, his voice just low enough for Newman not to hear. But it didn't matter. The Marine's thoughts were elsewhere.

●

If anything, Peter Newman was more proud of Captain James Bedford Newman, U.S. Army, West Point class of '84, than he was of his own military résumé. His brother had indeed been a Ranger, just as Harrod said. But in 1992, after serving in Desert Storm, the soft-spoken, lanky officer with the big shoulders and even bigger smile had quietly volunteered for Delta Force, the Army's elite, supersecret, counterterrorist outfit. The "Dreaded-D," based at Fort Bragg, North Carolina, selected only the best for its ranks. After months of harsh, grueling training, during which all but 9 of the 103 soldiers in his class dropped out, Captain Jim Newman became a Delta Force team leader. And little more than a year later, he was dead—killed on the night of October 3, 1993, during the bloodiest twenty-four hours of combat that the U.S. military had experienced since the Vietnam War.

The thirty-three-year-old officer had been part of a specially organized unit comprised of more than 450 Rangers from Fort Benning, Georgia; Newman's Delta Force Squadron from Fort Bragg, North Carolina; Navy SEALs out of Norfolk, Virginia; USAF para-rescue jumpers (PJs); and airmen of the 160th Special Operations Aviation Regiment—the "Night Stalkers."

Dubbed "Task Force Ranger" by the Pentagon, this extraordinary group of highly trained specialists had been secretly dispatched to war-torn Mogadishu, Somalia, in August 1993. Their mission: to capture or kill the murderous Somali warlord Mohammed Farrah Aidid, or, failing that, to disable his brutal Somalia National Alliance (SNA). In his bid for power, General Aidid had declared war on anyone and everyone and didn't care that he was now fighting the most powerful nation on earth.

When Captain Jim Newman and his Delta operators had deployed, he and all those with him were confident that they would deal with this petty, tinhorn despot in short order. It had all seemed so easy when they arrived at the sunbaked airport beside the Indian Ocean, less than 250 miles north of the equator. But when they landed and the airplane's door opened, the rush of hot air—literally like an oven—seemed to suck their breath away.

And from then on, it only got worse. Intelligence on Aidid's whereabouts and those of his key lieutenants was as scarce as a cold drink of water. The CIA and the Army's Intelligence Support Activity, called "ISA" by the Delta shooters, had a presence in Mogadishu, but they weren't located at the airport with Task Force Ranger. Instead, they were at the bombed-out, windowless, and vandalized former residence of the U.S. ambassador.

In his letters to his older brother back home, Jim Newman had written that there were other problems as well—the kind of problems that both Newman boys had learned to avoid at their respective service academies. In one of his early missives, shortly after arriving in Mogadishu, Jim had written, *"Get this. We're the only outfit on the ground in Somalia that reports directly to U.S. command authority. All the other military units here report to the UN. God help us if we ever need real backup. I wonder if anyone back there remembers those lessons from Clausewitz on unity of command!"* In the aftermath, Peter Newman would re-read his brother's words and wonder if anyone in Washington had had the same misgivings.

In his last note to his brother, written on September 20, Jim Newman had shared more of his concerns and uncertainties than ever before. Newman kept the letter in a folder in his desk.

Dear Pete,

Greetings once again from the armpit of Africa. They are calling this mission "Operation Gothic Serpent." It's appropriate because this guy Aidid really is a snake. He not only has the home-field advantage, but he's getting outside help. Our intel guys say that Aidid is getting a big boost from a Saudi exile named Osama bin Laden. It looks as though this guy bin Laden has used his own considerable bankroll to send in a bunch of his hired guns, who have been itching for a fight ever since the Soviets pulled out of Afghanistan. The ISA guys say that bin Laden's thugs are the ones who taught the Somalis how to tinker with the fuse on an RPG so that it can be used to shoot down helicopters. It has certainly made life very interesting for all of us.

Last week the blue bonnets at the UN really botched one up big-time. Somebody told 'em that Aidid was holding a big powwow downtown, so the UN—that's right, the UN—sent six gunships in to take the building apart with TOWs and Hellfire missiles. Killed about a dozen of Aidid's cronies, but the boss was a no-show.

Aidid and this Osama guy have now declared that it's payback time and they have their "technicals"—Somalis in Toyota pickup trucks with .50-cal machine guns in the back—racing around town shooting at anything with a UN or U.S. flag.

*As if that wasn't bad enough, when the UN
"peacekeepers" from Saudi Arabia, Pakistan, and
Malaysia aren't shooting at Somalis, they are
holding intramural fire fights with each other. Our
boss has asked for some armor to help get things
back under control, and your Marines have some
offshore, but apparently nobody at the Pentagon's
puzzle palace wants to tell the folks at 1600 PA
Ave. that this little nation-building exercise is
coming unraveled.*

*That's it from the "war is hell" and the
"disasters-in-progress" departments. Give Rachel
my love. Tell Mom and Dad when you talk to
them that little Jimmy is doing just fine and that,
in exchange for two camels and a goat, I have purchased eleven beautiful Somali wives to look after
me in my old age.*

He had signed it *"Rangers lead the way. Love, Jim."*
And then at the very bottom of the page, he had penned:
*"P.S. Tell Mom and our sister that I am saying my
prayers!"*

Less than two weeks after he sent that letter, forty-
two days after he and his comrades arrived in Somalia,
Jim Newman and seventeen of his fellow Delta Force
operators, Rangers, and airmen were dead and seventy-
three others were wounded. The next communication
that Peter Newman read about his brother was the stark
Mailgram that his parents had received on October 5,
the day after a ritual visit by an Army colonel and a military chaplain to their home along the Hudson River in
upstate New York. The Mailgram left them with more
questions than answers:

DEAR BRIGADIER GEN. AND MRS. NEWMAN:

THIS CONFIRMS PERSONAL NOTIFICATION MADE TO YOU BY A REP-
RESENTATIVE OF THE SECRETARY OF THE ARMY THAT YOUR SON, CAP-
TAIN JAMES B. NEWMAN, DIED AT MOGADISHU SOMALIA ON 3 OCTOBER
1993. ANY QUESTIONS YOU MAY HAVE SHOULD BE DIRECTED TO YOUR
CASUALTY ASSISTANCE OFFICER. PLEASE ACCEPT MY DEEPEST SYMPA-
THY IN YOUR BEREAVEMENT.

SINCERELY,
WILLIAM E. WILKES, COLONEL, U.S. ARMY

Peter Newman didn't have to turn to the casualty assistance officer for answers to his questions, for he
knew much more about his brother's death than the
terse official Army notification had revealed. At Headquarters Marine Corps—"HQMC" to Marines—Newman had been responsible for briefing the Marines'
senior officers on all issues regarding "Special Operations," the euphemism to describe activities conducted
by units like Marine Force Reconnaissance, the Navy
SEALs, and the supersecret Delta Force.

The military's Special Operations units are comprised
of highly trained warriors, all volunteers, handpicked to
do the most difficult and dangerous tasks in the U.S.
armed forces. They are the ones called upon to conduct
deep reconnaissance, collect covert intelligence, rescue
hostages, operate "behind the lines," "take out" terrorists, and succeed in real-life "impossible" missions.

Newman's job at the HQMC had required that he
pore over highly classified after-action reports and
back-channel cables between the commanders of these
units and their home bases, extract "lessons learned,"
and incorporate them into Marine Corps doctrine.

Many of the reports he had sent in from the field years before, when he had commanded the Second Force Reconnaissance Company, were still in the locked files of his office at HQMC.

Now, thirteen months after his brother's horrible death, here he was sitting in the White House Situation Room while his new boss prattled on over the phone. Newman could still vividly recall how he had learned the terrible news.

❂

At 6:55 A.M. on Sunday, October 3, 1993, the Marine Headquarters Command Center duty officer had called Newman at his home in Falls Church. Newman was already up, and as was his practice when his wife was out of town, he'd already been out for an early morning three-mile run in the crisp, early autumn dawn.

"Major Newman? Warrant Officer Davidson, here at the command center. Sorry to bother you on the weekend, but NMCC has advised us that a hostile-fire event is going down in Mogadishu. There's a lot of secure traffic coming across, and CMC is going to want a brief on this in the morning."

"Roger that, Gunner. I'll be there in about forty minutes." Newman knew that's how long it would take him to shower, change into his uniform, and drive to the Navy Annex, the official name for the five-story, World War II–era, faded yellow brick row of warehouses that the Marines called HQMC.

Rachel was due into Dulles that afternoon, inbound on a flight from London, so Newman left a note for her before heading into town. He turned his radio to 1500 AM, Washington's all-news station. There was a report on rumors of a coup being plotted against Boris Yeltsin in Moscow, a story about the President's travel itinerary for a trip to the West Coast, and a sports piece hyping Monday evening's Washington Redskins game in Miami. There was nothing at all in the newscast about events happening a third of the way around the world in Somalia.

It was shortly before 7:45 A.M. when Newman arrived at the HQMC security gate, and it was immediately obvious to him that he wasn't the only one to have gotten a call from the command center. On a Sunday morning in peacetime the headquarters parking lot should be nearly empty. Instead, several dozen cars were parked inside the fence surrounding the building. He noticed that his boss, Lieutenant General George Grisham, the deputy chief of staff for Operations and Plans, was already there. Clearly, something big affecting the U.S. military was happening. Newman recognized the feeling that was growing in his gut. It wasn't hunger from not eating breakfast. It was dread.

Newman bounded up two flights of stairs to what everyone else in the world would have called the third floor. But not the Marines. In keeping with the tradition of the naval service, the ground floor was known as "zero deck," the second floor was first deck, the third floor was known as the second deck, and so on.

Most of the "heavies," or the general officers, had their offices on the second deck, as did the commandant, the top Marine. Because the corps was so very small, they all knew Newman, and even though the assignment was highly classified, they also knew he had a brother serving with Delta who had been dispatched with Task Force Ranger to Mogadishu. Newman went immediately to the command center and presented his ID card to the sentry, a Marine corporal.

After checking the ID card against a list of names on

a clipboard and making sure that the photo on the card matched the officer standing in front of him, the corporal hit a button beneath the counter. There was a buzzing sound as the electronic lock on the door opened and Newman stepped into the command center.

Inside, he was greeted by a quiet hum of activity and a dozen people—five more than the usual contingent of watch officers, noncommissioned officers, and communicators. Two technicians were bent over one of the secure video receivers. The screen was mostly a mass of visual static, but occasionally it would shimmer with the aerial view of a sunbaked city and its streets and buildings. Even from the intermittent images, Newman knew what he was seeing: the city of Mogadishu from several thousand feet in the air, captured by high-powered video cameras mounted on a Navy EP-3 Orion surveillance aircraft. The images flickering on the screen were beamed from the plane flying at ten thousand feet over eastern Africa, up to a satellite, and back down to U.S. military commanders and intelligence centers at the airport in Mogadishu, and to intelligence and command centers in Florida, North Carolina, Washington, and other sensitive military installations.

As Newman leaned over the monitor in hopes that the adjustments made by the two techs would bring up a steady picture, his boss hung up one of the secure phones—the direct link to the National Military Command Center at the Pentagon.

"Pete, I'm glad you're here," said General Grisham. "I'm not going to beat around the bush. About two hours ago your brother's Delta team was sent into the Black Sea in Mog to snatch a couple of Aidid's thugs. His D-boys got to their objective and took the target subjects into custody, but two Black Hawks have gone down and now ninety-nine Delta operators and Rangers are stranded in a really bad part of town.

"Bad part of town" was putting it mildly. The Marines, first sent to Somalia in 1992 and then pulled out in May of 1993, had irreverently started calling the area around Mogadishu's Bakara Market the "Black Sea." It was a stronghold for Mohammed Farrah Aidid and his Habr Gidr clan, and the place where he recruited thousands of young fighters for his so-called Somali National Alliance. The "Black Sea" handle stuck, and it was now commonplace to refer to the neighborhood by its racially tinged nickname. It was not the place for a gunfight.

Newman listened as General Grisham continued. "I've reminded the Joint Staff that in addition to help from the Tenth Mountain Division Quick Reaction Force, they also have a Marine Expeditionary Unit with tanks, light armored vehicles, helos, gunships, and Harriers aboard the amphibious ready group offshore. It's almost 1600 hours out there now. They think that they will be able to get everyone out before dark, but I'm not so sure."

Newman wasn't so sure either. He had been to Mogadishu twice with his Force Recon Teams—but that was before the new commander in chief had rolled into town with his team of "nation builders." Since then, things had gone from bad to worse in Somalia, and now, of all things, the UN was in charge!

The general looked down at his notes, then back at Newman. "The chairman has called for a planners' meeting in the Tank at 1300. I want you and Colonel Weeks to work up some options for us, and let's see if we can help them figure a way to get your brother out of this mess without getting him or any more Americans hurt."

The next twenty-four hours were the worst that Peter Newman had known in all his thirty-seven years. He'd been shot at and hit more than once during his fifteen years in the Marines. Yet, even when things had been critical in combat, he felt like he was always able to do something to alter the outcome, no matter how dire the circumstances. But now he was in an intolerable situation: stuck in a high-tech command center in Washington, but unable to command anything. The room was full of electronic gadgets that allowed him to monitor events as they occurred; yet he was helpless—relegated to playing the role of a long-distance, impotent witness to a personal horror. For only the third time in his life, he thought to himself, *If I knew how to pray, I would.*

For the rest of Sunday and on into the predawn hours of Monday, Newman spent nearly every minute in the HQMC command center, piecing together bits of message traffic, fragments of desperate radio calls, and occasional pictures on the secure video link. By the time General Grisham had returned from his meeting at the Pentagon, it was dark in Mogadishu, and the intermittent signals received on the secure video link were no longer in color. Instead, the infrared, heat-sensitive cameras mounted on the EP-3 surveillance planes sent video pictures that showed up on the monitors as an eerie, green monochrome. Yet, because of its resolution and clarity, thousands of Somali guerrillas and civilians could be seen moving around the tiny perimeter in the heart of a hostile African city where Jim Newman and ninety-eight other Americans were slowly being cut to pieces by Somali machine guns, AK-47s, and rocket-propelled grenades (RPGs). It vaguely occurred to Newman that William Travis and his 182 Texans hadn't been this outnumbered at the Alamo.

General Grisham called Newman aside and said quietly, "This is a real mess, and it's gonna take a lot of prayer to get those boys outta there. Even though the White House sent the D-boys and Rangers in to get Aidid, they are now saying that the UN needs to find a political solution!" Then he added, "I wish that the guys who think they're running this war knew what end is up. From the beginning, the troops in Mog have had no decent intel, and every time the orders are cut, they get conflicting signals. Now that we've got a bunch of troops on the ground in big trouble, nobody over at the White House seems to know what to do. All they seem to know is what they *don't* want us to do—and that's send in a whole lot more Americans to rescue the Rangers and Delta. When I suggested that we land the MEU sitting offshore, the chairman called over to the White House, and the National Security Advisor told him to let the UN work it out. They're smoking something other than tobacco at 1600 Pennsylvania Avenue if they think the UN can get their act together in time to save these guys in the Black Sea!"

After delivering this appalling assessment, the general turned to Newman and the senior watch officer, Warrant Officer Bill Sturdevan, and said, "I'll be down in my office. Let me know if there are any developments." Newman went back to his lonely vigil, monitoring the satellite communications and incoming cables, and hoping that his brother would come out of this alive.

Shortly before dawn in Mogadishu, a rescue force of Rangers, Delta Force specialists, Tenth Mountain Division soldiers, Malaysians, and Pakistanis punched through the three miles from the airport to the surrounded Rangers and Delta Force operators dying in the "Black Sea." But by then, though his brother didn't know it, Captain James Newman, dehydrated, bloody from wounds received during nearly eight hours of battle, hoarse from shouting above the din of nonstop gunfire, was dead. He had been killed instantly by the earsplitting, flesh-searing burst of a rocket-propelled grenade. As the blast of the RPG snuffed out his life, James Bedford Newman was trying to protect one of the grievously wounded crewmen from the first of the two downed Black Hawk helicopters.

At the Marine command center, the watch officers and duty section shifts had changed three times by early Monday. But other than taking time out to refill a large mug with coffee and the inevitable call of nature that it produced, Newman stayed glued to a communications console in the corner of the room. In addition to all the secure communications gear, the center had several standard television sets tuned to normal cable and network broadcasts, which stayed on, muted in the background, throughout the long day and night.

But until early Monday morning there had been no mention of the horrible battle under way in Mogadishu.

And even the first news broadcasts simply said that "several American soldiers" had been killed and others wounded in an "exchange of gunfire" in Somalia. There were no names or units and no footage, only a map on the screen so Americans wouldn't have to consult an atlas while they prepared breakfast.

At the Pentagon and other military command centers in the U.S., casualty reports had been coming in throughout the night—with estimated numbers of killed and wounded but no names. Then, just before Monday's sunrise in Washington, the National Security Agency alerted all U.S. military commands that a European TV crew was sending video to their network in Paris on a United Nations press uplink. The message simply stated, "The video purports to depict U.S. casualties." No one, certainly not Peter Newman, was prepared for what was on the video.

Less than five minutes after NSA's alert notification, the intercepted signal came up on one of the command center's secure video links. The audio portion was unintelligible, but the video was unmistakable and grotesque: the bodies of two American soldiers were shown being dragged down dusty streets and mutilated by mobs of jeering Somalis. In the two-minute-forty-second-long videotape, the cameras captured the unforgettable images of enraged crowds jabbing the corpses with AK-47s, beating the bloody bodies with sticks, kicking them, all the while chanting and screaming. Some were laughing crazily.

The entire command center duty section gathered in front of the monitor and watched in horrified silence, utterly sickened. Master Sergeant John Murphy, a tough veteran infantryman who wore a Silver Star and a Purple Heart from Vietnam along with a Bronze Star from combat in the Gulf War, sat at one of the consoles and said, "Oh, dear God—how can this be happening? We were sent there to help those people!" Newman felt bile rising in his throat as his near-empty stomach reacted in revulsion to the images on the screen, his heart racing with adrenaline as he peered at the bodies, telling himself that neither looked like his brother.

When the transmission was over, Staff Sergeant Janet Howard, the only woman on this watch, had tears flowing down her face. Her husband, a gunnery sergeant, was assigned to the MEU aboard the Navy Amphibious Ready Group lying off Mogadishu. "They won't let those pictures be broadcast here, will they?" she asked no one in particular.

"Top." Murphy looked up and with burning cynicism born of too many years in uniform replied, "That videotape will be on every network by tonight's evening news." But he was wrong. Every network had the tape by noon and repeated it *ad nauseum* for days.

Just before noon the first confirmed names of the casualties came in on a classified message from the Joint Special Operations Command. When the message popped up on the screens in the center, there was a sudden hush as though all the air had escaped from the room. Everyone knew why Major Peter Newman had been there day and night for almost thirty hours.

The message was preceded by the ominous admonition:

CONFIDENTIAL
CASUALTY REPORT—NOT FOR RELEASE TO PUBLIC AFFAIRS.

And immediately below:

WARNING: UNDER NO CIRCUMSTANCES MAY SPECIAL
MISSION PERSONNEL BE IDENTIFIED BY UNIT.
ALL PERSONNEL SHALL BE DESIGNATED AS
"RANGERS" IN NOK NOTIFICATIONS AND ANY
SUBSEQUENT PAO RELEASES.

Finally, just above the list of names:

THIS CAS REP IS ACCURATE BUT INCOMPLETE.

His heart racing, Newman scanned down the alphabetical list to be used for notifying next of kin of those who were killed in action. His emotions were both hopeful and fearful. And then his eyes stopped, and he read the horrible words: NEWMAN, JAMES B., CAPT. U.S. ARMY, KIA. NOTIFY NOK.

Peter Newman had been in the Marines too long to hope that this was some kind of error. He stared in shock at the screen for a moment and then, without a word to the others in the command center, got up from the communications console, and with his jaws clenched, bolted for the men's head down the hall. He held himself in check until the door swung closed behind him. First his stomach ejected what little it had in it. Then came the tears.

When he regained his composure, he went down the hallway to his office, ran an electric razor over his face, and walked down the corridor to General Grisham's office. He was ushered in without fanfare. That kind of word spread quickly in the Corps, the "Band of Brothers."

"Pete, I'm sorry about Jim. He was a good soldier," said the general. His face was a mask of sorrow and sadness.

"Yes sir, he was, and a great brother too. I think I'd better take a day or two of leave and go up to New York and see my folks. I'd like to be there when the casualty assistance officer makes his call. My mom is going to take this awfully hard." Newman's voice, despite his efforts to control it, cracked as he spoke those last words.

"Go ahead, son. Have Staff Sergeant Winsat take care of the paperwork. Please give your parents my sincere regrets."

Newman went back to his office. While he waited for Winsat, who was the Ops & Plans administration chief, to bring down the leave papers, he called TWA Operations, Rachel's employer, at National Airport to see if they could help him make reservations for the next available flight to Albany, New York. He had no trouble getting a seat on such short notice. One of the advantages of marrying an airline crewmember was the courtesy extended to employees—even of a different airline—when there was a legitimate emergency. The death of a brother certainly qualified as such a priority.

After reserving his seat, Newman drove home, shaved and showered, and packed an overnight bag. Before heading to the airport, he wrote a note to Rachel, informing her what he was doing. They had talked on the phone briefly when she had returned the night before from London. Now she was at a special crew training session out at Dulles Airport. Newman decided that he wanted to deal with his brother's death alone, and instead of asking her to go with him, he merely wrote:

> *Rachel,*
> *Thanks for calling last night when you returned from your flight. I just learned that Jim was killed in Somalia. I'm headed to Albany to break the news to Mom and Dad. Hope to be back on Wed. morning. I'll try and call you tonight. Love, P. J.*

He contemplated calling his parents to tell them he was coming but decided that such an unexpected call would forewarn them that something was wrong. They knew that their youngest son was in Somalia. They watched the news. They also knew Jim had been doing dangerous things. Though Newman dreaded the task, he knew that he should be the one to deliver this terrible message.

★

Pete and Jim Newman had been inseparable as kids. Though three and a half years is not a small gap between siblings, the brothers had hiked, hunted, fished, and canoed together from the time the younger one was old enough to keep up. There was hardly a spot in the Hudson River Valley, the Adirondacks to the north, the Berkshires to the east, or the Catskills to the west that the boys hadn't explored.

The Newman boys grew up outdoors. They were both Boy Scouts; Jim had gone all the way to Eagle. Their career military father taught them how to bait a hook with a worm or a minnow, how to tie flies, and how to cast them into the riffle of a quick, cold stream so that the wild trout would invite themselves to dinner. He taught them how to lead a fast-flying pheasant with a shotgun, how to stalk a deer in the cold autumn air, and how to dress out the game they bagged.

When they weren't in the woods, the brothers engaged in various entrepreneurial ventures: they shared a paper route, mowed lawns together in the summers, raked leaves in the fall, and had a thriving walk-shoveling business every winter. They pooled the money they earned and bought a third-hand, wooden-strake Olde Towne canoe and more hiking, camping, hunting, and fishing gear than a small sporting goods store could hold. When they were older, they acquired an old 1951 Ford from a junkyard. To their mother's great anxiety, they abandoned their bicycles to become amateur automotive engineers and vacant lot stock-car racers.

The boys were indivisible until Peter went off to the Naval Academy in 1974. When Jim graduated from high school three years later, he enlisted in the Army, qualified for Jump School, and earned an appointment to West Point from his father's World War II outfit, the

Eighty-second. And even then, whenever they managed to get home together on leave, Pete and Jim put on their backpacks and took off for days to hike the Appalachian Trail. On each of those treks, they renewed their pact to someday hike the whole 2,043 miles of the trail, from Maine to Georgia. They just couldn't figure out when. Now it would never happen.

○

Before boarding his flight at National Airport, Newman tried to call his sister in Newport, Rhode Island, to tell her the awful news about their brother. Nancy had followed her mother's footsteps into nursing—but in the Navy instead of the Army. Now Nancy was a lieutenant in the Navy and was running a ward at the Naval Hospital where her husband was a doctor. Newman secretly envied his sister for finding a mate who seemed to love her as much as she loved him, for being able to see each other every day, and for having two great kids. Trying hard not to let the sadness in his heart be heard in his voice, he left a message on Nancy's home phone, asking her to page him as soon as she got the message.

Exhausted from his desperate all-night vigil, Newman did what most professional soldiers do aboard ships, planes, or vehicles in which they are merely passengers: he was asleep before the wheels were up on the U.S. Air commuter jet. He awoke with a start almost two hours later as they began their descent into Albany. Whether it was the brief nap or the effects of the adrenaline that had been coursing through him for the previous thirty-two hours, Newman felt strangely alert. It was the kind of thing he'd experienced in combat—an extra measure of awareness, a sharpening of focus. Colors were brighter; sounds he would normally have ignored in the background were pronounced.

When the cabin door opened, Newman grabbed his overnight bag out of the overhead compartment and made his way to the Hertz counter. He signed the paperwork and walked hastily outside into the crisp, early autumn air. Finding the numbered space for the car he'd rented, he threw his bag into the Pontiac and exited the airport toward N.Y. Route 9, heading south for Kinderhook and a meeting that filled him with dread.

It was almost 4:00 P.M. when he pulled into the driveway of the little farm he still thought of as home. The sun, almost down in the west, was hitting the two big maples that stood like sentinels at the entrance to the drive. The trees were just beginning to change from green to what would soon be riotous hues of red, orange, and yellow. *How many times did Jim and I rake those leaves together?* he thought to himself.

As Newman rounded the curve in the drive, he could see the old, white farmhouse surrounded by the white picket fence that he and Jim had been press-ganged into painting during a high-school summer vacation. There was the red barn where he and his brother had played in the loft, and from which they had been summoned to meals, arriving with hay hanging from their hair. Behind the house and barn was the little apple orchard where on long summer days the Newman boys had played soldiers, cops and robbers, cowboys and Indians, and capture the flag—always on the same side against other boys in the neighborhood.

Newman felt a deep sickening feeling in his gut as he remembered his brother, and he choked back the sob that caught in his throat.

And then he noticed the strange car in the driveway. It wasn't his dad's big Lincoln or his mother's red Jeep Cherokee. If they were home, their vehicles would be, in accord with "Newman Family Standard Operating Procedures," parked in the garage.

Newman pulled up beside the dark-green Ford Crown Victoria. The plate on the back read, *U.S. Government GSA-3721*. But on the door in small block printing it said, *U.S. Army*. He felt at once sick and then a little ashamed. He felt guilty because he had a sense of relief that he didn't have to be the one to tell his parents that their son was dead.

Instead of going around to the front entrance, he let himself in the back door without knocking and walked into the "the boys' mud room" as his mother called it. Once inside, he walked quietly through the kitchen, dining room, and front hallway into the living room. His father was seated on the couch, leaning forward, elbows on knees, talking quietly to two men in Army dress green uniforms who were seated on straight-back chairs. His mother was nowhere to be seen, although Peter could detect the faint scent of the only perfume he could ever remember her wearing, Chanel No. 5. He recalled that when he and Jim were little boys, they would chip in every Mother's Day to buy her a bottle of it.

All three men looked up and rose as one when Peter entered the room. The younger Newman walked up to his father, and without a word, embraced the older man as both began to cry unashamedly.

Neither of the Newman boys had ever seen their dad cry. He was their hero. He had been wounded leading a platoon of the Eighty-second Airborne Division in France in World War II. During Harry Truman's "police action" in Korea, a Chinese communist bullet had punched a hole in his gut and a grenade had mangled his legs. While the doctors were trying to patch him back together in a hospital in Japan, a pretty Army nurse named Alice Atkinson was working to mend his shattered spirit.

By the time Major John C. Newman was well enough to go back to the States, he and the pretty nurse were in love. And even though she was almost nine years younger than the badly wounded soldier, she agreed to marry him. Alice Atkinson and John Newman were married in the chapel at Fort Meyer, Virginia, in April of 1955. His colleagues from the Army staff, in their dress uniforms, formed an arch of swords for the bride and groom to walk beneath as they exited the chapel under a hail of rice thrown by her fellow nurses.

The birthplaces of the Newman children reflected the nomadic odyssey of a typical American military family. Peter was born the following May in the Army hospital at Fort Drum, New York. Nancy, the only girl, arrived in 1957 in the Army hospital at Crailsheim, Germany. And Jim was born in 1960 in Italy while their dad was commanding the Airborne Brigade at Livorno.

When the Vietnam War began in earnest in 1965, the now Brigadier General John Newman volunteered to lead one of the first Army units to deploy from Fort Benning, Georgia. But when he went to get his prede-parture physical, the doctors found that adhesions from his old stomach wounds were obstructing his intestines. Two bouts with the Army surgeons were followed by a quiet retirement ceremony and a family move to a small farm along the Hudson River, north of Kinderhook, New York. The reluctantly retired brigadier general took an executive position with General Electric in Schenectady.

Now, holding his father this way—feeling the convulsions of the older man's chest against his, his dad's once-powerful shoulders shaking uncontrollably beneath his arms—it abruptly occurred to Peter Newman that his father was suddenly an old man. It had been only four months since they had last seen each other. His father and mother had stayed with Peter and Rachel for a night when they were in Washington for a reunion of the Eighty-second Airborne, the unit he'd fought with at Normandy. In the brief time since he saw him last, Brigadier General John C. Newman had seemingly aged dramatically and was now showing every one of his seventy-two years.

The two men stood like this for several moments, and then, despite their grief, began to collect themselves. Still holding the older man, Peter spoke over his father's shoulder. "I'm so sorry, Dad," he said, the tears still streaming down his own face.

He could feel his father's whiskers against his cheek, his father's hair against his forehead. The hint of Old Spice mixed with the witch hazel his father always wore as an aftershave reminded the younger man once again of countless camping and hunting trips with "the three Newman boys" huddled against one another in the darkness.

"Thank you for coming, Peter. Your mother will be pleased. She's upstairs in the bathroom. She'll be back down in a few minutes," the old man said, his voice constricted, barely controlled and hardly above a whisper. And then, after standing this way for a few more moments, the officer and gentleman in him reasserted control over the grieving father, and he broke the embrace with his son and said, just barely composed, "Gentlemen, this is my son, Peter. He's a major in the Marines. Peter, this is Colonel Edward Robertson. We served together in the Airborne. He's now the chief Army inspector at the GE plant in Schenectady. Major

Olson here is the chaplain for the Army Reserve district in Albany."

The two men in uniform shook hands with the younger Newman, and they all sat back down, Peter taking a place on the couch beside his father. Colonel Robertson spoke first, following a script as old as warfare itself: "Major Newman, I am the casualty assistance officer for your brother. As you apparently already know, Captain Newman was killed in action last night by hostile fire in an engagement in Mogadishu, Somalia. The Secretary of the Army extends his sincere condolences . . ."

Peter sat numbly through the ritual: the intonations of sympathy, the declaration that details would be forthcoming, the chaplain's offer—politely refused—to pray with the family, and finally the promise to be in touch to make arrangements for interment.

Then, just as the two uniformed officers stood to take their leave, Alice Newman entered the room and choked back a sob as she saw her sole surviving son. Peter rushed to her, and the tears came again as he embraced his mother, her head on his chest. The colonel and the chaplain stood, looking down at the carpeted floor as the son tried to console his mother.

Alice Newman had opened the door to the two officers a half hour before Peter arrived. Even before the sad-eyed Colonel Robertson could utter a word, she knew why he and the chaplain were there. She had spent too many years as the wife of a career soldier to have any hope that this was anything but the worst news a mother could ever get—that one of her cherished children had preceded her in death.

With a gasp, her hand flew to her breast where she had nursed her children, and she turned and shouted in a voice that sounded almost strangled, "John, come quick! Oh dear, John . . . hurry! Something terrible has happened!" And then, with the two officers still standing silently outside the door, the afternoon sun shining on their uniforms, she leaned against the door and began quietly sobbing.

Brigadier General John Newman had rushed to the front door from his study off the living room. When he saw the two officers, he too knew in an instant the purpose of their visit, but other than putting a consoling arm around his wife, his demeanor hardly changed. "Gentlemen, please come in," he said as he escorted them to chairs in the living room.

Alice Newman had quietly endured the terrible, emotionally wrenching brief from the colonel and the chaplain for fifteen minutes, saying nothing as her husband, a comforting arm around her shoulders, asked questions about their son's death, for which these officers, as yet, had no answers. Then, convinced that a mistake had not been made, she had excused herself. "I must get another handkerchief," she said, holding out the balled-up white cloth she'd been using to soak up her tears.

Alice Newman had gone upstairs and sat on the bed she shared with her husband, cried some more, then gone to the bathroom, washed her face, applied some fresh lipstick, a touch of color to her cheeks, and had come back down to attend to the men in her living room as was expected of a general's wife.

Now, in the arms of her oldest son, she was crying again. It broke Peter's heart to hear his mother cry. And again, just as had happened minutes before when holding his grieving father, Peter Newman realized that his mother, now sixty-three, would never be young again.

His mother's greatest happiness had always been her

children. Even when her "kids" were grown, she still craved the holidays—especially Thanksgiving and Christmas—times when they were all together, when parents and children, and now grandchildren, gathered with joy and laughter in her big country kitchen. They would all take turns chiding Jim about getting married before he got too old. Now he never would, and those family gatherings would never be the same. They would always be tinged with sadness from the searing loss of Alice Newman's second son.

And in that instant, arms around his devastated mother, anger began to merge with the grief in Peter Newman's heart. A two-bit African gangster had stolen his only brother and his mother's happiness. It was then that a craving for vengeance began to smolder in his gut.

For the Newman family, the next ten days were a haze of tears and grief. His sister Nancy paged him that Monday evening, shortly after the colonel and the chaplain had departed. On Tuesday, October 5, mother, father, and son drove to the Albany airport and met her when she arrived on a flight from Providence, Rhode Island. The Mailgram from the Secretary of the Army was waiting for them when they got back to the farm.

Later that night, after their parents had gone to bed, Nancy confronted Peter in the kitchen. "Why didn't Rachel come up with you?"

"She had crew training. I didn't have time to track her down."

Nancy glared long and hard at her older brother, who finally said, "Sis, this isn't the time to talk about it."

She continued to stare until the Marine shrugged and went upstairs to bed.

★

"P. J., I'm so sorry about Jim," said Rachel as she came out of the kitchen to greet her husband when he arrived home from the airport.

"Yeah, so am I," Newman replied, brusquely brushing by his wife who had reached up to embrace him.

She reacted with anger at the rejection. "Why, P. J., why? You didn't give me a chance to go with you on Monday. I should have gone to your parents with you," Rachel said as he walked upstairs to change into his uniform.

"You had crew training," he replied without stopping.

"Crew training! Sure I had crew training, but if you had simply paged me at Dulles, you know that I would have met you at National and flown up with you. I loved Jim, too, you know," she said, following him into their bedroom.

"Look, this is a family matter," he stated with a flat tone of finality, not noticing the tears starting to well up in his wife's eyes.

"A *family matter!* What are you saying? I'm a Newman, too, for heaven's sake. I'm your *wife,* Peter! *Your sister* introduced us! What could you have been thinking by shutting me out of your life at a time like that?" Rachel picked up a book from the dresser and threw it at her husband. It hit him squarely in the chest, but he merely caught it and tossed it onto the bed, acting as if it had never happened. In her rage, Rachel turned and left the room, crying. He heard the front door slam as he buttoned up his uniform shirt. He checked the alignment of his shirt, belt buckle, and trousers in the mirror and headed back down the stairs, out the door to his car, and set off for HQMC. He noticed as he backed out of the driveway that his wife's Chevy Blazer was gone.

✪

The funeral service for Captain James Bedford Newman was held October 14 at the Old Fort Meyer Chapel—where John and Alice Newman had been married thirty-nine years before. It was a cool, clear day, and the church was filled with his parents' friends and comrades from wars and duty stations past. Jim's Delta Squadron commander was there, along with a heavy contingent of generals and colonels—some retired, others still on active duty—with whom father and son had served. The Secretary of the Army offered a eulogy and read Jim's citation for the Distinguished Service Cross. The blue-and-white medallion and a Purple Heart were affixed to the American flag that draped Jim's government-issue, gunmetal-gray coffin.

The words of the presiding chaplain weren't much of a solace to Peter, although he noticed that his mother and sister somehow seemed buoyed when one of his brother's fellow Delta troopers described how Jim had "come to know the Lord" a few months before his gruesome death in Somalia. Newman vaguely wondered what the young man meant.

As they always do on these solemn occasions, the Army's old guard provided a fitting send-off for one of their own: the pallbearers and honor guard in dress uniform; the horse-drawn caisson with the flag-covered casket aboard; the Army band, slowly leading the entourage through Arlington Cemetery's winding roads, flanked by row after ordered row of white stone grave markers. "So different in life, so much the same in death," they seemed to say.

When they arrived at Jim's gravesite, Peter and his father were seated beneath a white awning on either side of the grieving mother. Nancy and her husband, Dan, in their Navy dress uniforms, sat to her father's right. Peter in his Marine dress blues and Rachel in a black dress sat to his mother's left. After the chaplain read again from the Scriptures, they concluded with the Lord's Prayer. Then a bagpiper—a tradition in Jim's Delta Squadron, one of his mates said—played "Amazing Grace." As he did so, the captain in charge of the honor guard presented Nancy and Rachel each with a rose from the floral display at the foot of the bier.

Immediately after the piper's rendition of the ancient hymn came three volleys of gunfire—the final salute for a fallen warrior. Then, in the sudden silence, the mournful, haunting sound of "Taps" wafted over the green hillside where Jim's body would be laid to rest. As the bugler played the last, lingering notes of the military requiem, Peter could feel more than hear his mother weeping silently beside him. His father, stone-faced and wearing his dress uniform with a brigadier's single silver star on each epaulet, held her hand.

Peter watched, almost detached, as the honor guard smartly removed the colors from atop Jim's coffin, folded the flag in a ceremonial triangle so that only the white stars on the blue field showed, and handed it to Lieutenant General Paul Stenner, the commanding general of the Joint Special Operations Command, one of the Army's most distinguished soldiers. The general gently reattached the Distinguished Service Cross and the Purple Heart to the folded flag and then bent over and presented the banner to the grief-stricken mother. Only then did he speak, and his words surprised Newman: "Your son was a very good and brave man, Mrs. Newman. You have much to be proud of. We shall miss him, as I know you will. I look forward to seeing him again. Until then, I shall pray that our Savior—in whose presence your son now rests—will ease our pain and grief."

At that, the highly decorated officer, who had bent before the weeping mother who clutched the flag to the front of her black dress, stood erect and saluted. As he did so, Peter noted that the tall, thin general had two thin trickles of tears running down his face.

Although he had been present at a number of military funerals, Peter had never before seen a high-ranking officer make such deeply personal spiritual comments. It made him a bit uneasy.

○

There was no obituary published for Captain James Bedford Newman, or for any of the other Delta operators who died in Somalia. The government that had sent them there wasn't willing to admit, even when they were dead, that their unit even existed.

The week before Jim was buried, the President ordered fifteen thousand U.S. reinforcements—including a new Delta squadron—to Somalia. But it was all for show. By the time the leaves from the trees in Arlington Cemetery had fallen onto the fresh sod covering Jim Newman's remains, the withdrawal of those same units would be under way and a new UN emissary would be negotiating with the brutal warlord, Aidid.

Before those same trees over Captain James Newman's grave would bear the first buds of spring, the "massacre in Mogadishu" would have far-reaching consequences. The Secretary of Defense, who had presided over the debacle, would resign in disgrace. Mohammed Aidid, the target of the operation, would be invited to Egypt to present his ideas for "peace" in Somalia. And Osama bin Laden, the mastermind of the carnage in the "Black Sea," would quietly return to Khartoum, Sudan, to plot his next assault on the Americans, whom he described as "Satan's agents in the world."

❂

Back at his desk at HQMC, across the street from his brother's grave, Peter Newman was still filled with quiet rage. Even more than a year following his brother's death, he couldn't decide whom he despised more, the politicians who had sent his brother to his death and then abandoned the mission, or the man whose thugs had killed him. He did not know then that there might be another target for his willful vengeance—a charismatic Saudi millionaire and militant Islamic radical who had declared *jihad*, a "holy war," against the United States.

CHAPTER THREE

Vengeance Is Mine!

Situation Room
The White House
Washington, D.C.
Tuesday, 29 November 1994
1520 Hours, Local

Newman, are you still with me?" the National Security Advisor asked. Harrod had finished his phone call and was back, sitting across the Situation Room's long, mahogany table. Harrod had been watching from across the room while the Marine major wrestled with his inner demons.

"Yes, I'm with you," Newman answered as he regained his composure. "Exactly how do you propose that I can make sure that Aidid is caught and made an example to others, Dr. Harrod?"

"Do you know what the Special Projects Office does, Mr. Newman?"

"No. Special Ops, sure, but I've never heard of the Special Projects Office."

"Good. That's the way it's supposed to be. Officially it doesn't exist. In fact, it really hasn't existed since your predecessor left here exactly eight years ago this week." Harrod was riffling the corners of the pages he had shoved into the green-covered file labeled *TOP SE-CRET*. He had yet to open it again since Newman walked into the room.

Newman looked puzzled. "My predecessor?"

"Yes, your predecessor, another Marine—Lieutenant Colonel Oliver North."

For the second time in ten minutes, Newman was stunned. "Oliver North?" Newman's mind quickly analyzed the situation before him and said sharply, "Look, if you think I'm going to accept a job only to go down in flames like he did, you'd better think again. I'll resign my commission first."

"You don't have to do that. But I was led to believe that you wanted to see your brother's killers punished, to avenge his death," Harrod replied calmly.

In the nearly fourteen months since his brother had been killed, Peter Newman had indeed said those exact words countless times. And now he was wondering how the National Security Advisor to the President of the United States would know that. After pondering the question for a moment, he stopped trying to figure out how this sentiment had gotten across the Potomac River and decided to see what it was all about.

❂

What Newman didn't know, and what Dr. Simon Harrod didn't tell him, was that the Marine had been selected for this assignment based on a very sophisticated screening process that had begun twenty-one days earlier, on November 8, the "off-year" election day. The Republicans had won in a landslide, seizing control of the U.S. House of Representatives for the first time in forty years and sending the White House into the political equivalent of shell shock. Late on election night, the President had called Harrod and summoned him to a rare 8:00 A.M. meeting in the Oval Office.

The meeting lasted only a half hour, and when it was over, Harrod returned to his own office down the hall and summoned Arnold Granish, the man who had installed and now operated the high-powered computer system that was euphemistically known as the White House database, or WHDB. Granish and eleven bright young technicians were toiling in Room 208 of the Old Executive Office Building. The facility had been constructed during the Reagan administration as a crisis management center—a totally secure, TEMPEST-protected complex—meaning that it was electronic-emission-proof. Nobody outside the space could monitor any electronic device being used inside. This space, with its sophisticated equipment, was where Vice President George Bush had directed the planning for the Grenada rescue mission (dubbed Operation Urgent Fury) in October 1983. Though a person walking down the corridor wouldn't know it, the complex occupied nearly the whole south side of the OEOB's second floor.

Harrod had earlier ordered the Reagan-era equipment removed and the very best new, high-speed equipment installed by CompCo, one of the new tech-giants on the President's "major donor list." But the WHDB equipment and the personnel who ran the machinery were far more than an information management system for the executive office of the President. The WHDB facility was actually designed to reach into every possible civilian and government computerized record system in the U.S. and even some overseas—normally the purview of only the National Security Agency. And like the people who worked at NSA, Arnie Granish and all of his "data dinks" had been subjected to a rigorous background investigation. Their loyalty to the President and his goals was unquestioned.

Early on the morning of November 9, the thirty-four-year-old Granish, clad in a black sweatshirt and jeans, his ponytail pulled back with a rubber band, was sitting in the office of the National Security Advisor to the President of the United States. The rest of the West Wing was as quiet as a tomb—things usually didn't begin to happen until 9:30 or 10:00 on a good day. Granish figured that given the results of the election the day before, the rest of the place might never get going this day.

Harrod looked over his notes and silently appraised the skinny little man who sat across from him; he then shrugged and decided to press on. The President wanted to rebound from this defeat, and Granish was the key to doing so.

"Arnold, I have a crash project for you. I want you to set aside everything else you're working on and focus on a personnel matter."

"OK. Who do you want me to get the dirt on this time—the guys who won yesterday?" replied Granish, who had perfected the art of finding vulnerabilities in political opponents and potential donors.

"No, it's not that kind of project. I'm looking for a very special person to head up a sensitive assignment for the President. I want you to start with a detailed search of all government and open-source databases for any current or recent government employee who has lost a family member or a loved one in an act of foreign perpetrated violence or terrorism. Once you have identified that 'universe,' bring it to me and we'll go from there."

Granish looked up from the notes he was making on

the back of an envelope that he'd pulled from the pocket of his jeans. "When I set the parameters of the search, how recent is 'recent' when it comes to government employment?"

"Make it the last three years," replied Harrod.

"Do they have to be American citizens?"

"Yes," said Harrod.

"Do you want the usual info on these people?" asked Granish.

"Yes, again," said Harrod. "How long will it take?"

"Don't know," said the computer expert, standing and heading for the door. "I'll get it to you as soon as I can. Do you want these people to know we're looking at them?"

"No, absolutely not."

"It'll take a little longer then," Granish said as he exited without asking to take his leave.

It took less than thirty hours for Granish and his team—working around the clock in the WHDB—to search all government personnel records: Lexis-Nexis, Database-Tech, Choicepoint, CDB Info-Tech, D&B, AP, UPI, Reuters, FBIS, and the Transunion databases. They ended up with the names, social security numbers, addresses, phone numbers, bank accounts, driver's licenses, marital and medical records, vehicle registrations, insurance claims, court proceedings, and credit records on 2,317 Americans who met the basic criteria established by Harrod.

The National Security Advisor then had Granish purge the list of all who did not have a current or recent security clearance. The pool of "eligibles" was reduced to 487.

The "data dinks" on the second floor of the OEOB were then told to screen this smaller list and eliminate anyone who was not a current or former member of the armed forces; federal, state, or local law enforcement; or one of the intelligence services. This cut the "universe" down to 102. After that they were directed to eliminate all those younger than thirty and older than forty and any who were not in superb physical and medical condition; there were sixteen men and five women remaining. The entire database search had taken just four days.

Harrod then told the FBI and CIA to send him their top specialists in human behavior. When they arrived, he swore them to secrecy and put them to work in a cubbyhole office next to his in the West Wing of the White House where he could keep an eye on them.

The FBI sent Dr. Robert Davies, their chief "profiler." The CIA dispatched Dr. Eugenia Prados, their top inhouse psychiatrist and expert on foreign leaders.

The National Security Advisor gave these two experts in human behavior the complete personnel and medical files of the twenty-one individuals who had been selected by Granish's database search. Harrod also gave them the detailed FBI interview reports on what others had said about them when they had been "vetted" for security clearances and told the two "shrinks" that they were to give him the top five candidates for a sensitive job. He didn't tell them what the job was, only the qualities for which he was looking:

"From this group of twenty-one, I want you to identify the top five persons who meet the following criteria: he or she must be intelligent, fearless, a risk taker, but not foolhardy. I am looking for an individual, and maybe a deputy, who is smart, creative, innovative—someone who can think outside of the box but who will still follow orders. I want the top person to be someone who has a Type A work ethic, a multitasker—someone who can juggle a lot of things happening at once and who can still get the primary task at hand accomplished. The top candidate for this position should probably have a high anger quotient that can be directed by a competent superior." And even though he wasn't used to working with such people, Harrod added one other criterion: "This ought to be a person who can't be compromised because of an integrity or moral problem."

On November 23, after ten days of perusing all the data, the two doctors were in agreement. Of the twenty-one candidates, the person who best matched Harrod's criteria was a Marine major: Peter J. Newman.

○

"What is it I would have to do to avenge my brother, Dr. Harrod?" Newman countered.

That's when the National Security Advisor knew he had his man. But he decided to ease into it gently.

"Newman, what you will be doing is orchestrating the most sensitive covert actions against America's adversaries that have ever been undertaken." He paused. Newman appeared to be deep in thought.

"Excuse me, Dr. Harrod, but I thought that this kind of action was the mission of the CIA, or the SEALs, or Delta units like the one my brother commanded in Mogadishu."

"I'm not talking about special forces operations that are conducted by the military. They still have their job to do. The missions you'll be heading up are those that our active duty military units aren't allowed to undertake through the normal chain of command because of various restrictions—including Executive Order 12333."

Like all military and intelligence officers since 1975, Newman was familiar with EO-12333—the presidential directive specifically forbidding the assassination of any foreign leaders, be they civilian, military, or even criminal drug lords or heads of terrorist organizations. "This is a *legal* authorization that gets us past that one," Harrod said, a plume of cigar smoke rising above his head. The National Security Advisor deliberately didn't mention the handful of other laws and congressional prohibitions that would also apply to what was being contemplated.

But then the Marine asked the question anyway: "How about the CIA?"

Harrod paused before answering. He didn't want to scare off the number-one candidate for this assignment, but he realized that the man sitting across the table from him was smart enough to figure it out in short order anyway. The elections twenty-one days earlier meant that in January the Republicans would be in charge of every committee not only in the Senate but now in the U.S. House of Representatives as well. That meant that both the Senate Select Committee on Intelligence and the House Permanent Select Committee on Intelligence would be controlled by people who had enormous animus toward this President. Worse yet, the heads of the committee staffs—the people who did all the work and who made all the trouble—were now going to be picked by the opposing party.

And Harrod knew, just as surely as the sun was going to rise in the east tomorrow morning, that with "those people" in charge on "the Hill," there was absolutely no way they would get congressional consent for a Covert Action Finding to do what the President wanted done. He decided to tell Newman the truth—but not all of it.

"Look," said the National Security Advisor, his heavy

jowls hanging over his wrinkled shirt collar, "ever since the Iran-Contra hearings in 1987, it has been a requirement that before covert activities can be undertaken by the CIA, the intelligence committees have to approve a Presidential Finding. If you don't know it already, the Hill leaks like a sieve. If we submit a Finding to go after the people who killed your brother, it will leak before the CIA can even gear up to do what needs to be done."

What he didn't tell Newman was that one of the first actions of the present administration was to dismantle nearly all of the CIA's clandestine services. What little covert action capability the agency retained was now nearly all engaged in counterterrorism intelligence collection and a handful of operatives trying to keep track of Russian nuclear weapons. Other than that, the CIA— for all practical purposes—was out of the "spy business."

"Well then," said Newman, "it sounds to me like what you are asking me to do is against the law."

"No, it isn't," replied Harrod, speaking slowly again. "We have something going for us that those cowboys Reagan, Poindexter, North, and that crowd didn't have. They were off on their own. Nobody on planet Earth backed what the U.S. was doing in Central America back then. From the top down, the Reagan White House acted as though the rest of the international community didn't matter—that the U.S. could do whatever it pleased, anywhere it wanted.

"Look at the arrogance of that administration, sending ten thousand Marines and our soldiers to invade the peaceful little island of Grenada. Nobody believed that those medical students were in any danger. And how Reagan kept from being impeached when those 250 Marines were killed in Beirut in '83 is beyond me."

"It was 241," corrected Newman. He knew. He had been there. Newman had been a captain then, dispatched with a ten-man team from Second Force Reconnaissance Company to Lebanon to establish covert locations from which to adjust air strikes and naval gunfire from the battleship USS *New Jersey.*

"Whatever," said Harrod carelessly. "The point is, Reagan and those loose cannons on the deck of state seriously damaged U.S. prestige with their attitude of superiority. If it hadn't been for Thatcher—sitting there on her duff at 10 Downing Street, still licking her wounds from the Falklands—those international adventurers wouldn't have had a friend in the world."

The National Security Advisor was back in his Harvard classroom as he continued his lecture, barely pausing for a breath. "Things are different today. This President talks about a global village—and he's right. That's why the rest of the world leaders admire him so much. He knows we just can't go our own way. It's a new era. We have global trade, global communications, and global security interests. It really is a new world order.

"Given these new realities, we have to act multilaterally. We're just one of many actors on the stage, Newman. Reagan and Bush blew off our friends in the United Nations. But not this president—he knows that a strong UN is the key to peace. And thanks to his close relationship with the UN Secretary General, he's personally worked out a means to enhance the UN's authority for dealing with those who refuse to accept the decisions of the community of nations. It's something that's long overdue. And Newman, you ought to be very proud that you have been chosen to head a handpicked group that will enforce and carry out UN Security Council directives."

"The UN?" Newman interrupted, his eyes wide. "I'm going to be working for the UN?"

"No, you'll be working for the President of the United States—through me, of course—to carry out various sensitive missions as required by the Secretariat of the United Nations. It's simply part of our new responsibilities in this new world order. Things aren't as simple as they once were. We can't act unilaterally like we used to. We've got to have international backing—we've gotta have the support of others with like interests. We can't just go swashbuckling around the world."

Harrod finally paused long enough for the Marine to get a word in. "Look, Dr. Harrod, I just want you to know, I'm not going to do anything that's against the law. And I don't want to be involved in anything that someone else might even *think* is against the law. I've been on covert assignments before, as you probably know from my military record.

"I want to get whoever killed my brother so bad I can taste it. But I also know from what Colonel North went through that all it takes is for someone to *think* you've done something wrong and that's the end of your career. I'll carry out my lawful orders just like any good Marine, but I don't want to get cross-threaded in this town."

"You're right, of course," said Harrod, "and the only way I work is on the up-and-up. That's why everything you will be doing is fully covered by treaty and approved by the new executive committee of the UN Security Council—so there'll be no violation of law to worry about. Neither U.S. law nor international law. We're *complying* with international law, not breaking it." Harrod didn't bother to mention that the Attorney General had privately advised him that such activities were more than likely against U.S. law *if not approved by Congress*. That argument was for another day.

"Now, are you ready to proceed?" Harrod put on the smile he usually reserved for campaign contributors who were attending a "private" national security briefing.

"I suppose so, but I want to be sure we understand each other," said the Marine, looking into the eyes above the Cheshire-cat smile. "What I hear you saying is that the White House has a Special Projects Office that responds to tasking from the UN Security Council and that everything it does is fully legal under U.S. and international law. Is that right?"

"Yes, you've got it. That's absolutely correct. And you are, if you want the job, the new head of that office," replied Harrod.

"And where is this Special Projects Office?"

"Across the street—room 306 in the OEOB. Come on, I'll show you," said Harrod, struggling to haul his considerable girth out of the cloth-covered swivel chair. At the last minute, he turned to grab the green-covered file folder and his coat before his leading candidate had a chance to turn down the job.

The two left the Situation Room, walked past the White House Mess, and exited the West Wing beneath the awning, which pointed like a green finger toward the Old Executive Office Building. The rain had stopped and the afternoon was turning cool. Newman knew it was going to be a cold night.

Before crossing West Executive Avenue toward the OEOB, Newman stopped and said, "Just one more question: Does this Special Projects Office have the authority to 'take out' terrorists like the one who killed my brother?"

"Take out?" Harrod feigned a confused look.

"You know what I mean," said the Marine.

"Oh, I see," said Harrod. " 'Take out.' Well, let me put it this way. The UN Executive Order has designated certain individuals who have refused to accede to international law and flaunt their lawlessness before the international community. Those individuals are to be *removed,* as threats to international order. It's a short list. But the man who killed your brother, General Mohammed Farrah Aidid, is on it."

"Who else is on this list of people who are to be removed as 'threats to international order'?" asked Newman, relishing the idea of exacting vengeance on his brother's killers.

"Later," said Harrod, more sure than ever that he had just the man he wanted.

CHAPTER FOUR
The Special Projects Office

Room 306
Old Executive Office Building
Washington, D.C.
Tuesday, 29 November 1994
1605 Hours, Local

As the two men approached the portal of the Old Executive Office Building, they were confronted by a flood tide of mostly young people in what appeared to be a mass exodus from the ornate structure. Most were clad in jeans, various forms of athletic footwear, and nondescript outer jackets as a hedge against the damp cold. One of them carried a skateboard under his arm. To Newman it looked like an abandoned ship drill or perhaps more like the exodus of fans from a rock concert. Several of them recognized the National Security Advisor and said "Hi," or "Hey, man." As one of the precocious youngsters swept by on his way to the South West Gate, he hollered out, "Hey, Simon—waddayasay, big guy?"

Apparently unperturbed at the extraordinary familiarity, Harrod waved back with the file folder in his left hand, the green-bordered *TOP SECRET* cover sheet flapping in the breeze. He turned to Newman with a sheepish grin and said, "You can tell it's quitting time, can't you?" The Marine simply nodded, wondering for at least the fortieth time that day what he had gotten himself into.

When the two men finally made it into the building, Harrod pointed to an elevator, walked over to it, and punched the "up" arrow next to the door. As they waited to board the elevator for the ride up to the third floor, the National Security Advisor took on the role of tour guide. In point of fact, he wanted to avoid discussing any more details about Newman's assignment until they were back inside a secure space.

"Until the Pentagon was built, this structure was the largest office building in Washington, and even today it is one of the largest granite structures in the world. The outside walls are granite blocks, four feet thick. The interior is all granite, cast iron, brick, and plaster. When you look at how ornate it is, you can see why it took seventeen years to build. The building was supposed to house the Departments of State, War, and Navy. As an afterthought, someone decided that the Vice President should have his office here. Even then, vice presidents were useless, eh, Newman?" Harrod laughed at his own joke. Newman smiled politely but said nothing.

Harrod continued talking as the two men boarded the elevator. "The experts describe the architecture of the building as 'Second Empire,' which was apparently pretty popular for about two weeks after the Civil War. It doesn't fit with anything else in the city. It has nearly two miles of black-and-white marble on five floors, all connected by eight ornamental staircases. Above each staircase are stained-glass skylights. During World War

II, they also dug a bomb shelter beneath the White House and a tunnel in the basement that runs all the way from 15th Street to 17th Street, connecting this building, the White House, and the Treasury. Crazy, isn't it?" Newman realized by now that these kinds of questions didn't require an answer.

When the elevator door opened on the third floor, the two men exited. Harrod pointed them down the empty corridor toward the southeast corner of the building, saying, "The room right next to your office—room 308—used to be the State Department Library. The Declaration of Independence and the Constitution were stored there before they were transferred to the National Archives."

The two men stopped in front of a heavy, dark-stained oak door that looked identical to all others in the hallway, except this one had the standard, government-issue combination lock mounted at eye level on the door *and* an electronic keypad on the wall beside the doorjamb. On a plate above the keypad was the number 304-306.

Harrod terminated his historical treatise, tucked the classified document he'd carried from the Situation Room under his arm, and removed what looked like a credit card from his shirt pocket. Reading from the combination printed on the red plastic card, he spun the black combination knob first to the left, then to the right, and finally back to the left again. Then, after consulting the card in his hand one last time, he rotated the small, silver-colored, raised, arrow in the center of the knob with his thumb and forefinger. There was a satisfying *click*. Harrod then turned the outer black knob a quarter-turn to the right and was rewarded by the sound of a heavy mechanical bolt sliding open on the other side of the door.

"Well, that's the first step," said the National Security Advisor, obviously pleased with his prowess as a lock-pick.

Next, Harrod removed a sealed envelope from the breast pocket of his rumpled suit coat and, ripping it open, extracted another plastic card—this time a green one. He proceeded to press the numbers on the keypad next to the door slowly and deliberately, according to the sequence on the card. Once again there was the sound of a bolt moving and a heavy *thunk* as it unlocked.

"Well, Newman, I'm told that the last sequence is done from inside the door. It's a security system with an electronic keypad and a retina scanner to verify the person who is disarming the security system. If you do that part wrong, we'll probably have a whole lot of company in very short order.

"According to these instructions, the keypad is to your left as you enter the door and the retina scanner is directly above it. As soon as you open this door, you have fifteen seconds to enter the access code for the system before the alarm goes off. Here's the code."

Harrod handed Newman yet another plastic card—this one was yellow. On the card were the numbers 30671489. "Any questions?"

"Oh yes, Dr. Harrod, I have a whole lot of questions. The first of which is, what's on the other side of this door? Second, why am I going in but you're staying out here?"

Harrod's loud chuckle echoed off the black-and-white marble floor of the long, ornate, and empty corridor. "What's on the other side of this door? *Your office*, Mr. Newman. Why am I staying out here? Because, according to these very precise instructions, in order to disarm this ridiculously complicated security system, the door has to be closed behind you, and only one person can be inside at that point. Apparently your very paranoid predecessor, who designed this system, was worried that some spy could be holding a gun to the head of a person with the combination, and he wanted to guard against that."

"Oh," said Newman. It didn't sound particularly paranoid to him, but he didn't want to debate the point with his new boss.

Harrod continued. "Since your retinas have been scanned into the WHDB security parameters and mine have not, you should be the one to disarm the system. Now if it's all the same to you, how about opening the blasted door and going in? After you close the door and enter the access code, open the door back up and let me in so I can finish briefing you sometime before midnight."

As Newman opened the door, a subdued electronic chirp began to sound inside the room. He closed the door, groped in the near-darkness until he found a light switch, and entered the eight-digit code that Harrod had given him on the keypad.

The chirping continued as though he had done nothing. Only then did he remember the retina scanner. The Marine found the retina console, pressed his forehead against the panel, and peered into the glass screen that looked remarkably like a supermarket bar-code scanner. The chirping stopped. He opened the door. Harrod was standing there looking like an insurance salesman at the back end of a bad day.

"Nice work, Newman. Let's see what's in here. I've wanted to get into this place ever since I got here. Man, the crimes that were committed in this room."

Stunned by the statement, Newman could only manage, "What?"

Harrod looked at Newman as if he were a recent arrival from another planet. "Well, Newman, this is the scene of the crime—this was North's office. This place has been sealed up tighter than a drum ever since 1987."

The two men looked around, the door they had just entered now behind them. The dull late-afternoon winter sun barely lit the space in front of them. They were standing in an anteroom. Opposite, a window looked south toward the Washington Monument, which was already bathed by bright floodlights in the gathering darkness. In front of the window was a standard wooden secretarial desk. To their right stood a row of seven matching, government-issue, four-drawer combination-lock safes, the drawers open and apparently empty. To their immediate left, a circular stairwell went up to a suite of offices overhead. And just in front of the secretarial desk was a sliding door to an interior office. The door was open. Harrod walked over to it, flicked on the light switch, and entered. Newman followed.

There was a large mahogany desk in the southeast corner beside a window that also overlooked the memorial to the first president. Beside the desk was a built-in counter that, judging by the wires running like spaghetti from fixtures in the wall, once held banks of computer terminals and phones. Against the interior wall was a large circular table with six chairs around it.

Everything in the room was covered by a thin film of dust, but there wasn't a single scrap of paper, nor so much as a paper clip, left anywhere in the entire space. Whoever had cleared out the office had even removed the picture hooks from the walls. The only thing in the entire suite that appeared to be out of place was the large fireplace built into the east wall of the room. It had a large, ornamental mantel above the brick face. Newman could imagine some senior government bureaucrat warming his fanny against the flames in that office a century ago.

"Nice digs. No wonder they were out to get him," Harrod mused.

"Who?" asked Newman, feeling as though he had been reduced to monosyllables in order to learn anything.

"North. When all the systems are hooked up, this is the best office in the NSC besides my office," said Harrod, gesturing. "It must have driven the striped-pants peons from State, DOD, and Langley nuts to have this prime piece of real estate occupied by a Marine lieutenant colonel."

"Surely you don't mean to put me in here?" Newman asked.

"I do—but I'm not going to put you in the same predicament as your predecessor," replied Harrod. "You're not going to be chairing any of those interagency groups like North did. Your job won't require you to cajole State and Defense and the CIA into cooperating in anything like those crazy schemes they cooked up back in the Reagan administration."

"Well, what *am* I supposed to do in here?" asked Newman, his uncertainty evident again.

Harrod didn't answer the question. Instead he said, "Patience, Newman. Go down the hall to the men's room and get some damp paper towels so that we can wipe the dust off these chairs and sit down. Here's the combination so you can get back in." Harrod handed Newman the three plastic cards they had used to gain entry to the office. "Memorize these things, then bring them back over and run 'em through the 'confetti-maker' in the Sit Room."

"Confetti-maker?"

"The microshredder. It turns paper and those cards into pieces so small that they can never be re-created. North had one up here, but the special prosecutor seized it as evidence." Harrod chuckled again. "I'll have one installed up here tomorrow. Now, how about getting those damp paper towels?"

Newman did as ordered, and when he returned, he and the National Security Advisor began to wipe the accumulated dust off two of the chairs and the top of the circular table. While they worked, Newman asked, "Why has this place been sealed up since 1987?"

Harrod, his beefy face beginning to redden from the physical act of wiping the furniture, replied, "I don't know the full story, but I'm told that nobody was ever certain that they understood all that North had done in this office. First, the NSC, FBI, and CIA all laid claim to all the paperwork; then the congressional investigators and the special prosecutors fought over it.

"The papers and stuff were finally boxed up and sent over to archives when the Bush administration left town in '93, but then the Attorney General told us that the FBI forensic people needed to keep the place from being 'contaminated' and that they needed to come in here periodically and check for fibers, dirt, hair, and God only knows what else. I finally got tired of their fooling around and told the AG that we needed the space. I got the access codes last Friday. And here we are."

The two men sat in the chairs they had just dusted and put their forearms on the now-glistening table. Harrod placed the file folder with its *TOP SECRET* label in front of them but made no effort to open it or show it to the Marine.

For his part, Newman wasn't interested in what had gone on in this office before. There had been a dozen books written about the Reagan administration's efforts to rescue hostages and help Nicaraguan Contras. As far as Newman was concerned, that stuff was ancient history; it didn't affect him. He was much more interested in what *he* was going to be doing here. As soon as the National Security Advisor paused for a breath, he said, "Let's go back to my last question. What am I going to be doing in here?"

Harrod was suddenly all business. "You are now the head of the NSC's Special Projects Office. In here," Harrod gestured around the office, "you will have three assistants and an admin-secretary-classified records clerk to handle whatever paperwork gets generated. There won't be much.

"Your assistants have been handpicked, one each from the Army, Navy, and Air Force. The Army captain served in Delta with your brother. The Navy guy is a SEAL. The Air Force officer flies special missions aircraft. All of these guys served in the Persian Gulf War. They are waiting down the hall in Carol Dayton's office. She's the one who checked you in this morning." Newman nodded but said nothing.

Harrod continued, "We don't have the secretary-admin person yet. I have asked the Pentagon and the CIA to send us a list of names of people with the right clearances so that we can pick one and get them detailed over here.

"All these people will work for you. *You* work for me."

Harrod paused, so Newman jumped in. "OK, that's a

THE SPECIAL PROJECTS OFFICE | 89

nice chain of command, but, again, what exactly will we be doing in here?"

"As I told you over in the Sit Room, your job is to co-ordinate the implementation and enforcement of special sanctions imposed by the UN executive. The actual enforcement operations will be conducted by a thirty-eight-man group of handpicked U.S. and British specialists—consisting of twenty-seven Americans and eleven Brits, on loan from the Special Air Services by private arrangement between the President and the Prime Minister of Great Britain. He and our President are very close and in full agreement on all of this.

"The U.S. personnel are all on detail from Army Delta, Navy SEALs, the Air Force, and the Army's Intelligence Support Activity. Except for sending you over here, the Marines decided they didn't want to participate," Harrod concluded. Newman wondered why, but he said nothing. As the Special Operations coordinator at HQMC, he hadn't heard about a request for Marine personnel for this kind of unit. But before he could ponder the question further, Harrod opened the file folder with the *TOP SECRET* label and took out several sheets of paper.

Harrod began to read from one of the pages: "The International Sanctions Enforcement Group—we're calling it ISEG." He continued reading, "The ISEG consists of a three-man headquarters element—a U.S. Army captain, a British SAS lieutenant, and a U.S. Navy chief. The group is divided into five, seven-man teams—we call them 'ISETs,' which stands for International Sanctions Enforcement Teams. They are organized based on various regions of the world where the UN has a sanctions regime in place: ISET Alpha is assigned to Asia and the Pacific. ISET Bravo gets Africa; ISET Charlie has Eastern and Central Europe; Latin America and the Caribbean are the purview of ISET Delta; and finally, ISET Echo covers the Middle East, Southeast Asia, and the Persian Gulf region. Each of these five teams is headed by an American. The deputy team leaders are all SAS."

It occurred to Newman that the five regional teams Harrod described pretty much covered most of the planet. "OK, Dr. Harrod, I understand the organization, but what do the regional teams in this Sanctions Enforcement Group actually do? Do they gather intelligence and file reports? Do they go out in the field and observe possible violations—what?"

Harrod looked up from the papers in his hand. "No, Newman. They make sure that those who *do* violate properly imposed UN sanctions do not *persist* in efforts to thwart international laws and the will of the international community."

"Exactly what does that mean? Does it mean these teams go out and apprehend sanctions violators? Do they have the authority to kill people like Aidid?"

"Let me put this as straight as I can, Newman. Once the UN executive has determined that an international lawbreaker is repeatedly violating UN resolutions and is a threat to international law and order, and this international criminal refuses to surrender himself to the justice of the UN's tribunals in the Hague, then the ISEG is authorized to take whatever means necessary to stop the violations. As I said before, that includes people like Aidid, who so brutally murdered your brother. You will have total authority to 'take out'—as you so colorfully phrased it earlier—such people. Do you understand?"

Newman did. And he suddenly realized why someone very high up in the Marine Corps had decided not to assign any young Marines to the Sanctions Enforcement

Group. Newman knew that the Marine Corps had an inherent distaste for this kind of clandestine project because it came so close to crossing the line of Executive Order 12333 forbidding assassinations, signed by President Gerald Ford in 1975 and ratified by every president since that time.

If, as Harrod had explained, such acts were permissible when sanctioned by the UN and this new protocol, this ISEG team would be able to circumvent the executive order. And if what the National Security Advisor said was true, there was really nothing to keep Newman from killing the terrorist leader responsible for his brother's death in Mogadishu.

Harrod noticed that Newman didn't flinch. He didn't even blink. But Harrod watched the Marine's eyes, which told him all he wanted to know. When Newman didn't say or do anything, after a moment, Harrod said, "We don't have phones in here yet, so I'm going down the hall to admin and get your colleagues. I'm sure Ms. Dayton has had them long enough to take care of all their paperwork. While I'm gone, go get some more damp paper towels and wipe off three more chairs. This will take a while."

"Wait a minute, Dr. Harrod. Before you get the others, who were those guys following me when I went home to change clothes? You said you would tell me later. Well, it's later."

"Fair enough," said Harrod. "They were part of the ISEG, specifically the European team. All five teams are here in Washington right now for training exercises. Part of their training requires that they be able to tail a target without being observed. Since you were able to observe them while they were following you, they apparently need more training."

Before Newman could ask another question, Harrod said, "Look, I've got other things to do today besides answer questions that are going to get answered anyway over the course of this week. Get these chairs clean while I get the others."

By the time Harrod returned with the men—all wearing civilian clothes and short hair—Newman had wiped down the remaining four chairs around the circular table and had started on the desk he would soon be using. The National Security Advisor brusquely performed the introductions without the benefit of military rank. "Peter Newman, this is Thomas McDade, Navy; Bartholomew Coombs, Army; and Daniel Robertson, Air Force. Sit down, gentlemen."

The three each shook hands with Newman and sat down around the table. "Hi, Pete. I'm Bart," said Coombs. The other two men offered their less formal first names as well. "I'm Tom," said McDade, and "Call me Danny," proffered Robertson.

Coombs, the Army officer, reached inside his suit coat and took out a small notebook and pen, as if preparing to take notes.

Harrod looked at the young Army officer with the same disgust Newman had witnessed all day: "Put that notebook away. I'll tell you if you need to make a record of something around here. Just pay attention."

Coombs did as ordered, but his face began to color beneath his tan. Newman couldn't figure out whether it was anger or embarrassment.

Harrod continued. "You are here because each of your service secretaries has determined that you are the best people to carry out a very sensitive assignment here at the White House. I am told that you are all on the fast track in your respective services. If you want to stay on that fast track, you will be discreet about the activities you will coordinate. There can be no communications about your work other than to me or to others as I direct. You may not talk to your wives, parents, siblings, girlfriends, or boyfriends about this job. You shall not communicate back to your services about what you do here. If you do so, you will be fired, and I will see to it that your career gets derailed from that fast track. Am I making myself clear?"

The three newcomers all nodded. Newman noted that the three young officers were wide-eyed. He wondered if they knew the National Security Advisor's nickname.

"Newman here reports to me. You report to him. That's the chain of command. Here's what you'll be doing." Harrod dug again into the file folder with the green *TOP SECRET* cover sheet that he'd been carrying since he and Newman had left the Sit Room. He pulled out a piece of paper and set it down on the table so that they all could read it:

TOP SECRET
NATIONAL SECURITY DIRECTIVE 941109

Date: November 9, 1994
Subj: United Nations Sanctions Enforcement

1. (TS) In accord with the Classified Annex to United Nations Security Council Resolution 1606 [RESTRICTED DISTRIBUTION], the United States and the United Kingdom are designated as the International Sanctions Enforcement Powers.

2. (TS) The International Sanctions Enforcement Powers shall establish an International Sanctions Enforcement Group (ISEG). The Enforcement Powers shall provide such personnel, logistic, command, control, communications, and intelligence support to the ISEG as needed to carry

out the mandates of the United Nations executive in accord with the Classified Annex to UN Res. 1606 and international law. The functions and activities of the ISEG shall be undertaken in such a manner that they do not bring discredit or disrepute to the Enforcement Powers or the United Nations executive.

3. (TS) The United Nations executive shall communicate specific requests for action by the ISEG directly to the heads of state of the Enforcement Powers or to their mutually agreed-upon designees.

4. (TS) The Prime Minister of the United Kingdom has designated Sir Reginald Bomphrey, secretary of the cabinet, as the UK designated Point of Contact for all ISEG activities.

5. (TS) The President of the United States has designated the assistant to the President for National Security Affairs, Mr. Simon Harrod, as the U.S. Designated Point of Contact for all ISEG activities.

6. (TS) By mutual agreement of the United Nations executive and the International Enforcement Powers, the existence and activities of the ISEG shall be held at the highest levels of classification and nondisclosure. Accordingly, all communications pertaining to the ISEG shall bear the following legends:

U.S.: TOP SECRET. CODE WORD ACCESS REQUIRED, NO DIS.

UK: MOST SECRET. LIMDIS BY ORDER OF THE PM.

UN: SEC GEN RESTRICTED. SPECIAL HANDLING REQUIRED.

7. (TS) The secretaries of state and defense, the director of central intelligence, and the director of the FBI shall provide such support to the ISEG as requested by the National Security Advisor to carry out the terms of this directive.

8. (S) This directive is exempted from routine downgrading and declassification and shall not be reproduced except by order of the President.

The document bore the President's signature. There was silence while all four men read the directive through a second time, each trying to figure out how he fit into the words in front of them. Newman finished first and asked the question on everyone's mind. "Dr. Harrod, how is all this going to work?"

Harrod glanced at his watch. It was approaching 6:00 P.M. and it was already dark outside. He shrugged and started to describe what it is they would do and how they would do it.

●

By the time Harrod finished describing how these four officers would coordinate requests from the UN Secretary General for sanctions enforcement, and answering their questions, it was almost 7:30.

As they concluded, Harrod swept up the classified documents that he had shown them and replaced them in the file folder. "Tomorrow morning I've made arrangements for you to meet the ISEG. All thirty-eight members of the group are being housed in a secure facility at Andrews Air Force Base for this phase of their training.

"You should arrive at the main gate between 6:00 and 6:15 A.M. That way you won't have to fight the traffic on the Beltway. Tell the security people that you need to be escorted to Area 35. Show them your White House pass. All four of you, spend the day over there with the team; get to know them. They are scheduled to fly back to Fort Bragg tomorrow night at 6:00 P.M. You should all be back here tomorrow night at 7:00 P.M.

"Bring some jeans and casual clothes to change into when you get back here. Why?" he asked, reading their questioning eyes. "First, you'll fit in better around here. Second, the team from WHCA will be here at 7:30 to install your communications equipment, secure phones, and the rest of the stuff you're going to need in here. I want to get that done after the rest of the crowd is gone. I don't want people asking too many questions about what you're up to here." As he said this, Harrod gestured around the office. "Any questions?" he asked.

"Many, but only two for now." It was Newman again. "How do we get funding for these activities? There must be some kind of congressional oversight."

Harrod looked at Newman with new regard. "Very sharp, Newman. Of course you four continue to draw your normal military pay. As far as your services are concerned, you're on detail to the NSC staff. The U.S. personnel in the ISEG are all carried as 'detached duty' with their parent departments and agencies. I suppose the Brits do it the same way, since all their people come from the SAS where they've been doing it this way for years.

"As for funding the training and operational activities of the ISEG and the ISETs, that's all handled by a special allocation from the British prime minister and the UN Secretary General. Unlike us, the PM and SG both have discretionary accounts that don't have to be reported to anybody. They both have contributed cash to fund the accounts that you'll be handling from here. Any expenditure of more than $100,000 has to be approved by me. I expect the books to balance. And I will periodically conduct an audit of how you are managing the funds.

"As of right now"—at this point Harrod consulted a piece of paper from his pocket—"we have a total of $7.47 million in three overseas bank accounts to last us until the end of the year. The secretary general has assured the President that on January 1, the accounts will have an additional $240 million placed in them for ISEG activities."

Newman and his staff looked at each other. Did Harrod just say 240 million?

"Now, as for congressional oversight, we won't be going up to Capitol Hill to describe any of what the ISEG does. In fact, as far as the foreign relations committees, the armed services committees, and the intelligence committees—and all their staffs—are concerned, the ISEG doesn't exist." Harrod stopped to see how the men reacted to that statement. He could see the wheels turning in their minds, but no one spoke.

"And, if push comes to shove, we still have some friends up there on the Hill, in both parties and in both houses of Congress. These friends share the President's vision for a well-ordered new world. But we'll cross that bridge when we come to it.

"Meanwhile," Harrod said, turning to McDade, Coombs, and Robertson, "have you taken care of all the paperwork?" All three nodded. "And you have your White House badges and parking passes for the Ellipse?" They nodded again.

"Good. Newman, make sure they know the combinations to all the silly locks on the door so that somebody can get in if you get run over by a truck tonight. I'll see you all here tomorrow at 7:00 P.M. when you've finished at Andrews."

○

After the National Security Advisor trundled out, the four officers sat back down at the round table to exchange phone numbers and addresses, explaining as they did so what they had been doing the previous Friday when they were abruptly jerked out of their assignments and ordered to duty at the NSC.

Lieutenant Tom McDade had been an instructor in Coronado, California, at the Basic Underwater Demolition/ SEALs School—known throughout the Navy as BUD/S. Harrod had said that all of the officers were veterans of the Gulf War, and they were. But McDade had also been in the Panama dustup back in December '89. His SEAL team had been hastily dispatched to Rodman Naval Station in Balboa Harbor, and given the mission of making sure that Manuel Noriega didn't manage to slip away from Panama on something that flew or floated. McDade and his fellow SEALs had managed to disable all the escape crafts of the former dictator. But the drill had cost the lives of four SEALs. McDade said somewhat wistfully, "I've been hoping for orders to join SEAL Team 6. Instead, it looks like I'm gonna be pushing papers at the White Palace."

Until the previous Friday, Captain Bart Coombs had been limping around on a crutch, the result of a parachute mishap during a Delta training operation at Camp Dawson in West Virginia. Until his knee fully healed, Coombs had been temporarily assigned to the Delta headquarters staff at "Wally World," the nickname the Delta operators gave to their flashy new Special Operations Training facility at Fort Bragg, North Carolina. During Desert Shield/Desert Storm, Coombs had been a "Scud Buster," dropped deep into Iraq to pinpoint mobile SCUD launchers for air strikes before the Russian-built missiles could be launched against Allied troops or Israel. His Delta squadron had deployed for six weeks to Somalia after the shoot-out in October '93 in which Jim Newman had been killed. Now he was also anguishing over the prospect of being shackled to a desk at the White House for two years. "I'd rather be in Mogadishu or some other cesspool," he groaned.

Captain Dan Robertson was the only one who wasn't going to grouse about the assignment. He had been an MH-53 Pave Low Special Operations helicopter pilot since graduating from the Air Force Academy and follow-on flight schools. During Desert Storm, he had taken his "Big Bird" deep into occupied Kuwait and Iraq to insert and extract Delta operators, rescue downed Navy and Air Force pilots, and, on one occasion, pull out a Marine recon patrol amidst heavy enemy fire.

He would have kept doing that kind of flying for the rest of his life, but Special Ops in the Air Force was a dead-end street. The most he could hope to command would be a squadron—and then what? He had two Distinguished Flying Crosses, a Purple Heart, and a broken marriage. He hadn't told anyone up the chain of command, but he had been planning to put in an application with U.S. Air when the orders for the White House landed on his desk.

Although none of the three young officers knew it, all of them, like Newman, had been "profiled" and then selected by name for the NSC. The WHDB computers had picked them out of more than a million men and women in the military based on criteria established by Harrod with the help of Admiral Wilburn Robbins, the former chairman of the Joint Chiefs of Staff and the only current or former member of the top brass to back the President's candidacy in 1992.

The President had rewarded Robbins for his political fealty by naming him the ambassador to London. From there, Robbins stayed in touch with Simon Harrod on a near-daily basis. The portly old admiral had negotiated the deal for the British to participate with the U.S. in the formation of the ISEG and had told Harrod what qualities he should seek in those who would be coordinating the ISEG's activities.

Harrod had taken the admiral's criteria, including the requirements that the people selected be single or divorced and have served in combat, to Arnold Granish and his data dinks in the WHDB facility. Less than forty-eight hours later, Harrod had the names of nine officers, three each from the Army, Navy, and Air Force, who met the selection criteria. After reviewing them, Harrod had chosen these three because they simply looked better than the others from their respective services. His only regret was that none of them had turned out to be a woman or a minority. He knew that an all-white, all-male Special Projects Office didn't meet the President's diversity goals, but he had to work with what he was given.

After the round of introductions, Newman began to think that this assignment might not be so intolerable after all. At least he would be working with kindred spirits. If nothing else, this little office in the southeast corner of the OEOB would be a place where the military was respected. He contemplated inviting his three new colleagues to walk across Lafayette Park and join him at the Army & Navy Club for a drink and the telling of a few lies and war stories—but then he checked his watch. It was nearly 9:00 P.M.

"Let's make a break for it," he said. "We have an early day of it at Andrews and probably a late night tomorrow night. Does anyone need a lift in the morning?"

No one did, so they all lined up silently at the door while Newman punched in the code to rearm the security system. Then they all piled out the door and waited while he spun the combination lock on the door and reset the lock on the wall panel.

As they headed down the silent corridor and the elevator, they joked quietly with each other about what the penalty might be for forgetting any of the combinations to the various locks. The ribald speculation continued all the way out onto West Executive Avenue.

It had gotten cold enough that each breath produced a billow of vapor that shone in the bright lights illuminating the white mansion just a few yards away. Newman headed for the Situation Room to run the "credit cards" with the lock and security system combinations through the microshredder. The other three waved good-night and walked toward the South West Gate and their cars on the Ellipse.

After a few minutes, Newman came back out and went to his car. As he headed slowly up West Executive Avenue toward the North West Gate, it occurred to him that he was glad his wife wouldn't be home for two more days. That would give him time to concoct an appropriate answer to Rachel's inevitable questions: "What's your new job at the White House like, Peter? What do you do there?"

He wanted to have an answer better than the truth. He just couldn't tell her that he would be planning assassinations for the United Nations.

CHAPTER FIVE

Rachel

The Barclay Suites Hotel
14th and Pine Street
Chicago, IL
Tuesday, 29 November 1994
2214 Hours, Local

Rachel Newman stood in front of the spacious tenth-floor window of the hotel suite. She had a commanding view of Lake Michigan and Grant Park. Across the street in the Sheraton Plaza she could see that few of the windows were still lit, and as she watched, occasionally the shadows of the occupants would move past. A few of the windows were dimly lit by the blue of flickering television screens, most of which were airing the local news.

The weather had turned colder since she had checked in. Snow flurries had been falling on the way from O'Hare in the TWA van, and she wondered if her flight out in the morning would leave on time. Rachel shivered as she stood by the window. The room was nicely warmed, but the glass pane did little to shut out the chill that was making the night outside so frosty.

As she stood there gazing out the window of the parlor, her unfocused staring was broken by a man's shadow moving across the drapes. As he came nearer, she turned to face him. His two strong arms enveloped her and held her tightly. Then Rachel took his face in her hands and reached up to kiss him. They lingered in the embrace for a long moment. Then, smiling mischievously, the man released his hold and from behind her back produced a small, exquisitely wrapped gift box and extended it to her with obvious anticipation. Rachel undid the wrappings and, with a little embarrassment, pulled out a bright-red garment, just a wispy piece of lingerie, meant for only one thing. She giggled and said, "Just what is it that you have in mind, Captain Vecchio?"

❂

Mitch Vecchio was an eighteen-year veteran pilot. He had met Rachel three years earlier when they were assigned to the same crew. All that spring they seemed to fly together often. Some of her fellow flight attendants noticed the interest Mitch paid her, and one friend even cautioned her, "Watch yourself with that guy, Rachel. I know him. He may be a nice package, but he's a married man with a roving eye and fast hands, if you know what I mean."

Rachel did, and though she enjoyed the flattering attention Mitch bestowed upon her, she kept him at arm's length until little more than a year ago—shortly after Jim Newman was killed in Somalia. A week after her brother-in-law was buried at Arlington, Rachel and Captain Vecchio were paired on the flight to London. While the two were alone in the TWA flight crew office at Heathrow, completing the postflight paperwork, a CNN broadcast announced that the U.S. was considering pulling its troops out of Somalia. Mitch turned to Rachel and said, "It's about time. We had no business being in that sewer in the first place." Rachel burst into tears.

Mitch, with what seemed to be genuine concern, hastened to comfort her. "What's wrong, Rache? What did I say?"

She tried to respond but was so wracked with sobs that he handed her his clean handkerchief, and while she dried her tears, he put his arm around her. Then he said with great sincerity, "I'm so sorry, Rachel. I didn't mean to upset you. What did I say?"

With those words, the handsome pilot unwittingly opened the floodgates for Rachel. She told him about her brooding husband's rejection and anger, how all he talked about was revenge, and how cruel he had been to her when his brother was killed. Mitch Vecchio was a willing and sympathetic listener. And over the course of the next two hours, he let Rachel unload on him.

Rachel told him how her husband seemed to shut her out of his life and how he seemingly had no love for her. "It's like he has a mistress that I can't compete with," Rachel told him.

"What do you mean you can't compete?" Mitch asked. "You're a smart, gorgeous woman. You're fun to be with . . . you have a great personality. And did I mention gorgeous?" he added with a smile.

"It's no use, Mitch. I can't compete with his mistress," Rachel said. She was no longer sad. Her voice now had an angry edge.

"Your husband really has a *mistress*?" he asked.

"His mistress is the Marine Corps. It's a crazy love that he has for the Corps and its people and the things they do. I once thought I understood him, but if I ever did, I don't anymore. And I sure don't understand the military," Rachel added through clenched teeth.

They were seated now on the leather couch in the lounge. Mitch reached over and put his arm gently on her shoulder and said, "You shouldn't have to understand, Rachel. You aren't in the military, and you shouldn't be expected to act like you are. You deserve to have a life of your own—and you deserve to have a man who loves you just the way you are."

Two months later they shared their first hotel room during a layover in Chicago. In fact, it was at the Sheraton Plaza, the building on East Superior just across the street from the Barclay. For eleven months now, Rachel had rationalized cheating on her husband by telling herself that theirs was "equal opportunity infidelity." He found affirmation, satisfaction, even affection in his Marine Corps. So why shouldn't she find that same kind of intimacy with someone else?

○

Rachel awoke with a little start. She turned her head and looked at the alarm clock on the nightstand beside the bed. The red numbers glowed dimly: 4:15.

Her lover's arm was across her, so she gently removed it and slid quietly out of the bed. Mitch rolled over on his back, snoring gently. She picked up the bedspread that had fallen to the floor during the night and wrapped it around her shoulders as she walked over to the window and looked out.

The lights and flickering televisions that had illuminated windows in the hotel across the street were now all off. In the glow of the cityscape outside, snow was falling, and Rachel leaned forward, her forehead touching the cold pane of glass, to see what was accumulating on the street below.

In the pools of light made by the streetlights, she could see white on the pavement. She wondered if their 0950 flight to San Diego would be departing on time. Then, as she watched the white flakes being tossed by the wind outside, she had another thought: Christmas. And suddenly hot tears were flowing down her cheeks. She didn't make a sound, but her mind was racing: *What in the world am I doing? It's almost Christmas, and here I am in a hotel bedroom with another man! What am I going to do, give both Peter and Mitch Christmas presents? What would Mom and Dad say if they knew where I am right now? What would Peter do if he knew? Oh dear God . . . where is all this taking me?*

After contemplating these questions for a few minutes and without coming up with any satisfactory answers, Rachel wiped the tears off her face with the edge of the bedspread. She went into the bathroom and closed the door before she turned on the light so as not to awaken her lover. *Lover. Is that what Mitch is? Is he my lover? No . . . he doesn't love me—and he certainly has no intention of leaving his wife and two kids for me.*

For all his other faults, Mitchell Vecchio had at least been forthright about that. He had made certain that Rachel understood that their relationship was open and nonexclusive. Mitch was honest with her—if not with his own wife—and he let Rachel know right from the start that their affair was for pleasure and could have no commitment beyond that. Rachel had agreed to those terms because she held out hope that the man she had once loved would somehow come to his senses. *But what do I want him to do? I'm not even sure I know myself, so what should I expect from Peter?* Rachel asked herself.

As she bent over the sink to splash cold water on her face, she tried not to think about her husband. Thinking about Peter too often reminded her of her many betrayals. But then she remembered that he was to have started a new job today at the White House. Rachel wondered what kind of a position he held now and what he'd be doing.

How she wished he'd share his life with her. She didn't want to go on punishing him by having an affair. She smiled to herself at the irony of that thought. *How can I be punishing him when he knows nothing about it?* Rachel thought. It was true. She was the one who felt the punishing guilt every time she spent a night with the pilot who was sleeping soundly in the bedroom on the other side of the bathroom door.

Mitch couldn't care less about guilt or morality and almost seemed to enjoy cheating on his wife. During one of their trysts in Houston, the pilot had explained his philosophy of life: "Rachel, life is like a string that's only so long," he said, holding out his arms. "You can either tie that string up in knots and always worry about how you're going to untangle it, or you can stretch it as tight as you can and make it go as far as possible. I don't like knots. I aim to have as much fun as I can, and when the string runs out, that's it." But he also told Rachel that he was driven to distraction by his wife's materialism and how he was always stressed financially because of her shopping and spending. Someday he'd have to deal with that knot, but for now he'd just have fun.

✪

Rachel didn't go back to bed. She knew she wouldn't be able to go back to sleep, so she took a long hot shower, washed her hair, and took her time brushing it out and putting on her makeup. At 6:00 A.M. she finished packing her black, TWA-issue tow-along bag, and while Mitch was in the bathroom shaving, she slipped out of the room and headed for the Barclay's fifth-floor dining room.

She intended to grab a bagel, some yogurt, and a cup of coffee before joining the rest of their crew across the street at the Sheraton, where the TWA shuttle would meet them for the trip back to O'Hare. But as Rachel walked into the dining room, she saw a familiar face across the room. She walked over to the table.

"Inga? Inga Linstad?" she said. "Hi, remember me— Rachel Newman? We were classmates in Saint Louis at the flight attendants' course."

"Of course, Rachel. How are you? I remember—you were the only nurse in our class. And I see that you are still with TWA. Do you still enjoy the work?"

"Most of the time," replied Rachel. "There are good days and bad days—you know how it is—but I've never had a day as bad as the ones you had over there in the Middle East. Where was it— Egypt?"

"Close," said Inga, softly. "It was Lebanon. We sure could have used your nursing skills on that trip, Rachel."

Inga Linstad was a virtual legend in the airline industry. She had been the senior flight attendant aboard TWA Flight 837 when it was hijacked out of Athens by Hizballah terrorists. The plane had been forced to land in Beirut, and for six days, the passengers and crew were subjected to terrible brutality. By the time the terrorists were granted safe passage off the plane and disappeared into the chaos of Lebanon, three American passengers and two crewmembers were dead and seven others aboard the aircraft had been wounded. The surviving passengers and crew credited Inga Linstad's calm demeanor, firmness, and courage with saving their lives.

Since then, though Inga was still officially on the TWA roster, she had been employed throughout the industry to train new pilots, flight attendants, even airline executives on dealing with these types of crises. Her face was well known to almost everyone in the airline business. At TWA she was their heroine-in-residence.

The waiter came to the table to take Inga's order. Inga looked up at Rachel and asked, "Won't you join me for breakfast?"

The two women placed their orders and settled in to catch up on each other's lives.

"What brings you to Chicago, Inga?" asked Rachel.

"Oh, I had a briefing for United yesterday out at O'Hare. I'm headed out today for more of the same on the West Coast. They were nice enough to put me up here instead of across the street, where our crews normally stay, so I can avoid the crowds. I really don't much like all the attention, Rachel. I was just doing my duty. Yet everyone makes such a fuss about it."

"But you're a real hero, Inga," protested Rachel. "That's why everyone wants to hear what you have to say."

Inga shrugged and tried to change the subject. "So, is TWA now putting up flight crews here at the Barclay Suites?" she asked innocently.

Rachel felt the warmth rising in her cheeks. She and Mitch were staying in this hotel for the same reason as Inga—but with different motives. Inga wanted to avoid being seen by her airline colleagues out of her inherent modesty. Rachel and Mitch were staying here to avoid the wagging tongues of their colleagues, out of Rachel's sense of guilt. No matter how much they tried to convince themselves otherwise, they both knew what they were doing was wrong.

Unable to fabricate a plausible lie fast enough, Rachel ignored the question and asked one of her own: "Tell me, Inga, I've seen the training video TWA did about the incident on 837, but it didn't really give me a sense of what it was like when it happened. Weren't you terrified when the terrorists started killing people?"

"Yes, it was a terrible thing," Inga replied softly. "Lori, the flight attendant who they killed first, was a very close friend. She and I had flown together since she came out of training, and we roomed together on every trip." Inga paused, then continued even more softly than before, her voice just barely above a whisper. "I haven't told this to many people, Rachel, but Jerry, the First Officer, who they killed second, had asked me to marry him. We were going to see my parents when we got back to St. Louis so Jerry could ask my father for my hand. Sometimes I feel very sad because even though it's been eight years, I miss him so much."

Rachel was shocked. "Oh . . . Inga, I'm sorry . . . I didn't know. Weren't all the killings on the first day? How were you ever able to do what you did after that? How could you even function or stay so calm? You even talked the terrorists out of killing more people." Rachel's curiosity spilled out.

Inga shook her head and said, "It wasn't me. I don't know where the words came from. I am not a brave person. I don't know what possessed me to stand up to the ringleader and tell him to stop the shooting and torture. I do know that I prayed. And I know that God gave me the words to say . . . that's all I can tell you."

Rachel felt awkward, and her questions seemed forced and stilted. She desperately needed to keep the conversation about Inga and not about her. Yet even as she clumsily asked questions, she was fascinated by Inga's story. She didn't want to cause her former classmate more pain, but she couldn't stop now. "In the training video that TWA put together, there is some newsreel footage showing one of the terrorists holding you against the bulkhead by the open door. He has a gun underneath your chin. It looks like you're going to be the next one killed. It's clear in the video that he's saying something to you and that you say something back. But in the video, there is no sound. But a few moments later, he stands back and takes the gun away. And it wasn't much longer after that that the terrorists left the airplane. What was he saying to you, and what did you say back to him?"

Inga looked as though she was far away. "He was the ringleader. It was right after he had shot another American in the foot. I don't know what made me do it, but I got up from my seat and told him he couldn't do that anymore. That's when he grabbed me and pushed me up to the cabin door. He jammed that enormous gun hard under my chin and screamed that he was going to kill me. And I said, 'I hope you will find forgiveness.' And then he said—this is the part you see in the video—'Why aren't you afraid to die?' And all I said was, 'I'm not afraid to die because I know where I'm going and I know why I'm going there.' That's when he backed up and let me go. And as you know, an hour or so later it was all over."

Rachel was puzzled. "That's it? What made you say that, Inga? Where did he think you were going?"

Now it was Inga's turn to be puzzled. She looked at her classmate and said, "I said what came to mind, even with that gun jammed into my throat—it's the essential truth of Christianity. There is no need to be afraid of death if you know where you are going after you die. And all true Christians know where they are going—it's just that most of them don't know when. At that point, I was sure that I knew." Inga said this last part with just the faintest hint of a smile.

Perhaps it was Inga's subtle smile, maybe it was the guilt Rachel was feeling from the night's activities with Mitch, but Rachel reacted with some irritation. "Of course you're a Christian. I'm a Christian too. My parents are lifelong Methodists—so were my grandparents. We've always been Christians, but I'm not sure I know what difference that would make in a situation like yours, on that hijacked plane," Rachel said, shaking her head.

"You know, Rachel, I used to think the same thing, but a year before the Beirut incident, a dear old lady was on one of my flights. She was on her way from California to bury her daughter who had been killed in New York in some senseless street shooting. This young girl had been a totally innocent bystander who got in the way of a bullet that killed her instantly."

"How awful!" Rachel exclaimed. "I'll bet that poor mother was a basket case."

"That's what I'd have thought," Inga said, "but she wasn't. She had such composure and peace in spite of what had happened to her daughter. She told me, 'I've had some time to get used to the idea. The police called to inform me about the shooting two days ago. Since then my husband and I have tried to make sense of it all.' I asked her where her husband was, and she told me that he had gone on ahead to make funeral arrangements.

"I couldn't get over her composure, and so I asked her about it. She told me that she was a Christian, like we thought we were, too, you know? But she explained that your faith has to be personal in order to be real. She said, 'I trust God—even in this tragedy. I know that He has not abandoned us, and He has promised to give us peace and comfort.' Then, since we still had over an hour of flight time left, and I was caught up on my cabin duties, I sat down beside her. I thought I could console her. But she ended up consoling me."

Rachel was intrigued. The waiter interrupted their conversation as he brought Rachel's order along with Inga's breakfast. The two women thanked him in unison and began to eat.

Inga took a sip of her orange juice. "Anyway, this sweet little lady told me how, though she grieved for her murdered daughter, she didn't despair because she knew that her daughter was a true believer and follower of Jesus Christ, and she knew that her daughter was in heaven."

"I've heard people talk like that," Rachel said quietly, "but it's always kind of put me off, you know? I mean, it sounds kind of arrogant to me. Like there are different levels of religion and theirs is more real than mine. And how can anyone *know* that they are going to heaven?"

"I know what you're saying, Rachel. I was like that, too," Inga replied, "but deep down I knew I didn't have anything like that inside me. I mean, the faith of that lady was real. *It really was personal.* I wished I had that kind of faith, and I told her so. Then she spent the next half hour telling me how I could have *real* faith in God. That made me wonder what would happen to me when I died, something I'd never really thought about. Have you ever really thought about what will happen to you when you die?"

Once again, Rachel could feel her cheeks beginning to flush. Suddenly the spacious dining room seemed too hot, too small. She had the horrible thought that Mitch might come bounding in and say something that would reveal their secret to Inga. Rachel interrupted her friend. "Uh . . . listen, Inga. Sorry—I just noticed the time . . . and I'm running late. I need to get my things and catch the shuttle to O'Hare. It was sure nice seeing you again. Let's try to stay in touch," she said as she rose to pay the bill.

"What flight are you on today?" Inga asked.

"Chicago to San Diego, then back to Dulles. I'll get to sleep in my own bed tonight," Rachel said with a smile that she didn't feel. The words *my own bed tonight* seemed somehow out of place, embarrassing.

"The nine-fifty flight to San Diego?" Inga asked.

"Yeah . . . flight 1529."

"I'm flying standby to San Diego on that flight. Unless it's completely booked, I'll see you aboard the flight. Maybe we can talk some more," Inga said, excited at seeing her old friend and hoping they'd be able to spend some more time together.

Rachel smiled sheepishly and waved as she put her credit card back into her purse. "Great—I can't wait," she said without much sincerity as she turned to leave.

CHAPTER SIX

Baghdad

Office of the Commander, Amn Al-Khass
Special Security Service Headquarters
Palestine Street, Baghdad, Iraq
Tuesday, 29 November 1994
2305 Hours, Local

Hussein Kamil was unhappy, almost despondent. The first cousin and son-in-law of the country's Supreme Leader, The Defender of Islam, Secretary General of the Ba'ath Socialist Party, Head of State, and Commander of the Armed Forces surely had his benefits, but connection to all those titles also carried its liabilities. One of the benefits was that in exchange for marrying Saddam Hussein's only attractive daughter, Kamil got to be the Minister of Military Industrialization and commander of the *Amn Al-Khass*—the SSS, Iraq's Special Security Services and one of the world's most feared organizations. But as far as Kamil was concerned, one of his most serious liabilities—and perhaps his greatest threat—was sitting opposite him right now: his brother-in-law, Saddam Hussein's second (though some said favorite) son, Qusay Hussein.

Although they were in his office, Kamil had diffi-
dently escorted his brother-in-law to the seat at the head
of the oval conference table where the second son of
Iraq's Supreme Leader could feel in charge. Kamil gestured for Qusay to take the favored chair.

"My father is not pleased," Qusay said sharply as he sat.

"What do you mean, he is not pleased?" queried
Kamil, trying to control his nerves as he took a seat on
the corner of the table nearest the dictator's son. *It is
always like this,* he thought. The phone would ring late
at night. A meeting—always a very late-night meeting—
would be ordered. The caller would invariably be
Qusay or his older brother, Uday, or it might be Saddam's personal secretary, Abd Hamid Mahmoud.

The meeting—no matter where it took place—would
invariably start with a series of open-ended statements
that sounded more like accusations. There was never a
correct reply. The best that you could hope for was not
to say something that could be used against you in the
many paranoid purges that characterized the Supreme
Leader's regime. Tonight's inquisition appeared to be no
different.

"He is not happy with your efforts at identifying and
dealing with traitors," continued Qusay. "He is especially unhappy that Khidir Hamza has still not been
found and eliminated. It has been too long! What are
you doing about him?" On a hot August day four
months earlier, Khidir Hamza, the number-two man in
Iraq's supersecret nuclear weapons program, had
walked out the door of his house in Baghdad's high-
security palace compound and disappeared. Since he
was a walking repository of secrets and information of
great value, especially for the West, tracking him down
and killing him was Kamil's personal responsibility.

"My people are working on it. We have arrested scores of people, tortured dozens, and interrogated his wife and children. We will find him. Please assure our father that Hamza will be tracked down and punished for his ingratitude," replied Kamil.

In truth, Kamil had no real idea where Hamza was, but he didn't want to admit that to anyone, least of all Qusay Hussein. Hamza's defection, if that's what his disappearance was, could be fatal for Kamil—if he failed to find and silence him. He hoped that Qusay wasn't about to deliver a deadline by which the traitorous scientist had to be found and eliminated.

More than anyone else in Iraq, Kamil knew how valuable Hamza would be to the West—particularly the hated CIA and British intelligence. Hamza knew everything about the Iraqi efforts to build the ultimate weapon of mass destruction. And Hussein Kamil was the person who had hired him to build it.

"I am absolutely confident that we shall soon have him in our hands," Kamil said, though he felt anything but confidence. Professional torturers in the bowels of the Al Ranighwania prison had produced "testimony" from other poor souls that Hamza had been seen in the company of Iraqi dissidents in the mountains not far from the Turkish border. But by the time the assassination teams Kamil had dispatched arrived in Zakhu, deep in the Kurdish-controlled territory north of the Tigris, the traitor had disappeared, assuming that was where he had been in the first place. When the assassination teams returned to the SSS unit in Mosul empty-handed, Kamil had them shot for failing their mission. It occurred to him that Qusay and his father-in-law might be considering such a fate for him since he was the ultimate authority to whom the Amn Al-Khass teams reported.

Qusay grimaced. "I am told that Hamza was seen over two months ago in the North where the American swine recruit traitors for their puppet opposition. The Iraqi National Congress resistance wouldn't exist but for the American dollars they are spreading around like camel dung in a corral. What are you doing about it? My father wants to know if you can be trusted to do your job," he barked.

Then why doesn't he ask me himself? thought Kamil. But he didn't say it. He knew better. Kamil was, of course, recording this conversation. He audio- and videotaped nearly everything that took place in this office. Except, of course, the visits by the Filipino and Thai prostitutes sent by the Japanese ambassador. So he naturally assumed that Qusay was also recording this conversation for his own use—either with a radio microphone hidden beneath his robes or in his attaché case that he had placed so strategically on the table. It was all part of a lethal game of cat and mouse, a game that every senior official in Iraq played. It had been so even before Saddam Hussein had seized the reins of power in 1969. It got worse after Saddam proclaimed himself president in 1979. And, since the 1990–91 war, spying on one another had become a full-time, and essential, part of staying in power—and staying alive. Kamil wondered if Qusay had obtained one of the new laser listening devices that could be beamed against an unprotected windowpane and tuned to vibrations caused by the voices inside. Kamil had recently acquired such an apparatus, made in Sweden and delivered to him courtesy of a Saudi prince whom he was blackmailing.

Kamil also knew that the brothers, Uday and Qusay, both resented his power. As Minister for Military Industrialization, Kamil was responsible for building

Iraq's arsenal of mass destruction weapons—biological, chemical, and nuclear. And as the commander of the Amn Al-Khass, he was given the vast resources, both human and financial, of the Amn Al-Khass to run a global arms and technology acquisition network and, along with it, an extensive stable of agents, spies, and assassins. He also knew that if the brothers Uday and Qusay were able to convince their father that Kamil was incompetent or somehow disloyal, nothing except a capricious whim of Allah could save him.

Qusay's challenge hung in the air like the smell of garlic. Kamil sighed deeply and looked around his opulently appointed office for an appropriate answer.

The Persian carpet was a two-hundred-year-old treasure from Tabriz. The German pharmacologists from Frankfurt, who were helping to concoct Iraq's next generation of toxic nerve agents, had given it to him as a gift. The unique hand-rubbed mahogany for the walls had been delivered by Li Hoia Shan himself on one of his many trips to bring surface-to-air missile components and telemetry systems from Beijing to Baghdad. The desk, big as a battleship, and the matching conference table at which they now sat had been flown here by Giuseppi Rinaldi when he delivered the last batch of communications and computer equipment direct from Genoa. *In fact,* thought Kamil, *about the only thing in this office that is native to Iraq is the enormous painting of our magnificent leader adorning the wall behind my desk.* Its artist had used great license in portraying Saddam; Kamil thought it caricatured his father-in-law's eccentricities, but Saddam loved it. *That pompous fool can't be properly captured on canvas,* Kamil thought. But now he had to answer the question of his brother-in-law, who had begun to tap incessantly on the table.

"Please, Qusay, think of what you are saying," began Kamil in a soft but authoritative voice. "You are looking at the negative side. Think positive. The Amn Al-Khass is totally loyal to your father—the father of my wife, *my* father-in-law, the grandfather of my children and your nephews and nieces, our nation's greatest leader." His emphasis on family ties did not register with Qusay, so Kamil took a more businesslike stance. He leaned across the table and spoke to Qusay with sincerity and authority. His tone and body language were assertive as he said, "I created Amn Al-Khass and have made it work. I run it to protect *our* father, the Ba'ath Party, and the state, and it will always be so. This organization is not yet five years old, but already we have had great success." Kamil waited for his words to take effect before continuing, as much for the reaction of anyone else who might be listening to his conversation as for his brother-in-law.

"When the American president tried to provoke a rebellion among the Shia after the imperialists were driven from our homeland in 1991, your father, our great leader, gave me the task of eliminating the threat they posed to him and to the Ba'ath Party," Kamil reminded Qusay. "As you know, I personally saw to it that more than *ten thousand* of those Shia gangsters were exterminated at Al Ranighwania. The mullahs next door and their Shia lackeys have been completely eliminated as a threat. And I am talking about one man, Qusay—*I* have purged those ten thousand enemies for your father!

"Since then, the Amn Al-Khass has grown to become our glorious nation's most effective instrument for dealing with traitors and spies." Kamil decided that if Qusay or someone else was indeed recording all this, they ought to get an earful. He continued. "Of course I mean no disrespect to the members and leaders of the Mukhabarat. They are certainly courageous defenders of the Party and your father, our great leader. But Qusay, you and I both know that the General Intelligence Directorate is not what it used to be. Back in the old days, when it was just the *Jihaz al-Khass*—the Special Apparatus—we could all count on the loyalty of *everyone* involved. You know that it is no longer the case."

Kamil paused so that his brother-in-law could make a decision as to whether he wanted the conversation to continue in this direction. Qusay only nodded, so Kamil continued. "When Fadil al Barak was under consideration to head the GID, I told your father that he could not be trusted." Here, Kamil knew he was treading in dangerous waters. But he wanted this on tape, so he forged ahead, choosing his words carefully. "There were . . . uh . . . *some* around your father who dissuaded him of the accuracy of my information, and Fadil was appointed despite my warnings." Again Kamil paused, for Uday, the exalted leader's eldest son, had been one of those who had urged the appointment.

Qusay said nothing, but nodded again. Kamil pressed on. "It took until 1989 to verify that my information was indeed correct. And, as I am sure you remember, it took almost two more years of 'interrogation' to convince Fadil to admit that he was loyal—not to your father—but to the KGB. I was given the honor of personally executing the traitorous pig," Kamil added proudly, but with just the right amount of humility.

What Kamil did not mention, for he did not have to, was that he had also personally tortured Fadil al Barak on an almost nightly basis in the bowels of the large, fortress-like, Amn Al-Khass building behind the Palace of Meetings. When the wind was blowing right, guests enjoying the cool night air on the balconies of the nearby Rashid Hotel thought they could hear what sounded like the screams of a wounded animal. What they were hearing was the effect of Kamil's "gentle persuasion" that ran the gamut from pliers applied to fingernails, teeth, and genitals to the use of a cattle prod.

In his agony, Fadil eventually realized that "confession" was the only way he could escape the daily torture, so he gave them one, and that gave Kamil the privilege of putting a bullet in the head of the former head of the General Intelligence Directorate. For his loyalty and determination in ferreting out the "traitor," Saddam Hussein had named his son-in-law as the head of the new Special Security Service. As the commander of the Amn Al-Khass, Kamil's mission was to provide personal protection to Saddam and his family, an appointment with the means and authority to deal mercilessly with any perceived threat to the regime. In fewer than four years, Kamil had built the SSS into the preeminent intelligence/security organ in Iraq.

Now, in late 1994, Kamil had the authority to investigate and, where necessary, eliminate members of Iraq's other security and intelligence services for any real or imagined disloyalty. Yet even this authority did not guarantee his continued tenure if Saddam or his sons perceived that he was somehow becoming a threat to them or their regime. Kamil decided that a further litany of successes was in order. He knew that Qusay would soon tire of this and tell him what was really on his mind.

Kamil continued in the same assertive tone. "You must know that our recruiting drive is going well. Soon the Special Security Service will have five thousand members, all of whom are either loyalists from the Al Delaim tribe or recruits from Hawuija, Samarra, or Tikrit, our family's hometown. All of them have but one goal: to ensure your father's continued safety and success. And as evidence of this loyalty, each man has pledged his life.

"The Political Branch has begun issuing every Iraqi citizen an identity card that soon will be integrated into a new national database managed by the SSS," Kamil said. "Very soon, every police station in the country will have a Special Security Service unit assigned to it, with instructions to monitor the loyalty of all police and militiamen.

"Thanks to our friends in Beijing, we have nearly completed our Plan 858, the Al Hadi Project, which links five new listening stations to the center at Al Rashedia, so that we can monitor all electronic communications coming into or going out of the country—even satellite calls. Also, as I reported to you last Thursday at our weekly meeting in the Joint Operations Room—"

"Enough!" Qusay said sharply, interrupting his brother-in-law midsentence. "I already know all this. My father knows all this. That is not why I am here."

Kamil sat back in his chair. "Then to what do I owe the pleasure of your visit?" he said with a forced smile. His head might ache and his gut might churn, but his face would betray nothing.

Qusay was silent for what seemed to be several minutes but was probably only one at most. Finally he leaned forward and stared intently into the face of his brother-in-law and said quietly, "My father wants to broaden the effort to punish the Americans. We must bring into our cause others who have a common purpose. We need to find new allies."

"I do not understand . . ." Kamil said.

Qusay seemed to have trouble getting the next sentence past his lips, since it had to give credit to Kamil. "My father says that he wants to make use of the many advances that you have made in rebuilding our chemical and biological weapons following our war with the West. With the progress that you have made, these weapons can now be used against the Americans."

As Qusay spoke, Kamil didn't know whether to be gratified or terrified. After every hard-won success, Kamil was asked to do another "impossible" assignment. As Minister for Military Industrialization, he had indeed accomplished the extraordinary feat of rebuilding Iraq's nuclear, biological, and chemical weapons programs. And he had done it in just four years! The infrastructure for constructing these weapons of mass destruction had been severely damaged, but not destroyed, by the Allied bombing campaigns during what they called the Gulf War. The United Nations had tried in vain to locate and destroy any efforts to rebuild the Iraqi arsenal; yet despite sanctions and inspections, Kamil had achieved the impossible and spent billions in black-market oil revenues resurrecting the former laboratories, assembly plants, and storage depots—right under the UN noses.

Qusay continued. "I must admit I was skeptical, but your decision to reconstruct the weapons program at my father's palaces was brilliant. The UN inspectors cannot visit these sites. Now we must put the good work that you have done to its intended use. It is time for our glorious nation to strike back—not just at the American planes that violate our airspace, not just at their bases in Kuwait or Saudi Arabia, but at their very homeland. Women and children in the United States must suffer and die, just as ours have."

The statement took Kamil's breath away. It was a bold idea, but in his mind, impossible. True, the compliment from Qusay concerning his work and success would ordinarily have given Kamil great pleasure. But it was connected to some wild-eyed plan to use the nuclear bombs and other weapons of mass destruction on Americans—in their homeland.

"But how?" Kamil asked his brother-in-law. He chose his words carefully and thought of the implications of his questions. "How can we do this? The weapons that I have built are defensive and short range. We cannot deliver these weapons against the Jews, much less the Americans living in another hemisphere. Our planes would be shot down in minutes, and we do not have enough rocket capability for long-range destruction. It is true that we will soon have enough sarin gas and anthrax to kill many Jews, and perhaps many Americans, but how are we to deliver these agents?"

Qusay only smiled as if he had all the answers.

Kamil continued to ask the serious questions. "And the personnel. Think of the cost in having our technicians and scientists trying to put these agents into warheads. They are highly toxic and dangerous. More than likely, anyone using these agents would die in the process of using them against our enemies. We have so few skilled workers now that I am afraid that—"

Once again Qusay interrupted his brother-in-law. "Do not worry so much; we will not have to sacrifice your precious scientists and skilled technicians," he said.

Kamil looked morose. "That must mean, Qusay, that you are thinking of our nuclear weapons. I must tell you, that is even more difficult. We have only two nuclear bombs, and we haven't been able to test them yet.

Besides, none of our aircraft is big enough to carry such a weapon, even to Tel Aviv. Maybe in a while, a couple of years, we might be able to do something. Once the UN inspectors leave—"

"Forget the atomic weapons, my dear Kamil," Qusay said. "You are quite correct. The time for using them is later, not now. But we can use the other weapons to kill many Jews and Americans—your chemicals and germs. This is the time for using them."

"But how? Who will deliver them if we do not use our scientists and technicians? And how will we get them to Israel and America? These are nerve agents and biotoxins. They have to be delivered and used in specific ways, mainly in confined spaces. Men will have to be recruited to take these weapons to the enemy, knowing full well that they themselves will be killed in the process. They will die a horrible death. Where will we find people to carry out such an order?"

"That's just the point, my dear Kamil," Qusay replied. "We do not have to. Others will do this for us— others who will be glad to die a martyr's death just to have a chance at killing many Americans or Jews with the materials that you provide." Kamil noticed that Qusay had a cruel smile beneath his mustache. *It is the first time I have noticed how much he looks like a younger version of his father,* thought Kamil.

It was a startling revelation. Kamil stared at his brother-in-law, wondering if he had taken leave of his senses. They both knew, though no one would ever say so openly, that there was no one in Iraq willing to die for Saddam Hussein. Certainly there were Palestinians in the Hamas organization who strapped on blocks of C-4 plastic explosives and blasting caps and blew themselves up in crowded Tel Aviv markets and restaurants.

But these "martyrs" were killing themselves for a cause in which they believed. Nobody in Iraq believed in Saddam enough to do something like that.

And both men knew about the zealots of Islamic jihad and Hizballah, who built "suicide" cars and trucks in Lebanon's Bekaa Valley so they could blow themselves up in front of an Israeli military checkpoint, school, or shopping center. But these were young Shiite men who killed themselves willingly at the direction of the mullahs in Tehran.

"You said, 'others will do this for us,' " Kamil said. "What others, Qusay?" He leaned forward now, elbows on the table. "Who are these 'others' who will take these nerve agents and biological toxins to America? Whom do you know who would kill themselves by releasing these poisons in American cities? This is an evil plan, to kill thousands of innocent people . . ."

Kamil stopped himself midsentence, realizing that he was going too far. If Qusay was here delivering a decision his father had already made rather than a self-concocted, harebrained scheme, what he had been about to say could be used to try him for treason. He took a deep breath and tried a different approach.

"What I mean to say, Qusay, is that I have never considered using these weapons in that way. I built these weapons to defend our homeland against the Jews and Persians and their Shiite hordes. They are *defensive* weapons. I never imagined that . . ." He didn't need to complete the thought.

For an awkward moment neither man spoke. Then Kamil said, "When your father asked me to rebuild these weapons, he told me that we should be prepared to use them against the Jews if they ever attack an Arab nation again. Now you tell me that he wants to use them to punish the Americans in their homeland. Honestly, Qusay, I do not know how to do that. And I don't know who *does* know."

Qusay's smile quickly turned downward. He had never liked his sister's husband. Yes, Kamil was bright, but he was weak. He was a technician, well educated in the ways of the West, and thus able to do things that others could not. But he lacked courage, and courage in these times was a most essential quality. Up to this point, Qusay had tried to be patient with this overcautious weakling. But the hour was late and he was losing patience. His face flushed with anger, Qusay spat out curses in guttural Arabic, the language he had learned from his father, and which his father had learned as an urchin in the dusty, filthy streets of Tikrit. "Kamil, you useless eunuch! You miserable woman equipped like a man! Where is your courage? Did you lose your courage with your manhood? Who is the father of my sister's children? It couldn't have been you!"

Kamil sat back in his chair and stared at his brother-in-law, stunned by the outburst.

Qusay sighed deeply as if to demonstrate unusual patience and then spoke again, this time with his voice once again under control. "I will tell you, dear Kamil, who will do this for us. He is a man with a thousand times your courage—Osama bin Laden."

Kamil was aghast at what he had just heard. Osama bin Laden was a charismatic, ruthless, and uncontrollable fanatic. He and his Al-Qaeda organization had betrayed everyone with whom they had ever worked. Kamil drew in a deep breath to frame his next words mentally. He could think of nothing better than the blunt question that first came to him: "Do you think that is prudent?"

Qusay looked up at Kamil, puzzled.

Getting no verbal response and misunderstanding his brother-in-law's quizzical expression, Kamil continued in his normal, analytical tone. "Except for those closest to bin Laden himself, his people are zealous but not wise. Most are barely educated. Do you not remember what happened last year in Mogadishu? He sent two dozen of his Mujahedeen into Somalia to help Mohammed Aidid drive out the Americans—their Rangers killed nearly ten thousand Somalis. Osama bin Laden's men were useless in Africa and indirectly caused the death of thousands. How many of us will die if he comes to help us?" Kamil asked.

Qusay's impatience was near the boiling point, but he clenched his teeth and spoke slowly and deliberately, as to a child. "You do not understand, Kamil. Who cares how many Africans died? What does it matter? What matters is that Osama sent his people to organize and train the Somali fighters, and they killed nineteen of the arrogant U.S. Army Rangers and the Delta Force butchers."

"Yes, and the television pictures showing their bodies being dragged through the streets of Mogadishu provoked the sympathy of the entire world," Kamil reminded him. "Besides, it was a terrible violation of Islamic laws and teaching against the desecration of the dead."

Qusay erupted. Kamil had an excuse for everything. Pounding the table with his fist, Qusay shouted, "Kamil, you weakling! Where is your spine? You don't have an ounce of the courage that Osama bin Laden has in his finger! You talk of fear, but he talks of power and might. Don't you see, by dragging those bodies through the streets of Mogadishu, Osama proved that the Americans are not invincible! He did what our own Republican Guard divisions could not do in 1991. *He killed their soldiers!* And seven months before that, at their Trade Center towers in New York, Osama killed Americans *where they work!* Because of him, Americans are no longer safe in their island of conceit. Their towers can be humbled."

Qusay was shouting now, though his listener was only four feet away. He rose to his feet, gesturing dramatically and spewing spittle on the polished tabletop as he sneered at Kamil. "This is not a matter for you to determine," he informed his brother-in-law. "This is not some German scientist that you are bribing to help you redesign one of your laboratories. This matter has already been decided!"

Kamil looked up and blinked. Qusay continued his tirade. "Yes, it is true. It is already decided. Osama has been invited here. I have already dispatched two trusted officers of the Mukhabarat to Khartoum to extend my father's invitation. When they return from the Sudan, you will make all the necessary arrangements for bin Laden to visit your chemical and biological research centers. You are to provide him with whatever information and materials that he needs. You will use only your best and most trusted officers in Amn Al-Khass to oversee this process. Be sure to tell them that if the American swine or the British vipers or the Israeli scorpions ever learn about Osama's visit here, I will personally torture and disembowel their children while they watch! Those are my father's orders. Do you understand?"

Kamil nodded and stood up as Qusay grabbed his attaché case and stormed out the door.

It was then that Kamil Hussein realized that his days in power were numbered. That night he considered how he could escape Saddam's clutches. Though he did not know it then, his escape plan would cost many Americans their lives—and Peter Newman would be right in the middle of it.

CHAPTER SEVEN

Andrews Air Force Base

Area 35
Andrews Air Force Base
Wednesday, 30 November 1994
0700 Hours, Local

Newman, McDade, Coombs, and Robertson were being given the royal treatment. All four had arrived at the Andrews Air Force Base main gate within minutes of one another at 0600 hours. Newman had traveled the farthest, leaving his house on Creswell a little before 0450. As he'd turned right onto a quiet residential street, he had looked back to see if he was once again being followed. He couldn't tell.

Once he was headed west on Arlington Boulevard, Newman had a straight shot to I-495 and the "outer loop" of the Washington Beltway, which would take him across the Potomac and into Maryland and the sprawling Andrews Air Force Base. The eight-lane highway that encircled Washington was both a blessing and a curse. When traffic was moving, it couldn't be beat. But as Newman knew well, the slightest "fender bender" could shut the whole thing down, leaving people stranded for hours in both directions.

This morning, the Woodrow Wilson drawbridge didn't stop traffic across the Potomac, there were no accidents, and while it was cold from a hard frost, at least it wasn't snowing. Newman made the twenty-eight-mile trip in just over forty minutes. As he turned off Exit 9 onto Allentown Road, he checked his watch and the rearview mirror, once again trying to see if he was being followed. Since it was still early, he pulled into the McDonald's directly across from the large sign that read *ANDREWS AFB—MAIN GATE.*

Newman was a big believer in that old infantry axiom: "You never know when or where you'll get your next meal. Eat when you can." He ordered a breakfast sandwich, an orange juice, and a cup of coffee, and ate in his car. At exactly 0555, he pulled up to the sentry booth at the main gate, flashed his White House badge, and was directed by the sentry to a small parking area off to the right. McDade, Coombs, and Robertson pulled in behind him a couple of minutes later.

The base duty officer, an Air Force major, had met them there and directed them to some VIP parking behind a brick building labeled *BASE SECURITY.* There, they boarded a dark-blue Air Force van. Newman jumped into the front seat of the van before the others could lay claim to the seat. He wanted to see where they were going. Their escort climbed in the back with the others; Newman could hear them as they struck up the usual conversation, using the starter line soldiers and sailors have uttered ever since there have been armies and navies: "Where are you from?"

Newman had been to Andrews dozens of times. But

he'd never been to where they were headed now. To their right was an orange glow from thousands of sodium-vapor lights. Newman could see the long North-South runway, enormous hangars, maintenance sheds, and barracks buildings. Soon they were headed back to the south. He kept track of the names of the streets, memorizing them as he would terrain features on a reconnaissance patrol: Tyler Road, Patrick Avenue, Fechet Avenue, Trenton Street, Pearl Harbor Drive, Watson Drive—all famous people and places in military aviation history. And then, after driving for a good fifteen minutes, they were well south of the main runway. As the van rolled past the intersection with Wisconsin Road, he could see a lake off to their left. The rest of the base had been well lighted, but as the van turned left off the main road onto a smaller road, there were no lights at all except for the van's headlights. As they pulled through a stand of large pines, they came upon a number of low brick buildings and what looked like a small hangar, surrounded by a chain-link fence topped with razor wire. An armed Air Force security man dressed in a parka, his breath billowing out from beneath the fur-lined hood, admitted them into the compound.

Once inside the main building they were met by a wiry man in a dark-blue plaid wool shirt, jeans, and chukka boots. His dark brown eyes, longish dark hair, and beard made him a dead ringer for a member of Hizballah—"the army of God."

"Good morning," the make-believe terrorist said, holding out his hand, "I'm Captain Joshua Weiskopf, U.S. Army." Then he took a swing at Coombs, barely missing his jaw. Coombs instinctively pulled back and grabbed the man's wrist, grinning at the bearded man who had offered this bizarre greeting. The bearded one laughed. "Bart, looks to me like you're hanging around with bad company," he told Coombs.

Coombs also laughed, shook his head, and said, "I don't mind hanging *around* with them, I just don't want to be *hung with* them. How did you land this gig, Josh?"

"Well," the grinning beard replied, "after you got hurt on that jump, I guess the big brass at 'Wally World' figured they needed some adult leadership, so they put me in charge of this lash-up. Which one of you is Bart's boss?"

Newman smiled and said, "I guess that would be me. Major Peter Newman, Marines."

"Well, I guess that makes you my boss, too, but I'll give you some free advice, Major. Look out for that one." He pointed a finger at the grinning Coombs. "He's a wild one."

Introductions out of the way, Captain Weiskopf motioned for the men to follow him. "Come on, let me introduce you to the finest group of operators I've ever met."

❂

The bearded Delta Force captain walked them into the rear of what was clearly a pilot's ready room. There were fifty seats in five rows of ten—actual commercial airliner passenger seats, complete with tray tables, bolted to the green tile-covered floor.

Newman counted the backs of thirty-six heads in the occupied seats, their tray tables opened with some of the occupants making notes on yellow legal tablets. At the front of the classroom, an instructor clad in a red-and-black plaid lumber shirt, jeans, and chukka boots was holding forth on the topic he had written on the green chalkboard behind him: "Surveillance Techniques in Urban Areas."

"He's the CIA's expert on how to conduct surveillance without being observed," Weiskopf whispered to Newman. The instructor noticed the visitors in the back of the room but continued with a PowerPoint presentation that included a digital display of the Washington, D.C., area. As the four men standing quietly in the back of the room watched, the image on the screen shifted and an aerial photo appeared on the screen of the area around Newman's home on Creswell Drive. He strained to listen.

". . . and here's where you made your mistake," the CIA instructor continued, using the cursor on the PowerPoint display to highlight the photo of Newman's neighborhood. "You were too close to the subject's vehicle when he made the turn off Sleepy Hollow onto Carolyn. There was no other vehicular traffic in the neighborhood, and when he made the turn off Carolyn onto Creswell, you followed right into a cul-de-sac. You should have stopped at Sleepy Hollow . . . or at least should have driven past Creswell when he turned off Carolyn. The vehicle you were in was inconsistent with others in the neighborhood, and he probably noticed it immediately. Now if there had been a countersurveillance operation, you'd have alerted the subject. At that point your only option would have been to take out the subject to avoid compromising the entire mission."

Newman nodded his head in agreement with the instructor's assessment—even though he was "the subject" who would have been "taken out." Newman also reflected on the fact that he had seen the team that had followed him home from the White House the day before, but he hadn't detected those who had been following *them*.

Before he could dwell on that unsettling thought,

Weiskopf tapped him on the shoulder and nodded his head toward the door they had entered a few minutes before. The four men quietly exited and walked down the hallway to a small conference room where the bearded captain had established his office.

Once inside, Weiskopf said, "If it's all right with you, sir, we'll let him finish, and then after they have a ten-minute break, we'll make introductions. Meanwhile let me fill you in on what we've got here. Coffee?"

Newman, McDade, Robertson, and Coombs took mugs of hot, black coffee to their seats around a government-issue gray steel table. Weiskopf began, "On 10 November . . . the Marine Corps' birthday, right, Major Newman?"

Newman nodded and Captain Weiskopf continued. "On 10 November, I was ordered by SOCOM to set up a special billeting area down at Fort Bragg for a new task-organized, thirty-eight-man, joint U.S.–UK counterterrorism unit. At the time, I was working in the JSOC S-3 Detachment at Bragg, waiting for a slot to open up in one of the Delta squadrons. I had been with your brother Jim in Mogadishu, Major Newman, and would have been with him the day he was killed except that I had been wounded the week before and had been medevaced to Germany. Sorry for your loss, sir."

Newman nodded, with a new respect for this very intense and businesslike bearded captain. Weiskopf continued. "Anyway, they sent me . . ."

Newman interrupted. "They?"

"Sorry . . . SOCOM, at McDill down in Tampa—they sent one of those 'Eyes Only/Special Handling' cables giving me the task of organizing this new unit and assigning me as the CO. They assigned British SAS Captain Bruno Macklin as XO, and gave me Sergeant

Major Dan Gabbard, a Marine out of SOCOM, as the unit's sergeant major. He's the only non-Delta guy in this lash-up. I saw you counting heads in the ready room, Major Newman . . . he's the one who's missing. He's over at main side with the Andrews Base Ops people right now arranging for us to go out the back gate here so that we don't have to keep using the main gate. This crowd looks strange to begin with, and I don't want to attract any more attention than we have already."

"What do you mean, 'more attention'? Has there been any?"

"Well, yesterday . . . while we were running surveillance drills all over Washington . . . I'm told you picked up one of them tailing you. The base public affairs officer asked if she could send over a photo team and a reporter so that they could put a story in the base newspaper about how Andrews Air Force Base and Air Force One were now being protected by a 'special detachment of undercover Air Force security specialists.' It took me a half hour to get rid of her; I finally told her that all this was so secret that she might find herself transferred to Minot Air Force Base in North Dakota if she breathed a word of it."

"Anyway," Weiskopf continued, "SOCOM assigned, by name and by billet, every one of the personnel you see in that ready room. In all, twenty-seven Americans and eleven Brits. Gabbard, Macklin, and I are the command group, and the other thirty-five are organized into five seven-man teams. Everybody reported aboard at Bragg by the seventeenth. We spent the next eleven days getting used to working together—range time, PT, parachute jumps, the shooting house, weapons training, demo, night ops—the usual. I brought them up here on the twenty-eighth for some of the stuff that the agency does—like that class in there—and was told that you guys will be bringing us some special equipment tomorrow.

"I can tell you this, Major, these men are the best-trained troopers in the world. They are all experienced volunteers, mature men who have proven themselves as top performers and leaders in other units before they screened for Delta or the Navy SEALs. It's the same for the British Special Air Services. Every one of them has been in combat in some part of the world or another and, in many cases, multiple times. I know most of them personally, and you can put your life in their hands."

Newman was impressed—with the captain, with what he had accomplished, and with what he had said about the tough, hard, lean, and gutsy young men in the room down the hall. Except for the unconventional, unmilitary-like attire, haircuts, and beards, they were just like the Recon Marines he'd spent his best days leading.

But for this work they weren't supposed to look like U.S. servicemen. Each team would have to be able to blend in with the indigenous population in whatever part of the world they worked.

It was also clear to Newman that this whole organization had been in the planning stages for a considerable length of time.

"You've done one fine job, Captain," said Newman. "How long do you think it will be before your teams will be ready to deploy? Nobody wants these guys to go out before they're able to work well with one another. Teamwork on these missions is going to be essential."

"Well, that depends on how we're going to operate. I was told coming up here that effective Saturday, 2 De-

cember, we become the International Sanctions Enforcement Group, and I can tell you that there has been no
small amount of grumbling about whether they have to
wear UN insignia and that sort of thing."

"Don't worry about that. Nobody is going to have to
wear a blue beanie," Newman said with more convic-
tion than he felt. "But getting back to my question—if
we have to send the teams out independently, how long
'til they're ready?"

Weiskopf paused before answering and then said,
"ISET Alpha—the Asia and the Pacific team—could
easily pass for native Koreans, Chinese, Japanese, or Pacific Islanders, depending on how they were dressed. It
turns out that they not only look the part, but every one
of them can speak several Asian dialects."

Newman only nodded, still waiting for an answer, so
the Army captain continued, "The same is true of ISET
Bravo—the group assigned to Africa. As you'll see, they
are all very dark-skinned with distinctive African features."

Newman resolved to look at this particular team
extra carefully, for they were the obvious choice for
going with him into Somalia after his brother's killers.

"The entire group of men in ISET Charlie—the team
assigned to enforce UN sanctions in Eastern Europe and
the Balkans—look Slavic. In fact, one guy is from
Chicago and speaks Polish, and another hails from Mil-
waukee and is fluent in Czech. Two of the Brits are actually Scots." At this, McDade smiled for the first time
since coming into the building.

"The members of ISET Delta certainly look like they
were all from somewhere south of the Rio Grande, and
indeed, most of them have Spanish surnames. But the
team leader, who looks like he should be named Gon-

zalez, is actually named Wilson." All four of them chuckled at the way the American melting pot made life so interesting.

"The men of ISET Echo—the team assigned to the Middle East, Persian Gulf, and Southwest Asia—could blend in at an OPEC meeting or a Mujahedeen tent camp. In fact, the only ones of this entire group who appear to be Anglo-Saxons are the members of the command group—those of us who won't be going 'on the ground' if an operation ever gets launched."

The three officers from the White House were clearly impressed. But Newman noted to himself that Captain Weiskopf still hadn't answered his question, so he asked it again, slowly and with measured emphasis. "When will they be ready to go?"

Captain Weiskopf, looking very uncomfortable, said, "Look, these guys have all been on tough missions before—but they went with lots of backup. I think I could take these guys anywhere we have to go *tomorrow* and get the job done. But I'm not comfortable in just putting a seven-man ISET down in some faraway place without an Extract Plan, a Quick React Force, and some designated sanctuaries where they can at least get to some friendlies if things go sour."

"I understand," said Newman. "But that may turn out to be necessary. As I understand things right now, the people we work for don't yet have a clue as to where or when we're going to be used. When I go back to the White House tonight, I'll tell our boss that I need to go up to New York and talk to the people at the UN who are calling the shots. Until then, unless Harrod asks, I would recommend that you don't say one way or the other as to whether the entire ISEG is going to deploy or whether the ISETs are going in-country individually."

The Army captain looked long and hard at Newman, then his three colleagues from the White House nodded heads in agreement. Captain Weiskopf said, "OK, if that's the way you want it, but I'd like to get this settled as soon as possible."

The four men got up from the table and walked back down the hall to the ready room. It was 10:15 hours. Thirty-seven men—all but one assigned to the UN's International Sanctions Enforcement Group—were filtering back in from their briefing and into their seats as Weiskopf walked to the front of the room with Newman, McDade, Robertson, and Coombs behind him.

Newman looked them over as they moved to their seats and thought, *Talk about racial profiling! Isn't this the administration that wants everyone to take sensitivity training so that we're more "tolerant" of one another? Man, it's no wonder ol' Jabba the Hutt didn't want Congress to know about this outfit.*

Special Projects Office
Old Executive Office Building
Washington, D.C.
Wednesday, 30 November 1994
1905 Hours, Local

In Washington's heavy rush-hour traffic, it took Newman, McDade, Robertson, and Coombs more than an hour to make the trip from Andrews back to the White House for their meeting with Harrod. By the time they had completed the day with Joshua Weiskopf and his thirty-seven ISEG operators, Newman had developed the outline of a plan for training, deploying, supporting, and communicating with the force, and he told them that he aimed to have it approved at the White House before the unit returned to Fort Bragg.

Prior to departing Andrews, Newman told Weiskopf and the others how he planned to structure his tiny headquarters: Coombs, who had been part of Delta before his exile to the White House, would be his operations and training boss—the S-3 for this outfit. Robertson, the Air Force officer, would manage all logistics and transportation requirements—the S-4 for the ISEG—because, Newman reasoned, the USAF would have to be the ones to move the unit to wherever it was going to be used. And he put McDade, the frustrated Navy SEAL, in charge of intelligence and communications—combining the S-2 and S-5 functions.

Five minutes after the four officers arrived at their office in the OEOB and gathered around Newman's round conference table, there was a furious banging on the thick wooden door at the entrance to their office suite. They looked at one another and shrugged. McDade, who was closest to the door, got up and opened it to the full wrath of Jabba the Hutt.

"Where have you guys been?!" the National Security Advisor shouted. He was wearing a tuxedo, and to the four physically fit military officers, their boss looked like an obese penguin on the verge of what doctors would call a major cardiac event.

Behind the red-faced penguin, standing in the ornate, marble-tiled hallway, were half a dozen young men and one young woman, all wearing dark-blue coveralls. Three of them were leaning against four-wheeled steel carts like those used by baggage handlers at airports. The carts were stacked high with cardboard boxes and what appeared to be a mobile electronics shop.

"These people are from WHCA, and this is your

communications equipment. I told you yesterday to be back here at seven. Where have you been?" Harrod demanded.

All four of the military men looked at their watches simultaneously. It was not yet ten minutes after the hour. "Sorry, sir," Newman said, stepping between the penguin and McDade, "we just got back from Andrews."

"Don't call me 'sir.' I don't care where you just got back from! I'm late for a dinner the President is giving for the diplomatic corps, and I'm tired of waiting around for people who can't tell time."

When no one said anything in response, Harrod turned to the blue-clad WHCA techs and practically screamed, "Don't just stand there; get to work! Do you think I want to hang around with you people all night?"

The technicians began to unload the equipment and carry the components into the suite: computer terminals, a secure fax machine, encryption equipment, secure phones, and radio repeaters. Some of it went into Newman's office, and the rest went up the circular staircase to where Coombs, McDade, and Robertson officed.

"While they install this equipment, the four of you come over to the Situation Room so we can talk," said the National Security Advisor in a tone that proved he could calm down as quickly as his mercurial temper could be set off.

Harrod led the way to the elevator, out the ground floor door, and across West Executive Avenue into the West Wing. The four officers followed the penguin like his chicks. He didn't speak again until they were inside the Situation Room conference space. "Sit down. I want a full report on what you saw at Andrews today, your assessment on how ready this unit is, and what you think about their ability to carry out the UN mandate."

For the next hour, the man who had been in such a hurry to join the black-tie diplomatic party going on upstairs in the White House sat and alternately listened and interrupted the four military men with questions. Newman related how he planned to organize his office, the responsibilities he'd given to his three colleagues, and told Harrod about the additional training he planned for the ISEG.

At precisely 8:00, the Situation Room watch chief knocked on the conference room door and said, "Dr. Harrod, the President called down to ask if you will be joining them upstairs for dinner."

Harrod rose and said to the watch officer, "Tell him I'll be right up." Then turning to Newman and the other three, he said, "I have to go. The ISEG people will wrap up their D.C. briefings on Friday. They should then move back down to Fort Bragg and get out of here before they attract more attention. I have told the UN that they will be ready for operations in thirty days."

Newman stood up and interrupted. "That's not long enough. They have only been together for two weeks. They need to be able to do a whole lot more work together before they get thrown into something like chasing after Aidid. Furthermore, they can't just go from here to someplace like Somalia without getting acclimated."

Harrod stood quietly for a moment, contemplating Newman's walk to the edge of insubordination. Coombs, McDade, and Robertson sat in their places, contemplating the grain in the tabletop while awaiting the explosion.

Instead, Harrod replied quietly, almost in a whisper,

"Thirty days. That's all you've got. If Fort Bragg isn't good enough, figure out where else they have to go to get ready. Then get them there and work them as long as they and their mission are not compromised. If they need additional equipment, go get it. I want them ready to go before the first of the year. The UN and the President want results, not excuses. Now, I have other things to do besides baby-sitting the four of you. The WHCA people should be finished by now. Go back to your office and figure out what needs to be done—and go do it."

The four officers stood as Harrod turned to leave; but when he opened the door, Jabba stopped, turned, and said, "By the way, Newman, the secretary of defense called me this afternoon and told me that your Marine Corps selection board has decided that you should be a lieutenant colonel." With that, the National Security Advisor departed for the diplomatic reception.

✪

On the way back across to the OEOB, Newman was congratulated by his three colleagues with backslaps and ribald good humor. When the four officers punched in the security codes and reentered the office space they had left an hour before, they found that the WHCA technicians had all departed except for the warrant officer who had headed the installation team. In short order, he gave each man an inventory sheet, walked them through their spaces to show them what had been installed and where, and had them sign for every piece of it. Once he had officiously collected all their signature sheets, he walked to the door. "Thank you, gentlemen. If you have any questions or problems, please call me. My extension is on your copies of the receipts. And remember, gentlemen, WHCA is here to serve the President." And then he added cryptically, "We all have to do things we don't like to do. That's why we keep an eye on each other."

TWA Flight 324, 27,500 Feet Alt
56 Mi E of South Bend, IN
Wednesday, 30 November 1994
2030 Hours, Local

Rachel blamed her troubles on the Marines. "I'm clueless," she had admitted to her friend and fellow flight attendant Sandy when things slowed down in the cabin and they could catch a short break in the rear galley. They had begun their day aboard a flight from San Diego to Chicago, switched to another aircraft, and then continued east to Dulles with a stop in Cleveland that afternoon.

Rachel shook her head. "I don't have any idea what Pete sees in the military—I really don't. I remember one day after we'd been married about two years when he came home from something called jump school—"

Sandy interrupted. "Jump school? You mean they have a school to teach guys how to jump? Like jump rope or something?" she laughed.

Rachel giggled. "That's *exactly* what I asked him!" she exclaimed. "He didn't like that much. He was really miffed until I got him to explain. Jump school is where they learn how to parachute out of perfectly good airplanes!"

"Oh," Sandy said. "Isn't that kind of dangerous?"

Rachel laughed again. "Well, *I* think so. But P. J. likes that macho stuff, you know? He *really* got mad when he came home that December and showed me the 'jump wings' pin and emblem that he'd earned. He was so proud. And I spoiled everything by bursting out laughing as soon as I saw the pin. Boy, was he ever ticked!"

"What was so funny about it?" Sandy asked.

"Because," Rachel replied, "the pin looked almost like this." She picked up a cellophane bag with the words *Junior Pilot* on the front. Inside was a shiny, silvery pin for the flight attendants to hand out to little boys and girls who behave during the flight.

"All I could think of was someone pinning those jump wings on Pete and saying, 'This is for being a good boy,' " Rachel said laughing.

"I'll bet that went over like a lead balloon," Sandy observed. "What'd Pete say?"

"He never said a word—literally. He didn't speak to me for almost two weeks, even though I apologized all day, every day. Sandy, my problem is that I fell for a handsome guy in a uniform before I ever understood what his wearing that uniform meant. You and Tom have roots. Tom has a regular job. He comes home at night. You know your neighbors. You have friends where you live. We don't have *any* of that. Since we've been married, Pete has been gone more than he's been home. He proposed to me on the phone from Naples, Italy. A few months after we got married, he got shipped off again to the Middle East for six months. The Marines call it a 'Med cruise.' Some cruise! He was home for awhile, and then they sent him off to Beirut, Lebanon—where terrorists killed all those Marines. Then he was in Honduras—or somewhere in Central America—for months on end during all that Contra stuff. And then there was that thing in Panama. I couldn't believe that he actually *volunteered* to go to the Gulf War."

"Didn't he get wounded in Kuwait?" interrupted Sandy.

"No, it was actually in Saudi Arabia, at a place called Khafji, with one of his 'recon teams' that he loves so much. He was wounded when the Iraqi Army came across the border. They got trapped there when the Saudi Arabian Army retreated and P. J. and his nine guys stayed behind, surrounded, to 'call in fire,' whatever that means."

Sandy was wide-eyed. "Didn't he tell you about it?"

"No," replied Rachel, looking downcast. "He *never* talks about it. I didn't even know he'd been wounded. He had given instructions that he didn't want 'next of kin'—that's what they call *me* in the Marines—to be notified. The only reason I know any of this is because he was given a medal at a parade when he got back home to Camp Lejeune and they read some kind of a citation. That's how I found out that he had almost been killed!"

"Was it an important medal?" asked Sandy.

"I guess so. There were a whole bunch of generals and admirals there making a big fuss over him. His dad came down from New York and wore his uniform, and his mom said that the Navy Cross was like the Distinguished Service Cross in the Army. P. J.'s brother Jim was there in his uniform, and he told me that their dad got a DSC in the Korean War. And I had to ask him, 'What's a DSC?' And when he told me, I was so embarrassed because the Navy Cross and the Distinguished Service Cross are second only to the Medal of Honor."

"That must have made you very proud of Peter," said Sandy, trying to be helpful.

"You know, Sandy, I don't know what I felt," said Rachel, her eyes brimming with tears. "It was obvious that everyone there was making a big fuss over this medal and what P. J. had done. His dad was so proud. But I was so mad that Peter hadn't let me know anything about what had happened to him, or how close I had come to losing him, that I just felt empty. If his brother hadn't been there, I would have been lost. I could at least *talk* to Jim. Sometimes when P. J. was gone somewhere, I would call Jim just to get reassurance. I really miss his brother. He used to tell me, 'Rache, P. J. loves you. He just doesn't want you to worry.' And now Jim's dead, and I don't have anyone to talk to." At this, two tears streaked down Rachel's cheeks.

Sandy put her arm around her friend as they stood there in the galley of the aircraft. "Honey, there must be a reason why God kept P. J. alive through all of that. And there must be a reason why you guys are still together after all you've been through."

Rachel dabbed her eyes and after a moment said, "I must be a sight. I'll scare the passengers if they see me like this." She went into the lavatory across from the galley and washed her face, reapplied some makeup, and brushed her hair. When she came back out, Sandy had just returned from providing a blanket for one of the passengers.

"Sandy, I know what you said about Pete and me still being together, but I'm not so sure that this marriage ought to continue." Rachel's moment of sadness had passed. She now had a determined set to her jaw.

Rachel continued. "I wish there was a way for me to understand his work and why we have to pick up and move nearly every other year. It's impossible for me to put down roots. I've almost lost track of how many times we've moved. But even if I don't have to go, one day he would just come home and say, 'I'm being deployed.' And if I asked him when, he'd say, 'In two days.' And if I asked where, he'd say something like, 'I can't say.' And I'm supposed to get used to that uncertainty—gone for a month, six months, or a year, and I don't always know where he goes or what he does. It's just an absolutely impossible life for me."

Sandy nodded sympathetically. "Have you talked with some of the other military wives?" she asked.

"Yes. Some of them are just as frazzled over this as I am. But some of them are just so focused on serving their husbands that they don't care—they need to get a life, is what I think."

Rachel began to empty the coffee grounds from the pots in the galley and dump the remaining coffee down the drain. As she stowed them in their compartments prior to their landing at Dulles, she decided to confide in Sandy, to get her input on something that was troubling her.

"Sandy," she said quietly, "I need your advice. I haven't shared this with anyone, but I really could use your input."

Sandy nodded and moved closer so Rachel could share her comments in privacy.

"Pete has just taken a new assignment. He says he can't tell me anything about it, and it's for at least two years. The good news is we won't have to move for two years. The bad news is that I don't have a clue where he will be during those two years.

"I'm really getting so sick of this that I'm ready to end this marriage," she said.

Sandy took her friend's arm and said, "Oh no—don't give up yet."

"I'm not kidding. In fact, I've made an appointment with a lawyer to discuss a divorce as soon as I get back from the London assignment on Friday. I'm really fed up."

"I know, Rachel, but . . ."

"Remember when Peter's brother was killed last year? He went up to his folks' house to break the news to them and didn't even make any attempt to get hold of me and let me go with him. He said it was a family affair, for heaven's sake! I was so angry at him after that happened that I would have divorced him that very week. But I couldn't go through with it. I mean, with his brother dead and his parents so hurt—if I'd have served him papers then . . ."

"You guys need to get away and talk these things through. Before you and I met and got to know each other, Tom and I were having problems and went to a Marriage Encounter weekend. Neither one of us wanted to go, but we each felt that we had so much invested in our marriage that we couldn't throw it away without at least trying to understand our problems and see if we could fix them," Sandy said.

"And . . ."

"Well, it worked great for us. We're still together, as you know. We still have some bumpy rides, but each of us knows that we aren't going to walk out on the marriage, and that helps us work things out. I think you need some kind of a structured setting like that to get you on track."

"I don't know . . . we've got so much emotional baggage. P. J. would deny it—he'd say that I'm the emotional one and he's the logical one and that he doesn't have any emotion at all. But I've seen how he reacts when I hurt him—I know he has feelings."

"Listen, Rachel," Sandy suggested, "when we get home, let me give you some stuff to look at from our

Marriage Encounter weekend and their 800 number. You should at least check it out. Please tell me you'll do that instead of filing divorce papers."

Rachel smiled appreciatively. "Thanks for your concern. I promise to hold off on serving them, but I think it's time to look at all the options. I'll look at your stuff. But I'm also going to meet with the lawyer and explore the divorce options too."

Area 35
Andrews Air Force Base
Friday, 2 December 1994
1700 Hours, Local

Newman was alone with Joshua Weiskopf as the young Delta Force captain packed up his gear for the quick trip out to the runway to board the C-130 that would take him and the ISEG back to Fort Bragg. Weiskopf jammed a rolled-up pair of jeans, a dark-blue flannel shirt, a black Gore-Tex parka, a small notebook, and his 9mm Beretta pistol into the parachute bag that served as his "flyaway kit." Everyone in this line of work kept such a bag, always packed, full of the gear they would need to sustain them for several days. Newman certainly knew; he'd lived like this for sixteen years.

The last item into the bag was the EncryptionLok-3 that Newman had given him that morning. "This is quite a piece of gear, Colonel," said Weiskopf, holding the device and smiling at the Marine.

"Yes, it is, Josh—and speaking of code-breaking, I'm still trying to figure out how you all got the word on my promotion before I got back here yesterday."

When Newman had arrived at the Area 35 restricted compound on Thursday morning, the whole group had stood and applauded when he walked into the small mess hall where they were having breakfast. And in spite of it being just 6:30 in the morning, the five team leaders insisted on a traditional celebration. Someone produced a bottle of brandy and added a dollop to everyone's coffee cup and raised a toast. They then proceeded to sing several ribald verses of an old barracks ballad having to do with the honoree's dubious lineage.

As he thanked them, Newman wondered how they had learned what had yet to be announced officially even within the Marine Corps. McDade, Robertson, and Coombs, who had heard Harrod the night before, denied telling anyone. But Sergeant Major Dan Gabbard, the only other Marine and the senior enlisted man in the ISEG unit, knew before Newman that he'd been selected for promotion. He had heard the scuttlebutt from the "sergeant major's network" at HQMC and had passed the word to Weiskopf and the rest of the unit. Gabbard had also taken it upon himself to inform the group about all he knew of their "White House boss."

After Newman, Coombs, McDade, and Robertson had departed Andrews to get back to the White House for their Wednesday night meeting with Harrod, Gabbard had sensed that the troops had questions about the man who would be sending them into harm's way. After dinner in the mess hall that evening, the sergeant major had assembled all thirty-eight men in the ready room to cover some administrative matters: how their pay, life insurance, next-of-kin notifications, and the like would be handled in this international unit. He used the occasion to tell them that he and Newman had served together off and on ever since Third Battalion, Eighth Marines back in '79 and '80. For more than an hour, he regaled them with accounts from Newman's extraordinary career as a recon Marine, about his exploits in Central America, Beirut, Panama, and especially how he won the Navy Cross at Khafji during Desert Storm—knowing that Newman would never tell these stories himself. Even these hard-bitten veterans of covert combat had been impressed and had a new sense of confidence in their leader.

✪

Weiskopf finished packing and slung the parachute bag over his shoulder. "It's been a good three days. We all got a lot out of the briefings and the surveillance drills that the CIA put us through, and the intelligence briefings were top-notch. I'd feel better if we had more, but that's always the way it is. Do you still think that our first target is going to be Aidid?"

"It sure looks that way to me. Most of the intel that they've fed us is oriented on him."

"Yeah," said Weiskopf, "but they've also given us a big pile of stuff on Saddam Hussein, Milosevic, and a whole bunch of those thugs in Yugoslavia, or whatever it's called today. All I'm saying is that we've got a lot to get ready for and not much time to get it all done."

"Josh, all I can tell you is that I'll give you the best info I get and give you as much advance notice as I can."

"I know you will," said the Army captain, holding out his hand. Newman shook it, clapped the bearded

Delta officer on the shoulder, and the two men walked out of the building together into the darkness.

Weiskopf had come to respect and admire the newly brevetted Marine lieutenant colonel in the three days since he had first met him. It was clear to all the members of the unit, Delta, SEALs, and SAS, that Newman was deserving of one of the greatest compliments they could offer: "He knows his stuff."

For his part, Newman quickly realized that the small task force at his disposal was perhaps the most skilled and experienced group of military men in the world. Few of his well-trained recon Marines possessed the language skills, foreign experience, and maturity of the men in the ISEG. Every one of these men knew what it was like to be shot at. Some of them, like Newman, knew what it was like to be shot at and hit. All of them knew what it was like to kill other human beings in moments of extraordinary violence. All of them knew the terrible rush of adrenaline in the gut when you realize that some other human being is trying to kill you. And all of them knew the awful frustration of having those who were closer than brothers die beside them.

Newman knew that these qualities made these men a remarkable collection of individuals. Now it was Joshua Weiskopf's job—with the support of Newman and his small team at the White House—to turn these individuals into an effective team and to do it in thirty days.

The task was so daunting that Newman had simply decided to stay at Andrews and save himself the time of the commute to and from Falls Church. After the Wednesday night meeting with Harrod and WHCA's installation of equipment in the Special Projects Office, Newman had returned home to his empty house, grabbed his own "fly-away kit," and headed back to Andrews.

It was after midnight when he arrived at the Air Force base main gate, and this time he drove his own car all the way around the base, up to the chain-link fence in the woods bearing the white sign with black letters: *AREA 35—RESTRICTED.* He moved into the spartan room next to Weiskopf's in the one-story brick billet and had just laid down on the steel military cot to catch a few hours sleep when he remembered that he had forgotten to leave a note for his wife.

He got up, grabbed the mobile phone out of his kit, and called home to leave a message on their home answering machine. After telling the machine where he was and of his plans to stay at Andrews until Friday, he also left his new office telephone number in Washington at the OEOB. Then surprisingly, even to him, Newman concluded his message with a change of tone in his voice, from the businesslike update on his plans to a softer, more intimate voice. "Hey, babe . . . I miss you. I'm really looking forward to seeing you soon. I love you, 'bye."

Each evening he'd check in with Harrod and his teammates at his office in the White House. In less than forty-eight hours, Coombs had built a detailed, thirty-day training plan that had the unit practicing everything from High Altitude-High Opening (HA-HO) parachute jumps over the forests of North Carolina and West Virginia, to rubber boat drills in the frigid waters of Onslow Beach at Camp Lejeune, North Carolina. But his training schedule had one gaping hole in it. He had reserved the final week of the month-long program for getting the unit acclimated to wherever they would be conducting their first operation. And until the UN made up its collective mind about who their first target would be, he didn't know whether to book the unit for its final week of training at the NATO cold-weather site in Narvik, Norway; the Royal Marines Jungle Warfare Training Center in Malaysia; or the British SAS Desert Warfare Operations site in Oman. Just in case, he also informed the Naval Undersea Warfare Center on Coronado Island off the coast of San Diego that they might have thirty-eight unexpected guests for the last week of December through the first week of January.

Newman had put Robertson to work on finding an aircraft that was both big enough to haul the unit and their gear and could pass for something less military than a C-130 or a C-17. The Brits offered a Nimrod long-range patrol aircraft that had been repainted to look like a civilian airliner, and Robertson had put it down on his list as a possibility, but he wanted something that really could pass for a civilian aircraft. If the ISEG had to deploy in a hurry to some hostile location like Mogadishu, Somalia, nobody wanted their presence to be announced by arriving in a military transport. Then, late Thursday night, the Air Force captain found what they needed. In the Civil Reserve Air Fleet "boneyard" inventory—the list of aircraft out in Yuma, Arizona, waiting for a major mobilization—Robertson found an MD-80 that had been converted from passenger aircraft service to a "Nightingale" flying hospital. Once the plane had an appropriate paint job and tail number, no one would be able to tell from the outside that the plane was anything but a civilian airliner. Best of all, the MD-80 had a rear exit hatch. The tail cone, below the rear-mounted twin engines and the vertical stabilizer, could be jettisoned and the hatch opened to serve as a parachute exit. He issued instructions to have the CRAF aircraft inspected by maintenance experts from his old squadron and, if it passed muster, have it put back in service and flown to Atlanta for repainting as an Aer Lingus cargo aircraft on charter to the UN.

McDade, serving as the unit's intelligence and communications officers rolled into one, had been busy as well. On Thursday morning, he had gone to WHCA and, using their "Presidential Priority 1" authority, had placed an order with the Defense Communications Agency and the National Security Agency for every piece of communications equipment that the ISET team commanders envisioned that they might need, anywhere in the world. Included in his wish list were EncryptionLok-3s—two for each ISET, two for the ISEG headquarters element, and one each for use by Newman and the three officers in the Special Projects Office. McDade was amazed late that afternoon when he was already summoned to the WHCA office on the fifth floor of the OEOB to sign for a vanload of equipment. He did so and promptly dispatched the truck to Andrews Air Force Base to turn the equipment over to the ISEG. As soon as the truck left, he called Newman to tell him it was on the way.

While the Americans were familiar with the EncryptionLok-3s, the British SAS troopers were not, and they were fascinated. The device, no bigger than a TV remote, could be plugged into any communications gear—radio, telephone, computer, wireless, satellite phone, video—and have the communications traffic transmitted between two devices completely and permanently encrypted. Weiskopf's executive officer, or

"Number Two" as the Brits said, was SAS Captain Bruno Macklin. His assessment of the EL-3's ability to be plugged into anything from a phone to a computer signal pretty much summed up the British operators' appraisal: "Bloody well amazing, it is. Sure hope the bad boys don't get their hands on one of these."

Once they were comfortable with the operation of the devices, Newman instructed their use for all communications pertaining to ISEG operations or activities to ensure that no adversary could intercept and decode their communications.

"This is critical," he told them. "If you discipline yourselves to use the EL-3 for all your communications, you can avoid compromising a mission."

By working almost nonstop for three days, Newman, Weiskopf, Coombs, McDade, and Robertson had developed detailed plans for how the ISEG would work once a mission assignment came down from the UN. The concept was as simple as it was audacious, and it was constructed with input from all involved, particularly the highly experienced Delta, SEAL, and SAS senior noncommissioned officers. Sergeant Major Gabbard reduced it to a single page on his laptop computer:

CONCEPT OF OPERATIONS

1. WHEN THE UN DESIGNATES A TARGET FOR SANCTIONS ENFORCEMENT, THE ISET APPROPRIATE TO THE REGION WILL BE DESIGNATED AS THE PRIMARY TEAM TO CARRY OUT THE MISSION.

2. ONE OF THE FOUR REMAINING ISETS SHALL SERVE AS A QUICK REACTION FORCE (QRF) FOR THE PRIMARY TEAM.

3. ONE OF THE THREE REMAINING ISETS SHALL SERVE AS AN ADVANCE PARTY FOR THE OPERATION.

4. THE ADVANCE PARTY SHALL IDENTIFY, ESTABLISH, AND SECURE A

COVERT ADVANCED OPERATIONS BASE (AOB) FOR THE OPERATION AS PROXIMATE AS POSSIBLE TO THE OBJECTIVE.

5. THE TWO REMAINING ISETS SHALL PROVIDE COUNTERSURVEIL-LANCE, SECURITY FOR THE AOB, AND PROTECTION FOR THE ISEG COM-MAND ELEMENT.

6. ONCE THE ADVANCE PARTY HAS IDENTIFIED AND SECURED THE AOB, THE REMAINDER OF THE ISEG SHALL DEPLOY TO THE AOB TO PRO-VIDE INTELLIGENCE, LOGISTICS, MEDEVAC, AND COMMUNICATIONS SUPPORT TO THE PRIMARY TEAM AND THE QRF.

7. UPON COMPLETION OF AN OPERATION, THE QRF WILL ASSIST IN EXTRACTING THE PRIMARY TEAM FROM THE AREA OF OPERATIONS.

8. IN THE EVENT THAT THE ISEG HQ ORDERS AN EMERGENCY TER-MINATION (E/T) FOR AN OPERATION, ALL ISEG PERSONNEL WILL EXFIL-TRATE TO A PRIMARY OR SECONDARY RENDEZVOUS POINT (RP) DESIGNATED BY THE ISEG HQ.

9. IF THE ISEG ORDERS THE EMERGENCY TERMINATION OF A MIS-SION, IT SHALL BE THE MISSION OF THE ADVANCE PARTY ISET TO SAN-ITIZE THE AOB.

10. ALL COMMUNICATIONS WITH AND AMONG DEPLOYED ISEG UNITS SHALL BE SECURED BY USE OF THE ENCRYPTIONLOK-3 DEVICE.

Newman Home
Falls Church, VA
Friday, 2 December 1994
2033 Hours, Local

Rachel Newman fumbled with the key to what she and her husband called the "side door" of their home in Falls Church. She felt a sense of relief that she was fi-nally here. She unlocked the door, disarmed the alarm system, pulled her wheel-on luggage through the kitchen into the hall, and groped for the light switch.

The house was chilly—a sign that her husband had

not been here in awhile. She turned up the thermostat and was glad to hear the furnace start up right away. She browsed through the mail that she had brought in with her—only junk mail and a few bills. Rachel put the mail on the kitchen counter with the pile of unopened mail that Peter had left. Then she pushed the Play switch on the answering machine and turned up the volume before heading toward the bedroom to unpack her things. "You have four messages," the machine announced in its crisp, artificial voice. "First message, Tuesday, 10:34 P.M." The voice was Rachel's: "Hi, it's me. I'm at the airport. Just got in and have to turn around on a flight to London tomorrow night. I'm staying at the Airport Marriott tonight so don't wait up. I'll probably be up for another hour or so. Give me a call if you get home before then." The machine beeped and went on to the second message. This time it was Peter: "Uh, hi Rachel, it's me. I just finished up my first day of orientation, and I'm heading home. It's about midnight, and I have to leave home really early, so I won't wake you. I'll bring you up to date on everything when I see you." *Click*, and *beep*. The third message was from Rachel, calling Wednesday afternoon to remind Peter of her flight to London and her return Friday night.

Rachel was hanging up her clean clothes when the fourth message started. "Hi, it's me. I forgot to leave you a note when I zipped in and out of the house tonight. I heard your call on the machine saying you'd be heading for London. But in case your flight's canceled, just wanted you to know where I am. Uh, actually, I'm staying at Andrews until Friday night when the folks I'm working with head back to where they are based. Use my cell phone number if you need to reach me." In his usual, businesslike way he continued, giving her the office number for his new job. "But I probably won't be at that number until Monday," he added. Then he paused, and the tone of his voice changed to one that was at once more friendly and somehow vulnerable. "Hey, babe . . . I miss you. I'm really looking forward to seeing you soon . . . I love you, 'bye."

Rachel was both startled and pleased at the intimacy of his voice. It had been a long time since he had sounded so open and romantic. She went to the machine and pushed the *Rewind* switch and played the end of the message again.

Amazing. She wondered if there really might be some hope for their marriage after all. She was filled with guilt for cheating on him. Rachel also realized that she was too tired and emotionally drained to think much more about it right now. She finished unpacking and undressing, tossed her dirty laundry in the hamper of the master bathroom, and donned a clean, terrycloth robe.

The furnace still had not warmed the house. Shivering, she decided to take a hot shower. After a minute or two of waiting for the water to heat, she eased out of her robe and into the large, glass-walled shower.

Rachel took her time showering. She scrubbed off her makeup, letting the steam and hot water melt the cramps in her neck and shoulders.

She didn't hear the door open and close downstairs.

From the bedroom, Peter Newman had an unfettered view into the shower of the master bath. He stood for a moment, gazing at his wife, transfixed by her beauty. She still had not seen him. Peter undressed quickly and strode toward the shower.

As she was rinsing her hair, Rachel felt a cool blast of air when the shower door opened. Then two arms grabbed her and she jumped, screaming.

"Hey, babe . . . easy . . . It's just me." He laughed.

"P. J.! You scared me! I didn't hear you come in."

Peter smiled and kissed his wife. "I must have been just a few minutes behind you," he said. "I saw how beautiful you were in the shower, and you looked so inviting that I thought I'd join in."

"We haven't taken a shower together in a long time," Rachel observed.

"We haven't done much of anything together in a long time," Peter replied.

❂

Both Peter and Rachel lay in the quiet of the night, sleepily savoring their recent pleasure. They drew instinctively closer to each other for warmth, warding off the chill of the night. Rachel drifted off to sleep with the bittersweet memory of Peter's kisses and the realization of how much she had missed them.

But Peter was still wide awake. He lay there as a recurring fear gnawed at him—fear that had eaten at him quietly for months now welled up as anger.

He suspected Rachel was having an affair. It surely wouldn't surprise him if she was, nor could he really blame her. He knew that he had not been all she wanted or expected in a husband. Plus, the demands of his career were often contrary to the needs of his marriage. He could almost understand why she might be drawn into an affair with someone else. They had had many serious arguments over these matters over the years, and finding resolution for the two of them often seemed to be hopeless.

He wondered if he should confront her. He decided not to. He had enough of his own problems to work out right now before bringing someone else into the picture.

Office of the National Security Advisor
The White House
Washington, D.C.
Saturday, 3 December 1994
0821 Hours, Local

As usual, Newman arrived early for his 0800 meeting. And, as usual, the National Security Advisor was late. The wait gave the Marine time to think about the events the night before, and he suddenly realized that he hadn't even told Rachel about his selection for promotion to lieutenant colonel.

Harrod came bustling in past Newman who was waiting in the outer office, and without so much as a hello, threw open the door to his inner sanctum, tossed his overcoat on a chair, and roared, "Martha, where's the coffee?"

The National Security Advisor's long-suffering assistant looked at Newman, made a face and rolled her eyes, and went to get Jabba the Hutt his first cup of caffeine. Newman took the cup he'd been drinking and the National Security Advisor's copy of the *President's Daily Brief*—which was the CIA's overnight summary of what was happening in the world. Then he walked uninvited into Harrod's office.

"You're not cleared for that," said Harrod, holding his hand out to take the document.

"Yes, I am, Dr. Harrod. I'm on the access list. So is my whole office," replied Newman, handing over the red-white-and-blue–bordered document with the large notations, *TOP SECRET: EYES ONLY FOR THE PRESIDENT.*

Harrod ignored the rebuff, took the document, and reached to take the coffee cup that was being offered to him on a small tray by his secretary. "Have they gone back to Fort Bragg?" he asked without preamble.

"Yes, and we've devised a workable concept of operations that someone ought to take a look at to make sure we're planning this out the way you want."

"I don't want a lot of paper floating around on this," said Harrod, looking up from his coffee. "Where is this 'concept of operations' or whatever you call it?"

"Right here," said Newman, removing from his suit-coat pocket the single-page document Sergeant Major Gabbard had printed out of his laptop the day before. He handed it to Harrod.

The National Security Advisor skimmed the page and looked up at Newman. "So, you plan to send all thirty-eight of them on the mission?"

"Yes. There has to be some way of supporting the seven-man team that actually does the mission. This is the only way we can do it—unless someone is willing to dedicate more assets to us for our missions."

"That's out of the question. But this option may work. I want you to run this by General Komulakov," said Harrod.

"Who?"

"Dimitri Komulakov. He's in charge of the UN side of this sanctions business. He's a deputy secretary general. I've set up an appointment for you to fly to New York on Monday to meet with him. He'll brief you on their part in this."

Newman felt a little uneasy. *Their part in this* . . . he thought. *How much of a part are they going to have in this operation?* Yet he said nothing to Harrod.

"Now, when will they be ready to deploy?" asked Harrod.

"You told us to be ready in thirty days. We've built a

plan to do that, but it really isn't enough time. If we were doing a proper work-up for this kind of mission, we shouldn't commit them until March at the earliest. That would also create less of a problem with other units. We can't train just anywhere with this outfit. And if we start pushing other military commands around and bending their training schedules out of shape, there will be a fuss, and the ISEG will be liable to get more visibility than it should have."

"Who's giving you a problem?" asked Harrod.

"Captain Coombs ran into some resistance when he was making plans for Fort Bragg, and he knows the people down there pretty well. They've already got the place booked with a SOCOM exercise for the next four weeks, so I thought—since we're still in the starting blocks— that we could release our guys for the Christmas holidays and pick up the schedule in January. And if we're going to go after Aidid first, we've got to get this group acclimated. Even this time of year, the temperature in Somalia is better than ninety degrees Fahrenheit every afternoon. I want to take them to the British base in Oman for at least a week, but I'd prefer a month. Unfortunately, the Brits are in a holiday stand-down through the end of the year."

"What kind of a war is this?" Harrod bellowed. "These guys can always do their fun and games training nonsense. Do they want us to postpone all wars so they'll fit in with their training schedules?"

"No, sir, but I—" Newman started to say, but Harrod interrupted him.

"Well, never mind. Two weeks won't make or break our schedule. I'll call the Pentagon tomorrow and give Fort Bragg two weeks to get things straightened out. You make your plans to have your men at Bragg on the eighteenth, and get things moving. I want Aidid's head on a stick. You have no idea the humiliation he has caused this President. I'm counting on your team to get him. Have you got Oman confirmed following the training at Bragg?"

Newman nodded. "I originally had them at Bragg after New Year's, but we can push it up and finish there a little early. We should be ready to ship out for Muscat by mid- to late-February—providing everything else stays on schedule and we don't have any other problems."

"Good," Harrod said. "Then I'll see you when you get back from New York."

UN World Headquarters
Manhattan, N.Y.
Monday, 5 December 1994
1054 Hours, Local

Newman could see the UN headquarters building looming thirty-nine stories into the sky a block east of them as soon as the driver turned left to accommodate the one-way street that the UN building faced. When the vehicle pulled up to the main entrance at First Avenue and Forty-sixth Street, Newman hopped out and headed up to the entry doors.

Although he was early for his appointment, Newman still walked briskly up the expansive area leading to the doors to the building instead of taking in the sights—he had seen the huge building pictured in so many books, newspapers, magazines, and on TV that it had almost become a visual cliché. The cold wind set up a racket with every gust, making the flags of nearly two hundred nations ripple and snap in the breeze and causing their halyards to rattle against their respective metal flagpoles.

Inside the building, scores of visitors and others with business in the building moved about the vast entrance hall, some resolutely, others at a more leisurely pace. An elementary school group was queuing up with a tour guide as several teachers tried in vain to maintain order. Newman's heels clicked against the beautiful imported marble floors, and the sound echoed across the lobby. He had already noted the contemporary sculpture of a handgun twisted into a knot on the way into the building. Now he was confronted by a large glass case full of similarly destroyed guns of all makes and calibers. *Well, I can see that their politics aren't all that subtle,* Newman thought.

He walked up to the uniformed security guard at the desk and presented himself.

"Do you have an appointment, sir?" the guard asked.

"Yes," Newman answered. "I want to go to Operations, thirty-eighth floor."

"Identification, please." The security guard took Newman's Marine ID, punched a number on the telephone console in front of him, and waited for an answer. Then he said, "There's a Major Newman here. It says in the appointment book that he has an appointment to see General Komulakov. Uh-huh." Then he covered the mouthpiece and asked Newman for his rank again. Newman realized what the problem was. He hadn't yet been officially promoted and wouldn't be until the Senate confirmed the promotion list, but Harrod had likely identified him as a lieutenant colonel when he set up the appointment. Newman said, "The ID card says I'm a major, so I'm a major." The security guard shrugged, and he repeated it into the phone and hung up.

"Someone will be right down to escort you upstairs. You can wait right here."

Newman nodded and looked around at the architectural beauty of the place and the extravagant artwork. He picked up a brochure from the security desk. As he thumbed through it, he saw pictures of the art displayed throughout the building—original works in such wide-ranging styles as Chagall, Picasso, and Norman Rockwell.

"Major Newman?"

"Yes . . ." he said as he turned toward the man who was asking.

"I am Major Suva. I will escort you to your appointment." Major Suva identified himself as an officer in the Fiji Army and an aide to the man Newman had come to see. He turned and walked briskly toward the bank of elevators. Newman followed. But Major Suva walked past them and continued around the corner to where a single elevator was located. On the door was the lettering, *UN STAFF ONLY.* The officer took out a plastic, coded key card and swiped it through the magnetic stripe reader. The elevator opened immediately. The two of them got on and the door closed. The first thing that Newman noticed was that there were no buttons in this elevator for stopping on other floors. It was an express elevator that went only to the thirty-eighth floor. But it wouldn't move until Major Suva used his key card again to activate it.

The Fijian officer was friendly and almost made a ceremony of welcoming Newman as they got off the elevator. Newman could see that they were in an interior hallway, facing a double set of doors that led into an office area. Major Suva bypassed the receptionist's desk and walked straight to the double doors. Once again he used his key card. As they walked through, Newman considered the expansive, wide hallways with plush carpeting, the mammoth offices with breathtaking views, the original artwork—not just on the walls of the posh offices, but even in the hallways—and he tried to imagine the millions of dollars that had gone into building and furnishing this place. *No wonder the interior decorators who did this place ran out of money before they got to HQMC,* Newman thought, contrasting this opulence with the Marines' cramped, spartan offices with their drab walls and linoleum.

Newman and Major Suva turned left again and went through an arch with a sign above the entrance: *Offices of the First Deputy Secretary General of the United Nations and Director for International Peacekeeping Operations and Military Observers.* Newman had to break stride and stop in order to read the entire sign. He smiled and muttered to himself, "Now that's a mouthful!" He chuckled, remembering his briefing on the UN, when he discovered that most of the officers had exceptionally long titles. *It must be that the bigger the big shot, the more words he has in his title,* he thought. Major Suva escorted Newman into a huge anteroom outside the first deputy's inner office. Again Newman was struck by the extravagance.

At the Fijian officer's request, Newman sat on the leather couch that made a soft *whoosh* when he sat down. The coffee table in front of him must have been six feet square, an artistic piece of furniture that was part marble and part wood and glass. The one-piece, glass slab for the table was more than an inch thick and was balanced on five round marble balls almost twenty inches in diameter, which acted as legs and a center support. It was truly a work of art. On the walls he saw huge oil and acrylic paintings, wall hangings and tapestries of exotic fabric, and a huge portrait of the UN Secretary General.

On top of the wall-to-wall carpeting was an enormous Persian rug, probably twelve-by-twenty feet. *Good grief,* Newman thought, *Rachel and I couldn't afford carpeting that cost thirty dollars per yard, and these characters are covering stuff that's even more expensive with another carpet.*

On the office door, Newman saw a smaller-sized version of the wordy sign he'd seen on the way through the arch, this time inscribed in gold letters on black marble. And below the sign was the name of the first deputy, *DIMITRI KOMULAKOV,* in raised black letters an inch high on a gold plaque.

Newman was kept waiting for nearly an hour before the door opened and a tall man stepped briskly toward him, his arm extended for a handshake. Newman stood and extended his own hand. The handshake was firm and friendly. "Major Newman, or is it Lieutenant Colonel? I'm so sorry to have kept you waiting, my friend," he said in fluent American English. "I'm General Dimitri Komulakov."

The man did not look like a typical general—he was wearing what appeared to be a one-thousand-dollar-plus dark-blue suit. Nor did he sound like a Russian. Instead of answering the man's question, Newman asked one of his own: "You're an American?"

Komulakov laughed. "No, I am originally from Minsk and served in my government for the past thirty-one years. I was based in your country for most of that time. I wasn't much more than a kid when I started, and

I guess by now I've all but lost my accent. It's gotten to the point that I even think in English now."

Newman nodded. "Were you in the diplomatic service?"

"Yes, something like that," Komulakov answered. "A decade ago, we were adversaries in the Cold War. Now here we are."

Newman understood the subtext. Komulakov had worked for the KGB as a spy in America. The Marine lieutenant colonel had trouble thinking of the Russians as good guys yet, and wasn't quite as willing as his commander in chief to let bygones be bygones. Newman was ushered into the man's office; its opulence made even Harrod's posh office look frugal. Komulakov looked like he belonged here. He was tall and trim, his hair was dark blond and styled, and his skin was tanned to a deep bronze. Komulakov sat in a morocco-leather chair and reached for a Limoges cup and saucer sitting by a silver carafe on his desk.

"Please, sit. Would you like some coffee?"

"No thank you, General. I had plenty on the plane on the way up from Washington."

"Then let's get down to business," Komulakov said, gently placing the expensive china back on the corner of his massive desk.

"I'm told that you've had a rather broad base of experience in military matters," the general said.

"Yes, I guess you could say that. I'm a United States Marine," Newman said confidently.

"I see," Komulakov said without inflection. "And you have been briefed thoroughly on your assignment?"

"Yes. And for the past three days I've been briefing my men. But as I'm sure you understand, there is much work that they have to do before they will be ready to be committed. But, if you don't mind, General, I would like some confirmation that all that we're being prepared to do really does have the backing of international law, as Dr. Harrod has said."

"You don't trust your own National Security Advisor?" Komulakov asked incredulously.

"It's not about me trusting anybody. I'm responsible for the lives and safety of thirty-eight very good men. I've met them all. I just want to be sure that what we're engaged in is all 'legit,' if you know what I mean. Can you reassure me along that line?"

"Reassure you?" For an instant Komulakov's eyes squinted, and Newman saw in that brief microsecond an element of something he didn't like. But just as quickly the Russian composed himself and leaned forward. "Yes, of course. We all get a little suspicious, I suppose. Maybe it's because of the paranoia and suspicion of our former occupations and the innate cynicism and distrust that we previously had for each other. But it truly is a new world order, and some things will take a little getting used to.

"But to reassure you . . . yes, I can do that. The world is getting smaller, and all nations are beginning to want peace. War is too expensive, and in our era it's also terribly ineffective. It used to be that you simply put two mighty armies on a battlefield and let them fight it out. To the winner went the spoils, eh? Not anymore. You may be surprised at what I say, but the dominance of America and the collapse of the Soviet Union were inevitable. Right now, my country is in disarray and struggling to find itself. But thankfully, now we can do it without the Cold War pressures, and through workable United Nations political processes, we will do it.

"Now, the UN International Sanctions Enforcement

Group. I'm sure that my friend, Dr. Simon Harrod, told you that you were specifically selected for this assignment—from among thousands of possible candidates. That should give you some confidence."

Newman waved his hand and interrupted. "No, that's not the kind of reassurance that I want. I have no lack of confidence, General. In fact, I know that for whatever reasons—fate, luck, bad luck maybe, whatever—I am the best qualified on the basis of my record and where I've been. No . . . what I'm looking for are specific written orders—official recognition that what we're being asked to do is legal under international law and that the UN has the authority to issue these orders to me."

"I see," Komulakov said thoughtfully. "I'm sorry. I thought Dr. Harrod had covered all of that with you."

"No, I'm the one who's sorry, General," Newman said. "Dr. Harrod was very *thorough,* and I don't doubt for an instant that he was telling the truth. But, well, I'm a cynic—I want to make sure that this mission is on the up-and-up—there are no surprises. All I want is written confirmation from the very top. Now I'm smart enough to know that you can't put these things in circulation, but I just want to see it for myself. Is it possible to humor me so that I can go on my mission with no doubts hanging over my head?"

"You have my word, as well as Dr. Harrod's."

Newman grinned and looked askance at the man behind the desk. Komulakov laughed. "I suppose that does sound rather silly, in light of what we were just talking about—our past occupations and the like," he said, smiling.

He pushed a button on his desk and said, "Captain Sjogren, please come in."

The office door opened and an attractive blonde woman, in a well-tailored Swedish Army uniform that fit her lithe body like a glove, gracefully entered the room. Newman could smell her perfume almost instantly. Komulakov motioned for her to come near to him. He whispered instructions to her; then she nodded and left the room.

Komulakov poured himself another cup of coffee and gestured toward Newman with the carafe. Newman shook his head. "No thanks."

"You find my aide attractive, Major—or is it Lieutenant Colonel—Newman?" asked the general again, his eyebrow raised inquisitively.

"Major . . . the promotion isn't final yet. And, yes, she certainly is attractive—" began Newman, but the general interrupted.

"If you are staying here in New York tonight, I'm sure she would be pleased to prepare some dinner for you. She has a lovely apartment in Soho. And after that, who knows?"

"Thanks anyway, General, but I'm married. And I'm sure you know the meaning of the Marine motto, *Semper Fidelis*. I take it seriously in everything I do."

Before he could reply, Komulakov's intercom buzzed. He pushed a button: "Yes?"

It was Captain Sjogren. "Sir, I have the file ready on your computer. You can call it up with file number 'ZZ 744809.' "

"Thank you, Captain." He turned to his computer and typed in the file number and opened it. It popped instantly onto the screen. Komulakov hit the "print" command with his cursor, and the document began to print. After a minute or so, he retrieved ten sheets of paper from the laser printer and brought them over to Newman.

Newman began to read. The first two pages were a copy of the National Security Directive that Harrod had shown him. The second document was an almost identical UK *Cabinet Minutes,* bearing the signature of the British prime minister. And the third item was a copy of the secret UN Security Council Resolution that sanctioned it all. Newman read all three documents, just to make certain that nothing was included or left out that conflicted with Harrod's orders. Newman saw that the UN Secretary General had signed it.

"Thank you, Mr. First Deputy," Newman said, smiling. "I had full assurance that the action that I'm about to take on is right. But now I have reassurance that we have international law and the authority of the UN behind us. Thank you, sir." He handed the pages back to Komulakov who put them through a shredder behind his desk.

"Now, let's go look at the equipment and meet the people with whom you will be in contact in our UN command center," Komulakov said. Then he led Newman to a door in the right-hand corner of the office. It led into the command center itself.

"And all the while I thought this was a door to your private john," Newman said with a grin.

The huge room was without windows and darkened. Video and computer terminals glowed in rows on top of other rows. High-intensity flood lamps that focused only on the desk area and kept the light away from the terminals and monitors illumined individual workspaces.

"I'm impressed, General," Newman said with a soft

whistle. "Man, this room must have at least three thousand square feet."

"I suppose you're right," Komulakov said with a shrug. "I've never thought of it. But we use every square inch of space and could use more. This room primarily houses just the brains of the command center. It's where we gather all of the intelligence."

Newman looked around the room housing the command center operations—he looked slowly to take it all in. He had a strange feeling of *déjà vu* after seeing what was there. The computers were state of the art, and Newman was sure their servers must have had a "zillion" gigabytes each. Newman could see how fast the various computations were happening on the computer monitors and knew this was highly sophisticated stuff— like the equipment he'd seen at the NMCC at the Pentagon. Then he remembered. No wonder this all seemed familiar—*it was*. This command center could have been a clone of the one he had seen in the Pentagon, and it was a much larger and more sophisticated version of the one in the White House Sit Room.

Komulakov permitted Newman to stroll through the room at will. He took his time, making mental notes of everything he saw. From the banks of video screens he could see by their various labels that they were live video feeds coming from East Timor, the Golan Heights, Bosnia, Kosovo, Haiti, the Congo, Rwanda, Sinai, Angola, Namibia, Zimbabwe, Afghanistan, Bogota, Iraq— everywhere the UN had a peacekeeping mission, an inspection team, or a monitoring post. And then he noticed that there must have been at least a hundred "live" video cameras trained on potential trouble spots around the world, being watched by people on banks of twelve-inch video monitors.

On the opposite side of the room were computer monitors, which contained such things as temporary downloads of after-action reports, status reports, daily action reports, and all kinds of lists—including the dispositions of military and naval forces all over the globe. Remarkably, Newman saw his own name on one of the monitors. Unlike the other monitors, which had printed labels describing the content on-screen, this one, handwritten with a felt-tip pen, bore the same "ZZ 744809" code that Komulakov had used to open the file that Newman had read a few moments earlier. Below his name on the screen were the names, ranks, military branch, and home country for his three deputies at the White House and each of the thirty-eight members of the ISEG. Newman suddenly had conflicting feelings— excitement, recognition, uneasiness; he wondered how many other screens were lit up in *other* parts of the world showing these names—and who was watching them.

There were also larger video screens that showed weather displays around the globe and others with detailed military dispositions on tactical maps. There were monitors for receiving images from space satellites, some even offering infrared pictures of areas that were in total night darkness.

"Let me show you the comm center—the communications part of this outfit," Komulakov called to him from the raised carpeted walkway surrounding the room. It was some six feet higher than the floor of the command center operations, giving Komulakov and other planners or decision-makers a panoramic view of what was going on. "Come," he said, with a wave for Newman to follow him.

Newman followed him to an unmarked door at the

far end of the room. The two of them went inside, shutting out the buzz of activity in the larger area. As soon as they stepped inside, a British SAS major jumped to his feet at attention.

"Please," Komulakov said softly, "don't let us disturb you. I'm just taking Lieutenant Colonel Newman here on a little tour of our toy store. Major Ellwood is the watch chief for this section. We have seven other sections, each one covering a designated geographical area. You'll no doubt be communicating with Major Ellwood and his counterparts here when your people are overseas."

Newman shook the hand of the major. He smiled and nodded to Newman, "Glad to meet you, Lef'tenant Colonel Newman," he said, using the British pronunciation. "It's nice to be able to put a friendly face together with a voice when the messages come in." Ellwood then gave Newman a tour of his comm room operation. Newman surmised that the word of his promotion had now spread internationally—yet his own wife didn't even know about it. He drove the thought from his mind and said, "It looks to me like you have nothing but the best in here, Major. I'm impressed. Is there any piece of the most recent technology that you *don't* have here?"

"I don't think so, sir. All we have to do is ask, and the SG gets it for us."

Newman was puzzled. "The 'SG'?"

"Why that's the secretary general, sir. We all work for him, don't we now?" replied Major Ellwood.

As the British major was talking, Newman absently ran his hand over the smooth console. Suddenly an alarm buzzed on one of the machines. Newman drew his arm back quickly.

Ellwood chuckled. "That wasn't you, Colonel. It's the

signal that we have an outgoing message that we have to transmit. I'll have to encrypt it first. Excuse me, please."

He squeezed past Newman and reached beside one of the computers that was linked with video feeds to a small, covered box with an electronic lock on it. He took his plastic key and swiped it into the front of the box. "This just records who serviced this message and who encrypted it before transmission." A green signal light came on after Ellwood passed his plastic key through the reader. He opened the door to the protective cover, reached inside, pulled out an EncryptionLok-3 device, and made sure it was securely interfaced with the feed coming into the comm unit from somewhere else in the UN's vast command center. Ellwood checked the message on the screen for correct addresses and then put the EncryptionLok-3 back inside its housing and pushed the *Lock* key on the touch-screen computer monitor. Then he pushed the icon on the screen for *Encrypt,* and immediately the screen was filled with letters, symbols, and digits. Without any spaces, punctuation, or even comparative words or sections, code-breakers would find it impossible to make sense of it.

The mathematical algorithms used for the EncryptionLok-3 were so unique that every letter or number could have a totally different replacement even if the letter was a repeat. Most of the codes from World War II used a basic template to decipher words. It was a rather straightforward process; for example, whenever you used the letter *a* in your code it was meant to read as another letter, say *k.* But the EncryptionLok-3 had 56 billion equivalents for a replacement for just the twenty-six letters of the English alphabet if it were transmitted as a message.

Newman, of course, knew that the EL-3 was an absolutely superb device for keeping communications from the enemy. But now, as he had just witnessed its use in the comm room of the UN Security Council Operations and Command Center, directed by a former Russian KGB agent, the significance of the event nearly bowled him over. *What other U.S. top-secret equipment is being shared with these people?* he wondered.

"Major, how long have you been using the EL-3?" he asked as nonchalantly as he could.

"Well, let's see . . . I started this tour in July of '92. We didn't have 'em then. If I remember right we got 'em just about a year ago. Yeah, that's right—last November. They're really remarkable little assets, aren't they?"

"Yeah," Newman muttered, not knowing what else to say. "Remarkable."

CHAPTER EIGHT

The Device That Betrays

Corporate Headquarters
Silicon Cyber Technologies International, Inc.
Newport Beach, CA
Monday, 5 December 1994
1500 Hours, Local

Marty Korman, founder and CEO of Silicon Cyber Technologies International, Inc., had to be convinced that hiring high-profile military retirees to shepherd the company's sales efforts through the government bureaucracy was a good idea. It was SCTI's cofounding partner, Stanley Marat, who insisted that they follow existing protocol to get things done in Washington.

Marat and Korman had been classmates at Cal Poly, and after graduation when Korman went to Los Alamos, Marat had been stolen by one high-tech firm after another, always with the enticement of greater and greater compensation. He had been with six different companies over seven years until the two old friends had bumped into each other in 1981 at a high-tech seminar in Vail, Colorado. Over drinks the two twenty-nine-year-olds decided that if they continued to work for other people they would never get rich. Three months later both quit their jobs, mortgaged their homes and marriages, rented a warehouse in Paramount, California, and started Silicon Cyber Technologies Inc., then later adding the word *International*. And the rest, as they say, is history.

The match was perfect. Korman had a genius for every kind of communications technology. Some in the industry said he could "make electrons dance." And Marat, it turned out, was a master salesman. He took their ultrasophisticated digital encryption algorithms, with complementary hardware and software, to the master communicators at the Pentagon, the Defense Communications Agency, the National Security Agency, and the White House Communications Agency. Marat convinced them that if they wanted to protect their classified communications from the Soviets and Chinese, they absolutely *had* to have SCTI's equipment.

By 1983, the company's little prototype Encryption-Lok-1A device, no bigger than a TV remote, was being alpha-tested in the most sensitive sites in the U.S. government: the National Military Command Center at the Pentagon, North American Air Defense Command out in Colorado, the State Department, the CIA, the National Reconnaissance Office, the National Security Agency, NASA, the FBI, and, of course, the White House. Shortly thereafter the Pentagon ordered that they be put on every nuclear submarine and in every ballistic missile silo. They were purchased through a $288-million secret defense appropriation tacked onto another bill at the last minute that passed without fanfare.

But SCTI's big break came just a year later when the company won another multimillion-dollar sole-source classified contract to produce major quantities of the little secure communications devices for the most highly classified undertaking in the U.S. government: the supersensitive Continuity Project. President Reagan was adamant that, before he could enter into talks with the Soviets aimed at reducing nuclear arms, we had to ensure that the Soviets could never "decapitate" our government. He sought and received from Congress billions of dollars for the highly classified construction and deployment of covertly pre-positioned mobile command-and-control facilities for use in the event of a Soviet attack so the U.S. would never be without a civilian president.

The Project required *thousands* of the little EncryptionLok-1A devices so that a president, even in the most difficult of circumstances, could still transmit and receive secure communications—data, telephone, and video—to and from U.S. military commands, the State Department, CIA, NSA, the Secret Service, and FBI. It was the break that Korman and Marat had been hoping for.

Because secure communications were so essential to the Project, Jules Wilson, a senior officer at the National Security Agency, was appointed communications czar and charged with the responsibility for certifying all equipment to be used in the "presidential emergency communications suites." Wilson put together a small team of communications, encryption, and security experts that he dubbed the "Comm Hawks" and set out to find the best means of ensuring that the civilian president would always have a secure means of communications—be it by telephone, fax, computer, radio, or video. The Comm Hawks unanimously agreed that nothing was better than the EncryptionLok-1A—which was the first time the device became known within the small circle aware of its existence as the more abbreviated "EL-1A."

The Project was coordinated at the White House by a single officer on the National Security Council staff. His office, on the third floor of the Old Executive Office Building, had an innocuous title on the door: Special Projects Office.

❂

Until the Continuity Project came along, SCTI had been building each EncryptionLok-1A individually as a discrete unit. But starting in 1984, the company had to gear up a full-scale production line so that each new unit would have a unique identifier code built into its encryption algorithm. This model would become the EL-2. However, before SCTI could start producing EL-2 units for the "presidential emergency communication packages," the company was told that they would have to satisfy Jules Wilson at NSC about a couple of major concerns. The Korman technology was so sophisticated that the information being sent through an EL-2 unit was impossible to decrypt, even with the most powerful computers and the government's best code people. National Security Agency scientists at Fort Meade, Maryland, using Kray supercomputers, spent several months trying to crack the EncryptionLok-2 codes. The experts were good. But Korman's software and ideas were better. So the U.S. government bought more of these wonderful devices, and SCTI logged hundreds of millions in sales of the EL-2s.

All went blissfully well until late 1988. Experts at NSA and the FBI turned in a top-secret assessment to the Vice President who was then, because of the recent elections, the Republican President-elect. The report may have been the first instance of intelligence cooperation between the agencies without threats or coercion. Whatever the reason, the NSA and FBI experts were terrified that if an EL-2 unit should fall into the wrong hands, an adversary or sophisticated criminal operation could reverse-engineer the technology, build their own version of the EncryptionLok technology, and then the secret military and government codes would be useless. Worse than that, America's intelligence community would forever lose the ability to crack *their* codes.

Jules Wilson, a code-cracker, and two security experts from the Comm Hawks went to see Korman in his new digs. SCTI had already made enough to vacate the shabby warehouse in Paramount and move the company into a new, shiny, silver-and-glass structure overlooking Newport Beach. Were it not for the twelve-foot-high security fence, the guarded gate, two K-9 security teams walking the perimeter of the building, and the armed guards at the front desk, the SCTI facility would look like any other California high-tech giant. Korman thought that his highly visible security measures would be the crowning touch, but the government geeks weren't impressed.

Nor were they impressed at Korman's responses to their concerns. So, because he couldn't offer them iron-clad guarantees for their reverse-engineering or penetration problems, they required SCTI to make two changes to the EncryptionLok technology as a condition of granting the company the contract for any more devices that they called "contingency communications packages."

First, they wanted Korman to build a GPS transponder chip into each EL-2 device and link it to that unit's identifier code so that NSA could "interrogate" any unit, anywhere in the world, to determine its location. That way if it ever found its way into the wrong hands they'd know it. Second, SCTI had to create an internal "command/destruct" circuit inside each unit so that, at a predetermined signal, the internal circuitry of the EL-2 would fry itself into a small pile of molten silicon, plastic, precious metal, and circuit boards. The command/destruct circuitry would permit a higher headquarters to send a coded signal to any EncryptionLok-2 device determined to be "out of location" and potentially in the wrong hands. If that were the case, the commander of that unit could instantly render the unit totally useless to anybody, forever, before the technology could be·compromised.

Korman's engineers struggled with the problems, believing that adding these features would also likely add size and weight to what was to become SCTI's model EL-3, posing other problems in retrofitting the devices into already customized communications equipment and military gear.

But it took Korman less than two weeks, working on his own, to come up with the modifications that Jules Wilson and the Comm Hawks demanded. Korman and Marat flew to Washington with three prototypes and demonstrated them to Wilson and his team. All three units performed perfectly, though when the command/destruct signal was sent to the third unit, it emitted a curl of black, acrid smoke and what sounded like a little high-pitched cry as its circuits immolated themselves. Korman almost cried as he watched the third prototype frying on an asbestos pad sitting on Wilson's conference table. It had cost them nearly $2 million of research and development to make them, and now they were just melted rubbish.

The generals and bureaucrats examined the burned device. It was perfect. All that remained was a small, greasy black glob of charred and melted elements. Korman had sealed some volatile chemical components in a hollowed-out composite sleeve. The chemicals were inert unless mixed as part of the command/destruct sequence, but then they were fatal to the unit.

One of the government dweebs took out some tools and tried to take the unit apart to see if any internal elements survived to enable someone to guess at reverse-engineering. Nope. Cross-section slices of the device further revealed absolutely no trace of identifiable components. It would be impossible to reverse-engineer a destroyed EL-3. Period. The matter was closed.

The government buyers were satisfied and asked how much these changes would cost. Stan Marat had already estimated that the work to produce the newly modified EL-3 on a quantity production run with the new specs might be one thousand more than they were costing them now. But Korman, sensing the government's urgency and the lack of any competing vendor, quickly blurted out that "the per-unit cost to the government for each EncryptionLok-3 will rise from forty-three thousand to fifty-eight thousand dollars." Nobody blinked.

By the time Korman and Marat got back to California that night, they had government authority to scrap the model EL-2 and put the EL-3 into production with a purchase order for eight thousand of the new units to be delivered over the next forty-eight months. The order had come over a fax machine that was hooked up to a new EL-3 unit in Korman's office, and across the top of the page in bold letters were the words *TOP SECRET* and below that, *SENSITIVE COMPARTMENTED*

INFORMATION and below that, in much smaller type: *Special Projects Office.* The next four pages detailed technical, payment, and delivery requirements, much the same as other purchase orders that they had received over the past three years.

There was one new stipulation in this contract, however: a strict nondisclosure agreement. If SCTI accepted this purchase order, there could be no announcement of any kind in any trade publication regarding the contract or the modifications that had been made in the EncryptionLok technology. SCTI was not even allowed to reveal to its other U.S. government customers that the improved model existed nor that they had received the contract award to make them. Only the National Security Agency, the National Security Council's Special Projects Office, and the SCTI founders were allowed to have this information under threats of imprisonment and fines. Jules Wilson had told them that they were privy to "the greatest national security secret in postwar history." While Korman and Marat doubted *that,* they weren't about to test their skepticism.

For Korman and Marat, this new nondisclosure stipulation was a problem. They had already figured out that if these GPS-locate and command/destruct features were so valuable to this one customer, then they should also be important to those government agencies that had already purchased thousands of units *without* these capabilities. But if they couldn't even tell their existing government customers about this upgrade, what good was it once this contract was done?

"I don't like it," said Marat. "It ties our hands."

"Don't like it? What don't you like about *$464 million?* That's what this contract is worth! Are you crazy?" shouted Korman. He always shouted when he was agitated. Marat was used to it.

"Besides, that's why I marked up the cost at the demonstration—to cover our R & D and future lost sales," Korman said. But both knew he was lying; he'd raised the price only because he knew that he could get away with it.

Korman initialed the corner of each of the first three pages, signed the last page on the line labeled "Accepts," and turned to Marat and said, "Now, find a way around that nondisclosure so that we can replace all those old EL-1As and EL-2s already out there with these new models."

It was while he was driving home that night that it occurred to Stanley Marat that what SCTI needed was a stable of "brass hats" to push their product very quietly through the corridors of the Pentagon.

Much later on, Marat admitted to friends that he should have quit that night. Quit while he was ahead. But he didn't because the money was so good. And so easy.

Up to this point, Korman and Marat had been operating within the boundaries of the law, if not full propriety. Sure, the price tag for the EncryptionLok-3 was a whole lot higher than it should be, but nobody else had this technology—*and so what?* They reasoned, if some plumbing company could get six hundred bucks for a toilet seat on a DOD contract, why shouldn't they be able to charge what the traffic would bear?

"Besides," roared Korman one day when Marat seemed to be feeling pangs of guilt over how much they were charging for a device that cost them less than five thousand dollars to make, "if those fools in Washington don't know enough to come back and ask for a lower price, why should we *offer* it to them?"

Marat shrugged, went out, and bought himself a new BMW, which he paid for with a check.

But they both knew that SCTI had a long-range problem. Once this eight thousand-unit contract for presidential contingency communications and our strategic nuclear forces was filled, how could they find other customers for the EL-3? They had been doing very well making one thousand units a year, but now they wanted to double SCTI's production. If they didn't find new customers, they'd lose their highly skilled force of technicians and programmers to some other high-tech venture as soon as this production run was completed. And without a highly skilled group of "techies" like they had out back in the manufacturing bays, the company would go belly up.

Both Korman and Marat knew they had created the problem for SCTI: the EL-3 equipment was so good and so reliable that once a customer had it, they didn't need to buy anything else. Another potential problem for SCTI had come during the Gulf War. Korman was convinced that Saddam Hussein's invasion of Kuwait would bring another boom to the company. But the people at the NSC who called the shots had deemed the EncryptionLok-3 technology too sensitive to risk and had barred it from overseas shipment or sale to its allies, even the British.

There was military logic in this policy, but only because the commanders fighting the war didn't know about SCTI's upgrade. The GPS and command/destruct functions built into the latest versions of the EncryptionLok-3 made it safe to use anywhere. But the generals and admirals fighting Iraq didn't know about the new and improved model because it was reserved only for the Contingency Project and the strategic nuclear forces.

It made Korman seethe. He knew he was missing a magnificent opportunity for enormous profits.

Marat tried a less mercenary, more human approach in his pitch to Jules Wilson shortly after the troops started deploying for Saudi Arabia: "Look Jules, those Marines and soldiers are going to have to hump around the desert in one-hundred-degree heat, wearing those NBC suits and carrying those ancient KY-38s on their backs. I think you guys gave it that number because that's what it weighs. Let 'em use our new EL-3s. You and I know darned well that it doesn't matter if a military unit operating in Kuwait or Iraq loses one of the new EL-3s in combat. It wouldn't even matter if the device were taken back to Baghdad. Constant monitoring of the EncryptionLok-3 units by higher headquarters will alert them to such an event. You can use the same protocol that the Special Project EL-3s use. If the person holding the device doesn't respond with the daily password in thirty seconds, the comm officer at the next higher headquarters can initiate the destruct sequence for that particular EncryptionLok-3."

Wilson gave him a one-word answer to the plea: "No."

Both Marat and Korman knew that the only solution was to make some of the top military honchos in the Army, Navy, Air Force, and Marines aware of their new and improved EL-3. They reasoned that if one of the generals or admirals with knowledge of and experience with the supersecret EL-3s worked for SCTI, there would be incentives to find ways of getting the NSC to relax their prohibitions on the newer devices, especially when there were so many of the older units in use by the nation's strategic nuclear forces that did not have the GPS locator ability or its command/destruct capability.

SCTI's founders were sure that if they found the right retired general or admiral, they could use him to get the word out about the upgraded device. And then, they figured, once the "non-nuke" side of the services knew about the device, they would clamor to have it made available to their troops.

But it turned out to be more difficult to hire brass hats than either Korman or Marat had thought it would be. They couldn't advertise because their only customer didn't want anyone else to know what SCTI made. It was hard enough going to colleges to recruit employees. By the terms of its contracts, everyone working at SCTI had to be an American citizen, and, on top of that, this arrogant Jules Wilson insisted that his Comm Hawks vet every applicant for top-secret security clearances. They had even moved two of their FBI security dweebs into the SCTI building to monitor security. It bugged Korman that no matter what time he arrived or left, one of them was always there. When Korman groused about it once to Wilson, the NSA spook simply replied, "Deal with it." Korman took solace in knowing that Wilson's and his two security dweebs' *combined* income was about that of a janitor at SCTI.

When Marat traveled back to Washington for meetings with the Defense Communications Agency, Pentagon, and White House Communications Agency though, he would routinely remind the senior officers with whom he met, "Now when you get ready to retire to sunny California, give us a call."

The overture finally paid off in 1991—just as the Contingency Project contract neared completion and

SCTI was getting desperate for another purchase order. Rear Admiral Frank Laughton, the man originally responsible for installing EL-3s in the U.S. nuclear submarine fleet, invited Marat to come see him at his office in Crystal City, south of the Pentagon.

"Stanley, I'm going to retire this summer. I've already put my papers in, and I'm putting out a coupla feelers to see what I might be able to do in the civilian sector." That was all the initiative Marat needed.

He took the admiral to dinner at Five Seasons, the brand-new but pricey gourmet restaurant across from the Renwick Gallery, just up from the White House and the OEOB. When the check came, Marat peeled three one-hundred-dollar bills from his money clip and placed them on the small silver tray that the waiter had brought bearing the check and a pair of Godiva chocolates.

Marat knew that such opulence impressed the admiral. A young woman came by their table and offered them cigars. The men selected from a choice of Latin specialties, and Marat recommended one labeled in Spanish. "It's called 'the woman with the fragrant body,' and it's almost as good as any Cuban cigar that I've tried. Kinda sexy, huh?"

Admiral Laughton pointed at the box, and the young hostess took out two cigars and presented them to the men as if they were made of gold. They lit up, and Marat felt that he had impressed the admiral enough to state plainly what he wanted.

"Look, Frank, I've got to tell you . . . you wouldn't be making a mistake in choosing SCTI for your next career . . . and you know that—"

The admiral interrupted him. "I've already made up my mind, Stanley. I looked into several other companies, but SCTI offers the best opportunity for me. You've sold me."

"Well, you know how much I'd like to have you aboard . . . but I'm afraid I shouldn't have been so hasty . . ."

Admiral Laughton was visibly shaken. There was something in the tone of voice that Marat used that said that he had changed his mind. "You see, Frank, I've got a real problem. You're one of the small handful of people out of the six billion on this planet who knows what SCTI does, what we make, and the special capabilities built into the newest EL-3s that allow them to be tracked, and if necessary, destroyed. You had the foresight to see what we could do for the U.S. Navy's strategic nuclear forces."

"That's right," the admiral said. "I saw right away that we needed EncryptionLok-3s on every one of our nuclear subs, and when you developed the tracking and command/destruct features, I insisted we replace the original models with the upgraded devices. Just think of what could happen if we had an incident like that German sub in World War II that lost the Enigma code device. Remember that? It helped us beat the Nazis years earlier than we otherwise could have, and it saved thousands of U.S. and Allied lives. But what if our enemies got their hands on one of our encryption devices today? Who knows what catastrophes that would bring about!"

"Frank, you're a very perceptive man. I wish you were working at the NSC office. Those guys don't have a fraction of your vision and wisdom. And it's because of that—and this is highly confidential, Frank—I can share it with you only because of your security clearance. The reason is, because of the shortsightedness of the NSC, SCTI will be out of business by this time next year." Marat sighed deeply and shook his head for added effect.

"What!? What do you mean?" Laughton sounded like he had just seen his cash cow drown.

"It's a catch-22 situation. We've got the only solution to safeguard our country's military secrets, and it's been provided to all of the government agencies that wanted it. Then, as a service to America, and at a *great expense* to our company, SCTI created a *better* EL-3, like the later versions that you're buying for your Navy subs. But despite our loyalty to our country and willingness to help, we paid an enormous price—the government now says that we can't sell any of our devices to anyone else. Well, Frank, I can understand why they wouldn't let us sell 'em to the Chinese or North Koreans. But for cryin' out loud, we can't even sell these new EL-3s to our own government agencies and our own *military*."

Admiral Laughton was fuming as much as his cigar. "That's asinine," he snorted.

"Just think, Frank," Marat continued, "I'm not afraid that any of your subs or the missile silos would lose one of our EncryptionLok-3s—you guys have great security, yet you still got the *upgraded* EncryptionLok-3s because you wanted to make sure no device could ever be captured." This wasn't exactly true, as Marat knew. Laughton had been *told* to take the newer devices because after the discovery of the Walker spy ring in the Navy, nobody trusted anyone.

Marat continued. "As it stands right now, only the nuclear forces and the Contingency Project have the upgraded EncryptionLok-3s. And—if this isn't really stupid, nothing is—none of our military units other than your subs and the carriers with nukes aboard can take the devices out of the country. But as you know, with the new models there's no need to fear losing one or having one captured in combat because of that built-in safety feature. Unfortunately, we're stymied. The NSC won't let us tell *anyone* else about the upgrades we've made. Frank, *every* device ought to be upgraded, and *every* military unit ought to have one."

"You're right! It's the only way," the admiral agreed. "Why does the NSC want to keep the rest of the military without them? It's un-American!"

"It's true," Marat said. "Yet, we have two very serious contractual stipulations that NSA . . . well, Jules Wilson at NSA . . . handcuffed us with. One is that we can't sell the new devices to NATO, even though we're common partners in policing the world. The second—and this is more terrible than the first, Frank—we can't even sell them to our own government military and security people, except the NSC and the ones that they approve or control. Wilson wants a monopoly on all of the new units, for whatever cockamamie reason. But I think he's wrong, Frank. And I think that it's a matter of patriotism. All of our boys in the Navy" (he put that one first for the admiral's benefit), "Army, Marines, and Air Force need to have these new models. Just think, Frank—why, you even said it a minute ago. What if one of the older models fell into the wrong hands? They can't be located by GPS and tracked down like the new ones can. And worse than that, they can't be destroyed by remote control to keep 'em from the enemy, like the new ones."

Marat had touched all the right buttons, and the admiral was shaking his head. "Does the President know about this?" he asked sharply.

"I don't know," replied Marat, adding, "probably

not. I think that Wilson is the only one in the administration who knows—outside of two or three other military leaders who had the foresight to ask for
improvements over the old EncryptionLok-3."

For a long moment neither man spoke. Then the admiral began to think aloud. "You know, I've got a meeting with the President on Friday morning. Wilson and
some of the other security council people will be
there . . . and I can tell the President. I won't compromise your trust, Stanley. I won't tell them that you told
me this 'cause it might get messy, with the contracts and
all. But how about if I just *ask*, out of the blue, you
know . . . 'Hey, Mr. President, the NSC has new
EncryptionLok-3s, but I haven't heard of any other military or security agencies getting the new devices that
prevent our codes and secrets from being compromised.
What if those old EL-3s fall into the wrong hands? We
won't be able to track 'em, and they don't have the new
command/destruct capability. I think that poses a serious security risk, don't you, Mr. President?' And then
I'll look him straight in the eye and ask, 'Are we working on solving that problem, Mr. President?' I'll guarantee you that he'll be interested. Not only that, Stanley,
every one of the military guys in the room will be gung
ho in favor of it. And if that's the way our meeting turns
out, it'll be tough for Wilson to jam it. No, Stanley, I
think I can take care of your dilemma."

"Well, Frank, if you can *do* that, I'll be forever in-
debted to you. And I mean it, Frank. If that happens,
you won't have to worry about your retirement. Your
401K will grow very fat, believe me," Marat said.

Admiral Laughton was true to his word. He appealed
to the President and to the patriotism of every military
man in the room at the Friday morning meeting. Few of

those in the Situation Room meeting knew that an EncryptionLok-3 with the new features even existed. By the end of the meeting, the President instructed Jules Wilson to follow through and make sure the new EncryptionLok-3s got on the classified portion of the pending Defense Appropriation Bill. There was no discussion. It all happened within eight minutes of the meeting.

Jules Wilson was furious at this end run and knew in his gut that SCTI was behind it. Yet, with the President's full support, as well as that of the military men in the room who were asking for wider implementation of the newest EncryptionLok-3 devices, Wilson was powerless. He could not make trouble now for the government's only vendor with such support for the company from across the military. Marat even endeared himself to his customers by promising no price increases. "With a large enough quantity, we should be able to hold the prices where they are now," he promised them. But back in California, Korman was furious when he heard that and went into one of his shouting rages.

○

By the end of 1992, SCTI had contracted for or sold the government just about all the EncryptionLok-3s they could use, and future sales orders dropped to a fraction of what they had been in prior years. Though the money was rolling in, Korman and Marat could see the handwriting on the wall. Unless they found a wider market for their only product, the future would be bleak indeed for SCTI and the company's founders.

Marat went to friends he had made in the FBI and NSA and convinced them that with a few minor modifications SCTI could make another device—a somewhat less sophisticated version of the EL-3. But with the defense cuts that were already happening, they sold fewer than six thousand of the little devices—a fraction of sales in prior years.

The drop in sales drove Korman nuts. SCTI had the only product of its kind in the world, but the U.S. government was his only customer. And his only customer wanted to keep his invention as its own toy. The bigwigs in Washington had made Korman, Marat, and their three hundred employees profligately rich, but Korman knew he was not as rich as he could be if he could sell his EncryptionLok-3 *commercially.* Businesses would love to have a virtually unbreakable encryption method for keeping their communications secret. And of course, there was NATO and the UN. Sales to these two organizations could even surpass everything that SCTI had done with the American government to date.

When a new administration came to Washington in 1993, Korman made sure that he was introduced to the new National Security Advisor, Dr. Simon Harrod, at a defense symposium in January '93, shortly after the inauguration. Korman found Harrod to be a kindred spirit, and while he had never paid much attention to politics, Korman found the things he heard about a "new era of international cooperation" and talk about "eliminating barriers to trading our technology around the globe" as music to his ears. At a "meet and greet" after the speeches, Korman introduced himself to Harrod and quickly told the National Security Advisor that he had warmed the hearts of everyone in the room with his comments about opening the doors to sell American products overseas. He then boldly asked, "How can I tell the President directly about what a great idea this is?"

Harrod responded just as boldly. "Were you a contributor to the President's campaign?"

Korman said, "No," and hastened to add, "I didn't give to anyone's campaign."

"Well, it's never too late," replied Harrod.

Korman took out his checkbook. "To whom do I make the check out?"

"Why don't you make it out to 'Scientists for World Trade,' " said Harrod. "It's a political action committee, so you can give only ten thousand dollars for now."

Korman wrote the check and handed it to Harrod, who looked impressed. "I'll see what we can do about getting you an appointment this week. Stay in touch."

The President saw Korman the next day for forty-five minutes in the Oval Office. On his way out the door, Korman gave him a check for $100,000 made out to the President's political party—just as Harrod had instructed.

After that, Korman was a regular at White House functions. He was invited to state dinners, receptions in the residence, and one time, for a flight on Air Force One.

And it wasn't only the President he was with. After a meeting in Harrod's office one afternoon, the National Security Advisor walked Korman down the hallway and introduced him to the Vice President. They also hit it off immediately, and before he left, Korman presented the Veep with a check for his reelection campaign. By the end of 1993, Korman had donated almost a million dollars to the President's party.

But despite papering Washington with his checks, Korman was no closer to getting any new contracts for his products. Finally, in near desperation, he invited Harrod to visit the SCTI plant while the National Security Advisor was on a trip to California. Harrod took up the invitation, and after walking through the facility wearing an extra-large hospital gown that made him look like a green snowman, he retired to Korman's office for a drink.

"Marty, I hear you," said Harrod after listening to Korman's complaint about not being able to sell his EncryptionLok-3 more broadly. "What you've got to do is make some contacts on the other side of the aisle. I suggest that you go see Senator James Waggoner."

"Who's he?"

"He's the chairman of the Defense Programs Subcommittee. That's the Senate subcommittee that regulates what can and can't be sold to our allies and others."

"But isn't he in the other party?" asked Korman incredulously.

"Yes, but we can work with him. So can you. If you know what I mean."

Korman knew exactly what Harrod meant. He made an appointment the following week to meet with the slow-talking, white-maned, aristocratic James Waggoner, the "senior senator" of the Eastern seaboard state he represented. Korman brought with him a check for $100,000 made out to the "Waggoner Science Foundation," an entity describing itself as "an educational charitable trust to benefit the peaceful uses of defense technology."

In a matter of hours, Waggoner had appointed himself Korman's political mentor. It was Waggoner who tutored the Californian on the ways of Washington. Waggoner and his aides taught the heretofore apolitical computer-scientist-turned-businessman on the subtleties of campaign finance—and how vast sums of money could be contributed to a candidate, a campaign, a cause, and a political party with minimal risk of getting caught violating federal election laws.

The senator had said, "Son, here's how it works. Every American is allowed to contribute one thousand dollars each time a candidate runs for federal office. That means you can write me a check for one thousand dollars for my primary campaign, and another grand for my general election. And every American is allowed to give five thousand dollars every two years to a political action committee. Now you're a bright young man—that means, in round numbers, you can write three five-thousand-dollar checks for my PAC and two one-thousand-dollar checks for my reelection."

"That's me personally," said Korman. "But can't SCTI contribute as a company?"

The senior senator's deeply lined face broke into a cadaverous grin. "No, son, that would be wrong." And a mirthless chuckle came from deep within his wrinkled throat. "But, there is nothing to stop all of the *employees* of your company from contributing, just like you do. And all of your family, and all of your friends, and all of *their* friends, and all of your friends' friends . . ." The senator checked himself to see if Korman was getting his drift and concluded with the obvious, "If you know what I mean."

The light had indeed gone on. Marty Korman nodded his head. The computer-scientist-turned-businessman, now turned major political player said, "Yes, Senator, I know what you mean. You can count on me and my employees and my friends—and I know we can count on you."

Marty Korman wrote checks that afternoon totaling seventeen thousand dollars to the senator's reelection campaign and his political action committee. Just to be on the safe side, he wrote an equal amount to the presidential and vice-presidential reelection campaigns and their PACs. And within a week of returning to California, checks for similar amounts began to pour in from the employees of SCTI—all three hundred of them. By the end of 1993, the "SCTI Club," as the donors were called at the White House, had contributed almost $5 million to the President's campaigns. Marty Korman was a regular on Capitol Hill and at 1600 Pennsylvania Avenue. And top-secret EncryptionLok-3 devices were being sold to customers who hadn't even known they existed the year before.

CHAPTER NINE

Learning Too Much

Special Projects Office
Old Executive Office Building
Washington, D.C.
Monday, 5 December 1994
2120 Hours, Local

It was late when Newman flew back from New York to Washington National Airport. He had left his car at the airport and shivered as he turned the key to start it up. It took almost ten minutes before the heater began working. He was finally beginning to feel comfortable when he pulled the Tahoe into his parking place on West Executive Drive. Then he became chilled again as he left his car and walked down the sidewalk and into the OEOB.

Newman plugged the codes into the various locks and performed the retinal scan as he flicked on the lights and opened the sliding door into his office. Once inside, Newman threw his overcoat on a nearby chair and checked his messages. Extremely fatigued, he sensed its source was more emotional than physical. He walked over to the huge fireplace and stood in front of it, debating whether to make a fire or not. Actually, he wasn't even sure the fireplace had ever worked. The logs were ceramic fakes placed atop a wrought-iron grate. He decided not to bother. Then he sighed and put his arms on the mantel to support his weight while he did some stretching exercises. Newman had missed his usual three-mile run that morning because of his trip to the UN, and he felt stiff.

With his hands still on the mantel, Newman stepped back a little from the fireplace and leaned into it with his torso. He felt the muscles in his arms and chest flex as he pushed. He was a little off balance in this position, so he shifted his arms a few inches farther out on each side. He did sort of a vertical push-up and stretched his back muscles as he leaned in. Suddenly he felt the mantel move. It slid into the masonry that supported it by nearly three inches. Newman nearly lost his balance but recovered quickly. He was perplexed; at first, he was afraid that he had broken something. But it didn't seem like the mantel had shifted because of faulty workmanship or wear. He stood up straight to look at the mantel more closely. Then he saw something that told him that the movement had occurred because of parts that were *engineered* to move.

When the mantel slid backward into the masonry, the firebricks that made up the rear of the fireplace also slid open, parting in the middle and leaving an opening in the rear of the fireplace that looked almost square, about two feet by two feet. Newman looked down and saw something in the hole, but his view was blocked by the grate with its fake logs. Newman quickly lifted them onto the floor in front of him.

He stepped to his left to let more light into the fireplace. Then, looking into the hole in the back of the fireplace more carefully this time, he saw a single-drawer GI field safe, complete with built-in combination dial and unlocking handle.

Then he remembered the office's former occupant—Oliver North. *This must be left over from North's days here,* he thought.

Newman tried the handle of the safe. Incredibly it turned. It wasn't locked. *That makes sense—you don't lock an empty safe,* was the next thought that came to him.

He pulled open the drawer and it nearly filled the fireplace. Then he reached inside to feel if something was there. His hand felt something, and he moved it around, feeling for an edge to grasp. When he had it, he brought it up and out into the light.

It was a dark-brown file pouch, tied around the middle. Newman opened it. Inside were several file folders. He took them out and laid them on his desk. They were all marked *TOP SECRET* and, as he looked them over, he discovered that the files contained dozens of memos and interoffice correspondence from the 1980s, more than a hundred pages in all. And as Newman read the documents, his eyes widened. Some of the memos were signed or initialed by former President Reagan and his national security advisors.

After a half hour of perusing the papers, it was clear to Newman that these documents were a bombshell. Some of the pages were authorizations for travel. Others were transcripts of conversations with foreign officials. Some of the papers pertained to the activities of others. One, a document initialed by the President, authorized a trip to Beijing (North had spelled it *Peking*) and directed the chairman of the Joint Chiefs of Staff to ask the Chinese to provide shoulder-fired surface-to-air missiles for the Nicaraguan Resistance. He also found documents he didn't understand, memos pertaining to the diversion of a Soviet munitions train in Poland and the subsequent delivery of its contents to the Contras. The papers Newman found stunned him. *Why hasn't anyone discovered these before?* he wondered.

Newman put all the papers back into the file pouch that he had pulled out of the safe and got up from his desk. He tried to think of what he should do with the find. He knew that simply turning them over to someone in the present administration had political ramifications, and the legal proceedings had ended several years ago so he wasn't concerned about "obstruction of justice" charges. Because he was tired and uncertain about what he had discovered, he decided to return the documents to where he had found them until he could think through the right thing to do.

He put the pouch back into the safe and closed the drawer, careful not to lock it. It took him a few minutes to figure out how to close the back wall of the fireplace for access to the safe. He had to find the exact spots where he'd placed his hands when the mechanism was triggered, and then he pulled forward on the mantel. As the mantel slid toward him, the back wall of the fireplace closed. He looked carefully, peering into the fireplace to see if he could detect that it had been opened. Nothing showed. It appeared as a soot-blackened wall of firebrick with no discernable sign that it had ever moved since being built more than a century before. He replaced the grate and logs. And then he brushed the little specks of soot from his hands.

By now it was 2230 hours, and he was exhausted. As he walked out to his car, it began to snow. *Why am I not surprised?* he thought, as he headed out the North West Gate onto an empty Pennsylvania Avenue.

Situation Room
The White House
Washington, D.C.
Monday, 5 December 1994
2300 Hours, Local

"You told me to call you anytime something of significance happened, Dr. Harrod, and this is sort of interesting. I thought you ought to see it." The watch chief of the White House Situation Room's communication center had phoned Harrod's cell phone number. The National Security Advisor was in the study, upstairs in the White House residence. He had just settled into a comfortable couch with one of the chief executive's good cigars, and the President had just started to say, "That was a great fund-raiser tonight, Simon. I thought I'd fall over laughing when you said—" Then the cell phone rang.

Harrod said, "Excuse me," and put the phone to his ear. "Harrod—what is it!" he snapped. He listened for a moment, then said, "All right . . . I'll be right there," and hung up. He excused himself from the President's study and headed for a meeting with the caller.

"Show me," Harrod said, huffing a little from his walk down the stairs from the residence to the Situation Room on the ground floor of the West Wing.

"I've got the surveillance tape in my office where you can see it," the watch chief said.

Harrod knew that his decision to place mini–video cameras in strategic places would one day come in handy. He just hadn't expected them to bear fruit so soon after being planted. The WHCA technicians had installed the cameras the previous Wednesday while they were hooking up the new communications equipment for Newman and his deputies in the Special Projects Office. There were two cameras hidden in Newman's office. One was integrated into the smoke alarm in the twelve-foot-high ceiling. The other was behind a cold air return at ceiling level in the other end of the two rooms.

The tape began with a fairly clear picture of Newman coming into his office and throwing his overcoat on the chair. The time-code at the bottom of the screen recorded the time and date and the running time of what Harrod was watching. Then Newman was partially out of view as he walked into the other room to stand by the fireplace.

"I need to switch tapes for the next sequences," the watch chief said as he ejected the first tape and put in a second one. "This is the camera behind the register up high in the corner. It's going to be kind of hard to see what's going on, but I think I've figured it out." The second tape began with Newman's back as he entered from the outer room and came into view for this camera. The view was looking down into the room, across the fireplace from the side, and from this angle it was not possible to see inside the fireplace.

"We can't see everything, but watch what happens when he starts to stretch by the fireplace. Right there— did you see it?"

"See what? I didn't see anything."

The man rewound the tape a bit and repeated the sequence. "There—did you see the mantel move?"

Harrod did see the movement of the mantel of the fireplace as it recessed a few inches into the masonry.

"Look at the way Major—I mean, Lieutenant Colonel—Newman reacted, Dr. Harrod. He stumbled and nearly lost his balance. It's clear that he didn't expect that to happen."

"Expect what to happen?"

The watch chief pointed to the monitor. Newman was quickly grabbing at the fireplace grate and the logs. Then his body blocked the camera's view. He seemed to be doing some kind of action inside the fireplace.

"What's he doing? Did he break something? What's so important about this surveillance tape?" Harrod asked impatiently.

Then the video screen showed Newman standing, then turning to face the camera, holding a package of some kind.

"What is that?" Harrod asked.

"It looks like a file folder, sir."

"Where'd he get it? It looks like he pulled it out of the fireplace."

The two men watched as Newman took the package to his desk and sat down, opened the file folder, and spread out the documents on his desk. The watch chief ejected the tape and put the first one back into the video player. He fast-forwarded the action to the point where Newman sat down at his desk. The camera was positioned right over the desk and gave a perfect view of the documents spread out on Newman's desk. All the men could read, however, were the *TOP SECRET* legends on the folders.

"Can you zoom in on those documents? I need to know what he's reading. It doesn't look like anything I gave him. Look, that blue folder is for the President— that's the presidential seal. He's got very sensitive, secret files in his office. I need to know what they are and how he got 'em."

"I'll get right on it, Dr. Harrod. You'll have my work on your desk when you arrive in the morning."

"Can you zoom in on that stuff now?"

The watch chief grabbed a patch cord to route the video through a video editor nearby. By the time he had finished the connections, the program was up and running. After keying in some commands, he cued the tape to the overhead shot of the office desk and did a freeze-frame of the scene.

He clicked the mouse and magnified the picture. It was now somewhat grainy, so he fiddled with it until the picture was clear. Then he magnified it once more, fiddled some more, and the documents were readable. The watch chief reached over and pushed the *Play* button on the video player, which then began to play back the surveillance tape on two monitors—the first one showing the wide angle of the room, and the second showing the highly magnified close-up of the documents on the desk.

"Well, I'll be . . ." Harrod said disbelieving. "Look at the dates. From the sixties . . . no, those are eights . . . from the eighties—that stuff is from the Reagan-Bush period." Then Harrod's eyes widened. "Of course," he grinned. "I forgot whose office that was. North must've hidden those files. There's a secret hiding place in that fireplace."

The two men watched awhile longer and saw Newman collect the files, put them back into the pouch, and walk into the other room. Then they switched tapes again to see if there was any telling detail as to where the hiding place was. The camera angle was still not positioned well enough to see inside the fireplace. Newman was bent over for nearly a full minute before standing again.

"He put it somewhere inside . . ." Harrod said.

"Yes, and I think I know where. Look at this." The watch chief rewound the tape to the place where the mantel first moved and Newman bent down. "See there, he grabbed the grate and logs and set them on the floor in front of the fireplace. The hiding place must be inside the fireplace, otherwise he wouldn't have moved the grate."

"Yes . . ." Harrod said slowly, still entranced with the tape. Then he said, "Who knows about this?"

"You and me, sir. I was watching the surveillance tape bank, and it happened just before the 2300 hours' shift change. I took out the tapes and put in new tapes because Lieutenant Colonel Newman had already left his office. I called you right after that. No one else knows."

"Keep it that way," Harrod ordered.

"Do you want me to have some NSC security people go up to his office and check it out?"

"No, don't do anything! I'll take it from here." Harrod knew that if some NSC operators swept Newman's office, Newman would know it. The National Security Advisor remembered how Newman had reacted to being followed, and he didn't want the Marine's over-active (*though accurate,* Harrod mused) suspicions to gum up works for the UN mission ahead. Harrod took the surveillance tapes with him, stopping only to put them in the safe in his office.

He reasoned that this would be a good test of New-man's loyalty. If he came forward and admitted to finding them, he could be trusted. If he didn't, well . . .

Harrod wasn't sure what he'd do about it if Newman didn't turn over those files. There was no hurry to get a look at them—they'd been buried in that safe for all these years; another few weeks wouldn't matter. He was sure of one thing, however. He would have to increase surveillance on his Special Projects officer.

Headquarters, Joint Special Operations Command
Fort Bragg, North Carolina
Saturday, 24 December 1994
0945 Hours, Local

Lieutenant Colonel Peter Newman hadn't planned on spending Christmas Eve at Fort Bragg, North Carolina, but when he accelerated the schedule at Harrod's urging, the training for the ISEG had started on Monday, December 5, rather than January 2, as Newman had originally planned. The team had been hard at it since they returned from Washington, but Harrod wanted them to be ready for deployment in thirty days, and that meant setting aside any thought of holidays. Newman knew that he could have simply taken a few days off for Christmas, but he'd never believed in asking his troops to do something he wouldn't do. So, if they had to train over the holidays, he would be with them. He had called his wife to tell her why he wouldn't be home with her for yet another Christmas. As he expected, she didn't understand and went to be with her parents in Culpepper, Virginia. The ISEG had begun their training using the Delta operators at Bragg as "aggressors." Based on the assumption that the ISEG's first mission would be to capture or kill General Mohammed Farrah Aidid, they didn't want to make the same mistakes that had been made in '93 when Task Force Ranger descended on Mogadishu. Thus, the input from those who had already been there was invaluable.

This time, ISET Echo would be inserted by parachute to establish an advanced operations base outside the city, somewhere in the Somali desert. Then ISET Bravo—the all-black unit and the one designated to carry out the hit on Aidid—would parachute in and join them. Once they had a secure base, ISET Bravo would don local garb and make its way into the city. According to the plan, the rest of the ISEG would proceed to Djibouti aboard the repainted MD-80, complete with an Aer Lingus tail number, ID markings, and a UN humanitarian relief logo. If all proceeded according to plan, the MD-80 would be pre-positioned at the airport in Djibouti, a field controlled by the French foreign legion. Newman, Coombs, and McDade planned to run the operation from there. Robertson, the Air Force officer detailed to the Special Projects Office, would stay in Washington and monitor the satellite phones at the OEOB and, at least theoretically, send help if needed.

Newman had been planning the operation for several weeks and was still not satisfied. The team would be at a distinct disadvantage on the ground without mobility, and in particular, without armor. The vague and uneasy similarity to the situation that his brother faced in 1993 made him concentrate on all their options and review them over and over. The last thing Newman wanted in the world was to have history repeat itself.

His three assistants each contributed to the overall plan, but it was Newman who took responsibility for the details. He reviewed the known facts with each of the men and sought their input. Then each night, Newman, Weiskopf, Macklin, Coombs, McDade, Robertson, and Sergeant Major Gabbard worked late into the night, searching for vulnerabilities and ways to reduce them. "I don't want to go in there without every man knowing not only his job but the job of each of his fellow team members. If things fall apart in the field, I want you guys to be able to pick up and fill in for any of your team members who might become casualties," Newman told them during training exercise one morning.

No one groused about having to train over Christmas. The consensus of the team was clear—to get the job done and come home as soon as possible. *Their* holiday would have to wait.

Earlier that morning, a CIA station chief from Africa had briefed them. "Things have gotten much worse since October of '93. When the President pulled out all American troops and closed the embassy, we had to go to deep cover operations," he said. "Our intelligence is pretty skimpy these days. But we've put a priority on it and will give it some intense coverage over the next few weeks while your guys finish training. The last thing any of us wants is another Mogadishu bloodbath."

Newman nodded. "Do we have any locals on our side—guys we can trust?"

The CIA man shrugged. "We like to think so, but in that part of the world, loyalty is a commodity often bought and sold. I wouldn't count on too much. Once you're there, and if a couple of these guys seem reliable, you can use 'em. If they stay with you, they won't be able to give you up to Aidid's mercenaries. If they buck at anything, you'll have to use your own judgment as to what to do. They might become 'casualties of war' if you feel they can't be trusted. Once they know you're there, you won't be able to let 'em out of your sight or your mission might be compromised. Remember that."

Newman nodded again. The CIA man gave him a CD. "There are some more up-to-date after-action reports, and stuff like that on here. I'm supposed to let you copy it onto your laptop and take it back with me." He handed it to Newman, who slid it into the CD slot on his portable computer and transferred the information to his hard drive. After Sergeant Major Gabbard did the same thing, the CIA man took the silver-colored disk back.

He then said, "When you're finished with the material, erase it right away. And remember, you won't be able to copy this to any other computer or e-mail it to another source. It's encrypted, but your EL-3 will open the file. Just remember, the computer files have a built-in destruct sequence that will do some nasty things to your computer if you forget and try to copy or even print out stuff. Then it destroys all the information that you imported from the CD, and after that it attacks your hard drive, just in case you tried to translate the material in some other form to disguise it."

"Yeah," Newman replied, "I've worked with these CDs when I was in Ops and Plans at HQMC. I know the drill . . . I forgot once—it only takes once," he smiled, "but thanks for the reminder."

"Uh-huh." The CIA man nodded. "By the way, speaking of the Marines, what's the deal on this mission? My call to come and brief you came from the NSC and not the Marines."

Newman looked at him with a blank expression on his face. "How long have you been with the agency?" Without waiting for an answer, he added quickly, "You ought to know the drill by now. You don't ask questions. If you weren't told what we're doing, it's because of a 'need to know' protocol. Sorry, but that's all you need to know."

"Yeah, I know. But this seemed kinda out of the usual SOP for these kinds of things. I mean . . . you're a Marine, and the CIA and the Marines work together a lot. But I noticed that some of the guys on your team are from all branches of the services. Sounds important—like something I'd like to be in on."

Newman didn't tell him that he had seen only the tip of the iceberg—in addition to people from all branches of the U.S. military, the British and the United Nations were also involved. When the CIA man left, Newman once again had an uneasy feeling. Because of the way the NSC had contacted the CIA for the intelligence they needed, they had sparked more speculation—and a potential leak—than if they had simply stuck to the normal way of doing things.

He called in Sergeant Major Gabbard and asked him to take care of several of the details relating to the team training and to send a vehicle to pick them up at noon for another daily briefing/planning session to be conducted after lunch.

Newman then shut his door and began to review the CIA intelligence reports, committing important facts and secret information to memory so he could relate them to troops and then delete the files on his computer. Ordinarily, with the EncryptionLok-3, he'd feel secure, but for the past couple of weeks Newman had sensed that he was being watched. At first he dismissed the feeling as just a normal case of nerves before a mission—or perhaps the kind of paranoia that General Komulakov had said comes with a history of cynicism and suspicion. Yet, since the days following his trip to the UN, he sensed that he was being followed. He had even "made" one of those who had shadowed him—a young man in his twenties tailing him in Georgetown when he stopped into a restaurant and checked on the wait for a table. Looking at his watch, Newman had felt that the forty-five-minute wait was too much and decided to try another place up the street. As soon as he left the restaurant and strode across Wisconsin Avenue, the man, who had been sitting on a park bench outside the restaurant, looked surprised and jumped up much too quickly. Tail suspected.

When Newman noticed his "shadow," he decided to cross M Street to a different restaurant to see if the man still followed. At first he kept walking on the same side of the street in the direction the two of them had been walking. But when Newman crossed back over to the north side of M Street, the shadow also turned and headed back in the direction from which he'd come. Tail confirmed. *No doubt one of Harrod's stupid tests,* he told himself. *Well, I won't give him the benefit of keeping me off balance—I'll keep this to myself.*

But the surveillance hadn't stopped after Newman confronted Harrod. When he drove to and from home, he was sure he was being tailed, alternating between a bronze Odyssey van and a white Olds Aurora. His travels were unscheduled and at various hours. The odds of their mutual commute being coincidental were too astronomical to consider. He concluded that it was not a coincidence.

He never got a good look at any of the drivers, but he recognized the cars when they appeared regularly. He wrote down the license number of the van when he saw it on the way home from the White House one night. Using the computer and data access system in his office, he traced the tag and found that it was an "unissued" number—it didn't exist. The next time he saw the van, he was leaving home to run an errand to the hardware store about two miles from his house. The van had pulled out after he passed it, and he slowed to let it creep closer. Then when he got to the main intersection, he sped up and did a 180-degree turn and raced back toward the bronze van. It turned right at the next corner before Newman could get to it. He stopped to write down the license—this time it had New Jersey plates—but he got only the first two letters.

By the time he flew from Andrews Air Force Base to Fort Bragg, Newman felt justified for his paranoia. There *were* people following him, watching him, and somehow they knew his schedule. If he left early, they were there. If he was late, they still appeared. It's likely that a less experienced person would not have noticed as many of the incidents as Newman did. The tails were good, but not good enough for Newman, who had spent most of his military career as a reconnaissance officer, trained to look for things that could get you killed. He knew the drill better than his hunters.

It has to be someone from the White House, he thought as he sat in his temporary office at Fort Bragg. *Or maybe somebody who has White House links—like Komulakov.* He had begun to make notes of who, where, and when during these incidents when he discovered he'd been followed.

He didn't know whether to confront Harrod. Newman reasoned that if he were wrong, then the National Security Advisor might take him off the mission, fearing that its leader had already been identified by unfriendly entities. If, on the other hand, it was Harrod or Komulakov, then the people who were shadowing him were likely countersurveillance or counterintelligence spooks—there to either protect Newman or finger him if he was disloyal.

After weighing it all for several days, he decided to say nothing and simply keep his eyes open. But he also made a mental note to check for bugs at both his home and his office when he returned.

CHAPTER TEN

Heating Up

Office of the Special Projects Officer
Washington, D.C.
Monday, 16 January 1995
0900 Hours, Local

Newman entered his office on the third floor of the
Old Executive Office Building with a headache and
hoped it was just a lack of caffeine to help him start the
day. He had returned late the night before on an Air
Force jet from Pope Air Force Base, which is adjacent
to Fort Bragg. He had gone home to an empty house—
Rachel was on a flight somewhere—done his laundry,
caught a few hours of sleep, and headed back into
Washington. On the way to his office, he had stopped
in the GSA cafeteria on the first floor of the OEOB and
picked up a cup of coffee. He pulled the plastic tab off
the lid to the Styrofoam cup and took a long sip of the
hot, black liquid. He sighed audibly. The coffee made
him feel better.

He took off his coat and hung it on the coatrack. As
he did so a bright, cheery female voice said, "Good
morning, Colonel Newman. There's a fax that you'll

have to authorize decryption for." The voice belonged to First Lieutenant Sonia Duvall, U.S. Army, Simon Harrod's handpicked choice for admin officer in the Special Projects Office. She had arrived while Newman was at Fort Bragg with the ISEG, and though Newman had talked to her on the phone, this was the first time he had met her in person.

"Thanks, Lieutenant. What else is happening?" he asked.

"Nothing much, sir," said the bright-eyed, dark-haired, very attractive young officer. "The fax is for your eyes only. I'm going to the Pentagon to get those maps you requested. Anything you need before I leave?"

Newman said, "No, but I'd like the maps before I leave today. And Lieutenant, I know that it's a nice view out there," Newman pointed out the window, "but I want to make sure that the blinds on these windows are always kept closed—and the drapes as well—day and night so that someone outside doesn't know when we're here. It's just good OPSEC."

Lieutenant Duvall nodded, closed the blinds, pulled the drapes, and then put on her coat. She smiled, waved, and he heard her punching in the exit code to leave the offices. The security door closed with a quiet *thud* behind her, and he heard the lock snap closed with a loud *click*. After she was gone, Newman went to the fax machine and attached his EncryptionLok-3 and got the message to print out from the machine's buffer. It was from General Komulakov, asking him to fly to New York on Wednesday for another briefing at the UN command center. This was the second in ten days, and it was clear to Newman that things were beginning to heat up now that the ISEG was completing its training in Fort Bragg.

He wondered why Komulakov just didn't call him—he could use the EL-3 for the phone as well as the fax. As far as Newman was concerned, flying to New York was a waste of time and money. *What's with this guy?* he thought. *What's so all-fired important that it requires "eyeball to eyeball" contact?* But he faxed back his agreement and shredded the general's message.

Newman returned to his desk and sat down with his coffee. But instead of picking up another revision to the ISEG training schedule that Coombs had placed there for approval, he leaned back and reflected on his nagging sense that something was wrong. He knew that this feeling was normal in combat, but in all his years in the Corps, he'd never experienced it on garrison duty. *But then again, this isn't really garrison duty, is it? Nope. It's duty in the snake pit. Maybe even my office is bugged,* Newman thought.

He made a mental note to give the office a thorough going-over after Lieutenant Duvall left for lunch. Then he edited that thought. *Maybe I'd better think about video and audio surveillance,* he mused. Taking another sip of coffee, he thought, *If I go rummaging around looking for a microphone, the cameras might see me and if there are any cameras, they will probably be wise to me.*

Newman looked around for where a camera might be hidden. He knew from the clandestine work he'd done in Panama when the U.S. military went after Noriega that the CIA had tiny fiber-optic lenses that were as small as a pinhole and could be installed virtually anywhere, but he intuitively decided that if such work was being done at the White House, it would have to be done by people with less field experience, and that they would perhaps be more obvious.

He looked at the cold air return in the other room. *Maybe it's in the register.* In his own office, there was not a register high enough where a camera would do any good. But there was such a register in the adjoining office. Then he saw the smoke alarm. *It could be there too. Or maybe in both places.*

There was a picture of George Washington on the far wall that he had inherited with the office—*It could be built into the frame,* he thought. As he drank his coffee, he saw three other spots that might have a camera hidden.

Even the fireplace, he thought. Then Newman remembered the discovery of the safe weeks earlier. He had not gone back into it since he first found the mysterious files. A sense of dread suddenly swept over him. Those files! They were marked *TOP SECRET,* and some of them were intended only for the former president. Even though he had the top security clearances, he could still get in trouble for having these files. It occurred to him that they had his fingerprints all over them. And if he *were* under surveillance, they'd be sure to question why he had looked at the files and done nothing to resolve the matter of their ultimate possession, control, and disposition.

It was truly a dilemma. As one Marine to another, Newman would like to have Oliver North's take on what the files in his old office safe meant and what he should do with them. If the National Security Advisor or the administration took possession of them, there was no telling what might be done with and to them.

Newman went about his business and waited awhile before doing anything. Then he surreptitiously took a paper clip and a new number-two wooden pencil from his desk. He held the items in his left hand under the desk while he used his right hand to pick up a copy of *Newsweek*, pretending to browse through it. He spread the magazine open on the desktop and slowly dropped his right hand underneath by the other one. Under the desk, his hands worked quickly and skillfully. First he spread the paper clip apart and jammed one end of it through the eraser on the pencil. When he could feel equal lengths of the paper clip on either side of the eraser, he bent the wire in half, into a V shape, so that it looked almost like a divining rod, with the pencil eraser holding the two prongs of the paper clip. As he bent over the magazine, he slipped the strange item into his shirtsleeve.

He sat there another few minutes, in case his movements had attracted attention. Then he got up and walked toward the photocopier. Its power source was plugged into a duplex socket next to the counter where the paper was stacked. He took his magazine and put it in the carrier, ostensibly to make a copy of an article. When the copier light went on and the top carrier moved forward to make the copy, Newman slipped the little "tool" out of his sleeve and down into his left hand. Feeling for the outlet behind him, he turned the pencil so that the twin metal prongs were spread toward the openings for the AC plug. When he was sure that his fingers were not touching anything grounded, Newman used the wooden pencil to push the paper clip ends into the twin holes. There was a *zzz-ttt* sound as the paper clip shorted the circuit. The copier made a *clunk* sound and stopped. In the same instant, all the lights and appliances were disabled with the resulting short circuit. In the panel down the hall in the service room, a circuit breaker popped.

Whoever had designed the Special Operations Office

had done a good job. Because the room was expected to be used during crises, it had been designed with both regular venetian blinds and then an inner set of blackout drapes so that anyone looking up at the room from E Street or the Ellipse wouldn't know that someone was in the office "burning the midnight oil." Newman's rule about keeping the blinds and curtains in the Special Projects Office always closed as a general security precaution now paid off. The room was in almost total darkness. A little light from the computer backup power source gave Newman enough illumination to do his search for surveillance mikes or cameras. He was betting (and hoping) that any cameras were hardwired into the ceiling lights or wall circuits and also went dark with the copier and lights.

If that were the case, someone watching the screens would notify the custodial crew that a circuit had blown in the offices and have someone check it and turn the power back on. If no one noticed the power failure, Newman would call it in himself. In any event, he now had maybe five, or at most ten, minutes to check out the place. First, he stood atop his desk and checked out the smoke alarm. He used the small screwdriver from his desk drawer to pry off the hinged cover. *I was right,* he thought, *and in such an obvious place.* He replaced the cover and went over to the portrait of George Washington. *Nothing there.* Then he checked the other places he'd picked. *Nothing there, either.* Finally, he took a chair from beside his desk and stood on it to reach the cold air register in the opposite end of the other office. *Bingo!* He found a second camera. Newman screwed the register back in place and got down from the chair. He went to other possible sites and found nothing. Then he checked his watch. Only seven minutes had gone by.

He gambled that he still had time to go get the files out of the safe and take them to a safer place.

He struggled for awhile trying to find the exact spots on the mantel that would activate the opening in the floor of the fireplace. After some forty seconds of pushing and pulling, the mantel finally moved. Once again, he had to grab the grate and logs and set them on the floor. Quickly he reached into the hole in the back wall of the fireplace and opened the drawer of the safe. Reaching inside, he felt for the edge of the file pouch and lifted it out. But as he was doing so, he felt something underneath the file pouch. He pulled out the files, then reached in again and pulled out something much thinner and smaller. He quickly stuck it into his pocket and closed the safe again. He hurried over to his credenza where he kept his briefcase. He tossed the file pouch inside and closed and locked the case.

He went back to the fireplace—now nine minutes had gone by. He had mentally marked the spots on the mantel when it opened so it didn't take as long to close it. When it was fully closed, he replaced the grate and logs, thinking to himself, *I'm glad this mechanism isn't powered by electricity, or I'd be out of business.*

Newman went back to his desk and dialed the number for the building's custodians. "Hello," he said when someone answered. "This is Newman in the Special Projects Office on the third floor. The power is off in my offices. Can you send someone up to fix it?"

Then the lights went on. "Wow, that was fast," Newman said, chuckling. "The power's back now."

The custodial supervisor replied, "I was just going to say that someone else phoned it in about five or ten minutes ago. We sent someone up to check the circuit-breaker box first. That's usually the problem."

"Yeah, I should have thought of that," Newman replied. "Sorry to bother you."

Well, now he knew. There were two cameras, and there was someone watching—someone who phoned in the power failure.

As he sat back down at his desk, Newman recalled the old joke that *even people who are paranoid have enemies*. It didn't seem so funny anymore.

Office of the Commander, Amn Al-Khass
Special Security Service Headquarters
Palestine Street, Baghdad, Iraq
Monday, 16 January 1995
2100 Hours, Local

"I know what your father wants. Please do not forget, my dear brother-in-law, I am married to your sister, but I owe it to her father and yours to tell you of my reservations about bringing him here," Kamil Hussein said, almost pleading.

Qusay Hussein looked at his brother-in-law, disgust plainly written on his face. "Just do what you have to do, Kamil. Osama bin Laden is coming. You are going to be the big man at the party. And in the end, when Osama's martyrs make history by attacking the Jews and their American and British friends, you will be a hero.

"He has demonstrated that he can kill Americans with nothing more than a few conventional explosives and a handful of loyal and dedicated followers. Your job is to make it possible for him to do even more. My father has decided that you will help him. The weapons in your laboratories are to be made available to him, and you are to give him whatever he needs. Is that clear?" Qusay spoke with a sneer that was now almost always on his lips when talking to Kamil. Qusay's operatives from the *Mukhabarat* had gone to Khartoum and made contact with Osama. They were now standing by in the outer office, prepared to brief Kamil.

Through these emissaries, bin Laden had boasted to Saddam of his accomplishments: the attacks on American troops overseas in Maadi . . . at Clark Air Force Base in the Philippines . . . a USO club in Barcelona . . . the October '93 attack in Mogadishu, Somalia . . . the kidnapping of Americans in Indonesia . . . the routing of the Russians in Chechnya . . . the bomb in Moscow that killed 113 Russian civilians . . . and, of course, the bombing of the World Trade Center in New York in February 1993. Although just six people were killed, more than a thousand were injured, and the pictures on TV and headlines in world newspapers gave credence to bin Laden's claim that he had brought fear to the United States as he introduced "war" with the infidel Americans in their own land. "Not even the Japanese or Germans in World War II, not even the Russians, were able to do that," he boasted. "Next time, we'll bring those towers to the ground," bin Laden told Qusay's Iraqi operatives. "All I need is a bigger bomb."

Kamil wondered if bin Laden's revelation might have been made in order to get Iraq to help him acquire a nuclear bomb—but they were still years away from that achievement. *Besides,* Kamil thought, *if the world ever found out that Iraq had provided bin Laden with nuclear weapons—or any other weapons of mass destruction, for that matter—the West would bomb Iraq into oblivion.* For that reason, Kamil was opposed to offering too much help to bin Laden.

The shabby-looking master of terrorism had even sent a videotape to be shown to his newfound friends in Iraq, prior to his visit. In it bin Laden, more than six feet tall with a stringy, unkempt beard, went on for the greater part of an hour reciting his many accomplishments, boasting that he had been appointed by Allah to destroy the Americans and British so that the Islamic world would finally be free of their satanic influences.

Kamil had said nothing while Qusay played the tape, but now he was expected to explain to Saddam's favorite son just what he, Kamil, head of the Special Security Service and, more importantly, the minister in charge of developing weapons of mass destruction for the Iraqi regime, would be doing for their "special guest" when he arrived in March.

Osama had made clear in the videotape what his expectations were. "I trust you, my Islamic brothers, to make sure that there are no traitors among you who would jeopardize our plans. I am telling you things that could compromise my plans and bring them and myself to destruction if word of them were leaked. However, we are brothers in the faith, and I trust you with my life."

I am not sure that I would trust my life to any of these men, Kamil thought, looking at his brother-in-law, who was sitting in the chair beside him in rapt attention as the tape played. Osama droned on in generalities about his future attacks. "Soon the whole world will watch as I make my boldest attack on the enemy to date. I will strike the great Satan where it will be felt the greatest and bring the nation to its knees with such fear and trembling that they will plead with us to let them surrender. My plan calls for loyal martyrs to bring about the destruction of various American landmarks—

one, a symbol of capitalism and wealth; one, a symbol of military power, and the other two, the very icons of their government and leadership. I will thoroughly cripple them and their entire nation—yes, even the entire Western world will fall to its knees in total fear and surrender. Praise be to Allah."

At this point, Kamil hit the *Pause* button on the remote. "Qusay," he said seriously, "does your father know that if Osama somehow manages to destroy America that he stands to lose a fortune, given all that he has invested in the American stock market?"

Qusay looked annoyed. "Of course. Osama has said that he will tell us before he attacks so that we may divest ourselves before the American market collapses. My Mukhabarat informants tell me that Osama himself is also heavily invested in the U.S. But I'll make certain he tells us before so that we can protect our assets."

Kamil hit *Play,* and the diatribe continued. "I have several options for carrying out these attacks on the Great Satan. If one plan fails, I have several backup plans so that success will be guaranteed." Kamil wondered if the man would ever stop to take a breath, but the tape continued. "For some of these, I will need your help. And in return, I will be your servant to help you, my brother Saddam, and your great country," bin Laden said. "But we must meet soon to plan these with some of my most trusted followers, and plan our objectives—yours and mine—for the assured destruction of our common enemies. I know that I can help you, and you have resources that I will need."

Qusay had been convinced from the beginning that bin Laden could be the spark that would ignite a resurgence of the recognition, power, and glory that Iraq had enjoyed before the terrible war that the Americans and

British had launched upon them. After hearing Osama tell plainly of his accomplishments, his father Saddam had also been convinced that Iraq should provide the terrorist with whatever he needed.

"Yes," Saddam had said loudly and forcefully after viewing the tape. "We will be partners. I believe that we each have something of significance to bring to the table. Yet the synergy of our combined efforts can have an exponential power. We will do it."

So now it was up to Kamil to see the partnership carried out.

"But we must meet within the borders of our country. The West will be tracking every move, every breath, of my father. He takes regular holidays at his palace in Tikrit, so that will make a perfect place. It is also heavily guarded, with air defense installations all around the area for hundreds of kilometers," Qusay told Kamil.

"I have sent a message to Osama informing him that my father's palace in Tikrit is where we will meet. The date is set for March 6, less than two months from now. He has agreed to create some diversionary events that would make the Americans and the rest of the West look away at things happening elsewhere."

"What kind of events?" asked Kamil, feeling the acid eating into his stomach ulcer.

"I don't know; he wouldn't share that with my couriers, although they have now been back and forth to Sudan three times. All he would say was that it would be a good time to kill Americans."

"Where?"

"Who cares?" Qusay shrugged. "Anywhere you can kill Americans is a good place."

"What does your father want me to do?" Kamil was now completely submissive. "The SSS will of course ensure bin Laden's safety when he's here, but how do you expect me to get him in and out of the country without the Americans or, worse yet, the Jews finding out?"

"I asked that question," replied Qusay. "Bin Laden told my most trusted courier, Jamal, the one who takes care of my father's investments, that he would take care of it. In fact, he wrote me a note," he said and handed Kamil a note written in flowing Arabic characters, which Kamil read:

> *Thank you for your kind invitation. Please allow me to make my own travel arrangements to your country. I cannot permit another to act for me in these matters. I must maintain autonomy. This is no reflection on you or your great abilities, my friend. But I always make my own plans for internal and external movement. I will be at the meeting in March, but you must let me make my own plans as a precaution.*

Kamil nodded. That was fine with him. If something untoward happened to bin Laden, he knew that he would be shot by a firing squad—his execution order signed by his own brother-in-law or Saddam himself.

The meeting ended without Kamil ever meeting the couriers who had traveled back and forth between Baghdad and Khartoum. As he rose to depart, Qusay said, "Kamil, when Osama arrives at my father's palace in Tikrit, he expects to see you there with at least two of each of your best chemical and biological weapons. And if you can build a nuclear weapon smaller than a truck by then, bring two of them." With that, the young man who was the heir apparent to the presidential palace walked out the door without bothering to say good-bye.

The commander of the Amn Al-Khass sat back down at his desk and put his head in his hands. But he wasn't thinking about the meeting with Osama bin Laden in Tikrit on March 6. Instead, he was hoping that he could find some workable way to get out of Iraq and seek asylum in the West.

Parking Garage, FBI Building
Washington, D.C.
Monday, 16 January 1995
1300 Hours, Local

Newman had just finished a briefing at the FBI offices and returned to his car. Inside he took out his wallet and fished out a business card that was stuck in an inside pocket. It said *Keller's Auto Repairs and Service.* As he exited the J. Edgar Hoover Building's underground parking garage, he took out his mobile phone and dialed the phone number listed on the card. A voice answered, and Newman asked, "Do I have time to get in today for an oil and filter change?" He paused for a response then said, "Great. Is two o'clock all right? Good. Oh, by the way, I want a wash and the inside swept out. Can you do that too? Excellent. I'll be there at two." He looked at his watch and saw that he had enough time to run through McDonald's for a quick lunch before heading for Keller's Auto Repairs and Service.

He pulled the Tahoe into the two-bay service station on Clarendon Boulevard just a few minutes before 2:00 P.M. As he got out of his car, Newman was met by a middle-aged man with the name "Ed Keller" embroidered over one pocket and a patch that said "Manager."

Keller led Newman over to a nearby empty bay, asking him what kind of work he wanted done.

"I need your help, Ed. You gave me your card when we worked together four years ago. You used our Second Force Recon guys to support your CIA team when you tried to spring some defectors from—"

"Yeah, I remember. Newman, right?"

The two men spent a few minutes with small talk then Newman told him about his problem. "Ed, I need your help. And I'll have to ask for your discretion on this. I'm not sure, but I'm concerned that my car may have been bugged. And I need to know, without anyone else finding out that I'm suspicious. I know this sounds a little paranoid, but in the line of work we were once in, a little paranoia can keep you alive. Can you check the vehicle and just let me know if you find anything? And if you do find anything, don't disarm it or touch it, just let me know. I don't want to let anyone else know just yet that I'm on to them."

"Gotcha, man. Any idea who planted 'em?"

"Yeah, maybe," Newman said. "It might be another set of good guys who are worried about a joint venture we're about to take together. Probably just want to cover their six, y'know?"

The CIA agent nodded and went over to one of the employees and showed him a box that he had checked on the clipboard list. The other man nodded, went into the supply room, and came back with a large, battered toolbox. He opened it and took out a small set of wires attached to a wand, which was hooked up to a small oscilloscope. While another worker lifted the hood and began to drain the oil out of the engine, the man with the electronic equipment searched underneath the vehicle. Then he came up from the pit and went inside the car—with a hand vacuum that he didn't turn on—and searched the inside for electronic bugs.

"You're clean, Mr. Newman," he said at last.

Then the other worker was done changing the oil and filter, and he closed the hood.

"That'll be $24.80. I'm giving you the senior discount," Keller said with a smile.

"Very funny."

"Will it be cash or plastic?"

"Credit card," Newman replied and handed over his American Express card.

"He's our best guy for doing a sweep," Ed Keller told Newman as he signed the credit card slip. "If he says it's clean, it's clean."

"Yeah, that's reassuring. But a guy has to be careful out there, right?"

"He sure does. Well, you take it easy, Mr. Newman. Stay outta trouble."

Newman nodded and climbed into his car while one of the workers wiped an oil smudge from the edge of the hood. As he drove out of the service station, Newman felt better. Tucking the credit card slip into his pocket, he felt the small object that he'd stuffed there when he took the files out of what he now mentally referred to as *the fireplace safe.*

He took it out and looked at it. It was an American passport. When he stopped at the light on Massachusetts Avenue he opened it to see whose it was. Inside was a photograph of Oliver North. But the name under the picture was "William P. Goode."

He was distracted from examining the passport by a horn honking behind him. The driver threw an obscene gesture his way, and Newman looked up to see that the light had changed. He put the passport back into his pocket and turned to head back into Washington. On the east side of the Roosevelt Bridge, Newman got in the left lane to pick up the expressway that would take him directly to the South West Gate at the White House. As he came to a halt for the light at Seventeenth Street, he made his decision. Before telling anyone else about the contents of the safe, he would find out once and for all what all this was about. But that would have to wait until he got back to Fort Bragg later in the week.

CHAPTER ELEVEN

The Postcard

Narnia Farm
Bluemont, VA
Monday, 30 January 1995
0900 Hours, Local

It was a postcard in a stack of Monday morning mail. Lieutenant Colonel Oliver North, USMC (Ret.), probably wouldn't have taken the time at that moment to read it except that it was a picture that every Marine knows well—a photograph of the statue at the north end of Arlington Cemetery, the Iwo Jima Memorial. North read the caption on the postcard:

> *Six men, in battle dress, straining to raise an American flag atop an extinct volcano on a tiny atoll in the Pacific on February 23, 1945. The moment captured in 1/400th of a second by Joe Rosenthal, an Associated Press photographer. The statue, sculpted by Felix de Weldon, is a five-times life-size, three-dimensional rendering of Rosenthal's Pulitzer Prize–winning black-and-white photo. The six Marines, intent in their purpose,*

stand like silent sentinels overlooking the nation's capital.

North turned the card over and read a carefully hand-printed note:

IRONHAND THREE ACTUAL, URGENT. REQ U RNDVU W/ FOX TWO ACTUAL AT SURIBACHI AT 1930 ON TUE, 7 FEB; WED, 8 FEB; OR THURS, 9 FEB. DO NOT BREAK EMCON. FOX TWO SENDS.

"Ironhand Three" had been North's radio call sign when he served as the Operations Officer—or the "S-3" in military-speak—for Battalion Landing Team 3/8 in the Mediterranean in 1980. "Fox Two" was the commander of the Second Platoon of Company F. The former Marine stood staring at the postcard for a full minute while he tried to wring from his memory banks which of the bright-eyed, young lieutenants had commanded the Second Platoon of Foxtrot Company.

He was about to give up when he remembered something. North strode over to the bookcase in his office and pulled a copy of the Third Battalion, Eighth Marine Regiment "Cruise Book" from the shelf. Much like a high school or college yearbook, it was a neatly bound collection of photos, notes, and memories of the unit's seven-month deployment as the landing force for the Sixth Fleet in the Mediterranean Sea in 1980. Best of all, it contained rosters and photos of every sailor and Marine in the command.

Next to the title "Platoon Leader, 2nd Platoon, Co. F, BLT 3/8" was the caption "2nd Lt. Peter J. Newman." And there were pictures of him—one staring straight into the camera and another in front of his platoon formation. He was tall, straight, thin, and fifteen years younger than he would be today. He looked like a Marine recruiting poster model. And there was a third black-and-white photo. In this candid shot, the camera had caught him giving an order during a live-fire field exercise.

North recognized the terrain: Capo Teulada, Sardinia—the NATO live-fire training area. In the photo, the young Lieutenant Newman was holding a map in one hand and pointing out in the distance. His helmet and flak jacket were covered with dust. His radio operator at his side, the four other men in the photograph must have been his platoon sergeant and three squad leaders. The caption beneath the photo said, "Lt. Newman prepares 2nd Platoon for the night attack exercise."

It all came back, unlocking North's memory. Newman had been leading a Marine rifle platoon in a simulated night attack when one of the Italian Puma helicopters flying over his unit had flown literally into the side of a mountain, six hundred yards off the Second Platoon's right flank. Lieutenant Newman, ten of his Marines, and a Navy medical corpsman rushed to the scene, and despite a fiercely burning fuel-fed fire, the lieutenant had personally rescued four of the helicopter's injured occupants before they could be immolated in the wreckage. He then skillfully directed medevac helicopters and rescue teams to the site.

Newman, two of his Marines, and the Navy corpsman all suffered burns themselves but refused to be evacuated until after the more seriously injured Italian troops had been flown for treatment to the ships standing offshore. A few days later, when the Amphibious Squadron pulled into Naples for a five-day port visit, Admiral Crannick, the commander of NATO Forces in the Mediterranean, awarded the Navy-Marine Corps Lifesaving Medal to Lieutenant Newman, Corporal Ronnie Evans, PFC Filipé Enriquez, and HM3 Harold Benn.

Not to be outdone, the Italians had insisted on presenting an honor of their own: the Military Order of St. Boniface. Unlike the U.S. award, which was a medal pinned above the left breast pocket, the Italian decoration was a large medallion, suspended by a broad, multicolored ribbon to be hung around the neck. An Italian admiral gave a lengthy speech that no one could understand and, at its conclusion, insisted on kissing Newman several times on each cheek after he hung the medal around Newman's neck. In keeping with Marine tradition, instead of congratulating Newman on his honors, his fellow lieutenants kidded him incessantly, asking if he and the Italian admiral were now going steady.

Holding the postcard and looking at the Cruise Book, North remembered that, shortly after the battalion returned from its deployment to the Med in 1981, Lieutenant Newman had received orders to the Basic School at Quantico as a tactics instructor. It was a plum assignment—one that North had himself held upon his return from Vietnam. In fact, before departing Camp Lejeune for Quantico, Newman and his wife had come over to North's quarters to talk about what the Basic School would be like.

North also remembered that his wife Betsy and Newman's wife Rachel seemed to hit it off at once. Neither of them totally understood what their husbands did for a living, and they laughed together when Betsy began sharing. Rachel seemed to enjoy talking to another woman who understood how frustrating it was to move four times in eight years and how she could never expect her Marine husband to provide her with a daily routine and schedule that she might depend on when scheduling important family events like birthday parties. Rachel had identified with all of Betsy's frustrations and offered several examples of her own of what it was like to be a junior officer's wife in the Corps.

Before Newman and his wife left that night, North had given Newman some of his old infantry tactics lesson plans that he'd used to good effect.

Shortly after Newman left the battalion, North was ordered to the Naval War College in Newport, Rhode Island, and then to the National Security Council staff at the White House. North recalled reading in the *Marine Corps Gazette* that Newman had been deep-selected—promoted early—to captain. And North had seen him briefly five years later when Newman had been a student at the Marine Corps' Amphibious Warfare School and North had been sent there by the NSC to give a lecture on counterterrorism.

When they met that day in 1986 at Amphibious Warfare School, Newman had a few more wrinkles around the eyes from too many days in the sun, but he had the same firm handshake and the same quiet confidence. That was the last time North had seen him. And he hadn't heard from him at all in the nine years since. But now he had this postcard with a cryptic note from him. At least North thought it was from him.

He looked again at the postcard. It was postmarked January 23, 1995—a week earlier—from Fort Bragg, North Carolina. It wasn't all that unusual to be getting mail from a Marine at an Army base—lots of Marines served in joint commands, attending other service's schools and going through their training. What made

North more curious was the cryptic wording of the card's message.

Newman, if it indeed *was* Newman who had sent the missive, was asking for an urgent meeting at the Iwo Jima Memorial, hence the reference to Suribachi—the mountaintop where the Marines on the postcard were planting the flag. And for some reason or another, Newman clearly didn't want North to contact him about the request to meet, hence the reference to EMCON.

North's curiosity was thoroughly aroused, so he decided to call an old friend to find out if Peter Newman really was at Fort Bragg.

The phone answered on the second ring: "Brigadier General Murray Stedner, Office of the Deputy Chief of Staff for Plans and Operations, Headquarters Marine Corps."

"Hey, it's North. Man, that's quite an impressive spiel. Do you feel important? You must be important, answering your own phone and all," he chuckled.

"Oliver—hey, it's great to hear from you. Important, eh? Well, nothing I'd rather be doing than pushing paper and kissing more senior generals' backsides ten hours every day."

Stedner hated duty at HQMC. He was known as a "Marine's Marine"—a troop leader who despised staff assignments. He and North had served together at Quantico, gone together to Vietnam, relieved each other in commands from the Western Pacific to the Eastern Mediterranean. They had served together in the Second and Third Marine Divisions. Their wives were thick as thieves, had given birth to kids in the same military hospitals—kids who had subsequently grown up with each other in the same military base schools. Their two families had shared the privations and pains of military housing as neighbors. To say that Stedner and North were friends was an understatement.

They had talked when North had been forced to retire in the aftermath of the Iran-Contra flap, and Stedner had cried right along with North. Only Stedner and other Marines could know the emotion that was attendant to North's forced resignation from the Corps. But Stedner didn't bring up that subject. He stuck to small talk. "What are you doing these days? How's Betsy? And the family?"

North kept the conversation on that level until the two of them were caught up on each other's career moves and family matters. Then Stedner got to the point: "How can I help you, man? I know you didn't call me just to chew the fat. What's up?"

"Well, I'm calling because I'm trying to track down one of my old lieutenants from Third Battalion, Eighth Marines," said North without mentioning the cryptic postcard.

"Who is it?" said Stedner. "I can call up the personnel records on every Marine in the Corps right here on this computer. Give me his name and horsepower."

North could hear his friend tapping the keys of a computer keyboard, shifting from the program he'd been working in to the personnel file. North told him, "I don't have his service number, but his full name is Newman, Peter J."

The clicking on the keyboard stopped, and there was a long pause before Stedner replied. "Why are you asking about Newman, Ollie?"

North, sensing that there was more here than he had at first realized, was suddenly cautious. He would trust Stedner with his life in combat, but who knew who else might be listening in on this conversation or what trouble Newman might be in? He offered a benign reply. "I'm just trying to track him down to rehash some stuff when we served together in the Eighth Marines. You know, I may have another book in me, old man."

"Well, I don't need to run through the personnel records on Newman. He worked here in Ops and Plans until last November. But he was transferred out, and my boss, General Grisham, is handling his assignment personally."

North knew Grisham well. He was one of the most respected officers in the Corps and widely rumored to be a future commandant. "I see," said North. "Can you tell me if Newman's in the area—is he in CONUS . . . is he overseas?"

"Ollie, I can't say. It's a classified assignment. And I know you've had all the clearances, but I don't want to get cross-threaded with General Grisham." Then, as if changing the subject, Stedner said, "Say, by the way, when you went on all those trips overseas, did you ever stop in London and go shopping at that big department store there?"

North knew this wasn't a change in course in the conversation. His friend was offering him information, if he could figure it out. "Uh . . . well I never had much time to go shopping," he said, adding, "I guess you can't tell me what I want to know."

"Sorry, Colonel," Stedner said, "I'm afraid that's all I can say. But it's been great to hear your voice. You know, you and Betsy ought to get together with Anne and me for dinner one of these days soon. I'll have Anne call Betsy and set it up."

"Great idea, buddy. I look forward to it. One thing's for sure—if our wives set it up, we had both better be there; we don't need them telling tales about us behind our backs. Good to talk to you. Semper Fi." North hung up the phone, wondering about the clue Stedner had buried in the conversation. "Harrod's . . . he probably meant the department store in London by that name. Harrod's . . . ?" North asked himself. Then he sat up straight. *Simon Harrod. Newman's at the White House working for the National Security Advisor,* North thought.

Then he began to wonder why. His thoughts came in quick succession. *He doesn't have a background in Russia, so it can't be the Yeltsin coup. What else is happening that the White House needs a recon Marine?* North exhausted the possibilities without coming to a logical conclusion. Still, North reasoned, maybe Newman just didn't want anyone at the current White House to know that he was contacting a controversial member of a former administration. But just to make sure, North decided he would be at the Iwo Jima Memorial at 7:30 P.M. on Tuesday, February 7.

Smiling Buddha Restaurant
Washington, D.C.
Tuesday, 7 February 1995
1820 Hours, Local

As Newman maneuvered his Tahoe through Georgetown's rush hour into the tiny public parking lot on Thirty-third Street, the wipers were working hard to keep the freezing sleet from sticking to the windshield. He was less than a block away from the little Thai restaurant on M Street where Coombs, McDade, Robertson, and he had come to celebrate his being "frocked" as a Lieutenant Colonel a month before. Newman had chosen the place then because he and Rachel had several times enjoyed dinner there and because the price of a good meal was affordable. Being "frocked" meant that if he ever got to don his uniform again, he could wear the silver oak leaves of a Lieutenant Colonel—but he would still be paid as a major until his promotion became official sometime later in the year. But he had chosen this place tonight for an entirely different reason.

Before he got out of the car, he took his gray Marine-issue military trench coat, folded it into the smallest bundle he could make, and stuck it, along with a small collapsible umbrella and the front section of the *Washington Times,* under his bright yellow windbreaker. He had chosen this *L.L. Bean* sailing jacket because it was easy to spot in a crowd. He was also wearing a red baseball cap emblazoned with the Marine Corps' eagle, globe, and anchor embroidered above the bill. He wanted anyone who might be following him to keep watching for the tall guy in the yellow jacket and red hat. He also wanted to be close to the Key Bridge, the shortest route to Arlington Cemetery. He dashed up the hill, around the corner, and into the restaurant between drops of rain.

As Newman entered the crowded little establishment, the proprietor saw him and motioned him to his favorite corner booth in the back.

"Good evening, Mr. Newman . . . no friends tonight?"

"Not tonight, Mr. Sudhap. I just came in out of the cold for a big bowl of your famous egg-drop soup."

"Coming right up!" The owner was as good as his word, and the soup appeared almost instantly, along with a generous portion of crispy rice crackers and a little pot of hot tea. Newman ate quickly, and in less than ten minutes, he placed a ten-dollar bill on the table and got up to leave.

Upon entering he had hung his yellow jacket, with the baseball cap tucked into a pocket, on the coatrack. But now, Newman unfolded and put on his gray military trench coat and a black Greek fisherman's cap that he pulled from its pocket. No one inside noticed that he was dressed differently than when he came in. "I'll just duck out the back way to avoid the rain," he said to the owner, who shrugged and pointed the way to the kitchen.

Newman made his way through the swinging doors at the back of the restaurant, past the chefs and servers stirring woks over a huge gas range with steam tables full of vegetables. As he stopped by the rear door to the alley outside, Newman unfurled his umbrella and stepped out into the darkness, wind, and rain.

Keeping the umbrella low over his face, Newman came out of the narrow alley behind the restaurant onto Thirty-third Street, just up from where he had parked his car. But instead of going to the parking lot, he jay-walked across Thirty-third, turned right, and walked up to M, pacing his stride so he'd arrive at the intersection just as the light changed. A crowd of other pedestrians surrounded him as he crossed M Street. Then he turned left on M, melding into the people dressed just like him, and walked briskly down the busy sidewalk toward Georgetown University. He dared not look back, but he was hoping that anyone who might have followed him to the restaurant would still be outside watching the front door of the place, waiting for a person wearing a yellow windbreaker and a red baseball hat to exit the way he went in. Newman also hoped that his pursuers were getting cold and wet.

When he reached the intersection of M and Thirty-fourth, there was a crowd queuing up at the Metro bus stop. He stepped beneath the awning of a jewelry store with a small knot of prospective passengers and removed the newspaper he had taken from his car. While he pretended to read it, he surveyed the busy thoroughfare he had just traversed, looking for any watchers. He saw none.

A few minutes later, a cab stopped on the corner and discharged a tired-looking, wind-whipped woman. While the woman made change, Newman bolted from the crowd and jumped into the cab before any of the waiting throng could lay claim to its warm, dry interior.

"Rosslyn—Pettyjohn's Sports Bar at the corner of Nash and Colonial," he said to the cabbie, who was glad to have another fare so quickly. The driver pulled back out into traffic and a block later made the left turn onto the Key Bridge and across the Potomac into Virginia.

As they traversed the span, Newman kept looking behind them to see if he had been followed, but all he could see through the fogged-up, sleet-spattered windows of the cars around him were the faces of weary commuters, fleeing home from another hard day in the nation's capital.

It was exactly 1845 hours when Newman stepped out of the cab in front of the bar. A boisterous crowd was standing inside by the doorway, waiting for seats. Instead of entering, Newman walked across Nash Street, down the hill, and turned right. Two blocks later, he entered the Rosslyn Metro station and trotted down the escalator to the platform labeled "Blue Line to National Airport." He slid his FareCard into the slot in the turnstile and stepped onto the crowded platform just as the sleek, rush-hour subway train arrived to discharge one load and take on another. Newman waited until just before the doors closed before boarding the train and pressed himself in with other standees, who were glad to be riding instead of fighting gridlock on the highways to get home.

At the "Pentagon City" stop, Newman got out, took the escalator up to the Mall level, turned left, and went right back down the escalator and turned toward the platform labeled "Blue Line to Addison Road." Once again, he unfolded his newspaper and pretended to read it while he scanned the crowd for anyone he had seen boarding the train in Rosslyn. Again, he saw no familiar faces.

When the train arrived, Newman retraced the route he had just taken and arrived back at the Rosslyn Station at 1915 hours. But when he exited the station on Moore Street, instead of returning to the sports bar where the cab had dropped him, he turned right on Moore and right again at the next corner, then left on Mead Street. As he crossed over U.S. Route 50, he checked his watch again: 1925 hours. He again checked over his shoulder and then slowed his pace to arrive at his destination at precisely the appointed hour.

It was exactly 1930 hours and the rain had stopped when Newman walked down the wet grass, through the pines, and into the shadows cast by the lights shining on the six men in World War II combat gear, straining to raise the flag.

For Newman, like most Marines, there was something wonderfully inspiring about seeing the six huge cast-bronze figures that replicated that stunning photo that is indelibly ingrained in the national consciousness.

He was standing there, peering through a light drizzle at the six men frozen in that unique, historical moment of exertion, when out of the shadows he heard, "Impressive, isn't it, Marine?"

Newman spun around. There in the shadows of the pines, he saw a figure approaching. Though he couldn't make out a face, he could see in the damp darkness the familiar outline of a Marine trench coat—turned almost black by the near-freezing rain and subsequent drizzle. As he walked nearer, the figure spoke again. "Well, Pete, you sure picked a nice night for an outdoor rendezvous."

Newman relaxed. "Hey, Colonel North, you sure got a kick out of my adrenal cortex. Thanks for coming. How are you?"

"Not bad, if I don't catch pneumonia out in this stuff. You know, retired grunts are supposed to be excused from night-training exercises."

Newman, unsure of himself for the first time, looked to see if there was a rebuff in that comment, but North was smiling with his familiar gap-toothed grin.

"I didn't know that the weather was going to be this bad, or I would have arranged to meet in a place more suitable to your advanced age and frail condition, sir," Newman shot back.

North smiled again at the younger man. "So what brings a knight out on a dog like this?"

The two men were now standing next to each other at the edge of the pine trees on the west side of the memorial. To the east, beyond the six men and their flag, the two living men could see Lincoln's rectangular memorial, Washington's tall pillar, with the White House just beyond—and to their right, the dome of the Capitol, all glowing white in the misting rain.

Newman didn't answer. Instead, he reached into his pocket and withdrew the passport he'd removed from the fireplace safe. He handed it to the older man.

Now it was North's turn to be surprised.

"Where'd you get this?" North said after looking at the passport with the name "William P. Goode" typed in beside the picture of a younger, thinner North.

"It was in a safe in my office, along with some files."

For a moment North said nothing. "You're in my old third-floor office?" he asked finally.

"Yes. I'm now the director of the Special Projects Office at the NSC. I report directly to the National Security Advisor."

North looked up from the passport. "Does he know—?" he started to say.

"No one knows, so far. At least I don't think anyone knows," replied Newman.

North's expression showed that he was trying to recall something from a long time ago. "This was in a safe built into a secret compartment in the back wall of the fireplace in my office. How did you know how to open the fireplace?" asked North, still holding the passport.

"Quite by accident . . . not long before I sent you that postcard to set up this meeting. I'd been stretching my back and had grabbed the mantel when it shifted and opened the concealed compartment. The safe inside was unlocked, and the passport was in the drawer."

"Was there anything else in the safe?"

"Yes, a file pouch full of documents. Over a hundred pages, I would guess. I skimmed through them. I couldn't help but notice that a good number of the pages had either been signed or initialed by the President," the younger officer said, his hands now thrust deeply in his pockets to ward off the cold.

"Hmm, that sounds about right. Man . . . after all these years—" North began.

Newman interrupted. "But that's not the main reason I asked you to meet me here tonight. I'm the one with a problem, and I need your advice."

"What's that?" said North.

Newman took a big breath. There was no going back now. But he could trust this man, and he knew it. "The National Security Advisor has directed me to set up a joint U.S.–UK covert unit to go after terrorists and what they call 'international lawbreakers' for the United Nations. The unit is supposed to hunt down individuals selected by the UN, and all of this theoretically has the backing of the President and the Prime Minister of the UK," Newman explained.

"And . . . ?" asked North.

"And I don't know how legal any of this is, but I've been sworn to total secrecy. I can't even talk about it with the commandant, General Grisham, my wife— anybody."

"And you thought that you could talk about it with me because you've come upon some of my old secrets in a hidden safe in my old office?" North put it as a question, but it could have been an accusation.

"No. It's not that at all. I'm looking for some guidance. Colonel, we've served together. I respected you then, and I do now. I'm in over my head in this, and I know it. But I'm thinking that this unit could be the means by which those who killed my brother in Mogadishu are brought to justice. Still, I don't want to get burned like you did. I need some advice."

North paused for a moment before responding. "Let's take these things in order. First, launching a personal crusade from the NSC isn't a very good idea. I got involved in trying to save Americans—some of whom I knew personally—from their being tortured to death in Beirut. Then I got personally involved in trying to help the Nicaraguan Freedom Fighters. I'd come to know and admire them in their fight against a communist regime, and I wanted to help. As a result, my wife and children were targeted by terrorists, and my career was finished. I guess that's the result of getting *personally* involved."

"Would you have done anything any differently had you known the outcome?" interrupted Newman.

North hesitated before answering. "I should have tried harder to get out of the NSC and back to the Marines in '83. But I fell for the line that I was 'invaluable.' Hubris—the great sin. Other than that, would I have done things differently?" He paused again, looking thoughtfully at the monument. "On the whole . . . no."

"Well then—" Newman started to speak.

But North continued. "Second, I think you're smart to have some real questions about this administration expecting U.S. military personnel to serve in some kind of United Nations covert action program. As I recall, the oath we take is 'to support and defend the Constitution of the United States against all enemies, foreign and domestic.' There's nothing in it about the UN Charter."

"But they keep telling me that everything we're being prepared to do is legal and that it's all covered by treaties and international law," said Newman, his breath shining in the light reflected from the six bronze figures.

"Who are 'they'?" asked North.

"The National Security Advisor to the President, Simon Harrod, and a deputy secretary general of the

UN, who's also in charge of all the UN's military and peacekeeping operations. He identifies himself as a Russian general, by the way. From the way he talks, he's former KGB or GRU, I would guess. Neither the CIA nor FBI have much on him. He's apparently spent most of his career here in the States. Talks like he was raised on Long Island."

"How was it pitched to you?" North asked.

"Straightforward. They tell me that what I'll be doing is sanctioned by Article 7 of the UN Charter. I've seen the UN Resolution, the joint U.S.–UK agreement, and the National Security Directive signed by the President. All of them are classified 'top secret'—all with restricted distribution."

"Do you have copies of any of these documents?" asked North.

"No."

North sighed deeply and said nothing for at least fifteen seconds. "How about U.S. law? Have any of the oversight committees given their blessing?"

"I don't know. Dr. Harrod wants me to go up and talk to Senator Waggoner on the Armed Forces Committee."

North snorted. "Senator James Waggoner? I wouldn't trust him any further than I could throw his wizened old body. But then again, I'm probably not the unbiased observer that you need for advice on Congress. I've got too much baggage up on the Hill to be of much help to you there. How about at Headquarters?" North gestured to their right. HQMC was a mile to the south, at the opposite end of Arlington Cemetery.

"As I said, I was told specifically *not* to talk to anyone about this. But I knew I could trust you."

"Well," said North after thinking a moment, "you

can trust General Grisham. If I have my facts straight, you were working for him at HQMC when you got orders to go to the White House. He was C. O. of BLT Three/Eight before you joined the battalion. I know him well. He could probably give you some good advice on this."

North stopped talking and looked at Newman. The younger officer was deep in thought for a few moments, and then he said, "I'll think about that. But for now, I'm going forward, since I haven't encountered anything that would tell me I'm not carrying out a lawful order. Besides, it's not just a matter of picking up the phone and making an appointment to see General Grisham."

"Why is that?" asked North.

"I'm under surveillance. There are two video cameras in my office, and I have lots of 'escorts' wherever I go that are trying to keep from being noticed. I think that Dr. Harrod is building a file that will protect him if the mission goes south. I haven't done anything unethical or illegal, but he can make tapes 'document' whatever he wants them to."

"Well, what about the files you found in the safe? Come to think about it, the guy who designed and built that office back in the Reagan administration, a Dr. Richard Bale, is now deceased. I doubt that any of the White House carpenters who actually did the construction are still around either. How did you get the combination? I left no record of it, and the guys in GSA probably have no recollection that the safe was even installed there, let alone what the combination was."

"As I said, the safe was unlocked," Newman replied. "I want to lock that stuff back in the safe until I can get to it later, after my mission. Do you still remember the combination?"

"After so many years? I'm good but not *that* good."

"Really? You're a Marine, remember? Think of all the things you've committed to memory . . . your serial number, MOS number, weapon's serial numbers. Surely that combination's in that brain, somewhere . . ."

North thought for a moment. Then he took out a pen and wrote on the palm of his hand. He muttered to himself, eyes closed, visualizing the dial on the safe. He did it in his mind three times and confirmed the numbers. "You're right, Pete," he said grinning. "I guess a Marine is like an elephant—he never forgets." Then he showed his hand to Newman, who committed the numbers to his memory.

"What are you going to do with the files and passport?" North asked him.

"Do you want them?"

"No. Why don't you put the files back in the safe and lock it? They really aren't mine. They are the property of the U.S. government. Someday they probably ought to be declassified and shipped to the Reagan Library. But they don't belong to me."

"But," Newman interjected, "they prove that you were authorized to do all that you did when you ran the Special Projects Office."

"So? That's all ancient history. Put the files back in the safe, close the drawer, spin the combination, and forget about it until we can think about how those files ought to be handled. But this passport . . ." North fingered the blue folder with some affection. "This holds a lot of memories for me, and the State Department has canceled it, so it's of no use to anyone. Since it isn't really part of the files, I think I'd like to keep it."

"It's yours, after all," Newman said. "But there is

something else about those files I'd like to know about before I lock them away."

"What's that?"

"A lot of the documentation deals with the activities of this guy, William P. Goode—the name on the passport. But the last memo in the stack, dated 22 November 1986, the day before you were fired, was a memo you wrote to William Casey—the director of the CIA at the time—warning him to get 'the real William P. Goode out of harm's way.' At least that's how I think you put it. So, there's another William Goode out there somewhere, isn't there?"

"Yes . . ." North said slowly, wondering how much he ought to reveal. Even after so many years, he was still wary. Yet, it really was all over now. He had been acquitted of all those charges, and most of the details had already been rehashed over and over in the press. "There is a real William P. Goode. And he's a remarkable man. He was older than I. We switched the years on the passport. He was born in Ohio in 1934, not 1943 like the William P. Goode in this passport. He was orphaned as a baby and grew up at the Hershey Home for Boys, an orphanage in Hershey, Pennsylvania. In 1951 he lied about his age to enlist in the Marines, was decorated for heroism in the Korean War, and in 1954 was recruited by the CIA. They put him through college and he went to work for the Agency as a clandestine services officer. And he stayed with it even though his family was murdered in the sixties in one of those communist-inspired African revolutions. He retired from the CIA in 1984 with a thirty-year pin and a bunch of medals no one will ever know about.

"Casey knew I was in over my head with the hostage

business and the Nicaraguan Resistance. I was trained as an infantry officer, not a spy. In '85 he called Goode and asked him to work with me. Goode agreed and became my mentor, as it were. He's one of the finest, bravest men I've ever met. That's the *real* William P. Goode. Thank God, after all he had been through, he wasn't dragged through the mud with me."

Newman was silent at the end of North's impassioned soliloquy. Then he said, "Is the 'real' Goode still alive? I could sure use some help like he gave you."

"Yes. He's still alive. But there was so much that went so very wrong late in 1986 that many of the friends he'd made were killed. When all that we were doing came unraveled, he dropped out completely. We stay in touch. He's deeply involved with a religious community based near Rome. He lives on his sailboat and does, as he puts it, 'good things.' "

"You mean he became a monk?"

"Well, not quite, but kind of. But during his long career in the CIA he had come across this nondenominational religious community . . . , a group of people that practices what they call 'basic Christianity' and live a communal life. They have a lot of missionary-type works, especially in the Middle East—like hospitals, orphanages, and hospices, you know? I think he was kind of burned out and found some kind of peace in this community.

"Now he lives on that sailboat—you should see that beautiful sixty-two-foot Tayana—and travels anywhere he wants, but mostly in the Mediterranean, looking for ways to help people," North said quietly. Then he got an idea. "You know, if you ever get into trouble in that part of the world, Goode would be a resource that might be of help . . ." North didn't finish the sentence.

"How would I reach him?"

North thought for a moment. "Here's my pager number. Call me—but never call me from your office or home or any other phone you use regularly. Go to one of the cell phone stores around here. Get yourself another cell phone under a fictitious name. Get a post-office box under that name somewhere away from where you live, but where it's convenient to pick up mail and where they can send the phone bill. Pay the bill with a postal money order. Use that new cell phone only to call me or someone like General Grisham. Never use it to call your office, the White House, your wife, your home, or anyone else you call from your office or home. Never use it from your office or when someone can see you use it."

Newman was wide-eyed. "And you just said you weren't a spy, you were just an infantry officer?"

"I haven't forgotten everything that the real William P. Goode taught me," said North with a smile. Newman had many more questions, but he didn't want to take a chance on being seen talking to North.

"Thanks," said North as he held up the passport, saluted with it, and put it into his pocket.

Newman nodded, and said, "I'm looking forward to our next meeting being held under more relaxed circumstances. Thank you for coming. I owe you big-time, Colonel."

"You don't owe me anything. You were a good Marine. I hope you stay out of trouble over there in that snake pit. Call me if you need me. Give my love to your wife." With that, he strode off and disappeared into the trees toward the Fort Myer Gate. Newman stood for a few minutes, transfixed by the six men frozen in the moment of raising a flag atop an extinct volcano. As he turned to walk back toward the Key Bridge, he could just make out the inscription, emblazoned in gold letters on the base of the statue. They were, as every Marine knew, the words describing the Iwo Jima landing by the very man who had ordered it, Admiral Chester Nimitz: "Uncommon valor was a common virtue."

TWA Flight 919
32,000 feet above Atlantic Ocean
GPS: 37° 12'03" W, 48° 23'14" N
Thursday, 16 February 1995
1333 Hours, Local

Rachel Newman had just finished the meal service for the first-class cabin of the flight from London's Heathrow that would be landing in Dulles in another four hours or so. She began to stow away the utensils and utility service materials in the tiny galley. Her friend Sandy was helping the other flight attendants in the back of the plane, but when they were caught up, she joined Rachel in First Class.

The last row of the front cabin seats were empty, so the two women sat down to catch their breath while the passengers, now fed and relaxed, made no demands.

"That's a pretty gold chain," Rachel said of Sandy's new jewelry. "What kind of stone is that in the mounting, a sapphire?"

Sandy nodded and smiled. "Yes, thank you. I love it. It was a Valentine's Day gift from Tom. He's a great husband," she said with a little giggle.

"Oh, yes . . . that's right. Valentine's Day." Rachel couldn't help herself. Her voice was tinged with disappointment, and maybe even a little envy. "I guess my guy has been so tied up on whatever he's doing in Washington—what am I saying? He's hardly ever in Washington. He's probably in North Carolina at Fort Bragg. In fact, he's been so busy and so exhausted, he probably doesn't know where he is, let alone what day it is." She forced a grin and added, "Well, I suppose I forgot his gift too. I did leave a 'Valentine' on his pillow though. I don't think he found it, or I'd have heard from him by now. But I'm not sure. We're like the proverbial ships . . ."

". . . passing in the night," they both said in unison.

"Most husbands tend to be forgetful . . ." Sandy said after a pause in the conversation.

"Uh-huh," Rachel replied. "But this one is hopeless." Only the dull, muffled sound of the jet engines and the *hiss-ssss* of the air outside the skin of the aircraft filled the air inside the plane. Occasionally the two women heard a subdued laugh from someone watching the in-flight movie, but things were really quiet.

Rachel closed her eyes and hoped Sandy would not stay on this theme. Sandy didn't take the hint. "Have you served him divorce papers yet?" she asked.

"Not yet. But I did see a lawyer about it."

Sandy turned toward her coworker and was wide-eyed. "Rachel, I was kidding! I was just trying to be clever because you said he forgot Valentine's Day. That's not grounds for divorce in any marriage."

Rachel sat back in the leather seat, angry for jumping to conclusions and revealing too much. "I . . . I told you on our last flight together . . . I've been thinking about divorce for more than a year," she said. "I even got up the nerve to test the idea with Peter when we were together after Christmas at his folks—I mean, he was in Fort Bragg over Christmas and didn't even call. He was 'kind' enough to give me two whole days the week after New Year's, and we spent that at his parents. I got mad and told him that our lives didn't seem to be in sync and that it's been like that ever since we got married. I asked him if he'd feel better if he were single again."

"What'd he say?" Sandy asked quickly.

"Nothing. He said he didn't want to talk about it while we were at his folks' house. Then I asked him when we should talk about it—he just said, 'Later.' But he never said *when,* exactly."

"Sounds like he isn't against the idea of divorce. Maybe he's been thinking about it too," Sandy suggested. "But you guys shouldn't give up. I mean . . . you can't just throw away, what is it—ten years?"

"It'll be fifteen years in June," Rachel sighed. "You know, Sandy, I really *don't* want a divorce. But I can't live like this anymore. He doesn't even try to make me a part of his life. He can't talk about his work. 'For security reasons,' he says. But surely there are *some* things he can share. He leaves me every couple of weeks or months, and he's gone for weeks and even months at a time. He says he can't tell me where he goes and what he does. I even accused him of having some bimbo on the side that he goes off to see. That made him mad because he couldn't sense that I was kidding. Oh, Sandy, it doesn't pay to marry a military guy—they just leave a girl in a constant state of frustration. I'll never understand the military. I know that I just plain don't get them."

"Have you guys sought help, you know, like a marriage counselor or a pastor?"

"I suggested a shrink once, but I couldn't get him to go," Rachel said. "But not a pastor . . . neither one of us is very religious," she added.

"So, how are you going to handle it?"

Rachel smiled. "You know that valentine that I put on his pillow? It was one of those silly ones. It said, 'I've decided that for Valentine's Day I'm giving you something you've always wanted.' And then you open it up and it says, 'A divorce!' I wanted to be there when he opened it so we could discuss the matter, but we just never connected. And I had to go back to work. But before I left Dulles, I met with an attorney, and she's going to draw up the papers so I can serve him when I get back."

"Listen to me, honey," Sandy said, suddenly serious. "You guys have got to get together and discuss this. Don't burn any bridges. Yeah, maybe he *does* want a divorce too. But I don't think that divorce is the answer."

Rachel didn't respond. She loved Sandy—she was in fact becoming her best friend. But she felt that Sandy would find a way to reduce all of Rachel's and Peter's problems to a simple formula, patched together with a couple of Bible verses. As if on cue, Sandy said, "I can make an appointment with our pastor, Rachel. Please look at another option."

In order to change the subject and end, or at least postpone, the discussion, Rachel said, "Yeah, maybe, Sandy. Anyway, I'm not going to smack him in the face with divorce papers the minute I get back."

"Honey," Sandy said in her sweetest Southern drawl, "I know you'll do the right thing. Just pray about it first. Ask God to give you wisdom." Then, sensing that Rachel did not want to talk about it any longer, she said nothing more.

Rachel, however, surprised herself. *She did* want to talk some more—but not about divorce. "We *have* had some *good* times, too," she recalled with a smile. "I remember when I first met him; he was so handsome and courteous. I'd never been shown such courtesy in my life. He was so sweet."

Rachel shook her head sadly and said, "I don't know exactly when things changed. I wonder if it wasn't just after my first miscarriage . . ."

Sandy said nothing. She sensed that her role now was to be a sympathetic listener.

Rachel continued. "I lost a baby when I was six months pregnant—a little girl. We even had a name picked out—Laurel Marie," she explained, adding, "I lost the baby in August, and in September—*just ten days later*—P. J. was assigned to the Second Force Reconnaissance Company as platoon commander and ended up spending more time at Fort Benning, Georgia, and Little Creek, Virginia, than he did at Camp Lejeune, North Carolina, where he was *supposed* to be based. I pleaded with him to postpone taking all those trips, and he told me it was impossible. I grieved for more than two years over the miscarriage, but Peter wasn't there. . . ." Her voice trailed off.

Sandy nodded to let Rachel know that she was listening but let her friend continue talking. "I went back to work six weeks after the baby died," Rachel said drearily. "Peter buried himself in his work too. That was when he went to Jump School and underwater swimmer's school." She giggled. "Doesn't that sound redundant—'underwater swimmer'? Where else does anybody swim?"

The two of them laughed. "Peter and I reconciled right after that. He came home—let's see, home *then* was in Virginia, back at Quantico, where he was when we first met—and we had a whole month together before we moved. The Marines call moving PCS, for 'permanent change of station.' We both expressed regrets at the way things were going and he apologized, said he wanted to start over, and we had a great reconciliation. That was in March and April. Sometime during that interval, we made another baby," she smiled.

Then her face darkened again. "But six months later, I lost a second baby," she said forlornly.

"Oh, I'm sorry, Rachel," Sandy said, putting her hand sympathetically on her knee.

"We—I mean the doctors and me—we were trying so hard and being so careful. But when this baby was six months along, she died too. Another girl. We didn't even have a name for her 'cause we were so scared that it might happen again. And it did . . ." she said.

"Peter couldn't understand it," Rachel added. "He thought there was something wrong with him—like 'toxic sperm' or something," she said.

Sandy looked puzzled. "Really? Is there such a thing?" she asked naively.

"Of course not," Rachel said. "But since the doctors had no physiological reason for my miscarriage, I suppose Peter suspected either a psychological reason on my part or something physical from him. I don't know. We never really talked about it.

"About ten years ago, though, I had had enough of constant moving and living in shoebox-size officer's quarters. I told Peter that it was hard for me to commute by air to my base at Dulles. I was having to fly commuter planes to St. Louis or some other place to get a connecting flight to Dulles. Sometimes I'd have to leave a day early just to meet my schedule. I told Peter that we needed to buy a place near Dulles and have a permanent home. He could stay in the Transient Officer's Quarters or the Bachelor Officer's Quarters or whatever they call it, if he wanted to, but I wanted something permanent, and I kind of hoped that maybe if we settled down, we could have babies—without the problems we had before."

"Is that when you bought the house in Falls Church?" Sandy asked.

Rachel nodded. "He commuted to Quantico every day all the way from Creswell Drive. It was quite a haul back and forth every day—and he had pretty lousy hours then, too, but he never complained. Still, things never got better between us. I don't get it. He's always ready to head off to trouble. Since we've been married, he's been to Beirut and Grenada. Then he went to all that stuff down in Central America and to Panama and then the Middle East—first in Desert Shield, then Desert Storm. He's always running off somewhere to save the world, but he never seems to want to stay home to save our marriage."

"Is he out now? When I saw you guys over the holidays, he was wearing civilian clothes and wearing his hair longer—well, longer for *him*," she laughed.

"No, he's still a Marine," Rachel answered. "He works at the White House," she added simply. "He says it's better PR if the public doesn't see a lot of uniforms running around. They might think it's a military government, I guess."

"Are you sure it isn't just the President?" Sandy asked. "My husband says that this president doesn't like to have uniforms around him because he hates the military. Maybe it reminds him that he was a draft dodger," she added.

Rachel shrugged. "Maybe . . . I've heard that, too, but never from Peter. He's always so loyal to everyone he works for."

Sandy apologized. "I'm sorry, I didn't mean to interrupt you. You were saying you got fed up with Peter always running out on you for another mission. That must have made you kind of lonely, especially when he was in Desert Storm and all those other things," she suggested.

Rachel nodded again, but she wasn't going to tell Sandy about Mitch, the pilot with whom she had been having an affair for the past eleven months. Instead she said, "Yes, it's lonely, but my job is just as much to blame as his. I'm gone a lot too. But I don't want to wake up one day and find out that I've wasted most of my years in a marriage that means nothing to either one of us. If that's really the case, we both need to make a clean break and start over."

Sandy bit her tongue. She wanted to say lots of things that she felt Rachel needed to hear, but now was not the time. She looked at her watch and said, "I'd better go back and help the crew in coach. We'll talk again, honey. Maybe on the next flight we have together."

U.S. Commerce Department
15th Street entrance
Washington, D.C.
Thursday, 16 February 1995
1645 Hours, Local

Bob Storey was a general's general. Everybody knew that. He looked like a general, talked like a general, carried himself like a general. That's why Silicon Cyber Technologies International had hired him. Marty Korman, SCTI's founder, CEO, and chairman of the board had hired Major General Bob Storey the day he retired from the U.S. Air Force for one reason: he wanted to round out his stable of retired military brass hats—men who looked good even out of uniform. Korman wanted men who understood the ways and wiles of Washington, who knew their way around the E-Ring at the Pentagon, who looked good at press conferences, and who could snow the pompous politicians in Congress with all kinds of military tech jargon if they got out of hand.

But now Storey was becoming a pain in the neck himself. Storey was asking questions—questions about the leading-edge technology SCTI was developing, questions about who was using the hardware and software that SCTI had developed, *and* whether the selling of this technology was truly in "the national interest of America" or even legal under the restrictions that Congress had placed on high-end computer technology earlier in the nineties.

Korman had just finished a humiliating hour meeting with high-level bureaucrats at the Commerce Department. And right now he was furious. They had turned down an export license for his nonmilitary SCTI software for the nations of Saudi Arabia and Kuwait. What galled him most from the meeting was not so much the denial of the license but that during the meeting, the Commerce Department weenies had produced a memo showing that his own General Storey *had recommended against granting the license*. The loss of a multimillion-dollar sale to a couple of Middle Eastern countries wasn't that important to Korman. What was important was that his trusted employee suddenly got a case of conscience.

Korman exited from his meeting at the Commerce Department and all but ran down the stairs from the building. He had called ahead to have his company jet file an earlier flight plan back to California, now that his trip to Washington was fruitless. As he sped down Constitution Avenue in the backseat of the Cadillac that had picked him up at Dulles, waited for him, and was now taking him back to the airport, Korman swore loudly to no one in particular, adding, "Who does this guy Storey think he is?"

The limo driver responded, "What was that, sir?"

"Shut up—just hurry up and get me back to where you picked me up."

"Yes, sir."

Korman grabbed his cell phone and scrolled through the tiny directory. When he got to his office number, he punched the *Call* icon. "Sally, get me Storey's personnel file and have it out on my desk when I get back to Los Angeles." While she had him on the phone, Sally Pearson, his personal assistant, quickly briefed him on other matters he needed to attend to when he returned to the West Coast. Korman dictated a few memos, asking Sally to cancel an appointment that he had forgotten about when he left the night before on his Gulfstream IV for the flight to his early morning meeting. "See if Jerry can reschedule for next Thursday at the same time," he told Sally, wrapping up the last of the urgent matters.

Marty Korman wasn't used to being told that he had a bureaucratic problem with an export license—or anything else for that matter. Korman liked to tell people that he could do anything, even the impossible. After all, he'd boast, hadn't he personally started SCTI in his garage after he left Los Alamos National Laboratories? That wasn't entirely true—he had a partner who deserved at least half the credit. But Korman had spent countless, thankless hours, two wives, and incredible sums of other people's money building his company, and now he had succeeded beyond even his own great expectations. It seemed ludicrous that a simple matter like government licensing should now control his opportunities for success. He made a note to call his "friends," Simon Harrod at the White House and Senator James Waggoner up on Capitol Hill, again on Monday. For a few seconds, Korman toyed with the idea of calling the President or the Vice President, but he had never done that before. The obese National Security Advisor was his access to all things at the White House. And he figured that POTUS and VPOTUS, as Harrod referred to them, were his silver bullets. He didn't want to fire those shots until he had to.

And then in disgust, he thought, *What good are the best politicians money can buy if you can't get hold of them when you need them?* As the car sped west on the Dulles Access Road, he swore again—but this time to himself.

CHAPTER TWELVE

The Mission Changes

Corporate Headquarters
Silicon Cyber Technologies International, Inc.
Newport Beach, CA
Friday, 17 February 1995
0745 Hours, Local

After his disastrous meeting with the Commerce Department the day before, Korman had gone directly to his office. The SCTI Gulfstream IV had landed back at John Wayne Airport in Orange County shortly after 8:00 P.M., and Korman jumped into his red Jaguar convertible. He sped to the SCTI headquarters in Newport Beach, making the trip down Jamboree Road in record time. The security guard waved him in, and Korman headed straight for the office down the hall from his, the one labeled *HUMAN RESOURCES*. He used his master key to let himself in and went to the locked file titled *EXECUTIVE*. Another key on his ring opened the lock. Thumbing through the files, he pulled the one with a plastic tab that read *Storey, Robert A, BG, USAF (Ret.)*, sat down at a nearby desk, and opened the file.

Fifteen minutes later he closed the general's file and

stood up. He'd made his decision. Korman returned the file to its drawer, closed and locked it, shut off the lights in the personnel director's office, and closed and locked the door. He then walked down the expansive, well-appointed hallway to his own office and called the head of security.

"Fred, this is Marty." Korman had a company-wide policy that everyone was on a first-name basis. He had read in some management book written by another Silicon Valley whiz kid that this kind of informality was good for morale and helped instill "team building." Korman didn't give a whit about building teams. All he wanted to do was to build and sell EncryptionLok-3s, but if other Southern California megamillionaires were using first names, he would too.

"Fred, I want you to call the night security people and have them change the locks on General Storey's office. I want it done before dawn. Got it?" Korman paused, said, "Good, I'll depend on you," and hung up the phone.

Korman then left the building, waved to the security guard at the gate, and went home. He grabbed a good bottle of wine, a glass, and a Cuban cigar and went out on the deck to watch the surf and the stars and drink the bottle of wine. It was after 1:00 A.M. when the wine ran out. Korman checked his watch and wobbled into the house. He called Storey at home, got him out of bed, and told him to meet him in his office at 7:30 in the morning.

Korman then called Marat, told him what he was going to do to Storey, and after listening for a minute or two, hung up and went to bed. The man who could "make electrons dance" slept for only a few hours before he got up. After showering and eating a bowl of cereal with a banana, as he did every morning, he roared off to his office. He was sitting at his desk when the general arrived, promptly at 7:30.

First, Korman flew into a well-rehearsed rage about how the general's disloyalty was costing the company and how everyone who worked there faced the possibility of unemployment and ruin. He also ranted about his betrayal of Korman's trust and the company itself.

Finally, at the end of the fifteen minutes, Korman called the general a traitor and said that he was no longer an active employee of SCTI. He knew that the wily general would either want to argue his way back into the company's good graces or threaten to go public and really raise a stink. So to ensure his cooperation, Korman presented Storey with a letter that made his "retirement" from SCTI effective that day *and* made his continued receipt of retirement benefits dependent on a total nondisclosure of any of SCTI's activities. That had been Marat's suggestion on the phone the night before. The nondisclosure agreement had more teeth than an alligator—but allowed the general to keep his retirement package of $300,000 annual compensation plus insurance. The general would, however, have to give up all of the perks that he had enjoyed as an active employee: credit cards for his unlimited expense account, a company car, and a luxurious $400,000 condo in Cabo San Lucas. On Korman's desk the general put the credit cards, car keys, and the special ID card that gave him access to all of the SCTI empire.

The chastised General Storey had a choice: either keep his mouth shut or risk losing his pension from SCTI. Marat was convinced that the general would play ball in order to keep the money coming in. But if he didn't, they'd cut the compensation in a heartbeat. As an added incentive for Storey to go quietly, Korman alluded darkly to the possibility of "evidence" of wrongdoing on the general's computer that might have to be turned over to Jules Wilson's Comm Hawks, or even better, to the FBI, pointing to the possibility that Storey was a security risk or even a spy. If convicted he might even go to prison. But if the general did as he was told, the pension would continue "for life."

And as insurance, Korman leaned over the man's chair and hissed, "But listen to me, you jerk, if you mess with me, your life may not be *that long*. I'll agree to this deal, and you can keep your pension *conditionally*. For all intents and purposes, General, I'm buying your silence. Now you can run to somebody thinking that it's in the 'best interests of the country' to cause me grief. But remember, letting you keep your pension is costing me a lot more money than it would if I just arranged an 'accident' and had one of our armed security guards put a nine-millimeter hole in your head while 'mistaking' you as an intruder. So don't think of messing with me, or your 'lifetime' pension may be worthless. Your family will have nothing if the money stops. And *you'll* be in even worse shape!" Korman then launched into another tirade of curses as the general squirmed in his chair.

"If I were you, General—if I were you, I'd take my retirement package and leave the country. You never know when some kind of 'accident' might happen. It might be better if you retired to someplace *safe*, don't you think?" Korman told General Storey. The words were quiet and his tone was even, but the real meaning of the threat was explicit.

General Storey signed the letter and other documents and hurriedly left Korman's office. He stopped at his old office to pick up his things, but when he couldn't get in, he called his wife from his mobile phone and told her to come and pick him up at the main gate. And then he was gone.

After the general left, Korman decided that Monday was too long to wait for a callback from Dr. Simon Harrod. He called the National Security Advisor's West Wing office and told Harrod's secretary, "It's extremely urgent that I speak with the National Security Advisor."

Less than two minutes later, the White House Situation Room senior watch officer called Korman's private line and said, "Sir, the National Security Advisor will be calling you in five minutes. Do you have an EncryptionLok-3?"

"Of course," snarled Korman. "I make 'em, don't I?"

"Very well, sir. The National Security Advisor will be using encryption algorithm X-Ray, Papa, Juliet, Two, Kilo, Seven, One, Lima, Niner. He should be calling in less than four minutes." Then the line went dead.

Korman reached into his briefcase, pulled out the EL-3 he always carried with him, and punched in the encryption code that had been read to him over the phone. He then disconnected the handset cord from the base of the phone on his desk, plugged it into the EL-3, and connected the other end of the device to the phone instrument. Two minutes later the phone rang. It was Simon Harrod.

"Marty, it's Simon Harrod. My secretary called and told me that you have an international crisis or something. What's going on?"

"Simon," Korman said, "thank you for calling. I need to meet with you about something important. Can you fit me in later today?"

"I'm on my way to Andrews Air Force Base—heading for Colorado as we speak, Marty. Can it wait?"

"Are you going to the 'Mountain' by any chance?" Korman asked, referring to the North American Air Defense Command Center buried deep in the Cheyenne Mountains outside the city.

"Yes, as a matter of fact, I am. I'm meeting with a few Air Force generals to see why, among other things, NORAD is dragging its feet on converting their EncryptionLok-3s. That ought to be of interest to you. Would you care to join me, in case they ask some technical questions?" Harrod proposed.

"That's perfect. Stan Marat was planning on going there next week to build a fire under them. I'll call my pilot and have him file a flight plan to Colorado Springs instead of Washington. That ought to save a few gallons of aviation fuel," Korman said with a smile. "What's your ETA?"

"Now you're sounding like the brass hats," Harrod laughed. "I should be at Peterson Air Force Base in Colorado Springs—it adjoins the municipal airport—by 2:00 P.M. their time. I guess the 'stripes and stars set' would call that '1400 local,' " he chuckled.

"Yes, I know where it is. How should we connect? I expect it's too late for me to get clearances to land at Peterson, so I'll have our jet land at Colorado Springs Airport."

"Yes. Good. Have your pilot radio our plane and give your time of arrival. I'll have someone pick you up at the airport and bring you to me. We can have a late lunch and head for the Mountain."

"Do you mind if I bring Stan Marat with me?" asked Korman.

"Not at all."

Korman hung up with a sense of euphoria. This was the break he had been waiting for. Harrod was clearly fully on board. The money Korman had been throwing around Washington was paying off. Harrod had already made it possible for SCTI to begin replacing the outmoded older EncryptionLok units with the new GPS–command/destruct model, the EL-3. Then Harrod had helped SCTI acquire contracts to produce them for the UN Security Council's military Special Force. As always, the contracts had avoided congressional scrutiny by simply keeping Senator James Waggoner "in the loop."

The UN deal was typical. When some bureaucrat at Commerce raised a stink about turning the devices over to the UN, Harrod and then Waggoner had landed on the man like a ton of bricks.

"This is not a matter for the Commerce people," Harrod had declared. "It's a national security matter." He'd reasoned that with seventy-five hundred of the new EncryptionLok-3 devices, mainly to equip UN peacekeeping troops around the world, maintaining world order and peace was a higher law than some archaic commercial regulation. For good measure, Harrod told the secretary of commerce that he had discussed the matter with the President and he had concurred: they would permit the sale on grounds of national security. Two simple phone calls—one from Harrod and another from Waggoner—had made it possible to bypass any internal or external controls, including Congress and the Pentagon, which kept the sale a matter of utmost secrecy. If all went well, there would be another order of 7,500 devices for the rest of the UN force during the next year.

And to show his gratitude, throughout 1994 Korman had kept the huge checks coming, and Harrod had promised to introduce SCTI to NATO leaders who would probably order (again, secretly) at least fifteen thousand total units. SCTI would be in business through 2006—giving Korman plenty of time to explore the possibility of selling some variation of the device to commercial civilian markets.

But Korman wanted to get started on the other overseas markets now, and that's why he had run into trouble with Commerce. Storey had poisoned the well with his whistle-blowing. Korman was coming to realize that there were three types of people in Washington: (1) those who had come into town with the President and his administration; (2) people like Senator Waggoner who could be bought no matter who ran the White House; and (3) career government employees—some of whom apparently took their jobs very seriously. For this third group, even the hint of impropriety was the kiss of death to a project or politician.

Korman buzzed Marat on the intercom and yelled, "Meet me at the car in two minutes; we're going on a little trip!" He pushed the *Off* button before Marat could answer.

He then grabbed his briefcase and buzzed his driver to meet him in front of the building for a race up Jamboree Road to John Wayne Airport and into the SCTI hangar he had left less than twelve hours ago. An hour and twenty minutes later, Korman was airborne. He slept in the Gulfstream's comfortable leather seat all the way to Colorado. Marat spent the trip looking out the window, wondering how much longer all this could last.

Municipal Airport
Colorado Springs, CO
Friday, 17 February 1995
1400 Hours, Local

Harrod's limo picked up Korman and Marat at a little after 2:00 P.M. local time and brought them to Peterson Air Force Base to the north of the commercial airport. Korman jumped from the limousine and trotted over to where Harrod was talking on his cell phone. The porcine National Security Advisor concluded his conversation, smiled, and extended his hand. "The President sends his best wishes," he said to Korman.

Korman laughed. "Yeah, right," he said. "My old buddy . . . what'd he want . . . to get together for poker tomorrow night?"

Harrod's face turned red and his expression was serious. "No, really. That was the President, and he recalls the time last fall when he invited you and Stan to the Oval Office to congratulate SCTI on delivery of the first three thousand EncryptionLok-3 devices to the UN."

"Well, I'll be . . . he really did remember me, eh?"

"I'm sure that he did. If not, he sure remembers that check you wrote out to the President's reelection campaign on the spot. Yes, Marty, *he remembers.*"

Korman remembered too. Afterward, in Harrod's office, the two SCTI executives had sat through one of Harrod's little speeches about how pleased he was that they were involved in the progress of something that he called "a new world order" and had said that the President and his administration would be remembered in history as the one that opened the door to a new era of world peace and harmony.

"Well, the thing is, Dr. Harrod," Korman had said

softly, using the National Security Advisor's title rather than the more casual first-name basis, "Stan and I really appreciate how you broke the logjam at the Commerce Department. I mean, Stan tried pushing our request through last year and didn't get anywhere. They really held onto that foreign licensing policy that restricts us from selling high-tech computer stuff overseas. They told me that our technology fell into that category. But apparently you found a way around it."

"It's better if we don't talk about it," Harrod had said. "Just let me take care of it. Let's just say that I've found a way to get around your Commerce Department problem, and leave it at that."

Now here they were with another problem at Commerce. Korman knew better than to try and make himself look good—Harrod would see through it.

"I screwed up, Dr. Harrod," Marat told him. "First, I got a call from Commerce that they were going to sic the FBI on us because we were trying to circumvent the export license on selling our devices overseas. I told you about that when you saved our butts with the UN orders. I suppose we got a little impatient trying to build something similar to the EncryptionLok-3 for the commercial market. We talked about that too."

"Yes . . . I recall that we did. What's wrong?"

At this point Korman cut in. "One of my lobbyists suddenly became patriotic and felt that America needs to keep anything related to the EncryptionLok-3 solely for the military and not overseas sales, and especially not any commercial venues. I fired him this morning," Korman added.

Harrod laughed. "You always have been the impetuous one, Marty. I don't know how you and Stan ever teamed up. Opposites attract, I guess."

"Well, I suppose I am impetuous. But I want to be careful and not expose this administration to anything that might get fuzzy. I need your advice."

Harrod stretched his neck and moved his head around to relieve the tension. Then he spoke. "Marty, just leave it alone. Be patient. Give me time to grease the skids. Don't jump in and make things messy. Call your guy at Commerce and tell him you appreciate what he told you and that you think it's so important that you've gotta revisit your proposal—that you'll get back to him later when you feel it'll pass their scrutiny. Meanwhile, we try another avenue altogether."

The three men went to the Officer's Mess on the base and were given the VIP treatment for lunch. During the meal, Korman and Harrod worked out a strategy for keeping the SCTI pipeline full of contracts and orders for the foreseeable future. Marat ate silently while the other two schemed. In less time than it took them to eat, they had a plan. And as evidence of their gratitude, Korman and SCTI would see to it that the President's re-election campaign fund would be kept healthy with some serious contributions.

Andrews Air Force Base
Washington, D.C.
Friday, 17 February 1995
2335 Hours, Local

When the Special Air Mission Gulfstream, with *UNITED STATES OF AMERICA* emblazoned above its windows, taxied toward the VIP terminal at Andrews Air Force Base, it was dark and Harrod felt drained. He'd begun the day with two meetings and flew to Colorado for three more, including the one with Marty Korman and Stan Marat. When the plane stopped, Harrod stood up, put on his jacket, and grabbed his attaché case.

The Air Force lieutenant who served as an aide to Harrod for the flight handed him his black cashmere topcoat and beaver hat, which he carried instead of wearing despite the damp chill in the air. He ambled clumsily down the steps of the plane's exit stairs and walked across the rain-dampened tarmac.

As he strode into the building, his driver reached for Harrod's coat, hat, and attaché case. Harrod nodded to him but said nothing. He was glad that his White House limo was outside and ready—he hated waiting around at these military installations when his limo got stuck in rush-hour traffic or delayed in some other way.

The driver led the way to the curb where the limo was parked, opened the door for Harrod, and closed the trunk since the National Security Advisor had no luggage. As Harrod was preparing to compress his enormous girth into the open rear door at curbside, he heard someone call his name. He turned to see General Dimitri Komulakov walking briskly toward the car. Harrod waited.

"How'd you know I was on this plane?" Harrod asked.

"Your deputy gave me your schedule. I told him it was urgent that I meet with you today. There's an important development that we must discuss."

"Ride with me back to the White House—we can have a snack sent up to my office from the White House Mess."

Komulakov shook his head. "I'm sorry, Simon. As soon as I brief you on what's happening, I must fly back to New York. My plane is parked over there." He pointed to a smaller twenty-passenger jet nearby. "Can you delay your trip back to the city by twenty minutes, Simon? It would help me a great deal."

Harrod nodded, then gestured for Komulakov to get into the backseat of his limo. "We can talk here. My car's secure," Harrod said as he climbed into the back of the limo with the Russian. The White House driver got out and returned to the terminal.

Komulakov leaned across the seat and lowered his voice. "Last week, the Mossad passed along an unsubstantiated rumor of plans for a major defection from Iraq," he began.

"Yes, the CIA briefed me about it on the weekend. Seems that Saddam's son-in-law Hussein Kamil wants to get out of Iraq."

"When I heard about it, I put one of my former comrades on the case just to see whether it is true or not. It *is!*" the Russian exclaimed. "Kamil sent some feelers through one of the German pharmaceutical corporations that make his chemical weapons. Kamil wanted the Germans to bring him to the West."

"Boy, I'll bet the German was happy—closing the door to one of his company's most lucrative contracts, having to give up those million-dollar commissions. What'd he say?"

The Russian shook his head, "Their conversations were not recorded, but the Mossad has information that the German turned him down. If he helped Kamil, he'd be a marked man. He felt that Saddam would send someone to assassinate them both."

Harrod laughed. "Saddam's so dirty that he'll probably terminate the German just for listening to what Kamil wants to do." Then he added, "Does anyone in Iraq know anything about this plan?"

"I don't think so. Kamil seems like a bright guy, but

there's a story going around that he's had a brain tumor or something. One thing is for sure, he's a survivor, and he's moved up the ladder over there after every purge. There's no doubt he's been around long enough to know his way around. Maybe because he's a relative he's not under suspicion."

Harrod laughed again. "Are you kidding? Saddam couldn't care less about that. He'd butcher his own mother and invite all of Baghdad to watch if he thought she wasn't loyal."

"So far there is no evidence of Kamil's plans. But if the Mossad, the CIA, and my operatives know about it, it will be leaked eventually," General Komulakov said, adding, "Here is what I think we should do. My agent is in Baghdad—"

"A double agent?" Harrod interrupted. "This could be a setup."

"Yes, my man is a double agent, but no, it is not a setup. He is to be trusted as much as you and I trust each other." Harrod wasn't sure that the Russian's assurance was worth much, but he knew that this game of intrigue had certain conventions, and he was willing to give the man the benefit of the doubt—for now.

The Russian continued. "My man has been working with Kamil for more than two years to try and sell him three nuclear artillery warheads that he claims to have in the Ukraine. It's not true, of course, but he is able to keep Kamil's interest and the pretense of working on the matter while he has a chance to gain some rather decent intelligence.

"I told my man to not let Kamil know that his message to the Germans was turned down and to say that they had contacted my man to get Kamil to the West. It's a dangerous move—Kamil could kill him for knowing too much. But my guy thinks he can string it along for a while, simply because he knows that Kamil won't kill him until he knows *who else knows*."

Harrod thought for a moment and wondered what his role in all of this should be. A Hussein Kamil defection would make for an interesting press conference, and he might earn some points for the President, who certainly hated Saddam more than Kamil ever could. Harrod made a proposal. "How soon can you find out if this Kamil guy has something to offer the West in exchange for getting him safely out of Iraq? I'd guess he figures that he's a pretty big fish and could ask for some serious cash and other perks in exchange for some state secrets."

Komulakov reminded Harrod, "Well, he is the head of their internal state security apparatus, he's the one buying all the parts for their nuclear programs, and he's the guy in charge of their weapons of mass destruction. Yes, I'd say that he could tell us a thing or two."

"I mean things that we don't already know," Harrod said.

The Russian reached for the door handle with one hand and extended the other to Harrod, who shook it. "I will call you as soon as we have something new," he said as he exited the limo.

International Scientific Trading Offices
17 Agricultural Circle
Baghdad, Iraq
Saturday, 18 February 1995
0955 Hours, Local

Leonid Dotensk liked working with Dimitri Komulakov. In their days together in the KGB's Department V,

Komulakov had referred to Dotensk as "my Ukrainian." They had retired together from the KGB in 1990 when the Soviet Union was breaking up, and Komulakov had used his well-honed diplomatic skills to land himself at the UN. Dotensk, on the other hand, had returned to Kiev and opened a black-market arms trading company—but stayed in touch with his old boss in his new job. Dotensk had offices all over the Middle East but particularly liked this one, in Baghdad, because the Iraqi's needs were so great—and their money was so good.

Dotensk was enjoying his morning tea when he heard someone enter the outer office area and talk to his assistant. The assistant quickly slipped into Dotensk's office and gestured that he had an important visitor. Dotensk recognized the voice and told his assistant, "Show him in. And bring some tea."

Then he got up from behind his desk to receive the visitor. "Ah, my dear friend. Thank you for coming. I am embarrassed that you have to see me in such modest accommodations. I should have met you at your office, but I must talk to you about very urgent and important matters, and I thought that my office might have fewer . . . uh . . . 'distractions.' "

The visitor, Hussein Kamil, entered the room. He was wearing his Iraqi military uniform rather than Arab garb, and he seemed less arrogant here than he did when Dotensk met with him at the SSS offices or at the presidential palace. Normally Kamil would have an entourage—mostly bodyguards—who accompanied him everywhere. As head of the Amn Al-Khass, he usually welcomed this protection, but today he wanted no one to know where he was or what he was doing. He had called his office and told them that he was coming in later, due to working all night. The next trick was to elude the security force that was guarding his mansion, which was no small deception. But with the help of his driver, he had pulled it off.

"You said that you have important information for me," Kamil said, not wanting to waste time with small talk.

Dotensk took the cue and led Kamil to a big leather chair. When Kamil sat, Dotensk leaned over and whispered, "Do you have my offices under surveillance? Because if you do, we cannot talk here." Kamil jumped up and gestured for the Ukrainian to follow him.

The two said nothing as they hurried down the stairs from the third-floor offices of the "trading" company that Dotensk used as a front for his arms deals. They used a back entrance and climbed into a waiting car. Kamil's personal driver was waiting with the motor running. The tinted windows of the Mercedes kept curious onlookers from knowing who was inside, but the late-model luxury car would hardly be inconspicuous. Only a few Iraqis would have the means to have such an automobile, and most of these would be among the trusted military and political elite in Saddam's crumbling empire.

The driver drove away from the office district at Kamil's order. Dotensk knew the Arabic language well, so when Kamil instructed his driver on their destination, Dotensk was surprised to hear him call the man "Abu"—a name when used with another name usually meant "father of . . ." but by itself was an honorific name that was often meant as a term of affection. Kamil seemed to sense the Ukrainian's thoughts. "Abu is like a father to me . . . his family has served ours for some forty years or more. I call him 'Daddy,' but his given name is Khalil al Hardi."

"Where are we going?" Dotensk asked as they approached the outskirts of town.

"We will drive a few miles into the desert. I cannot be too careful about spies and others who mean to know my business," Kamil said.

In another ten minutes they were several miles away from the city. Its skyline was still quite visible to the southwest, but there were no other roads within miles. The Mercedes came to a stop, and they sat there in the air-conditioned comfort inside the car.

"Now what is it that you wanted to tell me?" Kamil asked.

Dotensk glanced at the driver.

"It is all right," Kamil said. "Just speak to me in English or Russian. Abu does not understand either of those languages."

Dotensk chose to speak in Russian and began his narrative. "First, I want you to know that I have heard from one of my contacts in Germany that you have sent out feelers to his firm that you would like to defect."

Kamil seemed immediately agitated by this. "How? When did you hear? I only told one man whom I thought I could trust."

"Well, from now on you cannot trust anyone—except me. I know that you have suspected that I am a spy for the Russians. Well, that is only half of the story. I also have good connections with the American CIA. These are the people that you should be dealing with."

Kamil was interested. "Tell me more."

"The Germans will have nothing to do with you and your family. They won't even guarantee your safety or give you asylum. The people that you have been dealing with in Germany have connections with the far right, so the Bonn government won't even bother to talk with you. The pharmaceutical firm that supplies you has already seriously embarrassed them.

"But the Americans are different. Without divulging your name," Dotensk lied, "I have made some general inquiries. The Americans will help you to get a new identity and locate you wherever you want to go. And, they may be willing to pay for information that you can give them."

Kamil thought for a moment, then smiled. "I never thought I'd be able to make contact with the CIA. The Americans were my first choice. And you say you can help me contact them?"

"Before the end of the day I can have a plan for you. You will have extremely valuable information for them. Of course they will help you."

"What should I do?" Kamil asked.

"Nothing. Just leave everything to me. I am the only one that you can trust. Here are my terms: first, I want you to go forward with the purchase of the three nuclear warheads that I have offered to sell to your government. I want 50 million Swiss francs for each one of them. You can arrange for payment to be transferred into my account in Kiev. But since it will take some time to transfer the weapons to Iraqi soil without the UN or others knowing about it, you will have to trust me. You must have the funds transferred before you defect, and I will give you the arrangements you must follow in order for the CIA to get you and your family out of Iraq safely."

"I see."

"And there is one other thing," Dotensk added. "I must have something to give to the CIA that will satisfy them that you will be worth the money. Give me some information that I can take to them—something big—

that will give you great credibility and show good faith on your part."

Kamil sat there for a while thinking. Anything that he'd tell Dotensk would compromise him and his family and put them immediately at risk. He knew that his brothers-in-law would not hesitate to hang him, nor would Saddam for that matter. But Kamil also knew that Dotensk was right: the CIA would not pursue this deal without some kind of enticement. Then he knew exactly the right information to secure their interest and sincere help.

"On March 6, there is going to be a meeting at President Saddam's summer palace in Tikrit. It is for the purpose of enlisting help from a former Saudi exile named Osama bin Laden to carry out acts of destruction—upon the West. They plan to make those other attacks on their embassies and military bases look like schoolboy pranks. These will be well-orchestrated attacks by teams of commandos.

"I will also be at that summit, and I will make highly detailed notes for the CIA," Kamil explained. "This will be *my* first installment for bringing my family and me out of Iraq. But tell the CIA that information in the future will cost them. It will cost them plenty."

Kamil knew that this information was good enough to accomplish what he and Dotensk wanted. It would whet the CIA's appetite for more. He also knew that the CIA would not be able to infiltrate the March 6 meeting on its own. Saddam's Tikrit palace was surrounded for thirty kilometers on every side by Iraqi air defense sites and by the armored division of the Republican Guard—one of the elite units that had been spared destruction when the Americans had come roaring across the desert out of Kuwait. They were loyal to their benefactor, Saddam Hussein. Of any place in Iraq, here Saddam was most secure. No CIA operative could get past this security and gain access to the meeting.

The two men in the back of the Mercedes shook hands on the agreement, and Dotensk made arrangements to meet Kamil later that night if he could get an answer from his CIA contact that soon.

"Abu, please wait outside for a moment," Kamil said in Arabic, leaning toward the kindly old man in the front seat. Then he turned to Dotensk. "Will you please join me outside of the car for a moment so that we can formally seal our pact? I have some whiskey in the trunk, and we can toast each others' success." Kamil put on his sunglasses and curiously pulled on his black leather uniform gloves.

Warily Dotensk opened the door and stood outside. He loosened his suit jacket and surreptitiously removed his gun from its holster and slipped it into his coat pocket after flipping the safety off. Then he walked around the rear of the car to join Kamil and his driver. When his eyes cleared the roof of the sedan, he saw that Kamil was pointing a gun at him.

"What's this?" he demanded. His instincts were immediately focused, and the hair on the back of his neck stood up. Within microseconds his mind wrestled with counterprotective actions. But logic told him that he'd be dead before he could execute any of those options. He hated himself for not keeping his hand in his pocket around the gun and trigger. As least he would have had a more equitable advantage. Now he was helpless and felt fear stealing over him.

"Now, Leonid," Kamil said. "Hand me your gun—handle first. Don't be afraid. If I wanted to kill you, you'd be dead already. This is just a precaution to satisfy my paranoia. Your gun, please."

Dotensk knew that Kamil was right—he could have killed him before he walked around the back of the car if he really meant to do so. He smiled to ease tensions and handed the gun over to Kamil.

"Leonid, you said earlier that I must not trust anyone. You are absolutely right about that. But you also said that I must trust you, and I cannot do that with full assurance just yet. I need some insurance that I can trust you to stay here in Iraq, work with me in planning my escape, and not betray me. I need some insurance that you can be trusted."

After saying that, he took Dotensk's gun and looked at it. "My, this is beautiful. It's German, I see. Nickelplated . . . nine millimeter . . . a Sig automatic—beautiful." Kamil put his own gun back in its holster and played with the Ukrainian's pistol, feeling its heft, holding it out at arm's length, and squinting over the sight.

Then, while holding it up and sighting down the barrel toward the distant dunes, he slowly turned and fired two quick shots into the head of his driver. The sounds of the cartridges being fired were loud and reverberated across the sandy dunes. The first bullet entered the driver's left eye socket and exploded in his brain; the second smashed his nose and also entered the skull. The old man arched backward and fell heavily to the ground.

Dotensk was startled and was poised to act, but Kamil brought the pistol back and aimed squarely at his face. "What was *that* for!?" he asked Kamil.

"That is my insurance. It will help me to trust you, knowing that the Amn Al-Khass will have the bullets from the gun that killed my loyal and trusted chauffeur. And my agents will find that gun and it will betray you . . . and you will be executed," Kamil said in a matter-of-fact tone. "That will happen—unless everything goes as you have suggested," he added.

Then Kamil turned back to the man he called "Daddy" and fired two more rounds into his heart. "Some additional insurance," he smiled, "in case the ballistics on the other bullets are inconclusive after they broke through the skull."

Dotensk looked at the poor man lying in the sand, blood spilling from his body. *This man is an absolute madman!* he thought. *What have I gotten myself into?*

The hardened Ukrainian arms merchant said nothing, but this kind of evil was too much even for Dotensk.

"Can I depend upon your utmost cooperation to do as you have proposed?" Kamil asked him.

Dotensk simply nodded and said, "I will call you tonight . . ."

Harrod's Apartment
Washington, D.C.
Saturday, 18 February 1995
0145 Hours, Local

Harrod had just undressed and was brushing his teeth to go to bed when his phone rang. It was Komulakov again. He explained that he had just gotten back to New York and had some further word on their conversation.

"Let me call you back," Harrod said. "Are you home or at your office?" After a momentary pause, Harrod scribbled the number on a pad on the nightstand and replaced the handset. He ambled into his office and attached his EncryptionLok-3 to the telephone in his office and called the number written on the piece of paper he carried from the bedroom. As soon as the call was ringing, Harrod shredded the piece of paper in his hand into a nearby wastebasket.

Harrod turned on the EL-3 and heard the metallic *ping* as the device engaged to make their conversation indecipherable. The Russian began to speak quickly, and Harrod could tell by his voice that he was excited. "My guy called me by satellite phone when I was on the plane to New York. He had anticipated our scenario and had already done the prelims for what we wanted to know.

"He says that he told Kamil that he was connected to the CIA through one of his contacts—me, but he didn't tell him where I work—and that he could see if the CIA was interested. Kamil seemed overjoyed at that. Apparently he doesn't hate 'the great Satan' enough to not want to enjoy its riches."

"Yeah, aren't convictions wonderful?" Harrod said wryly. "What did your operative tell him?"

"He said that he would start the ball rolling and see what could be done. And he told him that in the meantime, he wanted Kamil to cut a check for 150 million Swiss francs for those warheads. That way he keeps his credibility alive—as well as his own rear." Komulakov had told Harrod earlier about the warheads but had convinced the National Security Advisor that they were dummies and were just being used by his agent to gain Kamil's confidence.

What Komulakov specifically did not tell Harrod was that he had instructed Dotensk to expedite the delivery of the warheads because of the information Kamil had passed along about the meeting that was to take place on March 6. Komulakov wanted to make sure that his portion of the 150 million was safely in his Swiss bank account before Osama bin Laden showed up in Iraq.

"Did your man ask Kamil what he had to offer the CIA in return?" asked Harrod.

"As a matter of fact, he did. Kamil told him that on March 6 Saddam and a bunch of his cronies are meeting at the presidential palace in Tikrit. There are going to be other notables there who are also on our short list of 'lawbreakers.' And there is supposed to be one very special guest attending in whom I know you will have great interest. I'll send you a secure message in the morning with the full details.

"But the most important reason for this call, my dear Simon," the general said, "is that I think that we should change the mission for our International Sanctions Enforcement Group and your little Special Projects Office."

"What do you mean?"

"Send them to Iraq instead of Somalia," Komulakov suggested. "The SG is having some second thoughts about the Somalia mission anyhow. He doesn't want to be embarrassed again, as he was when the U.S. Rangers and UN peacekeepers were killed in Mogadishu in '93."

"Hmm . . . I think our president might have some second thoughts about that himself. But can we pull this one off so quickly?" Harrod asked. "I mean, this team has been training to go into Africa, not Iraq."

"Simon, don't worry. Leave the military questions to me—I know that's not your specialty. In some ways it will be easier than the Africa assignment. The U.S. and Britain are already doing flights over Iraq, and the infiltration can be worked out a lot better with that cover. Besides, we'll have the element of surprise. Hussein Kamil says that he's going to be there at the meeting to gather information for his new benefactors—the CIA. But I haven't told the CIA about this . . . yet. Our mission will have the element of surprise."

"How do you figure?"

"Kamil will be there. He won't be expecting an attack because he'll think the CIA wants him back alive to spill his guts about his infamous poppa-in-law. And that means that the Iraqi security services won't be as alert as they otherwise might be. This is perfect."

"That's pretty good," Harrod chuckled. "But maybe we do want to keep him alive. If he defects, it'll look good in the President's news conferences if we can parade him or his information to show how aggressive we are at fighting international terrorism and dictatorships."

"I'm not sure that we *need* his information," the general said. "I think that the Mossad, CIA, and the other intelligence reports that we are receiving will be more reliable. Can you imagine the husband of the daughter of Saddam burning all bridges in getting out? Is she that estranged from her father or that much in love with this guy she married? He might want to go back some day, so he's not likely to give us stuff we don't already know, and we already know a lot," said General Komulakov.

"About that list you're going to have to me by morning . . . is Aidid on it? Is he going to be at Saddam's little party?" Harrod asked.

"No . . . why?"

"Then put his name on the list."

"I don't understand."

Harrod explained, "I've got Newman hooked on going after Aidid as vengeance for his brother's death."

"Ah, I see. If Aidid's going to be one of the players at the meeting in Iraq—"

"Bingo," Harrod interrupted. "Put Aidid's name on that list. It'll be easier to sell a change in the mission to Newman. And I need Newman totally psyched for this mission so the rest of the team will be. They'll follow him into hell with just a wink from Newman . . . but if they sense he's not sure of the mission . . ."

"All right. Aidid is on the list. Anything else?"

"I'll let you know in the morning."

Office of the National Security Advisor
The White House
Washington, D.C.
Saturday, 18 February 1995
0810 Hours, Local

Jonathan Yardley, the senior watch officer for the Situation Room, had called Newman at 0500 hours sharp. Yardley told him that Dr. Harrod wanted him to be in his office at 0730 hours for an urgent meeting. "Are you sure that he didn't say '7:30 A.M.'?" Newman kidded Yardley, knowing Harrod's abhorrence of military expressions.

"As a matter of fact, sir, he did say 7:30 A.M. . . . but we both know that he meant 0730 hours," Yardley chuckled.

"OK, I'll be there. Did you say we were meeting in the Sit Room or his office?"

"He said his office, Lieutenant Colonel Newman."

"Right . . . thanks." Newman hung up the phone and thought of taking an extra twenty minutes of sleep, knowing he hadn't gotten to bed until after two-thirty, but he didn't. He got up, careful not to wake Rachel, and got into the shower.

That was nearly three hours ago, Newman thought. He was on time for the meeting, but Harrod was, as usual, late. Tardiness was one inconsideration that really got to Newman. He fidgeted in his chair in the reception area outside Harrod's office. Other employees were just now drifting in to work, and the receptionist saw him sitting there and offered him some coffee. Newman shook his head and mumbled a quiet, "No thanks."

The clock above the receptionist's desk read 8:10 when Harrod finally walked through a back door down the hall. Newman saw him stop to sweep his card key to let himself in, and he did so quickly.

Five minutes later he came out of the front door to his office and waved to Newman. "Come on in. I've been on the phone for forty-five minutes," he said to the Marine. That lie exasperated Newman's already deep lack of respect for Jabba the Hutt.

It took about twenty minutes for Harrod to bring Newman up to date with all that had transpired the previous day and the information from Kamil about Saddam's meeting.

"Just who is this Hussein Kamil character?" Newman asked.

"He's Saddam Hussein's son-in-law."

"Oh, yeah . . . I thought his name sounded familiar. And this intelligence about a big terrorist gathering in Iraq came from him firsthand?"

Harrod nodded. He didn't tell Newman about the fact that Kamil wanted to defect and that this information was his down payment on an agreement to get him safely into the West. Instead, Harrod blurred the edges of the truth by telling him that a double agent had received this information. "This guy's Ukrainian—I think he used to work with Komulakov in Moscow, but now he works for the West," Harrod explained.

"You mean the UN," Newman said.

"Yes, but he's in *our* pocket too. His stuff is reliable. He can be utterly trusted."

"Uh-huh," said Newman, not as convinced. "But what does all of this have to do with me or my team?"

Harrod acted impatient. "Judas, man, I just told you. Weren't you paying attention?"

"You're talking about a big meeting in Iraq in a little less than three weeks from now. When are you going to drop the other shoe?" Newman asked somewhat impatiently himself.

"Your orders have been changed. Instead of going into Somalia, your team will be going to Iraq. We're going to take out the whole lot of them! You see, here's the clincher. *Aidid* is gonna be there too! There are at least *twelve* names on that short list that I was telling you about—twelve of the world's most brutal terrorists that we want to eliminate."

"Why not just send in the U.S. Air Force and level the building that they'll be meeting in?" asked Newman.

"Because this has to be done as a UN operation. That's what the ISEG was set up to do. And it has to be done without any U.S. fingerprints on it," replied Harrod.

"How are we going to do that?"

"I've been thinking about all this," said Harrod. "Yesterday I was out in Colorado for a briefing on our UAV program—you know, those unmanned aerial vehicles."

Newman nodded, listening.

"We're about to start using a few of them over Iraq to see if they can cover the no-fly zones with them. I think if we put one of your ISETs on the ground in the vicinity of the meeting, they can confirm Saddam's guests, and when they all are inside, 'paint' the place with one of those new Laser Target Designators. Your guys can 'fly' a UAV rigged up with a warhead by remote control and send it right in the window of where this 'terror summit' is being held." Harrod stopped and leaned back in his chair, pleased at his mastery of the military terminology.

Newman pondered what the National Security Advisor had just said and then asked, "I've never seen a UAV big enough to do really serious damage. Is there such a thing?"

"Yes, I just saw some video of it yesterday. It's called 'Global Hawk,' and it can carry a payload of more than twenty thousand pounds," said Harrod with a smile.

"Well, that would certainly do the job," said Newman. "But how do we avoid the U.S. fingerprints on this? We're the only ones who have such a thing."

"Right," said Harrod, still smiling. "And when it kills Saddam, Aidid, bin Laden, and all those other terrorists, we'll simply say that it went out of control and we regret that it crashed." Harrod was now smiling like the Cheshire cat.

"When is this meeting in Iraq?" asked Newman.

"March 6. And it's in Tikrit—at Saddam's summer palace. It's his hometown," said Harrod.

"Well, I have confidence in my guys . . . they'll get your bad guys. But, that doesn't give us much time," Newman observed.

"Yes, I know," Harrod said. "But everything that your guys have trained for in the Somalia plan will have tuned the guys up for this. So the plan will have to be tweaked a little, but it's still the same kind of mission. You need to tell your team about the change in plans. Where are they, still at Fort Bragg?"

Newman bit his tongue to keep from saying something he'd regret. He took a breath and spoke slowly and evenly. "No, Dr. Harrod," he said, "my team completed their training at Fort Bragg and have been training at the British SAS site in Oman since the end of January."

"Whatever . . ." Harrod said dismissively. "I want you to take this file of new intel and digest it. Then I want you on a plane to brief the ISEG, wherever they are, ASAP, preferably before dark. Do you understand your change in orders, Lieutenant Colonel Newman?"

"Aye-aye, sir!" Newman replied instinctively.

Harrod had chosen this specific moment to actually recognize the military considerations that would draw this response from the Marine. Distasteful as it was for him, he felt good about the response he got.

"Oh, Newman, by the way . . . there's one other detail."

"Yes?"

"I remind you of the guidelines for these missions. You are not to accompany the units that go on the ground for this mission. I want you in Kuwait or Turkey, or wherever you decide is best to control this operation, but under no circumstances are you to go on the ground in Iraq."

"I understand, but I remind you, Dr. Harrod, the SOP that you approved for these missions provides for me to ensure that they are properly inserted. If we have to use that converted MD-80 to put them in by High Altitude–High Opening parachute insertion, I plan to accompany the aircraft to determine that they're in the right place. Otherwise, we've wasted a well-trained team."

"You may go on the insertion, and no further. No heroics. Is that clear?"

"Yes," said the Marine, biting off the "sir" before it escaped his lips.

"How will you get them out, once the job is done?" asked Harrod.

"I don't know yet. I'll have to look at the intelligence, get some satellite photos of the terrain, analyze the enemy situation. The rear hatch on the MD-80 is too small to drop vehicles. I don't even think we can get the dirt bikes we've trained with through that hole. I don't know. I'll have to think about that. It may be necessary to use some U.S. air assets after all."

"Well, let me know what you need. Remember, there cannot be any evidence of U.S. involvement when this whole thing is over," Harrod warned him.

"I understand."

"Good," said Harrod, getting up from behind his cluttered desk. "Incidentally," he said looking up at the Marine, "even if this all goes perfectly, there are likely to be some after-action reports prepared, and I'll need you back here filling in the blanks."

Newman had mixed emotions about this change in plans. It didn't really matter where he found Aidid—that wasn't the issue. Right from the start, Harrod had made it clear that he didn't want Newman, Coombs, Robertson, or McDade going "in country" after Aidid. But right from the time he had begun planning for the Somalia operation, Newman had been hoping that the murderous warlord would be captured alive and brought to his command post in Djibouti by the ISEG when they extracted. He had long savored the thought that he would be able to look his brother's killer in the eye—before he killed him.

Now, with this new scenario, Aidid would simply perish in a ball of fire from the warhead of a high-tech machine—a robot programmed to kill. It would have to do.

Something else bothered the Marine: Harrod's comment about "after-action reports" and "filling in the blanks." Newman thought, *If Harrod has said it once he's said it a thousand times: he doesn't want a lot of paperwork floating around on this stuff. Now all of a sudden the mission has changed from Somalia to Iraq—and there are going to be questions to answer. I have no doubt that I'll have to answer the questions . . . I just wonder who will be asking them.*

If anything went wrong, he knew who the fall guy would be.

CHAPTER THIRTEEN

Mission Doubts

Headquarters of Amn Al-Khass
Baghdad, Iraq
Monday, 20 February 1995
0910 Hours, Local

The phone on Hussein Kamil's desk jangled.

"Leave," Kamil said to the two ranking officers sitting in front of his desk. "I must take this call."

"Who are you and what do you want? And how did you get the number of my private line?" he said as soon as they had shut the door behind them.

The voice on the other end of the line did not identify itself and ignored the questions. "I must talk to you. Your three nephews are planning to visit. We must make arrangements."

Kamil recognized the voice of Leonid Dotensk. He sat up straight in his chair. *The warheads must be ready.*

"I will meet you where we last met," Kamil said, glancing at his watch. "At the same time. I will come with two of their uncles who will be anxious to make sure they are healthy."

"No . . . I'm afraid they are not *here*, but merely

ready to visit. That is why I want to make arrangements with you."

Kamil did not say anything for a moment. "All right. I'll meet you anyway."

He hung up the telephone. He smiled, again enjoying the brilliance of shooting his chauffeur, then blackmailing Dotensk. He had even given the Ukrainian his handsome pistol just before dropping him off a block from his office—and after removing the remaining bullets from the magazine. He realized that even if Dotensk got rid of the gun, the Ukrainian knew Kamil could "find" other evidence to use against him.

Unfortunately, there were questions about the disappearance of the chauffeur. Abu's wife and son worried when he did not return that evening; they went directly to Hussein Kamil himself to ask about his whereabouts. He had to give them a line about a special mission and "national security" to keep them quiet. He reassured them that they would see him soon, but he told them not to speak about the matter to anyone in the meantime.

Kamil picked up the phone again to call one of his security officers. "Bring Abu's wife and son to my office. And get me a car from the palace motor pool. No, I don't need a driver. And no bodyguards." It wouldn't do to have witnesses to his meeting with Dotensk.

When the wife and son arrived, Kamil escorted them into his private office. He gave them refreshments of tea and date loaves. Then, when the large shelf clock across the room began to chime, he said, "I will take you to see Abu now." He led them to the rear entrance of the building where the Mercedes was parked, its motor running.

He leaned toward them as they approached the car. A

motor pool driver was holding the door for them. "Say nothing, get into the car," he whispered. They did as they were instructed, happy at last they would see their loved one who'd been missing for almost a week.

The trip took about forty minutes. Kamil saw the Ukrainian's car parked near the spot they had last met. Dotensk opened the door and got out as Kamil's Mercedes pulled up. He held up both hands in greeting so that the Iraqi could see that he was unarmed.

"I am afraid that I have bad news for you," Kamil said when they were standing in front of the car. "Abu has been killed. Come, I will take you to his remains."

Abu's wife screamed and fell into her son's arms. Kamil took one of the woman's arms and her son took the other and they half-led, half-carried her to where her husband's body was. Animals had been at the body and the wind had coated what was left with sand. The widow and son both dropped to their knees beside the corpse and began to wail. Kamil pulled on a pair of calf-skin gloves, walked over to Dotensk, and said, "Give me your pistol."

"No . . . don't do this," said the Ukrainian, backing up against his car.

"Give it to me or I shall kill you here and now," said Kamil, his hand on his holster.

Dotensk handed over the gun and looked away. Kamil lifted the pistol and fired two shots. The son and his mother dropped on top of the corpse of the man who had served Kamil so faithfully.

"Dear God!" Dotensk cried out. "What are you *doing*? Must you kill someone every time we meet?"

"It had to be done."

Kamil ejected the clip from Dotensk's pistol, cleared the round out of the chamber, and handed the weapon back to the Ukrainian. "They were the wife and son of the chauffeur, and they would have begun to ask more questions."

The Ukrainian was trembling. He wasn't sure whether it was because of fear or rage. *This man is a lunatic!* he thought. *He is evil—even by my standards.*

"Two birds with one stone. Or, more correctly, three birds with one gun," Kamil said. "Now there is no one who will ask questions. *And* I have added to the means that will ensure your trust and loyalty."

"You didn't have to kill *any* of them for that. I told you, I *do* trust you and you can trust me."

"Nothing like honor among thieves, eh?"

"Well, let's get down to business," Dotensk said. "I do not have much time. If I am to complete the arrangements, I must leave this evening. Here is the plan. Make arrangements to have your scientists in Damascus by Wednesday noon. There will be a plane there to take them to the place where the three warheads are hidden. Your experts will accompany me there and be able to make their tests. I will provide the test equipment—they will have trouble getting their own equipment out of Iraq."

"Where will all of this take place?"

"I cannot tell you. It's better that no one else knows."

"I understand, but my scientists cannot get back here in time to be in Damascus when you want them to. One will be coming from Montreal and the other from Bonn. Can you arrange to meet them somewhere closer? And they will have their own equipment."

Dotensk looked at the three bodies grotesquely sprawled in a pile and decided not to push his "customer" any further. "All right. Tell them to meet me in Kiev, at the Izakov Hotel. You can't miss it—all the other buildings are painted in soft pastels; this is the only white building. They call it *Aqmola*—The White Tomb. It's right on the main street, Khreshchatyk. Tell them to leave a message for me at the same hotel when they check in, and I will meet them. All in all, the trip will keep them in and around Kiev for a little more than forty-eight hours."

"And, assuming all is well and the scientists give me a favorable report of their inspection of the warheads, how will you get them to me?"

"I can't tell you the details just yet, but I am working on a way that will enable us to fly them into Iraq under the very noses of the United Nations inspectors."

"That sounds risky. Why not bring them to Karachi or Istanbul and have them smuggled into Iraq along one of the regular land routes?"

"And they take weeks, sometimes months. Trust me, my way is faster and safer. The less time that they are en route reduces the chance they will be captured or observed by unwanted eyes. This much I can tell you: the shipment will come into Iraq aboard a United Nations airplane that we will be controlling. If you will look at the schedule, you will see that UN inspectors are to be here on the first of March to inspect your Al Atheer site. And since you have advance notice of their schedule, I'm sure the inspectors will find no evidence of nuclear weapons. But unknown to them, they will be bringing in as cargo the very thing that they will be looking for!"

Kamil did a little dance in the sand and laughed. "Audacious! I *love* it!"

The Ukrainian smiled. "You can tell Saddam it was all your idea."

Kamil liked that part of the plan even better. At last he would have some kind of parity with his troublesome brothers-in-law. "But how will you manage to do such an incredible thing?" he asked.

"You can do anything if you have enough money. I'm bribing an entire Ukrainian brigade," Dotensk said.

"Well, I don't care how you do it or how much it costs. I'll be ready with your money as we agreed. After the inspection I'll wire 50 million Swiss francs to your account in Kiev, and the other 100 million will be transferred to your account as soon as I take safe delivery."

"Agreed. And here is the number of the account to wire the funds into. On the first of March, when you take final delivery of the complete package, you need to wire the funds before the close of banking activity for the day. On the following day, there will be a number of transactions to move those funds where they cannot be traced. The same will be true of the first deposit, but it is important that your second deposit is received on time because after I move the money, the account will be closed."

"I will do as you say. Can you get me more of these warheads?"

"Not right away. It is too risky. In a year or two, perhaps. But even if we can locate some, they will be more costly."

"I cannot wait a year—or did you forget? You are also making it possible for me to defect," Kamil reminded him.

"I have not forgotten about your defection. I am making arrangements with the CIA for you to go to Jordan. It would pose too many political problems for the American president to bring you to America right away. They will listen to what you can tell them and give it a value before they determine how far you will travel with them."

"Well, no matter—I may just decide to stay in Jordan . . . but I want to leave no later than August of this year. That gives you at least four months to find me some more nuclear weapons. I don't care what they cost. Just get me some more," Kamil ordered, sounding again like the ruthless man that murdered so carelessly.

"I'll . . . I'll get right to work on it."

Muscat, Oman
Thursday, 23 February 1995
1330 Hours, Local

Customs control in Muscat was a mere formality. An official stamped Newman's passport and waved him through with a pleasant smile. "May Allah grant you a profitable stay, Mr. Newman."

Once outside the double doors that enclosed the customs area, Newman spotted Bruno Macklin, the SAS captain who served as Weiskopf's second in command on the ISEG. Standing with him was a wiry, well-tanned Anglo-Saxon who could have doubled as Macklin's brother. "Welcome to our little bit of heaven, Peter," said Macklin. "Meet me brother, Harry."

Newman shook hands with the two men. "Bruno, is this really your brother?"

"Aye, that he is. Da' made sure all of his sons went into the oil business."

They went outside and climbed into a dusty, well-used Land Rover emblazoned with *ANGLO-AMERICAN PETROLEUM—EXPLORATION DIVISION* in neat green lettering on its dented side. Within a half hour of leaving the airport, they were off the paved road, headed almost due west on a well-traveled dirt track, toward a range of mountains.

Harry drove, Newman rode shotgun, and Bruno Macklin took on the role of backseat tour guide. "The base we're headed to, up in the Al Jabal Al Akhdar mountain range, is one of seven bases that the regiment has run here in Oman ever since World War II. Qaboos bin Sa'id Al Sa'id knows how important his little sultanate is to keeping the Straits of Hormuz open for oil shipments. He's also smart enough to know that having us here is a hedge against Iranian mischief and the crazies of the Popular Front for the Liberation of Oman, which is based next door in Yemen."

Harry crashed through the gearbox and rode the brakes to avoid the ruts and potholes in the deserted road. "Yeah, and the sultan also knows it's a lot safer and cheaper to have us here than it is to hire more soldiers for his own little army," he said.

For the rest of the seventy-eight-kilometer trip to the inland SAS base, the two brothers talked while Newman reflected on how he had come to be sweltering under the equatorial sun with these two tough characters.

✪

The OEOB was mostly empty on Saturday mornings, Newman and his team had learned. Coombs, Robertson, and McDade were the first people he saw after leaving the National Security Advisor's office. The other three looked at him when he shut the door behind him.

"We have a change of mission," he told them.

They all groaned. Their Christmas and New Year holidays—and most of the preceding month—had been devoted to little else but planning the mission to go after Mohammed Farrah Aidid in Somalia. "How did I know this was going to happen?" said Coombs as all four men filled their coffee cups and sat down around the conference table in Newman's office.

The operation had been coming together well. All thirty-eight members of the ISEG had been deployed to the British base area in Oman, and the MD-80 aircraft that Robertson had ordered had been repainted as an Aer Lingus cargo plane on charter to the UN. As specified by the "Concept of Operations" drafted at Andrews Air Force Base back in the first days of December, an advanced operating base had been designated—the old French foreign legion facility at the far west end of the airport in Djibouti. ISET B had been tagged as the primary team to carry out the mission of capturing or killing Aidid in Somalia. ISET E had been told to prepare for departure to Djibouti as the advance party to establish the AOB. ISET C had been ordered to serve as the Quick Reaction Force, and was working on how to respond if the primary team ran into trouble. The two remaining International Sanctions Enforcement Teams and the ISEG headquarters were gearing up for the move to Djibouti aboard the MD-80. Newman's announcement meant that all this would now change.

Newman told them about the expected gathering in Iraq on March 6. When he had filled in the three officers on the new mission and listened to their complaints about how little time there was to do all that was necessary, he said, "Here's what we need. First, Bart, you get off a flash SatCom message to Weiskopf and tell him that the Somalia mission is off and that I'm headed his way with new orders. Tell him that the new target is Iraq and that it includes our present target and a whole bunch of other bad actors—including Saddam himself. That should make everyone in the ISEG happy since they all fought against him in the Gulf War."

"Where do we put the AOB?" asked Coombs.

"Harrod said he didn't care if it was in Turkey or

Kuwait," said Newman. "All other things being equal, we ought to try for Turkey. If I remember correctly, Tikrit is in the north-central part of Iraq, on the Tigris River. It's closer to Turkey, and the Turks may not even notice if this can be made to look like it's part of the normal northern no-fly zone operation.

"Second," continued Newman, "Tom, I need everything you can get on the presidential palace compound in Tikrit. We'll need maps, the latest satellite coverage, nearest friendlies, Republican Guard dispositions—the works." McDade scribbled on his legal pad.

"Dan," said Newman, turning to the Air Force officer, "I need you to find out what we have available in nonattributable guided ordnance—something that can be laser target designated by our guys on the ground and big enough to bring a building down on the bad guys while they have tea. Dr. Harrod mentioned using a UAV he called 'Global Hawk.' "

"Does it have to be U.S.?"

"I don't think it matters as long as we can get it by next week and nobody cares if we don't bring it back."

By 1400 hours the three men had rung enough bells in the U.S. intelligence and Special Operations community to have answers to most of what Newman wanted to know. They gathered again around the conference table.

McDade began: "I've put together a map package for you that shows everything we know about Tikrit and Northern Iraq to the Turkish border. It isn't bad. I've also scheduled seven passes with various assets between now and the fifth of March so we'll know the latest." He laid out the disposition of two Republican Guard armored-mechanized regiments and the nearest locations for Kurdish rebel operations along the southern side of Iraq's border with Turkey. His computer-generated map showed the location of all known Iraqi and Syrian antiaircraft sites, air-search radars, and signals intelligence sites.

Next, it was Coombs's turn. "The best site for an advanced operations base is the Turkish Air Force Base here at Siirt," he said, pointing to the location on the map, west of Lake Van and along the north bank of the River Nehri. "Unfortunately, we're not likely to get clearance to go in there and set up much more than a communications relay on such short notice. Our best bet is to base at Siirt or out of Incirlik. All the U.S.–UK northern no-fly zone ops are being flown out of Incirlik. I like it because there are plenty of U.S. and British assets available on site in case our units on the ground in Iraq get into trouble."

"How do you recommend that we get 'em in and out?" asked Newman.

Coombs looked at Robertson, who signaled for him to proceed.

Coombs continued. "Dan and I think we ought to pre-position the MD-80 at Incirlik, and once everything is set up, pull the tail cone off the aircraft so that we can use it for a High Altitude–High Opening insert of ISET Echo on the night of March 1 or 2. Depending on the weather and winds, we could drop them from thirty thousand feet up to twenty-five or thirty miles west of Tikrit. That would give the team a minimum of three and one-half nights to get into position to set up an LTD to illuminate the target."

"What are we going to use for the strike?" asked Newman.

Robertson spoke up. "Since this can't look like an intentional U.S. attack, all our laser-guided bombs are ruled out, as are cruise missiles. It'd be too hard to explain how a Tomahawk just happened to kill the president of Iraq and a room full of terrorists. In order to deliver a big enough payload, that leaves us just two options: one U.S., the other is Russian."

"Russian?"

"Yes, sir. The Russians have a handful of TU-123 UAVs sitting around." The Air Force officer put a picture in front of Newman. "As you can see, these things are big. They're truck-mounted and launched, and they travel at Mach 2. Max altitude is sixty thousand feet, and they have a range of better than one thousand miles. There are four of them at Factory N-135 in Kharkov that could be modified to accept our telemetry, GPS guidance equipment, a laser targeting terminal control system, and up to three thousand pounds of explosives. The advantage of using a TU-123 is that there would be no U.S. fingerprints. The downside is trying to get the Russians to buy off on it and get it rewired and ready for launch between now and the sixth of March."

"What's the U.S. option?" asked Newman.

Robertson put another photo in front of Newman. "This is what Dr. Harrod described to you. It's called Global Hawk. It's very big; its wingspan is 116 feet, it's 44 feet long, and more than 15 feet high. It's difficult to tell by this photo because it was taken at an altitude of 65,000 feet over Groom Lake Airfield at Area 51 in Nevada, and there's no perspective."

"Good grief," said Newman as the others craned their heads to see. "It looks like a cross between a U-2 and a whale."

Robertson shrugged. "Right now there are three of these things. Two are at Nellis Air Force Base, outside of Las Vegas; the third is undergoing payload tests at the Area 51 site at Tonopah. I talked to one of the engineers at Teledyne-Ryan about an hour ago, and he said that if they had to, they could outfit the telemetry suite the way we want. It already has X-band, UHF, and KU-band satellite radio command uplink equipment aboard. A GPS navigational cross-check system is built in. All they would have to add is the laser designator terminal guidance-control interface so that once it picks up the reflection from the designator our ISET puts on the target, it just follows the laser reflection in through the window. But here's the really good news: the thing weighs only 8,900 pounds empty. It's built to take a 2,000-pound instrument payload and—get this— 14,700 pounds of fuel!"

McDade, the SEAL, couldn't understand Robertson's excitement. "So what's the big deal about that?"

"Typical squid! If it doesn't swim, you guys don't get it. Look, all that fuel is so that Global Hawk can stay airborne for forty-eight hours! Think about it, man. If we put this thing at Incirlik—or better yet—up at Mus in Turkey, we can replace the fuel we don't need with a corresponding weight in C-4 plastic explosives. I've already run the numbers. The flight time from Incirlik at 350 knots is only an hour and forty-five minutes. From the Turk Air Force Base at Mus West it's less than an hour. Build in a margin of error of ten hours to account for wind, weather, or the team being late getting in position if you want. That gives us a ten-thousand-pound bomb, with some fuel left over to burn down the wreckage after it hits." The Air Force officer sat back in his seat with a smug smile on his face.

"What about the U.S. fingerprints problem?" McDade said. "That thing has 'Made in the U.S.A.' written all over it. Nobody else has anything like it. How could they not tie it to the U.S. after the international press corps gets in there to count the bodies?"

"That's right," interjected Newman, trying to smooth over the budding interservice rivalry. "That's why we're going to have a little disinformation campaign after the mission to deal with the back blast.

"We're already flying all kinds of UAVs over Iraq to enforce the so-called no-fly zones and the UN sanctions," Newman said. "The Turks know that our little Predator UAVs launch almost every night out of Incirlik to fly east along the Syrian border and then down into Iraq."

"Yeah, I know about Predators; the SEALs are using 'em for real-time OTH imagery in training, but this is a whole lot bigger than Predator—and the Predators don't have ten-thousand-pound warheads."

"That's why Jabba the Hutt will already be prepared with a press release that says something like, 'The USG deeply regrets that one of its unmanned aerial vehicles conducting reconnaissance in support of the UN sanctions program went out of control on March 6. We regret that it came down on Mr. Saddam's house, et cetera, et cetera.' "

"How does this thing take off and land?" Newman asked Robertson.

"It takes off and lands in five thousand feet, like a conventional aircraft. It just needs a normal, paved runway."

"I think this is exactly what Dr. Harrod had in mind," said Newman. "The only question is, how do we get it there?"

Robertson smiled again. "The wing comes off in two pieces, each fifty-three feet long. It all fits easily inside a C-5. And best of all, the one at Tonopah is already apart. Just in case, I put a C-5 out of Charleston, South Carolina, on standby in case we need a quick trip to Nevada and then to Turkey."

"Well done, gentlemen. I like the Global Hawk option. We have more control over getting it there when we need it. Does anyone have any reservations about this course of action?" Hearing none, Newman said, "I'll check with our boss and see what he says." He picked up his direct line to the Sit Room.

Fifteen minutes later the Sit Room watch officer had found the National Security Advisor, asked him to call Newman using an EL-3 for secrecy, and the two men held a brief conversation. When he hung up, Newman called the team back together.

"It's a go. Bart, you and Tom book yourselves to Incirlik the fastest way possible. Dan, you call whomever it is I need to talk to out in Nevada. I want to know all I can about this Global Hawk thing of yours. I plan to head out there tomorrow to take a look at it. Then I'll go to Oman and pick up the ISEG. Dan, I want you to stay here to act as liaison between Harrod and the rest of us in Turkey. Take care of getting that MD-80 down to Muscat to pick us up and then get it delivered to Incirlik."

He saw Robertson grimace at the prospect of missing the action, so he said, "Look, we need someone here to make sure that the story comes out right. You did a great job pulling all this together as fast as you did. Someone has to stay back on each one of these missions. Next time it will be Bart or Tom."

"Yeah, if there is a next time," said the Air Force officer.

Early Sunday morning Newman flew from Andrews on a USAF Special Air Mission Gulfstream direct to

Nellis Air Force Base in Nevada. The balance of Sunday and all of Monday morning were consumed with briefings set up at the Air Force Air Combat Command's Eleventh Reconnaissance Squadron at the Indian Springs Satellite Airfield. Just before dark on Monday afternoon, they took him over to the Tonopah site, inside Area 51. Engineers from Teledyne-Ryan brought him to a hangar to see the weapon he had chosen for this mission. The black-skinned Global Hawk was being worked over by at least a dozen white-coated technicians. Then, after darkness fell, they took him to one of the towers and spent the next six hours or so showing off the Global Hawk's radar-avoidance capabilities.

Exhausted but satisfied, Newman returned to Nellis shortly after dawn on Tuesday morning. There, he delivered the verdict to the Eleventh Recon Squadron commander: "The President has ordered that on Saturday, 25 February, Global Hawk 3 will be loaded aboard a C-5 for delivery to a Special Projects Office unit at Incirlik, Turkey. Send with it whatever personnel may be necessary to prepare the UAV for a highly classified mission to be conducted not later than 6 March. If all goes according to plan, the UAV will not return. If you have any complications or questions, here is your point of contact." Newman gave them Dan Robertson's NSC phone number.

At 1000 hours, the Gulfstream was wheels up off runway 36 at Nellis, banked hard right, and headed east. Newman slept almost all the way to Dulles, but by the time they landed at 1700 hours EST, he was rested—if rushed. At the Hawthorne FBO the ground-support personnel put him in a van and rushed him over to the main terminal. McDade had booked him on United

Flight 40, the overnight run from Dulles to Paris, and he had barely an hour to get to the gate after mailing to his office anything that would identify him as a Marine assigned to the White House. The only identification he kept was a single dog tag, hanging on a stainless-steel, government-issue chain around his neck.

When the Boeing 747 lifted off at 1800, Newman was seated on the aisle in business class, not as a Marine officer, but as Peter J. Newman, "Deputy Director of Security for Geological Exploration Operations, Anglo-American Petroleum." The business cards he carried had a phone number in Maryland that would ring in the Sit Room, where a watch officer would answer, "Anglo-American Petrol." If there was a problem, the watch officer was instructed to call McDade. Newman was pretty sure that his cover story would work, but he was glad the elderly woman seated next to him was engrossed in an in-flight movie.

The flight landed in Paris at 0715 hours Wednesday morning, and Newman had to hurry between terminals at Charles de Gaulle to catch his Air France flight to Dubai. Remarkably, the flight took off on time and he settled in for another flight across four time zones. It was just after 1800 hours in the Emirates when Newman stepped off the Air Bus and headed toward the immigration and customs control kiosk. Because he had only his carry-on bag, his laptop computer, and the EncryptionLok-3, he breezed through the checkpoint and headed outside into the sweltering heat to get a taxi.

He spent an uneventful but restless night in the Intercon Hotel. From his room, he sent an EL-3 encrypted e-mail to Robertson back in Washington and Captain Joshua Weiskopf in Oman, giving the Air Force officer and the ISEG commander his location and anticipated arrival time in Muscat, Oman, the following day.

Newman arose early the following morning, did some calisthenics to loosen up his cramped muscles, and checked his e-mail again. He had a message from Dan Robertson in Washington, advising that the Global Hawk deployment was proceeding as planned; another from Coombs in Incirlik informing him that he and McDade had leased two large commercial hangars at the east end of the Incirlik Air Base to use as an advanced operating base; and a third from Joshua Weiskopf, telling Newman that when he arrived in Muscat he would be met by a British SAS captain, accompanied by Bruno Macklin. The two Brits would be driving a Land Rover with the "Anglo-American Petroleum" logo painted on the side, Weiskopf said.

At 0900 Thursday morning, Newman checked out of the hotel and went to the airport for his Gulf Air flight to Muscat. This time, the flight didn't take off on time, and it was almost noon before the aircraft finally rolled down the runway for the one-hour flight to the capital of Oman, the strategically located sultanate perched between the Arabian Sea and the Persian Gulf and the unofficial guardian of the crucial Straits of Hormuz, through which pass nearly half of the world's oil.

It was almost 1600 by the time Newman and the Macklin brothers traversed the seventy-eight kilometers from the airport in Muscat to arrive at the front gate of the SAS compound. The base was situated on a desert plain with stark, sheer mountains to the north and west. The mountains made access from the outside almost impossible unless an infiltrator was willing to brave days of wearying, thirsty travel by foot. An aggressor would be discouraged on other approaches as well—first by an ordinary wire fence surrounding the place with numerous "no entry" and "no trespassing" signs in Arabic and English. And inside that fence was the real deterrent: a twelve-foot chain-link fence topped by coils of razor wire. Newman noted video cameras and sensing devices—infrared motion detectors, sound detectors, and alarms that would sound if someone tried to cut the fence links. As a final disincentive, the innermost fence was lighted and electrified with enough volts to kill anyone who touched it.

Newman nodded with approval at the security measures and handed his passport to the guard at the gate. Harry volunteered that Newman had an appointment with Colonel Kensington, the base commander. The vehicle was waved through, and the captain drove to the main headquarters building. As he approached the building, Harry explained that this was where the main contingent of SAS men were housed. It was spartan—little more than plywood barracks—but it was still better than what Newman's ISETs were assigned to. Weiskopf had sent an encrypted e-mail when the ISEG had arrived, reporting that his thirty-eight men were billeted in three hardback tents, large canvas enclosures that provided shade but little else. They were sauna-hot during the day and nearly freezing at night, Weiskopf said.

The British captain led Newman inside the building. It, too, was austere. The building was air-conditioned, but for the sake of the communications equipment, not the personnel. Newman could hear a diesel-powered generator humming somewhere in the distance.

Colonel Richard Kensington was prompt for the meeting, something that immediately endeared him to Newman.

"I understand you're trying to break the British record," the Colonel said, smiling.

"British record?" Newman asked.

"Yes . . . you know . . . those chaps back around 1880 who went around the world in eighty days, don't you know. Seems you want to do it in thirty hours."

"Well, I didn't quite make it. I think I've spent at least that much time in the air, but I've still got a trip to . . . to the north of here."

"Yes . . . well, I know your time is brief, so let's get right to it, shall we?" The colonel handed Newman a glass of ice water. "You chaps would rather have tea, I would guess, but in Her Majesty's service, we consider putting ice in good tea to be a sacrilege."

Newman smiled. "Thank you."

"I'll give you the tuppence tour." Kensington stood and walked toward a large map on the opposite wall. "As you can see, this is one of seven SAS bases here in Oman," the colonel said, using a pointer on the topographic map. "This particular installation was built during World War II for parachute training and desert maneuver exercises. This is the main base, really," he said. Then he pointed to an unpopulated area of the desert in the shadow of the mountains. "This is your team's base. We weren't able to offer them much in the way of hospitality, I'm afraid. Just three big tents." Newman shrugged and nodded.

"The tents aren't fancy. And they don't have toilets or running water. We keep mosquito netting over the cots in the tents," Kensington continued. "We have to be careful here about contracting malaria. We also gave your men a kerosene stove—it gets rather beastly chilly at night in these parts."

The colonel walked back to the small conference

326 | MISSION COMPROMISED

table across the room and handed Newman an envelope full of loose papers. "You'll find in here some additional documentation to support your cover. There are some real geological survey reports in there along with some meaningless drivel about personnel problems, missing equipment, and the like—all very authentic, I'm told by the intelligence chaps. It is of course the same kind of material that we gave to your Captain Weiskopf and his boys. By the way, my compliments, Colonel Newman, on the quality of the men you have selected to do whatever it is you have to do. Your man Weiskopf seems to be tip-top."

Newman could tell that the British officer was digging for information on their mission. A knock on the door spared him the difficulty of telling the British colonel that he simply wasn't cleared to know what the ISEG was doing and where they would be doing it.

The knock was followed by the voice of the camp's sergeant major. "Captain Weiskopf, sir." The deeply tanned and bearded Delta Force officer entered. Weiskopf was wearing a foreign desert camouflage uniform and his side arm.

Weiskopf saluted the British colonel. "Colonel Kensington, good day, sir. Lieutenant Colonel Newman, welcome to the best amusement park in the British Empire. I've commandeered a vehicle, and I can take you to our camp whenever you're ready."

"Well, I think we're done here, Lieutenant Colonel Newman," said Kensington. "Let me know if you need anything. When you're ready to move your boys down to Muscat for the trip out of here, just give Sergeant Major Wilcox a few hours to round up some lorries." Kensington stood and extended his hand.

The two Americans walked out to a canvas-topped

Land Rover. Newman tossed his carry-on and computer bag into the backseat. As they got under way, Newman briefed Weiskopf on the change of mission and his meeting with the other team leaders.

"How far away is your camp?" Newman asked. There was no sign of any tents as far as his eye could see.

"About thirty klicks northwest. So I hope your kidneys are in good shape, 'cause they're about to take a beating."

"Well, I've already seen the downside . . . tell me the good points of this place."

"It's quiet. And almost always sunny. No bad neighbors—in fact, no neighbors at all."

Newman's stomach reminded him he hadn't eaten in fifteen hours. "How's the food?"

"Food's OK . . . we've got our own mess tent. The SAS gave us a couple of their regular Army cooks and the food isn't half bad—if you like canned meat of indistinguishable origin and canned vegetables of uncertain pedigree. The cooks aren't all that experienced, but they can't go wrong just opening a can or a freeze-dried packet. They have the usual powdered eggs, milk, and something they claim is ice cream. The cook says, 'These eggs are just like your mother used to make,' but Sergeant Major Gabbard says, 'Yeah—if your mama was a sadist!' "

Both men laughed. Newman said, "We had a cook like that at Camp Lejeune."

"If it's GI food, it's either canned, packaged, or imaginary," Weiskopf said. "The only fresh food is the bread. Every day some guy brings in a loaf of bread for each of us. The cooks pick 'em up when they go back to the base for supplies. I'm guessing that some local who's on the tab of the Iranians or the PFLO is bringing it in. I think that he reports every day to his handler how many people are in the camp, based on the number of loaves he delivers here."

"I saw quite a few civilians back there at the headquarters area. What's their story?"

"Well, in typical British fashion, the base is totally supported by local 'businessmen' who contract with Her Majesty's armed forces to do everything—haul away the trash, provide motor oil for their small fleet of four-by-fours, Land Rovers, and motorized mountain bikes—all painted with camouflage like this one. These civilians also work on the generators, pump out the latrines, and things like that. The only place that they can't roam is our end of the base. I guess the SAS is kind of sensitive about people finding out that Americans are being billeted and trained here. Oh, and they don't allow civilians near the planes at the RAF air base on the other side of the mountains out in the desert, south of Ibri. They've got British AV-8 Harrier jump jets and some helos over there, and the C-130 that we use for our HA-HO jumps. They've got a whole company of Marines from the 40 Commando guarding the place.

"Since they keep us segregated from the main base, we don't get involved with the guys at the garrison. Sometimes the locals invite the Brits to a little party— they call 'em *haflas*. Not all that great by our standards, until you've gone awhile without fresh meat—then you're drooling. So we twist these guys' arms and ask them to bring us back some roasted lamb, goat, camel— or whatever it is. On occasion, they'll bring us back some roasted meat over some rice. Sure beats the stuff the Army cooks bring on," Weiskopf said.

"Speaking of goat meat," Newman interjected, "have

you guys had any of the local goat sausage? I hear it comes highly recommended."

"Are you kidding? Colonel . . . do you know how it's made?"

Newman shook his head. Weiskopf told him. "Well, they don't have a grinder to grind the meat, so the older women cut up the raw meat in chunks. Then they chew it up the best they can with their mostly toothless gums until it's nice and tender. Then they squeeze it into goat gut and tie off each link of sausage with a hair that they pluck from their own heads."

"Stop . . . you're making me hungry."

They drove another several kilometers. "Is it always blowing sand like this?" Newman asked. "Man, it must get real hazy sometimes."

"It's mostly like that during the day. By night, the wind goes away and the sky becomes brilliantly clear. This far away from the lights of the base, we get some terrific celestial viewing. And it's been good for navigational training."

"How's that going?"

"Excellent. In addition to parachute and navigational, we've spent a lot of time on the ranges. They've got things set up so we can test-fire all our weapons. The guys really wanted that 'cause they didn't have time for much of that at Fort Bragg. We've also been working the bugs out of setting up the new, enhanced Laser Target Designators."

"Good . . . that's going to be critical for the mission. Well, it sounds like you've got things under control."

"How was your trip from the land of the free and the home of the brave?"

"Not bad, just long. I started in D.C., went to Nellis to see the UAV we're going to use for this mission, then back to Dulles, on to Paris, Dubai, and now here. Any complications in getting your ISEG in?"

Weiskopf told him that all thirty-eight team members came in from different places, in twos and threes, on different flights. Some came through London to Nairobi and direct to Muscat. Others came in from Amman, Jordan, and into Abu Dhabi. One team came in via Frankfurt to Riyadh, Saudi Arabia, and then to Muscat. One three-man team flew into Dubai from Instanbul and drove overland to Muscat on the coast road.

Before they left Bragg, the SAS had secured paper to support their cover as part of a BP geological exploration team. So far, no locals had questioned the cover, Weiskopf said.

"Everyone but you has either a Dutch, Irish or British passport plus the usual pocket litter—business cards, photo-ID badges, and other proof that we are who we said we are. If somebody ever asks us about geology or oil exploration, the boys have been briefed to bluff and tell 'em that we were sent in to look for some lost equipment left by a previous expedition. If they wonder about us, we give 'em business cards and ID. Then they call 'our' phone number to check us out . . . and if everything goes the way Captain Coombs and Lieutenant McDade planned it . . . somebody in London or the White House answers the phone, 'Hello, British Petrol. . . . '"

"Is that your camp up ahead?" Newman asked after another lull in the conversation.

"That's it—still about seven klicks away. Before we get there, can you tell me why the Somalia mission got canked?"

"All I know is that last Saturday, the National Security Advisor called me in and said that he had intel that

Aidid was going to be at some big terrorist summit in Iraq on March 6. Our mission is to crash the party. The upside is that if we succeed, we get Saddam, Aidid, and a whole bunch of black hats all at once. The downsides are that we have very little time to prepare for the mission, we'll be using unproven technology, and we have to change the Primary Team from Bravo to Echo."

Newman didn't mention to Weiskopf the other concern that had been nagging him since Harrod had changed the mission: McDade had been ringing every bell he knew at the CIA, NSA, NRO and DIA trying to get more intel on the March 6 pow-wow in Tikrit. None of the intelligence agencies knew anything about it.

Office of UN Force Command
UN Headquarters
New York, N.Y.
Friday, 24 February 1995
1035 Hours, Local

"General, call for you on the encrypted line from Baghdad."

Komulakov looked up from the report he was reading. "All right, Major Ellwood, route it into my office. I'll take it in here."

In ten seconds the phone rang. Komulakov switched on the EncryptionLok-3 device wired to his telephone. If, in the unlikely event that anyone was tapping the phone and listening, they would hear only garbled noises. The same was true at the other end. Leonid Dotensk also had an EL-3 device, provided to him at General Komulakov's direction as a "UN contractor."

"Why are you calling me? I told you not to call here

except in emergencies," Komulakov said curtly in Russian.

"This is an emergency," Dotensk replied. "You told me to push up the delivery schedule and I am flying to Kiev in an hour. I just want to make sure that the plan is still 'go.' I need to know the details because their scientists want to examine the goods before the money is sent. What happens after I get to Kiev?"

"Things are still on track. When you get to Kiev, Colonel Murat Kaszak will meet you at the airport. He will have a large Ukrainian military van and an official escort vehicle that will take you and your scientists out to the old military air base. You know the place?"

Dotensk sighed. "Yes . . . I know it well."

Dotensk had been stationed there with a KGB Department V detachment during the Russian-Afghan war. By the time the Afghan debacle ended, he'd become totally disillusioned with the Russian military machine, especially its neglect of the military men who served in that conflict. Before a major in his unit defected to the West, he had told Dotensk that it was a sin how the Russian people and even the Ukrainians had such disrespect for the veterans of the Afghan war. "The Russians started this war only to test new military weapons. They had no real purpose or plan. Such a government does not deserve anything from us but our contempt." Two weeks later he was in the West.

It was shortly after this that Dotensk became a double agent, working both sides of the street. He had not defected—but he was paid handsomely as a freelance operator by the CIA and occasionally gave them good information. He maintained an office and residence in Kiev. Dotensk had set up a bogus trading company that permitted lots of travel without serious scrutiny. And he was also an agent of the UN, working directly under the First Deputy, General Komulakov. Komulakov was also a friend of the Russian major who had defected, and apparently all of them were playing every authority for what they could get out of them.

Dotensk and Komulakov had a unique partnership. The general was still a Russian-Ukrainian citizen (no one knew for sure where he was born since he had birth certificates and passports for both nations) and he had a lot of contacts from the former Communist apparatus—ex-KGB officers like himself, military men and ex-military men—he even had ties with the Russian mafia.

Dotensk had similar ties from his own background. Between the two of them, Dotensk and Komulakov were able to recruit the renegade soldiers who had helped them locate and hide nine 177mm nuclear artillery warheads. During the chaotic transport operation to move the stockpiles of Soviet Army, Navy, and Strategic Rocket Force weapons from the Ukraine back to Russia in 1992, the redirection of the nine warheads was almost too easy. Overlapping bureaucracy and the haste of the whole operation made the thefts virtually undetectable.

Dotensk got some UN money from Komulakov through the International Atomic Energy Agency, ostensibly grants for research on reducing the nuclear weapons stockpile of the former Soviet Union. And, he could honestly say that he was reducing the number of Russian warheads—but Komulakov was the only person who knew the Ukrainian was reducing Russia's nuclear warheads by selling them to Iraq.

Dotensk listened carefully now as Komulakov filled him in on the details of retrieving the stolen warheads.

"At the air base outside of Kiev, Colonel Kaszak will

take you all to a building at the air base and outfit you with decontamination suits. You take these suits with you and the colonel will have someone drive you north to Chernobyl. The driver will take you to the southern entry gate of the Chernobyl Restricted Zone. There you must don the protective suits and that is where my men will meet you and let the Iraqi scientists examine the three devices. The site is abandoned because it is still very contaminated—making it the safest place to store your devices. When Kamil's experts are satisfied, have them call their employer so that the first payment can be made. Then, on February 28 I have made arrangements for UN IAEA inspectors to fly in to Chernobyl for a routine inspection of radiation levels. While the UN inspectors are doing their work, my men will load our special cargo onto their plane. It will be packaged with 'contaminated soil samples' from the Chernobyl site, so even if the lead-shielded crates give off some radiation when the plane lands at our client's airport, no one should have to wonder why."

"There is one other matter," Dotensk said. "The client wants more product. Is it possible for us to supply him with more warheads before he leaves town in August?"

"Hmm . . . Perhaps. Did you discuss costs?"

"Only in general terms. But I thought because of supply and demand, the price ought to be two or three times our current price."

"I agree. I think he will be good for it. I'll talk with you after this sale has been completed."

Komulakov had a sudden thought. Unlike Dotensk, he knew that if things went as currently planned, their best—and thus far their only—paying customer would die in a fiery explosion on March 6 when the ISEG guided an explosives-laden UAV through a window of Saddam Hussein's palace. And then it occurred to the Russian general that even if Hussein Kamil somehow avoided the holocaust, a successful attack could still precipitate enough of a shakeup in the Iraqi regime to preempt any further sales.

"Uh . . . one more thing," Komulakov said. "You need to warn your client not to leave Baghdad on March 6. There is . . . a possible incident that could create insurmountable problems for future sales. He must not go to Tikrit for the meeting with bin Laden."

"He will want to know why. Do you want to tell me the reason?"

What could he tell Dotensk? Komulakov glanced at the doorway leading to the communications suite and Ellwood's desk. "I . . . don't think I should say. But plans are made and even now are being implemented . . ."

The slight electronic rustle on the phone told him Dotensk was running possibilities in his mind. Would his partner get scared, so late in the game? Another sale could easily net them several hundred million Swiss francs each.

"All right, then, listen carefully." Komulakov glanced again toward his closed door and lowered his voice. "The British and Americans are planning to assassinate Saddam and the others on that day. If Kamil is there, he will die with the rest of them. You must make it a priority to protect our client. If you can get him to stay away from Tikrit on the sixth, it will be best."

"But if Kamil stays away, and this attack goes forward, he will immediately be suspect," replied Dotensk. "As I see it, if Saddam is assassinated there will be an immediate struggle for power—and if that is the case, it is unlikely that we will be able to sell any more merchandise to Iraq."

Komulakov thought for a moment. "Then we must look after Saddam as well as our client . . . even if it means, uh, compromising the other plans."

Komulakov hung up the secured telephone and sat very still for several minutes. He had just severely compromised a top-secret mission sponsored by the most powerful nation on earth and one of its closest allies. But . . . surely there would be other opportunities to eliminate this handful of terrorists. And why should Komulakov be concerned for Harrod's plan to make the American president a hero to the international community? Public approval was fleeting. But 500 million Swiss francs . . .

Yes . . . he would have to abort the mission. However, he'd have to keep up the pretense—at least until he collected the payment. There were many arrangements to make. Komulakov sat back in his chair, bridged his fingers in front of his face, and stared into the middle distance, deep in thought.

CHAPTER FOURTEEN
Bartering Lives

Incirlik Air Base
Adana, Turkey
Monday, 27 February 1995
0530 Hours, Local

The U.S. Air Force C-130 had just been given clearance to land at Incirlik Air Base, ten kilometers east of the city of Adana—one of the most ancient sites in Turkey. Even at this early hour, Newman could see the base was a buzz of activity. Ordnance carts and "follow-me" trucks crisscrossed the aprons. Since Desert Shield in 1990, Incirlik had been the hub of NATO's patrols over Iraq's northern no-fly zones.

Aboard the plane, in addition to the five-man USAF flight crew, were Captain Joshua Weiskopf, the thirty-seven men of his United Nations International Sanctions Enforcement Group, and Lieutenant Colonel Peter J. Newman, USMC, head of the White House Special Projects Office.

As the lumbering transport banked to the left to commence its final approach, Newman climbed up into the cockpit. Below them in the predawn glow of the lights, he could see the two runways—one nearly two miles long, and the other only a bit shorter. Between the concrete strips, he could see the concrete and steel-reinforced aircraft shelters protecting American F-15 "Screaming Eagles," F-16 "Fighting Falcons," British Tornados and VC-l0s, along with Turkish F-4Es, F-16s and HC-135s. On the parking ramps and spread out in revetments around the field were U.S. C-12s, HC-130s, KC-135 mid-air refueling tankers, a giant C-5 cargo transport, helicopters of various sizes and shapes, and a British VC-10.

Newman knew that, in one of the large hangars that surrounded the base, a team of Air Force and Teledyne-Ryan engineers and technicians were reassembling the Global Hawk that had been shipped in from Nevada.

The strategic base at Incirlik had been activated in 1954 and served all through the Cold War as a listening post as well as a site well suited for the launch and recovery of NATO surveillance and reconnaissance flights. Many of the American U-2 flights over the Soviet Union had originated here.

The horizon glowed red over the Nur mountain range to the east by the time the wheels squealed onto the end of the runway. The heavy craft slowed, turned left onto a high-speed taxiway, and came to a halt beside one of the large hangars at the southwest corner of the base.

Newman climbed back down into the cavernous cabin feeling a sense of exhilaration. Ever since he left Washington a week ago, he had felt a renewed sense of balance. He was with a group of military men engaged in a challenging series of tasks. He was making things happen—and he was in charge. However, the knowledge that he was involved with similar-minded men in a difficult and potentially very dangerous endeavor heightened his natural sense of responsibility. Despite the fatigue and frequent time zone changes, every time he thought about being one day closer to evening the score with his brother's murderer, the adrenaline would kick in and he would feel even more alert.

"OK ladies, pick up your purses and follow me to the loo!" Sergeant Major Gabbard yelled as the ramp at the back of the aircraft dropped down. There were a couple of scattered *hoo-rahs*. The men grabbed their kits and shuffled toward the tarmac. They had been packed into the back of the aircraft since they boarded in Muscat just after dark at 1900 hours; they hadn't even been allowed off when the C-130 landed at Amman, Jordan, to take on fuel.

One of the SAS troopers stood at the base of the ramp and delivered an impromptu courtesy speech in a Cockney baritone: "It's been a pleasure having you aboard Air-sick Airways. If any of you weirdos have to travel to hell and back again, we hope you'll fly with us. Please take all your personal possessions with you. Don't leave any guns or grenades on the airplane. They scare the cleaning crew."

Newman smiled. He knew he had a well-honed, high-spirited group. Despite the quick change in their mission, the operation was going well. In fact, the only glitch since the change in target was the unexpected delay in getting the MD-80 out from the States. He had wanted to use it to transport the ISEG from Muscat to Incirlik, but Dan Robertson had sent him a coded e-mail explaining that the USAF Spec Ops people wanted to change out the pilots for the new mission and the new crew had to practice flying the commercial airliner without the tail cone and with the rear hatch opened as it would be for parachute inserts.

Somehow, Robertson had diverted the C-130 to Muscat from courier service for the U.S. embassies in Africa. Newman vowed to call Harrod if the UN-marked MD-80 wasn't on base at Incirlik by Monday night.

At first, Newman had been concerned about the morale effect of the change in Primary Team for the mission. Had they gone after Aidid in Somalia as originally planned, the all-black Team Bravo would have carried out the hit. Newman was afraid the quick substitution of the Middle Eastern Team Echo might have hurt the ISEG's focus.

Echo had been looking forward to the planned capture of Mir Aimal Kansi, a Pakistani terrorist who had murdered two CIA agents in a brazen ambush near their Langley, Virginia, headquarters in 1993. Kansi was reportedly holed up in Afghanistan, suspected of being in league with Osama bin Laden, who was known to also have terrorist operations in Sudan. Echo would have been the point team in that operation. Some Afghanis who had heard about the $2 million reward for Kansi were willing to turn him over to the Americans.

Though Harrod and the CIA wanted Kansi's head, they would wait if the ISEG wanted to deliver bin Laden's first. If they could kill Saddam, bin Laden, and their key terror-planners, then people like Kansi would be like a hand without a brain to instruct it. To a man, Newman believed, the ISET understood the importance of the current mission. Bravo knew their turn would come, and Echo would be ready to do the job at hand. Every indicator of the mens' attitudes looked good to Newman.

Coombs and McDade met Newman and the ISEG on the Tarmac. They ushered the men into the hangar. The yawning interior had been quartered off with portable partitions. One corner had been converted into a billet, complete with military bunks and lockers. Beside it were piles of boxes, ammunition cases, and a miniature armory. The left front, near the big doors, was a well-equipped gym, complete with free weights and benches. And next to it was a briefing area with five rows of folding chairs facing the wall where maps of Iraq, Syria, Jordan, Iran, and Turkey were tacked to sheets of plywood.

"On the far side, through that door, we have offices for the commanders," said Coombs, pointing. "As soon as the troops find their assigned bunks and get their gear stowed, we've arranged for them to eat breakfast at the USAF mess, just beyond the next hangar."

"Your toy from Area 51 in Nevada is in the big hangar right next door, nobody around here even bats an eye when people like us or equipment like that shows up in the middle of the night. They're so used to this stuff around here," McDade added.

Newman nodded in approval. "Good work, guys. Let's get the troops fed and then back here for a brief. Has anyone heard from Dan Robertson on the whereabouts of our MD-80?"

McDade and Coombs looked at each other and both said almost at once, "You don't know?"

"Know what?"

"About the change-out in the pilots for the MD-80," said Coombs.

"Yeah, I got that message from Dan Robertson before I left Muscat. What's the problem?"

"Well," continued Coombs, "it looks like the President has gotten involved. He found out there are no female shooters in our operation, and he told Harrod he wants a woman involved in this mission. Jabba the Hutt has the Air Force scrambling around trying to find a female pilot who can fly the MD-80."

"Over my dead body," said Newman, heading off in the direction of the offices.

After breakfast, Sergeant Major Gabbard had the teams square away their billeting area, then he took them into the hangar next door to show them the Global Hawk. "All right, kiddies, remember," he said, sliding the door open, "you can look, but don't touch."

The all-black UAV was situated sideways on small dollies in the hangar; its 116-foot wingspan was too wide to fit through the hangar's doors. The ISEG officers and men gaped as two white-coated civilian engineers explained to them how they had replaced more than half of the fuel with a corresponding weight of C-4 plastic explosive . . . how the craft would be slid out of the hangar . . . how it would be launched under its own power, guided by radio and computer to the target area . . . and how the new sensor in its nose would seek out the reflected beam of a Laser Target Designator.

An hour later, the ISEG filed back into their hangar for the mission brief from McDade, Coombs, Weiskopf, and finally Newman. As the two-hour briefing and discussion wound up, Newman stood in front of the map of Iraq and the surrounding region. "Let's run over the high points one last time. If all goes according to plan, the MD-80 will enter Iraqi air space behind a flight of F-16s and EA-6Bs. We believe Iraqi radar operators will think the MD-80 is the tanker that normally accompanies the no-fly enforcement missions. We'll drop ISET Echo from thirty thousand feet. The Exit Point for Echo is here, about forty kilometers west of Tikrit and ten klicks north of Lake Tharthar. In theory, we'll be well to the west of any SAM sites, and the hope is that the EA-6Bs will guide a HARM down the throat of any Iraqi crazy enough to keep their radar on.

"Echo, your mission is pretty straightforward once you're on the ground. You move under cover of darkness as close as you can to the presidential palace at Tikrit, ID the building where the terrorist convention is taking place, and illuminate the building with the LTD. Once the target is lit, call us and we'll send the Global Hawk to make a house call. Then be prepared for the havoc that'll follow.

"Once you're out the rear hatch, the MD-80 will return here and fuel up. We're going to try to re-position it at Siirt, the closest Turkish air base to the Iraqi border, as a mobile command post. If the Turks agree, ISETs Bravo, Charlie, and Delta will move up there with Captain Coombs and me. Delta, you'll provide counter-surveillance and security for the command post. Bravo and Charlie, you're the QRF. We're going to beg, borrow, or steal some four-by-fours for you in case you have to make a dash across the border to help Echo. Alpha, you will remain here at Incirlik with Lieutenant McDade to assist in securing and launching the Global Hawk. Once the UAV is gone, you will help in extracting Echo if we have to use our fallback option.

"We have two methods for getting Echo out of Iraq. The preferred method applies if the UAV works as planned and there's a subsequent power struggle for control of the Iraqi government. Under those circumstances, Echo will simply don native garb, commandeer a vehicle, drive north to Mosul, and link up with the QRF in the area between Mosul and Zakhu. Once you're north of Mosul, you're fairly safe because the Kurds and the Iraqi National Congress resistance forces control the territory.

"*Our* fallback plan is a whole lot more complicated, but we may need it if Saddam somehow survives and there is a full-scale manhunt for Echo. If that happens, Echo will go underground in the daylight and, after dark, head due west to this area here, marked on your maps and preprogrammed into your GPS receivers as 'Checkpoint X-ray.' You'll notice on your maps that it's slightly higher ground, hill 837, in the desert about 125 klicks east of the Syrian border. That's where Echo will call in the air drop for Fultons."

"Hey, at Disney World they make you pay for rides like that," cracked someone in the back of the room.

They all knew about the Fulton Surface-to-Air Recovery System, and each had been trained in how to use STARS, though having done it once, few ever waited in line to do it again. The device was so high-risk that it was used only to extricate Special Ops teams so deep in enemy territory that there was no other way of getting them out.

Each STARS canister contained the equipment to extract two men and it could be dropped from almost any tactical aircraft. Once dropped, the canister deployed a small parachute to prevent damage to the equipment inside. Each canister contained helium bottles, a balloon, and a five-hundred-foot nylon line with one end affixed to the balloon and the other fastened to parachute harnesses sewn into two recovery suits for the personnel to be rescued. The procedure required the men to inflate the balloon with helium after strapping themselves into the suits. Then an MC-130, equipped with guard cables and a V-shaped nose yoke, would swoop in low, snag the nylon line, and snatch the harnessed troops off the ground. The men would then be hauled into the rear ramp of the rescue aircraft.

"There are other contingency plans, rendezvous points, emergency exfiltration orders, and the radio frequency plan for the operation in the packets of materials Captain Coombs put on your seats. Are there any questions?"

"Yes, sir," it was Specialist First Class Maloof, of ISET Echo. "What altitude did you say we're going to be at when we exit the MD-80?"

"Depending on wind and weather, between twenty-five and thirty thousand," Newman replied. "You'll have internal oxygen on the aircraft until we arrive in the vicinity of the exit point. Then you'll switch to your personal oxygen bottles for the ride down."

"How far are we going to have to hike to get to Tikrit?" asked another Echo trooper.

"Well, I'll put you out as close as we can without risking the bird. Once you're out, glide as far as possible toward Tikrit. When you get on the ground, bury your chutes and start overland. You have the photos of the building you have to illuminate. Remember, you have to have everything set up by the morning of the sixth."

There were no other questions, though Newman knew from experience that there would be hundreds more as the men went through the op plan and thought about the things they'd have to do in the next week. Just before they were dismissed, McDade came up again and reminded them to read carefully the intelligence material in their packets.

As Newman and Weiskopf walked back to the office space on the other side of the hangar, the Delta Force captain said, "You think we'll get the go-ahead for this, or will some whiz kid in Washington pull the plug on us again?"

"I sure hope this is a go, Josh. I can't tell you how much I'd like to be on the ground at Tikrit when that Global Hawk slams into the palace. I have to admit: for me, it's personal. I want to get Aidid for killing my brother, *and* bin Laden, for helping him do it."

"Bin Laden. Isn't he the guy that was behind the New York Trade Center bombing in '93?"

Newman nodded. "But this time we're gonna get him."

"Well, I'll drink to that," Weiskopf said, raising his half-empty plastic water bottle and taking a swig.

Newman Home
Falls Church, VA
Saturday, 25 February 1995
2230 Hours, Local

Rachel wondered what her husband was doing right now, and where he was. He had taken her out to dinner the Saturday night before he departed, and apologized profusely for being so caught up in his work that he was neglecting her. "I'm planning on being back no later than the middle of March," he had told her. That was more information than she usually got from him. Rachel didn't have the heart to tell her husband of her discussions with Sandy and her attorney about a possible divorce. Later that evening, she and Peter had enjoyed a romantic and passionate night.

And then, on Sunday morning, he had gotten up at 0600 and asked her to drop him at Andrews AFB. As usual when they were together, he drove, and even though the Washington Beltway was virtually deserted, she noticed that he was constantly checking the rearview mirrors.

"What's the matter P. J., afraid of getting a ticket?" she had asked playfully. His only response had been to put a finger to his lips mysteriously and to turn up the car radio.

A short while later, after crossing the Potomac on the Wilson Bridge, he exited onto Indian Head Highway. "Rache, let's stop and get some breakfast. My flight isn't for another hour and I'm hungry."

They pulled into the McDonald's at the intersection with Brinkley Road. Instead of getting in line to order, he headed to a seat by the window. "I'm going to make some notes for while I'm gone," he said. "Would you order for us, please?"

By the time she returned with the food, he was staring out the window at the parking lot where they had left their car. The fast food restaurant was getting busy, and she thought he was worried about his car. "Hey big guy, relax. If somebody hits that old Tahoe of yours, it'll give us an excuse to buy a new one."

He didn't even smile. Instead, when she sat down across from him, he slid a cell phone across the table to her. Underneath the cell phone was a three-by-five card with his writing on it.

"Listen to me, Rache. This cell phone is for you to use if for some reason you don't hear from me by March 8. On the card are three numbers. The first number is for that cell phone. The second number is for Lieutenant Colonel Oliver North—you remember him from Camp Lejeune, when I was in 3/8, ten . . . no, eleven years ago. The third number is for Lieutenant General George Grisham, my boss at HQMC, before I got sent to the Snake Pit."

"Snake pit?"

"The White House."

"P. J., what's going on? Are you in some kind of trouble?"

"Not yet, and I don't intend to be either. But I am concerned about what this White House has me doing—not because I'm in physical danger, but because I don't trust these people one iota. Don't use that cell phone for anyone but those two men. And don't call either of them on any phone except that cell phone. Also, don't use it inside the house. I don't know whether the house is bugged or not."

"The house is *bugged*?" Rachel gasped. "What kind of people are you working with that would bug our house, Peter? What are you doing? Where are you going?"

"I'm going on a very secret mission to Turkey. It's not dangerous, but it's politically very risky. If something goes wrong, I suppose I could end up in Turkish custody, and you might not hear about it until it hit the news. If I haven't contacted you by the eighth, call Colonel North. He'll know what to do. That number is his pager. Leave the phone on, and if he doesn't call you back in three or four hours, try General Grisham's number—but only if North hasn't called you back. Knowing North, he probably sleeps with his pager."

Peter managed a little smile then, but it did nothing to reassure her. An hour later, she had dropped him at the VIP terminal at Andrews and he had kissed her goodbye.

Now, six days after that surreal departure, the breakfast sandwich she hadn't touched was still in the refrigerator downstairs. She was sitting on the edge of their bed while outside a late-winter storm pelted the windows with freezing rain. Rachel couldn't shake the cold she was feeling; having already put on a robe, she now went to stand under the overhead sunlamp in the bathroom.

She sighed. Rachel felt totally off balance in their relationship. Peter had said some special things to her at dinner last week—and now she was even having second thoughts about whether to move forward with the divorce and a life and career of her own. He had confided in her, something very rare for him. He told her that he wasn't happy in his new assignment, and he was beginning to see what really mattered in life. He had confessed to thinking long and hard about their marriage following their disastrous Christmas. He said that she really mattered most to him—and she had melted in his arms.

But after he had gone, some of the same doubts resurfaced. All week she wondered what she should do.

Her friend Sandy hadn't been much help. It turned out that Rachel didn't realize what a religious zealot Sandy was.

First she had pressured Rachel to admit it was wrong to get a divorce. She told Rachel that God hated divorce—He loves people, she was quick to add, but He hates divorce. "The Bible encourages people to work out their problems with God's help. Just stay committed to making the marriage work. If two people want a marriage to work, it will," she had told Rachel.

Rachel told Sandy her advice sounded kind of naïve, that Sandy was operating on a different wavelength. Still, she was persistent, and Rachel finally gave Sandy a reluctant commitment that she would postpone any move regarding a divorce for at least a month.

Rachel walked back into her bedroom and sat down on the bed once more, still thinking about what her friend had said. "Well, what am I supposed to do in the meantime?" Rachel had asked her friend.

"Why, just use that time to pray and trust God."

I don't even know what that means, Rachel thought. Sandy had invited her several times to attend an evening Bible study with some other career women in her church. Finally Rachel got so weary of saying no that she went just to keep Sandy from nagging her.

She reflected on that experience. *Wasn't as bad as I thought,* she told herself. *In fact, I kind of enjoyed it. It sure was different than I expected.*

For one thing, there was no pressure. None of the other women made Rachel feel uncomfortable. For about forty minutes the women read from one of St. Paul's letters in the New Testament, and then discussed its relevance for their lives. Then they prayed. The group leader had asked for requests that could be shared with the women, but Rachel felt too self-conscious to say anything. The other women were not as reserved. Without embarrassment they offered several explicit, personal prayer requests—a son on drugs, a husband who spends his evenings watching pornography on the Internet, a sister facing a mastectomy, another woman facing a layoff. Rachel was amazed at the ease with which they laid bare their hearts.

Interestingly, some of the women said that they wanted to praise God for answers to prayer—and they told how things had improved in their lives.

Yeah . . . I wish things were that simple, Rachel thought. She remembered how she had admired those women for their faith, all of them Christians like Sandy. But Rachel didn't even know what it meant to have faith. She wasn't a religious person, having grown up in a more or less secular home. Neither of her parents had been to church much, although she had memories of her grandmother being that kind of person—one who claimed to know God and felt at ease talking about that aspect of her life. Rachel identified herself as a Christian, in the way one would say, "I'm an American" or "I am Scots-Irish." It had more to do with her family background and overall culture. She felt that she was a Christian because she had grown up in "Christian America" and held most of the same values as those who had more clearly identified themselves as Christians—like the Golden Rule or being against murder and other crimes, and obeying the Ten Commandments. Rachel wondered parenthetically how many of them she'd broken.

Her husband was no help when it came to personal faith in God. Peter had always been such a self-sufficient person that he'd probably never considered God as having any particular relevance to his life. And his parents were much like her own—not religious, and only in church on special occasions like Easter and Christmas because it was traditional—not because the family drew any other meaning from it.

Yet . . . Rachel recalled how, at the funeral of Peter's brother Jim, there was an officer who had presented the family with the folded American flag and took just a moment to share details of Jim's odyssey of faith. *How could that officer know for a fact that there was a place like heaven—and that Jim was there? How can anyone be sure?*

Sandy is like that, she recalled. Sandy had that same quiet, inner assurance and seemed to be at peace with herself.

Rachel stopped brushing her hair and stood up. She glanced at the small alarm clock on her bedside table and decided to give in to an intuitive persuasion. She reached over and picked up the phone. After two rings she heard a familiar voice.

"Hi, Sandy, it's me. . . . I hope I didn't wake you."

Sandy laughed. "Are you kidding? Our teenagers are still doing homework, and my husband is watching a *Seinfeld* rerun. What's up?"

"Oh, nothing . . . just wanted to talk. Peter's still away and—"

"I hope you're not still thinking about divorce."

Rachel chuckled. "The way you came at me the other day, I don't know if I have what it takes to fight *God* over divorce."

There was a moment of silence on the other end of the line. "Rachel, honey . . . I didn't mean to come down on you with all that fire and brimstone routine, but I was so scared for you . . . and what you were going to give up. And I had just heard Dr. Dobson or somebody on the radio that morning talking about how God hates divorce—"

"No, Sandy, you didn't hurt my feelings. I can understand how God—assuming there is one—would be against divorce. I guess . . ."

"What is it you're *really* afraid of, Rachel?"

"I don't know . . . honestly, Sandy, I don't know. I'm really mixed up. I guess I'm scared because I don't have the kind of assurance that you have, you know? I mean . . . when you asked me that question the other day—"

"When I asked you, 'If you died tonight, do you know for certain that you would go to heaven?' "

"Yeah, that one, I got kind of mad at you for asking it. I thought you were being pretty presumptuous. I mean, how can anyone know for sure?"

"Well, do you believe that there is a God?"

"Yeah . . . I suppose I do, y'know? I mean, look around at the universe and everything—how could it all just happen? I guess that deep inside I *do* believe in God."

"OK, and do you remember what we were talking about in Bible study when you went with me?"

Rachel tried to recall the subject that evening. "Wasn't it about what St. Paul said in . . . uh . . . was it Romans? In the Bible?"

"Hey, you *were* paying attention!" Sandy said, then added, "Do you remember those verses where Paul talked about how everyone in the world, not just churchgoers, have sort of a built-in antenna that tells them that there really is a God?"

Rachel laughed, "Is that what it says in the Bible—built-in antenna?"

"I'm paraphrasing," Sandy said with a chuckle. "Anyway, what he said was that everyone knows at least *some truth* about God because God has revealed His existence and something about Himself to every culture. There's something within our hearts that understands that God exists—that the invisible qualities of His infinite love, eternal power, and righteousness all have a ring of authenticity in our hearts and minds. That's because He established something called 'moral law' in us. Deep down, we know the difference between right and wrong because God is righteous and we aren't."

"OK, I think I understand that and can accept that."

"Well, Paul says that if God exists then so does His righteousness. And he says that the trouble with human beings is that not one of them has ever measured up to God's standards of righteousness. Paul says in chapter 3—do you remember this part?—that we've all sinned and fallen short of God's expectations and demands. And that brings up the reason for the Christian gospel. He says—in that same chapter 3—that God 'came by

Christ'—that is, He became a man—the Son of God . . . and well, you know the rest of the story. Jesus lived a perfect life, preached against living contrary to God's standards—St. Paul calls it sin—and then He was crucified. Paul says, 'God presented Jesus as a sacrifice of atonement,' and he said that *through our faith in Christ's sacrifice,* we can have forgiveness."

"How?" Rachel asked bluntly.

"Through repentance, and faith in the fact that Christ really did die for you and your sins."

Some of what Sandy was saying was still going over her head, but that last statement seemed clear enough. Rachel didn't understand it all, but one thing that she did relate to was the innate ideas of right and wrong. It didn't take Sandy to point out the wrong things going on in Rachel's life. She knew intuitively that although she probably wasn't as bad as a lot of other people, she could certainly, and accurately, be called a sinner. She began to weep quietly, overwhelmed by a sense of guilt. Tears of regret ran down her cheeks but she made no noise and her friend didn't know that she was crying.

"It . . . it's a lot to take in," Rachel said.

Sandy began telling her again how *everyone* is guilty—that nobody is better or worse in sinning. "Sin is sin, whether it's a biggie or some little one," Sandy told her, adding, "No one is exempt from the fact that he or she has broken God's laws." Rachel felt the weight of her enormous guilt. She thought of her adulterous affair with Mitch . . . of her anger and resentment toward her husband . . . and she felt absolutely helpless.

"I don't want to live this way," she admitted to Sandy. "Can you help me?"

"Of course. Do you want me to come over—to talk and pray with you?"

"Not tonight . . . it's too late, but are you still off the flight schedule tomorrow? Can we meet for lunch?"

"Yes, honey, I'd love to."

The guilt that Rachel had been feeling gave way to a sensation of being bathed in feelings of love—Sandy's love as her close friend, but it was something more than that—something vague and unfamiliar. It was a perceptible and real feeling. And Rachel recognized it, even though it was impossible for her to describe or quantify it.

She hung up the phone and broke down even more. Her feelings had taken control. Feelings of guilt . . . pain . . . loss . . . then feelings of love . . . hope . . . and the sense that at last she might even be able to forgive herself.

Rachel was looking forward to tomorrow with Sandy.

Saddam International Airport
Area 12
Baghdad, Iraq
Wednesday, 1 March 1995
1000 Hours, Local

Hussein Kamil had made arrangements for considerable pomp and ceremony when the UN nuclear inspectors arrived in Baghdad. There was a band and a news conference to greet the officials and let them—and the world—know that Iraq had nothing to hide.

Kamil summoned one of Iraq's top generals to escort the inspectors to the Al Altheer site they had demanded to see. They would, of course, find nothing at all suspicious. The UN personnel insisted on bringing their test equipment and video cameras. There was no objection by the Iraqis, and the general led a procession that even included TV journalists. They were under way in less than an hour after the UN plane landed.

Leonid Dotensk's flight from Kiev had arrived a day earlier in Damascus, and he had flown into the Baghdad airport, three hours ahead of the UN aircraft. He had also checked in with General Komulakov, who reported that the first wire transfer of 50 million Swiss francs had cleared at the Kiev bank.

Dotensk looked for Kamil in the crowd, but decided to try and meet him when he left the entourage. Dotensk went toward the UN aircraft parked on the tarmac. Security was everywhere at the airport, but some of the elite officers knew Dotensk on sight, and knew that he was an important man who often met with their commander. When the Iraqi Army major saw Dotensk trying to get past the guards, he waved him in.

Dotensk and Kamil got to the area beside the plane at about the same time.

"Good day, my friend," Dotensk said. "I want to introduce you to your nephews."

Kamil smiled and looked among the faces in the hangar until he saw his two nuclear scientists. He motioned for them and the four of them walked out to the portable cargo ramp leading into the plane. Kamil strode up the ramp into the plane's cargo hold. Dotensk and the two scientists followed.

A platoon of soldiers armed with AK-47s formed a perimeter, and Kamil instructed them to shoot anyone who tried to board the plane.

Inside the cargo hold, the two scientists lost no time opening the shielded tops on the wooden crates. First they lifted off the canvas bags marked *RADIOACTIVE SOIL SAMPLES* that had been taken from Chernobyl.

The bags covered a shelf that hid the real cargo. The workers took the plywood shelf out of the crate. Each of the 177mm nuclear artillery projectiles was wrapped in plastic film and lead sheets. As soon as the scientists uncovered the first warhead, they set up their testing equipment and examined the weapon.

After an hour of extensive inspection, the scientists assured Kamil that the goods were as advertised.

Kamil smiled broadly and pumped Dotensk's hand. "All right . . . check the other two crates," he said to the scientists. He turned back to Dotensk. "If they are the same, you will get the rest of your money."

Café al Balad
Palestine Street
Baghdad, Iraq
Wednesday, 1 March 1995
2015 Hours, Local

After the final payment of 100 million Swiss francs had been wired to the Kiev bank, Leonid Dotensk told Hussein Kamil that he had another urgent matter to discuss. "Meet me at the Café al Balad," Kamil told Dotensk. "I need to make sure my 'nephews' are sent to a safe place. I'll see you there in half an hour." Dotensk left. Two of Kamil's most trusted Amn Al-Khass officers then removed the shelves from the UN crates and filled the void with bags full of common dirt so that when the crates were opened at the IAEA laboratory in France, no one would wonder why there was so much Chernobyl soil missing.

The Café al Balad was just down the street from Kamil's office. His bodyguards stood at the front of the café and steered customers away from the small room where the two men were having a quiet but animated conversation.

"What are you saying—that I should *not* go to the summit with Osama bin Laden on Monday in Tikrit? That's madness!" Kamil said sharply. "Why!?"

Dotensk motioned for him to lower his voice. "I have learned that there may be a problem."

"What kind of a problem?"

Dotensk sighed. He knew of no other way to deal with the problem than to be up-front with his client. He told Kamil of the plans for British and American commandos to attack Saddam's palace in Tikrit.

Kamil jumped up as if he'd been jabbed with a cattle prod. He paced for a few seconds, then sat down and swore through clenched teeth. "Why are you telling me this? Did you give information to the CIA so they could come and kill us!?"

"No, I assure you, I did not. The intelligence came from the Jews. The Mossad found out about it and told the British intelligence and CIA. I swear I had nothing to do with this plan."

"Don't you know that if I permit this meeting to go on as planned, and do not show up myself, I might as well carry a sign that says, 'I killed Saddam'? I will be a dead man—*whether or not he survives.*"

"No . . . *I* also have a plan," Dotensk said. "Remember, your well-being is in my own interest. You have asked me to bring more . . . uh . . . 'nephews' from abroad. I have found some more, but it will take a few months to get them to you. This deal, obviously, means a great deal to me and to my associates. If the March 6 summit goes on and there is a major attack, our plan to sell you the additional merchandise will be lost.

"So you can see why we are not the ones behind this planned raid . . . but we *do* have the ability to make it *fail*. And you must help me because it is in your best interest to do so. Your father-in-law will shower you with praise—just as he will when you show him those 'little nephews' that were delivered today. His respect for you will soar after what you will do to *abort* the attack that has been planned for Monday."

Kamil waited for Dotensk to continue.

"We will keep you, your father-in-law, and his guests safe from any harm. After all, I want to add to your family of 'nephews' and collect my money. As I have already told you, it is absolutely in my best interests for the raid on Tikrit to fail and I am going to make sure that you have it within your power to see that it does. And you, Kamil, will emerge the great hero for having discovered the plot and exposing it—and in the process, saving your father-in-law's life.

"On Sunday night they plan to parachute in a team of commandos. Their mission is to set up a laser-targeting device aimed at the palace. Then on Monday afternoon, while your father-in-law and his guests are in the Tikrit palace, an attack will be mounted by some kind of missile or aircraft loaded with explosives and guided to its target by these laser devices."

Kamil nearly shuddered at the thought of it all. He had been terrified by the bombs and missiles they had unloaded on Baghdad when the West launched the war on Iraq—the one they called the Gulf War.

"How do you propose that I stop it?"

"You will let the assassins get in place and set up their targeting equipment, keeping watch from a distance so they cannot see you. Then when you have them all together, it will be like shooting fish in a pond. *I* will know the exact position where they will rendezvous after their parachute jump. Your men can be hidden not five hundred yards from where the Americans and British are set up. There will be only a handful of them, so as soon as they assemble, your men can kill them all. Then you can move the laser-targeting device and use it to aim at one of those old abandoned buildings along the Tigris River. When the laser-guided weapon arrives, it will hit the building by the river instead of your father-in-law's palace. You can even make propaganda capital by bringing in a few truckloads of prisoners from Al Ranighwania Prison. Put some cots in the building, make it look like a hospital or something. All of them will be killed in the bombing. Think of it—you can bring in CNN, BBC, and Al Jazeera Television cameras to film it. Saddam can hold a press conference and tell the whole world that the Americans, with no provocation, bombed an Iraqi hospital.

"Finally, you can alert your anti-aircraft installations to bring as many of the Americans' planes down as possible when they come to search for their missing commando team. Now, it is important that this be coordinated, so I will be with you. I will be in touch with my associate, who can eavesdrop on their command center and intercept and decode the communications of the Americans."

A smile spread across Kamil's face. "You are in contact with someone who can plug in to the command center of these Western commandos? You never fail to amaze me, Dotensk." Then the smile turned into a grimace as he leaned across the table and aimed a finger at the Ukrainian's face. "This better be as you say, or you will have signed *both* of our death warrants."

"Listen to me. I could have left immediately after you

took delivery of the merchandise that I brought you today; my money is already in the bank at Kiev. But I am a practical man, a businessman. I want to sell you more merchandise before I help you defect. That is why I have told you about these plans and have agreed to be with you in Tikrit on Monday when the attack is to be mounted.

"Now remember," Dotensk went on, "in order for this to work, everything must go according to plan. On Monday, after your special guests have arrived, tell your father-in-law about the imminent attack you have just discovered and of your plan to use the knowledge against the Americans and British. Tell Saddam that this action will make him appear as the innocent underdog who is constantly bullied by the Americans. He will get enormous public relations advantage from this—and the sympathy of the entire world. And, of course, my dear Kamil, *you* will be the one who will uncover, expose, and foil the entire plot."

By the time Dotensk finished his pitch, Kamil was smiling again, and nodding his head. He shook Dotensk's hand and watched the Ukrainian walk out of the café. It would be a busy few days, he realized. But it would be worth it.

Office of Dimitri Komulakov
UN Headquarters
New York, N.Y.
Thursday, 2 March 1995
1035 Hours, Local

General Komulakov hung up the phone and switched off the EncryptionLok-3. He smiled; the news from

Dotensk was even better than he had hoped. Everything was under control.

The Russian got up from his desk and went into the command center. Walking over to the operations board, he admired his handiwork. When he had assumed this post four years ago, this room was nothing—a few phones and some sleepy Third World watch officers who spent most of their time reading newspapers and practicing their English. But now, with the encouragement of the SG and the support of an internationalist American president, the UN had a real command center— one befitting a global government with its own military forces in the field. Komulakov had his own intelligence gathering capabilities, even his own state-of-the-art encryption equipment—instead of having to rely on hand-me-downs from the British and Americans. General Komulakov looked up at the new, flat-screen plasma display boards, *Quite a step up from the chalkboards they had when I got here.*

The Russian general reviewed the location of the UN's far-flung military forces and the readiness status of each. On the screens were displayed the details of UN contingents in Haiti, East Timor, the Philippines, Sinai, the Golan Heights, Jordan, Lebanon, Gaza, Bosnia, the Congo, Kosovo, and a host of others. Some had only been at these locations for a matter of months. Others had been on UN maps for decades. The screen also showed, in different colors, the most recent disposition of U.S., NATO, Russian, Chinese, North Korean, and other military forces. Each country, as a "confidence-building measure," provided most of this data voluntarily. And now there was a new designator, a small blinking label reading "UNISEG," next to Incirlik, Turkey. Komulakov smiled again at the thought of how few of the countries represented in this building knew that the ISEG even existed.

Major Ellwood was looking over the general's shoulder as he reviewed the latest reports from the ISEG. The unit was required to send in a situation report every twenty-four hours, more frequently if there were an incident or crisis. In response to instructions from Komulakov, Ellwood had instituted a procedure so that every night, Sergeant Major Gabbard would send him the report in a formatted, encrypted e-mail. And though he and the Marine sergeant major had never met, the two of them had established a bit of computer rapport—an informal, back-channel exchange.

The general turned and saw Ellwood watching him. "Major Ellwood, who generates these reports?"

"Sergeant Major Gabbard, the senior enlisted man with the ISEG, sir."

"Are there any other copies of this floating around?"

"Not that I know of, sir."

"And how do you receive them?"

"By encrypted e-mail, every night."

"I see. And does the sergeant major keep a copy of them on his hard drive?"

"I would assume so, sir. But I would also assume that he's very conscientious about classified material."

"Quite so, Major, quite so. But just in case, send out an order to the ISEG that they are not to keep any classified materials of any kind, on paper or on any laptop computer, other than that which is essential to the immediate operation. We can archive anything they might need right here. Can't risk this information falling into the wrong hands."

"No, I suppose not, sir." Ellwood walked back to his carrel overlooking the command center. His computer station was the center's main IT station. As comm chief,

Ellwood had computer access to any of the other terminals within the center.

Ellwood keyed in a password and a command before complying with the general's edict. His terminal screen gave him a list of options for checking access and protocol for the various other computers. He typed in the assignment code for the first deputy's computer and did a summary review of his incoming messages. Although he knew that the general had just received another call from Baghdad, there was no such call on the file listing. It had been erased. In fact, Ellwood speculated that almost half of the incoming and outgoing messages had been deleted from the general's computer.

Major Ellwood thought that strange. It was one thing to delete files in a sensitive environment, where they might be compromised. But here? Why would General Komulakov delete the records of his overseas messages and calls in his own command center?

The general finished his review of the plan Newman had submitted for the March 6 mission and then returned to his office. For the past day and a half, he had been thinking over how to keep the mission on track without betraying the fact that it was already compromised. He was glad that the deadline was so close. *As long as the Iraqis don't do anything stupid,* he thought, *the mission won't be called off.*

Komulakov had considered a preemptive leak, so that the mission to Tikrit *would* be canceled. It would be a way of saving the lives of the ISETs. Yet, how could it be leaked? Turkey was one of the few places where Komulakov lacked the ability to plant information to be read by various agencies and military organizations and then interpreted and analyzed—in time for it to be useful. In the end he decided it was not practical to leak

word to the West—it would be just another messy com-
plication to worry about.

And speaking of messy complications, he thought,
there is one more item I need to take care of. He knew
that Newman had been ordered by Harrod to stay out
of Iraq and to command his ISETs from the command
center in Incirlik. Harrod wanted Newman where he
could control him—or where the Marine could be the
fall guy in case the mission failed and there were political repercussions. But General Komulakov knew that it
would be impossible to control Newman; he was no au-
tomaton, like many in the military who blindly followed
orders without questioning. Newman already knew
more than Komulakov wanted him to.

Someone like Newman, after a foiled mission like this
one was going to be, might raise a great many questions . . . unless *he did not survive the mission.* Yet, the
general knew that Harrod had forbidden him to parachute in with his team.

Komulakov picked up his phone. "Major Ellwood, I
want you to locate Lieutenant Colonel Newman for me.
Try him at HQ in Incirlik first. Yes, I know there is a
time difference. Just track him down and get him on the
phone."

ISEG Tactical Operations Center
Incirlik Air Base
Adana, Turkey
Thursday, 2 March 1995
1654 Hours, Local

"Uh, guys . . . take ten. I've got a call coming in from
General Komulakov, our 'other boss' at the UN—I'd

better take it," Newman said to the others around the folding table he had set up in the small office on the east side of the hangar. On the door he had put a handwritten sign, written in black felt-tip marker: "Ops Center." He waited for them to leave, then checked his EL-3 to make sure it was in the "on" position.

"How are things coming together?" the general asked.

"Well, everything here is ready to go except that I don't have the insert bird yet. The UAV is ready to go. The troops are ready to go. The comms relay site is up and running at Siirt, but the MD-80 still isn't here. If it doesn't get here in the next twenty-four hours, we're not going to be able to get the team on the ground and near enough to Tikrit with enough time to get to the objective while the big pow-wow is still going on," Newman said.

"Pow-wow?" asked the Russian.

"Sorry . . . the big terrorist summit. I don't want to go through all this just to find out that Aidid, bin Laden and Saddam have all packed their bags and gone home before we get there to spoil their party," replied the Marine.

"Ah . . . yes, now I understand. Pow-wow," Komulakov replied, seemingly more concerned about learning a new American slang expression than about solving Newman's lack of an insert aircraft.

"What about the MD-80?" said Newman becoming somewhat exasperated.

"I'll call Dr. Harrod about it immediately. Now, as I understand your last message, you have added one person to the mission, but it is not you?"

"Yes, I've added one person to the ISET going in on the ground. Captain Weiskopf wanted to go because he's concerned that when the mission changed from Somalia, the work-up for ISET Echo just wasn't long enough. I agreed because Weiskopf has a lot more time on the ground in Iraq than any of the men in Echo. That'll give us a total of eight men on the ground for the mission. If we have to extract them with the STAR System, we will still only need four canisters—since each device extracts two men.

"Now, as to my not going in, that wasn't my doing, General. Harrod told me I wasn't to parachute in with my men, that I'm supposed to stay back here in the command center. I don't know why—I suppose he has his reasons."

"Hm-m," the general mused. "Is that typical?"

"I don't know if it is or isn't. Most of the time I go in with my guys. Sometimes I stay back. It varies."

"I see. . . . Do you have a preference?"

"Well, on this mission I had asked to go in with the team."

"But Dr. Harrod told you not to?"

"Yes."

"I think that I sense your problem," the Russian said after a pause. "It appears that Dr. Harrod wants to make sure nothing happens to you—you are, after all, indispensable. Yet I think that you have an eagerness to go so that you can make certain that the man who is responsible for your brother's death is found and dealt with."

Newman thought about how to respond. "I suppose there's something to that," he said in a neutral voice.

"Well, Colonel . . . perhaps I have a solution that will satisfy both you and Dr. Harrod. As I understand from the mission planning thus far, you are going to be aboard the aircraft when it inserts the ISET team in Iraq, is that correct?"

"Yes, sir. But then I'm going to return here to Incirlik or to Siirt to coordinate the operation."

"Why don't you set up your command center aboard the aircraft that actually goes into Iraq for the parachute drop? And then re-position the aircraft at Siirt so that it is immediately available to launch in the event that something goes wrong. That way you will be 'on site,' as it were, to make sure personally that everything goes as planned. Yet, because you won't be actually parachuting in with your team, you are living up to the letter of the law with regard to Dr. Harrod's instructions. If there is any question about it, I will tell him that I overruled his orders. We won't say anything more about it—Dr. Harrod will not be directly involved with the planning and execution of the mission. I will be briefing him and you need not worry about staying in touch with him until after the mission."

Newman was beginning to like this Russian. "General, I will take that to mean that you will approve my decision to put my command center on the plane."

"Well, you know the old adage, Colonel—sometimes it's easier to get forgiveness than permission."

"Thank you, General. Is there anything else?"

"Yes. I don't want you to make any changes in your mission planning. It is important because there are so many countries and organizations involved. Before you change anything—even adding a single minute to a procedure—you must clear it with me first. Is that understood?"

"Perfectly, General. I hear you."

"Yes, thank you, Colonel Newman. And good luck."

"Thank you, sir. I'll be in touch."

Newman got up and walked over to the hall where his team leaders were taking a break. He no sooner waved them back into the office than his satellite phone rang again.

"Newman," he said into the mouthpiece after checking again to make sure the EncryptionLok-3 was still engaged.

"Colonel, it's Dan Robertson."

"Robertson, where the devil is my MD-80? Why can't your Air Force find a pilot to fly this mission?"

"It's inbound to Incirlik as we speak," Robertson said. "Harrod released the plane eight hours ago, and I just found out about it. If it isn't there by now, it should be any minute. I don't know what kinds of games the powers-that-be are playing, but I'm sorry. I asked to brief the crew and was told that would be impossible. Anyway, it should be there within the hour.

"I know it's late, but there's a little good news," Robertson continued. "They tell me that it has a complete communications suite aboard so that you can use it as a flying command post if you want."

"Good. That's exactly what I want. Send Sergeant Major Gabbard an encrypted e-mail with a complete list of what's aboard so that I know what comms and frequencies to set up for the mission. We're going to have to go tomorrow night at the latest."

"Will do. Anything else?"

"No. Well done, Dan. I know the delay wasn't your fault."

The men sat back down at the conference table, and Newman told them about the slight change in plans regarding his staying behind in Turkey. "I've been given the OK to put my command center on board the aircraft. After dropping in Team Echo, we'll take the MD-80 to Siirt. I'll command from there, and will be a lot closer than I would be back here," he told them.

Weiskopf grinned and gave him a high five and the others followed suit. "Way to go, Colonel," said Weiskopf. "I'll feel a lot better having you up top than back here, I'll tell you that!"

There was a knock on the door and Sergeant Major Gabbard walked in. "Sir, the MD-80 is taxiing up to the front of the hangar right now. Shall I ask the pilots and crew to come in?"

"By all means, Sergeant Major," replied Newman. "Bed the crew down with the troops or the senior NCOs, as appropriate, and send the aircraft commander and copilot over here right away. We're down to hours to get this mission under way."

About ten minutes later, the sergeant major returned, knocked on the door, opened it, and announced, "Gentlemen, please greet the Air Force pilot who will be flying our troopers into Iraq." All eyes turned and almost immediately every man's mouth dropped open.

Standing in the doorway, dwarfed by the sergeant major, was a five-foot-six-inch African-American woman wearing a big smile and an Air Force flight suit with pilot's wings and gold oak leaves.

"Good afternoon, gentlemen. I'm Major Jane Robinette, USAF Reserve. I have thirteen years of service and various tours of combat experience and served most recently in Operation Desert Fox, and I'm flight-certified in the MD-80 aircraft. In fact, in my civilian life, that's what I fly. And I can just tell how glad you are to see me."

Newman was stunned. He knew that women were becoming more and more commonplace in the military, but he had strong feelings about bringing a woman into combat. As far as he knew, the Air Force was the only branch that assigned women to combat duty.

"Uh . . . welcome, Major Robinette," he said, finally. "Forgive me . . . but I didn't really believe that a woman would be assigned to such a dangerous mission. This will be combat, Major. Did you get a briefing on the mission?"

"Yes, sir, I did. Not all of it, of course. But I do know that the mission is dangerous, and that it involves flying into Iraq."

"Who's flying the plane tomorrow night for the parachute drop?"

"I am, sir."

"But this is a very difficult and dangerous mission. Very high risk."

"Yes sir, I know. That's why the Secretary of the Air Force picked me. He said that the mission deserved the very best that the Air Force could give you guys—and here I am."

The men in the room laughed at her chutzpah.

Newman was still uneasy. He was also honest and decided to voice his more conservative viewpoint. "I suppose I'm a dinosaur, and old-fashioned about women serving in the Armed Forces. Actually, I don't have a problem with women serving. But I *do* have a problem with a woman going into combat."

"You got that right," one of the men muttered under his breath.

"Are you sure that you know what you're getting yourself into, Major?"

"Do *you*, Colonel?"

"What's that supposed to mean?"

"Well, sir . . . I don't think anyone ever knows exactly what's going to happen on *any* mission, whether it's a routine one, or if it's a mission like this one. I've learned that it's best not to dwell on what *might* go wrong and to concentrate on making it go right and doing my job better than anyone else."

"Sounds like you've heard these complaints before, Major."

"Yes, sir . . . just about every time I fly with someone who doesn't know me."

Only now did Newman realize why it had really taken so long to get the MD-80 out here—they had been looking for just the right pilot to meet the President's diversity goals. "Well, Major, what planes do you feel you're proficient in flying?"

"I have more than a thousand hours in F-15s and F-16s, sir. I've got nearly as many hours in C-130s, KC-135s, and the B-52—all together."

"Have you seen any combat action?"

"Yes, sir. I was called up from the Air Force Reserve for Desert Storm and Operation Desert Fox before this mission. In Desert Storm, I flew fifty-six missions in an F-15 fighter jet, all of them in the same neighborhood we'll be going to on this mission. Later, in Operation Desert Fox, I flew seven missions in the two days of that campaign . . . hitting the targets determined to be Saddam's industry for weapons of mass destruction. I had the second-highest number of kills and second-highest number of successful missions."

"Who was number one?" Newman asked.

"The guy who flew *eight* missions—but I beat him in average number of kills per mission."

"She's a regular top gun, Colonel," Bart Coombs said with a grin.

Major Robinette also grinned, but it was more forced. "Like the Colonel says, I've heard these complaints before."

"Just want to make sure you know what you're getting into," Newman mumbled.

"Uh-huh. Colonel, can we get on with the briefing? I simply *must* get back to my quarters to rinse out my panty hose."

The room rocked with laughter.

Newman, still laughing, rose from his seat and pulled out the empty chair at the table. He bowed grandly. "Major, it is with great pleasure that I welcome you as one of the guys."

The others clapped and cheered as Major Jane Robinette took her seat at the table.

CHAPTER FIFTEEN

Mission Compromised

Incirlik Air Base
Adana, Turkey
Friday, 3 March 1995
1745 Hours, Local

For twenty hours straight, the ISEG teams rehearsed their mission—in the hangar during daylight hours, and at night, at the far end of the air base. Newman then insisted they all get a few hours' rest—even though few would sleep, especially the eight men who were going on the ground inside Iraq.

Now, after months of planning, training, changes, and more planning, it was finally time for the mission to depart. The delayed arrival of the MD-80 had forced Newman to make further adjustments to the plan.

The seven men of ISET Echo plus Weiskopf would be the only ones to go into Iraq, unless there was trouble. And even though the others moaned about "being left in the rear with the gear," he ordered ISET Delta, along with Sergeant Major Gabbard, to remain in Incirlik as security and support for the UAV technicians and to guard the thousands of pounds of gear that wasn't going on the operation—equipment that was now staged in the hangar.

Newman had already displaced ISETs Alpha and Bravo forward to Siirt as the QRF. He placed Bart Coombs in command of the QRF, with Captain Bruno Macklin, the SAS officer, as Executive Officer. Newman told them to locate enough four-by-four transportation to get the two ISETs across the border somehow and into Iraq if ISET Echo ran into trouble. ISET Charlie would remain with Newman and the airborne command post—to be parachuted in to help Echo if necessary.

Finally, Newman decided that because of the belated arrival of the MD-80 and the delay in getting the operation under way—at the most it should now last just seventy-two hours from insert to extraction—he and McDade would simply stay aboard the converted MD-80 and use it as their mobile command and communications center. His plan was to return to Siirt after ISET Echo parachuted into Iraq, from which he would then control the operation. All these plans were dutifully transmitted back to Deputy Secretary General Komulakov at the UN and National Security Advisor Simon Harrod via encrypted e-mail.

Counting the six UAV technicians who had delivered the Global Hawk, the three-person MD-80 crew, Newman's two-man command element, and Weiskopf's thirty-eight ISEG operators, there were only forty-nine people involved in carrying out this complex and dangerous operation. But, Newman reasoned, *that's enough to get my brother's killer—and if we get Saddam or any of those other thugs, all the better.*

Just after the sun's light was replaced by the bluish-white glare of the mercury-vapor lamps surrounding the hangar, Captain Joshua Weiskopf and the fourteen men of ISETs Charlie and Echo boarded the MD-80, headed for the back of the aircraft, and started strapping on their SVX-30 steerable parachutes. A few minutes later, Newman and McDade climbed aboard and took up their stations at the communications consoles that had been installed on the left side of the aircraft, directly aft of the forward cabin door.

Major Robinette, First Lieutenant Charlie Haskell, the copilot, and Master Sergeant David Maddox, the crew chief, were already aboard, checking and double-checking the engines, oil pressure, and hydraulics; testing the communications equipment, navigation, and avionics displays; making one last inspection of the flight maps; and getting the latest weather updates. They had completed their pre-flight checklist by the time the men in back were 'chuted up and strapped into the two rows of web seats secured to the sides of the cabin.

Though from the outside this MD-80 could have passed for a civilian airliner, the interior was pure military transport. Not only had all the regular airline passenger seats been removed and replaced with two long rows of standard military red nylon benches, but numerous other changes had been made as well.

The forward galley had been removed and turned into the crew chief's station. Only the coffeemaker and sink remained of what had once been a mini flying kitchen. Where once food and beverage carts had been stowed for serving passengers, green oxygen bottles were now strapped in place. A system of tubes affixed to the interior of the fuselage carried the oxygen to those in the passenger cabin. Every two feet or so, all the way to the back of the aircraft, there were quick-connect fittings so that each passenger could be assured of a place to hook into the oxygen.

As the aircraft's twin tail-mounted engines started, Master Sergeant Maddox walked down the cabin between the two rows of men, making sure that each was strapped in, hooked up to the aircraft oxygen system, and had a working intercom connection. He got a thumbs-up from each man. Before strapping into his own seat, he checked the gauges on the green bottles once again to make sure they were fully charged. Satisfied, Maddox keyed the microphone on his headset and said, "All set back here, Major Robinette."

As the aircraft began to taxi away from the hangar that had been their home, Maddox threw a switch on a console in his compartment to turn off the incandescent lights and turn on the bank of special night-vision lighting, giving the compartment an eerie, red glow.

As the MD-80 reached the end of the taxiway and began the right-hand turn onto the runway, Newman could see four USAF F-15s, two F-16s, and a Navy EA-6B Electronics Warfare aircraft to the left of their aircraft, all poised to follow them down the runway and into the night sky. Newman heard Major Robinette's voice in his headset: "Ready to go, Colonel?"

"We're ready to roll, Major."

With that, he heard the copilot's voice, "Switching to channel 21." Then, "Tower, this is Picnic One. Permission for takeoff."

Newman heard the voice of the air traffic controller in the tower give the aircraft its clearance as they turned onto the runway. As the plane began its takeoff roll, Newman flicked a switch in at his console and a video monitor came on, displaying the ground racing past the rear of the aircraft. A miniature video camera, equipped with a low-light lens, was mounted at the base of the tail so Newman would see the jumpers go and ensure that they didn't get fouled with one another.

As the aircraft cleared the ground, there was a loud "clunk" as the landing gear retracted into their housings and then the whine of hydraulic pumps over the roar of the engines while the flaps retracted. In the cockpit, Major Robinette reached up and flipped down the night vision goggles mounted on the front of her helmet. Lt. Haskell kept his goggles up so he could monitor the instruments.

Newman switched his intercom to the channel designated for communications among the passengers. Unlike a standard military aircraft rigged for parachute jumping, this one had an intercom station for everyone aboard. He keyed his mike and said to no one in particular, "I was thinking . . . with all that extra cargo space back here, maybe we should have brought some Harleys."

"That would have been a great idea if we could have gotten a hog out that rear hatch," Weiskopf said. "I'd much rather roll out of Iraq on a Harley than ride the upchuck snatch on Monday afternoon." Despite Weiskopf's carefree tone, Newman knew he was concerned about using the STARS system. They had all seen it demonstrated while they were training in Oman, and they had all practiced deploying the helium-filled balloon with its nylon tether and donning the two-man rescue suits with their sewn-in harnesses. Having demonstrated the device once to his own Recon Marines, Newman could understand why the Harleys sounded better.

As the MD-80 headed east toward the mountains shadowing Lake Van, the banter over the intercom slowly sputtered out as each man dealt with his own thoughts about what might lie ahead. Some fiddled with their equipment as though some last-minute change in rigging might have monumental consequences. Others attempted to doze, leaning back in the webbing of their seats with their eyes closed. The plane turned right to a heading of 120° south to follow the Tigris River.

As they crossed into Iraq at the junction of the border with Syria and Turkey, there was a flurry of radio traffic from the F-15s and -16s, now ahead of them near Mosul. A USAF KC-10 tanker had met the war birds over Siirt, and they had gone screaming off to the south to take out any Iraqi missiles that might try to acquire and target the MD-80.

As the MD-80 passed west of Mosul at thirty thousand feet, headed for the drop zone ninety miles to the south, fires could be seen burning off to their left, near an Iraqi air base. From the radio chatter, Newman and the others could tell that the strike aircraft had engaged an Iraqi radar site and scored a hit, probably on a surface-to-air missile site. *They aren't supposed to have SAMs this far north,* Newman thought.

He checked the navigation plot and his watch, confirmed the heading, and said into the intercom: "Gentlemen, forty miles to the DZ, in ten minutes. Check your portable oxygen bottles. It's almost time."

Each man disconnected from the intercom, took a few last deep draughts from the aircraft oxygen system, and switched over to his own portable oxygen bottles. The jumpers moved to the back of the plane where the rear hatch opened to the cold night air. The noise of the wind rushing past the aircraft and the roar of the two engines mounted above the tail were deafening. The temperature gauge on the GPS strapped to Weiskopf's wrist said that it was minus eighteen degrees Fahrenheit near the open hatch.

Timing for the jump was critical. This was no standard combat jump. Even though the MD-80 was going to nose up and throttle back to slow down briefly, the jumpers would still be spread out over miles if they didn't exit within seconds of each other. Behind and slightly above the MD-80, two F-l6s were lined up as if preparing to refuel and would so appear on Iraqi radar.

"Thirty seconds to the 35th parallel," Newman shouted to the last man in line. He in turn tapped the man in front of him on the shoulder and the word was passed instantly to the front of the column with a hand signal. Weiskopf stood poised in the mouth of the hatch. He had elected to be the first man out. Each man behind him would count to two and throw himself out the hatch.

The backup team, shifted forward to compensate for the weight of the eight men, gathered in the tail of the aircraft. Newman helped clear the area by the cargo bay door and wished each man good luck.

"Ten seconds!" yelled Newman. Once again the hasty series of shoulder slaps and Weiskopf turned and leaned into the hatch, his gloved fingers gripping the aluminum skin as he waited for the light above his head to go from red to green. Newman could hear the whine of the engines diminish and felt the deck tilting as the nose of the aircraft came up, bleeding off airspeed.

Newman heard Major Robinette's voice on the intercom: "Go!" The light over the rear hatch flashed to green and in less than fifteen seconds, all eight men had disappeared into the night sky thirty thousand feet above Iraq. Newman ran forward and resumed his seat at the command and control console.

Within a few minutes, the four F-16s peeled out of formation and headed east. The MD-80 banked and turned back to the north, heading for the "Three Corners" junction of the Iraqi, Syrian, and Turkish borders.

It took Weiskopf and his seven teammates more than twenty-five minutes to glide the twenty miles to their target, the drop zone eighteen miles west of Tikrit. There was little wind, so they flew their chutes in on a fairly straight path and managed to land a mile or so from their objective. Within an hour, all eight men had buried their parachutes and high-altitude jump suits, regrouped, and headed off at a dog-trot for the small rise north of Lake Tharthar where they planned to hole up until the next night's movement. Their escort, an F-117A "Nighthawk" stealth fighter launched from Incirlik, picked up their radio acknowledgment that all had landed safely, and it stayed high overhead, invisible to Iraqi radar, refueling from a real tanker when necessary, until the ground team arrived at their safe-haven just before dawn. After dark on Saturday and Sunday, another F-117, also invisible to Iraqi radar, would show up to orbit overhead like a guardian angel to provide fire support if the eight-man unit was detected by an Iraqi patrol while on the move.

Now, as Weiskopf and his team moved across the desert floor, the F-117 was overhead. Though neither the small patrol nor the aircraft pilot broke radio silence, they were acutely aware of each other's presence and confident that no Iraqi knew they were there. At least, that was the plan.

Parkside Community Church
Dulles, VA
Friday, 3 March 1995
1930 Hours, Local

Rachel sat in a back pew of the church that she had seen from the highway many times on her commutes to Dulles. She had simply intended to drive by the sign at the entrance to the parking lot to check on what time services were on Sunday but had found lights on, the parking lot almost full, and people walking up to the front door. She had come inside as much out of curiosity as anything else. *Why,* she wondered, *would all these people be going to church on a Friday night?*

This question was answered as the meeting started. The pastor welcomed the people in the congregation and said how pleased he was that so many would come out for "the final night of a week of special meetings designed to help people discover God." He had called it an evangelistic meeting. Rachel was uncomfortable with the word *evangelistic* but soon settled into her seat anyway.

It had been almost ten minutes since the church service had ended—yet she still sat there contemplating what had just taken place.

Sandy had been encouraging Rachel to "find a church where you can hear the Word of God." Rachel didn't quite know what that meant. Sandy had tried to explain what it meant to be a Christian, but that had also sounded confusing to Rachel; in fact, there was a lot of terminology Sandy used that Rachel didn't understand.

She had planned to simply show up at a Sunday service, but here she was on a Friday night in a suburban Virginia church surrounded by people she didn't know. When she had entered, she had found a place to sit, not far from the rear of the sanctuary, and moved in to take a seat. An usher had handed her a printed program, which she read before the service began. On the back cover was printed:

GOD'S PLAN OF SALVATION

THE NEED: "For all have sinned and fall short of the glory of God." (Romans 3:23)

THE CHOICE: "For the wages of sin is death, but the gift of God is eternal life in Christ Jesus our Lord." (Romans 6:23)

GOD'S PROVISION: "But God demonstrates His own love toward us, in that while we were still sinners, Christ died for us." (Romans 5:8)

CHRIST'S SACRIFICE: "For God so loved the world that He gave His only begotten Son, that whoever believes in Him should not perish but have everlasting life. For God did not send His Son into the world to condemn the world, but that the world through Him might be saved." (John 3:16–17)

YOUR PART IS FAITH: "For by grace you have been saved through faith, and that not of yourselves; it is the gift of God, not of works, lest anyone should boast." (Ephesians 2:8–9)

"He who believes in the Son has everlasting life; and he who does not believe the Son shall not see life, but the wrath of God abides on him." (John 3:36)

IT'S UP TO YOU: "Behold, I [Jesus] stand at the door and knock. If anyone hears My voice and opens the door, I will come in to him." (Revelation 3:20)

"For with the heart one believes unto righteousness, and with the mouth confession is made unto salvation." (Romans 10:10)

It struck Rachel as peculiar that so many of the verses listed were ones that had been discussed in the Bible study she had attended with Sandy, and she felt this was more than coincidence. And then the pastor got up to begin the service with prayer, which he introduced with another Bible verse: "Draw near to Him, and He will draw near to you." Rachel felt he was speaking directly to her. She was here because she wanted to get nearer to God and know more about Him. The congregation rose, sang the Doxology, and sat down again.

Then the pastor quoted from the Scriptures: "Being confident of this very thing, that He who has begun a good work in you will complete it until the day of Jesus Christ."

When the music started, Rachel was still thinking about those words from the Bible—everything she was hearing seemed directed at *her*. Then she focused on the choir and the words they were singing. It was an anthem of praise, and she strained to understand the words: "Amazing Grace, how sweet the sound that saved a wretch like me. . . ." It was the familiar tune the bagpiper had played beside Jim Newman's grave at Arlington Cemetery, and its old melody stirred her.

There were other musical selections; some were sung by a small group of singers and others by the congregation. Then the pastor prayed again, an offering was taken, and he began his sermon. As Rachel listened, she prayed silently. *God . . . if You're there . . . I want to understand. I want to know about Jesus . . . and all the other things I've been hearing about since Sandy and I went to that Bible study. I know I don't have any right . . . I feel really guilty now . . . but if that song means anything, God . . . can You . . . would You save a wretch like me?*

The sermon also felt directed to her. At its conclusion, the pastor said that he'd like to pray for anyone who wasn't sure about his or her spiritual condition. "If you're seeking God and want Him to change your life, I want to pray for you," he said to his listeners. When he prayed, Rachel felt the love that he had been telling her about flow over her; tears began to course down her cheeks as she stood with her head bowed in the back of the church.

The service over, Rachel still sat by herself in her seat. Most of the people had left the church or were chatting in the vestibule of the sanctuary. Though her thoughts were still a jumble, some things were starting to make sense. Then, as if on cue, a woman sat down beside her. "Hi, I'm Lucy, Pastor Brooks's wife. I saw you sitting here, and you looked like your heart was breaking. Would you like me to pray with you?"

Rachel looked at the woman—attractive, about forty, with eyes that were full of sympathy and concern. And suddenly, Rachel couldn't hold it in any longer. She poured out her thoughts in a torrent of frustration and regret for the life that she had been living. Rachel also expressed hope that she hadn't gone so far away from God that He might abandon her. Mrs. Brooks assured her that God's love was still available. For about twenty minutes they talked, and then, with the church nearly empty, Lucy Brooks said, "I want to pray with you, Rachel. You're in real anguish and you don't need to be. You don't have to say a thing. Here, give me your hand."

Rachel put her hand in Lucy's, and the pastor's wife quietly prayed. Once again the tears flowed down Rachel's cheeks as her new friend ended her prayer with a plea: "Lord, help Rachel to see that Your grace is sufficient, that all things work together for good for those who put their trust in You, and most importantly, Lord, help Rachel to know that the salvation You offered all of us on Calvary is available for her as well."

Lucy reached in her purse and pulled out a little package of tissues and handed them to Rachel. "Do you have plans for Sunday after church? Could you join my husband and me for brunch at Terranova's?"

"Oh, that's kind of you but—"

"Please, if you have no plans, we'd be delighted if you'd join us. My husband is a wonderful teacher and counselor, and I know that he'd be pleased to help you deal with what's weighing you down."

Rachel smiled and nodded. The two women stood and walked toward the front doors.

Baghdad-Mosul Highway
5 km S of Tikrit
Friday, 3 March 1995
2000 Hours, Local

As Leonid Dotensk bent to tighten the lug nuts on the left rear wheel of his Mercedes, he added this tire change to the long list of reasons why he hated Americans. The tire he had just changed—as he'd done with so many other tires in Iraq—had gone flat from running over a piece of shrapnel, a shard of razor-sharp steel from an American bomb dropped more than four years ago. *This filthy country is covered with American scrap metal, and now they have made me late!* he thought. As Dotensk stood up, a jet aircraft roared over his head at both a very high speed and very low altitude. The Ukrainian double agent threw himself on the ground in terror and started to crawl toward the ditch beside the road, trying to get away from the car. As he did so, a second aircraft passed right behind the first.

Immediately after he reached the ditch, an anti-aircraft gun opened up from Tikrit South, the air base directly to his north. *The fools; what do they think they are going to hit?*

Dotensk spent ten more minutes huddled in the ditch and then, when the firing stopped, he climbed out, brushed himself off as best he could, got back in his car, started it up, and began driving very slowly toward the small city of Tikrit, claimed by Saddam as his hometown.

The Ukrainian was driving on the only four-lane highway in the country. Saddam had constructed it as a showpiece, widening the roadbed that the British had built along the west bank of the Tigris River after they inherited Iraq from the Ottoman Empire at the end of World War I. In the fashion of dictators the world over, Saddam had made the highway a monument to himself, connecting Karbala and Al Hillah in the south through Baghdad with Mosul in the north. For most of its route, the road paralleled the Tigris.

What made the going so slow were the craters and blown bridges left unrepaired from American and British bombs during the Gulf War—and the millions of pieces of tire-shredding sharp steel strewn on and in the pavement from hundreds of bombs, rockets, and missiles. Dotensk proceeded at a snail's pace. He didn't have to worry about holding up any other traffic—in fact, the Ukrainian didn't even *see* another vehicle until he was stopped at the checkpoint just south of Tikrit. As he pulled out his documents, he could see flames and sooty black smoke rising from the Tikrit South Air Base to his left.

The Republican Guards officer who examined his paperwork gazed carefully at the Amn Al-Khass seal on Dotensk's travel permit, pointed his flashlight at the Ukrainian's face, looked again at his passport, and said, "You are to report to His Excellency, Minister Hussein Kamil at the presidential palace. You are late."

Dotensk checked the impatient words that leapt to his mind. "I know. I was held up by the air raid."

The officer shrugged and said, "You will need an escort from here." He called out to a sergeant who got into a BJC Beijing Jeep and led Dotensk up the highway, into the city, and to the gates of the palace grounds.

Saddam's palace at Tikrit was one of his most lavish. Set well back from the road and surrounded by trees, a small lake, and lush gardens, the seventeen structures on the grounds were constructed of marble over reinforced concrete and designed to send an unmistakable signal: "Local boy makes good." Everywhere Dotensk looked there were armed men patrolling.

The escort vehicle stopped at one of the buildings near the towering palace structure, and the sergeant got out and talked to the uniformed guard at the door, who then called to someone inside. Two strikingly handsome young men in shirtsleeves came rushing out to help Dotensk and take his bag out of the trunk.

This is more like it, he thought. They brought him into a large, well-appointed waiting room. Somewhere within the building he could hear voices and music. Then, down the long carpeted hallway, came Kamil. At first Dotensk did not recognize his co-conspirator. Kamil was not in uniform but was instead garbed in a white *thobe* covered by a brown *mishlah* trimmed with gold. He had sandals on his feet and was wearing the traditional Arab *gutra* with a black *igal* wrapped around it. "Good evening, my friend," said the Iraqi, holding out his hand. "Thankfully, the Americans waited to bomb until after the Sabbath. Had they come earlier, so many of our brave soldiers would have been at prayer that we would not have been able to shoot down many of them."

Dotensk wondered for whose benefit this propaganda was recited, but decided to say nothing. The Ukrainian had learned that with Kamil there was always a hidden, complex agenda. The man was, on the one hand, planning to defect while, at the same time, spending hundreds of millions of dollars to acquire stolen nuclear weapons to arm his nation. He was playing host to Osama bin Laden and the other terrorists and concurrently planning to become a hero by "saving" his father-in-law from a UN-directed assassination. Dotensk wondered how the Iraqi kept all four initiatives separate in his mind. But about one thing, the arms dealer had no doubt. He had already witnessed the merciless killing of three people by Kamil and so he had no illusions about Kamil's ethics.

"Kamil, can we talk?"

"Ah yes, but first, you must shed the desert sand from your clothing and have some food. They will show you to your room, and after you have had a chance to cleanse the dust out of your eyes, you will join me for some refreshment." At this, Kamil clapped his hands twice and the two young men who had met Dotensk at the entrance appeared from an anteroom and guided him down the hallway to a luxurious suite.

Dotensk removed his soiled suit, showered, and changed into a pair of cashmere slacks and tailored cotton shirt. A half hour later, a knock on his door introduced another young boy—*he can't be twelve years old*—thought Dotensk. "His Excellency, Minister Hussein Kamil, has instructed that I am to be at your service this evening," said the child in perfect Russian.

"Yes, well thank you," said Dotensk. "But all I desire is a chance to talk to the Minister, if he's available."

"Of course," said the child. "I shall take you to him. Please follow me.

The Ukrainian followed the boy down the hallway to a large room made to look like an enormous Bedouin tent: muslin was draped from the ceiling; sidewalls of silk reached the floor; there, seated on cushions, and surrounded by voluptuous women, was Hussein Kamil. Music from several stringed instruments was playing softly, and the pungent odor of burning hashish mixed cloyingly with the scent of incense.

"Welcome, my dear friend," said Kamil. "Come sit here beside me and we shall eat. Then we shall talk."

Dotensk was astounded. An hour ago, enemy aircraft, undoubtedly American, had bombed an air base not five kilometers away. He knew from information provided by General Komulakov that the UN assassination team was planning to parachute into Iraq tonight, and the arms dealer strongly suspected that the air strike he'd witnessed was a diversion for the insertion. And here was his co-conspirator in the entire plan, splayed out like a desert sheik.

As Dotensk took a seat on one of the cushions, he hissed, "We must talk!"

For nearly a minute, Kamil seemed not to hear. He sat with his eyes closed as the music continued. Then his head snapped up abruptly, and he clapped his hands three times and motioned for all those attending him to depart. They disappeared immediately, though the music continued to play. Dotensk hoped that it was a recording and that it was loud enough to mask the conversation they needed to have.

"Can we talk here?"

"Certainly, these are my private quarters. We are protected by Amn Al-Khass officers totally loyal to me."

"Good. You know that the air strike was very likely conducted to mask the insertion of the assassins?"

"Yes, I thought the same thing myself."

"Is everything in place for Monday?"

"I have made all the preparations we agreed upon," said the Iraqi security chief. "I had my people paint the interior of the large abandoned brick Ba'ath Party building beside the old aqueduct northeast of the city. It took almost two hundred gallons of paint just to make it look like a hospital. And, as you suggested, I had 247 prisoners trucked there from the Special Security Service prison at Al Ranighwania. Unfortunately most of the prisoners were uncooperative so they— died."

"But if you shot them—"

"Ah, you always underestimate me, my dear little arms dealer. I ordered some to be beaten to death, a number to be stoned, others to be burned alive, and some dropped from the roof of the building. When the international press corps goes to see the ruins of the 'hospital' destroyed by this UAV thing, all they will find are dead patients, killed by the explosion and the collapse of the building."

Dotensk was feeling ill and contemplated taking a hit from the hash-filled water pipe that had been offered earlier. But realizing he needed a clear head, he decided to press on. "Does anyone else know about the UN attack on Monday?"

"Of course not. If Qusay or my father-in-law had any

inkling of what was about to happen, they would call off the meeting with bin Laden or move it to another location and all this planning would be for nothing."

"My contact told me just before I left Baghdad that the commandos are to move overland for the next three nights so they can be in position by Monday morning. How do you plan to interdict them?"

"I have a brigade of Amn Al-Khass troops and Republican Guards deployed to the west of here in the direction from where you said they will come. They have seven hunter teams of twenty men each. Each man in the hunter team that finds the British and American killers will get a new Mercedes. I have set up a command post in hangar 3, the least damaged structure at Tikrit South Air Base. Inside the hangar, invisible to the American satellites, I have placed two MI-27 HIND attack helicopters—yes, the pilots are loyal to me. You told me that you would be able to give me the exact location of the assassins once they establish their observation post. If that's true, we will quietly go there and kill them, take their targeting device, and point it at the fake hospital."

Dotensk was impressed. "How about their quick-reaction force? It's now deployed just across the border in Turkey. According to the British-American plan, they are to cross the border between Silopi and Zakhu to rescue the assassination team—if they run into trouble. Since that part of the border is controlled by the Kurds and the Iraqi National Congress, how do you plan to stop them?"

"What is this QRF—fourteen or fifteen mercenaries? That is nothing. I have an Amn Al-Khass office in Mosul. The colonel who commands that detachment is one of my fiercest officers. He assures me that when you provide the location of where this QRF will cross the Tigris, he'll eliminate them in a matter of minutes."

Kamil had been busy. In less than a week, he had taken delivery of three Soviet-made nuclear artillery warheads, transported several biological and chemical weapons samples from his laboratories to the presidential palace for examination by Osama bin Laden on Monday, and still found time to position forces to disrupt the planned UN assassination of his father-in-law. "Now," he said, pushing his finger into Dotensk's chest, "it is all up to you to tell me where these killers are so that they cannot escape. If you fail me, I will kill you." And then he smiled and handed the Ukrainian a plate of figs and dates.

Command Center
UN Headquarters
New York, N.Y.
Sunday, 5 March 1995
0825 Hours, Local

General Komulakov strolled slowly around the command center operations area and observed the activities there—busy for a Sunday morning. He stopped occasionally to watch as operators keyed in the latest data downloaded from satellite communications. He watched—but his mind was elsewhere.

Ever since Captain Joshua Weiskopf and the seven men of ISET Echo had parachuted into Iraq, the Russian had been passing to Dotensk regular updates on their movements. Now the team had reported to Newman— and Newman had dutifully informed Komulakov—that the ISET was nearly in position, having hiked nearly eighteen miles in two nights from their drop zone west of Tikrit. The Russian knew he was taking a great risk in passing along information to Dotensk. If anyone suspected he was involved in sabotaging the first International Sanctions Enforcement Group mission, particularly given its targets—Saddam Hussein and Osama bin Laden—all his plans for a luxurious retirement would be traded in for an eight-by-eight-foot cell.

Komulakov also felt conflicted because compromising the ISEG mission would mean that, instead of a UN commendation and perhaps even international recognition for helping to rid the world of Saddam and one of the world's most ambitious terrorists, he would spend the next few months answering inquiries as to what went wrong and why—all the while having to cover his own tracks.

After mulling it all over again, the Russian shrugged and walked back toward his office. He concluded again that there was no other choice than to proceed as he and Dotensk had planned. The ISEG mission had to be compromised. Otherwise he would lose the only client he and Dotensk had found who could afford to pay for the nuclear weapons they had stolen.

He knew that he could never find other buyers for his stolen weapons at the price Iraq was willing to pay for them. None of the other rogue nations with which he and Dotensk dealt had anywhere near the resources of Iraq. However, thankfully for Komulakov, there was no one else standing in the wings to offer Iraq such weapons. If another seller did exist, Kamil would have been able to "haggle" and get the price dropped. But Komulakov knew he was the only seller of such a prized commodity. The potential cash from this sale would enrich him beyond his imagination, and he could retire at the ripe old age of forty-six.

Actually, his share of the 150 million Swiss francs that they already had in secret bank accounts would enrich him enough to provide wealth for several lifetimes, but this had now become a contest for more than money. It was a dangerous game of peril, of risking everything, and there was no other competition that was worthy of his participation.

Komulakov thought that if he could maintain his good relations with so many Western leaders and the respect and associations with the United Nations, it was conceivable that he might amass sufficient wealth to one day return to Moscow and announce that he was a candidate for president of Russia. To become the chief of state for the world's second great power would be a wonderful addition to his list of glories.

Major Ellwood interrupted the general's reverie. "General, the Baghdad channel is calling you. Do you want to take it in your office or here?"

"Send it to my office."

Komulakov had been getting regular updates from Newman on the status and location of the team on the ground inside Iraq. To ensure he was getting real-time information, the Russian had also directed that the UN Communications Center be patched into all satellite communications traffic between Newman, aboard the MD-80; on the ground in Siirt, Turkey; ISET Echo in Iraq; and the UAV element back at Incirlik.

There was no risk in this—such monitoring and reports were expected, and the USAF Satellite Relay Station at Incirlik had dutifully complied with the White House directive to keep the UN command center in the loop. The risk for Komulakov was in passing this information on to Dotensk.

And now, with Weiskopf and ISET Echo nearly in position in Tikrit, the risks to Komulakov were about to increase considerably. He would have to be in near-constant communication with Dotensk. The ISEG operations plan called for the ISET in Tikrit to establish a satellite video uplink so that, in addition to the audio description of the mission, a visual record could be made, confirming the results of the UAV attack and to document every effort that had been made to avoid collateral damage. Once the ISET was at its final location, they would set up a miniature camera pointed at the target, position their flat-plane satellite antenna, and dial into the USAF Satellite Relay Station just as though they were making a telephone call. Komulakov planned to use this visual connection to confirm the ISET's GPS location by using the coordinates displayed by the team's EncryptionLok-3. He would then pass these coordinates to Dotensk, who would in turn give the information to Kamil for his Amn Al-Khass hunter teams. If everything worked as Komulakov planned, Weiskopf's ISET Echo, the QRF crossing into Iraq from Turkey, and Newman and the crew and team aboard the MD-80 would all be dead within hours.

Al Fuhaymi Oasis
Euphrates River
Western Iraq
Sunday, 5 March 1995
1345 Hours, Local

Eli Yusef Habib was sitting in the shade of a date grove, isolated from the hubbub of the oasis activity just a few hundred meters away. Al Fuhaymi was a tiny retreat in the vastness of the Iraqi desert, enriched by the waters of the Euphrates River that ran from northern Turkey, through Syria, and into Iraq, where it joins the Tigris River just north of Basra.

Habib was sixty-eight, born in 1927—not far from where he sat—when the British ran the country through a monarch they imported after they took possession of Iraq under a mandate from the League of Nations.

In the many years since, Habib had seen governments come and go—some kind, some cruel, like the present regime. Yet he had survived them all and even prospered. And despite his age, he was still strong and nimble. He was taller than many of his neighbors. Habib's wife of forty-four years let it be known she thought her husband was also quite handsome. His beard was still black, like the thick black hair on his head—although within the past two years, some white hairs were beginning to grow on both.

As a young boy, Habib had spied for the British in World War II. It was dangerous, and he was nearly shot on at least four occasions by the Gestapo in the North African desert. It was during his three years of wartime activity with the British that he learned to speak English. When the war ended, Habib found that this skill was extremely valuable. The world was becoming smaller by the '50s and '60s, and international industries were looking for ways to sell their merchandise and products in the Middle East, where oil revenues were helping many Arabs become rich. Radios, TVs, Levis, and other consumer products found new markets—in places off the beaten path in Turkey, Syria, Iraq, and Iran, the area he considered his sales territory. Habib had established contacts in many of the small towns along the Euphrates River. And like most successful salesmen, he had spent much of his life on the road. There was hardly a paved highway or dirt track in four countries that he did not know—and his smiling face was well known. Habib was respected everywhere as an honest man who could deliver a portable radio here, a hard-to-find part for a diesel engine there—or, nowadays, a microwave oven almost anywhere. His integrity, perseverance, and willingness to trust a customer's word that he would pay on delivery had made Habib a wealthy man.

Habib was also something of an anachronism. He had roots going back in the region more than seven hundred years. His ancestors were among those who traveled the ancient trade routes between Persia and Eurasia. And today, seven centuries later, he was a man who had the same occupation as his forefathers. He even dressed as he might have seven hundred years ago.

For nearly fifty years, Habib had plied the craft he had learned from his father and his grandfather before him. And since 1970 Habib had been teaching his sons—and more recently, his grandsons—how to carry on the family business. He had four sons and three daughters. They had given him and his wife twenty-one grandchildren. All of the sons, daughters, sons-in-law, daughters-in-law, and grandchildren, to some extent, helped with the business. Some, along with their own families, had established homes and businesses along the route. They acted as warehouses for their wandering father. Habib would find those who needed merchandise, and they would locate it, procure it, and deliver it to the buyers.

But Habib was different from other Arabs. He stayed mostly to himself and his family. Like other Arabs, Habib was deeply religious and prayed many times each day, stopping his work one day a week in observance of the Sabbath. What made Habib different from his Muslim neighbors was that he was a Christian. The followers of Christ were a tiny minority in Arab countries. Many times they were tolerated without problems, but often they were verbally and physically persecuted. Arab Christians like Habib had learned to be cautious in practicing their faith. Even in these modern times there were some places, Habib knew, where a practitioner of Islam could legally kill a Christian if the Muslim felt threatened by the Christian's belief. Christian believers were considered to be outside the true faith, and as such, they were infidels.

Another thing that set Habib apart was that he was a lay preacher. He was a self-taught pastor-theologian and as he traveled for his business, he had a preaching itinerary that enabled him to mentor other believers as his business took him back and forth through the countries of Syria, Iran, Iraq, with sometimes stops in Turkey and even trips to Cyprus and Greece when a particular product could only be found there.

Habib was a happy, contented, and gentle man who had mastered the harshness of the desert and the eccentricities of its towns and cities. He had also come to terms with people.

And now he was sitting by himself, praying. His prayers grew longer with each passing year. He had many petitions that he brought to God on behalf of his growing family. He also prayed for wisdom for himself—wisdom to know how and when he might share his faith so others could find the peace and solace that he had through belief in God through Christ. Habib was not really a mystic, but his devotion to God, along with his sincere and continual prayers, seemed to put him into a trance whenever he rested like this. He liked to tell his family that prayer was conversation with God, and that conversations were two-way avenues of communication. That's why, sometimes when he prayed, he had his Bible open in his lap. He prayed for God to answer his prayers, then he read, to hear what God was saying to him. Occasionally he had received what he believed to be specific instructions directly from God. Sometimes he just sat still and prayed with his eyes closed, but without conscious thoughts. Instead, he tried to be receptive to other thoughts that he believed God might put into his mind.

His family was used to this routine. Sometimes Habib would come home and announce, "I believe that God wants me to go to Chanam" or some other place—perhaps a place that he may have just left. They would shrug and say, "I understand, Father." What else could they say? They seldom argued with the old man. For, more often than not, he'd go and learn that someone was in great need, and he was the only person who could help. "A miracle," they'd say. "No, God told me that I should come to you," he'd say.

For the past half hour, Habib had had the distinct impression that God was telling him to turn back from the direction that he was headed and follow the pipeline road that led to Laqlaq, a small town on the Tigris River more than 170 kilometers away. He knew there was little trading to be done in that direction, and it was definitely out of the way. Given the state of the roads, few of which had been repaired since the 1991 war, it would take him the better part of two days to make the round trip. Who knew how much *additional* time would be required for whatever God wanted him to do?

For some reason, God never told Habib what He wanted him to do. Habib just felt led to go in one direction or another, and did so. Then, God always led him to the divine appointment.

This time he thought that he ought to wait before driving his Toyota two-ton truck toward Laqlaq, this being the Christian Sabbath. But the impression came to him more clearly than ever—*Now! Go now!*

Habib gave instructions to his oldest son, who had accompanied him on this leg of the journey, to stay at the Al Fuhaymi Oasis until his return "in a few days." Then he packed his few belongings, some food, water, and his Arabic Bible. Within ten minutes, the Toyota truck—its four spare tires, drum of gasoline, and extra water in the bed—was kicking up clouds of sandy dust behind him as Habib drove toward the road that paralleled the underground pipeline to Lake Tharthar. He expected to reach the north end of the lake by 8:00 P.M., and perhaps Laqlaq shortly after midnight.

"Picnic Base" Alpha
10 km W of Tikrit, 5 km S of Al Sahra Iraqi Air Force Base
Sunday, 5 March 1995
1933 Hours, Local

For three days, Weiskopf and the seven men of ISET Echo had been living on long range patrol rations, minimum water, and maximum adrenaline. It had started to pump as the MD-80 had approached the drop zone on Friday night, and it hadn't stopped in the seventy-three hours since.

"Picnic Six, this is Picnic Base . . . over." Captain Joshua Weiskopf released the button on the side of the satellite radio handset and waited for a response. It came in less than two seconds, with a slight audible ping

as the EL-3 on his radio decrypted the voice of Lieutenant Colonel Newman.

"Picnic Base, this is Picnic Six, go ahead, over." Newman's signal was strong, though he was likely sitting at
the communications console of the MD-80, more than
250 miles away on a taxiway at the Turkish Air Force
base outside of Siirt.

"Roger, Picnic Six. This is Picnic Echo Actual,"
replied Weiskopf. "I'm sending my twenty hundred
SitRep early so I can get under way and get the Lima
Tango Delta set up at the objective. I know it's only a
few klicks, but I want to get under way ASAP so we can
move in quietly. There has been heavy road movement
in and around the objective. There is also a lot of traffic on the highway, so it may take us awhile to get ourselves across."

"Roger, Picnic Echo Actual. If you have to split up, be
sure to let us know where you all are so that we can
keep track of where everyone is, over."

"Roger. Everything set with the UAV at Incirlik?
Over."

"Yeah, Josh, I just talked to Sergeant Major Gabbard," said Newman, reverting to plain English over the
encrypted satellite link. "He says the techs will have
that puppy ready to roll as soon as you say so. How are
you fixed for water?"

"We're fine," replied the Delta commando captain.
"We still have four quarts apiece of what we brought
with us, and there is some water here that we've been
able to filter and put some purification tabs in."

"Roger," Newman said, and then added, "Be careful,
Josh."

"Wilco. Out." Weiskopf put the handset down,

turned to Lieutenant Kenneth "Key" Palmeri, and said, "Before we get under way, send out the twenty hundred SitRep by digital burst over the Sat Com, letting Picnic Six know the exact location and status of everyone here."

As soon as the message was sent, the Army captain motioned to the seven others standing at the mouth of the cave with their packs on. They headed out on to the penultimate leg of their mission. If all went as planned, they would only need to evade enemy patrols to get back to this little base and either wait out the palace coup or inflate their STARS balloons and get snatched into the air by the passing C-130.

Picnic Base Bravo
1.5 km W of the Presidential Palace
Tikrit, Iraq
Monday, 6 March 1995
0558 Hours, Local

Weiskopf had taken the last shift of watch so the others could get a few minutes of sleep. Now, with dawn just breaking in the sky, he quietly awakened the other team members.

The hike from "Picnic Base Alpha" to this new site, designated as "Picnic Base Bravo," had been the most difficult movement of the three nights that they had experienced so far on the ground in Iraq. The closer they got to Saddam's hometown and the Tikrit palace, the more Iraqi patrols they spotted.

Though the ISET's night vision goggles gave them an extraordinary advantage, they still couldn't take needless risks. Traffic on the highway between the Al Sahra and Tikrit South air bases had been so heavy and frequent that it had taken them nearly two hours to cross the road. Then they had almost stumbled over a four-man Republican Guard outpost outside the palace. Had the Iraqi soldiers not all been asleep, the ISET would have been forced to kill them.

Finally, at about 0415 they had found a small cave in a small outcropping of rock less than two kilometers from Saddam's summer palace. They had studied photos and videos of the palace, so it seemed quite familiar when they finally saw it. Their observation post was nearly perfect. They were slightly above and west of the palace with a clear view of the main structure where the terror summit was to take place later that same day.

Within a minute of Weiskopf's silent reveille, Lieutenant Palmeri was awake and eating something from his rations pack. He kicked the leg of Fernandez while Weiskopf woke Turner and Diberra. Lieutenant Watson, the British SAS officer, arose and began to assemble the satellite video equipment while Maloof, the only real Arab in the team, got to work sighting in the Laser Target Designator. Sears, the SAS sergeant, stood watch at the mouth of the little cave, scanning the terrain through the scope of his sniper rifle.

Since they had parachuted out of the MD-80 on Friday night, the men had only gotten a few minutes sleep in short snatches. They all hoped to have the chance to catnap a bit during the day while they waited for Saddam's guests to show up.

Apartment 2, Hussein Kamil Family Pavilion
Presidential Palace
Tikrit, Iraq
Monday, 6 March 1995
0600 Hours, Local

Despite the luxurious apartment Kamil had provided for him, Leonid Dotensk hadn't gotten much sleep since Friday night. On an almost hourly basis, he'd been calling UN headquarters in New York to get the current position of Weiskopf's ISET from Komulakov. Now, sitting at a desk in the apartment with a map provided by Kamil, he had just plotted the ISET's latest location—as Weiskopf had reported it to Newman at 0500 hours—and as Newman had transmitted it to New York—and as Komulakov had relayed it to the Ukrainian arms merchant. Now, staring at the coordinates, Dotensk shuddered at the thought of how close they were. From where he sat, they were 1.5 kilometers distant—a little over a mile away.

Dotensk got up, went to the door, and opened it. There, across the hall, was one of the many young men who staffed the building, dozing in a chair.

The boy snapped awake and stood up. "May I help you, sir?"

"Yes, please ask His Excellency, Minister Hussein Kamil, to join me."

"Oh, I cannot disturb him, sir."

"Look, I don't care what he's doing right now. If you don't go get him right away, I'm going to shout at the top of my lungs until he shows up. Do you understand me?"

"Yes, sir."

"Well . . . go!" A few minutes later, a bleary-eyed Kamil was at the door.

"You look awful," Dotensk said. "You had better get a grip on yourself. The UN assassination team is in position." Dotensk put his finger on the map to show Kamil the team's location.

"That close? By Allah, we should be able to see them from here." He opened the draperies covering the western windows and peered out into the growing light of dawn. "I must go get my binoculars," he said and turned to leave.

"Stop, you fool!" shouted Dotensk, grabbing the sleeve of Kamil's wrinkled, white *thobe*. "If they see you peering at them, they may call for their pilotless bomb now and kill us."

Kamil looked down at the hand on his sleeve. Then he looked at Dotensk.

Dotensk moved as if struck by a snake "That was very rude of me. I apologize. Please forgive me."

"Certainly," replied Kamil, calmer now that he had reestablished the hierarchy.

"May I suggest that you and I go to your command post at the Tikrit South Air Base?" said Dotensk.

"Yes, I was thinking the same thing myself," said Kamil, still looking out the window to the low hills west of where they stood. "We have good communications there, and you can continue to talk with whomever it is that provides this information. Please be prepared to drive over there in ten minutes." Kamil turned and walked out the door.

Ten minutes later, Dotensk was seated in Kamil's Mercedes as they pulled out of the palace driveway toward the main highway. The president's son-in-law was once again dressed in clothing familiar to the Ukrainian—the uniform of an Iraqi general.

The guards at each checkpoint saluted them—none of

which Kamil bothered to return—and they drove into the air base. As they approached hangar 3, the evidence of the American raid on Friday was still visible. Dotensk could see the remnants of old Soviet equipment—some of which he had most likely sold to them.

Beside one of the "impervious" French-built concrete hangars that had been destroyed by a single laser-guided U.S. two-thousand-pounder in 1990 was a wrecked 36N85 "Flap Lid" Fire Control Radar, destroyed by an American missile just three nights ago. And behind another destroyed hangar was a burned-out hulk that had once been an SA-6 "Gainful" elevator/launcher. Obviously, the Americans had perfected their anti-SAM capabilities. Dotensk made a mental note to report these results to his friends in Moscow.

Kamil pulled the car into hangar 3 next to one of the MI-27 HINDs, jumped out, and started giving orders in Arabic. He grabbed the map out of Dotensk's hand and spread it on a chart table.

Kamil ordered a team of snipers to position themselves. One sniper was dressed in workman's coveralls and given a hard hat. He climbed a nearby communications tower that was only seven hundred yards away from where Dotensk said the ISET team was hiding. The sniper carried his weapon dismantled in a tool case so that if the intruders were watching they would not have their suspicions aroused.

Now, as the sun crawled above the horizon, Kamil ordered an entire company of his Amn Al-Khass commandos, along with one of his hunter units, to begin a systematic approach to the ISET team. If they followed his instructions, they would take hours to crawl inch by inch through the sand and not be seen until they were on top of the ISET.

"You are sure that there are only eight of them," Kamil asked as the eager commando unit set out.

Dotensk looked at his watch. It was nearly 0700 in Iraq. In New York, it was nearly 2300 the day before. He dialed the UN number anyway and switched on the EncryptionLok-3. Komulakov was on the line in seconds. "My host, who is standing here next to me, wants confirmation that there are only eight intruders at the location you gave me an hour ago." Dotensk listened for a moment, said "thank you," and terminated the call. "Yes, it is only eight," he said to Kamil. "But he is concerned that you may have sent your commandos in too soon. They will have to wait out there in the hot sun until the ISET team gets its equipment set up—that may take hours. Will they be all right out there for so long?"

"Of course. They are the best."

Dotensk shrugged. "I hope so."

CHAPTER SIXTEEN

Disaster!

Laqlaq, Iraq
34 km N of Tikrit
Monday, 6 March 1995
1230 Hours, Local

Eli Yusef Habib sat cross-legged on the carpet of a shabby inn—it was the only one in town. He had arrived late the previous night and was having his midday meal and tea. He had arisen at dawn, and he had spent most of the time since then in prayer. Still convinced that God was leading him here, yet finding no obvious connection to that impression, Habib took his time with his meal and tea.

Ordinarily this place would be a sleepy little town. Yet that morning Habib noticed that a military convoy had gone past just before he left his room. He wondered why such a strong military presence was necessary. It made him nervous to be around either the Iraqi or Iranian soldiers. Neither liked outsiders, and Habib, who felt at home in many countries, was to them an outsider.

For some reason he did not feel as if this were the place he was supposed to be.

Lord, do You want me to stay or go back? Habib had prayed earlier. He had no immediate sense of what to do.

Now it was just after 1:00 P.M. and as he finished his midday meal, Habib prayed again. This time he was impressed with the idea of leaving Laqlaq right away. He paid for his meal and room and carried his things to his Toyota truck.

"What was the commotion about this morning? I saw several Army trucks," he said to the Iraqi owner of the inn, sitting nearby in the shade, out of the mid-afternoon sun.

"You should wait until it is cooler to go," the man said.

Habib tried again. "The Army trucks—what were they doing?"

The man shrugged. "Who knows? But my brother just returned from Tikrit, and he told me they have roadblocks around the town. No one is allowed in. Are you going that way?"

Habib shook his head. "I am driving to Jisr Al Tharthar—about fifty kilometers due west of Tikrit."

"Ah, yes, the way you came last night. I remember you told me."

"Saddam must be at his summer palace," Habib guessed. "The roadblocks must be for his security."

"Yes, no doubt that is it."

Habib drove about a kilometer to the town's only petrol station and filled his tank. He also filled two spare gas cans and two five-gallon water cans. His route was mostly deserted; it was the road alongside the petroleum pipeline, and there was seldom much traffic.

He also purchased some dates and cheese in case he did not arrive at his destination before nightfall. But what was his destination? He had no idea. He was simply following the leading of God.

It was almost two o'clock in the afternoon by the time Habib was ready to leave. But before he did, he spread out his prayer rug in the shadow of the truck and prostrated himself in prayer. It was 2:15 P.M. when he got up again and climbed into his truck. It was finally time to go.

MD-80 Command Center
Siirt Air Base, Turkey
Monday, 6 March 1995
1313 Hours, Local

"Colonel Newman, sir. Captain Weiskopf has just sent the signal to launch the UAV. Shall I call Incirlik and tell Sgt. Major Gabbard?"

Captain Ben Phillips, one of the British officers assigned to ISET Charlie had been manning the Comm Station aboard the MD-80.

"What's the latest, Ben?" Newman asked.

"Picnic Base reported in via satellite link. They have everything set up and have been checking in every half hour as instructed. They just sent the launch order three minutes ago, while you were off the plane at the head. They said they're about a klick from the target; they have the laser-targeting device tested and in. Everything is go. Captain Weiskopf said they were going off-air so the Iraqis wouldn't intercept their transmissions. Even though we've got the element of surprise, he says that we can't presume that Saddam won't be on alert—if for no other reason than the company he has for the weekend."

"Is Josh sure that he has a good angle on the target so that the UAV will be able to pick up the reflection from his LTD and not the designator itself? We don't want that thing to fly up his nose."

"Affirmative, sir. They're just sitting and waiting for the guests to show up at the palace."

"All right, let's do it!" Newman said. "Alert the QRF to start moving toward the Iraqi border in case they're needed. Call Sergeant Major Gabbard and tell him to launch the Global Hawk. Get Major Robinette out of the powder room or wherever she is and tell her to get this crate into the air. I want to be airborne in case something goes wrong. Ben, have your ISET suit up for a jump just in case we have to drop Charlie in to help Echo out of trouble. Call General Harris down at the 331st Expeditionary Air Group and tell him the fireworks are about to start in Tikrit and remind him that the contingency plan calls for his F-15s and -16s to fly cover for the exfiltration."

The men all stood and grabbed their weapons and gear. Jane Robinette boarded the plane wearing her flight uniform and helmet. Newman noticed she was packing her side arm. While the men inside prepared their weapons and equipment for takeoff, Major Robinette and her crew made a hurried last inspection of the aircraft.

Newman climbed into his seat at the command console, where he had directed the insertion three nights ago. Tom McDade settled himself into the electronic warfare station. Strapped into the red nylon web seats, three on one side and four on the other, were Capt. Phillips and his ISET Charlie men.

As the engines spooled up, the electronics on the consoles in front of Newman and McDade flickered on. Because it was midday instead of the middle of the night, the video feeds were much more visible than they had been when they had dropped Weiskopf and his ISET Echo three nights ago.

It took less than fifteen minutes for the crew to finish its pre-flight checks and for McDade, acting as the EWO, to make sure that all the necessary data was uploaded into the plane's computer.

In the cockpit, Major Robinette and Lieutenant Haskell were checking their instruments, as was Master Sergeant Maddox, the Crew Chief. Some smart aleck had hung a sign over Maddox's little compartment: "Galley Slave."

Haskell's copilot seat on the right side up front had been slightly reconfigured by the spooks out at Nellis Air Force Base when the MD-80 was borrowed from the "bone-yard" for this mission. On his side of the cockpit Haskell had a complete navigator's station with video displays for radar, altitude, VORTAC navigation, GPS, heading, and two radios—one of them an ARC-210 for secure voice transmissions.

Just as they completed the pre-flight check, Lieutenant Haskell said into Newman's intercom, "Sir, there's a call coming in on the ARC."

Newman flicked a switch on his console and keyed his mike. "Picnic Six, go ahead."

"Colonel, I'm glad I reached you."

Newman recognized Major Ellwood's voice.

"What is it? We're about ready to leave."

"I know that, sir. That's why I called on the secure channel. I just wanted you to know there are some suspicious happenings here. I don't have anything specific to tell you, except that there is a live *audio* feed of the RF transmissions between you and your units that is being fed back to here. Did you know about this connection, sir?"

"Are you sure? How are you picking me up?"

"It's being fed to us from your Air Force sat com link at Incirlik, apparently at the direction of the White House," the British major replied. "Every time you communicate with one of your units, we're picking it up here. And I'm concerned that the information we're receiving may be getting fed to Baghdad."

"Baghdad! Major, are you sure?"

"I'm not positive, but I have noticed over the last three days that after every MoveRep and SitRep from your unit in Iraq, within minutes there has been a call to a satellite phone number in Iraq—and none of those calls show on the communications log. I raised the matter with Deputy Secretary General Komulakov and he told me, in so many words, to mind my own business. Well, I'm making it my business now. We'll sort things out here, or when you get back. I just wanted you to know . . . and to watch yourself up there."

"Copy that . . . Let me know if anything turns up while we still have our guys on the ground. Newman out." He toggled the switch back to intercom. "I want you guys on radar and the radios to be extra alert. There may be someone monitoring our RF communications and passing info to the bad guys in Iraq. From here on out, I want to keep our radio communications to an absolute minimum.

"Major Robinette, hold our departure. Lieutenant McDade, I want you to type up a 'Top Secret' encrypted data message—no voice, no video—to Brigadier General James Harris in the 331st Expeditionary Group command center at Incirlik. Tell him we have reason to believe our RF messages to him and to the ISETs in the field are all being picked up by somebody at UNHQ in New York and being re-broadcast to someone in Iraq. Tell him that, if he is relaying our comms to the UN in New York at the request of the White House, that as the mission commander, I respectfully request he pull the plug on any feeds to the UN in New York until we can sort this out. I want to talk only to the faces I've been talking to the last three days . . . and shut down *every-one* else. Ask him to please keep *his* comms up with us, the EA-6s, F-15s, and with the F-16s, but no one else. Now, type that up, print it, and hand it to the nearest airman on the ground crew with instructions to get it to General Harris ASAP. Got that?"

"Yes, sir!" McDade began typing the message on his keyboard. He turned his monitor display so Newman could proof it before it was printed. Newman read it and nodded. McDade keyed in the print command and the document was ready in twelve seconds. He grabbed it from the console and opened the closest escape hatch. He waved to one of the ground crew. "Airman! Take this to General Harris as fast as you can."

Within a couple minutes there was another call on the ARC radio line. Newman took the call from General Harris and explained the situation. Then the general asked Newman, "When is the next time we're supposed to hear from your team on the ground in Iraq?"

"They're supposed to call me as soon as Saddam shows up at the palace with bin Laden, and then I'm to vector the UAV from its loiter station over Turkey on to the target. I'll fly it from here until it picks up Weiskopf's LTD reflection off the target. There shouldn't be that many radio communications with them until we pull them out after the UAV detonates."

"Roger that. What do you want me to do?"

"I don't know whether there's a problem, but I want to err on the side of caution. Please, General, pull the plug to New York now, before the call comes in from ISET Echo."

"You've got it, Colonel." Newman heard the general's voice giving the order to cut the feed to New York. "The guys are asking, 'What about Washington?' Is there a chance that the feed to the Pentagon or the White House has been picked up?"

"I don't think so . . . but use your own judgment. There's nothing we need from them, and they just want to know what's going on. But just to be safe, cut the audio feed only. Let them keep the video feed. That way they can still see what's going on."

"Lieutenant Colonel Newman, we have clearance for takeoff. Is it a go?" Major Robinette asked.

Newman paused for a moment. There was too much at stake not to go. "Yes, let's go!" he called to the pilot. The engines accelerated and the aircraft began to pull forward on the tarmac and move toward the end of the runway. Within three minutes they were airborne. Major Robinette retraced her flight path from the previous mission, this time filing an enroute flight plan as a United Nations humanitarian aid flight from Turkey to Yemen.

While they were climbing to altitude and awaiting clearance from the International Airspace Coordinator in Ankara, the Global Hawk's pre-programmed satellite radio queried McDade's console, seeking instructions, as its Rolls-Royce turbofan engine pushed it to 65,000 feet at 350 knots. Up to this point the UAV was simply flying a parking pattern pre-programmed into its GPS-guided memory.

McDade pushed a button on his terminal and sent a

stream of zeros and ones to the UAV's electronic brain, programming the huge flying bomb to head for the coordinates of Saddam's summer palace and then, at precisely 1500 hours, to activate the seeker head in its nose cone and search for a laser reflection at those coordinates. Once it found the laser reflection, the UAV was instructed to hurtle its 22,900 pounds of explosives and fuel at the point where the reflected beam originated— the building housing Saddam Hussein, Osama bin Laden, and, according to Harrod, the killer of Peter Newman's brother, Mohammed Farrah Aidid.

Ten minutes after Major Robinette had requested the over-flight clearance, Ankara granted it, and instructed her to contact Baghdad flight control. Even though United Nations sanctions limited Iraq to no more than one commercial flight in and out of the country each day, Baghdad was still required to maintain flight clearance facilities for other nations' commercial flights.

Robinette came up on the assigned frequency, contacted Baghdad, and switched her commercial IFF transponder to the assigned squawk. She then picked up a heading that would have taken the MD-80 roughly parallel to the Tigris, but twenty miles west of the river, and finally out over the Persian Gulf, west of Basra. Baghdad Center specifically instructed her to avoid Tikrit since it was a "Head-of-State Restricted Area."

At precisely 1415 hours, Newman saw Tom McDade signal him.

"Colonel Newman—I've got him!" McDade announced over the intercom. "Captain Weiskopf is on comm one."

Newman, not knowing whether the audio feed to New York from the Incirlik Air Base Command Center had actually been cut yet, asked if the call was on the

ARC secure radio. McDade nodded. "The call is being relayed from a satellite in earth orbit."

Weiskopf's voice was clear and crisp. "This is Picnic Base. We are go for video in ten seconds . . . switching to video feed in . . . five, four, three, two, . . ."

On "one" the video monitor on Newman's console flickered and a picture flared on-screen. There was too much light, but the camera quickly compensated and the image cleared up.

"We've got your pictures," Newman told him. "Are you guys set?"

"Affirmative. The finger is pointing and ready for your model airplane."

"It's on the way. It should be in your area in another forty minutes if it's working right. Do you have guests at the hotel?"

"Do we have guests? It looks like a used Mercedes auction over there. We saw Saddam with bin Laden and a whole raft of straphangers. Couldn't pick your buddy Aidid out of the crowd, but he's probably one of the dozens dressed in the Ali Baba and the forty thieves' outfits."

"Any unwanted visitors to *your* location?"

"Funny you should mention that. I'm going to take the camera and give you a tour. We've noticed some activity. There's a bunch of Iraqi soldiers—maybe a platoon or as much as a company—that have spread themselves all around us. I don't think they've made us; I think they're just a security force connected to the summit."

Newman watched as Weiskopf slowly panned the video camera from the northeast where it had been pointing to the right in a clear visual panorama of the summer palace and nearby air base. Newman saw a tower at the edge of the air base, and a curious dark spot near the top. Weiskopf must have noticed it too; the camera jiggled slightly as he stepped just outside the cave. The picture zoomed in on the mysterious spot on the tower. As Newman and the flight crew watched, the image became clearer, and it was obvious that it was a person with a rifle. Newman's mouth went dry as he realized the rifle was aimed at Weiskopf's location.

As if in slow motion, Newman watched as a sudden puff of blue-white smoke and a flash obscured the face of the person on the tower.

A fraction of a second later, Weiskopf's body collapsed, as a bullet smashed through his forehead adjacent to where he had been holding the camera's eyepiece. The video picture slewed as the camera fell to the ground. It ended on its side, pointed at a tilted view of sky, rock, and what looked like part of Weiskopf's camo uniform. "Oh, God, please," Newman prayed. "Please . . ."

Within seconds the other ISET Echo team members were spread out in defensive postures, weapons at the ready. "Key" Palmeri crawled to the side of Captain Weiskopf, still crumpled on the ground below the camera. Palmeri checked the captain for vital signs, found none, then carefully turned him to check for the exit wound—and grimaced as he saw that most of the back of Weiskopf's head was missing.

Palmeri eased the camera from beneath Weiskopf's arm and turned it so he was staring into the lens. He shook his head. He reached for the mike switch on his headset radio and took over the transmission. "He died instantly, sir. Sniper. We're going to have to focus on what's outside . . . I'll try to get the camera re-mounted and leave it running."

Back on the flying command post, Newman switched on the intercom and spoke to McDade. "How far out is the UAV?"

"It's still thirty minutes out before it can acquire the LTD."

Those guys won't be there in thirty minutes. Newman locked eyes with his EWO. "Call back to General Harris and tell him that our guys on the ground are in contact. Tell him they already have one dead and he needs to send in the F-15s and -16s. We can act as airborne FAC if they can't talk to the guys on the ground."

Amn Al-Khass Operations Center
Hangar 3, Tikrit Air Base
Monday, 6 March 1995
1434 Hours, Local

Hussein Kamil was furious. He shouted at a nearby colonel. "Who authorized that sniper to shoot?" Then he unleashed a torrent of obscenities. "Bring that man to me."

A few minutes later the sniper was brought in to the hangar. The soldier looked confused—was he being congratulated for the first kill of an American?

"You idiot! Who told you to fire?" Kamil screamed. "Are you the one running this operation?" He drew his automatic pistol and shot the man dead as his stunned and frightened aides looked on. "I will not waste my breath on this pile of camel dung. That bullet is my reminder to the rest of you to *follow orders!* I do not want anyone to act without my authority. Do I make myself clear!?"

Dotensk, who had seen two similar demonstrations

of Kamil's cold-blooded rage, could not disagree with his actions this time.

Kamil whirled on Dotensk. "What do you hear from your all-knowing source? Can he tell you what the assassins know?"

"I don't know." The Ukrainian was hesitant to tell the Iraqi security chief that just moments before the sniper fired, Komulakov had called on the satellite phone to advise that New York had lost the audio feed from Incirlik. "Just as you were dealing with the incident, the audio feed . . . it went silent. It may be a temporary loss, but I don't know for sure."

"Well, stay with it. Try and get it back. We need to know the plans of these people!" *The risks of failure were coming more and more into focus now,* Dotensk thought. With the trained infiltrators out there and the raging, murderous security chief in here, he knew he was now fighting for his own life.

Kamil took a breath and walked over and picked up a phone. "Get Qusay on the phone for me." There was a brief pause. "I know he's in a meeting, you fool. I'm supposed to be there myself. Get him on the phone now. Tell him his father's life may be in danger."

A moment later, Kamil said, "I have discovered a plot against your father. I'm dealing with it, but for his safety and that of our very important guests, it would be best if you would please immediately escort the President and his distinguished guests away from the palace and to the safety of the secure bunkers at Al Sahra Air Base."

There was another long pause as Kamil listened to his brother-in-law. "I suspect the Americans or perhaps the British," Kamil said. "I believe it is an effort to kill many people—including you. I urge you to take the

President and our guests out of the palace and to the bunker at Al Sahra immediately. If necessary, I will have the demonstration materials for the guests delivered there."

Kamil hung up and turned to Dotensk. "If what you told me earlier is correct, there are seven of them left. We must take them out, and then we have to capture the laser-targeting device and aim it at the site where we want their weapon to hit. There is still enough time to do that. Have you been able to re-establish the audio link so we can know exactly what they are up to?"

"Sorry . . . not yet. Nothing."

"Then we must act on our own. Major Shahir! Come here."

The officer hurried over to Kamil.

"Take the company of sharpshooters that you have in position . . . and more if you need them. Bring in two or three squads with grenade launchers and mortars. Begin now to encircle the assassins and destroy them. But do not destroy their equipment. I need it. Do you hear? Make sure you do not harm their equipment."

Major Shahir saluted and turned to obey his orders.

✪

A little more than a kilometer west, ISET Echo was dug in and carefully hidden. The seven surviving members had slipped away from the cave after Captain Weiskopf was killed.

With their commander dead, Key Palmeri assumed the leadership position. "We'll stay on headsets to communicate but try and get as far apart as you can. We have to make sure the LTD does its job. After the UAV hits, there should be enough confusion for us to E and E to the west, toward the rendezvous point. If we can hold 'em off until dark, we'll be able to get to the extraction site. If you end up alone—if no one answers your radio signal—then you know the E and E route to link up with the QRF. By my reckoning," the lieutenant said, checking his watch, "the UAV ought to be here in twenty-one minutes, right at 1500."

Palmeri had just gotten into a prone position and wiggled into as much sand cover as possible when a mortar round exploded some thirty yards to his right, just outside the rock outcropping where they had spent the night. A second one followed, and this one detonated right at the mouth of the cave. Rocks and pebbles showered down all around. Two more rounds struck the cave. Now there were rocket-propelled grenades. The explosions continued for several minutes.

When there was a break in the shelling, Palmeri did a radio check to find out if everyone was OK. They were. Palmeri had stayed closest to the laser-targeting system. They had covered the equipment with a small camouflage net and had covered that with scrub vegetation. Just the laser lens itself was visible, and only from a few feet away.

Captain Weiskopf had wisely chosen to separate the antenna for the UAV terminal guidance system and those for the video and audio uplinks that were located near the cave. Palmeri was hopeful that the mortar and grenade explosions had not destroyed the UAV uplink.

He raised his head slowly and for only an inch or so in order to see over the rise in the sandy terrain. What he saw made his guts turn to liquid; the Iraqi troops who had been deployed around the cave were now crouching and moving forward in a wide semicircle. They were being joined by what looked like a company of reinforcements. Soon their ranks were filled so that they appeared as a solid line of soldiers—it reminded

Palmeri of an infantry line of the Napoleonic era or one from the Colonial wars. He exhaled so that there was no air passing over his vocal cords when he talked into his headset. "Spray 'em," he commanded the others. "Try to get as many as you can. Maybe it'll scare 'em back."

There were muffled sounds as the ISET sprayed the oncoming line of troops with their automatic machine pistols. The flash suppressors and silencers on their weapons all but eliminated the noise and flash of the muzzle bursts; the Iraqis never saw where the shots came from. More than two dozen fell, and the line hesitated.

The seven men replaced magazines and rolled into new positions, still not visible to the soldiers approaching up the slight incline. Suddenly, a squad equipped with RPGs fired a volley in a pattern with each burst some thirty meters apart. Five or six rounds exploded close to four of the men. Each of them scurried on their bellies toward the nearest explosion, trying to reduce the odds of being hit by the next round.

Palmeri switched on his helmet-mounted radio. "Picnic Base calling Watchdog," he said as quietly as he could, and hoping that a friendly USAF or Navy aircraft somewhere in the area was listening.

"This is Watchdog. I'm ten klicks from your finger-pointer. Advise."

"How close is the big bang? We're in a mess of trouble with a company of bad guys coming on strong." The others continued to fire on the advancing Iraqis, but now ammunition was becoming an issue. They fired in short, well-aimed bursts. Whole squads fell dead and the Iraqis fell back, but only until their officers urged them on.

"Picnic Base . . . stand by."

Another volley of RPGs slammed into the hillside. Palmeri saw Sears and Maloof go down. Then Diberra and Fernandez were overrun. The ISET couldn't fire fast enough to stop the vastly superior numbers of Iraqis. A moment later, twenty meters to his right, the lieutenant saw Turner, grievously wounded, rise up from his concealed position and stumble toward his attackers, firing his MP-5 from the hip and then, when his ammunition ran out, tossing hand grenades. They cut him down, but not before he had taken eight or ten of them with him. Now, only Palmeri and the Brit were left.

"Picnic Base . . . be advised that ETA for the firecracker is sixteen minutes. What can we do to help you while you're waiting," the F-16 pilot asked.

"There are only two of us left, and we have no smoke to mark our pos. If you can home on the UAV beacon, drop down low, you'll see the bad guys. They're coming at us like some Civil War infantry line. Can you lay down some fire and take out enough to make the odds a little more even?"

"Picnic Base . . . Watchdog responding. Keep your head down; I'm coming in!"

Seven seconds later the F-16 screamed out of the low hills to the north, releasing a GBU laser-guided bomb directly into the line of Iraqi troops. The fighter plane whooshed over Palmeri's head. The plane was so low that when it banked away, Palmeri could see the pilot's face.

The F-16's wingman then made a pass and decimated another line of troops, by now scattering for cover.

From his command post in hangar 3 at the abandoned air base, Kamil watched as the U.S. plane dove and sprayed his troops with devastation. He screamed at the nearest officer to bring some anti-aircraft weapons to bear. Meanwhile, the pilots for the two MI-27 HIND helicopters that would have been able to provide support for his Amn Al-Khass troops were nowhere to be found.

After two passes each, the flight leader of the two F-16s called down to the ISET Echo base. "Picnic Base . . . this is Watchdog. Advise."

There was no answer. He climbed in a roaring, soaring arc to thirty-four thousand feet and tried again. "Picnic Base . . . give me your status. Please advise, Picnic Base."

Still no answer.

The flight leader then broke away, did a tight turn five miles to the east of the contact, and came back at rooftop height. He aimed his video cameras at the site of the battle and zoomed in. The images were not very stable, but he knew where the ISET team was located. It had appeared to him that the two of them were either dead or wounded. And now . . .

"Watchdog . . . we're all dead." Palmeri's weak voice came through the pilot's headset. "The Brit took a grenade hit . . . and I . . . uh . . . I c-caught a couple rounds. I'm bleeding bad . . . won't make it . . . tell Picnic Leader . . . a grenade took out . . . took out the LTD. The laser's gone and I—" Palmeri stopped in midsentence, choking on his own blood.

"Picnic Base . . . can you repeat?"

All the pilot heard was static. He reported back to Newman aboard the MD-80 that his team and the laser-targeting device were lost. He flew north to rendezvous with the others.

Aboard the MD-80
28,000 feet, 20 miles E of Mosul, Iraq
Monday, 6 March 1995
1451 Hours, Local

Newman had listened in helpless horror as the action took place 125 miles away. "How long to target?" he asked Charlie Haskell.

He looked at the airspeed and ETA readout and responded, "Twenty-one minutes, sir."

Newman turned to McDade and asked, "Can the UAV still do some damage without the laser?"

"Yes, sir. We know the GPS of the team . . . and the target. They're already programmed in. I think I can disable the instructions we gave it earlier, slow it down, and re-program it to follow guidance from here based on what we see from its onboard camera."

"Do it," ordered Newman.

While McDade worked out the instructions to the UAV, Newman thumbed his intercom switch. "Major Robinette, break off your course and head straight down the Tigris to Tikrit. I want to see the UAV hit the target."

"Roger that, sir."

"Everyone aboard," Newman ordered into the intercom, "make sure your parachute harnesses are tight. You may need your chutes before this is over."

Robinette had no sooner made the turn back to the east than an alarm sounded both in the cockpit and on McDade's console.

"It's an Iraqi radar and missile site," said Haskell. "They've locked on."

Newman heard Robinette's voice on the air-to-air net.

"Watchdog, this is Big Bird. I'm being painted by a target acquisition radar, over."

"Roger, Big Bird, we're on the way."

Seconds later an F-16 came whipping in from right to left across the front of the MD-80, talking to the other F-16 escorts. The fighter banked hard to the right in front of the MD-80, found the site, and locked on. A few seconds later, a guided missile blazed from beneath the fighter. The missile took out the site with an explosion the crew in the MD-80 could see from miles away.

The alarm sounded again. Another Iraqi radar site was locking on to their aircraft. And another F-16 banked and dived, and another Iraqi site was destroyed.

Five minutes later, as they approached the defensive zone surrounding Tikrit, three different Iraqi radar sites locked on to the plane. One site was destroyed right away, but since there were three different immediate threats, it required precious seconds for the F-16s to coordinate their response. A second site was destroyed before it could launch, but the third site had enough time to fire four missiles at the MD-80. Two F-16s streaked out in front and dived toward the oncoming weapons ready to use defensive armaments and missiles of their own.

Two of the Iraqi rockets were destroyed while they were still almost thirty miles away, but the other two continued on their course toward the lumbering MD-80. One of the two was just under two minutes from their plane when an F-16 downed it, but its twin kept coming. Another F-16 released a Sidewinder missile and eliminated the incoming threat.

On the flight deck, there wasn't time for even a sigh of relief. More and more Iraqi radar sites were coming alive. Two F-16s took up defensive positions off the wings of the MD-80.

Alarms sounded again. This time the threat was from a single site, an easy target for one of the F-l6s.

The MD-80 was approaching the 35th parallel, still some thirty-eight miles north of the target. McDade shouted, "I've got the Global Hawk under positive control. I'm getting imagery from its onboard camera and can make out the buildings on the palace grounds, but I don't know which one is which."

Newman jumped from his seat to look at the display on McDade's console. As he did so, he could hear the F-16 pilots talking to Major Robinette.

"We're out of bullets, babe," one of the fighter pilots said. "I recommend you break away now, 'cause if they shoot anything else, all we can throw at 'em is chaff."

Suddenly, the missile warning alarm sounded again. This time three other sites were coming alive. The Iraqi radar stations west of Tikrit, responsible for protecting Saddam's palace, had acquired the MD-80.

"What do you want me to do, Colonel?" It was the voice of Major Robinette from the cockpit, calm and measured.

"Can we hold this course for just a minute more while we get the UAV homing on its target? If they are paying attention to us heading at 'em from the north, maybe they won't be able to pick up the Global Hawk coming in from the west."

"Roger that," replied Robinette, the sound of the alarms bleeding over her mike.

"What are you guys doing?" It was one of the now-toothless F-16s.

"We're going to hold this altitude and heading for another fifty seconds and then skeedaddle," replied Robinette.

There was a momentary silence on the radio and the

intercom while Newman bent over McDade's video display and tried to pick out the right building on the palace grounds so McDade could put the cursor over it and hit "Enter," for the UAV's memory. But before they could act, he heard one of the F-16 pilots: "SAM! SAM! SAM!"

One of the fighters broke hard to the right and dived for the deck. But his companion, instead of following the prescribed SAM avoidance maneuver, continued on course, looking visually for the missile that had been fired at the two fighters and the ungainly MD-80.

From the MD-80, the surface-to-air missile looked like a telephone pole riding a column of fire and smoke, racing toward them. The fighter pilot kicked in his afterburner and flew straight for the oncoming missile.

"Oh, dear God," said Haskell, "he's going to take the bullet for us."

They watched in horror as the F-16 purposely ran into the incoming missile about seven miles ahead of them. There was a huge fireball as the F-16 disintegrated. No ejection seat, no parachute. And then as they watched with a feeling of nausea in their guts, their eyes widened in sheer terror. Coming through the smoke and fiery wreckage was a second missile, still hurtling toward them. Major Robinette's voice came over the intercom, "He only got one! A second one's coming at us!"

Haskell was frantically calling for the EA-6 or more F-16 support, but there was no answer. The oncoming SA-6 would strike them in less than thirty seconds.

Robinette shouted into the intercom, "Gotta go, gang, sorry 'bout this. Hang on in back." She pushed the nose of the passenger jet hard over and dived for the ground.

Everyone but Newman was strapped down. They grimaced as the MD-80 pulled negative g's and tried to throw them against the ceiling. Newman, bent over McDade's console one second, was flat against the ceiling the next. It probably saved his life.

When the Iraqi missile struck the MD-80, it ripped off the bottom of the plane. The ISET and McDade, strapped in their seats, disappeared in the conflagration. There was a gaping hole where the bottom of the cabin had been, and what was left of the fuselage was beginning to tumble. Out of the corner of his eye, through the cracked lens of his full-face oxygen mask, Newman could see a body, incinerated beyond recognition.

Major Robinette was somehow crawling out of the cockpit, trying to make her way to either an emergency exit or the hole in the floor.

As the aircraft did another 360-degree roll, Newman pushed himself off the ceiling and grabbed the injured pilot. In what seemed to his oxygen-starved brain like slow motion, the two of them tumbled out of the hole in the fuselage just as it was pointed toward the earth. Still clutching one another, they fell clear of the plunging wreckage. Just before he passed out, Newman jerked the d-ring of Robinette's parachute, then his own.

Underground Pipeline Road
Lake Tharthar, Iraq
Monday, 6 March 1995
1512 Hours, Local

Eli Yusef Habib had hoped that he might reach the pumping station oasis on the Euphrates River by nightfall. He did not like to sleep in his truck on this stretch of deserted highway. There were robbers and Army deserters who would think nothing of slitting a throat for a little food and water, not to mention the truck.

Nevertheless, when he stopped for his afternoon prayers and a bite to eat, he felt he needed to stay there, where he had stopped. "All right, gracious God. I will give myself over to Your protection as I sleep here tonight."

Habib stopped his truck alongside the road and offered his prayers outside, as was his preferred way. He always felt distracted by the smells and touch of his mechanical transportation. Outside, in the air, he felt closer to God. He could smell the humid scent of the lake just to the south and the faint fragrance of the few desert flower blossoms.

Habib finished his prayers and stood to go back to the truck for some food and something to drink. The sound of aircraft high overhead caused him to look up just in time to see a huge fireball in the sky; many seconds later he heard the explosion.

Perhaps they are having military maneuvers. That is probably why they had roadblocks set up near the air base.

He was still looking at the burning wreckage falling from the sky when a second, larger fireball erupted—the sound was much louder. This time the explosion seemed much closer to where he stood. Habib suddenly feared that he was in the path of an attack. He had witnessed many such engagements from a distance during the 1990–91 war and in the years since. The Americans and his old friends the British were always flying their jets overhead. That's why he tried to avoid areas where Saddam had his military forces. They were the real targets, not an old man and his truck.

As Habib watched, he strained his eyes to see two small, dark spots in the sky above the flaming wreckage falling to earth. Suddenly, first one and then the other object stopped in their fall, then began to fall again, but much more slowly. As he squinted, he saw that two parachutes had opened.

He knew about parachutes. As a boy he had seen the Nazis jumping out of airplanes into the desert. It had been a frightening sight for a fourteen-year-old boy.

Habib watched them drift lower. Most of the wreckage had already dropped into Lake Tharthar. He regretted he did not have a boat so he could row out and see if there were any survivors. He looked up again at the two parachutes. Unlike the German paratroopers he had witnessed in North Africa as a youth, one of these two, the smaller one, did not seem to be doing much to control the direction of descent.

Habib looked at the wreckage splashing into the lake and wondered if there had been others aboard who had not managed to extricate themselves from the flaming hulk. The old man said a quick prayer for them. Then he looked back over his shoulder for the two parachutists—but he saw nothing. He said a prayer for them as well.

✪

Newman regained consciousness as he descended below ten thousand feet. He remembered the missile hitting the aircraft and the explosion and seeing the gaping hole in the bottom of the fuselage, but he couldn't immediately recall how he had gotten free of the wreckage.

As he hung in the harness, he shifted his legs, moved his arms and feet and tested his shoulder muscles to feel if anything was broken or if he was injured. He smelled smoke and realized his jacket was smoldering. He beat at the spot with his hand. Beneath the charred leather, he could feel his arm was burned. He had no idea where his gloves went. His helmet face-protector was coated with oily soot, and he could hardly see. He rubbed it with the back of his hand and saw pieces of his skin stuck to the plastic. His hand was badly burned.

Newman flipped up his face protector and felt the icy wind; the blast of cold air helped to revive him. He could see now, and looked all around him as the parachute drifted lower. He spied wreckage beside a large lake below him, but he could see no sign that McDade or any of his ISET team had escaped. He felt an awful sickness in his stomach as the reality of their deaths hit him. Two teams . . . everyone killed.

He turned and looked around some more. Maybe he missed them; maybe they jumped earlier, he hoped. Then he saw the lake, and he was heading right toward it. He grabbed the harness and pulled the parachute lines to keep himself from sailing into the water. It wasn't the kind of high-performance parachute he'd become accustomed to while jumping in Force Recon, but the aerodynamic principles were the same.

He let what little wind there was work for him. By creating a parasail effect he was able to maintain his rate of descent.

"How do you do that?" a thin voice yelled at him. He turned and saw, slightly above him, another chute. It was Jane Robinette. He was glad she was alive. Newman yelled back at her, giving instructions on how to use the lines to guide her descent.

Newman estimated that by turning into the wind and using the chute as a brake they could traverse at least a mile to the west and perhaps avoid the water altogether.

As he looked at the expanse of Lake Tharthar, he saw bits of wreckage and what looked to him to be at least two bodies floating in the water some four hundred meters from the shore. From the looks of things, Newman guessed that only he and Robinette had gotten out of the flaming MD-80 alive.

The ground was approaching quickly now, and Newman started looking for a landing site. He anticipated the impact and did a near-perfect landing fall, allowing his bent legs to take the initial shock and then rolling left onto his calf, thigh, hip, and shoulder. He quickly got up and collapsed the chute to keep it from dragging him along the rocky ground. As soon as he had unsnapped his harness, he looked around to see where Major Robinette had landed.

At first there was no sign of her, and he stood there, revolving 360 degrees until he spotted the light green billow of a USAF parachute blown by the wind on the other side of a small rise. He ran to the top of the elevation to see the smaller, lighter pilot being dragged, face down, along the rock-strewn surface. She finally came to a stop when her body slammed against a boulder. Newman ran down the slope to free her from the chute.

He grabbed the lines, pulled them down, and collapsed the canopy. He unbuckled her harness and knelt beside the injured pilot to assess her injuries.

She was unconscious. Newman eased her onto her back and examined her for injuries. Her right arm was twisted at a grotesque angle—probably a multiple fracture. She had some burns on the side of her face and on her left cheek, and when he removed her shattered flight helmet, Newman saw a fairly large swelling on the right side of her head. There was blood on her lip, and Newman prayed she had bitten her lip—that the blood wasn't coming from an internal injury.

He reached into her parachute pack for the first-aid kit, wondering what he could use as a splint for her broken arm. He unzipped her flight suit to ease her broken arm out of the sleeve. Newman put some disinfectant on the wounds on her arm and bandaged them. He could feel the edges of the shattered bone just beneath the skin of her forearm. *Thank God the skin didn't break. Who knows how long until we're rescued?*

Newman saw blood oozing through her T-shirt. He lifted it carefully and grimaced again when he saw the wound. It looked fairly small, but he couldn't tell how deep it was. He pulled out a four-inch piece of shredded aluminum from between two of her ribs, just below her right breast. He used some gauze to stop the bleeding and bandaged the wound. She probably needed some stitches, at least.

After about half an hour, Major Robinette started to regain consciousness. She moaned quietly.

"I'm here, Jane . . . it's OK. We made it."

"A-anyone else?"

"Not as far as I can see. I had hoped the team got out the back door in time, but it doesn't look like it. Master Sergeant Maddox didn't make it. Do you know if Charlie got out before you did?"

Robinette shook her head as tears filled her eyes.

He told the major that she had a broken arm and probably a concussion. She also had a puncture wound in her lower chest.

"That's probably what hurts so much. I may have cracked a rib or two. It's even more painful than the arm. I hope you've got something in that first-aid kit that looks like a pain killer."

"There's morphine, but I don't think I should use the styrette with your head injury. How about if we try the Tylenol? There should be some emergency water in the bottom of your parachute pack." He dug down in the pack until he found it, opened the small can, and offered her a sip along with two of the pain pills. "I was looking for something to make a splint for you," he said. "Maybe I can find something over by the water."

"Any idea where we are?" she asked.

"Yeah, I know exactly where we are. We're at the north end of Lake Tharthar. There's a road that goes east to the Tigris River. We can wait until after dark and head that way and hopefully link up with the QRF coming down from Turkey if they can make it past Mosul."

"At least my legs aren't broken."

Their first option would be to trek parallel to the Tigris and keep out of sight, using the emergency radio from the kit. If they could reach the Kurds or someone from the Iraqi Resistance in the north, it might be possible to arrange an evacuation. Judging from Jane's injuries, it needed to be by helicopter—and soon. The alternative plan consisted of a two hundred-mile hike to the Turkish border. Newman looked at his injured companion. It was possible he could make it in ten or so days if he were traveling alone, but that wasn't an option. He would carry her out if he had to.

Newman cut some small branches from a stunted tree he found along the lakeshore to fashion a splint for Major Robinette. The pain pills were having little effect, but she was trying to be stoic. She suggested he cut strips of parachute fabric to make a sling for her arm.

"I'll go look around and see if I can find other survivors and anything from the crash we can use," he said. "You stay here and gather your strength. You'll need it for our walk. We should try to cover five or ten miles tonight. We need to get as far away from here as we can. Try and eat some of those rations from the kit, if you can."

Newman walked for nearly a mile in the gathering darkness before he saw anything that looked man-made. Newman trotted toward the object. As he drew closer he could see that it was part of the MD-80, though it was so badly charred it was impossible to tell exactly what part it had been. He also found another parachute—or what was left of it. It was almost entirely burned. Even the lines were blackened.

The body in the scorched harness was so badly burned it must have died in the explosion before it dropped from the sky. He checked the dogtags: "Haskell, Charles M."

Newman removed his helmet and then his dogtags and dropped them into his pocket. Then he untangled what was left of the harness and pulled Haskell's mangled body clear. He dragged the remains several yards and used the copilot's battered flight helmet to scoop out a grave in the sand.

He covered the body with the parachute and removed Haskell's wedding ring. He made a silent promise to the dead lieutenant that he would return the ring to the grieving wife who would never see her husband again. Newman choked up as he covered the young Air Force officer with a final helmet scoop of sandy soil. He went back to the parachute harness and gathered up all the emergency items—flashlight, rations, water, first-aid kit, water purification tablets, knife, pistol, ammunition, and a radio. They would all come in handy as he and Jane Robinette made their way back to Turkey. He stuffed the pistol and ammo into his flight suit pockets, along with the smaller emergency items. Then he gathered up the other items and wrapped them in the Mylar-backed thin blanket that would help them ward off the cold.

On his walk back, the full depth of the tragedy began to sink in. He tried to count how many deaths had occurred in this terrible place. He did not know for certain how many were dead. McDade and the seven men from ISET Charlie were missing, presumed dead. Master Sergeant Maddox and Lieutenant Haskell were confirmed dead. Captain Weiskopf and the seven members of ISET Echo were all dead near Tikrit. One F-16 pilot had been killed when he had sacrificed himself in a futile attempt to save the MD-80.

Newman had come to this forsaken place hoping to successfully carry out a mission that would eliminate some of the world's most notorious terrorists—and help him lay to rest the injustice of his brother's death in Mogadishu. He had hoped to make the world a safer place. Instead, nineteen of his men were killed—and he and Jane Robinette were in a desperate fight for survival.

There were other casualties that day, too, though Newman couldn't know it at the time. One hundred forty-seven Iraqis also died that day. The ISET team killed seventy-nine enemy soldiers, and the missiles and bombs of the F-16s killed the others.

It was for Newman a devastating day, full of blood and carnage. But he would have been *totally* demoralized if he had known the fate of the QRF, trying to make their way to Tikrit from the Turkish border.

CHAPTER SEVENTEEN

Closing the Door

Komulakov was tired, frustrated, and angry. The Russian general had been up virtually around the clock since ISET Echo had parachuted into Iraq on Friday. Now, after more than fifty hours with little happening, events were spinning out of control for his grand scheme to protect Hussein Kamil, his most valuable client. Then, he had lost communications with the units on the ground and Lieutenant Colonel Newman. He stared at the last entry in the watch officer's log:

0531: Lost all R/F audio signals from UN ISEG units in vicinity of Iraq.

He stared at the notation as if that might help, somehow. But Komulakov still had no clue as to why the audio feed through Incirlik had failed. All he knew for sure was that Dotensk was probably going insane with frustration, trying to keep Kamil in business—unless

Kamil had summarily executed the Ukrainian out of panic and outrage. Komulakov and Dotensk had such grand plans for making Kamil a hero in Saddam's eyes and persuading him not to defect—enabling them to sell him hundreds of millions' more in weaponry. But with no communication at such a critical juncture, those plans could very well be melting like ice cream in the desert sand.

Since the audio link had gone down, information was now flowing the opposite direction from what Komulakov and his co-conspirator had intended. Instead of receiving crucial intelligence on the ISET relayed through Komulakov's UNHQ communications link, Dotensk was now passing information to the Russian in New York.

Dotensk had called Komulakov immediately after the sniper on the tower had killed Weiskopf. And moments later he had called back to tell Komulakov that USAF F-16s had materialized out of the desert air to support the ISET—something Komulakov had assured Dotensk would not happen.

Over the course of the next forty minutes, Dotensk had called Komulakov a dozen times with blow-by-blow descriptions of events. Interspersed with Dotensk's telephoned narrative were Kamil's Arabic expletives as his best Amn Al-Khass battalion was decimated by the ISET and the F-16s.

Not only had Kamil's Amn Al-Khass hunter teams failed to quickly dispose of the eight man ISET, but the entire Iraqi Air Defense system was engaged, a half-dozen or more USAF aircraft were attacking Iraqi ground troops and SAM sites, and Komulakov had no idea where Newman or the QRF were. The last message from Dotensk on an EL-3-encrypted satellite telephone call at 0650, New York time, had only heightened his anxiety.

"I think the UN assassins must all be dead. The firing has stopped," the Ukrainian reported from hangar 3 at Tikrit South. "But our client is very agitated. Qusay, the number-one son, just told Kamil on the radio that Saddam is furious that his meeting was interrupted by the air strikes and wants to know how the mercenaries could get this close to the presidential palace. Kamil did not tell him about the unmanned bomber—what did you call it, a 'UAV'—the thing your assassins have headed toward the palace. You must stop it before it gets here or Kamil may be finished. And if he is finished, we're out of business."

Komulakov's heart almost stopped. Distracted by the furor of the engagement with Weiskopf's ISET, he had forgotten about the UAV winging its way at 350 miles per hour toward Tikrit. He saw his plans for the future going up in a blinding flash when the fuel- and explosives-laden Global Hawk detonated on the west wall of Saddam's palace. The Russian tried to remember what Newman had told him about the device and wished that he had paid more attention to the technical details. *Does this device have a command-destruct feature that could stop it?* the Russian general wondered.

And then it dawned on him: the technicians who had delivered and launched the device were still at Incirlik. If he could reach the people at Incirlik who had launched the device, perhaps they could send a signal that would destroy the thing or at least cause it to go off course.

But with the connection to Incirlik broken, the only way he had of reaching those who could stop the weapon was through Harrod.

He shouted at Major Ellwood. "Get the National Security Advisor at the White House on the secure phone and put him through to my office!"

Komulakov raced out of the command center to his office. By the time he reached his desk, the call-waiting light on his phone was blinking. He picked up the receiver with one hand and engaged the EncryptionLok-3 with the other.

"Simon, this is Dimitri. Are you aware of what's happened to the operation in Iraq?"

"Aware?" Harrod's voice blared in his ear. "Of course I'm aware! I've been in the White House Situation Room with the Director of Operations for the JCS for two hours! We saw the ISET team leader get killed, and before the video signal went out, it looked from here as though the whole team was killed. I can't raise Lieutenant Colonel Newman on any net and if we can't stop them, the QRF is probably heading into the same fate. This is precisely the kind of debacle you were supposed to prevent!"

Harrod was on the verge of losing it. "Get hold of yourself, Dr. Harrod. I don't know who else you have in the room there with you, but you must contact the team in Incirlik that launched your UAV. The aircraft has to be stopped before it—" Komulakov paused a beat. "Before it kills Iraqi civilians and makes a bad situation even worse."

"How am I supposed to do that?"

Komulakov considered how much he should reveal about what he knew of U.S. military command and control capabilities—information he had gleaned from the two highest-placed spies the KGB had ever recruited in the U.S. government. The Russian decided that he had to risk everything to save Kamil from humiliation or worse at the hands of Saddam.

"Listen to me, Simon. Press the phone tightly to your

ear so that others there in the room with you cannot hear me talking and just reply 'yes' or 'no' to what I'm about to tell you. Do you understand me?"

"Yes," Harrod replied, almost meekly.

"Is Lieutenant General Tatum, the operations chief of your Joint Staff there in the room with you?"

"Yes."

"Is anyone else in there besides the two of you?"

"No."

"Is this phone call being recorded?"

"No . . . I don't think so."

"Good. Write this down. Tell General Tatum to call your White House Communications Agency and have them immediately re-route your communications to Incirlik from your satellite system to your fiber optic emergency backup link at Sigonella, Sicily, and from there to the NATO hub switch at Ankara for a direct long-line connection to the 331st Expeditionary Air Group Headquarters Air Operations Center at Incirlik. Make sure you tell him to tell WHCA that he has FLASH traffic, presidential priority one. They will recognize it simply as 'PRI-1.' Did you get all that?"

"Yes."

"Good. As soon as he gets through, and it shouldn't take long, have him tell General Harris that the UAV has to be destroyed before it gets to a populated area. If that's not possible, tell him to divert it out over the Persian Gulf. Do you understand all that?"

"Yes."

"Good. Do it. And then call me back so we can work out the damage control on all this. All right?"

"Yes."

Komulakov hung up.

*   *   *

Harrod set the phone in its cradle and repeated the instructions he had just received from the Russian general to the incredulous three-star sitting before him.

General Tatum's first response was, "Who was *that?*"

Harrod had now recovered sufficiently to assert himself. "That's not important. What matters right now is whether you can follow those instructions and get General Harris at the 331st Expeditionary Air Group!"

"Of course I can, Dr. Harrod. That's the communications protocol we'd use to notify our NATO allies in the event of a nuclear attack on the United States. But who were you talking to that knows *that?*"

"General, I don't have time for Twenty Questions! What I can tell you is that if you don't find a way to get me through to General James Harris in Incirlik, thousands of innocent civilians are likely to die a terrible death in the next few minutes, and the United States of America will be blamed."

General Tatum sat down in the chair he had been occupying at the Situation Room's conference table and pulled out a drawer concealed in the side of the table. He picked up the handset of the red phone inside. There was no key-pad or dial on the face of the phone so the General said nothing until a crisp military voice spoke.

"This is Lieutenant General Tatum, Joint Staff, and this is a PRI-1 presidential call. I want the following FLASH routing. . . ." The general relayed the instructions as Harrod had given them, and just seconds later he said to the voice on the other end of the line, "Jim, this is Harry Tatum calling from the White House Situation Room. I have the National Security Advisor for you." Tatum handed the telephone to Harrod.

"Harris, this is Simon Harrod, National Security Advisor to the President."

"Yes, Dr. Harrod, this is Brigadier General James Harris, Air Force. What's happening? I was told this is a presidential PRI-1 call."

"General, the UN's International Sanctions Enforcement operation in Iraq seems to have gone seriously awry. The ISET on the ground at Tikrit has apparently been overrun. And there is great concern here that the Global Hawk due to strike the target in the next few minutes may go off course and kill innocent civilians. It has to be destroyed or vectored out over the Persian Gulf where it won't jeopardize innocent lives and cause a major diplomatic debacle. Can you contact those who launched it and give them those instructions?"

"Wait one."

Harrod could hear the Air Force general shout to someone, "Get Sergeant Major Gabbard on our internal UHF security circuit ASAP."

General Harris spoke to Harrod again. "We're trying to contact them, Dr. Harrod, but I have to tell you that the UAV was re-programmed by Lieutenant Colonel Newman from his airborne command post in the MD-80 just before they went down."

"Re-programmed? Went down? Who went down? Where?"

"Lieutenant Colonel Newman's MD-80 command aircraft has gone down over Iraq. We have also lost at least one F-16. Iraqi infantry has apparently overrun the ISET at Tikrit. The QRF is on the move into Iraq and should be fording the upper Tigris south of Faysh Khabur in the next few hours. Iraq's entire Air Defense system is fully alerted, so we can't put any SAR birds over either of the downed aircraft or the ISET until I can launch more F-16s with some AGM-88 HARMs aboard to deal with the SAM threat."

Harrod was barely listening. He had no idea what an AGM-88 was or did, and he couldn't care less. He only knew that his masterful plan to make his president look good in the eyes of the international community was going down in flames—just as Newman's plane apparently had done.

Now Harrod could hear the Air Force general talking to someone else. ". . . I understand Sergeant Major, thank you very much. Out here. Hello, Dr. Harrod?" the General said.

"Yes," Harrod replied weakly.

"Sergeant Major Gabbard tells me that they will try to divert or destroy the UAV, but they do not believe it can be done in the time remaining. The Global Hawk is due on the target in less than thirty seconds."

Harrod hung up the phone without saying another word. He stared at the wall. Then, remembering the Army lieutenant general standing on the other side of the table, he said, "The UN Sanctions mission has been terminated. You might as well go back to the Pentagon. I have to go brief the President."

Later, just before he was called to testify before a closed session of the Senate Armed Services Committee about the U.S. military role in the UN operation, General Tatum was instructed by Senator James Waggoner to "forget about the meeting with Harrod on March 6 in the Situation Room." The Senate committee would not ask about the meeting, so the general wouldn't need to testify about it. But he would never forget about it either.

Amn Al-Khass Operations Center
Hangar 3, Tikrit Air Base
Tikrit, Iraq
Monday, 6 March 1995
1501 Hours, Local

Dotensk was standing next to Kamil at the west end of hangar 3. Kamil was congratulating the commander of the Amn Al-Khass unit that had finally overrun the UN assassination team when the whine of an Allison Rolls Royce AE3007H turbofan jet engine passing almost directly overhead made them all instinctively duck. Once they realized that they were not about to die, they raced around the north end of the hangar and looked off toward the Tigris, in the direction the craft had flown.

In the river valley, a kilometer east of the hangar, they could see a huge, black, V-tail aircraft with extremely long, skinny wings, an engine mounted high and aft, and a whale-like nose, descending directly toward Saddam's summer palace. And on the highway headed south toward the same palace was the Iraqi president's twelve-car motorcade, returning from the bunker at the abandoned Al Sahra Air Base.

The Ukrainian arms merchant and his client watched in horror as the strange-looking aircraft passed just above and directly in front of the lead Mercedes in the motorcade and slammed into the west wall of the largest building in the palace complex—Saddam's personal residence. There was an enormous explosion that sent a huge fireball high into the sky. By the time the sound and concussion reached Kamil and Dotensk, flaming fuel and debris were falling on the vehicles in the motorcade. The lead Mercedes was on its side, tossed over by the explosion and totally engulfed in fire. The next three vehicles in line were also aflame, and the occupants could be seen jumping from the cars and running for the ditches on both sides of the roadway. And then, as everyone at the hangar watched, eight of the dark-windowed, silver sedans pulled around the four wrecked and disabled vehicles and sped south on the highway toward Baghdad.

Dotensk watched as Kamil raced into the hangar to the communications center and screamed at the radio operator, one of the few not to rush out of the hangar when the Global Hawk swooshed overhead. "Get me the President's security detail, now!"

The operator consulted a chart on the table in front of him, reached up to change the frequency on one of the radios before him, and handed Kamil the handset. Over the speaker atop the radio, the Amn Al-Khass commander could hear members of the security detail talking hurriedly to one another. He keyed the handset.

"Break, break . . . this is Commander Hussein Kamil! I want to talk to the senior Amn Al-Khass officer with the presidential motorcade. All others stay off this net."

After a moment of silence, a voice came over the speaker, "This is Major Khidan al Tikriti, over."

"Major, is the President all right?"

"Yes, sir. He and his special guests are unharmed. We were the last two vehicles in the motorcade."

"How about Qusay?" the Amn Al-Khass commander asked, more than half hoping his rival for Saddam's affections had been in the lead vehicle. Kamil knew that Qusay would try to blame him for the assassination attempt.

"He is here with me. We are now the lead vehicle. The President has ordered that we return to Baghdad. Our special guests want to go to the airport and fly out immediately. I was making those arrangements when your radio call came in."

Kamil paused, unable to think of a way to salvage his standing with Saddam. "Allah be praised. I shall proceed to Baghdad as soon as I have completed the investigation here."

Dotensk had walked back into the hangar and was now standing beside the dejected Kamil as he handed the radio handset back to the radio operator. The two men now walked off to the corner of the hangar out of earshot of the others.

"Now, Mr. Dotensk," said Kamil in a strangely calm voice, "the only thing that will keep me alive are those three nuclear artillery warheads you delivered. At this moment, I am the only person alive who knows where they are hidden. But that will only last for a short time. You must now find a way for me to escape to the West. Do you understand?"

What Dotensk also understood was that for Kamil to be the "only person alive" who knew where the three nuclear warheads were hidden had to mean that *he* had killed the subordinate officers who had helped hide them. He also understood that the elaborate plan he and Komulakov had concocted to make millions more selling weaponry was now in ruin. And finally, he understood that his own life was in greater jeopardy than ever if Kamil decided to offer up a "Ukrainian spy" as the reason for the assassination attempt on the Iraqi president, his son, and their prized guest, Osama bin Laden. But all Dotensk said was, "Of course, I shall start working on your escape immediately."

"Good," said Kamil. He started to walk away, then turned and asked, "By the way, you are sure that those warheads will work?"

In fact, Dotensk had no idea whether the warheads would still perform as advertised. He had gone to some lengths to get the PAL auto-arming keys for the three warheads, but he also knew that these old weapons were notoriously unreliable. One Soviet officer had told him that only one in ten would actually detonate properly with its full yield.

"Certainly," he told Kamil.

Situation Room
The White House
Washington, D.C.
Monday, 6 March 1995
0915 Hours, Local

The National Security Advisor came bustling, breathlessly, into the White House Situation Room and without so much as a nod to the watch officers, entered the conference room and closed the door. After leaving General Tatum an hour before, Harrod had gone to his own office and awakened the Commander-in-Chief with a phone call, convincing him of the urgency of the situation.

Now, having briefed the President on the catastrophe in Iraq, Harrod was back with a plan. Alone in the conference room, he sat down at the table, removed an EncryptionLok-3 from his pocket, attached it to the telephone cord on the same phone over which he had received the bad news from General Harris in Incirlik, and told the signal operator to get General Komulakov on the line.

When the Russian general took the call in his office on the thirty-eighth floor of the UN headquarters building, Harrod told him to engage his EncryptionLok-3. "Here's what we're going to do. There has been no press reporting on this incident yet. We think it will be several more hours before anyone in Baghdad or Turkey says anything. I want you to round up the Iraqi ambassador to the UN so that I can meet with him privately—preferably in your office. Tell him that an unmanned American reconnaissance vehicle doing surveillance for the UN Special Commission on Weapons of Mass Destruction went off course and crashed, and we deeply regret any damage or loss of life. Second, tell him that a USAF F-16 has crashed in the no-fly zone south of Mosul and that I'm coming to New York to negotiate for the return of the pilot. Don't tell him that we're already pretty sure he's dead. Third, tell him that a UN humanitarian flight transiting Iraq is missing and overdue. Tell him it was an Aer Lingus MD-80 chartered by the UN, and you want his help locating the aircraft if it's down. Finally, tell him that as a sign of good faith, the President is sending me up there to meet with him to do a rug dance."

"Rug dance?"

"You know, make apologies, and tell them how sorry we are. Let him know that when I get there I'll provide information we have obtained about a group of mercenaries that may be trying to stir up trouble in Iraq. Now, if I understand things, you have a secure way to get information to some of the authorities in Iraq, is that correct?"

Despite his fatigue, Komulakov, the disciplined KGB officer, was thinking clearly and he didn't want to reveal that his connection was through Dotensk. It raised too many other questions. So he simply said, "I . . . have a way of getting information to Hussein Kamil, the head of the Amn Al-Khass."

"Good. There is one final thing we must do if we're going to keep all this from blowing up in our faces. Neither the President nor the Secretary General can afford to have another counterterrorism failure on their hands. If there are survivors to talk about all this, it'll be worse than that fiasco in Somalia. You botched both attempts against Mohammed Farrah Aidid back in '93, and neither you nor I will be at our jobs next week if word gets out that this was a failed attempt on Saddam and bin Laden."

"May I remind you, dear Simon, that the twenty-three cruise missiles fired at Baghdad on June 26 of 1993 were all made in America. And when it comes to Somalia, on the twelfth of July '93, when the attack helicopters tried to kill Aidid, though the UN sanctioned the mission, the pilots were all Americans. And if memory serves me right, when the raiders were killed in Mogadishu, in October that year, they were all American Delta Force soldiers and Rangers. Your President's record at proving his manhood isn't very good, but I don't see what that has to do with me."

"Look, we don't have time for this. The QRF has fifteen men in it who know everything. If they are captured in Iraq, we'll be getting a bill from the devil himself. Contact your Amn Al-Khass commander and tell him that you have reliable information that a group of mercenaries has crossed into Iraq from Turkey and plans to cross the Tigris River near Faysh Khabur. If any of them are captured and expose my government's or the UN's role in what they are doing, we're finished."

Komulakov thought for a moment. Harrod was right. Though gratuitous killing had never been part of how the KGB operated, when it was a necessary means to an end, it was done with a minimum of soul-searching.

"You are correct, Simon. I will see to it," the Russian said quietly. "What about the one that's left at Incirlik? A sergeant major, I believe. And there's that officer you still have back there with you. Robertson, isn't it?"

Now it was time for Harrod to think. "I think I know how to take care of Robertson. Can you handle the sergeant major in Incirlik?"

"I suppose so, Simon. But it's getting very complicated. What if there are survivors from Newman's MD-80 inside Iraq? Do we have to hunt them down too?"

"We'll do what we have to do."

✪

After hanging up with Harrod, Komulakov had Major Ellwood contact Captain Bart Coombs, the QRF commander; the satellite radio had finally started working again. Komulakov told Coombs that ISET Echo was likely dead and he should try to rescue any survivors from the downed MD-80. He gave them the last known location of the aircraft from earlier in the day—east of Tikrit and almost due north of Lake Tharthar.

Coombs, the good soldier from Delta Force and close friend of Peter Newman's deceased brother, dutifully altered his original plan of trying to extricate the trapped ISET and set out to find Newman or any other survivors of the downed MD-80. As instructed by the Russian general in New York, Coombs kept in communication with his UN superior via sat comms encrypted with an EL-3. And, as Komulakov had planned, the GPS transponder in the little encryption device provided the exact location of the QRF every time Coombs communicated. After each radio call came in from the QRF, Komulakov contacted Dotensk, who in turn passed on the latest grid coordinates of the QRF to Hussein Kamil.

It was a little past 1300 hours in New York—2100 in

Iraq—when Dotensk called Komulakov. The Ukrainian reported that a company of Kamil's Amn Al-Khass had ambushed the fifteen-man QRF as it crossed the Wadi ath Tharthar, thirty miles east of Sahl Sinjar. There were no survivors.

The Russian general consulted the map spread out on his desk and was impressed at how far into Iraq the American-British QRF unit had gotten. *Those were good troops. A shame, somehow.* But he knew, just as he had back in 1986 when he'd ordered the assassinations of those who had diverted the munitions train in Poland, that sometimes people just had to die.

TWA Terminal Food Court
Dulles International Airport
Washington, D.C.
Monday, 6 March 1995
1520 Hours, Local

Rachel had left word for Mitch Vecchio to meet her for five minutes before she left on the overnight flight to London. She glanced at her watch. He was already twenty minutes late, and she had to check in at 4:00 P.M.

Then she saw him walk into the restaurant, between the "A" and "C" gates overlooking the runways and the new midfield terminal, look around for her, then cross the room to her table.

"Hey, babe, what's up? You sounded kinda serious."

"Mitch . . . I have to go in just a couple of minutes before checking in, but I had to tell you this face to face."

"Whoa . . . I'd better sit down. This *does* sound serious."

"Mitch . . . we can't see each other anymore. We have to break off our relationship."

"Oh? Why?"

"Well, for one thing, it's *wrong*. We're both being unfaithful to our spouses, and I'm not going to do it anymore."

"Why the sudden change?"

"Mitch, I . . . I've been thinking a lot about my life lately. And this past weekend everything all came together. My life was a mess, and I knew what we were doing was wrong. I think God is giving me another chance to get my life straightened out. To make a long story short . . . I committed my life to Jesus Christ, Mitch . . . and I can't do some of the things I used to do."

Mitch threw his head back with a look of surprise on his face. "Well, glory, hallelujah! Don't you think it's a little late in life to become a nun?"

"Please don't joke about it, Mitch. It was a serious step for me, and I know it's the right thing to do. I have such peace about my decision. It's really like they say— like being 'born again,' and I have been given a whole new chance at life."

Mitch grinned at her. "Rache, who are you trying to kid? Look, it's me, Mitch, your lover, your friend. Surely you can come up with a better exit line than that?"

"It's true, Mitch. It all happened over the past couple of days, and I made my decision to place my life in God's hands. That means I no longer decide what's right and wrong. And no matter what we think, adultery is wrong, Mitch. You must know that too. We both need to be faithful to our spouses."

"You're serious about this, aren't you? Well, listen Rachel, it's been a great ride. You can buy into religion if you want. Me, I'm not interested. I'm the only guy I have to be accountable to, and what I do is my own business."

They looked at each other for a long time without speaking. Then his face softened. "Look, honey, I know things have been stressful for you lately, with your husband gone off on some mission. But don't go off the deep end. Give it a little time . . . and then think about us. I'll be here if you change your mind. Just give it some time."

Rachel suddenly had doubts about what she had decided the day before. Her feelings were arguing with her intellect and winning. . . . *No! I know this is the right thing to do!*

She stood up. "Please don't call me again."

"Listen, Rachel," Mitch said, leaning toward her, "we both have to check in now. Let's leave it for now. I won't call you or bother you any more if that's what you want. Just remember, I'm here for when you need me. Just give it some time." Then he stood and took her hand with both of his. "Take care," he said, then he walked away.

There was something sad about their parting, but Rachel felt a sense of relief as well. She knew it was something she had to do. She had already started a daily journal listing all the other changes that she anticipated making in her life. This had been a suggestion from Pastor Brooks.

After the unexpected meeting with the pastor's wife on Friday, Rachel had decided to take up her offer to meet with them for brunch after the Sunday service. The pastor hadn't pointed the finger of condemnation at her, even when she told him about the affair she'd been having. Instead, he gently encouraged Rachel to break it off, to focus not on the past but on the future, and to start her spiritual journey by doing as much as she could to alter her old routine.

Part of her new schedule was to spend a few minutes every day reading Scripture. He had called it "the armor of God."

Reverend Brooks had also encouraged her to join a small Bible study in her neighborhood. That Sunday night she went back to the church—the first time in her life that she had ever gone to church twice in the same day—and signed up for a Bible study that met on Wednesday evenings in the home of a woman who lived less than two miles from their home on Creswell Drive.

The pastor suggested that Rachel find time to write her thoughts in a journal and list all the prayers that she wanted answered. That morning she had made a list of things that she wanted to do for Peter—including telling him about her conversion to Christ.

Rachel wondered if P. J. would have the same response to her newfound faith as Mitch just had. She decided to pray that Peter would understand and that someday he might make the same choice. But at that moment she also felt a sudden compulsion to pray for her husband, for his safety and protection.

N Shore of Lake Tharthar, Iraq
Monday, 6 March 1995
1915 Hours, Local

Newman was faced with a difficult choice; he was debating about whether they could take the risk of starting a fire. It was fully dark when he returned from burying the navigator. It took him nearly another half hour to make his way in the darkness to where he had left Major Jane Robinette. She had seemed to be OK when he left, but by the time he returned she was moaning and her breathing was quite labored.

He knelt down beside her and apologized for leaving. "I shouldn't have left you alone." Robinette was shivering with intense, wracking chills. Was she going into shock? He found the thin Mylar-backed blankets he had recovered from the survival kits and folded them over her. Newman saw that she had dropped the can of water he had left with her; whatever was left in it had run out. He opened a second one. He told her about finding Haskell's body on the ground about a mile from where they were. "I never even had a chance to learn anything about him," he told Robinette.

"He was a good guy," she panted. Her breathing was coming in quick, uneven gasps. "He has a wife and daughter . . ."

"Don't talk now. Try and get some sleep."

Newman wondered if he was far enough away from Tikrit that he could build a fire without attracting attention. Across the lake he could see some scattered lights, but other than that, it was a vast, empty darkness and it was rapidly getting colder. Even if he could gather enough fuel for a small fire, could he risk giving away their position to whomever might be out there?

He looked away from the lake, to the north. The highway was there, probably only two to three kilometers away. Wait—was that a fire? It appeared to be on or near the highway that he recalled from his descent. It had seemed to him then that the road ran from horizon to horizon in an almost straight line northeast to southwest. *Maybe someone stopped for the night, or perhaps a car broke down.* Newman thought it best not to make a fire.

He knelt to check on Major Robinette. She was shivering so much that her teeth were chattering. He wished he had more of the Mylar blankets. Her body couldn't afford the energy spent in shivering; he had to get her warm, somehow. Newman lay down beside her and took her in his arms. *Careful of her arm and chest.* She felt his warmth and instinctively moved closer.

"I—I'm so cold," she chattered.

The ground was still a bit warm from the sun's heat. For several hours they lay in that embrace, and eventually her chills subsided. Neither of them slept.

Newman was trying to form an escape plan. He did a mental inventory of their equipment: two parachutes; three survival packs, counting the dead navigator's; three .38-caliber survival pistols; two PRC-112V radios; two tiny little survival flashlights; three aviator's survival mirrors and three red pop-up flares for signaling; three collapsible water bottles; three survival knives; three first-aid kits; two survival compasses—but no maps—and the EncryptionLok-3 device he had jammed into a pocket of his flight suit before taking off from Incirlik. That was it. He had tasted the water in the lake; it was brackish, but drinkable. He decided to fill the three containers with lake water before they set out. The prearranged escape plan was to walk north into Turkey, a trek of nearly two hundred miles in a straight line, but since they had alerted the entire Iraqi military establishment, it was a safe bet the hike north would be anything but a straight line.

They had to get moving soon. It was only a matter of time before an Iraqi Army patrol came out here to investigate the wreckage. *In fact,* he thought, *this little rocky outcropping is probably the first place they'll search.*

Now that it was completely dark, Newman was listening for the USAF Search and Rescue birds that should have been in the air over them almost from the minute they had gone down. *Sure could use one of those para-rescue guys right now,* Newman thought, not knowing that the SAM threat had delayed any search and rescue attempt.

Jane Robinette's breathing was becoming more labored, and she was moaning almost constantly. Newman decided to try and distract her somehow. He asked about her family.

"My husband works for the post office . . . and we live near Chicago . . . Harvey, Illinois. We have a son . . . fourteen years old." She was gasping every time she tried to breathe. "My husband and I named him Dwight Moody Robinette."

Maybe asking questions wasn't such a good plan, Newman thought. "Jane, save your breath," he said. But she shook her head. She wanted to keep talking.

"Dwight was named after an evangelist . . . they call Dwight Moody 'the Billy Graham of the 1800s.' I wanted my boy to learn early about God . . . I prayed he'd go to the Bible institute that Mr. Moody founded in Chicago. Both his daddy and I wanted Dwight . . . to grow up and serve the Lord. His daddy—he's the part-time pastor of our little Baptist church—he hoped that Dwight might someday follow . . . in his footsteps."

Newman could tell she was weakening, "Please, Jane . . . just rest." He was still holding her close. Finally the wounded pilot fell into a fitful sleep.

Newman set one of the puny survival pistols beside them in case he had to get to it quickly. He resolved that he would not fall asleep, although fatigue was dragging at him like a lead weight. His joints and muscles were beginning to ache, and his body was crashing from the near-constant adrenaline rush of the last few hours.

He awakened with a start when Jane's body stiffened, wracked by a spasm of coughing. Newman knelt over her and shined a flashlight on her face. Bubbles of bright red blood were on her lips. She tried to sit up. Her gasps were much more panicked. She was at the point of choking. Newman could hear a gurgling sound with every breath she took. He put the back of his hand on her forehead, and it felt hot. *From chills to fever,* he thought, *that doesn't sound good.* Newman propped her up so she could breathe easier.

He shined the flashlight on her chest and felt a shiver of dread; her T-shirt was soaked with blood. She had bled completely through the bandage that he had applied earlier. The wound must have been much deeper than he realized. She was bleeding internally.

Gently he used his knife to cut off her T-shirt and he used it to wipe the blood from her chest. He put the flashlight close to the wound and tenderly pulled the opening to see if there was anything else in the wound. What he saw caused his chest to tighten. While there was no other debris inside the wound, it was deeper than he had first suspected. The piece of aluminum wreckage that had penetrated her uniform and skin must have also pierced her left lung, not far from her heart. He'd seen a similar wound when during the battle for Khafji during the opening days of the Gulf War one of his Force Recon Marines had been wounded by Iraqi shrapnel.

"What is it?" Jane asked, seeing the deep furrows of concern on his face.

"I . . . I think your lung is filling with blood."

"Am I going to die?"

"I don't know, Jane. I've seen this kind of thing before, and the guy lasted for three days. But if we can't get you to some real medical help pretty soon . . ."

"Well, we both know . . . I won't be seeing a hospital . . . anytime soon. It feels like my left lung isn't . . . really collapsed, but it's not working either. Seems . . . like there's an elephant . . . sitting on my chest."

"Let me try and blow some air into your lung," Newman suggested. He pinched her nose shut and blew into her mouth. He could see her chest rise considerably more than it had. He blew again . . . and again . . . and this time he could hear it—the sound of air escaping from the hole in her chest. He stopped and examined her chest wound, and saw bloody bubbles of air oozing out from her injured lung.

Newman felt absolutely helpless, but intent on putting to use every bit of first-aid training he'd learned in peace and war. He put some more disinfectant on the wound, then packed it with gauze and folded more gauze on that. Then he took the plastic wrapper from one of the battle dressings in the first-aid kit and taped it down to seal the wound.

He used her tattered T-shirt to wipe the blood from her chest and side. He gently lifted her to wipe underneath and was further distressed to see a pool of blood beneath her. The fragment of metal had apparently passed right through her; the lung was leaking from the back as well.

It was only a matter of time before she bled to death. Making a nighttime hike north toward Turkey was out of the question. In the reflected glow of the little emergency light, Jane saw the sadness and shock on his face. Surprisingly, she was more calm than he was, though she was the one in such a desperate situation.

"It's time to get real, Colonel Newman," she said between quick gasps. "I'm not gonna make it. I feel myself getting weaker . . . and I'm afraid that I'm not going to be able to keep breathing . . . seems like every time I try to breathe, my chest and lungs are fighting me . . . like a charley horse in my chest. I won't be able . . . to breathe."

"Jane, don't—"

"No . . . I have to. Please . . . tell my family how much . . . I love them . . . and how sorry I am . . . to leave them this way. But remind them that . . . I'm going to meet my Savior . . . and I'll be in heaven . . . waiting for them."

Newman envied her confidence, but knew that if that were he lying there, he would not have such assurance.

"You must have a lot of faith."

"Yes . . . I'm sorry that I won't get to . . . see my family again . . . but I'm not afraid of dying. I know where I'm going from here . . . and it's not scary. Can you hold me? I'm beginning to . . . get cold again."

Newman lay down beside her and held her as he had before.

"Are you a believer?" she asked Newman.

How to answer? "I . . . uh . . . I guess that I don't have your kind of faith. I believe in a Supreme Being . . . but, well, I'm just not sure what I believe about God."

"Will you let me pray for us both, Colonel?"

Newman shifted his weight on the ground nervously when she asked, but he replied, "Sure . . . of course."

"Lord . . . I know that all things . . . work together for good . . . for those who love You. You know my heart, God. I place myself . . . in Your hands. May I glorify You . . . whether I live or die, heavenly Father. I pray for my family just now . . . that You'll take care of them. I know that . . . my dear husband will be all right, but I don't know how my boy Dwight . . . will take the news of my death. Please be with him . . . protect him . . . and I pray that Your Holy Spirit . . . will fill his life with Your love and truth and purpose. There's so much more I could ask You . . . for my family, but I trust You, Lord. I know that You'll . . . look after them.

"And God, please reveal Yourself . . . to Lieutenant Colonel Newman. I don't know him very well, but . . . he seems to be a good man . . . for all the wrong reasons. I sure hope I'll . . . see him in heaven someday. So, God, please show him Your love . . . and introduce him to Your Son, Jesus. I pray for him with all my heart. Now Lord, I give myself to You . . . for whatever's next. . . ." Her voice trailed off.

Newman had closed his eyes reverently when she prayed and half expected Christ to be standing there when he opened them, so real was her prayer. But he was not a person of faith. In fact, he wondered why, if there really was a God, He would allow one of His own to suffer and die here. If any time and place deserved a miracle, this surely was it.

Dawn was coming. In the distance he could see some trailing smoke from burning Iraqi radar installations and, possibly, the wreckage of aircraft.

Jane's breathing became even more labored, the air husky across her vocal cords, rasping in and out with an awful hoarse sound. He agonized over her pain and the effort it took just to get air into her lungs. Then, as she had predicted, her chest muscles cramped and she writhed in panic as her lungs failed. Her eyes widened and she arched her back, then fell in place. Her eyes showed she realized what was happening.

She managed a small smile and mouthed, "Good-bye." She gave up her valiant struggle to live.

Newman began mouth-to-mouth resuscitation. He

kept it up for more than ten minutes before he gave up. He could feel no pulse, and when he shined the flashlight into her eyes, her pupils were dilated. She was gone. Newman hoped she was right about her faith.

Command Center
Incirlik Air Base
Adana, Turkey
Tuesday, 7 March 1995
0300 Hours, Local

General Harris walked into the ready room adjacent to his command center just as Lieutenant Douglas Hill, the assistant operations officer, was completing a preflight briefing. The pilots, in their pressure suits and carrying their helmets and kneepads, were just leaving. Hill shouted, "Attention on deck."

"Stand easy, men," Harris said. "I want you to do what you can to find these people, but I don't want to lose any of you. Be careful out there. Carry on."

As the pilots shuffled out the door to head to the flight line, the general went over to the lieutenant. "How does it look, Doug?"

"Well sir, we've got three different locations and a ton of people missing. In addition to Randy Jenkins's F-16, we've twelve people on the MD-80, and fifteen more that went across the border with their QRF. We've had no contact from any of them. There's no satellite readout from the E-PRB beacons on any of the aircraft and no comms from the QRF since shortly after they crossed the 36th latitude. That's not good."

"What are you sending up?"

"We moved three of our four MH-53 Pave Low SAR

birds, each with a para-rescue team aboard, up to Siirt at about midnight so they will be close if the over-flights pick up a beacon or a call on a survival radio. I've got two MC-130s up there with them to tank them if they need to stay up awhile. One of the Combat Talons is equipped with a STAR rig in case any of the folks we're missing have the pick-up equipment.

"The flight we just briefed consists of four F-l6s with AGM-88 HARMs aboard in case they encounter SAMs, two F-15s with the standard mix of air-to-air and air-to-ground ordnance, and one Navy EA-6 to jam Iraqi radar and listen for any noises from missing friendlies. We have two KC-10s on station to top off the fast movers on the way in and refuel them again on the way out if they need it. I've told them to stay north of the border unless we have a lot of action because we don't want to tip the Iraqis that we've got people down—if they don't know it already."

"You did well, Doug. I'm going to try to get a couple hours' sleep. Call me right away if our guys pick up anything or start getting shot at." The general returned to his office down the hall, turned out the lights, and stretched out, fully dressed in his desert camouflage uniform, on the military cot in the corner.

Office of Deputy Secretary General Dimitri Komulakov
38th Floor
UN Headquarters
New York, N.Y.
1912 Hours, Local

Dr. Simon Harrod had flown aboard a USAF Gulf-stream IV from Andrews AFB to New York and was

now sitting in the conference room adjoining Komulakov's office, waiting for the UN Ambassador from
Iraq to meet with him. He looked at his watch; the ambassador was late.

The door opened and Komulakov came in with the
Iraqi ambassador. Harrod stood. The Russian made the
introductions and asked, "Shall I stay?"

The ambassador shrugged, but Harrod shook his
head. "I think it is best if we meet in private," he said.
"We can talk more frankly." Komulakov nodded and
left the room.

Harrod had stood as a sign of respect when the ambassador had entered the room. Now he gestured for
the man to take a seat. Harrod had wisely taken a seat
on a side of the table and not at its head. The ambassador sat down across from Harrod.

"So, what brings the National Security Advisor to the
President of the United States all the way to New York
to meet with the lowly ambassador of the country
whose children are starving because of your embargo?"

Harrod looked at the man across from him. On the
flight to New York he had read the CIA's file on the
Iraqi. He was a career diplomat and had served among
Saddam's hierarchy for nearly two decades. As the pres-
tigious ambassador to the United Nations, Igouri
Rubariyah was a cut above Saddam's other political and
diplomatic underlings. He had studied in England and
held a Ph.D. in history. He had taught at the Baghdad
University for many years before joining Saddam's team
and was known to be one of the dictator's most intelligent strategists.

"Has your country briefed you on the events of this
afternoon in Iraq?"

"Of course."

"Well, there are some things you need to know. First, the President has instructed me to express our sincere apologies about the reconnaissance drone that went out of control and crashed in Iraq. It was conducting surveillance for the UNSCOM inspection program, and it apparently had a malfunction."

"Please, Dr. Harrod, do not play me for the fool. That was no reconnaissance drone. It was some kind of missile, and it was aimed at our president who, thanks to Allah, was not in the building when your weapon hit it. We reject your private apologies delivered in this imperious manner. When your president makes an apology before the world's TV cameras, then we will consider it, not until."

"Well, Mr. Ambassador, we can discuss that—and the political implications. But I do want to offer the condolences of our nation, expressed by the President himself."

"That's it? You could have done that by telephone."

"No, sir, there is more."

"Go on."

"The unmanned aircraft was being directed as part of a United Nations mission in response to Iraq's lack of cooperation with the UN inspections. It was to have over-flown specific sites that your country has not allowed inspectors to enter. It was—as much as anything—a symbolic indication of our resolve to enforce UN resolutions regarding weapons of mass destruction."

"Yes, I can see how an attack on the summer palace would be most symbolic."

"It was not an attack and the palace was not a target. It was simply a site to be inspected. We don't know why the aircraft crashed. Perhaps your anti-aircraft fire damaged it and caused it to crash, and the fuel aboard exploded."

"Is that the story you are going to tell at your president's news conference tomorrow morning? What about the F-16 that our valiant forces shot down just before your surprise attack on our president's home?"

"The F-16 was on a routine patrol of the no-fly zone when it was hit by an Iraqi missile fired from a SAM site north of the agreed-upon line."

"Is that so? And what about the other large aircraft that your friend General Komulakov says was a UN humanitarian relief flight enroute to Yemen or somewhere?"

"If that's what he said, that's what it was. That's not our concern. I am here to ask you to return the U.S. pilot from the F-16 if he is still alive, and his body if he is not. As a sign of good faith, I have asked Deputy Secretary General Komulakov to transmit to you information that we have obtained about a group of mercenaries who may be attempting to infiltrate Iraq to assassinate your head of state. All we want is our F-16 pilot back. All the UN wants are their air crewmen from their downed flight returned. Why do you think I came here?"

"Let me tell you what I think, Dr. Harrod." The ambassador leaned forward, his arms on the table. "I think that all three aircraft are somehow related. I think that the 'drone' as you call it, was an attempt to kill the head of state of my country. I think that the F-16—if that's what you say it was—and this larger so-called 'UN humanitarian flight' aircraft and this exploding drone thing are all connected. And I think that you also know a whole lot about a small, well-armed group of eight men who were detected and killed by our security personnel in the vicinity of our president's summer palace just before your so-called drone exploded. You see, Dr. Harrod, I think all these things are connected and I think you know how. It seems to us that this is your attempt to pull a 'Pearl Harbor' on the tiny unsuspecting nation of Iraq."

"Look, Mr. Ambassador, I came here in good faith. As I said, I brought with me information about a mercenary group that we believe may be attempting to infiltrate northern Iraq with the intent of killing your president. All we want is our pilot back. And as I understand it, all the UN wants is the return of their air crew."

The ambassador sat, staring at Harrod for what seemed like minutes, then he spoke quietly, "The F-16 pilot is dead. What's left of him will be returned through the International Committee of the Red Cross in Geneva. As for the crew of the UN plane, we will attempt to find them when daylight comes. What do you want done with the bodies of the eight 'mercenaries' as you called them?"

"Can you tell their nationality?"

The Iraqi ambassador opened a folder and consulted a piece of paper. "They have no identification. They appear to be Anglo Saxons. All but one appears to have been circumcised. Some of their equipment was American, some British. Some were carrying Israeli-made Uzis, others used German H&K weapons. One had a U.S.-made M-16. So, we surmise that they are either Israelis or westerners. Do you want their bodies? Or should I have them sent to Tel Aviv?"

"Why don't you have them sent to the Red Cross as well? We will, of course, provide all possible assistance in having their remains delivered to whatever country they came from."

"Of course. Now, let me tell you what else is going to happen. Go back and tell your president that starting tomorrow, two Republican Guard divisions and three mechanized divisions are going to move north into the hills between Mosul and the Turkish border, and we are going to eliminate once and for all your CIA-supported Iraqi National Congress. When we find your puppet Ahmad Chalabi, he will be tried and executed for treason. We are going to use all necessary force to accomplish this. We know that your government has promised these terrorist forces your air power to keep our patriotic armed forces from moving north of Mosul. If you lift one finger to help the rebels, or if we find any survivors from any of yesterday's attacks that tell a different story than the one you have told me here, we will ask that your president be charged with war crimes in the International Court in The Hague. Please relay that message to your president. Good day."

Harrod was stunned but had the presence of mind to stand as the Iraqi ambassador shoved the file back in his briefcase and walked out of the conference room. He was no sooner gone than General Komulakov walked into the conference room.

"How did it go?" asked the Russian.

Harrod looked at his co-conspirator. "What, you turned off your hidden mikes for this interview?" He struggled into his overcoat. "You know exactly how it went." He strode toward the door, then turned back toward Komulakov. "Dimitri, there had better not be anyone around who tells this tale any differently."

Lake Tharthar, Iraq
Tuesday, 7 March 1995
0555 Hours, Local

Newman had taken a wedding ring and a dogtag from the lifeless body of an American for the second time in less than twelve hours. The first one he barely knew, but his death still gave him feelings of sadness and sympathy.

Now he had to bury Major Jane Robinette. He had been drawn to this gutsy woman, barely more than five and a half feet tall. Though he was more convinced than ever about the issue of women serving in combat, he had to acknowledge that she had flown her plane with bravery and skill. She knew the risks inherent with such an assignment, and in the scant ten hours or so that they had spent together after parachuting into hostile territory, this courageous woman had given Newman a new understanding of how to face death without flinching.

There were tears in his eyes as he used her flight helmet to dig a shallow grave. After scooping out a hole about six feet long and almost two feet deep, he carefully carried her body, wrapped in a parachute, and laid it reverently into the dirt. He pushed the sandy soil over her.

He smoothed out the mound of dirt and stood up. He took off his helmet, held it under his arm, and bowed his head.

"God . . . Jane believed in You. . . . I'd be a hypocrite to say that I do too. I suppose the same thing could be said of any prayer I offer You. But if You are a God of love and compassion, as Jane said, I pray that You will take her soul to be with You. Amen." The words sounded awkward, even to him.

He checked his gear and made some decisions. He decided to bury his helmet; he wrapped a piece of parachute cloth around his head to protect him from the sun. His gray-green flight suit would protect his arms, legs, and body and give him some small amount of concealment from Iraqi aircraft or army patrols.

Newman took the remaining items from the three survival kits—signal mirror, compass, flare launcher, strobe light, and one of the survival radios—and jammed them into his flight-suit's numerous pockets.

He then took the Mylar blankets, the ammunition from the two pilots' pistols, and the three water bottles, now filled with the murky, silted water of Lake Tharthar, tinted orange by water purification tablets, and placed it all into the knapsack he had fashioned from his parachute and the harness webbing. Into this pack he also stuffed several survival rations, a full first-aid kit, water purification tablets, matches, and Major Robinette's radio. He had smashed the copilot's radio so it couldn't be used by the Iraqis to lure in a SAR flight.

About twenty minutes after burying Major Robinette, he was ready to start out walking back to Turkey. Even though he knew that daylight movement was risky, he wanted to put as much distance as he could between himself and this location. He didn't have a map, but he had memorized the important features and towns along the Tigris River between the Iraq-Turkey border and Tikrit. He headed north, keeping the rising sun on his right.

Newman had been walking less than an hour and was looking for a place to hide until darkness fell again when he saw the contrails of two aircraft heading south, high above him. The sound of the engines hadn't yet reached the ground, but to his unaided eye, the two specks far up in the blue sky appeared to be small aircraft—perhaps U.S. or British fighters, flying to enforce the no-fly zone. Newman decided to try the radio, using the pre-set emergency frequency. He knew from long experience that U.S. aircraft routinely monitored the channel, and he hoped that the aircraft high overhead would hear his distress call.

"Any allied aircraft, any allied aircraft, this is Picnic Six, over." He was startled when a voice immediately answered his call.

"Picnic Six, this is Fox Fire Three Dash One, authenticate, over."

Newman froze in his tracks and hunkered down to reduce his visibility. He began to fish through his pockets for the signal mirror from one of the survival kits while he called back to the aircraft with the authentication code for the mission: the initials and last four Social Security Number digits of the individual's next of kin. "Fox Fire Three, this is Picnic Six. Authenticate: Romeo, Sierra, November, Niner, Six, Two, Five, over."

"Roger Picnic Six, state your situation, over."

I might actually get out of here alive! "Fox Fire Three, I'm the sole survivor of the Operation Picnic C and C bird that went down yesterday. I'm approximately two klicks north of Lake Tharthar. I have signal flares and a mirror. No bad guys in sight, over."

"Roger, Picnic Six. This is Fox Fire Three Dash One. I'm a Foxtrot One Six at thirty grand headed due south with my wingman nine klicks west of the lake. Can you see me?"

Newman looked at the two sets of contrails as they made a left turn and started to rapidly descend toward him. "Roger, Three Dash One, if you're the two fast movers that just made a left turn and descent, you're headed toward me and will pass about three klicks north of my pos on your current heading."

"Roger, Picnic, I'll turn right. Tell me 'steady' when I'm headed directly toward you and give me a 'mark, mark' when I pass overhead."

Newman crouched in the desert dirt and watched as the two USAF jets swung back to the right. When they were headed directly toward him, he keyed the radio and said, "Three Dash One, steady . . . steady. . . . Come left two degrees . . . steady . . . steady" and then as the two F-16s flashed directly overhead, headed east at five hundred miles per hour and one thousand feet, he shouted into the radio, "Mark! Mark!"

The two jets waggled their wings and began to climb almost straight up, rolled upside down and headed back toward him from the east.

"Picnic Six, flash me with your mirror."

"Roger." Newman peered through the center hole of the little mirror and flashed it at the oncoming aircraft.

"I've got him," said a new voice. "Picnic Six this is Fox Fire Three Dash Two, flying wing for Dash One. I'm coming straight back over you so that Dash One gets a GPS fix as well."

One of the two F-16s now descended even lower. Newman thought he was going to plow into the earth, but as the jet passed overhead he said, "Mark, Mark."

Now the other F-16 came over, and as he did so, Newman heard, "Got it. Picnic Six, we've got your pos. We're going to call home base and see if we can get a bus driver to come by and pick you up. We'll stick around as long as possible to make sure no bad guys show up. Call us if you need any help. Out."

As the two F-16s climbed back into the blue sky, Newman looked around for any kind of cover or concealment that would allow him to avoid being spotted by the Iraqis before help arrived. About one hundred meters to the northeast, he spotted a rocky outcropping on a small elevation that would give him better observation and offer some protection against the sun and Iraqi eyes. When he got there, he crawled into the shadow of a small rock shelf to await rescue—surely only minutes away.

Apartment of Dimitri Komulakov
Waldorf Towers
New York City, N.Y.
Monday, 6 March 1995
2330 Hours, Local

The phone rang on the bedside table. General Komulakov awakened with a start and fumbled for the phone.

"Sir, it's Major Kaartje, the UN Forces Command Center duty officer. Sorry to call you so late, but you asked that we let you know if we hear anything at all about the Picnic mission from overseas. We were just informed by Incirlik that Lieutenant Colonel Newman is alive."

Komulakov sat up straight in bed and turned on the light, ignoring the protests from the young Swedish Army officer trying to sleep beside him. Captain Sjogren pulled the covers up over her close-cropped blond hair and rolled over.

"What? He's alive? How . . . where?"

"About an hour ago two USAF F-16s picked up his emergency radio call and have confirmed that he's alive and unharmed. That's the good news. The bad news is that he's apparently the only survivor of the MD-80. At least that's what Incirlik told us he said."

"Do they know where he is?"

"Yes sir, they saw him and have a GPS fix on his location."

"And you say there are no other survivors?"

"I'm afraid not, sir. Lieutenant Colonel Newman reported he was the sole survivor."

"I see. Uh . . . well, that's tragic. What are his coordinates?"

"Just a minute, I'll get that communiqué." The duty officer was gone for a few seconds and came back on the line and read the GPS coordinates of where Newman had been found.

Komulakov had the Norwegian duty officer read them back twice to make sure that he had written them down correctly and then asked, "Did the American Air Force say how long it will take them to mount a search and rescue mission to pick him up?"

"Yes sir, according to this cable, they have alerted their SAR aircraft in Turkey at both Incirlik and Siirt, and they are now deciding whether to try to rescue him right away or wait until cover of dark. Meanwhile they are keeping two F-16s up over him for protection in case the Iraqis start looking for him. That's great news isn't it, sir?"

"Yes, very exciting indeed, thank you, Major. Please call me immediately if there are any further developments, no matter what hour. I especially want to know right away if the Americans launch a rescue effort."

Komulakov hung up the phone and sat on the edge of the bed, thinking. He had to get this information to Dotensk so the Ukrainian could pass it on to Hussein Kamil. But he couldn't very well make that call with Captain Sjogren beside him. He patted her leg and said, "Duty intrudes. I must make some calls, my dear. I'll just disconnect the phone here in the bedroom so it won't disturb you." He got up, took the phone, turned out the light, and went into his study at the far end of the seven-room apartment. Ever mindful of the trade-craft he had learned as a young KGB officer, the general closed the bedroom door but left the door of the study open so that he could see if Captain Sjogren awakened and approached the study.

Just as the Russian was connecting his EncryptionLok-3 to call Dotensk in Baghdad, the phone rang. "Hello, Deputy Secretary General Dimitri Komu-lakov."

"Dimitri, it's Simon Harrod. Go secure."

Komulakov switched the EncryptionLok-3 and when he heard it engage, said, "Yes, Simon."

"Newman is alive. I was just called by the situation room watch officer."

"I know, Simon. I'm dealing with it."

"Good. There are issues at stake here more important than the fate of one Marine."

"I couldn't agree more, Simon. Do you know when your Air Force intends to mount a rescue attempt? It would be best if they waited until after dark over there so that I have time to make other arrangements."

"I'll call the Pentagon and tell them the President doesn't want to put any more of our people at risk and that he's ordered the rescue to be postponed until tonight."

"Very well. That should give me enough time. I'll call you back if I hear anything."

Komulakov hung up, then dialed another number. The phone rang only twice before Dotensk answered.

"Can you go secure on Alpha, Zulu, Two, One, Seven, Zed?" Komulakov asked.

"Just a minute." There was a brief pause as both men entered the new code into their EncryptionLok-3s, waited for the familiar "ping" and then Dotensk said, "Go ahead."

"Leonid, we have a problem that must be solved immediately. One of the Americans involved in the attack yesterday has survived. He was aboard one of the aircraft that was shot down. I have his current location. You must urgently alert Kamil to this situation and have him deal with it. If some other Iraqi unit finds this particular American, it will be devastating to our client and to you and me."

"But what is so important about this one American?"

Once again Komulakov hesitated. His entire career had been based on "compartments" where one only revealed to others what they needed to know to accomplish a particular assignment or mission. Now he judged that his co-conspirator needed to be fully motivated.

"The surviving American is the commander of the entire mission. He knows everything. If he is rescued or captured and confesses under torture to what he knows, he will bring us all down."

"I see. I will immediately try to find our client and advise him, but I warn you, his task will not be easy. The entire Iraqi military seems to be on the move. I'm in Baghdad, and all foreigners have been told to stay off the streets while the Army moves north. The rumor here is that when Saddam got back here yesterday he ordered a full-scale assault against the resistance forces north of Mosul. He was on radio and television last night telling his countrymen that he was going to crush the terrorists who have invaded Kurdistan."

"Yes, well, nevertheless, Kamil *has* to find a way. Tell Kamil the American knows he wants to defect and that if he's rescued by the American Air Force tonight or captured by the Republican Guards, he's likely to compromise Kamil's plans to escape Iraq. Kamil will believe all that, if you tell him."

"You say you know the location of the American?"

Komulakov took out the piece of paper on which he had written down Newman's GPS coordinates, and Dotensk wrote them down. Before hanging up he reminded the arms merchant, "Remember, tell Kamil—this must be done at once!"

Apartment of Leonid Dotensk
Rashid Hotel
Baghdad, Iraq
Tuesday, 7 March 1995
0810 Hours, Local

As soon as he hung up with Komulakov, Dotensk redialed the cell-phone number for Kamil. As the phone rang, the Ukrainian thought, *It's a good thing that those good communists from Beijing installed this cellular system, otherwise nobody in this filthy cesspool of a country could make a phone call.*

The commander of the Amn Al-Khass answered curtly in Arabic, "Kamil, who is this?"

"Hussein, it is Leonid; I must speak to you."

"After yesterday, I think I have listened enough to you. I am very busy right now. As you probably already know, the Republican Guards and several other divisions have been ordered to attack the pirates' den north of Mosul. I will be too busy to meet with you for the next several days. Do not call me. I shall call you when I believe it is safe to do so. Good-bye."

"Hussein, Hussein, your life is in danger!"

"What did you say?"

"There is an American from one of the aircraft downed yesterday who is alive, and if he is rescued or captured by a unit other than the Amn Al-Khass, he could tell everything about your plan to defect."

"An American now on the ground here in Iraq knows of what you and I have spoken regarding my family and me? What kind of fool are you, Leonid?"

"Not as big a fool as you, if you fail to hunt him down. I swear, Kamil, you must take action immediately, for your good as well as mine."

Dotensk could sense Kamil fuming on the other end of the line.

"Where is he?" Kamil snapped, finally. Dotensk gave the GPS coordinates.

The Iraqi wrote down the GPS coordinates that Dotensk recited to him and after consulting a map Kamil said, "Well, dear Dotensk, it appears that Allah may be smiling upon us. The two HIND helicopters you saw are still there. I am supposed to use them to provide flank security for the armored column as it moves north into the area where the American-sponsored puppet army is holed up. I will dispatch them to this location to see if they can find your American who knows too much."

"The sooner the better, because the Americans know where he is and plan to rescue him tonight. And please, Hussein, keep your phone on. If there are any changes, I shall call you at once. And . . . please forgive me for my intemperate words earlier. You are no fool. But you are my friend."

"Of course." The line went dead.

1400 meters N of Lake Tharthar
Western Iraq
Tuesday, 7 March 1995
0900 Hours, Local

"Picnic Six, this is Fox Fire Three Dash One, over."
The call awakened Newman from a sound sleep.
Though he had promised himself he would stay awake,
the heat and fatigue had won again and he had dozed
off, sitting upright, with the small radio on his lap. He
grabbed the radio.

"Fox Fire, Picnic Six, go ahead."

"Picnic Six, we've been advised that the bus won't be
coming to your stop until after dark tonight—unless
you have any unwanted company, over."

"Roger, Fox Fire. No sign of any unexpected guests
yet, over."

"Well, don't take it personally, but they may have bigger fish to fry. Our Navy friends with the rabbit ears say
they're picking up all kinds of traffic on the Baghdad-
Mosul highway—all of it headed north. For whatever
reason, we've been instructed to let it go. Meanwhile,
we've got to run up to the north to pay a quick visit to
a gas station. Think you'll be all right without us for a
while? Over."

"Roger that. I promise to be a good boy and stay
right where I am until you get back."

Newman understood the jargon. The "rabbit ears"
were the sensors aboard a Navy EA-6 flying somewhere
over Iraq and listening to radio "traffic." The "gas station" was undoubtedly a KC-10 or some other airborne
tanker, flying somewhere over Turkey. The F-16s would
fly up behind it, hook up to the fuel drogues, fill their
tanks, and then return. Meanwhile he'd sit tight.

What neither Newman nor the aviators above him understood was that the heavy radio communications being picked up by the EA-6 were emanating from the Republican Guards, armored and mechanized units headed north to crush the Iraqi National Congress resistance forces north of Mosul—the very attack that the Iraqi ambassador to the UN had told Simon Harrod about the day before. Just sixty kilometers west of where Newman lay hiding, the best units in the Iraqi military were jammed bumper to bumper on a single highway, headed north. Had Newman known that his failed mission was the cause for Saddam's decision to crush the resistance, he would have been sick. And he would have been further despondent to know that the Iraqi attack was being permitted to take place unhindered by U.S. airpower because of fears in Washington that Iraq would expose the mission's failure. But then, he also didn't know that his own life was in jeopardy of forfeit as well.

Because he had no knowledge of these things, Newman wasn't worried. Dusk—and rescue—were only nine hours away, and the F-16s would be back in thirty or forty minutes with full fuel tanks.

Underground Pipeline Road
Lake Tharthar, Iraq
Tuesday, 7 March 1995
0941 Hours, Local

Eli Yusef Habib was getting ready to go. He had slept overnight in his truck and took his time cooking an egg for breakfast and heating his tea over a small primus stove, one of the consumer products in highest demand along his "sales route."

He wondered why he was here. Could he have misunderstood his leading?

Habib was beginning to think it was dangerous here. A half hour earlier he had seen and heard two military jet planes swoop low out of the sky and fly over him, then they left the area.

Now he heard another noise and looked to the sky. As he watched from his position three kilometers north of Lake Tharthar, two helicopters roared toward him from the east. He reached into his truck and grabbed his Zeiss 10x56 binoculars. The aircraft were huge, bristling with guns and rocket pods. He recognized them as Russian-built HIND attack helicopters. The Kurds along his sales route called them "flying tanks." Even at this distance they looked fearsome as they skimmed along, just one hundred feet or so above the ground.

Suddenly, the lead helicopter unleashed a volley of rockets at a small, rocky outcropping about a mile or two away. The first helicopter swooped up to avoid the blasts and the second helicopter, slightly behind the first, repeated the attack, its warheads exploding at exactly the same point, just as the concussions from the first volley reached the old man. As Habib watched, the first helicopter came back around and though the sound had not yet reached him, he could see puffs of smoke from the gun pods and tracer rounds impacting where the rockets had landed.

Both helicopters went into a low hover, firing their guns at the same target, just a few hundred meters in front of them. The downwash from the rotor blades kicked up an enormous dust cloud and, where the rockets and 12.7mm exploding machine gun rounds were impacting, there was more dust and smoke. And now, Habib could hear what sounded to him like two chain saws running at very high rpm—the noise of the HINDs' revolving machine guns sending thousands of rounds a minute into whatever they were aiming at.

Suddenly, two jets roared over the old man from behind. They were the same planes he had seen earlier, but now were so low and so loud that Habib instinctively cringed, expecting an explosion. Instead, the two aircraft each fired two missiles apiece, almost simultaneously, at the two helicopters. He put the binoculars up to his eyes just in time to see both of the HINDs explode in mid-air. The rotor of one spun off at a high, crazy angle and they crashed to earth in a fiery tangle.

Habib was almost breathless at the spectacle being played out before him. He had seen war as a young boy. And he had certainly seen it again during the Iran-Iraq war of the '80s and the Gulf War in the early '90s. He had visited the Kurdish villages in the mountains and the Shia towns near Basra that had been attacked by Saddam's mustard and nerve gases. But he had never seen air combat at such close range. He didn't know who or what the helicopters had been shooting at and didn't know whose planes had shot them down, but he had no doubt that people had died. He lowered his glasses and said a prayer. "Lord, to You I commend their spirits. In Your merciful hands I pray that those who just died knew Your Son, our Savior. Amen."

As the old man prayed, high above him, Fox Fire Three Dash One and Fox Fire Three Dash Two were calling back to the tanker, asking for it to cross into Iraq and fuel them up so they could remain on station. They had been heading north to take on fuel when they had heard Newman's frantic radio call: "Fox Fire Three Dash One, Picnic Six, two HIND Deltas coming in low and fast from the east. I think they have me spot—"

That had been enough for both pilots to do a 180-degree turn and head back to where they had just left the Marine lieutenant colonel. The fighter jet pilots had no way of knowing that the HINDs had launched from Tikrit South while the USAF aircraft winged their way north to link up with the tanker.

Now both USAF aircraft were running dangerously low on fuel.

The two jets each made separate passes over the burning wreckage of the HINDs and fired on it with their guns, but it was clear to Habib there could have been no survivors in the helicopters.

From beside his truck, Habib watched the two aircraft make a few more runs over the wreckage of the burning helicopters and then turn and head north, once again passing almost directly over where he stood. As they passed by, he could see clearly, beneath the gray camouflage paint, the USAF markings on their sides. And then they were gone over the horizon behind him.

Who or what were the helicopters attacking? Did it have something to do with the parachutes he had seen yesterday? He concluded it did—and further, because the helicopters had been shot down by American jets— that the helicopters must have been shooting at any American survivors from the events of the day before. He chastised himself for not investigating last night. *Some poor souls must have spent a terrible night alone in the desert. And because I did not go to help them then, they may now be dead.* Once again he said a silent prayer as he threw his belongings into the truck and started down the dirt track toward the smoking wreckage.

It took him about five minutes to get near the place. The fire was parallel to the highway, but nearly a kilometer away—and still he could feel its heat. Habib stopped his truck and gazed at the destruction.

He was shaking. It had just occurred to him how vulnerable he would have been had the helicopters seen him, or if the American jets had mistaken him for an enemy. Habib uttered a silent prayer of thanksgiving to his merciful God and decided that he'd make a quick search for whatever the helicopters had been shooting at. If he found nothing, he would get away from this area before more helicopters or soldiers came.

And then it occurred to him that more American planes could come at any moment and mistake him for an Iraqi soldier. Looking back to the north, he didn't see the planes coming back, nor did he see Army trucks coming from the east. But it was certainly time for him to keep moving.

Habib drove as close as he could to the small outcropping where the helicopters' rockets and machine guns had hit. There was the strong scent of ammonia from all the explosions. Dust and smoke still hung thick. As he got out of the cab, he spotted what at first seemed to be a smoking bundle of rags. He looked again. Was it a person? Yes . . . it was a man! He was on fire—or at least his clothes were. The old man grabbed a five-gallon water jug out of the bed of his truck and scrambled up the slight incline.

✪

With the burned and blasted man now regaining consciousness, Habib began to examine his wounds. His right side was a mass of blood; the old man guessed he was wounded by fragments thrown by the rockets and stones chewed up from the machine gun fire. The old man firmly but gently examined the burns on the victim's neck, right arm, and leg. He scrambled down from the rock, ran back to his truck to find his first-aid kit, and then climbed back up the little hill. When he got there, the man was trying to remove what was left of his smoldering flight suit. Habib saw the charred U.S. insignia. *So—this man is an American.* Habib spread the ointment from his first-aid kit liberally on the ugly burns and bandaged the worst of the many puncture wounds on the man's torso, arms, and legs. As he helped bandage up the holes in his body, he removed and set aside a money belt strapped around the victim's waist.

Newman watched the old Arab as he applied the salve. His first thought as he had regained consciousness was that he was drowning. Water was pouring over him, and then he felt strong hands gripping his flight suit and trying to hold him upright. He had looked up through seared eyelids and could barely make out the silhouette of a bearded man wearing Arab garb. The man's lips were moving, but Newman couldn't hear a thing. He remembered that he had been on the little survival radio, calling the F-16s to turn back because two HIND helicopters had been approaching, and then there were explosions. He could remember nothing else. He assumed his eardrums had ruptured from the concussions.

The old man's hands were gentle and expert. "Thank God that you came by when you did," Newman said.

"Ah . . . you are a Christian," the Arab said with a broad smile as he worked away at Newman's wounds. "I am also a believer. I am glad to meet a Christian brother from America. But I must get you away from here. The army may return, if not with planes, at least with trucks and soldiers to find you. Come, climb into the truck with me. I will drive you somewhere where you can be sheltered and recover from your wounds. Yes . . . thank God."

Though Newman's hearing was still terribly impaired, he could catch parts of what the man was saying—and it was in English. The old man shouted, "You cannot walk. Put your left arm around my neck and I will carry you to my truck. We must get away from here."

Newman did as he was told, and to his amazement, the old man picked him up and lifted him in a fireman's carry. He took Newman down the hill to the truck and helped him climb in on the passenger side. Then, the old man ran back up the hill and picked up the burned remnants of Newman's flight suit, the charred pack he had made from his parachute, the money belt, and the shattered pieces of the survival radio the Marine had been using when the helicopters unleashed their deadly fire. Returning to the truck, the Arab threw all of Newman's possessions in the bed of the truck, jumped in, and slammed the door.

"We must go now." He put the truck in gear and drove back toward the highway.

Until they reached the road, the bouncing and jostling of the truck was extremely painful, but once they reached the underground pipeline road, the pain eased. The old man noticed as he drove that the American was dozing off to sleep. "Lord, let him sleep and kindly take away his pain," he prayed aloud. Newman appreciated the sincerity of the man's concern. He closed his eyes.

Newman was awakened three hours later when the truck came to a halt. They had traveled a little less than seventy-five kilometers.

Directly in front of the truck there was a sign in English and Arabic: "Pumping Station 3." In front of them was a long line of cars and trucks. And up ahead, Newman could see a wrecked bridge and another sign, "Euphrates Ferry—50 Dinars."

The old man turned right, off the main road onto a side street, stopped beneath a tree to shade the truck from the midday sun, and jumped out to rummage through some of the boxes he had in the bed of the truck. He fished out a white linen garment that looked like a woman's cool summer dress and handed it in to Newman. He then fished around in another carton and brought back a white skull cap, not unlike a yarmulke, and a large square red-and-white-checked cloth with a black cord.

He climbed back into the cab and leaned over near Newman's ear. "I know that this will be painful, but you must put these on. I will help you."

Newman nodded that he understood, and the old man explained that the long white garment was called a *thobe,* that the skull cap was called a *tagia* to hold in place the red and white *gutra* which in turn was held in place by the black cord, called an *igal.* All of this, the old man explained, was intended for a customer that he would see on some future trip.

With his passenger suitably attired, the old Arab turned the truck around, went back to the main highway, and took a place in the line of cars and trucks waiting for the four-vehicle ferry to take them across the Euphrates. Sitting in the seat beside the old man in the heat, as the truck inched forward in line, Newman dozed off again. He barely awoke a while later as the truck bounced off the ferry on the southeastern side of the river.

Because he had been asleep, he had missed the transaction when Habib had handed the Iraqi soldier collect-

ing tolls and checking identity papers and travel documents, ten 50 dinar notes.

As they pulled off the ferry, the sun was much lower
in their faces and Newman noticed that they once again
had left the main road and turned right, onto what was
barely more than a well-traveled dirt path. A handwritten sign announced, "Al Fuhaymi–30 km." He looked
at his wrist compass and then his watch. Both were
smashed, but from the sun's angle Newman could tell
they were moving to the northwest, parallel to the river
on their right.

Fifteen minutes later the old man again stopped the
truck alongside a building with a weathered hand-
painted sign in Arabic. Several other pickups and cars
were pulled up alongside and in front of the single-story
structure. The old man motioned for Newman to wait
where he was and went in through the front door. When
he returned, he had a pan of warm water and some
more ointment.

Once he had cleaned and treated Newman's burns, and
put clean bandages on both of his hands, his head, and his
back, the Arab returned to the establishment and this time
emerged with a bowl of steaming soup and several loaves
of flat bread. Newman finished the soup and took some
aspirin, helping them down with pieces of the flat bread.

"We must keep moving," the old man said quietly to
Newman as they noticed a few men some fifty yards
away who were looking at the truck. "Will you be all
right?"

"Yes, I'll be all right," Newman said to his new
friend.

"My name is Habib. We should go now." Habib
started the engine and pulled back out to the track taking them not northward but west. Newman could see

by the sun that they must be heading toward Syria. And while Newman was anxious about where he was being taken, he knew that his wounds were severe enough that he lacked the reserves to flee, even if he had known where he was.

Habib noticed Newman looking about and shouted over the noise of the engine, "That is the Euphrates. Do you remember? It is one of the two great rivers mentioned in Genesis. The other is the Tigris."

"Genesis?"

"In the Bible . . . Adam and Eve . . . Eden was somewhere between the two rivers. The earliest paradise was not far from where we are now."

"Ah . . . the Bible." But Newman's planned escape route followed the *Tigris* River, not the Euphrates. He knew the aircraft that had come to his aid earlier in the day would never think to search for him along the Euphrates. And the QRF, coming in from Turkey, was to search for anyone from the mission escaping and evading on the way *north,* to Turkey. Newman tried to push back the pain he was feeling to envision the course of the Euphrates.

The wounded Marine closed his eyes again. He had no choice. He had to trust that this old man who called himself a Christian would help him.

CHAPTER EIGHTEEN

The Believer

Road to Anah, Iraq
Tuesday, 7 March 1995
1600 Hours, Local

Newman awoke just as the truck passed through the little riverside town of Al Fuhaymi. His driver was listening to an excited voice talking in Arabic on the truck's radio. A sign on the outskirts of the village gave notice of the next settlement big enough at least to warrant a name: "Anah–25 km." The throbbing pain from his burns had subsided a little, and the breeze from the open truck window was a soothing, cooling touch to his face and upper arms.

The old man stopped the vehicle at an isolated bend of the sluggish river to their right. He took two gas cans from the bed of the truck and filled the gas tank.

"We must remove anything that would identify you as an American," he told Newman when he got back in. "There is a checkpoint up ahead with guards that may not accept my offering as an incentive to blind their eyes. We cannot take that chance."

He unloaded the remnants of Newman's uniform and equipment and headed for the river.

"Wait," Newman shouted. "There are some things there I simply must have. Please."

The old man came back and Newman painfully pawed through the charred remains of the parachute-material knapsack he had made. He removed a signal mirror, a flare launcher, a pistol, the extra ammunition, the money belt—into which he placed the dogtags and wedding rings of his dead crewmates—and the EncryptionLok-3. "I must keep these," he said to the old man.

Habib shrugged and proceeded to the river with the rest. Once there, he bundled everything with some heavy rocks and cast it into the water. He returned to the truck, took the items Newman had kept, and placed them under a load of sponges in the back of his truck. He then pulled back out onto the road.

Habib glanced over at the American. "Do you feel any better, brother?"

"Yes, a little. My hearing is coming back some, and the burns seem to be better. Thank you. I owe you a great debt for rescuing me back there."

"No, you must thank God. He sent me to you."

"What are you saying—that God sent you to rescue me?" Newman asked.

"Yes," Habib replied. "I did not know what He wanted me to do, but He called me to that spot and impressed upon me to wait there, that He would send someone who needed help."

"No kidding?"

Habib shook his head; he didn't understand the expression. Newman tried again. "Are you saying that

God specifically talked to you and told you to come and rescue me?"

"Oh, no." Habib laughed. "He is not always that precise when He calls me. I just felt He was calling me to a place. What He wanted me to do would be revealed. But I stayed one night in another town, and all night in that spot where we met, and nothing happened, no one came. I was just ready to get into my truck and drive away when the helicopters came. Then I knew why God told me to come there, to stay there, until He was ready for me to help."

"That's great," Newman said. *Guess he's never heard the word "coincidence."* If Habib wanted to give God the credit, Newman had no problem with it. He was too grateful for his rescue to argue about its cause.

"It must be very wonderful to live in America," Habib said after a while.

"Yes, it is. It's a great country."

"I should say. Imagine, living where all of the people are believers."

Newman thought carefully before he answered. *How could he tell Habib that not everyone in America had the kind of faith that someone like Jane Robinette had shown?* "I am afraid that you've been misinformed, sir. Not everyone who lives in America is a Christian. I . . . uh . . . I'm not even sure that I'm a Christian. You know, the way that you . . . and some of my friends . . . define a follower of Christ." This was getting uncomfortable. "Where are we going?"

"We are going to Anah today. My son and family will meet us there. We trade along this route, beside the Euphrates. After we get to Anah, I will introduce you to my son, and he will help you get to Turkey."

"What makes you think I'm going to Turkey?"

"You are not?"

"I . . . I'm not sure where I'm going. I was going to try and get back to Turkey by following the Tigris. But you don't seem to think that's very wise. I guess I'm open to suggestions."

"Your first concern should be of safety. Iraq is not a safe place for you."

"No kidding," Newman said, under his breath.

"The Euphrates will be a much safer way to get to Turkey than the Tigris. According to the radio, Saddam has launched a major attack against the Iraqi National Congress forces north of Mosul. The way to Turkey on the Tigris will be paved with the bodies of those who oppose Saddam if your Air Force does not help them."

"Oh, they will," said Newman, recalling the plans he had seen months ago when he worked at the Marine headquarters.

"Well, they had better come soon. According to the radio, Saddam has been attacking all day, and there has been no help yet."

Newman couldn't fathom why the promised help hadn't been delivered, but he decided it was best to avoid discussing such issues with a virtual stranger. He decided to concentrate on his own predicament. "How far is it to Syria from where we are going?"

The old man thought for a moment. "When we leave Anah it will not be far to the border of Syria. But Syria is not safe for you either. They might think you are a spy. They might even return you to the Iraqi border authorities. I am not sure which fate would be worse."

Command Center
UN Headquarters
New York, N.Y.
Tuesday, 7 March 1995
0830 Hours, Local

General Komulakov hadn't been able to get back to sleep after the calls to Dotensk and Harrod the night before. There were simply too many loose ends. Ironically, now the failed mission of Lieutenant Colonel Peter Newman had become the Russian general's nightmare. He had decided the UN command center was the best place to manage the rapidly unfolding events.

Shortly after he had arrived at the command center, Dotensk had called him to report that Kamil had launched two HIND helicopters to locate and kill the downed Marine. While he awaited a report on the outcome, Komulakov decided to take a shower, shave, and put on a fresh change of clothes. Just as he was turning on the faucet in his private lavatory, he heard a knock at the door. He turned off the water and opened the door a finger's width.

"Yes, Major Ellwood, what is it?"

"Sorry to bother you, General, but the line from Iraq again, sir."

"All right, I'll take it in here. Did he give the EncryptionLok-3 encryption password?"

"Yes . . . right here on this paper, sir." Ellwood hesitated a moment.

"Something the matter?"

"Uh . . . no, I—I mean, well, I was thinking how odd it is that you've been sending and receiving so many calls to Iraq during Colonel Newman's mission."

"I suppose it does. We are very fortunate to have an

operative on the ground, so close to the enemy. It will certainly prove to be helpful now that the mission is unraveling."

"I see . . . thank you, sir." Ellwood went away. Komulakov shut the door and took the call from Dotensk, after first keying in the encryption password.

"Yes, Leonid?"

"Things seem to be going from bad to worse. The HINDs went to where you told me Newman was hiding. As they launched the attack, two jets came at them from the north and shot them down. . . . Yes, yes, they're all dead. It was all observed on radar by the Iraqi Air Defense site at Tikrit South. Kamil now says that his HINDs were led into a trap, that they were ambushed. He thinks that I deceived him. He then sent a platoon of his Amn Al-Khass troops to the site. They got there just as the trucks from Tikrit were arriving with a company of Army regulars. They scoured the entire area for Newman's body. They found the body of a young black woman under freshly dug earth and the body of another male buried by the lake, but your man was nowhere to be found. They found tire tracks around the wreckage of the two HIND helicopters and some signs of blood beneath a rock shelf where the HIND munitions hit, but nothing else. Newman must have escaped.

"Kamil's men are checking to see if the tire tracks can give them some idea of the kind of vehicle it was. They now think that there are many more UN assassins on the ground and that they radioed for the American jets to attack the helicopters. Kamil's troops killed the one team yesterday, but there may have been another."

"Leonid, listen to me. That was not part of the plan. There are no other UN teams. Didn't you tell me yesterday that they had ambushed fifteen men who had crossed into Iraq from Turkey?"

"Yes, Kamil sent his men to the locations you gave me and they killed all fifteen of them."

"Well then, there are no more. The Americans would have notified me if they had any more distress calls from any of the others. And since I have had no calls, we must assume that the one who escaped the HIND attack is the only one left. Tell Kamil to keep searching. He can use the offensive against the opposition forces in the north as a cover for his efforts. This man is surely headed back to Turkey, and Kamil must find him.

"Tell Kamil to have his men keep searching a path ten kilometers on either side of the Tigris, all the way north to the Turkish border. Meanwhile, I'll double-check with Incirlik and anywhere else he's likely to check in, and get back to you.

"But, Dotensk, listen to me. We must find him and kill him. He can bring down the whole apparatus if he is captured by another Iraqi unit and tortured or, worse, rescued and begins to investigate why his mission failed. Be sure that Kamil understands the consequences of our downfall. If the American is not caught and killed, Kamil and his family will never get out of Iraq. Let him know that if they find out about us, then Saddam *will* find out about his disloyalty and treachery. If he wants those nuclear weapons, he must find and kill Peter Newman. I will do everything I can to help you, but it is really up to him. He must find him before he escapes from Iraq."

"Yes, I understand, General. I just hope we aren't already too late. If he has transportation, he could be across the Turkish border by now."

"Well, have Kamil set up more checkpoints on all the

highways going north from Tikrit. Use planes, soldiers, guard dogs, whatever he can. Just do it!"

Komulakov disconnected the EncryptionLok-3, thinking about the remark earlier by Major Ellwood. He thought his answer had convinced Ellwood, but how could he be sure? *Things are unraveling; I can't even control my own staff.* He wondered if he ought to have a little chat with Ellwood to try and determine the level of his concern. No, he thought, that would only draw more attention to the situation. *It may be that Major Ellwood will have to meet with an accident. . . .*

As he walked back in to take his shower, Komulakov's worries intensified. Here he was plotting the death of yet another soldier—he was spending all his time just putting out fires!

It was so much easier in the old days. He stepped under the showerhead and felt the hot water play over his face. *Back in '86, we took out all those operatives that hijacked the Polish munitions train: one in Poland, the priest; another in France, the banker boy; and that shipping tycoon in Lisbon. And all of it was done in the space of twenty-four hours, in three different countries.* The success of that operation had been the guarantee that he would be promoted to General.

Things were much easier in the KGB days. Loose ends were so much easier to tie up. Rolling up the Polish train hijackers in '86, for example, had been done when he could call upon dozens of Department V operatives in practically every country on earth. Now, he was reduced to using this petty Iraqi potentate who couldn't even find one Marine lieutenant colonel in his little desert country.

Sure, they might get Newman, and even kill him. But then there is Ellwood. What does he know? And are there others? What about Newman's wife—what does she know? It seemed to Komulakov that he could spend the rest of his life taking care of annoying details.

Newman Home
Falls Church, VA
Tuesday, 7 March 1995
0855 Hours, Local

The phone was ringing. At first Rachel thought it was part of her dream and wished someone would answer it. She had gotten in very late the night before because of a delayed flight into Dulles Airport and had hoped for the luxury of sleeping late. Then she awakened, cleared her senses, and reached for the handset.

"Hello?"

"Mrs. Newman?"

"Yes, who is this?" Rachel fumbled for the clock on the bedside table, trying to focus on the glowing red numerals. "Sorry to bother you, ma'am. I'm Sergeant Major Dan Gabbard, and I work with your husband. I found your telephone number in his things and—"

Rachel was suddenly wide awake. "Is he all right, Sergeant Gabbard?"

"Well, Mrs. Newman . . . we all sure hope so. I know I'm not supposed to call you, that there's a regular channel for handling this sort of thing. But I wanted to let you know what was happening before you saw it on TV or—"

"Saw what? What's happened? Where is Peter? What's going on?"

"Well, let me tell you the good news first: he's alive."

"Thank God!"

"He was on a mission. There was some trouble, and well . . . the plane was lost. But your husband parachuted safely to the ground. He radioed an American plane going overhead, and we got a message that he's OK."

"Where is he?"

"I'm sorry, Mrs. Newman. I'm afraid that's classified."

"Well, is he in the United States or overseas?"

Rachel could sense the pause, realizing her caller was calculating how much information he could divulge. "He's in the Middle East, Mrs. Newman. That's all I can tell you . . . sorry."

"How can I find out more?" Rachel asked, surprised by her own intensity. "I want to be there when you go in and rescue him."

"Mrs. Newman, I'm afraid that'd be impossible. But the bright side is that by the time you got here, he'll probably be rescued and on his way back there. I'll tell you what. I'll call you periodically to let you know what's happening. After all, we're family."

Family. Wasn't that the term Peter used for his compatriots in the Armed Services? She was beginning to understand the meaning.

"Sergeant, earlier you said something about hearing about it on TV. What did you mean by that?"

"Uh . . . well, you know how it is when a large plane goes down, it always makes the news. Especially when a U.S. plane goes down in another country—"

"Was Peter's plane shot down?"

"Someone else must have told you, ma'am. You didn't hear it from me."

"But he survived, right?"

"Yes, ma'am, he did. He called in, like I said, and said

he was OK. Let's just hope and pray that our guys can get him out of there before things get . . . uh . . . difficult."

"Yes, I agree. Thank you, Sergeant Major Gabbard, for thinking of me. I'll be depending on you to keep me informed. Thank you for calling. Good-bye."

As she hung up the phone, Rachel looked past the bedroom drapes and could see the rain pouring down on a gray early spring morning. She checked the digital alarm clock beside her bed. It would be late afternoon in the Middle East. She tried to imagine where her husband was, and what he was doing. She bit her lip. Rachel felt helpless and so far away. She also felt something else—deep inside she knew she still loved Peter.

Oh, God, please look after P. J. Keep him safe. And if he's in a place he shouldn't be, keep him from being captured. Help his rescuers to find him and bring him home.

Road to Anah, Iraq
Tuesday, 7 March 1995
1720 Hours, Local

Newman was once again in pain from his burns as the truck bumped along the rough road to Anah. It seemed like forever since their last stop and he was eager to get out of the truck. The salve Habib had applied to his burns had helped for a while, but now Newman couldn't sleep for the pain.

Habib sensed his new ward's discomfort and tried to take his mind off of the pain by carrying on a one-sided conversation. He told Newman a long story about how his family had been Christians for at least six generations. His ancestors were from Cyprus, and his family had lived variously in a number of places, depending on the needs of the family businesses. Habib was the current patriarch, and his sons and daughters were reaching the age where they could take over the heavier responsibilities of the businesses.

The one thing that Habib was most proud of was the fact that his children had all become followers of Christ. "God does not have grandchildren," he told Newman. "Each of my children had to make their own decision to accept the teachings of Christ and to follow after Jesus. It is a personal decision." He gave Newman a long look when he said that. He realized Peter was not a Christian, except in a cultural sense—it was merely a traditional label for someone with Peter's background. If Habib could, he intended to change Peter's view, he said. He would talk, not only about his family, but also about his God.

Newman had listened. He thought he would have to pretend to be sleeping in order for the man to stop talking. Still, there was something fascinating about the man's knowledge, as well as his faith. At first Newman thought Habib was a simple, unpretentious man—and that was true, up to a point. Yet Habib was also very wise. Newman figured he must have committed entire books of the Bible to memory because every time Habib needed an illustration for a point he was trying to make, there was a ready soliloquy from the Scriptures.

Newman asked questions—serious questions about God, Christ, and faith—and Habib was never without words. He seemed to understand what Newman wanted to know, and he shared his thoughts simply and humbly. Habib was not an intellectual, but he seemed to have great wisdom. Newman found this to be refreshing.

Most people who were infatuated with their own intelligence often turned out to be arrogant and conversant only in narrow, self-serving ways. But Habib seemed genuinely interested in Newman.

Newman found it awkward to discuss his family, because it occurred to him that he had almost nothing in common with Habib's wife and family. His brother was dead, and his sister was a Navy nurse married to a Navy doctor. They were focused on their careers and their children, and had little in common with him. His parents, of an entirely different generation, shared only a common background in the military. And as for his wife, Rachel . . . Newman found it hard to talk about her. He realized that, after fifteen years of marriage, he didn't really know his wife. He realized he had never bothered to think about her needs, her ideas, or her plans. The concept that he was basically selfish was something of a revelation—and Newman couldn't get away from this distinctly unpleasant thought.

The way Habib had talked about his wife of more than forty years—especially how they had learned to walk together in faith from the very beginning—he might have been speaking Farsi because Newman didn't understand any of it. *Faith, trust, love, peace,* and *God* were words that were essentially alien to Newman, but they described Habib's day-to-day existence. When Habib said words like "faith," "trust," "peace," "love," or "God," he endowed them with a sense that made them seem almost like foreign terms to Newman.

Newman said, "You seem to have different meanings for some words that I learned as a boy—take the word *love,* for example. To you it means something much more than affection or devotion for another person. Or *peace*—to you that word apparently means more than simple tranquility."

Habib nodded. "I understand, for it is as God has said in His Book, 'I love those who love Me, and those who seek Me diligently will find Me.' Man's love for another can never mean the same thing that God's love means. He is love. God demonstrated His love when He sent His Son, Jesus, to die. We use these words glibly, but they have such a depth of meaning when we think about them in the light of God's grace. Probably to you, my friend, these words have never had the meaning that God has given them, not until now. That is because now His Holy Spirit has come to you, and your soul is seeking meaning—it is seeking God, and if you seek Him diligently, you *will* find Him."

That sounds pretty simplistic.

As if reading his thoughts, Habib said, "But no doubt even you have noticed: *faith* is a simple word. Even children understand it. You believe in something; you trust that it is true. But this intellectual belief is only an abstract concept until it is acted upon. For example, I say to you, 'See that chair—go sit on it; it will hold you.' But you are not sure. The legs look weak to you. You do not understand how such a flimsy thing can hold you. But you already know that I sat on the chair, and it held me, so you say, 'If you say the chair will hold me, I believe you.' That is intellectual belief. But in fact, you really do not believe me. Not until you act upon that belief and put it to the test. You must go to the chair and try it, sit in it. You must find out for yourself that it will support you. Faith is like that. You cannot depend upon another's beliefs to work for you. You must come to God and test faith for yourself. You must make your own decision to walk in His path."

Newman noticed his pain had eased. The sun was getting lower in the sky, and Habib told him they would be in Anah in another half hour. But during that time, Newman plied his new friend with more questions about faith and the reality of his God. By the time they got to the outskirts of Anah, Newman's thoughts about these elemental issues and ideas concerning God, salvation, and eternity had more clarity than they had ever had before.

They drove into the small city just after dark. There were no streetlights, and only a few business buildings had lights outside. The houses along the streets were ancient, with stone and clay walls and flat roofs. They rode for another ten minutes along an unpaved road until Habib stopped outside a walled compound with heavy, wooden gates, got out of the truck and opened them; and then he drove into a small enclosed yard.

The high walls would make it difficult for outsiders to see inside the compound; that was a comforting thought to Newman.

Someone hurried out to pull the wooden gates shut, and then carefully locked them.

Newman was stiff and sore, and his burns were still rather painful. He climbed out of the truck. In the darkness he couldn't see much.

"May I present my son, Samir, and his wife, Halimah," Habib said as the man who locked the gates came over to the truck, followed by a woman. "This is Mr. New Man," he added by way of introduction to his family. Habib turned to Newman. "You never gave me your name, but I saw it on your uniform."

Newman laughed. "Well, it's Newman—one word—not New Man."

Habib apologized for the gaffe. "But if you keep seeking God, you can become what the Bible calls 'a new creature in Christ' . . . a New Man, Mr. Newman."

"Please, Mr. Newman, won't you come inside?" asked Samir. "It's dark and chilly out here, and we have our evening meal ready. You and Father must be hungry. Come, please."

They walked inside through a narrow corridor that had a wooden door framed into the old masonry walls. After about twenty feet, they came to another door that led into the small house.

Inside, there was what Newman would call a living room, a place with cushions, a few chairs, and a couple of other mismatched pieces of furniture. From that room, there were passages into other rooms, probably including sleeping quarters, and a kitchen, well-lit with mantled oil lamps. They had electricity, Samir said, but the delivery was spotty at best. Since 1990, they had learned not to depend upon it.

There were enticing smells coming from the kitchen. Newman remembered that he and Habib had not eaten in a long time.

Habib came in, tugging at the sleeve of a woman about his age. "This is my wife, Mr. Newman. Her name is Zahira—her name means 'intelligent.' She is very smart, Mr. Newman. She speaks four different languages and several dialects, but she does not speak English."

Newman smiled and bowed slightly in the Middle Eastern custom, and spoke a few words of greeting in Farsi. She smiled broadly and nodded her appreciation. Then Zahira noticed Newman's burned hands and arms, and the blisters on his face. She showed concern and asked her husband about the injuries. Habib explained how he found Newman.

His son, Samir, heard his explanations about the exploding airplane, the parachute, and the fire that had come raining down out of the sky and so he assumed that the American had been burned when his plane blew up. Habib didn't include the details that had to do with the Iraqi helicopters and the other aspects of intrigue.

The two women disappeared for a few moments, returning with a box of medications and first-aid items.

"My wife was a nurse when we married eight years ago," Samir said. "She says that we must treat you before your injuries become infected. Will you please permit them to help you, Mr. Newman?"

"Of course, and thank them for me. And please . . . call me by my first name, Peter."

"Ah-h," Habib said, his eyes widening, "Peter . . . like the apostle."

"Please, can you take off the thobe?" Halimah said. "We need to clean and treat your burns."

"Yes, thank you. Habib was very kind to me. I think I would have died if he had not rescued me."

They helped Newman pull the thobe over his head. For about twenty minutes, the two women worked gently to wash and disinfect the seared and blistered skin, applying antiseptic and bandages to the numerous puncture wounds he had received in the helicopter attack. From some of the wounds they pulled small pieces of metallic casings, and from others, bits of dirt and stone. Halimah said, "You have many burns and holes in you, Peter Newman. I am afraid of infection. Let me see if I have a better antibiotic ointment." She rummaged in the big medical box and found some. "It's only a month beyond the expiration date. It should be all right. I have several tubes. It should help."

Halimah went to get a bottle of white vinegar and

dabbed some of it onto his burns with a cotton ball. Newman could smell that it was vinegar, and at first he was afraid that it would sting. On the contrary, it was cooling and soothing. "It will keep the skin alive," Halimah said.

The antibiotic ointment also felt good when it was spread on his skin. "You must be in great pain," Halimah said. "You are shaking."

"It hurts pretty bad," Newman admitted. "Do you have anything for the pain?"

"Only aspirin, I'm afraid. But we will let you eat, and then take some aspirin. The food should help you get some strength back, and the aspirin will take some of the fever away, as well as the pain."

Habib's wife, Zahira, had prepared food and spread it on a low table in the living room, and the five of them went to eat. Habib took a piece of flat bread and held it up. He closed his eyes and began to pray in Arabic. He concluded his prayer in English: "Loving Father, God," he began, "we love You and thank You for Your bounty. We thank You for Your protection and blessings. Now we ask for Your help for our friend, Peter Newman. Please protect him and keep him safe until he can return to his dear wife and family. Bless now, we pray, this food. Amen."

Newman felt genuinely touched at the man's simple devotion and selfless charity. *He must know the risk that he is taking,* Newman thought. Once again Habib amazed him by reading his thoughts.

"We know that you are in trouble and that you must find a way back to your own people. We are helping you because of Jesus. He is concerned for you. Do not worry about us—we will be all right," the amiable patriarch said softly.

The meal was eaten leisurely, and Newman felt pleasure in sharing their food. After they ate, Habib told him, "Zahira went to prepare a place for you to sleep, Peter."

"Thank you for such wonderful hospitality. You have literally saved my life today, and I'll always be grateful to you," Newman said.

"You sleep, and Samir and I will talk about the best way for you to get back home. We will talk again in the morning. But first, we will pray for your healing."

Habib stood by the chair where Newman was sitting and placed his hand on Newman's head. His son stood next to him and placed his hands on Newman's shoulders. Each of the women placed a hand on his shoulders. Newman felt a little embarrassed and squirmed a little in the chair. Habib raised one arm toward heaven and began to pray in Arabic, with great passion in his voice. The prayer lasted for more than five minutes, and Newman understood none of it, yet he felt inwardly calmed and touched by their concern. When the prayer was concluded, Habib said simply, "We trust God to heal you."

Newman nodded and followed Zahira into a small room with a bed and small table. On the table was a large bowl of water and a nearby pitcher. He thanked her, undressed, blew out the lantern, and all but collapsed onto the bed. He was asleep almost at once.

Home of Samir Yusef
Anah, Iraq
Wednesday, 8 March 1995
0720 Hours, Local

Newman awoke the next morning feeling sore but refreshed. He got up gingerly, went into the bathroom next to his bedroom, splashed some water on his face, and looked into the mirror. The redness of his burns had receded and his face simply looked tanned. He looked at his arms and saw they were the same. Only his left hand still had sores where the top layer of skin had been burned off. Otherwise his burns were healing faster than they should be. He wondered what caused this— the vinegar used to clean and soothe the skin, the antibiotic ointment . . . or the prayer of the patriarch of this humble Christian family. Or, perhaps it was the combination of them all.

He walked outside into the courtyard and saw some fruit trees in blossom and several tomato plants. Songbirds sang in the foliage outside this quiet little home. The setting was so tranquil that it was hard for him to believe that he was still in Iraq.

Habib was sitting outside on a stone patio, enjoying the sun. The morning was still a little cool, but Habib appeared comfortable sitting there, reading from his Arabic Bible. When Newman came outside, Habib closed the book, stood up, and greeted him. He showed the American around and pointed out the small vegetable garden out back. Then he escorted Newman back inside, into the living room. He offered the American hot tea, some biscuits and honey, and some slices of cheese.

During the meal, Newman told them the cover story that he was told to give—that he was a worker with a UN humanitarian organization, and their plane was on its way from Istanbul to Pakistan when it must have been mistaken for an intruder and shot down. Now he needed to contact this humanitarian organization for instructions on getting back to Turkey. Newman asked if there was a public telephone in the town.

"Yes, but it is very public. You may not be safe using it. It is bound to attract attention."

"Please . . . can you think of one that is less dangerous to use? Maybe a friend or another Christian that you can trust?"

Samir said something to his father, in Arabic. The older man thought for a moment and then nodded his head. "Perhaps there is one. It is at a bank in Khutaylah. It will be on the way when we leave, and it will not take us long to get there."

"What is the plan?"

The two men explained how they would help him get to Turkey by following the ancient trade route to Iskenderun, a seacoast city in Turkey, just across the border from Syria. "It will be a long and complicated business, and will involve several changes of transportation," Samir told him.

While they were talking, Newman reached under his T-shirt and pulled out the cloth money belt that Habib had removed from the wounded Marine in the desert and later returned.

In the belt's scorched pouch was Newman's false passport for his identity as a UN aid worker, along with a Visa card with the same name, and an international driver's license with his picture. Newman peeled back the Velcro cover and pulled out a large wad of foreign currency—five thousand dollars in Iraqi, Syrian, and Turkish notes. "I can pay," he said.

Habib waved his money away. "Please, Peter . . . put your money away. You are my new friend."

Samir brought out a map of the region that he had gotten in an old *National Geographic* magazine some time earlier. "If we get separated for any reason, you should carry it," he said. Newman looked at the map. It was extremely detailed—showing roads, towns, rail-roads, rivers and streams, elevation—it was nearly as good as the military map that he lost when the MD-80 went down.

For nearly half an hour the three men discussed the preferred route. "I still think the best thing is to follow the Euphrates," Habib said.

"It is where the cities and towns are located, and they will help you to blend in. If you go on these roads," Samir said, pointing at the map, "you will be more readily detected."

"We will take you to the pumping station just before the border crossing. You can stop in Khutaylah along the way to make your telephone call.

"From the blacksmith at the pumping station, you and I will borrow some horses and ride across the border ten kilometers south of the guarded crossing. Father will drive the truck to Abu Kamal—inside Syria—and wait for us. We should be there by nightfall."

Habib nodded and said, "While I wait for you, I will also find a boat that you and Samir can use on the river—one with a good motor. The two of you can travel all night. It will take you about ten or twelve hours to reach Bahrat Assad—"

"Bahrat means 'lake,' " Samir interrupted. "There is a dam on the lake so when we reach it, the boat will go no farther. We will have a person we trust meet the boat before we get to the power plant at Tabaqah and take it back downriver to its owner. But I will call ahead and arrange for a second boat to wait for you at the top of the dam, in the water by the two radio towers. It will be waiting there beginning at 0600. They will be fishing near the shore. There will be a green sash tied on the front of the boat if it is safe. A red one, if it is not safe."

Newman committed the directions to memory and nodded. "How far up the Euphrates does the boat take us?" he asked.

Habib answered, "The first part of the journey goes as far as the dam at Bahrat Assad. The second part, the rest of the way."

Samir added, "It will take you all the way into Turkey. The border is not guarded well on the river, and you should be able to stay on it all the way to Birecik, about 25 kilometers north of the Syria-Turkey border, located right on the Euphrates River. The trip from Tabaqah to Birecik is about 180 kilometers and will take another full day, perhaps more if you have to hide. Adana, Turkey, is 250 kilometers due west by air. It may be possible to take a regional airline from Birecik to Adana. Otherwise it would be best to go overland to Iskenderun. There is a train that runs from there to Adana where the NATO base you call Incirlik is located."

"How soon can we leave?" Newman asked.

"Right away," Habib told him.

Office of Leonid Dotensk
Hotel Rashid
Baghdad, Iraq
Wednesday, 8 March 1995
0915 Hours, Local

It seemed to Leonid Dotensk that sleep had become as elusive as the American Marine he was trying to find. He had finally asked if this American had a name, and Komulakov had told him: "His name is Peter Newman. He's a lieutenant colonel in the U.S. Marines. He was assigned by the American government to head this mission. And you had better make sure that your friend Kamil finds him."

Dotensk had been trying his best to do just that. He had been here in his combination apartment-office ever since returning from Tikrit with Hussein Kamil on Monday. He'd been on the phone with both Komulakov and Kamil almost non-stop ever since.

Now, General Komulakov himself was on a special UN flight headed this way, ostensibly at the direction of the UN Secretary General, to investigate the Iraqi military incursion into the so-called "Kurdish Safe Area" in the mountains of Iraq, north of Mosul—an apparent violation of some UN resolution or other.

The Iraqi military operation, which had begun the day before, had been the usual bloody affair, with whole towns and villages being wiped out. Men, women, and children were dead in the streets, and Saddam was claiming over the state-run media that some CIA officers had been killed. Dotensk hoped that the elusive Peter Newman was one of them. The American air support for the Iraqi National Congress forces had never materialized. It must have been a rude surprise for the resistance fighters, Dotensk thought—just like the Bay of Pigs, decades ago. *Oh, well. That's what they get for making league with the Americans.*

Dotensk also knew that the real reason for the general's visit was to conduct a house-cleaning mission with a handful of retired KGB officers. Komulakov was having them fly to Damascus to meet him there the next morning.

When Komulakov had called Dotensk to tell him that he was coming out to supervise this part of the operation, the Ukrainian had noticed that his old KGB boss had sounded nervous. He had told Dotensk that the missing American Marine seemed to be always one step ahead of them.

When Komulakov called from his plane, he had not seemed surprised when Dotensk told him that there still was no sign of Newman nor the truck that seemed to have spirited him away from the helicopter attack.

Dotensk also sensed that Kamil was also getting more nervous—if that was possible. He had a dozen people working through the day and night to try and match the tire tracks at the place where Newman had disappeared. Unfortunately, all they had learned was that the tires were quite common, used on 80 percent of all trucks in Iraq. It would take them years to investigate everyone who owned a truck with such tires.

Kamil had abandoned that effort and committed even more military resources to the search of the area that was the most probable escape route to the north, along the Tigris River. Kamil had said, "It is the most logical route, and the shortest, which gives it more credence. Newman must have been planning to rendezvous with the fifteen-man unit that we ambushed coming into Iraq from Turkey."

Kamil then rounded up every guard dog he could locate. He sent the guard dogs and their handlers out, forming lines on either side of the river, and moving north, alert for the scent of the American. It may have been that the items from the helicopter attack site smelled of smoke too much to be of use; in any event, Kamil had told Dotensk that the dogs had not turned up anything.

Dotensk had not heard from either man in more than four hours. He got up from the couch where he had been dozing and cleared away the empty coffee cups and whiskey glasses, dumping them with a clatter into the small sink at the back of the office.

He was brewing another pot of coffee when the telephone rang again.

It was Komulakov.

"Listen very carefully," Komulakov began. "I am still aboard my personal plane and will land in Damascus late this afternoon, local time. Is there any word from Kamil?"

"No . . . nothing. The tire tracks proved to be a useless lead. Kamil is putting all of his efforts into finding the American somewhere along the Tigris River on his way back to Turkey," the Ukrainian told him.

"That's what I thought. And why I called you. Listen, this American is very smart. He would not take the obvious escape route. I think he will go west, into Syria, and try to make it back to Turkey that way."

"But that could take days . . . even weeks if he has no help. Why would he choose that way, unless—"

"Unless he does have help."

"The tire tracks."

"Yes. I believe that whoever is helping him is taking him across the country on a direct route, one that will not draw as much attention. Look at your map. If he follows the Euphrates River, he can go directly to Turkey. Once he gets into Turkey, he will be more difficult to capture or kill. I am going to take a dozen or so of our old associates with me. I have hopes that I may be able to borrow some helicopters from our friends in Damascus, and if he communicates with anyone before he gets back into American hands, while he transits through Syria, we will have him. Of course, he will try using his EncryptionLok-3 to call someone he trusts to get instructions for coming in," the general said.

"That device can help us track him. I had the UN communications people equip my plane with a direct link to the command center. If Newman uses his EncryptionLok-3 device, they can instantly check his GPS coordinates and tell me. And then, we can take him out," Komulakov told Dotensk. "I want you to stay in your office so when I call I can reach you right away. Do you understand?"

"Yes, General," Dotensk said in a flat voice.

"I will call you again in a few hours," Komulakov said, and hung up.

Dotensk wondered, *Will it never end?*

Newman Home
Falls Church, VA
Wednesday, 8 March 1995
0150 Hours, Local

Once again Rachel Newman was awakened by her telephone in the middle of the night. This time she woke quickly and grabbed the cordless phone on the nightstand.

"Hello?"

"Honey . . . listen, it's me—"

She screamed as she recognized her husband's voice immediately. She called out his name and began to cry. "Oh, P. J., I've been sick with worry. Are you all right? Where are you?"

Newman spoke quickly and distinctly because of the poor connection. "Rachel, I want you to use that phone I gave you the day I left and call the number on that card. And when that call is returned, tell the person on the other end that I'm in trouble and need some 'good' help. Give it to him word for word."

"Yes . . . I'll do as you say. 'You're in trouble and need help.' "

"No . . . word for word, Rache—I'm in trouble and need *good* help.' Understand?"

"Yes . . . all right. I'll say it just like that. P. J., what kind of trouble is it? Where are you?" she asked frantically.

"I'll tell you everything when I call back. It's going to be all right. Rachel, I miss you, and I'm realizing more and more just how much I love you. I have to go now." There was a click, and the line was disconnected.

Rachel sat in bed, shivering with anxiety and wondering what in the world was going on. She had never really taken that much interest in what Peter did in the Marines, but now she quickly grasped that whatever he was doing at the White House was even more dangerous than the things he had done in places like Beirut, Panama, and Honduras—and during the Gulf War, when he'd been awarded the Navy Cross.

Peter had just said that he'd explain everything when he called next time. When would that be? she wondered. He also told her to use the cell phone to call the number that he left with her. Rachel then assumed that he was on the run somewhere, and he had not yet checked in with his unit—at least according to Sergeant Major Gabbard, who had called her the night before.

Then she remembered the other instructions and went over to the dresser. Rachel rummaged through her husband's socks drawer and found the card he had mentioned. There was no name or address on the three-by-five card: only a toll-free number that Peter had said was Oliver North's pager number.

Rachel decided to wait until she left the house before calling the number. She wrote down the exact words that Peter had given her to pass along to North, so that she wouldn't forget them.

She tried to go back to sleep, but she was wide awake and her thoughts were racing.

Situation Room
The White House
Washington, D.C.
Wednesday, 8 March 1995
0210 Hours, Local

The White House watch chief called Dr. Simon Harrod at home and woke him up. "Sorry to bother you, sir, but this seems urgent," he said when the National Security Advisor answered.

"Sir, on the monitoring of Lieutenant Colonel Newman's house, there was a telephone call that came about fifteen to twenty minutes ago. The caller didn't identify himself, but according to what was said, and the way that Mrs. Newman answered the phone, it had to be from Lieutenant Colonel Newman."

The watch chief could hear a rustling sound on the other end of the telephone, as if Harrod was jumping out of bed and trying to focus more clearly on the call.

"What'd he say?" Harrod asked.

"I transferred the recording to a disk and have it in the MIDI player. Do you want me to play it for you?"

"No, I want you to whistle 'Dixie' for me—you idiot, of course I want to hear it. Play the blasted thing!"

The watch chief played the recording twice for Harrod, and when it ended the second time, Harrod said, "Put the recording and the disk in the safe. Give it to me in the morning. Meanwhile, patch me through to the

UN command center. Have them get General Komu-lakov on the line. Tell them it's urgent and to reach him at home or with whatever woman he's sleeping with tonight. I'll wait . . . but don't take your sweet time."

"I'm on it, sir." He pushed the speed dial on the telephone console and got the comm desk at the UN. When he identified the caller and asked for General Komu-lakov, he was told that the general was airborne.

"Stand by, please," the watch chief told the UN communications coordinator. Then he picked up the line where Harrod was waiting. "He's on a plane, Dr. Harrod. Shall I try and reach him there?"

"Well, what do you think I mean when I say the call is urgent?" Harrod said sarcastically.

"Please hold, Dr. Harrod." The watch chief then got back on the line with the UN. "Dr. Harrod says this is a matter of extreme urgency, and he must talk to the general now. Please patch us through."

After a moment of hesitation at the other end, the voice at the UN came back and said, "The general will call Dr. Harrod right back. Please give me his number." The watch chief gave the number and the man at the UN, in turn, gave an encryption password for the EncryptionLok-3 that the general would be using to call Harrod back.

The watch chief explained the situation to Harrod and read to him the list of code ciphers for the EncryptionLok-3.

✪

Across town in his Georgetown residence, Harrod had just hung up the phone after jotting down and entering the encryption code into his EncryptionLok-3. He waited only forty seconds before the phone rang again. It was Komulakov, who explained, "I didn't want to take a chance that my communications were being recorded at the Command Center and didn't want our conversations to be part of the archive. What did you want, Simon?"

"Where are you?" Harrod asked.

"I'm on my way to the Middle East. I should be in Damascus in another five hours."

"Well, that's good, because we've got a problem. It's Newman—he's alive!"

"I knew it!" Komulakov said. "I've been fairly certain of it since yesterday. I'm sorry I haven't called you to tell you, but we weren't quite positive ourselves. It seems he's a regular cat with nine lives. He survived the aircraft destruction, and the parachute fall that apparently killed his pilots, and then an attack by two of Iraq's MI-27 HINDs in which he somehow managed to bring them down instead of letting them kill him. Now, I'll just have to find him and I'll take care of him myself."

"He just called his wife, for crying out loud! He's on to something. He all but told her their house was bugged . . . told her about an accomplice of his for her to call . . . and said he'd call back."

"Interesting. I had no idea he was so inventive. How deep do you think this thing goes?" the general asked Harrod.

"I'll tell you what I think," Harrod snarled, "I think this thing's totally out of control. If this guy ever makes it back, he knows enough to create a real tsunami. We can't afford that. You need to make sure that he doesn't survive any more 'hardships' or—"

"Are you threatening me, Dr. Harrod? It seems to me that you are the nervous one. I haven't done anything that is in violation of any protocol. And unless you have been careless and allowed Newman to make some discoveries that could compromise you, you should be all right as well. Now simmer down. When is Newman supposed to call again?"

"He didn't say an exact time," Harrod replied.

Komulakov continued, "I think it's because he's on the run and has to make arrangements however he can. If he uses his EncryptionLok-3 to frustrate any attempts by the local constabulary to trace or eavesdrop on any calls he makes to you, the UN command center, or to the Search and Rescue center at Incirlik, we could locate him instantly—if I had the locator number for his EncryptionLok-3 unit."

Once again the National Security Advisor was astounded about the things that Komulakov knew about the U.S. command and control system. The knowledge that the newest EncryptionLok-3 devices had an internal "Locator-Command Destruct" feature was known to only a handful of people in the U.S. government. Most of the people *using* them didn't even know it. And now here was a Russian general, albeit one assigned to the UN, telling him things that even most American generals weren't cleared to know.

Still, Harrod knew immediately what Komulakov had in mind. Knowing the locator serial number could give him the ability to track the unit, and locate its user by the GPS internal software. The rest would be like shooting fish in a barrel. "I'll call the Sit Room and get that locator code. Call me back in fifteen minutes," Harrod said as he hung up.

The watch chief was still chafing from the chewing out that Harrod had given him just minutes earlier and had just locked the recording and its copy in the safe when Harrod called back with additional instructions. Harrod thought he could hear some sullenness in the man's voice, but he couldn't have cared less. He told him to get the codes for the encryption device.

"Dr. Harrod, I don't know where those records are kept. I think that's a function of the National Security Agency when they distributed them."

"Then use your blasted phone and get somebody out of bed. This is a matter of national security, and I need some answers right now! Now call me back when you have something besides excuses."

Twelve minutes later, Harrod's phone rang. "Dr. Harrod, the reason that we can't find a locator number for Colonel Newman's EncryptionLok-3 is that we didn't issue him the one he has. He was part of the ISEG, and they took care of that matter through the UN communications office."

Even Harrod could think of nothing to say. He hung up the phone. He sat on the edge of his bed and lit a cigar while he waited for Komulakov to call him back. When he did, Harrod explained the situation.

The general said, "Good. That's even better. I won't have to work through third parties to stay on top of this. I'll take care of it. I'll radio back to the command center to have them assign somebody to sit on Newman's EncryptionLok-3 and monitor any activity at all. That way, when it's activated, we'll know immediately."

Harrod flicked the ash off his cigar. "General, Colonel Newman must not survive his next near-death experience."

Pipeline Pumping Station Oasis
Khutaylah, Iraq
Wednesday, 8 March 1995
1315 Hours, Local

As Habib's truck pulled into the small city of Khutaylah, just twelve kilometers from the Syrian border, Newman tried to look inconspicuous sitting between the father and son as if he belonged here as much as they did. He thought he blended pretty well at a glance, but he was afraid he wouldn't pass anything like a detailed inspection.

✪

The three men climbed out of the battered vehicle and walked across the dusty road to the shade of a small tea stall where Habib ordered some food and tea. While they were waiting to be served, Samir looked around, studying the faces. "I don't see anything out of the ordinary," he told Newman. Then he left for a while. He came back about the time they were served their meal and he sat down. Samir leaned forward, put his elbows on the table, and leaned over close to Newman's least damaged ear.

"My brother-in-law runs the bank here. They are closing in a few minutes for the midday meal and will reopen at 2:30 P.M. I have told him that you want to make an international call, and I paid him for any line charges. He is waiting in his office. I will go with you and knock on the window—he will unlock the back door and let us in. You can use his private office while he goes to eat."

Habib stayed to drink his tea while his son and Newman walked about five hundred meters around the corner to the local bank. Samir knocked twice on the window of the one-story brick building. Beside the portal was a small metal sign in Arabic and English: *AL BURHATH REGIONAL BANK OF IRAQ*. Inside, a curtain was pulled back, then the door was unlocked and they entered the cool interior. The man who had let them in simply nodded at them and left by the door they had entered. He locked the door from the outside.

Samir was certain that no one observed them going in. After showing Newman the phone in his brother-in-law's office and reminding the Marine, "We only have ten minutes," he went to wait and keep a watch on the front and side doors in the small lobby. Newman plugged the telephone handset cord into the EncryptionLok-3, keyed in an encryption password, and pushed the "Standby" button on the face of the device. When he got a dial tone, he dialed the overseas code and the number for the White House.

It rang only once. "Signal," said a male voice into his one good ear.

"Please go EncryptionLok-3 secure on algorithm Alpha, Tango, November, Seven, Niner, Two," Newman said immediately.

"Roger," said the White House signal operator.

Newman pushed the "On" button on his EncryptionLok-3 and heard the metallic *ping* as the two devices, ten thousand miles apart, synchronized their electronic encryption software.

"How may I help you, sir?" said the operator.

"This is Lieutenant Colonel Newman of the Special Projects Office. I need to talk to Dr. Harrod, the National Security Advisor."

"Please wait one, sir."

There was a forty-five-second pause in which Newman heard nothing and then Harrod's familiar voice came booming over the circuit.

"Newman. Am I glad to hear from you—even if it is only 5:15 in the morning. Are you all right? Where are you?"

"I'm in Iraq, about to enter Syria, trying to get back to Turkey." *It's great to hear another American voice, even if it is Harrod.* "The MD-80 took a SAM and went down. Only the pilot and I survived, but she died of her injuries. I'm fairly certain that ISET Echo got wiped out as well. I'm concerned that the QRF may be searching for me at my last reported location and I'm not there."

"Don't worry about the QRF, I'll take care of that situation," said Harrod. *They're already dead, pal, whether you know it or not.* "Why don't you just stay put where you are? I'll contact the Air Force at Incirlik and have them work out an S and R plan to get you out of there. Where are you?"

Newman ignored the last question and said instead, "I don't want to wait here. It's too dangerous, Dr. Harrod. I'm concerned that our mission has been compromised somewhere—maybe it's our comms with Turkey, perhaps even in New York at the UN."

"Why do you think that," asked the National Security Advisor. *Oh, great. This guy has figured it out already. . . .*

"Because the ISET in Tikrit was ambushed," Newman said, "because the Iraqis seemed to know that the MD-80 wasn't a UN flight and shot it down out of hand, because right after I talked to some F-16s flying air cover after the shoot-down, two Iraqi HINDs showed up to take me out. That's too much coincidence and enough to convince me that the Iraqis know more than they should. Maybe we have a leak somewhere at the UN, at Incirlik . . . or even at the White House."

"Now don't get paranoid on me, Newman," said Harrod. *Gotta calm this guy down; gotta keep him on the line long enough to get a fix on his location. . . .*

"Look, Dr. Harrod, I think I can get myself out of here OK. I've got some help. Don't pass on to General Komulakov that we've talked, just in case the leak is at the UN command center. But please call my wife and let her know that I'm all right."

"Of course," said the National Security Advisor. "Uh . . . where are you headed? Perhaps we can get you some help if we know where to meet you."

"I'll call you again as soon as possible." Newman could hear someone knocking at the side door through which they had entered the bank. He saw Samir walk past the office door to let him know his time was up. "I've got to go. Please call my wife. Out here," Newman said as he hung up the phone. He disconnected the EncryptionLok-3 and slipped it into the pocket of the trousers he wore beneath the thobe just as Samir unlocked the door and admitted his brother-in-law.

Once again, the bank manager, now holding a plate of figs and brown rice and a paper cup of tea, nodded to the two men without saying a word. He pointed to the door and then turned to his two visitors and gave them a thumbs-up. They exited the door through which they had entered and were back on the street in the midday heat.

Instead of going back to where they had left Habib and the truck, Samir led Newman back a different way than they had used to go to the bank; they went down a narrow street that was more like an alley. They came to a large, wood-sided, rough-looking shed—Newman could tell by the smells there were animals inside. He waited beside an old delivery truck while Samir went to barter with the owner for two horses they could take to Abu Kamal, across the border in Syria.

Samir had told Newman that he and his father had done this with such frequency in the past that the man would not even question the proposition. He would tell Samir where to leave the horses when they arrived in Abu Kamal across the border in Syria, but of course would insist on payment in advance.

Newman and Samir walked the horses slowly down the street, past the petroleum pumping station, and toward the cluster of crude oil storage tanks for a refinery they could see off in the distance. Just beyond the tanks was a trail that ran parallel to the oil pipeline. They would ride horseback along that pipeline trail until they crossed the border, then head north to Abu Kamal.

They walked for several hundred meters and then prepared to ride into the desert to the west. As they climbed onto their mounts, Samir said, "We must stay away from the pipeline where it crosses the Syrian border. There are patrols out there that may ask more questions than you wish to answer. A few kilometers after we are over the frontier, we can cut back toward the north and pick up the track for Abu Kamal."

But as they began to make their way toward the trail, a Toyota four-by-four vehicle painted with the distinctive green of the Amn Al-Khass Interior Police—with five armed and uniformed men inside—raced past them and rounded the corner just behind them. Newman and Samir, riding slowly along the dusty track, looked at each other, then turned in their saddles to watch as the police vehicle stirred up a swirl of dust and sand as it braked to a stop in front of the bank. Four of the uniformed men jumped out of the police vehicle, carrying submachine guns. Two of them went to the back of the bank and two stayed out front. One of the two in front was banging on the door trying to arouse someone.

"I don't like the looks of that," said Newman. "Let's move a little faster."

Samir slapped the reins of his horse and turned between some of the small buildings and vendors' tents along the main road, trying not to attract too much attention. Newman was right behind him. There were other horses and camels just ahead; Newman and Samir eased into the crowd of six horses and four camels making the same journey. Samir and the American tagged along with them, just a few meters behind and out of earshot.

"Someone betrayed us," Newman said. "That was too much of a coincidence."

"Perhaps you are right, or maybe it was an alarm that Gudyl forgot to turn off when we came. Those men are local Amn Al-Khass. They will not follow across the border," Samir said.

Leonardo da Vinci Airport
Rome, Italy
Wednesday, 8 March 1995
1120 Hours, Local

General Komulakov's baby-blue UN Gulfstream IV with "United Nations" painted above the windows and the olive wreath, globe, and dove logo on the tail had just touched down in Rome for refueling. The Russian general was impatient; when they were two hours out of

New York, the pilot had informed him that they would have to make an unscheduled stop at Shannon to fix some problem in the cockpit—but at least they would finally be in Damascus in another few hours.

The plane was still taxiing when the satellite phone mounted beside his bulkhead worktable rang. The Russian picked it up.

"This is Deputy Secretary General Komulakov," he answered.

"Dimitri, this is Simon Harrod. Engage your EncryptionLok-3."

Both men entered the pre-arranged code and paused while the sets synchronized themselves. Harrod said, "I have had NSA track the GPS location of the EncryptionLok-3 serial number you gave me—and it tracks with what Newman told me. He said he was in Iraq, near the Syrian border—and the location for his EncryptionLok-3 is right at the border. Here are the GPS grid coordinates."

Komulakov wrote down the coordinates and said, "Thank you, Simon. Let me see what I can do to find your missing Marine. I'll call you back."

The Russian disconnected from Harrod and punched the speed dial for the satellite phone being carried by Leonid Dotensk in Baghdad. It answered on the first ring.

"Leonid, this is Dimitri. I have the GPS grid coordinates for the American we are seeking. Write this down."

Dotensk repeated the coordinates—accurate to within one meter of the place where Newman had made the call to Harrod—back to Komulakov and then said, "I will call Kamil immediately."

*   *   *

And now the cycle repeated itself. Kamil took the call from Dotensk on his cell phone, in his office at the Amn Al-Khass headquarters on Palestine Street. He, too, recited the GPS coordinates back to ensure accuracy, terminated the call, and walked twenty steps down the hallway to the Special Security Service command center.

After quickly consulting the large map of Iraq mounted on the wall, Kamil picked up the phone and told the operator, "Get me Major Mohammed Samarai, the Amn Al-Khass commander in Khutaylah." There was a brief delay and then he said, "This is Hussein Kamil. Write down these coordinates." He repeated the numbers yet again. Then he said, "There is an American at that location. I want you to go there and arrest him. He will have a UN ID with the name Gilbert Duncan. He will also be carrying an Irish passport in that same name. I want him arrested. If he makes an attempt to flee, kill him. And kill anyone who is helping him. Once you have him, or have killed him, call me back."

Meanwhile, back in Rome, Komulakov wasn't idle. First, he called Harrod back to tell him that he had passed on the GPS coordinates of where Newman's EncryptionLok-3 had been used—and to learn more about what Newman had said.

Convinced by what Harrod told him of the conversation, Komulakov was certain that his suspicions were correct: Newman intended to follow the course of the Euphrates northward toward Turkey, with the goal of getting back to Incirlik. The Russian checked his map and decided that if Newman slipped the noose in Iraq and made his way into Syria, the general was going to need more help on the ground than a handful of ex-KGB Department V thugs.

His phone rang again. It was Dotensk.

"The American got away," the arms merchant said. "Kamil's officers missed him literally by minutes, maybe even seconds. The GPS grid coordinates you gave me, I gave to Kamil, and he called his Amn Al-Khass detachment commander right there at the border outpost. He sent his officers to the location, using a GPS. Apparently all his units now have them. The location turned out to be a bank and the bank has a phone. The bank manager was eating his midday meal when Kamil's officers arrived, and he denied seeing anyone matching the American's description. But Kamil checked with his communications security people at Project 858—the Al Hadi unit—and they say someone made an overseas phone call from the bank only minutes before the Amn Al-Khass officers showed up. They have taken the bank manager to their headquarters for questioning."

Dotensk paused. "You seem to have underestimated this Marine," he said bluntly to the general.

Komulakov agreed with him. "Yes, I most certainly did. But now I know my quarry, Leonid. He is going to follow the Euphrates up through Syria to Turkey, probably with the goal of getting across the border to Birecik. From there he can catch a plane, train, or bus to Incirlik. He's trying to get back there, because he thinks that's where the rest of the members of his ISEG are and, of course, many other Americans. But I have an idea, my old friend."

Dotensk asked, "What do you want me to do?"

"Tell Kamil that you must go to Damascus to make arrangements for his defection. I will be there in three hours. If there is not someone to meet you at the airport when you arrive, meet me at the Russian Embassy or at the offices of the UNHCR. I will be staying at the Intercontinental Hotel. Before you leave Baghdad, I want you to contact Viktor, Pavel, Akhmerov, Borodin, and Veksel, from our days in Department V. They should all be in Sevastopol. Tell each one to meet us in Damascus. Tell them we will pay them five hundred U.S. dollars per day and a ten-thousand-dollar bonus if they succeed. Tell them to leave all their toys at home. I have plenty of weapons, radios, and other equipment with me on the aircraft to outfit twenty men—and this plane has diplomatic immunity so there won't be a problem getting the equipment to Damascus. Tell them I want them there tomorrow at the latest. Pay for their round-trip tickets."

"Is that all?" said the Ukrainian.

"Yes, Leonid, that is all," said the Russian. Komulakov hung up the phone.

He turned to Captain Sjogren in the seat nearest the cockpit and said, "Ilsa dear, tell the pilots to hurry up and get me to Damascus. There is a war going on in Northern Iraq and the international community expects me to stop it."

Next, Komulakov turned to his Dutch military aide and said, "Now, Major Kaartje, draft a message from me to the headquarters of Interpol and tell them to put out an international arrest warrant for a dangerous fugitive. He is suspected of planting the bomb aboard the United Nations Humanitarian Services flight that blew up over Iraq on Monday. All the essential information is right here. Include his photograph, UN Identity Disc data and his Irish Passport information." The Russian slid a piece of paper across the table to the young officer. At the top was the legend: "Wanted by Interpol for Terrorism: Gilbert M. Duncan." Below the legend and the other data was a picture of Peter J. Newman.

Abu Kamal, Syria
Wednesday, 8 March 1995
1620 Hours, Local

Eli Yusef Habib was sitting in his truck when two men in uniform approached him. They wore the badges of the Syrian Border Patrol and Habib knew that they had a detachment in this little village, just seven kilometers from the frontier with Iraq. They ordered him out of the truck for questioning.

"What are you doing here?" the taller of the two asked him.

"I am waiting for my son. He is to meet me and we will have our evening meal together."

"Where did you come from?"

"I was in Iraq on business," Habib replied.

"Were you in Tikrit on Sunday or Monday?" the soldier asked.

Habib replied, truthfully, that he was not. He prayed that the soldier would not ask him if he had been near Bahr Tharthar earlier in the week. They didn't. Instead the soldier asked, "Were you in Khutaylah today, in the early afternoon?"

"Yes," Habib replied. "I stopped for something to eat, then left to come here."

"Did you go to the bank while you were there?"

Habib could answer truthfully that he was not at the bank, nor did he go near it.

The other soldier began poking around in the cargo area of the truck. He stuck his rifle in the big cartons of sponges. Habib's heart began to race. He prayed that they would not discover the items that Newman had buried beneath the sponges. They did not.

The tall soldier asked for Habib's identification papers. He reviewed them, nodded, gave them back, and led his companion away to look elsewhere for the missing American.

Ten minutes later Newman and Samir rode their thirsty horses into the small city. As the two riders had entered the dusty little town, they had seen the soldiers approaching Habib, so they had waited in the shade of some trees about fifty meters away until the uniformed men continued walking down the dusty thoroughfare.

"There may be more of them," Habib warned as Newman and his son approached. "We should hurry and get to the boat."

"Yes, I agree," Samir replied. He turned to Newman and said, "My father will stay here awhile with the horses while we take the truck up the road to where the boat is waiting. One of our friends will meet him here and accompany him up to where we leave the truck and then his friend will take the two horses back to Khutaylah. But by the time they have done all these things, I hope we will be many kilometers up the river."

Newman looked at Habib. "Then this is where we say 'good-bye,' I suppose." He embraced the old man who had saved his life. "I will never forget what you have done for me, my friend. You, Samir, and your family are taking a great risk to help me." Newman was thinking of the brother-in-law banker, hoping he would not have to suffer for his small part in the escape plan.

"I will be praying for you every day, Peter," Habib said. "I will pray that you will find your way back to your home and your dear wife . . . and I will pray that you will become a believer," Habib said sincerely.

"Thank you . . . not just for your prayers but for everything. And who knows . . . you've given me a lot to think about. Perhaps one day I will be as convinced as you are. I hope that one day we'll meet each other again, maybe under better circumstances.

"One thing is certain," Newman continued. "I'll never forget you. I may have trouble remembering all that happened these past two days . . . but I'll never forget you. I'll always remember you as the man who saved my life—the man who knows God personally. I'll remember you as 'The Believer' for as long as I live. Thank you—" Newman choked on his words, and he felt his eyes stinging with tears.

Habib nodded and then turned to pray over his son, asking God to protect him and the American on this journey. Newman went to the back of the truck, pawed beneath the sponges, and retrieved the .38-caliber revolver and his survival equipment. He shoved the gear into the pockets of the linen trousers beneath his thobe. Then, as the sun began to duck behind the western hills, he and Samir climbed into the truck and drove up the road to where they hoped the boat awaited.

CHAPTER NINETEEN

Ambush

Euphrates River
15 km N of Abu Kamal, Syria
Wednesday, 8 March 1995
1830 Hours, Local

The tiny outboard motor ran smoothly and quietly, pushing the little *dhow* north, up the Euphrates toward Turkey. Samir sat in the stern and Newman in the bow. The Marine wished he had a GPS so that he could plot their course up the sluggish river with greater accuracy than he could manage with his little survival compass and the old *National Geographic* map. But now that it was nearly completely dark, he had put away the map and compass and both men were intent on watching the dark water for obstacles, police boats, and other watercraft—particularly smugglers.

Newman and Samir had found the boat tied up at a small dock at the river's edge, less than fifteen minutes after leaving Habib. They had rowed it out into the river before starting the ancient motor.

For a long time, neither man spoke. There were some other boats on the river. Samir had said that they were

likely fishermen. On occasion someone from another
boat would yell to them in the darkness. Newman
guessed it was the Syrian equivalent of the universal
fishermen's query—"Are they biting where you are?"
Samir would call back to them.

Samir had said they would motor until they reached a
small riverside inn at Dablan. The Marine had tried to figure out how long it would take them to reach the little
town. Though it was only fifty kilometers by road from
Abu Kamal, Newman could see that by following the
river's meandering course and endless switchbacks, and
estimating that they were making only about ten knots
headway, he computed they wouldn't reach their first
day's destination until midnight. Hunched over in the bow
of the little craft, he was once again aware of the pain of
his injuries. He was looking forward to lying down and
changing the bandages on his badly burned arm.

Fortunately, Samir had taken this river route many
times in the course of the family trading business, he
told Newman. He knew it well. He could tell how fast
they were traveling by checking his watch and noting
what landmarks they were passing. Now, for example,
he said, they were passing Saliniyah. Just ahead to the
northwest were the lights of Kharaij, and beyond
that—about fifteen kilometers in the distance—was
Dablan.

✪

Newman awoke with a start as the bow of the boat
touched the shore. Samir had stopped the motor and
was standing in the rear of the dhow. Newman, now
fully alert, jumped ashore and helped the younger man
tie the small boat to a tree at the river's edge. After a
short walk of about 150 meters, they stood outside a
tiny hotel—it looked to Newman as though it only had

seven or eight rooms—near the marketplace, which by morning, Samir said, would be bustling with buyers and sellers.

Samir went inside to make arrangements while Newman stayed outside and watched from the darkness of a small grove of citrus trees. The hotel looked at least a century old, with high ceilings and wonderfully carved balustrades and cornices on the balcony overlooking the Euphrates. The little cubicle, just inside the front door, was like something from a museum. Samir rang an antique bronze bell to summon the manager. A few minutes later, a portly, elderly man entered the lobby from his personal quarters across the hall. He was wearing an undershirt, black trousers, and was pulling up his suspenders as he squeezed into the small space between the tiny cubby holes for mail and the large guest register on the black marble counter. After registering, Samir was given a key by the manager, who went back inside his own quarters and closed the door.

Once the door to the manager's apartment closed, Samir stepped outside and motioned for Newman to follow him. They went up the stairs. The old wooden steps creaked and groaned as the two men climbed them. At the landing at the top, they turned down the hall, and Samir opened the door to the room with the number 3 painted on the jamb. He switched on the light. Samir gestured toward the two beds and offered Newman his choice. He chose the one in the corner, where he had a commanding view of the entire room, in case they had unwelcome visitors. Newman was surprised to notice that the hotel room had a telephone. He picked up the receiver and heard a dial tone.

"Hey, this is great. Do you think I can just dial out and make my call?" he asked.

Samir walked over and read the Arabic writing beside the telephone.

"Yes, it is like the big cities. You dial '9' for an outside line, then dial the country code and area code, then the local number. I, too, am surprised that this small hotel has such modern telephone service."

"Well, good. I'll make a call, but first I want to change the bandages on my hand. Do you still have some of that antibiotic ointment?"

Samir nodded and dug out a tube of the medication from his small bag. Newman unraveled the bandages, wincing a couple of times when the bandage pulled away the scab where the burn was healing. It was still red and there were small pockets of pus where his burned hand was infected.

As he pulled off the old bandage, he used a small towel to wipe it clean with some running water from the sink. Then he squeezed the ointment from the tube, rubbing it gently, but generously, into the open sores. He applied some ointment to a fresh bandage and placed it on the burn, wrapping it all several times with gauze around his hand. Samir ripped the end of the bandage into two strips so he could tie the bandage to Newman's hand.

As Samir was picking up the old bandages and disposing of them in the trash receptacle, Newman said, "What time is it?"

"Twenty minutes after midnight. You need to get some sleep, for we must be under way early in the morning."

"I will, but first I must make a phone call. It's only twenty minutes after 5:00 P.M. in Washington. I must call this person before he goes home."

After two rings, Newman heard, "Grisham."

Newman replied, "Please go EncryptionLok-3 secure on Papa, Yankee, Mike, Eight, Two, Seven."

The two waited momentarily as their devices synchronized.

"General Grisham! This is Lieutenant Colonel Newman. Am I ever glad to hear your voice!"

"Pete, is that you? Are you all right? Where are you? Oliver North just called and told me you were in trouble. Your wife called me too. What's going on?"

Newman quickly related the events since Monday and his concerns about a serious compromise of the mission. Most telling of all, he said, was what had happened earlier that day, right after he had been in contact with the National Security Advisor. "Iraqi authorities surrounded the bank from where I made the call. I don't know whom I can trust. I thought the problem was at the UN in New York. Now, I'm not so sure that it isn't at the White House. All I know is that I need some help."

Grisham paused a moment before answering. Then the General said, "It may be even worse than you think. About an hour ago I received a flash Interpol fax from our Marine security guard detachment in Paris. Interpol has put out an 'International Wanted Notice' for an IRA terrorist suspected of placing a bomb aboard an MD-80 chartered by UN Humanitarian Relief. According to the notice, the MD-80 blew up on Monday while transiting Iraq. The dead or alive notice is circulating all over the planet as we speak. Right above all the relevant details about age, hair color, size, and weight and the name, Gilbert Duncan, is your picture."

"Oh no," said Newman, a knot twisting in his stomach. "That's the alias documentation the UN issued to me."

"I know," said the General.

"If that's the case, I won't be safe even after I get to Turkey."

"I think you will. You see, Colonel, it's time for me to inspect our NATO contingency plans for Turkey. Saddam has apparently decided to create his own final solution to his problem with the Iraqi resistance. His Republican Guards are roaming at will all over the no-go zone north of Mosul. For whatever reason, the White House has decided not to give the INC the air cover they were promised, but I can certainly justify an urgent flight to Incirlik to make sure that our NATO preparations are in place in case Saddam sends his tanks across the Turkish border.

"By the way," General Grisham continued, "when your wife called she said that you wanted her to have North get hold of Bill Goode. How do you know him?" asked Grisham.

"I've never met him, General. Lieutenant Colonel North mentioned him. Said that Goode knows everyone out here and might be able to help if I get in a tight spot. I had already figured out that I was in a pretty tight spot before you told me about that wanted poster. Do you know Goode?"

"I know him," replied the General. "When he was with the Agency, he was the best they had. None better. He got put out to pasture when Colonel North got all cross-wired with the Congress back in the '80s. I'll try to find Goode and get him out there. It'd be good to see him again anyway. If I leave Andrews in the next two hours, I should be in Incirlik by noon tomorrow."

"General, may I ask a very big favor?" Newman asked.

"Go ahead, son."

"Is there any way you can bring Rachel with you? I'm concerned about her. I may have made a mistake calling to let her know I'm OK, and I may have placed her in jeopardy."

"Consider it done. She's a military dependent and is allowed to travel on space-A—and I've certainly got space available."

"Thank you, sir. Now, what about the rest of the ISEG? And is there any word on survivors from the ISET we put into Tikrit? Did Dr. Harrod at least get the QRF turned around and out of Northern Iraq before Saddam sent his Republican Guards up north?" Newman asked.

Again Grisham hesitated. He'd read the cable and hated the words that were about to come out of his mouth. "There is no pretty way to say this, Pete. They're all dead."

Newman was stunned. He had specifically asked Harrod to turn the fifteen-man force around and get it back to Turkey when he had called early that very morning. "What about Sergeant Major Gabbard?" asked Newman, hoping that someone in his small force had survived. "He was at Incirlik when I last talked to him."

"I'll call General Harris at the 331st Expeditionary Air Group right away and see to it that the sergeant major is protected," the general said.

"How about Captain Dan Robertson, in my NSC office—"

"He was killed in a one-car crash on George Washington Parkway on the way into the White House this morning," Grisham replied.

"Oh dear God," said Newman.

"Look, Pete," the General interrupted. "This isn't

your fault. I don't know what's going on here, but it's pretty clear that your mission has been seriously sabotaged. Keep making your way toward the Syria-Turkey border—but don't take any chances. If you can, contact General James Harris at Incirlik. I'll call him right now and tell him to expect your call. You call him in ten minutes. Use your EncryptionLok-3 on setting Yankee, Papa, Hotel, Four, One, Niner. I'll call him on secure right now to expect your call. Here's his phone number."

Newman motioned for Samir to give him a ballpoint pen and wrote the number the general gave him on the palm of his hand. When the two men broke the connection, Newman put the EncryptionLok-3 back in his pocket and said to Samir, "Tell me when ten minutes have passed. I need to make one more call." The young man nodded in response.

When ten minutes had passed, Samir sat up on his mattress and signaled Newman by tapping his watch. Once again the Marine connected the EncryptionLok-3 and dialed the number he had written on his unbandaged palm. The phone answered immediately.

"Harris."

Newman said, "Going EncryptionLok-3 secure."

"Roger. Wait."

When the secure connection was assured, Newman said, "General, this is Lieutenant Colonel Newman. General Grisham told me to call."

"Newman, I'm glad to hear that you're alive. I understand that you're making your way up the Euphrates. That's as good a route out of there as any. It's been a smuggling route for a thousand years, and the smugglers wouldn't still be using it if they couldn't get through. But I wouldn't try to get to Birecik. The Turks have a big military and police presence there. Instead, see if you can get to the port of Iskenderun. Make your way to the area known as 'The 25 Piers.' When you get to the piers, go to the one that corresponds to the date— if it's the tenth, go to pier 10 . . . the eleventh, go to pier 11. You got it?"

"Yes sir."

"Good. Now the number you just called is my satellite portable. I always have it with me and it's always on. That's how you get hold of me. If you get in a real bind, close to the border or on this side of it, maybe we can launch our Air Force SAR birds and come get you. I'd like to pull a Marine out of the soup and kill a few of Assad's goons in the process. OK?"

"Roger that, sir."

"Don't hesitate to call. Out here."

As Newman terminated the call, he looked across the room at Samir, who was flailing his arms wildly. Newman had been so engrossed in the phone call that he hadn't heard the sirens. Some kind of police, fire, or emergency vehicles were coming their way, and by the sound of the sirens, they were getting close—fast.

Samir grabbed the phone, slammed the receiver down, and pulled the EncryptionLok-3 from the wires. "This is how they find you!" he shouted. "You must destroy it." Samir threw the EncryptionLok-3 to the floor and stomped on it. As he was stomping the instrument, it suddenly began to smolder.

Newman stood there dumbfounded, but immediately knew that Samir's intuition was right. Somehow they must have changed the EncryptionLok-3s so that they could track him when he used it. He heard the police car squeal to a stop outside. Grabbing their things, Newman pointed Samir to their only possible escape—the window. It overlooked a flat roof that was thankfully over the empty kitchen and not the manager's quarters. The two men could hear the police or soldiers downstairs, banging on the manager's door. They dropped the five feet from their windowsill to the roof and then ran to the edge.

"It's too far down," Samir whispered to Newman as the two men peered over the edge. A puddle of light suddenly appeared on the ground below as a light went on in the manager's quarters.

"We have no choice," Newman said. He shuffled along the edge of the roof to where a large tree overhung the structure. He flung himself out, clawing for a large branch. Pain raced through Newman's burn-damaged arm as he moved hand over hand to the trunk and then slid down to the ground.

A few seconds later, he heard Samir grunt as his body hit the tree trunk—and then he, too, was down. The pain in Newman's injured hand was intense, but the sounds from inside the hotel were enough to motivate both men to keep moving.

They could hear the voices of the police shouting at the innkeeper to reveal what room the American was in. He knew of no American, the innkeeper protested, and told them that only two rooms were occupied, number one on the ground floor and number three, on the second floor.

The authorities then spent several minutes banging on the door to room one and rousting out the newlywed couple—who were terrified at the intrusion of their honeymoon.

The police finally burst through the locked door to room number three and rushed inside, guns drawn, ready to shoot. Finding the main room empty, they checked the bathroom. In a small wastebasket they discovered a pile of bloody, pus-encrusted bandages. In the bedroom, the telephone had been knocked from a small table on which it had rested, and some of its wiring looked as if it had been ripped out of the phone. On the floor beside the telephone was a pile of smoldering rubbish that smelled acrid and its lingering smoke hurt their eyes. Then they noticed the open window and went to look out.

Meanwhile, Newman and Samir were half-stumbling toward the river. They clambered into the boat and began to paddle as silently as they could toward the middle.

Their breathing sounded as loud as a sawmill to Newman. When they were in the middle of the river, Samir pulled on the cord to start the motor. Nothing. He pulled again, and the old motor caught. Newman thought its sound was as sweet as a symphony, right at that moment. Samir pointed the bow upstream.

By now there were more than a dozen Syrian Interior Ministry police officers searching the buildings adjacent to the small hotel. It did not occur to them to search the river until they heard the sound of a motorboat starting up, well out on the river. Several of the officers raced to the water's edge but when they arrived, though they could hear the faint hum of the motor, it was impossible for them to tell if the boat had gone north or south. The officer in charge of the police detail was furious. Damascus had said that an "American spy" was at the hotel. Clearly someone had fled the room that his men had searched. He had to bring back something to show that he had made every effort to capture the American. So he had his men arrest the night manager.

Newman sat in the bow with his head in his hands. They had escaped again—by an even narrower margin than last time. Would they be so fortunate next time?

National Security Agency
Fort Meade, MD
Wednesday, 8 March 1995
1750 Hours, Local

Jules Wilson hung up his phone and stared out the window, mulling over what he had just been told by an old friend.

Lieutenant General George Grisham had been brutally frank: "Jules, there is something terribly wrong with your EL-3 encryption systems, and I'm ordering all Marine units to cease using them effective immediately until you get to the bottom of the problem."

Grisham had gone on to specify for the number-two man at the National Security Agency what he had learned from Newman. Grisham was convinced that "his Marine in the field" was being compromised by the EncryptionLok-3 device that he was using. So, he had called Wilson to check on it.

Grisham's call didn't alarm Wilson about the EncryptionLok's cipher having been broken; he was convinced that was impossible. Instead, Wilson had asked where the Marine had gotten the device he was using.

Grisham replied, "I don't know. I'd guess that they got them from the NSC or the Special Ops people down at Bragg."

But a quick check of the EncryptionLok-3 inventory in the NSA's master computer index showed that Newman didn't have an EL-3 signed out to him. And then a subsequent call to WHCA confirmed that all of their EncryptionLok-3 devices were accounted for.

Could the UN have EncryptionLok-3s without our knowledge? Wilson wondered. He had come down hard on Silicon Cyber Technologies when they tried to sell the device to the UN and NATO, and assumed that was the end of it.

Now, alerted by General Grisham's call, Wilson swung into action. He picked up his phone and called the NSA Operations duty officer.

"Major Hammond speaking, sir."

"Major, Deputy Director Wilson here. I need you to check something for me. Within the last two hours, an EL-3 encrypted call was made from overseas to the deputy chief of staff for Operations and Plans at the Marine headquarters. I want you to find out the GPS location for that device—from the EL-3 systems tracking profile—and get me its registration number. . . ." Wilson gave the duty officer the phone number where General Grisham had received the call.

In less than fifteen minutes, Wilson had a computer-generated report:

EL-3 LOCATOR NO. DGL/94IS00033744 IS AN UNASSIGNED DEVICE. IT WAS USED FOR A TELEPHONIC VOICE TRANSMISSION TO THE NUMBER INDICATED IN THE TIME FRAME OF YOUR QUERY. GPS DATA FOR THE UNASSIGNED EL-3 UNIT INDICATES THAT THE CALL ORIGINATED FROM SYRIA. INITIAL INSPECTION OF DGL/94IS00033744 INDICATES THAT IT HAS BEEN MONITORED BY UNKNOWN SEQUENCER/INQUIRER LOCATED IN VIC OF 1600 PA. AVE, WASH, D.C.

IMMEDIATELY AFTER LAST GPS INQUIRY, THE WHITE HOUSE SITE EL-3 MADE A 2MIN 31SEC ENCRYPTED VOICE TRANSMISSION TO A SECOND UNASSIGNED EL-3, LOCATOR NO. DGL/94IS00033753, THAT APPEARS TO BE CONNECTED TO AN UNKNOWN MOBILE SATELLITE VOICE PHONE

IN VIC OF LEONARDO DA VINCI AIRPORT IN ROME, ITALY. AFTER TERMI-
NATING COMMS WITH THE WHITE HOUSE SITE, THE ROME DEVICE IM-
MEDIATELY MADE AN EL-3 VOICE-ENCRYPTED TRANSMISSION TO
ANOTHER SATELLITE PHONE CONNECTED TO A 3RD UNASSIGNED EL-3,
LOCATOR NO. DGL/94IS00033537, WHICH APPEARS TO BE LOCATED IN
BAGHDAD, IRAQ. UNKNOWN INQUIRER AT WHITE HOUSE MADE THREE (3)
GPS INQ LAST 48 HRS. OF DGL/94IS00033744. UNASSIGNED EL-3 NO.
DGL/94IS00033744 DESTROYED PER SOP 8331.

GPS LAT/LONG AND UTM COORDINATES WHERE DEVICE WAS LAST
USED ARE PRINTED BELOW UNDER 'SENDER'S LOCATION.' REQ ADVISE
ACTION TO BE TAKEN RE EL-3 DGL/94IS00033753 AND EL-3
DGL/94IS00033537?

Jules Wilson could not believe what he was reading.
First, the unassigned EncryptionLok-3 that Newman
was using had a serial number that was not even in the
range of those that the NSA had authorized for purchase. Second, there were other unassigned EL-3 devices
being used in that same serial sequence, and if those
numbers were correct, there must be additional thousands of them circulating in the world. He felt a shiver
of alarm running down his spine. "The UN has
EncryptionLok-3s!" he said out loud, though he was
the only person in the room.

The watch officer's initial assessment also indicated
to Wilson that the unassigned EL-3 that Newman was
using had been queried for its GPS location at least
three times in the past two days—from the White
House. The final piece of information was that the NSA
Operations Center had, in accord with established standard operating procedures, initiated a command-
destruct signal for the EL-3 since it was in an area where
no EL-3 units were authorized.

Jules Wilson decided to act. First, he called General

Grisham back and told him what he had discovered, and warned him to tell Newman, if he could, that up until the time it was destroyed, the Marine's EL-3 had been GPS-tracked by someone at the White House.

Wilson then made a second telephone call: to the senior FBI agent serving with his "Comm Hawks." When the agent returned his call, Wilson was customarily blunt: "David, I want you to quietly open an espionage case against the officers of Silicon Cyber Technologies, the manufacturer of the EncryptionLok-3 device. I have reason to believe that the company may have intentionally compromised U.S. encryption technologies in violation of U.S. law."

Newman Home
Falls Church, VA
Wednesday, 8 March 1995
2015 Hours, Local

General Komulakov didn't have many of his former Department V officers in the U.S.—but two Russians—who happened to be running drugs in Brooklyn for the Russian mafia—jumped at the chance to be of help—for a fee, of course. Aleksandr knew the general through a former colleague in his old Dzerzhinsky Square office. Aleksandr had provided the second man—his own son, Vasili. Komulakov had offered each of them one thousand U.S. dollars to clean the Newman house.

They knew, of course, what their assignment was and started immediately. Under his father's watchful eye, Vasili packed a small aluminum suitcase, lined with lead, that contained some unusual tools, along with their pistols, ammunition, and silencers—and checked it as baggage on their flight from Newark to Dulles.

They arrived a little after 2030 hours, rented a car at the airport, and bought a local street map at the Dulles Airport gas station. The father-son team then drove directly to Falls Church, found the Newman address, drove past it, and parked several doors away.

There was a light on in the Newman's bedroom, but none in any of the lower story rooms. They found where the telephone lines came into the home, and cut them, to forestall both a silent alarm to a security company, or a call to the police by a frightened victim.

Then, following his father's instructions, Vasili forced a basement window on the side of the house that was not illuminated by the street light three doors away. Aleksandr went to the back door of the garage and, using a large pneumatic tube wrapped in a piece of blanket, punched the dead bolt lock through the door with hardly a sound. A second punch took out the doorknob. In less than five seconds, he was inside the garage. He noted that there was no car parked there, and since there was none in the driveway or on the street, he didn't expect anyone to be home. But to be safe, he did his best to muffle the noise as he used the same procedure on the interior door from the garage into the kitchen. Ten seconds later he was inside the house and the kitchen door was swinging uselessly on its hinges.

The older man took out his silencer-equipped automatic pistol and quietly chambered a round. He switched on a laser-sight and crisscrossed the room with it, seeking a target. He began to silently climb the stairs. He was halfway up to the bedroom level on the second floor when Vasili came up from the lower level. There was enough light coming through the living room windows for them to see each other. The blond killer shook his head; no one was downstairs. Aleksandr pointed in the direction of the closet and bathroom doors off the kitchen. The younger man crept up on each door and, holding his Glock 9mm pistol in front of him, threw each door open. Both rooms were empty. Aleksandr continued up the stairway toward the lighted master bedroom. He had to be careful; military wives often knew how to use handguns. If the woman was inside, she might have a gun pointing at the door right now.

He crouched, away from the door, by the wall, and quietly listened for any sound coming from the other side. If Mrs. Newman had been aiming her pistol, she'd have three or four rounds off through the door by now. Or she might be in the bathroom and couldn't hear the sounds of their forced entry. Vasili was behind his father now and flat against the wall, covering the older man's back. They both moved away from the door, on either side of it. The son slowly and silently turned the knob. He dipped his head to mark the count of three, then swung the door open and they both raced into the room. The son fired four shots from his silencer-equipped automatic into the bolster lying lengthwise on the unmade bed.

The two of them looked in the bathroom, the closets, and then they went outside the master bedroom and searched the other rooms and closets, but found no one. Relaxing once they had confirmed that the house was indeed empty, Aleksandr took out his cell phone and dialed. He spoke briefly in Russian.

"Wait until she comes home? Why? We should leave immediately." He listened a bit longer, then shrugged and ended the call.

After he put his cell phone away, he said to his son, "Look around—find his computer. We will take it with us. You can take whatever else you see that you like. We are to make it look like a robbery. Her jewels are mine." And he turned to the task of ransacking Rachel's dresser and closet.

They waited until after 0300 and when Rachel still had not come home, the son left the house to bring back their car. He pulled it into the garage and closed the door while they put the computer, a TV set, VCR, some jewelry, and a few things from Newman's closet into the trunk of the rental car. Then they left for a local motel, to await further instructions.

Aboard USAF C-17, Special Air Mission Flight T-43
Andrews Air Force Base
Wednesday, 8 March 1995
2105 Hours, Local

Rachel heard the familiar sound of jet engines and felt the landing gear thump into the wheel wells as General George Grisham's C-17 lifted off the tarmac at Andrews Air Force Base. For a change, she hadn't had to give the pre-flight safety brief, and wouldn't have to get up to check on the passengers' comfort. As she leaned back in the comfortable executive package seats of the big U.S. Air Force transport, she contemplated her last twenty-four hours.

After the call from Peter, almost twenty hours earlier, Rachel had tried unsuccessfully to sleep for a few more minutes. After tossing and turning for half an hour, she had gotten up and taken a shower. By the time she had toweled and dried her hair, it was almost 3:00 A.M. She then decided to call the number on the card he had given her the day he left.

I'm supposed to use the cell phone, she remembered. She put on her jogging suit, slipped into her running shoes, went down the stairs, out the front door, and walked down Creswell Drive toward the cul-de-sac at the end of her street. Standing beneath the streetlight, she dialed the number. Oliver North's pager offered two options. "For a numeric message, press 1. For a voice mail message, press 2." Rachel pressed 2.

"Colonel North, this is Rachel Newman. My husband called me and is in trouble and he told me to call you." She gave her cell phone number and ended the call.

In less than a minute, North had called her back.

She had told him about Peter's call, and when she finished, North had asked where she was. When she told him, the retired Marine had given her very specific instructions: "Go back to the house, pack enough comfortable clothing for a few days—just as though you were making an overseas trip for TWA. Nothing formal. Pack for comfort. Go immediately to a hotel that you know. Get some food to eat in the room because you shouldn't be going out. Use another name. Pay in cash. I'm going to call a friend. After you get settled at the hotel, call me back using the cell phone." He gave her the number for his cellular phone.

Rachel had followed the instructions exactly. She raced back into the house, packed some clothing in her black TWA-issued flight bag, and grabbed the one thousand in cash that she kept in an envelope in a dresser drawer. She didn't even take time to make the bed. But just before running out the door to jump into her car, she stopped and ran back up the stairs to pick up the study Bible that her friend Sandy had given her several weeks before. *It's heavy, but I might as well stay with my new routine.*

Rachel drove along Broad Street to Old Town Alexandria. She knew of a Hampton Inn there where commercial airline flight crews often spent the night when they had a D.C. layover. Even though the streets had been empty, uncooperative traffic lights had turned the ten-mile drive into a half-hour trip. From Broad Street she had turned left onto King Street, past Dangerfield Road—seeing some irony in the street sign—and then one block past Diagonal Road to the Hampton Inn in "Old Town" Alexandria.

On the form provided by the bored young man behind the counter she printed her middle name and maiden name and her parents' address. She asked for a non-smoking room on the second floor, paid cash in advance for one night, and waited while the clerk made her room key.

When she went back to her car, Rachel saw the sign for the parking garage in the rear, and drove around and parked inconspicuously in a corner between two vans.

Then Rachel took her carry-on out of the back seat and headed for her room.

She took the elevator to the second floor, looked for the number plan on the wall in the hallway, and then walked to room 207. She unlocked the door, reached in and found the light switch, flicked it on, looked inside, and finding it empty, went into the room. Rachel tossed her carry-on onto the bed and double-locked the door.

Then, feeling a little out of breath, she sat on the chair by the desk and opened her purse. She took out Peter's cell phone and dialed Oliver North again. It was 4:10 A.M., but he answered right away. Once again, he had instructions: "In case someone else is listening on my line, don't mention where you are in the course of this call or any other until we know that we can get someone to you to protect you. I'm going to give you a phone number. As soon as we are done, I want you to call the number immediately. The last two digits of the number will be a kind of code that only you and I understand. If you understand my little code tell me 'yes,' hang up, and call that number. That way, you will have completed the call by the time anyone who might be listening can break the code. Tell the person who answers what you told me an hour ago. He will give you instructions. Do you understand?"

"I think so."

North gave her the first eight digits of a telephone number, but instead of the last two digits in the sequence, he then said, "And the last two are the numbers of the unit that Peter and I were serving in when you two came over and had dinner with Betsy and me."

His wife Betsy. We were at Camp Lejeune. . . . 1980, the 2nd Marine Division. . . . Third Battalion, 8th Marines. . . . three, eight!

"Yes! I've got it."

"Good," North had replied. "Call that number now, and do as he says." North hung up.

Rachel had called the number immediately. It, too, rang only once, and the voice said simply, "Grisham."

✪

In the hours since that first call to General Grisham, the sun had come up and the rest of the world had gone to work, braving the notorious Beltway commute. The general had told her to stay put, to get some rest, and to call him back at 4:00 P.M., using the cell phone. Rachel did as instructed. She had watched the news, studied some from her Bible and probably would have slept soundly for a few hours but for the maid who had come by to freshen the room. Rachel had sent her away and called down to the front desk to extend her stay. The manager had required her to come down and pay in advance for another day since she hadn't left a credit card. Other than the brief trip to the lobby office, she had been in the room all day.

At precisely 4:00 P.M. she called General Grisham. It wasn't a pleasant call.

"General, it's Rachel Newman again. Have you heard anything more about Peter?"

General Grisham's calm and reassuring voice came back on the line. "Not yet, Mrs. Newman . . . but I'm gathering a fair amount of information, and I'm hopeful that this is going to work out for the best. Unfortunately, there seem to be some other people in this government who want it to turn out differently. Mrs. Newman, are you somewhere where there's a TV?"

"Uh . . . yes, I have one here."

"Turn on the news. There's a press conference, and it concerns your husband. I'll hold while you turn it on," General Grisham said.

Rachel reached for the remote and clicked the TV set on. She found the news and turned up the volume just as the anchor said, ". . . has brought you this report live from outside the White House, and that was our correspondent, Brian Penner. We've just seen and heard the announcement that the United States government and the United Nations have joined Interpol in an international manhunt for the Irish Republican Army Terrorist, Gilbert Duncan—suspected of planting the bomb that brought down the United Nations Humanitarian Relief flight over Iraq on Monday. The U.S. government has offered a $2-million reward for Gilbert Duncan—dead or alive." As the newsman droned on about the IRA denying any connection to the crash that had supposedly killed all aboard, a photo of Rachel's husband was added to the top right of the TV screen, with the name "Gilbert Duncan" below the photo.

Rachel was flabbergasted. She had so many thoughts going through her head that she didn't comprehend half of what she heard. But she had seen the picture and heard key words that made her react with stark fear— "fugitive . . . terrorist . . . dangerous killer . . . fanatic . . . bent on a suicide mission . . . sought by U.S. agencies . . . Interpol . . . wanted dead or alive."

"Uh . . . General . . . what's happening? That was Peter—but not his name. Have they made a terrible mistake? I don't know what's going on. Why are they saying these things about Peter? And why didn't they use his real name?"

"Mrs. Newman, I don't know what's going on. I've known your husband since he was a second lieutenant. I do know that he's not a terrorist and I believe that someone is trying to frame him, and use him for purposes that are dishonorable at best, and treasonous at worst. I would very much appreciate it if you would stay in touch with me from right where you are. Would you please call me back at 6:00 P.M.?"

Rachel was sure that if she hadn't brought her Bible with her, she would have gone crazy watching the digital alarm clock by the bed slowly click to 6:00. By the time she called the general's number, the cable news networks had all repeated the story twice about the "terrorist Gilbert Duncan," each time showing a picture of her husband.

But despite what was on the TV, this time, when the

general answered his phone, the news was better. "Mrs.
Newman, I've talked to your husband," the General
had said. "He's all right, and trying to make his way
back to safety. I'm headed to Turkey this evening to
make sure that he knows he has friends out there. I
don't mean to intrude on your personal life, but he
asked me to bring you with me. I think it would be safer
for you. Would you like to go?"

"He called you? When? How long ago—did he say
where he was? Is he all right?"

"Mrs. Newman, I talked to him within the past thirty
minutes. He said he was all right, but I can't tell you
much more. That's when he asked me to bring you with
me—if you wish to go, of course."

"I'd like that very much, General."

"Good. Tell me where you are. I'm going to send
some Marines to pick you up right away and take you
to Andrews Air Force Base."

❂

For a few minutes after takeoff, General Grisham had
patiently answered her questions—and there were
many—right down to why a Marine General was flying
on an Air Force C-17 transport. He chuckled and said,
"This aircraft is actually used for Special Air Missions
by the Joint Chiefs of Staff. The pilots needed some
long-range over-water navigational experience so they
are making a 'training flight' to Turkey."

After they had been airborne for half an hour, the
stewards served a hot meal. Rachel turned on her reading light and opened her Bible. In minutes she was
asleep.

General Grisham motioned for the Marine major
who was sitting behind them and said quietly, "John,
ask the crew chief to dim the cabin lights and get a blan-

ket to cover her up. And when you get that done, have Staff Sergeant Winsat bring me those briefcases full of paper." The General spent the next four hours bent over his tray table reading "Action Items" under his purview at the Marine Headquarters. Despite the "URGENT ACTION REQUIRED" label on most of them, none seemed as pressing as the husband of the woman sleeping across the aisle.

International Airport
Damascus, Syria
Wednesday, 8 March 1995
2350 Hours, Local

General Komulakov's aircraft had arrived at Assad International Airport in Damascus at a little after 4:00 P.M. At his request, the airport authorities had parked it at the far end of the terminal, beyond the row of Syrian Arab Airlines planes.

Instead of going to the Syrian Foreign Ministry as would be expected of a senior UN diplomat in the region to help resolve the bloody conflict just across the border in northern Iraq, he went directly to the Russian Embassy on Omar ben Al-khattab Street in downtown Damascus in a shiny black Lada with Russian diplomatic plates. He told his aides to stay behind with the UN aircraft to monitor communications.

Komulakov knew this embassy well. He had been assigned to the KGB's Damascus Residency—here at the chancellery. As a relatively junior Line F officer in Department V—the Special Tasks unit—he had the job of recruiting terrorists to work for the Soviet cause. Komulakov had been credited with convincing Dr.

George Habash and Dr. Wadi Haddad—leaders of the Popular Front for the Liberation of Palestine—to ply their deadly trade in support of Moscow's agenda. Those who had succeeded Komulakov here in Damascus revered him for his skill and success. It was to them that he made his request. They owed him, and he knew it.

"Colonel Grankin, you are now resident here in Damascus. Do we still have the secure hangar at the airport?"

"Yes, General, though it is much in need of repairs," replied Russia's senior intelligence officer in Damascus.

"No matter," answered the General. *They changed the name from KGB to SVR and hired whiners. Where do they get these soft, mushy types like Grankin—from the Finance Directorate?* Komulakov said, "Please, dear Grankin, find for me ten well-trained PFLP members who can be trusted. Have them report to the hangar at midnight."

"Yes, General," said the SVR chief. Grankin had a doubtful look on his face, but Komulakov didn't care.

"And you, Major Radchenko, you are now the local representative of Department V?"

"Yes, General," said the incredibly large Russian with the huge head and extremely big smile.

Komulakov smiled and said, "You were one of my best captains. You handled some of my most difficult tasks—like that operation in Poland, with that Solidarity priest and that capitalist in Lisbon back in '86. You should be at least a colonel by now. Whom did you alienate to get assigned to this, ah, remote area?"

The big Russian stopped smiling. "Afghanistan."

"Well, not to worry, Major. This is your chance to improve your record," replied Komulakov. "Do you still have two helicopters available, or have Moscow Center's budget cuts eliminated your ability to do your job?"

"We still have two helicopters, MI-8s, and they both work—when the pilots are sober."

"Good. I am going to need them. We are hunting for a major international criminal. His name is Gilbert Duncan. He is a terrorist—he placed a bomb on the UN charter aircraft that blew up on Monday over Iraq. He is trying to make his way to Turkey, up the Euphrates River valley. On land or water, I don't know yet, but I will. I have some of our old colleagues coming down from Sevastopol to help take care of this problem.

"Colonel Grankin," said Komulakov, "there is to be no cable traffic back to Moscow Center on this operation. I shall see to it that the appropriate authorities are made aware. Also, I don't want the ambassador informed. Do you understand?"

"Of course." Grankin shifted uneasily in his chair.

"Now, Colonel, I'd like to borrow Major Radchenko here, and those helicopters, and those PFLP fellows for a few days, if that's all right with you. Please take care that the Syrian Interior Ministry, Border Police, Intelligence Service, and even their provincial authorities urgently distribute copies of this." He handed Grankin the Interpol notice with Peter Newman's picture on it and the particulars describing the crimes of "Gilbert Duncan." Then he said, "Come, Radchenko, we have work to do," and walked out the door.

By the time Radchenko and Komulakov arrived back at the airport, it was 1900 hours and the field was lit up with mercury vapor lamps. All the way to the field, the general gave the Russian clandestine service officer instructions on details that had to be covered: Dotensk's arrival from Baghdad, the plans for billeting and feeding the PFLP volunteers, and arrangements for meeting the Department V alumni when they arrived from Sevastopol.

First they stopped at Komulakov's UN aircraft, told Captains Kaartje and Sjogren to go into town and get rooms at the Le Meridien Hotel at City Centre. When the two officers had departed, Radchenko helped Komulakov remove the weapons, ammunition, and explosives from the back of the UN aircraft, load them into the trunk of the Russian embassy Lada, and take the entire load over to a hangar at the far end of the field.

Radchenko showed his Diplomatic ID disc to the local Syrian guard, went to a side door, and unlocked it. They had only been in the hangar a few minutes, admiring the two MI-8 HIP helicopters with Syrian Air Force markings, when the pilots showed up—both Syrians.

Komulakov shot Radchenko a look, but he said in Russian, "No worry, General. They are loyal to me, and they will take us wherever you wish to go."

At 9:45 P.M., Komulakov and Radchenko were drinking strong Arabic coffee and standing over a large-scale map of Syria in the windowless office of the hangar when they heard a commotion at the door.

"Get your hands off me, you big Russian lout!" The door flew open and both men reached for their 9mm pistols, as Dotensk came flying into the room, propelled by one of Radchenko's Line F Department V brawny heavyweights.

Radchenko's man, following instructions rather literally, had met Dotensk's flight, grabbed the Ukrainian arms merchant when he exited the terminal and, without telling him where he was going, had dragged Dotensk, kicking and pleading for his life, to the hangar.

Komulakov re-established order, and the three men talked until almost 11:00 P.M. when the twelve-man PFLP squad arrived, escorted by two more of Radchenko's thugs. They were soon bedded down on the opposite side of the terminal with instructions not to go near the helicopters until told to do so.

Shortly after midnight, just as Komulakov had decided to go get some sleep, an Aeroflot flight arrived from Odessa, carrying the six former Department V officers whom Komulakov had summoned earlier in the day. Following Komulakov's orders, the local SVR man issued each of the Russians weapons and ammunition and then took them into the hangar to introduce them to the PFLP shooters. The six Russians, all in their mid-thirties, were dressed like mountain climbers. In fact, their hastily-issued visas claimed that they were "archaeologists."

Each of them was given a Motorola UHF radio, a small backpack for carrying rations, water, ammunition, explosives, extra batteries, a small halogen flashlight, and a set of the latest Russian Army night-vision goggles.

While the six were getting to know the PFLP terrorists they would be leading, Komulakov's satellite telephone began to chirp.

"Deputy Secretary General Komulakov."

Harrod's excited voice came through the speaker, "Go EncryptionLok-3 secure, same encryption as last time."

The Russian reached into his pocket, clipped the little device to his phone handset, and said, "Yes, Simon."

"He just did it again."

"Who?"

"Newman—who do you think? He has called someone here in Washington, and right now he's on the phone with someone in Turkey. He used his EncryptionLok-3 on the first call, and he's using it right now. NSA got a GPS fix on his location. Copy down these coordinates. . . ."

Komulakov said, "Got it. I'll call you back." Komulakov wrote down the numbers of Newman's location. The general went to the map and yelled for Radchenko. The younger intelligence officer came running.

"Get on the phone to Grankin. Tell him to alert the Syrians that the terrorist Duncan is at the following location right now and that the UN has reason to believe he may be planning to blow up the hydroelectric dam at the south end of Lake Assad. Dotensk, use your best Arabic to wake up the pilots and tell our little group to get ready to go hunting."

The men hurriedly opened the hangar doors and began pushing the helicopters out onto the tarmac. Komulakov turned to Dotensk and said, "You wait here. Stay by that phone. I'll call you if I need anything."

The general hurried outside to join the others, who were already boarding. The helicopters lifted into the night sky. It was just a few minutes after 1:00 A.M.

Once in the air, Komulakov stood up and, in rusty Arabic, told the pilot where they were going—almost three hundred miles northeast—to the town of Dablan on the Euphrates River, where Newman had been on the phone using his EncryptionLok-3, just moments earlier. As the two helicopters raced toward the location, Radchenko leaned over and shouted in Komulakov's ear: "If Grankin followed orders, the Syrian Army unit at Dayr Az Zawr will get there well ahead of us. We're going to have to stop and re-fuel at Palmyra, but we should get to Dablan well before dawn." Komulakov looked at the map. Depending on the state of the road, he estimated that the Syrian Army units should beat them to Dablan by several hours. He only hoped that their quarry wouldn't elude them yet again.

○

Shortly before dawn, when the two Russian-built helicopters settled down on the dusty soccer field just outside the riverfront town of Dablan, there was a Syrian Army command vehicle waiting for them. Komulakov and Radchenko got in and went into the little village where they were met by the colonel who commanded the garrison, up the river at Dayr Az Zawr.

He saluted and said to the two Russians, "I regret that the terrorist Duncan and his accomplice have gotten away."

"Accomplice? What accomplice?" asked Komulakov in his heavily accented Syrian Arabic.

"He and another man fled as our Interior Ministry Militia approached. All they left behind were these, and this." The colonel held up the pus-covered bandages that had covered Newman's burns and the semi-melted remnants of some kind of electronic device.

Komulakov, the only one there who had ever seen one before, recognized it as an EncryptionLok-3. "Thank you, Colonel. Apparently one of them has been hurt," he said, pointing to the bandages. "And this," the Russian said, picking up the destroyed EncryptionLok-3, "this appears to be one of his bomb devices. I need to take this with me to see if it matches the parts we found in the destroyed MD-80. And, I'll be glad to have some DNA tests performed on those bandages if you'll let me have them."

The Syrian Army colonel then said, "The Interior Ministry officers don't even know what direction they went. They were in that hotel," he said, pointing across the dusty street. "Apparently the officers used their sirens when they approached and alerted them."

"Don't worry, Colonel, we know where he's gone. He's headed for Lake Assad, probably to blow up the hydroelectric dam," said Komulakov.

The Syrian's eyes widened. "In the name of Allah—how do you know?"

"Never mind that. But you have a chance to stop him," added Komulakov. "May I suggest, Colonel, that you take your men to the dam and make certain that it is safe and fully protected from any outside interference or attack? After the sun comes up, I'll take my UN counterterrorist unit aboard the helicopters to patrol the river north of here. I'm absolutely certain that he will stay on this river."

"It is a good plan," the Syrian colonel replied. He was going to order the UN force to stay away from the dam because he wanted to personally insure its ongoing safety, and their presence would be a complicating factor. "My men will guard the dam, and if we find him first, you may not have anything to do," he told Komulakov.

Komulakov said, "I know this man. His path has been very predictable. He plans to go to Birecik and try to get to Incirlik from there. This man Duncan is smart. He will likely travel on the river only at night, when it will be hardest for us to locate him. But by this time tomorrow evening, I shall be toasting you over his corpse. He will not outsmart me this time."

Euphrates River
12 km SE Dayr Az Zawr, Syria
Thursday, 9 March 1995
0545 Hours, Local

It was still dark but the dawn was overtaking the underpowered outboard. Newman and Samir had escaped capture at the hotel in Dablan, but barely. At about 4:00 A.M., just north of Bushayrah, they had run out of gas, and began to drift silently back down the river. The two men rowed feverishly toward the shore, and Samir went to see what he could scrounge up in the way of some petrol.

Newman waited with the boat for twenty minutes, until Samir returned with his prize. He had bargained with a fisherman for two plastic milk bottles filled with fuel, and before long, the boat was under way once again.

They had maneuvered the river, its currents, and shallow sandbars fairly well, despite the darkness. Only once did the boat get stuck in the muddy flats where the river became so shallow that the two men had to get out and pull it through what turned out to be knee-deep water. Finally the river got deeper, but was thick with reeds. The propeller kept getting tangled in them, and they had to stop frequently. Eventually, by towing the boat through the shallower water, and by rowing it in the deeper stretches, they finally got past the reeds.

All of this ate up precious time, however. Samir had said that there was an Army garrison at Dayr Az Zawr. They didn't want to transit that stretch of water in daylight and they knew that they would soon have to conceal themselves from police and military units using the highway that ran parallel to the river.

Here the Euphrates became much narrower: a twisted

sluggish stripe through the desert, snaking through the geography of the area and, turning back on itself several times each mile. For the two fugitives, this was also the most dangerous place on the river because it was impossible to see much more than a kilometer ahead—everything always seemed hidden behind the next curve.

Samir sat by the outboard motor and steered the small boat from one side of the river to the other, trying to enhance their view of what lay ahead. At the same time, he was praying aloud in Arabic. Newman couldn't understand him but figured the man's piety couldn't hurt.

As the boat rounded a wide curve, the sun burst over the horizon on their right like a searchlight shining across the Euphrates valley. They could now only hope that someone looking for them would be unable to distinguish them from the dozens of other small craft on the water. Newman squinted in the morning light as the sun's rays illuminated a rise about two kilometers ahead. He could make out a town at the west edge of the river, and just south of the town a number of trucks were lined up alongside the riverbank. Newman could also make out the figures of men standing, and walking around, by the trucks.

When they were less than half a kilometer away, Newman's blood ran cold. The trucks that he had seen were Army trucks, and the men were soldiers. He motioned to Samir to slow the boat so they could assess their next action. Two boats that had been a little way ahead of them going up the river were being hailed over by soldiers who had commandeered four larger boats. It appeared that the Syrian Army was stopping all river traffic going north.

Samir stopped the boat in the middle of the river as

they tried to gauge whether they should go forward or not. Newman shook his head. "These guys know what they're doing. They've got one part of their force on the highway with machine guns facing the river . . . and some of their men on the river checking the boats to see who's in them. We can't go ahead. We've got to turn around."

Samir made a wide turn and headed back downstream, increasing their speed as they went. Someone on the riverbank saw them and fired his rifle at them. Then another did the same. The machine gunner next began firing.

They got as low in the boat as they could. Samir tried to maintain speed, peeking occasionally over the low gunwale at the riverbank to their right. As the Syrian troops found their range, bullets began striking the water and snapping over their heads.

One of the Syrian soldiers must have had something more accurate than the standard Soviet-bloc AK-47, because bullets—big ones it seemed to Newman—began striking the boat, not in bursts, but one at a time. Water began to fill the boat. Newman grabbed one of the empty plastic gasoline bottles, cut it in two with the survival knife, and began to bail—even as the boat started to settle deeper in the river.

The firing continued until they maneuvered around a bend in the river. When they were once again obscured by the riverbank, Newman called out to Samir, "Steer for the east side of the river. Their trucks and troops are all on the west side of the river. There are no soldiers on the east side. If we can make it across before this boat sinks, we can make a run for it in the underbrush over there."

Samir did his best, but they sank about fifteen feet

from shore. The two men jumped into the water and half-swam, half-scrambled to the water's edge, then ran up the muddy slope and into the heavy underbrush.

Samir started to head south, but Newman stopped him. "They'll expect us to go south. They'll be looking for the boat until they get the bright idea that it must have sunk, then they'll start combing both sides of the river—hopefully from here south." Samir nodded his assent, too out of breath to speak.

They had lost almost all of their supplies and what little equipment they'd had when the boat sank, but Newman had managed to save the old *National Geographic* map. He stopped beneath the shade of a tree, opened the well-worn page, and pointed to a bridge just north of the garrison at Dayr Az Zawr. "Samir, is this bridge still here?"

The younger man looked at where Newman was pointing on the map and said, "Yes, it is a railroad bridge. It also has a pipeline beside the tracks across the Euphrates. I have never seen it guarded before, but then I have never seen river roadblocks before either."

"Well, let's hurry and see if we can cross there. They won't expect us to come back to their side of the river," said Newman, already starting a dogtrot.

They had gone less than a kilometer when Samir signaled a stop. He was out of breath and panting heavily.

Newman slowed down and plopped himself in the shade of a scrubby pine. Samir fell to the ground, exhausted from the run, gasping for breath. They both lay there for at least five minutes before Newman stuck his head up just enough to look across the river at where the soldiers were positioned. His hunch had been right; they were sending several truckloads of soldiers south from the checkpoint down the highway that paralleled the river on the west side. The trucks drove slowly, with soldiers standing in the back, their rifles pointed toward the river, looking for the boat that had fled. But when the trucks were about two kilometers downstream, the soldiers must have realized that the boat could not possibly have gotten that far and they stopped.

. Though they were too far away to make out the shouted commands, Newman and Samir watched as officers ordered the men out of the trucks. The desert khaki-clad Syrian soldiers dismounted and began to walk back north along the riverbank, sticking their bayonets into every thicket. Then, as the two fugitives watched from across the muddy watercourse, a third truck came south from the checkpoint. It halted where the other two had disgorged the troops, but this one didn't have soldiers aboard.

Newman and Samir watched as the soldiers unloaded a large rowboat. Again, the indistinct sound of shouted orders, and a squad of soldiers boarded the boat and started to row across the water to the eastern side of the river, just a few hundred meters downstream from where the two men were hiding.

"If they walk north when they get to this side, they'll find us in ten or fifteen minutes," Newman told Samir. "We need to get to that railroad bridge across the river. If we can get across the bridge and into Dayr Az Zawr, we'll stand a lot better chance than here by ourselves."

"With God's help, I am ready," Samir told him.

The two men climbed up from the riverbank onto the well-worn footpath between the water and the macadam highway that ran parallel to the river's eastern shore. There was no traffic on the road, and as they walked and ran north, they confronted only a few other locals, who paid them little heed, despite their now filthy garments.

Newman estimated that they had at most a ten-minute head start on the soldiers before they discovered their foundered dhow. The officers would take a few minutes to find their muddy footprints on the riverbank and figure out which way he and Samir had gone before they continued their pursuit. By now the sun was fully up, and the heat was bearing down. Samir kept up fairly well, but was gasping again by the time they had reached the brush along the eastern side of the railroad bridge.

As they crouched in the small copse of trees, they could hear a roaring sound coming from the river to the south. Newman looked out from their concealment and saw two MI-8 helicopters coming slowly up the river, one helicopter flying over the water along the right side shoreline and the other along the left. As Newman watched, the helicopter on their side of the Euphrates went into a hover, and he could see an arm extending from the troop door pointing down toward the water. Someone aboard had spotted their sunken dhow and was trying to signal the Syrian soldiers along the shore or in the boat.

"Quickly, Samir, we must hide before they get here!" said Newman as he scrambled up the embankment and toward an animal pen and shed not far from the tracks. Samir, barely recovered from their last run, sprinted after the Marine, and they bolted into the abandoned shed about ten feet from the tracks running across the bridge into Dayr Az Zawr. The rusted rails of a siding served by the switch just outside the building ran off to the east, parallel to the main tracks for about one hundred meters or so.

"There is nowhere to hide in here," said Samir.

The livestock shed was about fifty feet long and ten

feet wide. As the sound of the helicopters grew louder, Newman noticed a small office in one corner of the shed. As one of the MI-8s approached the shed from the river, they ran into the little office. It was empty except for an old train schedule tacked to the wall, a few loose papers on a heavy old wooden desk, and a dented metal trashcan on the floor. The two windows facing the tracks were cracked and caked with grime.

The helicopter was directly overhead. Roaring engines and the downwash of its rotor made speech impossible. The air inside the enclosed space was filled with dust and dirt that poured in through cracks in the walls. Samir motioned to Newman to push the battered desk up against the door.

They had just completed the task when the building stopped vibrating from the wind created by the rotors, and the screaming engines of the helicopter dropped to a low whine as the MI-8 landed in a cloud of dust in the corral.

Inside the office, Newman motioned, and both men sat on the floor with their backs to the wall and their feet braced against the desk. Suddenly outside the office, where they had both been just seconds before, they could hear the sound of men moving about, the occasional clink of what Newman knew was a weapon. And then, over the sound of the engine, they could hear voices, speaking in Arabic.

Samir whispered, "Palestinians." But before Newman could respond, the doorknob rattled as someone outside tried to open the door. When it didn't budge, the person trying to get in put a shoulder to the ancient wood and tried to force it open. As the battering continued, Newman and Samir pushed hard with their feet against the old desk and hoped that whoever it was would think that the door was locked, and that he wouldn't just start shooting. If that happened, the bullets would blow right through the wooden wall in front of them and the old desk wouldn't offer much protection.

Then, someone outside shouted in Arabic and the battering stopped. Newman and Samir could hear footsteps on the flooring outside and then a shadow filled the window over their heads, above where they were sitting on the floor.

Again, another voice, this time from farther away, also in Arabic, but with an accent. Newman thought it was Russian but couldn't be sure. The shadow disappeared. There were a few seconds of silence and then the pitch of the engine's whine increased, the roar resumed, and they could feel the building shake again as the MI-8 took off and flew back to the west, toward the river.

The two men, bathed in sweat and covered with dust, didn't move for a full minute after the helicopter left. Then, their legs shaking, they very quietly got back up off the floor, listened again for any sounds and finally, when they were absolutely certain that no one had been left behind for ambush, moved the desk away from the door, and slowly opened it. The other part of the shed and the corral were empty. But only after creeping outside did they breathe a sigh of relief.

"Come on, before they come back, we have got to get across that bridge and into the town," said Newman to Samir. The younger man could only nod his assent.

Much to their surprise, as they approached the bridge, there was a virtual traffic jam. To Newman it was as though the helicopters had awakened the neighborhood, and now the railroad bridge had become a pedestrian thoroughfare across the Euphrates. Even though there was no footpath on the bridge, the locals were using the rail bed and pipeline supports as a way to transit the river.

Samir and the Marine fell in, about twenty meters behind a family of five, and walked with them across the Euphrates as though they had made the same trek a thousand times. As they made their way from one railroad tie to another Newman asked, "Where do these tracks go?"

"They are for the Taurus Express. You may remember it when it was named 'The Orient Express,' and it used to go from Aleppo to Baghdad. But east of here, across the border with Iraq, much of the track was destroyed in the Gulf War, and Saddam has been slow to rebuild. Syria has kept up the tracks, as you can see, and there is a train that runs from Dayr Az Zawr to Aleppo," Samir explained.

"Does the train stop here to pick up passengers?"

"Yes, my father and I have taken it many times. The station is just over there"—Samir pointed ahead, in the direction they were walking—"just outside the town."

"If I take this train to— What is it? Aleppo? How far is that from the Turkish border?" Newman asked.

Samir said, "Not far. But let's look at the map." As the two men walked side by side, he showed the Marine, whispering so that passersby would not hear them speaking English. "If you take this train to Aleppo, you can take another train to Turkey. That train stops at El-beyli on the other side of the border and then heads through the mountains to Iskenderun, then goes up the coast to Adana, then—"

"Did you say Iskenderun?" Newman asked.

"Yes, you would have to change trains in Aleppo, but the second stop in Turkey is Iskenderun."

"Perfect. My bet is that they think I want to get to Incirlik—you call it Adana—by following the Euphrates all the way. I'll let them think that's where I'm headed, but if you can help me get on that train to Iskenderun, that's a much better way to go."

"Yes, I can do that. The route up the river is winding and treacherous. And, as we have learned, now they have helicopters. But the railroad can be dangerous too. They may have police or soldiers inspecting the trains," Samir whispered.

Newman said, "Samir . . . I think you've done more than you should already, both you and your father. Last night in Dablan, I was so engrossed in my phone calls back to the States that I didn't even hear the sirens coming. If it weren't for you I could never have gotten out of there safely. I can't put you in jeopardy anymore. If you can get me on the next train to Aleppo, I'll take it from there. I don't want to take any more chances of getting you hurt or in serious trouble with the government. Here is where we must part company, my friend."

Samir did not reply, but seemed deep in thought. Actually, he was praying about what God would have him to do. The two men pulled their dirty thobes up to make themselves a bit more presentable and let their gutras hang down across their shoulders to cover more of their faces. They followed the railroad tracks to the train station.

As they approached the station, Samir said, "I am very thirsty, and we have not eaten in almost twenty-four hours. Do you mind if we find a tea stall so that we can get some nourishment before going on?"

Newman was feeling parched as well. Their water and food had gone down with their little boat. They found a small eating place close to the train station and filled their stomachs with some bread, cheese, and roasted lamb. A nearby vendor was selling cans of soda;

Samir purchased one for Newman and he drank it as the locals did—warm. He would have preferred plain water, but the contents of the can were probably safer. Seventeen years in the Marines had taught him that bacteria could be as deadly as bullets.

After they ate, they walked over to the rundown train station, a stucco structure that looked like a smaller, less well-maintained version of the ones he had seen in the French countryside years ago. It had a few benches in the waiting room, with a few more outside along the walls. For such a small town, there were quite a few passengers waiting for the train. Samir went in, and when he came back out a few moments later said, "The next train to Aleppo is at noon—more than two hours from now. Of course, it is liable to be late."

Newman and Samir kept walking. There was a Syrian Interior Ministry soldier pacing back and forth outside the station, every now and then looking at the new people who arrived and occasionally asking them for identification. Newman did not want to have to answer any of his questions.

They walked around the corner, just out of his range of vision, and began to strategize on how to get the train ticket. Samir cautioned him, "I can buy the ticket for you here, but I fear for your safety when you get to Aleppo because you will have to buy another ticket, from Aleppo to Elbeyli on the border. And from there you will have to buy yet another ticket to Iskenderun. I do not know how you will do this without getting caught."

"Well . . . we'll just take one step at a time," Newman said.

South End of Bahr Assad
Tabaqah Air Base, Syria
Thursday, 9 March 1995
1130 Hours, Local

While Newman and Samir were quenching their thirst and avoiding the Syrian Interior Ministry police in Dayr Az Zawr, General Komulakov and most of his combined force of retired KGB Department V thugs and PFLP terrorists were enjoying the relative luxury of a Syrian Air Force hangar at the military installation protecting the hydroelectric dam at the south end of nearby Lake Assad. But the Russian general wasn't happy.

He knew that they had come very close to catching the American who could undo him. Earlier in the morning they had spotted the fugitives' sunken boat, and a search of the items left aboard the dhow by Newman and his accomplice had confirmed that the missing Marine had been there. The Syrians had found a USAF survival pistol, a signal flare, a strobe light, a signal mirror, and a first-aid kit. The fugitives had left their food and water behind.

"I'm telling you, Radchenko, we wasted too much time at that filthy camel loading station or whatever it was back there by the railroad tracks across the river from Dayr Az Zawr. Any fool could tell they weren't out there. The place was locked—they couldn't have gone inside without breaking down the door or a window. No . . . he's found another boat on the top side of the dam, and he's going north, up the Euphrates."

"Yes, General," the Russian SVR Major replied. "I have positioned two of the PFLP teams on top of the dam as you directed. The reaction force here with the helicopters will swoop down on the terrorists as soon as either ambush team spots them. It is a brilliant plan."

"Radchenko, don't play the sycophant with me. I've known you too long. Did you contact Dotensk, back in Damascus?"

"Yes, General, he is coming here with your UN aircraft and your two aides."

Not much later they heard the sound of a jet aircraft approaching the remote air base. It was Komulakov's UN Gulfstream. The two men watched as the plane touched down and taxied toward the hangar where they stood.

The engines were still turning when the passenger door opened, and Dotensk bounded down the built-in stairs. He rushed over to Komulakov.

"Grankin has been busy. He came to my hotel room this morning to tell me that he received a secure call from Washington Residency. Apparently the intercept site at the embassy overheard a non-secure call from the National Security Advisor to the Pentagon last night, trying to get them to stop some Marine general from flying to Turkey. The resident doesn't know if the general's trip has to do with Saddam's military move against the Iraqi National Congress or your trip, but Grankin wanted you to know."

"Hmm," said Komulakov, thinking. "I think I had better make a few calls."

Komulakov went into the hangar to the table where his maps were spread out and after connecting the small TV remote-sized device, picked up the handset on his satellite telephone. The Russian checked his Rolex watch—almost 0200 in Washington. He dialed the number anyway, and when the phone picked up on the other end after eight rings, he said, "Go EL-3 secure— India, November, Yankee, Seven, Niner, Four."

When he heard the electronic handshake, he continued. "Simon, what's the latest?"

"A Marine general named Grisham left here yesterday evening, headed your way. He's supposedly going to Turkey to check on NATO contingency plans for dealing with Saddam's effort to crush the rebellion in northern Iraq, but I think that's one of the other calls Newman made from Iraq after he called me. I think the general knows Newman is alive and is coming to get him."

"And why do you think that, Simon?" Komulakov tried to sound calm.

"Because he took Newman's wife with him."

"How do you know that?" asked the Russian.

"Because I checked with the White House Military Office liaison at Andrews Air Force Base. He checked the manifest for the general's flight. And what's more, the general's plane isn't flying direct to Incirlik, where the NATO planners are meeting."

"Where is it heading?" asked Komulakov.

"They filed a revised flight plan once they were airborne. The aircraft is headed for the British base at Larnaca, Cyprus."

"And you are sure that Newman's wife is with this Marine general?"

"Yes," responded Harrod. "The Air Force has no reason to lie about such a trivial thing."

"Well, then I must go there. When I find Newman's wife, I'll find Newman. He'll be headed for her. I'll call you back when I get there, Simon."

Komulakov terminated the call and summoned Radchenko. "Get the best four PFLP men you have, and get aboard the UN jet. I want you and them to come with me to Cyprus. I'll leave Dotensk in charge here with a satellite phone."

A few moments later, while Komulakov was briefing Dotensk on the change in plans, Major Kaartje came running up.

"General, there are Palestinians boarding the aircraft with weapons," the Dutch military aide said breathlessly.

"Yes, I know," replied Komulakov, irate at the interruption. "We're taking the aircraft to another location in an effort to deal with this international terrorist, Duncan."

"Sir, I must report this back to the Secretariat. This is a neutral aircraft and cannot be used to transport combatants. We're supposed to be on a diplomatic mission," the Dutch Army captain said.

"Ah, you are so correct, Major Kaartje," said Komulakov. He swallowed the rebuke that was on the tip of his tongue. He smiled at the Dutch aide. "Come, Major, let us confer with New York on my secure satellite phone. Excuse us, Mr. Dotensk."

He put his arm around the officer and led him outside the hangar and then around to the rear, facing the desert wasteland to the east

"You are a very bright young officer," Komulakov said. "Thank you for reminding me of my lapse in protocol." But as soon as they were out of sight behind the hangar, the general suddenly grabbed his junior officer by the head and jerked him with such ferocity that he snapped the man's neck, breaking the fifth vertebrae, which in turn severed the officer's spinal cord. The man fell dead at Komulakov's feet. The general dragged the body a few meters away and placed it facedown in front of a rock outcropping.

When he returned to the hangar, he said to Dotensk, "I am leaving for Cyprus. I'm taking Radchenko, the four PFLP he has selected, and Captain Sjogren with me. Continue the search of the river valley in case I am wrong. And after we are gone, take the body behind the hangar out into the desert to feed the vultures. Any questions?"

Dotensk shook his head.

Taurus Express Train Station
Dayr Az Zawr, Syria
Thursday, 9 March 1995
1145 Hours, Local

Newman feigned napping on some wooden crates in an alley near the train station while Samir went to buy his ticket. Samir was gone almost twenty minutes before returning. When he returned, he was smiling broadly. "I believe that God is watching over us," he said.

Newman raised his eyebrows.

He handed Newman a clean linen thobe and a brown wool mishlah. In the relative privacy of their hiding place, Samir helped Newman remove the filthy garment that he had swum ashore in earlier in the day and assisted the Marine in putting on the fresh gown. Then he showed the American how Arabic men wore the mishlah like a cloak in the cool night air. Finally, he pressed into Newman's hand a wad of currency, some Syrian and the rest Turkish. When Newman started to protest, the younger man simply waved a hand and shook his head.

"Now, do you see those two women and the two little girls over there, sitting on the bench?" Samir asked. "They are traveling to Elbeyli, Turkey too. I asked them if I could do them a favor and they could also do a favor for me. I said, 'Could my friend ride on the train with you as an escort, to fend off any troublemakers?' I told them that you were strong, but unable to speak—and that you were on your way to meet your family. I asked them, if, in exchange for being their escort, they could help you get the tickets you will need in Aleppo and El-beyli, since you could not read and write."

Newman smiled. "Well, my Arabic is pretty nonexistent, all right."

"They have agreed," Samir went on, "so I purchased a ticket for you and gave them money to buy your tickets in Aleppo for Elbeyli and Iskenderun. There was a fare chart posted on the wall, so I know how much it costs, but I added some to it, so they will feel like they are making something for their trouble.

"The older lady is the grandmother. The young mother is a widow, and those girls are her daughters. They are from the Christian community in Homs that Assad tried to obliterate years ago. Those who survived his purge and who did not flee Syria were sent to 'internal exile' out in the desert. They told me that they live not far from here and have just been given travel documents allowing them to visit their family in Turkey. They are going there for Passover and Easter, since they are Assyrian Christians and many of them celebrate both. When I showed them this, they gave their word that they will take good care of you," Samir said.

Newman looked down at Samir's open hand. He held a small metal fish, similar to the one Samir's father wore on a chain around his neck. But before the Marine could ask the significance of the little metal fish, the train sounded its whistle just outside the city. Newman looked to the east and saw it heading toward them on the bridge they had crossed earlier that morning. It was slowing to come into the station.

"It will stop only long enough to take on passengers. If you were thinking of waiting until all others boarded, you might miss the train," Samir said. "Please come and meet your new companions so you can all board together. That will make it less likely that the soldier will question you."

"But anyone who looks at me will see that I am not an Arab," Newman protested.

Samir shook his head. "God will show them what He wants them to see," he said simply. "Besides, the sun and burns have browned your face, and you have a good start on a heavy beard. Just keep your *gutra* loose around your face so that your blue eyes do not show. I will pray that God will keep those who are looking for you from seeing you.

"I will also hold you in my prayers every day from now until we meet again. My father and mother and the rest of my family will do the same. Have faith, Peter Newman. God answers prayers. Not always the way we think they should be answered—but He always answers. Now you must go."

Samir embraced Newman—with whom he'd had so many close calls in just two days. Simply because his father had asked him to, he had risked his life and possibly the lives of his wife and children, to—as Habib had said—obey God.

"I can't possibly thank you enough," Newman said. "I'd take your name and address so I can get in touch with you when I get home, but I'm afraid that if I'm caught, I wouldn't want to have that information on me. It would be too dangerous for you."

"Don't worry, Peter. We will see each other again. I

know it." Samir walked with Newman to where the women and girls were waiting. By now the train had pulled up beside the station, and passengers were boarding. Samir gave last-minute instructions to the women, and the five of them got on the train. No one seemed to notice that Newman's features were more Anglo-Saxon than Semite. Newman smiled and nodded at the women and helped them up the stairway into the coach. Then he lifted the two girls—about seven and ten, he estimated.

Newman watched as Samir turned and walked away, toward the center of town, where he could make a telephone call to his father to come and get him. As Samir disappeared behind a building, out of Newman's sight, the tough Marine felt a catch in his throat and knew that this loving, trusting man really was going to pray for him. He was overwhelmed.

Newman followed the women through the corridor of the railway coach. They had third-class tickets, and the coaches to which they were assigned were old and smelled of sweat, mildew, and animals. He followed them into a compartment where they could all sit together. The women sat on one side and he sat with the girls on the other side. He lifted the smaller girl onto his lap so she could see outside, just as the conductor was coming through to take their tickets. Newman took the tickets from the hands of the girls, put them with his own, then handed them to the grandmother. She held them with the others, outstretched for the conductor. Newman managed to keep looking outside, pointing to some camels for the girl to see. She began talking in her own language, excitedly, and he pretended interest and excitement, but without words.

With practiced boredom, the blue-uniformed conductor took the tickets from the grandmother, tore them in half, used an ancient hand punch to punch a square hole through all five stubs, and handed the punched paper sheets back to the oldest child. The blue uniform then moved off down the corridor beside the compartments, through the coach, and into the next one. *One hurdle passed,* Newman thought.

The train was moving fast on its way to Aleppo. Samir had told him that the trip to Aleppo, including stops, would take four hours and that they would have a one-hour layover in Aleppo for the train change to El-beyli, Turkey. Newman hoped that the train was able to stay on schedule. Samir had told him that there was a midnight train from Elbeyli to Iskenderun. *If all goes well, I'll be in Iskenderun by two o'clock in the morning,* thought Newman as the stark, barren desert flashed by outside their open window.

The little girl had relaxed and sat back in Newman's lap; she soon fell asleep. Her mother looked over and gestured as if to say, "Shall I take her from you?"

Newman smiled and shook his head. He sat back, cradled the girl against his chest, and rested his head against the window jamb, pretending to be asleep himself. Soon pretense gave way to reality, and he was sound asleep.

He didn't even wake up when the train stopped at As Salhabiyah, just east of the great Assad hydroelectric dam, and more passengers got aboard. Two heavily-armed militiamen boarded and moved from car to car, searching for a fugitive terrorist. With their weapons in front of them, and their fingers beside their triggers, they started at the front of each coach and began inspecting the papers of each traveler. In some cases, they even stopped to ask a series of questions: "Where are you going? Where do you live? What is your father's name?" And they asked, "Have you seen this man?" One of the armed men held out a copy of a poster describing the crime committed by Gilbert Duncan. In the center of the sheet was a picture of Peter Newman. No one questioned had seen the beardless man in the picture.

The train engineer blew two short blasts of the horn just as the soldiers reached the seats of Newman and his companions. One soldier reached for the identity papers from the grandmother. The soldier asked her where she was going and if they were all traveling together. She answered that they were going to Aleppo, and the soldiers seemed content with her answer. They joked about her daughter's husband, sound asleep with their little girl on his lap. There were several more passengers to check, and the two soldiers moved on as the train whistle sounded again—this time a longer, single blast: the signal that the train was about to depart.

The sound startled Newman, who woke up. He heard two men talking in the corridor outside the compartment, their tone officious. Newman resumed his sleeping pose. In another moment, the soldiers exited the rear of the coach and joined other soldiers standing on the wooden platform of the train station. Then Newman heard someone on the platform blow a whistle, and the train began to slowly move forward.

He decided that he would not fall asleep again, no matter how tired he was. He also hoped that the station in Aleppo would not have troops checking the train's departing passengers.

None of them noticed the large, heavyset man in European clothing who had boarded the train at As Salhabiyah.

CHAPTER TWENTY
The Goode Messenger

Aboard the *Pescador*
Eastern Mediterranean Sea
30 Nm NE of Cape Andreas
Thursday, 9 March 1995
1230 Hours, Local

The big blue hull cut like a knife through the gentle swells. With both the mainsail and the jib perfectly trimmed on the slightly raked seventy-two-foot mast, the twenty-knot wind out of the north-northwest had the sixty-two-foot-long sloop just slightly heeled to starboard. The white-haired, deeply tanned man at the helm checked his gauges and instruments and estimated. *If this wind holds all the way, I may make it to Iskenderun before 1800 hours.*

He scanned the horizon, checked his GPS, and put a tic mark on the chart with a notation, "1230," in pencil, verified that the Northstar Auto-helm was engaged, and after scanning the horizon one more time, got up and went below.

Standing at the chart table in the navigation cabin of the vessel, he again picked up the hard copies of the e-mails he had started receiving shortly after midnight, just a little over twelve hours ago.

The first contact had been through an e-mail message from Oliver North while the vessel had been at its berth, tied at pier 3 of the Royal Navy facility in Larnaca Bay, Cyprus. When North's e-mail had arrived with its "Urgent" heading, it had made the laptop computer on the chart table emit a series of electronic chirps until the light came on in the cabin and the "Read Mail" icon had been clicked. North's electronic communiqué had asked the sixty-four-year-old captain of the sloop to call another old and mutual friend, Lieutenant General George Grisham—and provided a number.

The satellite phone call to General Grisham had produced more e-mails and a request that he contact Brigadier General James Harris at the NATO Air Base at Incirlik, Turkey. Harris had then sent three e-mails of his own to the laptop in the sloop.

All these electronic exchanges in the middle of the night had prompted the captain to don his foul weather gear, climb up on deck, and commence preparations for getting under way. First he started the engine and when the big diesel began to idle smoothly in its compartment, he had jumped onto the pier, disconnected the shore power that charged the boat's batteries, untied the spring lines, then the fore deck line and finally the stern line, tossing each aboard the boat as he did so. Then, belying his sixty-four years, he had given the transom of the fifty-thousand-pound boat a healthy shove to push the stern of the vessel away from the pier. Then he jumped aboard like someone more athletic and fifteen or more years younger.

Back in the cockpit he had turned the helm hard to port, put the transmission into "Reverse" and slowly eased the throttle up until the boat's single large brass screw bit into the water and backed the big sloop away from the pier. Once he was clear of the pilings, the man at the helm throttled down, pushed the transmission lever forward to "Neutral" and then to "Forward." He again eased the throttle forward, straightened the rudder and the engine quietly pushed the vessel out into the darkened harbor. From his station at the helm he turned on the radar, his running lights, depth gauge, GPS, knot meter, auto-pilot and the wind-measuring instruments mounted high on the mast above his head. Then, as he headed for the breakwater at the entrance of the harbor, he picked up the handset of the ship-to-shore radio, pressed the "Transmit" button and once the harbormaster responded, said simply, "Sailing vessel *Pescador* departing Larnaca en route to Iskenderun, Turkey; Echo Tango Alpha, nineteen hundred hours, today, over."

The harbormaster acknowledged the message and Goode replaced the radio handset.

He had motored for less than an hour and a half until he cleared Cape Greco and then, after testing the wind speed and direction, he had decided to set the sails. He came up momentarily into the wind and pushed the buttons for the roller-reefed main and jib, then, as they deployed, he turned back to the right and let them fill. With the bow of the *Pescador* pointed for the mouth of Iskenderun bay on a heading of 040 degrees, he had expertly trimmed the sails, set the auto-helm, gone forward and stowed his dock lines, and gone below to make a pot of coffee.

Now, standing in front of the chart table, the sun was directly overhead and he was halfway to Iskenderun, making eleven knots under full sail with the engine adding a bit of a boost to what the breeze offered.

Goode once more read the e-mailed requests he had received from North and the two generals before leaving Larnaca. His dark brown eyes scanned the documents in front of him. Several of them he shuffled, comparing one message with another.

Grisham's first e-mail was very straightforward: a Marine officer named Newman was in serious trouble and trying to escape from Iraq through Syria. An Air Force general named Harris at the NATO Air Command at Incirlik had details and was expecting to hear from the captain of the *Pescador*.

General Harris had filled in the details of how Newman's UN mission had gone awry, about the Interpol poster with Newman's face and the name "Gilbert Duncan." A later e-mail from Harris had instructed Newman to proceed to the 25 Piers area in Iskenderun rather than take the risk of being apprehended as Duncan by Turkish authorities while trying to make it back to Incirlik.

Subsequent messages from General Grisham spelled out the Marine general's flight plan—and intention to be at the British base in Larnaca when the *Pescador* returned from Iskenderun—hopefully with Newman aboard. General Harris had provided the details of what he had told Newman in his last EncryptionLok-3 phone call about meeting his rescuers at the pier number that corresponded to the day of the month. And a final e-mail from Grisham before he took off from Andrews AFB had provided a satellite phone number for contact, and the advisory that he was bringing Newman's wife with him. What none of the messages could tell him was the answer to the uncertainty that nagged him now: who sabotaged this mission?

The white-haired captain of the *Pescador* had spent most of his adult life answering for others the question: "Who is the enemy?" And once again, as had happened to him back in 1986, he did not know the answer—and neither did the people with whom he was working now.

He gathered up the printed copies of the e-mails, and after assuring himself he had memorized all the important details, phone numbers, and e-mail addresses, he began running them one at a time through the small shredder beneath the chart table. When he reached the one on the bottom, the first message he had received, he looked at it, shook his head, and smiled. It was addressed very simply:

FROM: NARNIA FARM, OLIVER L. NORTH, LTCOL USMC (RET)
TO: SAILING VESSEL PESCADOR FOR WILLIAM P. GOODE

Taurus Express Station
Aleppo, Syria
Thursday, 9 March 1995
1600 Hours, Local

As the train pulled into the Aleppo station, Newman was relieved to realize it was exactly on time. The next moments would be critical. The little girls had napped most of the way, but for the past half hour, they had been playing with a couple of tiny dolls and talking softly with each other as they sat, polite and well-behaved, beside him.

When the train stopped, the women reached for their belongings and stood up to get off the coach. Newman picked up the smaller girl and carried her off the train, holding the hand of the other little girl and helping her down the steep stairs. The two women trailed behind, but they all stayed in a cluster and looked like a typical Middle Eastern family—at least Newman hoped so.

He saw the soldiers when he stepped off the train. There were several of them. This time they were only stopping people at random; some were questioned, and others were being shown the poster with his photograph prominently positioned in the middle. The two women separated and took up positions on either side of him. The mother took the other hand of her daughter, and they all crowded close together. They passed the first soldiers without receiving so much as a glance. Several other Syrian soldiers manned a second checkpoint, at the platform entrance. One looked directly at Newman, and smiled when the little girl in Newman's arms waved at him. Newman and his "family" went inside the train station, and the grandmother pointed to a nearby bench. They sat in the large waiting room while the older woman purchased their five tickets to Elbeyli and Newman's single ticket to Iskenderun. When she came back she handed them out with a smile.

Newman looked at the clock on the wall and then at the ticket. They had only an hour to wait for the train to Elbeyli. He fervently hoped that there would be no more questions or paperwork inspections from the Syrian authorities while they waited.

At one point, about ten minutes before their train was due, a Syrian railway policeman came into the crowded waiting room and began to eyeball the waiting passengers. The young mother of the girls, realizing that their inactivity was inviting scrutiny, opened up a tourist brochure for Aleppo, the second largest city in Syria and one of the most ancient cities in the world. She began using the pictures in the brochure to explain to her daughters the history of the region. Newman and the grandmother feigned interest in the presentation, and the policeman's gaze roved elsewhere.

Once he walked away, the young mother leaned back and let out a deep sigh. It was then that Newman realized what a great risk they were taking for him. By now, having seen the posters at every stop, they had to know that they were in the company of the man being sought by the authorities. Yet simply because Samir had shown them a little metal fish and asked for their help, they were placing themselves in jeopardy to help him.

He heard the whistle as the Elbeyli train approached. A wave of passengers pressed toward the door to the platform. Despite the efforts of the soldiers and railway police to inspect every person crowding out onto the platform, it was impossible, and Newman passed through the portal, bending over, pretending to smooth the collar of the older girl's blouse, his face obscured by the gutra draped over his shoulders.

They boarded the train and stayed in the middle of the crowd until they once again found a compartment to themselves. And again, when the conductor came to collect tickets, Newman was "asleep" with the little girl dozing on his lap.

Everything worked as it had before, and the little "family" avoided attracting the interest of any of the Syrian authorities aboard the swaying train as it made its way north to the frontier. None of them had taken note of the large, European-dressed man who had entered the station waiting area just prior to the arrival of the train and who had passed by their compartment.

As the sun was setting, Newman noticed that the train had slowed and he watched out the window as it pulled into the station at Elbeyli, Turkey. Once again the women gathered up their belongings and, as they had before, formed a phalanx around Newman and the girls. But this time there was a sign in Arabic, French, and English that said *CUSTOMS*. Newman's blood ran cold at being asked to produce documents. As he was looking warily about for a way out of the station without having to pass the booth where a dozen or more officials were checking identity papers and occasionally opening the migrants' bags, he noticed the same poster that had been so prominent on the Syrian side of the border. This poster, with his face above the name and the phrase "For Terrorism—Dead or Alive" in English, French, and Arabic, was hung on the wall opposite the customs inspectors.

As he stared into his own eyes in the poster, he felt a tug on the sleeve of his thobe. It was the young mother. She was holding up her Syrian passport, open to the first page. Inside was a picture, not just of her, but a family of four. In the photograph, her deceased husband sat beside the woman now holding the passport. In front were the two children—one of whom was now asleep on Newman's shoulder, while the other clung to his finger. Without attempting a word, the young mother looked from the photo to Newman and then nodded her head toward the customs queue. He understood immediately and seeing no alternative, proceeded toward the booth with his adopted "family."

When he had looked at the photo Newman realized that the deceased husband looked nothing like him, and the inspector would surely see that immediately. But for some reason, he recalled the words of Samir—"The guards will see what God wants them to see." Was it again time for him to have some faith?

The uniformed clerk took the grandmother's passport

and the one offered by the mother, and he opened them on the counter before him. He pored over them, flipping through the pages, looking for the appropriate exit stamps and visas. He flipped back to the front and looked at the pictures, then at the weary travelers in front of him, then back down at the documents.

Newman could feel the sweat running down his back as the uniformed man reached for something below the counter. Newman felt the muscles in his shoulders tensing for action. But then, with an officious flourish, the customs official took the hand stamp he had retrieved from under the counter and pounded it twice, once in each book, with the imprint of the Turkish government. He handed the documents back to the women.

By the time they exited the station and came out in the center of the little border town, it was dark. Newman walked with the women and the children for a block from the station, still carrying the youngest girl. As Newman put her down, he kissed his finger and tenderly placed it on her cheek. She giggled. He did the same for her older sister, who likewise giggled. The young mother reached out her hand to shake his. He took it and held it with both hands while he looked into her fatigued, attractive face. He tried to tell her with his eyes how grateful he was for their help. He did the same with the grandmother. The older woman nodded, bent down on one knee, and drew an outline of a fish in the dirt, then stood and pointed to Newman, then herself, and upward. She smiled broadly, then turned to lead her family up another street.

Newman watched them walk away—the girls looked back a couple times and waved—then he strolled toward what he thought was the business district of the little border town. As he walked he noticed that there were very few men wearing Arab garb on the streets. Nearly everyone wore Western-style dress. In a public rest room he disposed of the thobe, tagia, gutra, and igal he had been wearing since shortly after Habib rescued him in Iraq. Beneath the thobe he was wearing the brown cotton shirt and linen trousers Samir had bought for him back in Dayr Az Zawr. He wore sandals, and because the night was cool, he decided to keep the woolen mishlah to use it as a cloak. As he was changing, he heard the voices of two men entering the rest room. They were speaking a language Newman hadn't heard since parting company with Samir: English.

He let the two men exit in front of him and watched them walk up the street toward some lighted shops. He waited a few minutes and then went in after them. It was a restaurant, and there was a group of young people at a booth in the corner. One of them looked up, saw him, and waved him over.

"Are you an American?" one of the girls asked.

"Canadian," he replied.

"Come join us. We're going dancing later; you can come with us." The young blonde spoke English with a Nordic accent. She slid over and made room for him beside her in the booth.

Newman learned that they were part of an international student group that was studying ancient architecture. They were out for a "night on the town" before they took the morning train to Ankara and then to Constantinople. They had been here in the little town of Elbeyli for three days as they explored the ruins of old churches, castles, and forts in the area and they were ready to move on. Newman followed along as they barhopped from one establishment to another, drinking strong Turkish tea and an occasional beer when they could find it. But as the evening grew later, more and more of the restaurants closed. So the group decided that it was time to go dancing at the hotel where they were staying.

Newman walked with them. It was little more than a youth hostel as far as he could tell. Somehow, the students had convinced the management to let them haul the furniture from the courtyard and had brought the TV out of the common room to catch the music from American MTV, which the hostel was apparently pirating from the satellite. Someone else produced some beer. And thankfully for Newman, no one came around to bother him or the celebrants.

The Marine found a quiet corner as far away from the TV and dancers as possible. He sat back on what seemed to him to be something akin to a beanbag chair back home. There he kept out of sight until almost 11:30 P.M. when he quietly got up, slipped out the door, and walked up the street to catch the midnight train to Iskenderun.

Her Royal Majesty's Officers Guest House
U.K. Sovereign Base Area
Larnaca, Cyprus
Thursday, 9 March 1995
0015 Hours, Local

Even though she was familiar with the effects of "jet lag" from her years as a flight attendant, Rachel was exhausted. General Grisham's C-17 had flown straight through, thirteen hours from Andrews Air Force Base to the Royal Air Force facility at Akrotiri, on the western side of Cyprus. When they landed, one of the Air Force stewards had told them, "The local time is 1800." Rachel changed her watch to 6:00 P.M.

After a brief arrival greeting from a British admiral, General Grisham and his party of six, including Rachel, were loaded into two Suburbans. Two vans carried heavily armed men in front of and behind them and they drove seventy-five miles east to the British base at Larnaca. Rachel noticed all the security and the bullet-resistant glass in the windows of their car and asked why.

Grisham had replied, "Like so many other places in this part of the world, this beautiful little island is divided. In July 1974, Turkey invaded the island, ostensibly to protect indigenous Turks from the Greeks who have governed the island for centuries. Shooting started. The UN has a mandate to resolve the dispute—and they have hundreds of peacekeepers here. But like so much of what the UN does, it hasn't worked, and to this day the island is divided. Both sides still shoot at each other. All this extra protection is in case we get caught in the crossfire."

Rachel had been impressed with the answer. It was understandable, succinct, and spare. It was clear to Rachel that General Grisham didn't waste a lot of words. Yet, on the long flight here, he had been more than willing to talk to her and answer her every question.

In fact, she remembered that there was only one moment when she recalled him becoming just a bit impatient. One of his assistants had come into the VIP compartment and told him that he had a satellite phone call from Headquarters. The connection had been more than a little loud so Rachel couldn't help but hear both sides of the conversation:

The officer in Washington had said, "The National Security Council is making inquiries about your trip and wanted to know your itinerary. We haven't told 'em anything about your stop in Cyprus. But somehow the NSC is aware that you are at least stopping in the island. They now want to know when you'll be headed to Incirlik. What do you want us to tell them?"

Grisham responded, "Blast those people, who's asking—Harrod?"

"No, it was one of the hired help."

"Well . . . don't answer just yet," said the General. "If Harrod himself calls, tell him I'll call him back. Then contact me right away."

"Aye-aye, sir," said the voice coming from Washington. "Anything else?"

"You've had several telephone calls from a retired Army general. Says his name's General Bob Storey. Do you know him?"

"Name sounds vaguely familiar. Is he the guy that got that cushy job with that high-tech company in California? What's he want?"

"I don't know, sir. He wouldn't tell me. He just said that it was very important that he talk to you at your first opportunity."

"All right, I don't want to call him on this phone. Send me the number via secure e-mail at Larnaca and I'll call him when I get there. I'll call you after we arrive. Out here." And with that he hung up the phone, shaking his head.

But to Rachel, he had been nothing but patient and polite. Now, riding in the guarded and bulletproofed Suburban, she realized there was one more question that was burning in her mind. She decided to risk the general's patience an additional time.

"Is . . . is this going to turn out OK for Peter, General?" Rachel asked.

"I don't know. I don't have the gift of prophecy. But I do have a gift for solving very difficult problems, and if that isn't enough, we can also pray."

Her face must have registered her surprise.

"Rachel, I've learned that the good Lord welcomes people from every walk of life," Grisham said. "He doesn't want us to make war on each other, but He doesn't reject soldiers just because they serve in uniform. If you go to Matthew's Gospel in that Bible you have there, you'll find that Jesus commends a Roman centurion, a member of the occupying army, for his faith."

"Does your faith mean a lot to you?" she asked.

"It's everything to me. It's even the motto of our Corps—'Always Faithful.' "

Rachel paused a moment and said, "Well, when I started to think about God . . . and my life . . . and the things going wrong with my life, I began to see a lot of things coming together." Rachel wasn't sure why, but she felt such trust toward this kind general who was helping her, it seemed natural to tell some of her story. "It seemed like everywhere I turned, there was another Christian. All my life I wasn't sure what it even meant to be a Christian, and then my friend Inga told me how Christ had changed her life. Then another friend, Sandy, told me how she and her husband had turned their marriage around when Christ came into their lives and their home. It all began to make sense to me. Then, last Sunday I went to church and later went to lunch with the pastor and his wife. They showed me how Christ could change my life as well . . . to forgive me . . . give me peace of mind . . . and even restore my marriage," she said.

"You and Pete having some rough times?" the general asked her.

Rachel told him how she had given up on the marriage and had been looking for the right moment to serve Peter with divorce papers. "But you know, General, I had a chance to see that I was as much to blame as Peter for the problems in our marriage. When I prayed and asked Jesus to take over my life, to make me clean and right in His eyes, something happened to me. I can't quite explain it, but somehow I know that God changed me—He turned my life inside out and has given me assurance that everything that I read in the Bible, the things my friends have shared with me, and my own spiritual seeking have all come together with a clarity that I've never known before. Do you understand?"

General Grisham smiled, and then he reached across and patted her arm. "Yes . . . I do understand. I understand perfectly. Welcome to God's family." Rachel recalled that moment with fondness.

They reached the British base at Larnaca and now she was in the comfortable "Visiting VIP Quarters." It was just after midnight. An entire day of her life had disappeared in an aircraft on the way here. What would the next hours bring?

A maid tapped on Rachel's door and asked if she needed anything. Rachel smiled at the olive-skinned young woman and shook her head.

The maid left, closing the door behind her. Rachel thought it was odd that a maid would be on duty so late. *Maybe that's just how they do it here,* she thought as she got ready for bed.

25 Piers Dock
Iskenderun, Turkey
Friday, 10 March 1995
0300 Hours, Local

William Goode had arrived at the 25 Piers dock in Iskenderun at exactly 1800 the previous evening. He had berthed the *Pescador* between piers 9 and 10, so he could periodically check for Newman's arrival without attracting too much attention. He went to meet with an old friend, a member of the Intelligence Service of the Republic of Turkey.

They met in a crowded restaurant along Attaturk Street, a venue that the Turk often chose for meetings like this. As they shared tiny cups of strong Arab coffee, Goode handed the Turk intelligence officer a manila envelope. Inside were several photographs he had downloaded and printed from the e-mails he had received before leaving Larnaca, two lists of essential biographical data that he himself had compiled, and fifty one-hundred-dollar bills. The Turk asked a number of questions, noted Goode's answers on a slip of paper, and then excused himself, telling the white-haired American that he would meet him aboard the *Pescador* before midnight.

Goode had returned to the pier, stopping on the way to purchase some fresh fish, a loaf of good bread, some feta cheese, and several bright, red tomatoes. Back aboard, he grilled the fish over a small charcoal brazier attached to the transom of the boat, and while it was cooking, he sliced the tomatoes, drizzled some olive oil and tarragon vinegar over them, and added some crumbled feta cheese.

Shortly after sunset, the breeze softened and backed

around to blow offshore from east to west, making the night warmer. Goode ate on deck, from plates set on the foldaway table in the cockpit. By 11:30 he had finished his meal, cleaned up his dishes and utensils and was sitting on deck, listening to the Voice Of America news on the short-wave radio. He saw his Turkish friend walking toward his boat, along the pier.

"Request permission to come aboard, sir," said his smiling friend, standing beside the *Pescador* with the manila envelope in hand.

"Permission granted," replied Goode, and helped his friend make the short leap from the pier to the deck of the boat that had lifted with the rising tide.

The two of them sat on cushions in the cockpit, and as the Turk put the envelope on the table, Goode asked, "Any problems?"

"No. I made them Irish, as you suggested. Are you still certain that's wise?"

"I think so," replied Goode. "My supposition is that whoever did this to him wouldn't expect him to adopt the nationality of the poster. Hopefully, that will afford them a better chance of getting away, if that's what they want to do."

"I hope you are right," said the Turkish intelligence officer. "He should be here shortly. I have confirmed that your man made it onto the midnight train from El-beyli. My people didn't see anyone tailing him, but it is always possible. Even so, I would advise you to depart here as soon as he arrives. And in case he is tracked here, I have, as you requested, filed a sail plan for the *Pescador* from here, up the coast to Mersin. That is consistent with the word I let slip that you might be making an Easter pilgrimage to Saint Paul's hometown of Tarsus."

"As always, you do very good work, my friend," said Goode, patting his ally on the arm.

The Turk rose and headed for the narrow gangway that would take him to the pier. "I look forward to spending more time with you next time you visit and shall hold you in my prayers until I do."

"As do I." Goode rose to embrace his former agent, now his friend.

When he got to the rail and was about to descend to the pier, the Turk turned and said, "By the way, I am told that in Elbeyli, your Marine apparently had the help of an Assyrian Christian widow, her widowed daughter, and two grandchildren. I thought you told me that he didn't speak Arabic."

"I don't think he does," replied Goode.

The Turk shrugged and said, "Many, strange, and wondrous are the ways of the Lord."

"Amen." Goode smiled.

He spent the next three hours alternatively checking for the Marine he had come to rescue and watching the all-night activity in the busy port. Just a few hundred meters away from the *Pescador*, beneath huge banks of mercury vapor lights, husky stevedores used heavy transport equipment to load steel, grain, and ore into giant cargo ships. And at other piers, cargo from other parts of the world was being unloaded and placed aboard trucks to be shipped to cities throughout the Middle East. Goode watched as automobiles, giant Sea-Land containers and other crates, and all sorts of commodities were taken from the bowels of the huge ships. Just down the quay, fishermen were arriving with their catch, and seafood brokers, chefs, and wholesalers shouted out their bids.

Then Goode spotted his man, walking unhurriedly past the open-air seafood auction.

He was dressed in the rough linen trousers and cotton shirt of a backcountry peasant. He wore sandals and had a short, heavy beard. Over his shoulder he had a brown mishlah. All in all, Goode concluded, he looked like a man who might have come in from the mountains looking for work.

Once he had him spotted, Goode paid less attention to the man and more to what was happening around and behind him. From his vantage point on the *Pescador*'s deck, four or five feet higher than the pier, Goode looked carefully for anyone who might be following his intended passenger.

Seeing no one following the tall man headed toward pier 10, Goode grabbed a large plastic bag of trash, descended to the pier and started walking toward the large trash container at the landward end of pier 10. He timed his pace to arrive at the same time as his man.

As Goode passed within a few feet of him, he said in a quiet voice, "My name is William Goode. . . . Do I know you?"

"Man, am I ever glad to see you! Yes, I'm Lieutenant Colonel Peter Newman." The Marine never looked at Goode as he spoke.

"Great. I'm going back to that sailboat with the blue hull behind me. You walk on back down the pier behind me like you're one of the deckhands. Throw off my lines and take off the gangplank as though you're helping me make ready to get under way. As soon as I engage the prop, jump aboard. Got it?" said Goode.

"Got it," replied Newman.

Less than four minutes later, the big blue sloop was headed out to sea with the white-haired captain at the helm and his passenger below decks, watching the lights of the harbor falling behind them.

Neither man noticed the heavyset European with the binoculars amidst the crates and boxes at the seaward end of pier 12 as he made a call on his satellite phone.

Room 306
Hotel Kophinou
Larnaca, Cyprus
Friday, 10 March 1995
1525 Hours, Local

"Radchenko, tell me what you have learned," said UN Deputy Secretary General Dimitri Komulakov.

"Immediately after arriving in Cyprus aboard the UN aircraft the day before," Radchenko said, "I dispatched the four Palestinians to confirm some intel that a Marine general had arrived on the island with a mysterious woman. One of the maids who was assigned to her said that she is the wife of someone important."

"If I can find his wife, I can get him," Komulakov said.

Radchenko continued, "This is important. This U.S. Marine general is named Grisham. He landed last night aboard a U.S. Air Force C-17 at Akrotiri and came here to Larnaca by motorcade provided by the British security service. He has with him six aides and the American woman. I found out that she is registered as Rachel Huffman. She is right now in room 204 at the Royal Officers' VIP quarters, inside the U.K. Sovereign Base Area. The general is in a suite of rooms in the next building."

This confirmed the information Komulakov had received from Harrod while still in Syria. "Huffman" was obviously an alias. From his next-of-kin data, he knew that Newman's wife's first name was Rachel. He asked, "What are they doing?"

"Nothing," said Radchenko. "They appear to be waiting for something or someone. Earlier today, the Huffman woman asked her maid for a good place to buy a dress. She also said something about her husband arriving tonight."

"Will we know if this Rachel woman leaves the base to go shopping?"

"I can make it so," said Radchenko.

"See to it. Now, let me tell you what I have learned. While you were gone, I found the man we are seeking."

"Duncan? The terrorist? Where is he? What does this woman at the British base have to do with him?" exclaimed Radchenko, excitedly.

"His real name is Newman," replied Komulakov. "He is an American Marine. And I learned last night that he is right now headed here on a large blue sailboat from Iskenderun, Turkey. It took me all day to find out whose boat it is, but now I know: it belongs to a retired CIA clandestine services officer named William P. Goode."

"Goode . . . where have I heard that name before?"

"My dear Radchenko, now I know why you are not a colonel. Don't you remember the operation in '86 when we had to take down those who stole our Soviet Army's munitions train from the siding in Poland?"

"Ah, yes, General Komulakov. You got promoted and I got sent to Afghanistan. I personally killed that Solidarity priest in Poland and then delivered the bomb to Lisbon. And it was my PFLP guys who liquidated the Frenchman. But what does that have to do with this person named Goode and his sailboat?"

"The theft of the Soviet munitions train was his operation," replied Komulakov. "Think back to when Moscow Centre gave us the mission. They told us that Goode was that Marine at the White House who was helping the reactionary Nicaraguan terrorists over-throw our Scientific Socialist friends in Managua. He was running around to places like Beirut and Tehran and making all kinds of mischief for Moscow."

"I remember—but his real name was North," said Radchenko.

"Yes, that's correct. Yet all along there was another 'Goode.' He was the one who really orchestrated the train robbery and the theft of those whole carloads of weapons and munitions. I knew it then, but Moscow Centre wouldn't buy it. They said that North was the key to bringing down Reagan, the American president. So they let the real Goode slip through their fingers. Now we have a chance to correct that."

"It was a long time ago, and I'm not sure I remember clearly, but didn't this Marine, North, have false documents in the name of 'Goode,' as well?" asked the major.

"Of course, Radchenko, of course. That was all part of their plan. And it would have worked but for others we have planted in very important places in Washington. I was the resident there, remember? We have people very high up in their CIA, their FBI. I even have one of their very sensitive communications security devices." Komulakov showed the EncryptionLok-3 to Radchenko.

"So what do you want us to do?"

"What I want to do is to finish the job we started in 1986, and eliminate the real William P. Goode. And, I want to be rid of this Newman person forever. Here's how we're going to accomplish both. . . ."

U.K. Sovereign Base
Larnaca, Cyprus
Friday, 10 March 1995
1745 Hours, Local

General Grisham and Rachel Newman arrived at the little boat basin in the Royal Navy Yard just as the big blue sloop rounded the bar that protected the port from the Mediterranean's bitter winter storms. The general had called Rachel's room at 1730 hours and informed her, "I just got a call from the harbormaster. The *Pescador* is inbound and should be tied up at 1800. Do you want to go down to the pier and meet them?"

"Oh, yes!" Rachel had exclaimed. "But . . . good grief, I look a sight. I was going to go out and get a pretty dress, and my hair is a mess."

The general chuckled at her response. "You sound just like my wife and daughters. I think Pete will be glad to see you whatever you're wearing. But if you want, the waterfront shops are open until eight or nine—I think just on the other side of the fence where Bill keeps his boat. After you greet each other, you can run out and get something and then join us for dinner at the Officer's Mess."

✪

Early that morning, Goode had called on his satellite phone to both Grisham and Harris to inform them that he was on his way back to Larnaca and that "the fishing has been good." And during the fifteen-hour sail from Iskenderun, he had debriefed the Marine, asking him detailed questions as he tape-recorded the interview on a little cassette tape recorder.

When Newman's interrogation was finished, the captain fed the hungry Marine and taught him some basics of seamanship. And then, as the sun was rising behind them, he went below, emerging a minute or two later with two steaming hot cups of coffee and a manila envelope. He poured the contents of the envelope out on the table: two Irish passports, employment cards, drivers' licenses, and birth certificates. Newman looked at the documents and then at Goode.

"I don't know if you're going to need these or not," Goode said. "Nobody asked me to have them made for you, but they may come in handy."

Newman put the paperwork into a pocket of the linen trousers Samir had bought for him and asked Goode how it was that he had become his final rescuer. The old man explained how he came to know General Grisham as a Clandestine Services officer in Vietnam and how he and North had worked together in the '80s. But it was his answer to Newman's query about "family" that really grabbed the Marine's attention.

In response to Newman's questions, Goode had explained how he had been orphaned as a baby, raised at the Hershey Home for Boys in Pennsylvania, and how he had joined the CIA's Clandestine Services after serving as a Marine in the Korean War. With gentle affection, he described how for fifteen years he and his wife had enjoyed the challenges of overseas postings—until 1969 in Africa. And then, in a near whisper, the white-haired man at the helm described how his wife and daughters had been caught in one of the terrible tribal uprisings fomented by Soviet agents in the Congo . . . how he had returned to Brazzaville when the French paratroopers finally arrived, only to find his family slaughtered.

Newman finally asked, "Aren't you bitter?"

"I was, for a long time afterward," replied Goode. "But in 1975 I was posted to Rome as deputy station chief. While I was there I met a group of men—and some women, but mostly men—who met every Tuesday night at a little church just outside the city. One of the Italian security service people I worked with invited me to meet with them.

"This little group has no denomination, it has no priests or ministers—they're all laymen. They meet at this church to pray for each other and to try to get to know their Lord better. They read from the Bible and pray for each other every day. Well, it sounded like it would be kind of boring, and I kept declining his invitation. But I saw some qualities in the man that I admired, and decided to take him up on his offer. I went . . . and came back again . . . and again. It was through them that I met Jesus."

He said it so matter-of-factly that Newman wondered if the old man was describing an actual vision. But Goode explained, "I got to the point where I could no longer deny that Jesus Christ had come to this earth two thousand years ago, lived a sinless life, was seized and tortured to death—and then arose from the dead. Intellectually, I had no reason to disbelieve those facts. They're the basics of Christianity, but I had never really given these facts much thought.

"Once I accepted those events of Christ's coming to earth as fact, I asked, 'Why?' And the answer I got, every time I prayed about it, was, 'to save you, William P. Goode, you miserable sinner.'

"You see, Peter, I didn't think I was worthy of such sacrifice. My heart was still full of hatred toward those who had killed my wife and lovely daughters. And so, after I prayed about it some more, and talked about it more with my friends at this Tuesday evening gathering, I eventually concluded: No, I wasn't worthy of His sacrifice, but He had done it for me anyway—and that my hatred and anger were a repudiation of what He had done. It was that realization that changed my heart. It took me a long time to confess my rejection of Him and to ask His forgiveness. That's when I met Him. He was always with me. But now I'm with Him."

Lieutenant Colonel Peter Newman pondered all of this—deeply moved, but still uncertain of its full meaning. He asked about the group in Rome.

Goode responded, "Most are professionals: businessmen, doctors, lawyers, government workers, even members of the military. They have all kinds of different backgrounds. The group has spread. There are members in almost every country, though there is no membership card—only this." Goode held out his hand. In Goode's palm was an emblem of a little metal fish.

Newman was stunned. "What does it mean? The old man who saved me in the desert, Habib, had one of those. And so did his son."

"It's an *icthus*, the ancient sign of the Christian believer. It even predates the cross as a sign of Christian faith, though few people recognize it as such today." Goode and Newman were still talking about what faith really meant when they rounded the headland and sailed into the British base at Larnaca Bay.

❁

On the pier, Rachel and General Grisham watched as the main and jib were furled on the fly and the big sloop, now looking somewhat naked without her big white sails aloft, nosed expertly into its slip. Just outside the fence, a group of youngsters watched the boat as it docked.

Newman, on the foredeck, waved to Rachel, who was jumping up and down like a schoolgirl. Beside her, beaming from ear to ear, was Lieutenant General

George Grisham—dressed in khaki trousers and a blue blazer.

The lines weren't even made fast to the pier before Rachel had jumped aboard and flung herself into Peter's arms. Still on the pier, Grisham yelled out to Goode, "Hey, sailor, there's an old Marine out here requesting permission to come aboard."

"Welcome aboard, sir," called Goode as he lashed down the little gangway the dock boys had shoved across to the vessel's gunwale.

The two old friends embraced while Newman and his wife were wrapped in a much tighter grip, both of them now crying and laughing at the same time.

"Uh . . . listen," Goode said quietly to Peter and Rachel, "the general and I will walk on ahead. We've got reservations for dinner at eight. I'm going to take the general with me to my room up at the Queen's billet, and we'll meet the two of you at the Officers' Mess. That way, you can have some privacy while you get reacquainted." Newman and Rachel nodded from their embrace as the two men strolled down the pier.

When Peter finally opened his eyes, he noticed that the sun was about to set. He grabbed his wife's hand and said, "Rache, quick, watch this."

"What," she said, surprised at his sudden urgency. "What?"

"Watch the horizon, right where the sun goes into the sea," he said. He held her as the sun's bright orb dropped into the sea and suddenly, just as the top of the red ball lowered itself into the Mediterranean, there was a bright green flash at the point where the sun had sunk into the water.

Rachel was awestruck. "That was beautiful," she said in a whisper.

Her husband explained, "That green flash is caused by the bending of light waves as they pass through the atmosphere. The air, at different density and temperature, acts for an instant like a giant prism. At the end of a clear day, when the cool and warm air conditions are just right, the blue and green wavelengths refract more than the red and yellow—and for an instant—the blue bands are made invisible by the nitrogen in the atmosphere."

Rachel laughed. "You scientific types take all the romance out of everything."

And her husband, almost as though he was a thousand miles away, quietly responded, "Yeah, you're right. It is beautiful. My dad showed that to Jim and me a long time ago when we were little boys, on a fishing trip on the Oregon coast. Later that night, over a campfire, he told us of an old Irish—or was it Scottish?—legend, that God promised true love and happiness to all who are privileged to see the green flash."

The two of them sat there, close together in the cockpit of the big boat, until it began to get dark. Rachel said, "Look, we've got to go to dinner with these two men. And you didn't even bother to introduce me to Mr. Goode. Is there a shower down below?"

"Yeah," said Peter, "what do you have in mind?"

She punched him playfully on the shoulder and said, "Later, big boy. You go below and get cleaned up. I'll run over to one of those shops." She pointed beyond the chain-link fence fifty meters from the bow of the boat. "I'll get you a shirt, a decent pair of trousers, some shoes, and socks."

She pecked him on the cheek and ran down the gangway, headed for the gate about seventy-five yards up the quay from the slip. Peter watched the armed sentries salute as she presented her military ID card and saw her disappear into the traffic in the street. He then went below, found a razor and some shaving soap, and entered the head on the starboard side, just forward of the master cabin.

❂

Rachel had quickly found a men's shop and in no time had a shopping bag full of new clothing for her husband. But on her way back to the gate, she noticed a cute little boutique with a lovely print dress on a mannequin in the window. She paused, made her decision, and went inside.

The very helpful English-speaking sales clerk found what she thought would be Rachel's size and suggested that she go in the back and try it on.

Rachel set her packages on a table in the back of the little store and entered the nicely appointed changing room. She had just slipped the dress on and was admiring it in the full-length mirror when there was a knock on the door. Rachel turned the knob and started to say, "It fits just fine," but the door flew open and a large man charged in, pinning her against the back wall. Her eyes widened in terror as she got her first glimpse of the attacker. He grabbed Rachel with an arm around her neck in a chokehold, and then in the mirror she could see he had a knife in his hand. He pressed the point against her throat.

"Don't scream or I'll kill you," he growled, his breath foul and his voice heavily accented, as he put all his weight on Rachel to hold her down on the little seat inside the changing room. He reached outside the door with his right foot to pull the door closed behind him. But suddenly the man grunted as his leg was grabbed from outside. Rachel saw his foot twisted violently, then she heard the snapping of bone and sinew. Her attacker screamed.

As Rachel struggled to free herself from his dead weight, she looked over his shoulder and recognized, standing in the doorway, one of the Marines who had been aboard the C-17 with General Grisham. But he wasn't in uniform. The man who had attacked her was big—but her rescuer was even bigger; his build and appearance reminded her of George Foreman.

In what seemed to Rachel to be a single fluid motion, the civilian-clad Marine released the attacker's broken leg, reached into the little room, and grabbed the wrist of the hand holding the knife. There was a quick, twisting motion, and the knife tumbled from the attacker's now-useless hand.

The American then grabbed the man's hair, pulled his head back and slammed his left fist at the attacker's protruding Adam's apple. At the same time he jerked the man to his feet, spun him around, and kneed him hard in the groin. As the attacker fell in a heap at Rachel's feet, the Marine sergeant reached down and removed the man's wallet from his back pocket, then slipped it into his own. He reached down to help Rachel to her feet. It all happened so quickly that she was disoriented, almost dizzy.

"Oh, thank God you were right there!" Though Rachel hugged him, her rescuer still eyed the inert attacker. The Marine kicked the knife across the floor and said, "Got your things?" Rachel, still somewhat in shock at the sudden violence, nodded and picked up the dress she had worn into the shop. On the way out, he asked, "Are these yours too?" Again she nodded, and the Marine picked up the shopping bags of clothing she had purchased for her husband. "We probably ought to see if there's a back way out of here," he added. "I sent the store clerk to get the police. You can take care of the bill later. Let's go."

They exited the rear of the shop into an alley and headed in the direction of the gate Rachel had left a half hour before. At the end of the alley, they came to a busy thoroughfare full of pedestrians and joined the throng as they walked across to the gate. As Rachel and the sergeant showed their ID cards to the armed Royal Marine sentry, the U.S. Marine kept an eye on the passing traffic.

He walked her back to the boat, helped her aboard, and said, "Ma'am, I'm going to go report this incident to General Grisham and then I'm going to come back here with a car to take you and Lieutenant Colonel Newman to meet with the general up at the Officer's Mess. I know he's expecting you, but I think you need to get back up to the officer's billeting area. It's farther away from the street and safer."

"Do you think that man was sent to kill me?" Rachel's voice shook a little.

"I don't know, Mrs. Newman, but our guys will find out. I've got his wallet and ID. The general will know if we have to alert the local authorities. You're safe now . . . just relax. Tell Colonel Newman that I'll be right back with the car."

As he started to leave, Rachel said, "Wait. I didn't even get your name, Sergeant."

"Skillings, ma'am. Staff Sergeant Amos Skillings," he replied. "I served with your husband in Force Recon. Now I work for General Grisham. The general said I should make sure that nothing happened to Colonel Newman's lady," he said, smiling broadly.

Rachel was close to tears but managed to say, "Thank

you, Staff Sergeant Amos Skillings, for what you did back there. I'm still shaking, but more grateful than you'll ever know. Thank you."

"No problem, ma'am. Glad to do it." He came to attention, saluted, and said, "I'll be right back, ma'am."

❍

When Rachel went below deck, Peter was just coming out of the shower. He had a towel wrapped around his middle and for the first time Rachel noticed the extent of his injuries.

"Nice dress," he said. "By the way, who were you talking to up there on the pier?"

"Staff Sergeant Amos Skillings." She told him quickly what had happened on her shopping expedition while he dressed in the clothing she had just purchased.

"He's going to get us a car. He doesn't even want us to walk up to the Officer's Mess up on the hill without an escort. Peter, suppose there are more of them. Is Staff Sergeant Skillings going to be all right?"

"What do you think?" Peter replied with a hearty laugh. But then he said, "Seriously, I'm not worried about Skillings. It's *us* I'm worried about. This long ordeal may not be over. Come and sit beside me. Let me show you something."

Peter took out of a manila envelope the documents William P. Goode had given him earlier in the day.

❍

"May I take your order, sir?" said the tuxedo-clad waiter to the two men seated at the best table in the officers mess.

Grisham and Goode looked up from their menus and were about to tell the waiter their choices when the entire building shook as a tremendous explosion rocked the piers outside. The general could see a reflection of the huge fireball across Goode's face.

Both men were startled—it sounded and felt as though a one-thousand-pound bomb had been dropped directly in front of the restaurant. Several of the diners leaped under tables, and others screamed.

Both Goode and the general ran to the window. Despite being reinforced with Mylar film, it had a web of cracks from the force of the explosion. Through the shattered panes they could see outside and below them that the dock was a raging inferno.

Goode and the general raced down the steps from the officers mess toward the piers. As they did so, a black sedan sped down the quay, made a screeching turn at the gate, and raced past the Royal Marine sentry, ignoring his order to halt. And though he fired twice at it, the vehicle careened off up the hill and disappeared.

Goode ran toward where his sixty-two-foot sloop had been. Flames had already completely engulfed the vessel and were now consuming the teak deck and other wooden fixtures. There was a gaping hole in the starboard side into which seawater poured and pulled the beautiful blue hull into the harbor depths. The explosion had been purposefully set . . . obviously by someone who knew what he was doing. From the look of it Goode guessed that the bomb had been placed just below the waterline—and had probably detonated the propane cooking fuel.

General Grisham caught up with him and was equally shaken by the sight.

By the time the first firefighters responded, the deck of Goode's ship was almost completely under water and the flames were almost out. Only the mast protruded above the slip, canted at a crazy angle as though pointing toward the ocean it would never sail again.

Both men stood together for a long time without speaking, and before long there was a large crowd watching and waiting for the Royal Navy divers to show up and begin trying to salvage what they could. But aside from the mast sticking up out of the water, there was very little for the crowd gathered outside the chain-link fence or on the crowded quay to see. There was nothing left but a thin layer of floating ashes.

EPILOGUE

The package arrived in the morning mail, and Dave Smolinski, director of Corporate Security for North American Enterprises, was concerned. He was standing in the front office doorway.

"Colonel North, I told Mr. Smolinski that he couldn't interrupt you. I'm sorry." Marsha, my long-suffering secretary and guardian of the gate, apologized for the intrusion. She was standing behind Smolinski, glaring at the back of the security chief's head for having had the temerity to barge past her into the boss's office. But Smolinski was one of the few who could get away with it. Before leaving government service, he had been one of the federal agents detailed to protect my family after the Libyan assassination attempt in 1987.

"I've got to show you this package, Boss," Smolinski said. Marsha rolled her eyes in despair for the day's schedule and went back to her desk. "It's addressed to Lieutenant Colonel Oliver L. North, USMC (Ret.) at this address, but doesn't mention the company name, it doesn't have a return address, and it's fairly heavy. I had the dog sniff it and ran it through the X-ray. Both negative. In the X-ray it looks to me like it contains some kind of audio- or videotape, a pile of paper, and a 3.5-inch computer disc. There are no visible wires or detonators and no sign of any shielding to mask something from the X-ray. Oh yeah, it's postmarked APO, N.Y., on 11 March. I checked, and the zip code is for EUCOM, meaning that it was mailed in the military postal system from somewhere in the European Command."

"Well, go ahead and open it," I said.

"Uh . . . Colonel North, why don't I take it out back and open it in the cage?"

"Look, Dave," I reminded him, "Marsha is mad enough at both of us right now because she's having to re-jigger my whole day. Open it here. If it blows up, it'll be a minor explosion compared to the one Marsha's going to detonate if I don't get back on schedule."

Smolinski shrugged, smiled, and said, "Always nice to know who's in charge around here." He started to carefully cut around the packing tape with his penknife and peel back the several layers of brown paper.

As the security chief lifted back the brown paper wrapping, we could both see the corner of a thick file folder—with a distinctive red and white border and the words *TOP SECRET* emblazoned upon it. "It looks like someone's mailed you some classified documents, Colonel."

"Yeah, open it up."

Using his penknife, Smolinski carefully cut away the rest of the wrapper and slid the contents out onto the conference table. There was a fat file folder full of paper, a digital audiotape, and a computer disc. On the computer disc was hand-printed, "Read this first." And below that, an *icthus* was drawn with the same indelible marker.

"Let's load this disc in the old stand-alone computer down in the file room, just in case there's a virus on it," said Smolinski.

As we walked past her desk, Marsha inquired, "Colonel North, will you be keeping any of your morning appointments—or shall I just reschedule?"

"Don't know yet. I'll let you know in a few minutes," I told her and ducked out of her line of fire into the file room where Smolinski was loading the disc in the computer. He clicked the mouse to open the files. The index contained three entries:

"Read This First," a 19 KB file;
"National Security Directive 941109," a 36 KB file; and,
"ISEG Concept of Operations," a 22 KB file

All were dated 10 March 1996, one year to the day since Peter and Rachel Newman had disappeared in the fiery blast aboard the sailing vessel *Pescador*.

Smolinski clicked "open" on the "Read This First" file and we then bent over to read:

"Lt. Col. North,

"I pray this finds you well. I regret that it has taken me so long to get this material to you, but now that I have it assembled, I believe you to be the best judge of what should be done with it.

"Please note that this computer disc contains two other documents: a copy of NSD 941109, de-

scribing the U.S. role in a Top Secret United Nations assassination plan—called 'Sanctions Enforcement Operations' and a copy of The International Sanctions Enforcement Group (ISEG) Concept of Operations. The ISEG was a highly classified group of U.S. and British shooters commanded by Marine Lieutenant Colonel Peter J. Newman. Both of these documents were retrieved from a government-issued laptop computer issued to Sgt. Maj. Daniel J. Gabbard, USMC. I am told by friends still working for my former employer that the 'Gabbard computer' has since disappeared, that NSD 941109 does not exist, and that there never was any such thing as an ISEG.

"The audiotape included in this package was recorded on 10 March 1995 aboard the sailing vessel Pescador, *en route from Iskenderun, Turkey, to Larnaca, Cyprus. You will hear me asking the questions and Lt. Col. Newman answering. I believe that the answers he gave are truthful and accurately describe what happened to him and those who accompanied him on a highly sensitive, UN-directed assassination mission into Iraq twelve months ago. Newman did not know that all of the other members of his unit, except for Sgt. Major Gabbard, had been killed at the time of the debriefing. As you may already know, Sergeant Major Gabbard retired from the Marines last October and has dropped out of sight.*

"When you listen to the tape, you will find that your name comes up several times—to include references to the third item enclosed in this package—a photocopy of a classified file taken from

your office in the Old Executive Office Building. In the debrief tape, you will hear Newman tell me where this copy of your file could be found and that you alone know where the original is hidden. He also speculates correctly that you and I were both identified as William P. Goode during the 1985–86 hostage rescue and Nicaraguan Resistance Support Operations.

"Based on what I learned from Newman, your enclosed file, the information from the ISEG computer, and some short debriefs with Marine Lt. Gen. George Grisham, USAF General James Harris, and Sgt. Major Gabbard, here is what I surmise—though I caution you that I cannot prove any of it:

"Communications for Newman's mission—and our operations back in the 1980s—were thoroughly compromised, probably by the EncryptionLok communications devices. I suspect a long-term, high-level Soviet/Russian penetration of NSA, CIA, and/or the FBI.

"The Senate Armed Services Committee has purview over who gets the EncryptionLok-3s. Someone on that committee had to authorize transferring/selling these devices to the UN. I suspect that the company that makes the EncryptionLok-3 may be complicit in this technology transfer. Look for where the owners make campaign contributions.

"Newman and his team were set up by someone very high up in the U.S. government and the UN. My estimate is that the culprits are at the White House and at the top of the UN. Newman's two primary points of contact are obvious suspects:

National Security Advisor Harrod and this fellow Komulakov at the UN. They may have had different motives, but they seem to be the people responsible for this tragedy and for sweeping it under the rug.

"I don't know much about Harrod except what I read about him resigning from his post as National Security Advisor to go back to teach at Harvard last year. He undoubtedly knows enough to be considered dangerous. Whether he could be convinced to talk to the appropriate authorities, I don't know.

"The UN official is General Dimitri Komulakov, who was the head of KGB Department V back in 1985–86. It was Department V that destroyed the European supply line for the Nicaraguan Resistance in Nov. '86. My sources tell me that Komulakov is involved with former Department V officers and the Russian mafia, trying to sell Soviet-era weapons and technology. As long as he is free, neither you nor I are safe.

"I'm forwarding all this to you in hopes that you may be able to find some responsible officials in the Department of Justice or up on Capitol Hill to look into what really happened to the brave Americans and British involved with this operation. The present British government apparently doesn't want to open an investigation, but maybe someone in Washington will care to try to find out why all these good people were killed carrying out what they believed to be a legitimate counterterrorist activity. At the very least, if the guilty can't be punished, those who died ought to be remembered for their courage instead of the phony story

*that they were all killed by accident on some UN
humanitarian flight over Iraq.*

*"As for me, I'll be taking delivery of a new
sloop in the next few weeks. After a shakedown
cruise, I may head for the Caribbean for a while.
If you need to contact me, use the new e-mail address that I will send you separately.*

*Semper Fidelis,
William*

When we finished reading all that was in the first file
on the disc, Dave Smolinski looked at me and said,
"Look, Boss, there's a whole lot here that I don't understand and it's none of my business. Why don't you
just keep this stuff, and if you want me to do anything
with any of it, just let me know?"

I thanked him, and after Smolinski left the file room
and returned to his office, I re-read Bill Goode's communiqué. As usual, Goode was right. Someone at Justice or up on the Hill ought to look into what happened
to Peter Newman and his UN International Sanctions
Enforcement Group. Unfortunately, nobody would.

✪

For the better part of a year, efforts to get the attention
of anyone who would listen at the Department of Justice were stonewalled. No one at the Attorney General's
office wanted to touch the matter. And up on Capitol
Hill, it was even worse. Several calls and letters to Senator James Waggoner's office eventually provoked a
curt note in reply:

*"The matters you have raised have been fully
investigated by the Senate Armed Services Committee and the matter is closed. Senator Waggoner*

*has personally looked into the unfounded rumors
that you are spreading about current and former
U.S. and UN officials and regards them to be potential violations of law."*

That's the note that prompted this book. It was the
only means for the real story of Peter Newman to be
told. As for the others:

Mir Aimal Kansi, the Al-Qaeda terrorist who assassinated three CIA officers in the 1993 ambush at Langley,
was apprehended in Pakistan and returned to the U.S.
to stand trial. A jury convicted him, and he is presently
on Death Row in a Virginia prison.

Senator James Waggoner continues to serve as his
state's "senior senator" on the Armed Services Committee.

General Bob Storey, formerly employed by Silicon
Cyber Technologies International, at the urging of General George Grisham, testified before a closed session of
the House Permanent Select Committee on Intelligence.
His testimony concerned the EncryptionLok-3's wide-
spread distribution to non-U.S. government entities. As
a consequence of General Storey's testimony, corrobo-
rated by that of Jules Wilson, all government funds for
EncryptionLok-3 production were terminated in July
1996.

Peter and Rachel Newman were honored at a memorial service in the Old Fort Meyer Chapel in April 1995.
General George Grisham delivered the eulogy and presented Newman's mother with the flag that would have
covered his coffin had his body been found. A marker
was erected in Arlington Cemetery, next to Jim Newman's, with Peter's and Rachel's names and birth dates

inscribed upon it, along with the notation: "Killed by terrorists on 10 March 1995."

Lieutenant General George Grisham, USMC, was named Commander in Chief, U.S. Central Command in April 1996.

Jules Wilson retired as Deputy Director, National Security Agency, in October 1997 and moved to Coronado, California. He serves as a consultant to the FBI and the U.S. Navy on matters pertaining to communications security.

Dr. Simon Harrod, National Security Advisor to the President, resigned his post suddenly in early April 1995 and returned to Harvard. In a written deposition submitted to the House Permanent Select Committee on Intelligence in June 1996, he denied "categorically that the U.S. government had any role in the creation of a United Nations assassination program." He currently teaches a course entitled "U.S. Responsibilities in the New World Order."

Marty Korman and *Stanley Marat,* the founders of Silicon Cyber Technologies International, dissolved their partnership in September 1996 as a consequence of the U.S. government decision to buy no additional EncryptionLok-3s. In January 1997, the company's remaining assets were sold at auction to pay taxes and legal fees. In May 1997, Korman was allowed to plead guilty to violating various campaign contribution laws and regulations relating to selling national security equipment to foreign entities in violation of Commerce Department and Department of Defense regulations. Marty Korman is currently serving a fifteen-year prison sentence at a minimum-security facility in Marion, Illinois. Stanley Marat teaches computer science at a high school in Nebraska.

General Dimitri Komulakov resigned from his post as Deputy Secretary General of the United Nations in June 1995. He announced that he was planning to retire in Sweden, but in November of that year he returned to Russia to "develop new business ventures."

Lieutenant Colonel Wilbur Ellwood, the senior watch officer at the UN's command center and the man who detected Komulakov's calls to Baghdad during Newman's mission, returned to duty with Her Majesty's Special Air Service in June of 1995. Once back in England, he formally requested that the British Defense Ministry initiate an investigation into the calamity of March 1995. In August, just as the investigation was about to commence, Lieutenant Colonel Ellwood was killed in a training accident.

Leonid Dotensk, Dimitri Komulakov's Ukrainian business partner, is still selling former Soviet-bloc weapons to the highest bidder. After the botched effort to kill Peter Newman in Syria in March 1995, he traveled to Amman, Jordan, to facilitate the defection of Hussein Kamil from Iraq. He currently maintains offices and residences in Bern, Switzerland; Damascus, Syria; London, England; and Kiev. However, he no longer travels to Iraq.

Hussein Kamil, his brother, their wives, and families defected from Iraq in August 1995 and sought asylum in Jordan. He had several meetings with the CIA, but it was determined by the agency that his information was unreliable and they were reluctant to pay him for it. On February 23, 1996, following a promise from Saddam Hussein to pardon Kamil and other family members, they returned to Baghdad. Upon arriving at the airport, the two brothers were taken into custody and immediately assassinated.

Mohammed Farrah Aidid, having eluded two UN assassination attempts, died on August 2, 1996, as a consequence of wounds received during an intertribal military action in Somalia. He was sixty-one years old. He was not invited to, nor did he attend, the March 6, 1995, "Terror Summit" in Tikrit, Iraq.

Saddam Hussein crushed the INC/Kurd Northern Opposition Coalition in the aftermath of the ill-fated UN assassination attempt on March 6, 1995. The promised British and U.S. air support for the opposition forces never materialized. Thousands of CIA-supported opposition fighters and their families were killed.

Osama bin Laden flew from Baghdad to Khartoum, Sudan, on March 6, 1995, within hours of the UAV attack on Tikrit. When he arrived in Sudan, he ordered a new round of terrorist attacks on Americans. Two days later, Al-Qaeda terrorists killed two American diplomats and wounded a third in Karachi, Pakistan. Charges that he was able to acquire weapons of mass destruction from Iraq have never been proven, though bin Laden's subsequent attacks on U.S. citizens and property have killed thousands.

Eli Yusef Habib and his son Samir returned safely to their homes along the banks of the Euphrates after helping Peter Newman escape from Iraq. Both men continue to ply their risky trade in hard-to-get consumer products along a sales route that takes them from the Mediterranean to Pakistan. In December 1995, Eli Yusef Habib celebrated Christmas in Bethlehem. With him at the midnight service in Manger Square was a couple from the Hospice of Saint Patrick in Jerusalem, John and Sarah Clancy, who entered Israel in March on Irish passports. After the service, Habib took great pleasure in playing with their infant son, James.

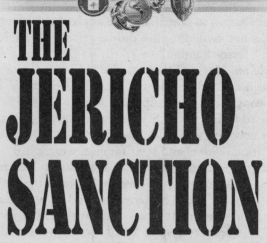